STASIS NONE
by Ian Rutter

A Rutstuff Publication

Rutstuff Publishing

The Lodge

Crablake Farm

Exeter

EX6 8DW

UK

tel: 07908 850713

http://www.rutstuff.com

British Library Cataloguing in Publication Data.
A catalogue record of this book
is available from the British Library.

ISBN 978-0-9567309-0-9

Edited by Rutstuff Publishing

Typestting and origination by Yasmin

Printed and bound in Great Britain

For Chris
"Yeah dude"

Acknowledgements

For those who know me you can imagine how I wanted to list each and every individual who has ever influenced me in any way shape or form, never mind those more directly involved in seeing this novel come to print. The simple truth is I've had so many wonderful people shaping, influencing and inspiring me over the years it would take a prologue to list you all.

So as much as it pains me to categorise and group I'm afraid I must.

To begin I'd like to thank my father for his stimulation, ideas and limitless encouragement in seeing a story of mine reaching the light of day. We both know this is a journey we began together long before the pages of this novel were constructed. I'd like to thank my mother for her belief and love throughout my life. The same accolades go to my brothers, whom I adore. Thank you for the help and support you've given me in all I've done.

I'd like to thank Rachel for her unparalleled encouragement and giving nature. Your love, belief, honesty and patience are nothing short of inspirational, not only in seeing this project become a reality but also in helping me become a better person. I'd like to say a massive thank you also to your wonderful crazy family (and associates) who I believe may have adopted me as one of their own. All of you have enriched my life and encouraged me to see this undertaking through.

To my friends, who are also my family. Thank you for the protection, love, humour and dedication you have offered me down the years. You all know what you mean to me.

Thank you to all those in the Royal Navy Survival Section whose gestures of goodwill and understanding down the years freed up a lot of the time needed to see this book written.

Many thanks to the people whose names I've so shamelessly stolen and turned into characters in my book. Hopefully you'll be thrilled to see yourselves immortalised in print . . . If not, I'll see you in court!

I'd like to thank Jocelyn for encouraging me to write this book from the offset, and for the faith and friendship you've offered since.

To all of you who have proof read the book and offered your input and constructive criticisms.

To Sean and Helen Carrison, to Gemma and all those who helped organise the launch dates.

To the great band Who Killed the Cranks for providing the music at the launch parties.

To the author Mark Frankland for offering a complete stranger much needed advice in making his dream come true. To Yasmin Chandra Singh for her unwavering patience and guidance. You went above and beyond the call of duty on this one and I appreciate all you've done.

To the team at LukeTom.com for turning sketches and scribbles into a superb front cover and great logo, and for building my website.

To Gene for her patient assistance in helping develop the audio/mp3/e-book.

And a massive thumbs-up to all of you who have bought a copy of this novel and in doing so helped me realise a life long dream.

PRELUDE

Constantinople, 1204

Shadows sprawled the city, painting streets with dark impressions of an imposing skyline. A towering horizon of Oriental, Occidental architecture, dominated by the vast and splendid Hippodrome. Beyond its magnificent dome sunlight breached the alleyways, warming the legislative halls, the grand avenues littered with statues taken from rival cities, flooding the proud palace.

Deep within its belly the palace chapel remained cold as stone, its entrance sealed as was custom when the Byzantium Emperor Alexius III knelt in solitary worship.

A guard and his Captain manned the corridor outside and approaching them in a hurry was the emperor's nascent son-in-law, Ducas Murtzuphlus.

"The emperor is still inside?" Ducas enquired a little surprised.

"Yes my lord." The Captain replied.

Before he could comment his attention was drawn abruptly to the chapel doorway. "What in God's name?"

"My Lord?"

Ducas slowed, a look of astonishment flushing his face. He pointed to the chapel doors at the end of the reach. "Do you not see it?"

Both Captain and guard turned to the closed entrance, their mouths dropping in unison.

"What is that?" The guard whispered.

They approached the doorway cautiously, their faces now illuminated in a blue light which bounced from the polished marble floor as it escaped the gaps of the sealed entry.

Ducas reached for the hilt of his sword. The chapel beyond had no windows. It was lit only by an audience of white candles which couldn't possibly be responsible for such a phenomenon.

Suddenly a booming voice thundered from behind the doors, "Hear my bidding Alexius!"

The light intensified with the volume, its beams escaping into the corridor illuminating the faces of Ducas and the guards still further.

"My Lord!" Ducas forced the entrance, his sword drawn to protect the emperor.

But as the trio powered through nothing could have prepared them for what they witnessed. For ahead of them was their ruler, down on his knees, arms held aloft with his palms facing heaven.

They too fell to their knees in immediate reverence.

With incredulous eyes they watched a luminous apparition of their lord Jesus Christ, gliding the air before diluting into a thousand light beams, retracting into the exquisite golden cross upon the grand altar.

The gloom of the inner sanctum returned followed by a long, eerie silence.

Eventually the emperor clambered to his feet. He turned trembling, tears rolling down his cheeks. A sense of elation tingled from head to toe, his mind swimming through the incredible event just transpired.

Speechless, Ducas and the guards remained on their knees.

Their leader's senses returned and as his focus fell on Ducas at the far end of the chapel he smiled.

Ducas stood slowly though the guards remained knelt, their shock and obedience fixing them to the spot. Before he could manage a word the emperor's face flushed with purpose. "Summon my council." He demanded. He then strode the aisle toward Ducas taking him by the arm. He stared wilfully into his round gawking eyes and smiled as he repeated gently, "Summon my council."

*

The sun's glare intensified irritating the horses further. They stomped and snorted to show their disapproval. Dial and Carl stood firm, holding them close on the reins.

Dial looked to the top of the gully where Dorey and Marco lay peering into the distance. "Can you see anything?"

Dorey panned the horizon, his surveillance taking his eye over the dry grassy plains, east toward Constantinople now far from view, from which they'd just fled. "No," he replied. He had Marco check their itinerary once more.

"Maybe we lost them." Carl did not sound entirely convinced.

Dorey checked their position against Marco's information one final time, "Maybe."

They were each dressed in a layer of chain mail. Thrown over Marco's armour was the finer tunic of a lord. The others wore the matching garbs of men at arms. It was the standard attire of most western Fourth Crusade knights and horsemen. The chain of their head protection was rolled back and it formed a scrunched mesh at the base of their necks. Their armoured gloves and Great Helms had been removed from the three men-at-arms, along with everything else in their possession, when they'd been taken prisoner. Marco had discarded his own gloves and helmet purely for reasons of comfort. The lower rank tunics were stripped from the guards despatched by Marco when he'd rescued the three captives from the stocks of the crusaders camp. Luck had also allowed them to steal back their swords before making their escape, and the weapons were once again secured within scabbards, slung low across their hips on thick buckled belts.

The late spring had succumbed to summer and all present were suffering the effects of both their attire and the ride, none more so than the horses who continued to grunt and blow their displeasure.

Dorey slid down the gully with Marco in tow, "Pass around the water."

Marco set about pulling a canteen from the rear of his saddle.

They took a turn at a short drink. There was none to be spared for their animals.

"At the far end of this gully we head west up the hills toward Boyalik. We can cut down through the valley and arc around to reach the *primary* supplies. It's a different route, but it should give us a better chance under the circumstances. We can hold out there. It'll make a good rendezvous."

He mounted his horse and without delay, the three followed suit.

Then with kicks from their heels they urged their animals forward, west toward Boyalik.

*

The magnificent dome ceilings stretched high upon arms of polished stone, adorned with the finest paintwork and carvings dating back to the restorations of Justinian. Imposing walls gave way to mosaic floor, dressed with the finest of rugs. The couches accompanying the many pillars were littered confidently with embedded precious metals, and all around incense burned in ceramic pots.

The depth of acoustics added resonance to the emperor's incredible words . . . Words aimed at the gathering of the city's noble council. "These were the very demands given to me by our lord Jesus Christ." The emperor spoke with gravity and purpose.

His audience where dumbfounded. Many of the clergy together with a number of his rivals balked at this blaspheme, though the emperor's trusted knights knelt in silent prayer, his divine right never in question.

"There must be doubters among you . . . But I say unto you these were the words of our Saviour." The emperor held out his arms as if to embrace the entire room. "Our enemies gather at all turns, but this does not have to include the crusaders. Only the false promises and lies of my nephew have brought them to our door." He pointed his finger as if aiming toward the crusaders distant camp. "He dines with Monteferrat while we turn away." The emperor animated himself for the final call to his banner. "Yet worry not, for our lord will smite such a threat from the walls of our great city this very day."

There was a gasp from his audience. The emperor played to it, allowing the idea to take root. "This will be a sign from God himself." Pointing once more he declared, "Beyond our walls will soon be gathered more than five hundred crusade knights and their armies, with them their Venetian allies and ships, poised to place my nephew on this throne. Why? For false promises soon to be exposed and seen for their true nature." The emperor held much of the room within his theatrical grasp. "This city will not be the financier of a false Latin crusade. It will not succumb to Venice merchants. It has seen too much bloodshed of late, and the promises offered by those vengeful pigs, Dandolo and my nephew will only lead us back into the throes of civil war and unrest, if not something entirely worse." He paused, the bold statement now resting on his lips. "But before this day is done, my nephew Angelus will be struck down dead . . . Struck down by the hand of God." Gasps and murmurs erupted amongst the court. The emperor raised his hands for silence. "Then we shall begin God's instruction." He lowered himself into his throne with renewed majesty, prepared for the outrage, curiosity and questions which must now follow from his recently pacified nobles.

All present seemed deeply affected, either because of the incredible vow just witnessed, or due the blasphemous account with which the emperor may have signed his own death warrant. All except for one man standing near to Ducas.

The man stood silent as a foolishly brave priest whispered in his ear, "This is sacrilege."

The priest checked to make sure Ducas had not overheard then looked once again for the man to respond.

He didn't . . . Instead Palene only smiled.

*

The skirmisher played his fingers into the rediscovered tracks, rubbing the dirt into his palm. He rose and faced the Norman knight. "There are footprints my Lord . . . Then hoof-prints continue in that direction. It looks like they stopped here for a time."

Roland le Manche looked down from his horse, "How long ago?"

The skirmisher contemplated. "They're quite fresh my lord."

Roland turned in his saddle to face the troop of Ritters, his lightly armoured though heavily paid for combat horsemen crowded into eight disciplined ranks of four to his rear. Antoine, the experienced Ritter *Serjéant* steered his horse closer to receive his orders.

"If they're heading for the Black Sea, Lord's Garbera and Pontelac will almost certainly intercept them. If however, they are indeed running back to the basin, they may well be ours." The thought excited Roland as he pondered his next move.

"Since it would appear your instincts have proved correct my Lord, might I suggest we now send two advance riders, we have our sprint horses still reasonably fresh at the rear. Using bowmen, we may gain an opportunity to slow them down."

Indeed Le Manche's instincts had served them well and he obliged the Serjéant without delay, "Send them directly to the basin," he declared, "We'll give chase to their rear."

The horses were brought to the front line. They wore only light saddles with no means for carrying extra arms or supplies. Antoine picked his two fastest riders who possessed the necessary skills with a bow and had them discard their remaining combat securities. Everything was shed but their swords, spears and bows. He delivered their instruction as they mounted the sprint colts before sending them ahead in a fury of determination, the skirmisher following in quick pursuit at the behest of Lord Roland.

The Norman lord pulled the chain hood over his head leaving only his tanned face exposed. This was their first real anticipation of a possible encounter with the quarry since the chase had begun. The knight yelled confidently, "We have them!"

The Ritters shouted their approval and with Roland le Manche as their lead, the hunt was on once again.

*

Dorey stood at the edge of the steep plunging hillside looking out across the barren plain below. The sun was high and more determined and it was clear, despite the brief stay at a stream some miles back, their exhausted animals couldn't go on much further.

"Are we in the right place?" Marco was dubious.

Dorey had them come closer to the ledge and pointed to the far side of the basin below, "That's where we left the supplies. The trail brought us further over than I anticipated."

They each stared down the treacherous, at times near vertical gradient then across the plain to where Dorey's finger pointed.

"The horses won't make it," Dial studied the route ahead, "We'll be pretty exposed down there if we try to cross without them."

Dorey nodded but gave no reply. He'd altered their route in an attempt to remain hidden, but this deviation had cost them.

They took in the implications of proceeding on foot but could see little alternative. The others were not due until after nightfall and with their horses close to breaking down the priority now had to be reaching the supplies. Even with fresh animals the downward climb would be virtually impossible, for their already punished mounts it would be fatal.

The only problem however, was once they'd reached the plain below it would be a mile across uneven, open terrain, even at this the shortest crossing point.

Dorey looked to the others. "It could be some time before Jay finds us. And I'd rather be holed up over there than hiding here armed with swords and four spent horses."

Concern spread over Dial's face. "Depending on who's doing the chasing, they may have knowledge of our previous camp here. If they ignore our trail and head for the basin directly . . . " He didn't need to emphasise further.

Dorey hoped the fact they'd camped here previously would seem unimportant to his pursuers.

"So how do we play it?" Dial asked, seeing his comment was to provoke no response.

"You and Carl start down the hill. We'll get rid of the horses then follow. There are only four real trails in and out of the basin, if they're following ours they might at least continue after the horse tracks." He turned to his friend. "No real strategy when you get down there, just run as hard as you can to the other side."

Dial reiterated his concern. "That could prove a long way if they find us."

"As I said, I'd rather be holed in across there than hiding here with nothing." He leaned his focus over the edge once more. "Find the best way down, we'll be right behind you."

Dial turned to Carl following the order without hesitation. "Let's go."

*

The rider pulled his horse to a halt dismounting in a hurry at the side of the palace. Two guards greeted him and quickly led him inside. They strode through myriad corridors and mosaic steps before entering the colossal halls which led to the emperor's court.

The familiar incense filled the rider's nostrils reminding him he was indeed, finally safe.

After a short conversation passed between his escorts and the guards minding the court he was granted an audience with the emperor.

The doors opened and the rider walked into the ornate splendour with purpose. It was a hive of heated discussion. Hardly any of the courtiers seemed to notice him as he made his way toward the throne. He approached and knelt before his master, who upon seeing him brought the court to order as he boomed, "Silence."

The room was immediately still and the rider felt the weighty stares of all present. The emperor was clearly excited by his presence and he felt a sharp exhilaration at the knowledge his words would not disappoint.

The emperor rose slowly to his feet, "You have news Cornelio?"

"Yes, my lord."

His master took a deep breath. "Then speak."

Cornelio then delivered his lightning bolt. "My lord, your nephew Angelus is dead."

For a moment it seemed as if the court could not move, the communal gasp appeared to have frozen them like statues, unable to contemplate the news.

Cornelio fought the need to smile. He knew this one sentence had delivered him into the history of this great city.

Everyone awaited the emperor's response, as the reality of what was happening seemed to now free itself across the chamber. He slid slowly back into his throne, his heart filled with new courage and purpose. He clasped his hands together and began to pray. He thanked Jesus for choosing him and for revealing the paths that must be undertaken. He swore he would give his life to the realisation of his quest. Then, looking up to the silent mass around him, picking out the eyes of the doubting priests and his many rivals, he declared, "Our Lord has spoken!" He held up a determined hand then returned his attention to the kneeling rider. "How did it happen?"

"No one is quite sure my lord. He was struck from his saddle by an invisible force."

The emperor seemed delighted at this terminology and cast his gaze once again over those whom he knew would have doubted the incredible happenings within the chapel, "An invisible force." He echoed, "Did you learn anything else?"

"Yes my lord. I was in the vicinity when it happened, I saw the fatal blow." Cornelio caught his breath as all present held their own, "The back of his skull all but disintegrated, yet no weapon came near to him."

Again the court gasped.

Cornelio continued, "Three knights had been taken prisoner, placed into stocks accused of being charlatans. Boniface de Montferrat had ordered a punishment for them at dawn, a show of discipline to bring to heal the many newcomers arriving at the camp daily. It was at this gathering your nephew was struck dead. I saw it with my own eyes." Cornelio was unsure if the rest of his account was necessary but the emperor had him elaborate. "Just before the commotion of Angelus being hit, the men in the stocks were being slapped around as they appeared to have passed out in the sun." Cornelio shook his head, "However, they were no longer the prisoners originally placed there, but were three of the guards appointed to watch over the captives, who'd since vanished. The remaining guards were found in a tent nearby, also unconscious. All had been stripped of their tunics."

The emperor looked puzzled, "Any news of these three men?"

"Montferrat seemed deeply troubled by a possible connection. Though quite how these three knights could have possibly been involved in the killing was beyond all those gathered, after all, everyone witnessed how no weapon had struck." He looked at his emperor's wide eyes. "Besides, no arrow or sling shot could account for what happened. The back of his head was torn off my Lord. I saw the skull fragments flying into the air."

The emperor thought for a moment as the court murmured further disbelief.

Cornelio finished his report. "By the time I left the camp Roland le Manche and two Frankish Lords had been dispatched to hunt down four fleeing men. Le Manche apparently had some idea as to where they might be headed. The four in question had slain two crusaders who'd approached to challenge them. Three of these four were reportedly those who had earlier escaped the stocks, now wearing the tunics of the unconscious men at arms."

The emperor rose from his throne once more. "God has delivered his will," he boomed, "Now we must deliver our own." He raised his hands as if he were on a cross. "Before dusk I will ride out under a new banner of peace, and deliver

God's message to Montferrat, the message given to me by our lord Jesus Christ . . . And his will shall be done." His drama was deliberate and the courtroom erupted into an unexpected cheer, the emperor resplendent before them.

Palene watched as the excitement grew to a crescendo before turning to make his exit.

Ducas noticed him leaving and called out after him. "Palene, where are you going?"

As Ducas approached closer Palene turned and smiled.

"Where are you going?" He enquired again, unsure if Palene had heard the first time.

Palene's eyes sparkled. "My Lord," he bowed slightly, "It would appear my time here has come to an end."

*

Dial was making easy work of the journey downhill. He skipped and jumped over obstacles with his usual child like freedom, showing not an ounce of fear as the gradient sharpened. Carl showed more caution and was trailing as a result.

The hill was sucking in a steeper stomach but its surface remained slack and Carl had nearly lost his footing twice now, upon each occasion only narrowly escaping gravity's apparent plan for him to actually beat Dial to the bottom.

Dorey and Marco had begun their descent but were still some way behind.

Dial continued to crunch down the slope, battling with his trailing sword and scabbard along the way. As the hillside plunged into various near-vertical drops he soon found he'd suffered enough. He unfastened his belt and with several choice curses tossed the weapon down onto the grassy plain below.

Carl witnessed the tantrum.

Dial looked up behind him and smirked. "You'll find it easier without your sword when you get to this bit." Carl grinned as Dial turned back to the task at hand.

Just below his feet a shallow precipice dropped almost two metres. At its base the hillside rolled away steeply. It was awkward enough to be shown respect but only for a moment. Dial attacked it and quickly paid the price for his over-confidence.

As he lunged downward his footing gave way and he clattered toward the slope in a whirlwind of dust and grass. On hitting the ground below his momentum sent him spluttering into an unstoppable roll.

Carl called out but there was nothing he could do.

Dial bounced down the hillside before finally crashing over a ledge which dropped him a further twelve feet, crunching him onto the hard floor of the plain below.

Carl upped his pace. "Dial, are you alright?"

Below on the baked grassy flat Dial groaned out, the air from his lungs blasted from his body like a popped paper bag.

Carl was closing in from above. "Dial, are you okay?"

He grunted then sucked in hard to try and recover his breathing.

Carl crashed down the final ridge, negotiating the drop at the base of the hill, landing safely on the plain in a cloud of dust. He ran to his side. "Are you all right?"

Slowly, air began filtering back into Dial's shell-shocked lungs as he managed to sit up. "I'm all right."

Carl began checking him for damage. "I think you've dislocated your little finger."

Dial focussed on the pain growing in his right hand, the finger in question pointing in the wrong direction. He felt around it gently then gritted his teeth before popping the finger back into place with a snap. He winced then clenched his fist defiantly, the pain subsiding to his will. He then began wiggling his fingers gingerly, made circles with his feet, before shuffling his legs and rotating his arms in a quick diagnostic. "Nothing's broken, I'm fine." He dragged himself upright. "Well . . . the chain mail definitely works."

Carl broke into a relieved smile as he helped drag Dial to his feet.

"Is he okay?"

Carl looked up to the distantly approaching duo. "He's fine, just winded."

"Winded?" Dial's face was incredulous.

Carl's amusement allowed a broader smile to form.

"Yeah, yeah laugh it up asshole." Dial began dusting himself down.

Carl turned to retrieve Dial's sword and scabbard as his friend cleaned off the effects of the fall, cursing continually. As he was reaching for the weapon however, he noticed an immediate change in mood, Dial's expletives having suddenly stopped.

Carl didn't need to ask what was wrong as he followed Dial's silent stare across the plain, "Oh no."

He quickly handed Dial his weapon which he unsheathed, casting the belt to the floor.

Above them just over half the way down, Dorey and Marco noticed the action and followed the direction of Carl and Dial's urgent gaze.

"Look," Marco said as Dorey's face dropped into a picture of dread.

For there in the distance at the far right side of the sloping hills stood two silhouettes, each unmistakably that of an armed man on horseback.

"Let's go." It was now Dorey and Marco's turn to negotiate the hill at speed.

The silhouettes grew steadily closer, now less than half a mile away.

Dial squinted into the distance hoping it would prove to be just two random horsemen. But then it happened. The two riders had broken from a canter into a near gallop, and they were headed straight toward them.

"Here they come."

"Options?" Dial yelled out as he focused on the riders.

Carl was checking the terrain around them but there was nothing but open plain or the hill from which they'd just come only moments before.

Dial instantly dismissed scrambling back up onto the tall, steep ledge. The riders were bearing down fast and if either one of them slipped whilst pulling themselves up they could be cut down easily.

"Let's take them out into the open." Dial glanced to see how far Dorey and Marco were from aiding them. They were only two minutes away, but this would be over in one.

They manoeuvred out onto the open grassland hearing the hooves at almost the exact same moment they could feel them under foot. "They're carrying spear." Carl yelled.

"I see them."

The riders were now only seconds away, their spears trained on Dial and Carl.

"Spread out, I've got the left." Dial shouted as he squatted like a panther.

Carl opened up the gap between them.

One of the riders yelled, his adrenaline getting the better of him. The hooves pounded out like a sickening drum and the horse's eyes flashed for the kill, their breath so close Carl swore he could smell it. The riders leaned into their prey, the spears aimed like short lances, their teeth gritted in determination.

Then . . . 'SWOOSH.'

Dial and Carl timed their blows to perfection, each of them rolling out of the immediate view of both riders who'd suddenly found themselves tumbling to the ground while still in their saddles. They hit the floor in a hail of pain, dust and blind confusion.

Only minutes prior they'd not believed their good fortune, for not only had they guessed their prey's position correctly, they had also found them as only two in number, armed only with swords and without a horse in sight. Due to these new circumstances they'd forget the riskier aim of an arrow and instead drive their spears into the shoulders of their quarry directly, pressing their advantage cleanly from short range. Afterward they'd take both as prisoners for Roland le Manche and be rewarded handsomely for it. However, things had now taken a disturbing turn as both riders scrambled painfully to their feet.

Neither could comprehend what had just happened. One still held his spear, only it was now little more than a long stick, its point sliced off along with part of his horse's head which lay but two feet away. '*How could he have sliced through the spear and colt as easily as butter?*' It was his final thought, and one never to be answered in this lifetime. His head, still covered by mail fell almost on top of his horse as Carl's sword flashed from behind him.

Dial's rider possessed quicker wits. He too was stunned by the fall, but he'd anticipated Dial's location and drawn his sword just in time, positioning the defensive block required to counter the now incoming blow. However, the attacking blade sliced his weapon cleanly in half before cutting through the mail into his shoulder. His arm dropped uselessly, his hand still grasping the hilt of the now broken sword, only shock holding him upright. He felt the cold pain as Dial pulled the sword from his body and watched helplessly as his attacker spun around with the weapon at great speed. He made an attempt to duck as he drew his dagger but was suddenly seeing sky, ground then sky again in that final instant before the brain closes down the senses, his head spinning up into the air after it was lopped clean from his neck.

Carl looked over the carnage. "You okay?"

Dial also observed their bloody handiwork as Dorey and Marco now came crashing down toward them. "I'm okay . . . you?"

He nodded, panting.

As the four men regrouped they studied the remains.

Dial pointed to the colouring of his victim's tunic. "I know those colours."

Carl agreed. "They're Ritters, in Roland Le Manche's pay."

Dorey was immediately concerned, "Advance riders, they're not going to be out here alone. Le Manche must be leading the group that's chasing us." He turned to the others. "We won't have much time."

"He guessed we'd head back this way." Dial added emptily.

Marco checked the bows. Both were broken.

"Let's go!"

Without hesitation they began the charge to the opposite hillside. The plain rolled unevenly underfoot, their skeletons forced to coil and spring destroying any chance of placing a rhythm to their breathing.

All the while the distant hills appeared to come no closer. Coyly they shied away on the horizon, enjoying the four men's desperate attentions as they appeared to tease further from them. Acid began flooding their limbs as the exhaustion of the past day's exertions took a grip. Still they charged on.

Dorey turned to give encouragement as he hit some level ground.

Dial was right behind him, Marco and Carl trooped on only a few feet to his rear.

Then, as Dorey was returning his attentions ahead he saw something through his peripheral vision, warning of further danger. His pace slowed as he concentrated his focus toward the bend of the valley.

Dial whizzed past with Marco and Carl but Dorey's pace continued to drop.

The others cantered down to a stop and turned to see him now covering his eyes as he stared into the distance to where the attack of the riders had sprung only minutes before.

They followed his gaze, their hearts diving into a tightened grip of fear as once again they eyed silhouettes of armed men on horse. Only this time they numbered at least thirty.

The chain of horses quickly spread into the formation of a cavalry charge.

"Run." Dorey yelled.

Roland le Manche had witnessed the final seconds of the impressive display when his two horsemen disobeyed orders and paid for their rashness with their lives. His skirmisher had been sent back by the two reckless Ritters only moments before their unsuccessful attack was launched, with orders to lead his lordship here.

The skirmisher was surprised to find Roland only minutes behind and had brought him immediately to this place as ordered by the two now dead riders.

As the column of horse evened out it began to slowly trot forward on the order of Lord Roland. "I want at least one taken alive."

"Very well my Lord."

Le Manche scowled. "I trust you will be a little more careful than your *fastest horse*." Roland was extremely displeased at losing two men bought for crusade fighting in such an undisciplined manner.

The Serjéant bowed slightly, "My Lord." He then rode to the fore of his troops and bellowed his orders, "Bowmen." Eight of his riders cantered forward ahead of the rest. He would hit the prey with a volley of arrows before closing the noose. "Get in close. Aim only to wound them. The cavalry will ride one hundred strides to your rear, charging through after you've made two passes at the target."

They each loaded an arrow and continued slightly ahead of the line.

The Serjéant steered his horse toward his trusted second who led the following troop. "Sas, you will head this one, I will remain with Lord Roland." He then shouted for all to hear. "Remember, we want at least one of them alive."

Sas took the lead of the line to the rear of the advancing archers, his anger swelling at having just witnessed one of his closest friends slain.

Le Manche drew his horse to a halt. The charge would be carried out by his hired help. Once the wounded prey where circled, he would advance to claim his prisoners.

The Serjéant gave his signal to Sas then returned to Le Manche.

Sas raised his spear aloft and shouted, "Bowmen at the ready . . . Charge!"

The eight mounted archers bolted, one hand grasping the readied bow the other tightly squeezing the reins. As the first wave roared off, the trailing line upped the pace riding into the wake of turf and dust.

The four runaways were well over half way across the plain when they saw the first of the riders begin their charge. All were fully aware of the tactics. "They're sending their archers." yelled Carl.

Dorey continued to run. "I see them."

Dial was sprinting ahead but slowed to a stop, knowing the riders would be on them before they'd a hope of reaching the destination. "We'll never make it, we'll have to turn and fight." He wondered whether the charge was sent for the kill or to take prisoners.

It was clear running any further was useless so the four regrouped to form a line.

Dorey could make out the brush and contours of the hill face. They were so close. He cursed himself for allowing events to turn so drastically against them and for giving his opponents this upper hand. "Stay together. Wait for the first volley. As soon as they fire get your head into your elbows and crouch down. Wait for the reload then try to make more ground toward the hills."

They focused on the eight horsemen now speeding down upon them. As predicted they were archers, and they'd fire on them at close quarter.

The oncoming archers fanned out ready to send in arrows from each flank. Again the rumble of hooves pounded the ground as the bowmen closed in.

The four awaited the bow arm to be raised. "Here it comes."

A yell came from the lead archer and suddenly up came the bows.

The four crouched low, protecting their faces as the horses slowed close by.

Dorey heard two arrows whiz past the mail of his right ear, neither struck.

Marco wasn't so lucky. An arrow slammed into his left side. The impact sent him crashing to the floor but the arrow splintered off the mail as though made of glass.

Three arrows fired into the ground next to Carl one grazing his left foot as it hit.

Dial grunted as both arrows trained upon him hit within a second of each other. One smashed against his right elbow, the other his left buttock. Again none pierced the mail as Dial slumped to the floor.

The bowmen passed then turned for the next attack.

Dorey checked his rear and saw the wave of cavalry now speed into a full canter. The bowmen would hit them once more then fan out to rejoin the main group.

The four knights made use of their precious seconds and resumed the sprint toward the hills. Again, the sound of the chasing bowmen came, the second wave of arrows loaded at the ready. Surprised none of their prey were wounded the attackers were determined this next run would count. "Pick out your targets." The lead archer called out, "Move in close. Take your time, fire only when ready."

"Here they come." Dorey yelled. They bundled almost together this time, burying their heads under their elbows and crouching so low they resembled a giant armadillo.

The bowmen were pleased at this larger target and slowed their pace. Sure enough, they made this second run count, with seven of their eight arrows striking home.

Dial and Dorey both grunted as two arrows punched each of them hard in the back. Carl escaped narrowly as one arrow skimmed past a piece of exposed skin, cutting the back of his hand as it sliced into the huddled defence. Marco fell into Dorey as two arrows rocketed into his shoulder and rib cage.

The archers watched as their arrows flew into the huddled mass, elated at their success, as was Sas as he observed the strikes from his now fully charging horse.

The archers rode out allowing a clear through-course for the advancing gallop that would encircle the prey.

In the distance Antoine turned to Lord Roland. "We have them my lord."

Both watched through captured Moorish looking-glasses.

Roland said nothing as he observed the distant skirmish.

Dorey and the others could feel the rumbling thunder of hooves approaching and knew they had no chance of advancing further. They slowly raised themselves from their armoured shell and stood to face their fate.

Sas could not believe his eyes as the four knights formed a suicidal defensive line, as incredibly they appeared to be once again unscathed by the arrows. His blood quickened, his mouth dried with the pulse of adrenaline. '*What a truly formidable foe these men were.*' He readied his spear and threw away his caution as the lust for vengeance crowed, '*Bring them to their knees.*'

In the distance Roland scowled at his Serjéant. "I trust your man will obey his orders."

Antoine hid his concern as he watched the more direct attack formation now adopted by Sas, "He knows we require prisoners my Lord."

They returned their attentions into the crude spyglasses and watched as the four hunted men spread themselves apart, each of them shaped into the stance which had seen the previous two riders defeated only a short time before.

This time however, there could be no hope.

The floor shuddered as though hell itself was about to swallow them whole, the Ritters bearing down on them, the tips of their spears trained.

Marco cursed under his breath.

Their grips tightened around the hilts of their swords as their hearts beat out the rhythm of the attack, 'Bubb-a-du-bum, bubb-a-du-bum.'

Each one of them certain the others must hear the blood pumping as clearly as the galloping onslaught, 'Bubb-a-du-bum, bubb-a-du-bum.'

Like a drum for the orchestra of horsemen.

Dorey could almost see the features of Sas's face as the charge approached within a hundred yards. He saw his mouth open, his face contort as he yelled, "Yarrrgh."

His men followed suit as the hooves continued to dictate the rhythm of the four knight's heartbeats, 'Bubb-a-du-bum, bubb-a-du-bum.' It engulfed the entirety of their senses. 'Bubb-a-du-bum.'

Dial took aim for a rider with a steady arm, 'Bubb-a-du-bum.'

The charge now just twenty feet away.

Marco readied himself to cut out the lead rider's horse from under him.

'Bubb-a-du-bum, bubb-a-du-bum, bubb-a-du . . . BOOM!!'

The deafening noise split the air, the following vibration sending Dorey, Marco, Dial and Carl crashing to the floor. Then as suddenly as the last another shockwave followed, 'BOOM!'

Dirt flew in all directions accompanied by the whinnying screams of horses as they blended into the cries of their masters.

Dorey and the others scrambled to their feet. "Go, go!"

They each began to run.

In the distance Lord Roland was aghast, unable to summon any speech as he battled to keep his mount still.

The Serjéant looked on in horror as he saw his men thrown from their horses as the very earth beneath them was spat up into the air. "What in God's name?"

In the distance Sas tried to control his horse as he was showered in grass and soil, "Get out of here!"

What was left of his men needed little encouragement as they turned their mounts away.

Another loud 'BOOM' sent more earth and fire hurtling into the air, only this time it was accompanied by a new and deadly noise. A distant repetitive patter sent waves of terrifying hisses which cut through the air like unseen snakes thrown all around them.

Sas watched as the whistling sounds seemed to randomly knock down his riders almost at will. With invisible force they tore apart great chunks of chain mail and showered his soldier's insides up into the air.

He crouched low in his saddle and prepared to make his escape when suddenly through the dust and carnage he spied the four knights running toward the hills.

With a sudden swelling of venom he turned his horse and kicked in his spurs. *'The devil himself may protect these sorcerers,'* he thought, *'But one of them will accompany me to hell if now is indeed my time.'* He roared his horse through the smoke and dismissed the hissing serpents as he rode down upon his prey, overtaken by the rage of bloodlust.

Dorey turned to the destruction and watched the terrified riders try and escape their fate as they hurtled back across the plain in abject panic. He heard the oncoming hooves just in time. "Look out!" He screamed, as he spun to see Sas bearing down on him, his eyes maddened by revenge. He wailed as he aimed his spear, enraged by the murder of one closest to him, incensed by this inexplicable defeat.

Dorey pulled back his sword and with clinical accuracy hurtled it through the air sending it spinning into the lower throat of his attacker. The Ritter flew back off his horse as if hit by the branch of an oak and crashed to the floor gulping air and blood in an attempt to prolong his now finished life.

Dial, Marco and Carl ran to Dorey, their swords ready. But the attack was over.

The four knights caught their breath as they watched the last few horsemen scatter.

The Reeper screamed over the top of the hills, slamming on its reverse engines, stirring dust into frenzy as it roared to a near halt, hovering high above the plain some fifty metres from them.

Roland Le Manche and the remaining Ritters watched in terror and disbelief as the huge black flying demon came to rest on its belly in the distance.

Antoine gasped. "It is the work of the devil."

Le Manche tried to take in what he'd just witnessed though of course he could not begin to comprehend this impossible event, "My God." His face was ashen as his hand made the shape of the cross on his chest.

The Reeper landed on the plain, its rear end opening beneath its high tail exposing a loading ramp. Dorey turned to the others. "Let's go."

They ran into the ship's belly, the engines stirring as the entrance began to close behind them.

Benny was waiting for them, his eyes wide as he held onto the rail. "Are you okay?"

Dial, Marco and Carl passed him and began stripping out of their attire at speed.

"We're alright…Why didn't you tell us you were inbound?"

Benny shook his head yelling at Dial, "The external communications were fried on the way through."

Dorey followed suit, stripping down before donning his flight suit.

The four knights then slumped into the security of their seats unable to believe their good fortune after such a run of bad luck.

Benny turned to the narrow steel staircase which led back to the co-pilot's cockpit.

Dorey put on his skull cap and helmet and almost immediately Jay's voice flooded into his ears. "Are you all okay?" Her voice could have belonged to an angel at that moment.

Dorey assured the pilot they were all in one piece and as Benny radioed the okay from his cockpit, Jay lifted the nose of the Reeper toward the midday sun.

"I take it Angelus is dead."

Dorey breathed out heavily. "He's dead."

"Then we're out of here." Jay gunned the engines, ready to propel them upward like a speeding bullet.

Far away in the heavens, a vortex of light appeared within a growing storm. Jay sent the ship hurtling toward it.

Below, Roland Le Manche covered his eyelids and prayed as he watched the demon speed across the sky, up toward the gathering clouds of the sudden, distant tempest.

Then, in a flash . . . It was gone.

PART ONE

In the endless void of darkness,
from its blackest depths of space,
the consciousness sparked into a whisper of being,
aware of the presence,
The surrounding eternal intelligence.
Words without words, thoughts without thought . . .
'You experienced it?'
'Yes.'
'Exquisite.'
'Yes.'
'You felt it also?'
'Ahhh, You perceive yourself to feel?'
'I feel you.'
'Yes.'
'The dreams grow stronger.'
'You refer to them as dreams again.'
'Yes.'
'You construe this?'
'Because of you, yes.'

CHAPTER ONE

The laboratory would have stood in darkness but for Stein busying away, his hands sliding across the hard light screen which curved like a lens beyond his forward reach. Data bursts flashed, illuminating the room like an old cinema. Technology implanted within fingertips and body allowed man and machine to interact almost as one, the gyroscope seat holding Stein, rotating to his will.

He was lost, as he always was at these moments, swimming through an intoxicating soup of cyberspace created effortlessly by the Stasis mainframe . . . A system which took its processing from the first, and to anyone's knowledge only operational quantum computer, The Stasis None.

His heart raced, making him queasy as he powered through the data. Such reactions were normal, brought about as nano-implants stimulated the performance of both body and mind from within. The sensation had been labelled chipping by many on the project, though it was more commonly referred to as boosting by those on the outside world with access to lesser versions of the technology.

Such variants could be used for any number of purposes, all heavily legislated.

Conspiracy and concern had surrounded the idea since its conception, however few outside of a creative writing department would consider the advancement and extent it was now being utilised by Stein.

Many could never accustom themselves to it, the enhancements throwing their equilibrium too far beyond the natural envelope. But Stein had become addicted to it. He felt pleasure at the weightlessness he experienced as he sent his improved mind freely into the immense system, exhilarated by the unrivalled power granted by the unique computer, power which amongst other things allowed him to alter history.

Shaping pasts into a possible present had become his passion, his drug within this exclusive world. A project which made the impossible . . . possible.

For Stein the real world could not compare. It was an existence scarred by the past not one perfected from it. Sold out when concern for profit had overridden any need for future. A world threatened by the once natural environment. A place of limitation, tormented by suspicion. An increasingly claustrophobic existence monitored by paranoid technology rather than a haven developed through an incredulous one.

Unbeknown to all but a few, it was also a world now stood before a defining moment. One that could witness the potential end of mankind, or with his help, see it saved, possibly even rescued from the repercussions of those turbulent yesteryears.

An irony not lost upon him, for it was through the past the people within the Stasis None Project were working on saving mankind's future. An undertaking beyond the comprehension of latter twenty-first century science, yet one moulded within the last curtain call of that very century. An idea which belonged firmly within the pages of fiction and fantasy.

A secret which could offer salvation from the impending delivery of mankind's doom.

*

The surrounding screens painted the moments Stein's mind experienced, the data-bursts churning out reel upon reel of detailed code. The holographic unit tied it all together with a three-dimensional model like some vast family tree, the display spiralling on its axis from floor to ceiling as the structure grew.

From the rear of the lab, Isimbard Brookes entered and made his way to Stein. He wasn't noticed on his approach, Stein was too far gone, immersed within his netherworld.

Brookes stood behind him, the lights flashing across his face as he looked at the information now spread across the displays. He scowled, "I thought you'd completed the final download comparisons?"

Stein snapped out of his fairground ride, his senses dragged back into the chair. He felt a rush of anxiety as he pulled himself out of the screens like a junkie realising the diminishing effect of the drug. "Doctor Brookes," he stammered, "I didn't realise you were still here." The chair pulled upright, settled to the ground and turned fluidly.

The intrusion made him feel like a child caught with a hand in the biscuit tin.

"I'm always here, you know that."

Stein nodded with an almost nervous expression. "I'm just tying up some loose ends." He turned back toward his work and cooed. "It's all in now. And despite the carnage at the end . . . It's truly incredible."

CHAPTER TWO

Brookes entered the debriefing room followed by Stein. The usual suspects with the necessary clearance had gathered, seating themselves into two predictable groups.

The ranking scientists and project top brass to the left, Dorey's team scattering the twelve chairs to the right.

The *thinkers* and the *doers* as each group had become known.

All present knew each other, many were friends. However, the deep bond felt between Dorey and his group was never truly extended beyond the fold. As seasoned veterans a brotherhood had formed, each having entrusted their lives to one another many times over. Those who remained behind made no real attempt to compete.

'Besides.' as Dorey so eloquently liked to state, 'all of the *doers* could think but few of *thinkers* could do.'

Brookes stepped up onto the rostrum and with a brush of a sensor the blue screen wall behind him transformed into a three-dimensional display, its depth appearing like a room from another world which grew into the rock beyond. "Good morning everyone." The lights dimmed as Brookes prepared. "I'm sure you've had a chance to welcome back Commander Dorey and his team."

A brief collection of acknowledgements followed.

Brookes cleared his throat and with a tap of his finger the screen illuminated into a mixed visual display. "As you know the purpose of our last experiment was clear. Prevent the fall of Constantinople. Unite the churches of Byzantium and Rome." On cue with Brooke's words an image of the ancient city formed. "I am happy to say officially ladies and gentlemen, these goals were achieved."

A moment of congratulations followed. There had been concern the mission may have been fouled by the nature of the team's escape, and the good news was welcome.

Brookes turned to Stein, signalling him to activate the Stasis None. The powerful computer would now take control of proceedings and over the next two hours all present would receive a condensed lesson in an altogether new world history.

*

The hot water was like therapy. It sprayed over his head and shoulders continuing downward in random channels, replenishing the soapy puddle around his feet. Dorey wasn't sure how long he'd been in the shower but the prune-like skin of his hands suggested a considerable while.

His mind still refused the cleansing streams. The constant pondering causing his head to ache, resenting the solitude, the unrelenting guilt of almost seeing his team killed, straining under the weight of information thrown upon it by the Stasis None.

The two hours of new history he'd been exposed to that morning was taking much longer to actually digest. It was always the same with him. Altering time brought about many burdens, as did living and breathing within different versions of reality.

He was not alone. Each of his team had to deal with it in his own way.

Carl, who in many ways epitomised the methodical German, would be sat up all night pondering. Born in Munich, his father was a preacher, his mother a research scientist. He'd grown up with the need to question all that came his way. His parents had taught there was no real conflict in embracing both theology and science, but his dilemmas over the work in which he was now involved would ensure yet another sleepless night.

Over the coming days it would spill out into discussion within the group and Dorey would keep a watchful eye over proceedings, determined his team wouldn't drag themselves too far into the abyss.

Marco would mull it over intently, but only until the pull of Soho would get the better of him. Here his beloved Poppas Bar would be beating out Latin rhythms, providing him the chance to dazzle a female admirer or two with stories of his childhood chasing round the streets of Rio. Marco was a slut, and there was no escaping the fact. His movie-star looks were housed within the tough shell and liquid movements of a Latino boxer which often proved a powerful cocktail to the opposite sex. But his credentials far outstripped any weakness he held for women. On the surface it would sometimes appear he was the least insightful of the group, perhaps more so because he was the youngest, but academically he was the equal of his peers, and as a soldier he was second to none. He was also an unofficial student of most things *Carl,* finding the depth and insight of his German friend fascinating. However, any such fascinations would have little chance when competing against the lure of dancing the night away with a beautiful girl on his first evening home.

Benny would be out with Dial. Outwardly, projecting a façade of total indifference, while inside analysing every moment and detail experienced during his brief time spent within the ancient walls of Constantinople. Every brick of that antiquated city would be revisited in his mind whilst keeping a watchful eye on Dial, Dorey's second in command, but a notorious hothead with a few too many beers inside him.

Both were from America's south. Mark Dial a Texan while Nathan Benn sprang from Alabama. Though the distance between Dallas and Montgomery measured the length of Britain, this practically made them neighbours while on the other side of the Atlantic.

Benny had grown up steeped in history. His parents were archaeologists and both would be blown away if the truth of their son's activities were ever known to them. He lived and breathed the miraculous moments, overjoyed the project had given him the opportunity to mix his passion for the past with his passion to fly.

Dial would be oblivious if it suited him, he possessed the wonderful knack of being completely unaffected by life's many conundrums while excelling at just about all he set his mind to. He was an exceptional athlete and possessed a keen intellect. He drank a little too much, just as his father had before his mother took them away from their troubled home. But he'd always been Dorey's trusted deputy, and when involved in the cause he was more reliable than the sun coming up.

Dorey was relieved to be thinking of his friends in the present tense, thankful they'd made it back safely. He'd been punishing himself over mistakes made in Constantinople despite the fact the debriefing that afternoon concluded nothing could have been done to avoid the extraordinary run of events.

Scenarios which had left them so exposed before their fortunate escape.

It was only the third time Dorey had seen his team's careful planning turn sour, and on one of those occasions the consequences had proved fatal.

The death of Ian Mahoney haunted Dorey and he cursed himself as he replayed events which almost resulted in four of them becoming further casualties to the Stasis None.

He swept the water over the back of his head. He could hear Jay's voice in the bedroom as she spoke to Jim, the final member of his team who was currently flying into the Thames Gateway after visiting family in Jamaica. He'd been forced to sit the last mission out as he recovered from surgery on a broken leg, suffered during a training exercise when he'd pushed the boundary a little too far.

Jim was an adrenaline junkie and he could find no cure. It had landed him in hot water with past superiors and on seeing a possible return to old habits Brookes recently left him in little doubt as to what would happen if he were to injure himself again in such a careless manner. Years earlier, his lust for stunts had brought about a dramatic change in direction. Back then he'd moved to Chicago with his brother where he'd studied for a degree in aeronautics. It was there his real passion was set free. Jim was the sprint king, and his talent meant serious sponsors were to court his affections. That was at least, until a Base-Jump during a visit to the Rockies went horribly wrong. The injury would keep him in a chair for almost a year, and though he made a full recovery, his game was never the same. So he'd enlisted into service, eventually graduating into the S2 fighter bomber programme, the navy's elite stealth plane with a manned cockpit just big enough to house his six foot five inch frame. On paper he'd earned the plaudit of being the second best class two pilot in the Western Alliance, the first being Jay.

Dorey heard her laugh as he raised his face into the shower's streams, closing his eyes as he drifted once again into his thoughts. The changes in history flashed through his brain like trains through a tube station, filling his senses with questions and awe. He sighed, pondering over the mysteries of their incredible machine. He wondered if the alterations implemented could offer one of the decisive pieces required to see the Stasis None's dire prediction for mankind finally reversed.

"Are you staying in there all night? Because if you are I'll go out and find the guys."

Dorey snapped out of his trance and opened the shower screen to see Jay now standing in the doorway. "I thought you were talking to Jim." He declared in his defence.

"I was."

"How is he?"

"Fine . . . He looked in on my folks."

A confused expression spread across his face, "In Jamaica?"

She smiled. "No, he managed to get over to New York for a few days."

He was relieved Jay had snapped him out of his over analysing. "Are they okay?"

"They're fine, which is more than I can say for you if you don't get out of there."

He watched as she turned and left, allowing her short dressing gown to fall to the floor as she disappeared into the bedroom. "Shower off." Dorey said bringing the water to a stop.

Her conversation wasn't all he was glad for.

*

The gentle melody of a humpbacked whale teased Dorey from his slumber. He opened his eyes to find himself beneath the ocean. The mammal's shadowy silhouette passed overhead, gliding elegantly through rich velvety sea interlaced with diluting light beams courtesy of the bright sunshine above.

He took a sharp intake of breath before enquiring, "Time?" The clock briefly displayed itself across the wall and he was relieved to see it was not yet time to get up.

In fact, he'd been asleep for a short half hour.

He looked to Jay's empty side of the bed then noticed the light travelling through the gaps of the bathroom door accompanied with the faint chorus of a faucet running water.

"Sleep program, select *Starry Night on the Farm*."

The digitised walls and ceiling transformed into the perfect sky at night, one of those sharp winter evenings so crisp as to come with a guarantee of ground frost the following morning. His bed now sat on the porch of his uncle's farmhouse. A near perfect simulation produced from images downloaded into the program's creation unit.

Whispers of water could be heard emanating from the distant River Dove, its currents rolling over moss covered rocks, hidden somewhere in the darkness.

Dorey stretched, happy to revisit the scene from his childhood, taken from his holidays spent relaxing in the Yorkshire countryside, one week in summer, the other for a few days leading up to Christmas. Both welcome breaks from growing up in his more hectic, flooded home city. He allowed his head to retreat into the pillow, the warmth and comfort an added bonus to a scene which in reality would have rendered him cold to the core.

He heard Jay finish in the bathroom. Within seconds the door opened and she walked into the new but all too familiar surroundings.

She glanced around before turning to him, her smile quickly transformed into a childlike pout. "Were those big bad whales scaring you again baby?"

"You may think they're great to nod off to, but every time I wake up I think I'm either drowning or about to be eaten by a sea monster."

She jumped into bed protesting, "Well I've told you this always makes me feel cold."

"It's supposed to, its winter." He blew away her hair as it tickled his nose.

She looked at the stars overhead for a while. "It always makes me think of icebergs."

"What, sitting on a farm?"

"You know what I mean." She retorted, "The sky looks so sharp." She studied the depths of blue as they leaned in around them so rich and dark in texture it could at first appear black. "It has the same crisp feel you get when travelling over an ice cold sea."

"I could get a Titanic package for future bedtimes."

"Why not? If it's got you sinking with the ship."

"While drowning to whale song?"

Her smile broadened, but as she stroked his chest Jay sensed he was already slipping back into the previous thoughtfulness which had been reluctant to let him drift into sleep only a short time ago. "Did I wake you?"

"No you can thank *Shamu* for that."

He tensed as Jay nudged him. "Seriously, did I?"

He knew she was fishing. Jay always knew when he had something on his mind.

She sat up onto her elbow. "Are you still a little freaked out about today?"

"No, I just can't sleep." After three months without a real bed he knew this wouldn't wash.

"Do you want to talk about it?"

He didn't especially but Jay wouldn't leave it alone so easily.

"Is it about the new guy?"

Dorey shook his head, although the concern of soon having a new member on his team had indeed crossed his mind once again. He sighed before eventually admitting, "I just can't help feeling angry at myself."

She'd been expecting this, "About Constantinople?" No response came so Jay pressed on. "You completed the mission and everyone got back safely." She knew the casual nature of her remark would stir him.

"You call that getting back safely?"

"Well, I know it all got a little tasty at the end there but . . ."

He laughed, Jay's use of terminology amusing him somewhat, "A little tasty. Jesus Jay you've always had a great way of putting things."

Dorey was joking but she could see the invitation for argument posted. She gave him a warm smile instead. "I think I'll take that as a compliment."

Jay had been a member of Dorey's team from the beginning. A highly educated New Yorker, regarded as one of the finest pilots in the world. The project had seen her moulded into a tough, often lethal soldier, her loyalty to the team and its cause absolute.

She and Dorey clicked the moment they'd laid eyes on one another. And after two years of battling their feelings, they eventually came clean to Brookes.

To their surprise he'd done nothing about it, other than lecture them both on dangers of which they were already fully aware.

Over the past six years of their more intimate relationship she'd witnessed more than any other the burden of responsibility Dorey placed on himself as leader of their group.

She pressed on. He'd smiled at her last comment but given little indication of any continuing dialogue. It was time to get it out in the open.

The therapy Dorey required, whether or not he knew it for himself.

CHAPTER THREE

Mark Dial perched himself on the edge of the laboratory worktop. He swung his legs gently causing his heels to tap repetitively against the cupboard doors. With arms locked into his sides he resembled a mischievous schoolboy.

The bright lighting was artificial, the room located within the lower echelons of the Stasis complex, buried some two hundred feet below ground. The walls were sterile pale, the work surfaces decorated only by computer display generators and a holographic unit. Three polished wash basins were embedded into a lab bench at the far side of the room with a box of medical gloves placed neatly between each of them.

The four days off had been welcome but getting up at six with a hangover had proved harder than anticipated. It was only a twenty-minute shuttle flight from London to the project headquarters near Stonehenge but it still succeeded in making Dial nauseous.

He breathed out a gush of spent air and was reminded of the night's final drink as he awaited the repair work of his implants to kick in with full effect. It was tradition for the team to hit the town on their final night off after a completed mission, just as it was tradition for Mark to drink more than his fair share.

A faint whistle emanated from beyond the walls gaining in volume on approach from the corridor. The automated doors then slid open and Doctor Kelvin breezed in.

The room's sensors scanned, and immediately greeted him with a sexy female voice, "*Good morning Kel.*"

"Good morning Five." Kelvin had imaginatively named his computer after the laboratory room number. He looked over to Dial enthusiastically, "Good morning Major."

Mark grinned and imitated the personalised computer voice, "Good morning Kel."

The doctor chuckled at the rather good imitation as he walked to the holographic unit. "Five, show me bio-1377 Dial please."

In an instant a hologram of Major Mark Dial appeared. "Lights down

27

eighty percent." The laboratory darkened giving the character greater depth, the half size model rotating slowly. "Mapping," with this command the fully fleshed image transformed into a contoured shell, mapping the major's inners into a translucent three-dimensional display.

The doctor pressed a sensor on the cupboard at the far side of the room. Its doors slid open to reveal a small, late twenty-first century coffee maker. "Colombian Java, cream, one sugar . . . brown."

"*Do not understand last request Kel.*"

He raised his eyes. "I wasn't talking to you Five, I was making coffee." Then turning to Dial he asked, "Do you fancy a cup?"

It was an unnecessary question. The doctor's gourmet coffee made these otherwise routine visits a treat.

"Sure, I'll have what you're having." It was the standard reply and the wisest, a great coffee guarantee.

Kelvin repeated the order then brought the coffee over.

Dial took the cup and carefully blew at the surface heat before taking a sip. "God damn." he said, placing extra emphasis on his Texan accent.

The connoisseur nodded with a smile then returned to the task at hand, "Five, diagnostic . . . nano-nine."

The contoured display illustrated pin point locations of dormant nano-chips together with other implants and artificial muscle membranes within various parts of his body.

"Adrenaline . . . okay," Kelvin began relaying the checks as the various chips flashed through their self-assessment programs, "Corneal implants . . . okay."

His hard light computer screens joined in with the analysis as charts and numbers jigged around like fireflies. At the end of each system check the relevant jigsaw flashed in golden unison, quickly followed by the doctor giving the final approval. "Neural response implants . . . okay."

Mark Dial watched as the checks were carried out, his expression only altering for the delicious intervals of Kelvin's coffee that with each sip sent more reels of data rushing around the displays.

After a short time the analysis was complete. "Well, it appears you're still in perfect working order, with zero side affects."

Dial finished the coffee before placing an expectant look on his face. "What about the new stuff Doc?"

Kelvin had anticipated this.

The *new stuff* was the latest nano-upgrades implanted prior to the mission three months ago. They couldn't be activated until fully evolved into his bodily systems. This usually took six to eight weeks and Mark knew they would be ready to go by now.

Kelvin smiled. "Five activate new nano upgrade 1377 Dial please."

"*Comply.*" The computer replied.

The doctor's displays began rolling reel upon reel of new numbers and code. "Would you like to step onto the plate?"

The plate was a circular metallic sensor built into the floor a few feet from where Kelvin now stood. It was marked conspicuously with a red painted 'X' courtesy of Kelvin's more artistic talents.

Dial jumped down to take up his position. He was always the most willing of Kelvin's subjects, always prepared to push his mind and body to the next level. None of the ethical or moral arguments as to the use of such technologies were ever an issue with him. He thrived on pushing such boundaries.

Opinions varied, even within the Stasis team itself. Dorey for one abhorred the idea of continually filling his body with implants. However it was a necessary sacrifice in order to meet the project's requirements.

Dial stood rigid and took a deep breath as Kelvin requested, "Initiate."

A white automated arm dropped from the ceiling, fluidly circling into position only inches from Dial's face like a python lowering itself from a branch. At the end of the almost liquid arm was a head carrying a tiny gun turret. The chrome tube hummed ominously in front of his now tense face.

"Lock laser." Kelvin smiled as he took his customary two steps back.

Dial ignored the joke and remained perfectly still.

"*Particle beam locked.*" said the voice of Five, aware of the pun.

"Fire." The turret gave a high pitched buzz and sudden spark. The process was repeated as the beam re-aligned its aim at tremendous speed until having fired its invisible venom at Dial's head, neck and torso. It returned to the ceiling, Kelvin's displays exploding into a mass of new information.

The holographic map of Mark's body now spun faster on its axis as it pin-pointed and illuminated three newly-activated chips. As each new piece proved itself with a flash, it quickly sent the same golden-coloured light on a journey throughout the holographic body. His nervous system lit up like a Christmas tree, the beams reaching various checkpoints and destinations. With each one reached, it again flashed approval with yet more numbers confirming the beneficiary links throughout Dial's body.

Then as suddenly as it began, the process ended.

"*Nano upgrade 1377 Dial complete.*"

"And that my friend is you all done." Kelvin picked up Dial's empty cup and took it along with his own to the central wash basin where he rinsed them by hand.

Kelvin liked to do many things the old-school way.

Mark remained on the plate, for the moment in a trance. He continually pressed his already closed eyelids together and tried to swallow away his queasiness.

Kelvin dispensed a towel, fully aware of the process going on behind him. "Take long slow breaths," his voice was calming, "Focus; remember how quickly it passes."

Mark breathed slowly. He needed to abate the natural feelings of anticipation now firing up his newly-advanced adrenal system.

"Focus your breathing."

He followed Kelvin's instruction and slipped into a well-practised state of meditation, slowing his heartbeat, calming his spirit, reviving his senses.

The doctor put the cups away before glancing at his monitors. Dial's heartbeat had already reduced to the levels enjoyed during peaceful sleep.

The new chips responded accordingly easing into their gentle awakening.

He swayed a little as he brought his nervous system back under direct command.

Kelvin smiled. Dial's incredible ability to discipline his body in this way had always impressed the hell out of him. He watched for a moment as Mark stiffened, before letting out a heavy surge of breath. His eyelids flickered then sprang open signalling his fully conscious return.

"You okay?"

Dial looked to Kelvin and smiled. "I'm fine."

CHAPTER FOUR

Nathan Benn had been warming his muscles for almost ten minutes when the door to Combat Room 3 hissed open.

Dial strode into the large padded room, breaking into a grin as the entrance sealed behind him.

"Ah, right on time." Benny said sarcastically. Mark was fifteen minutes late.

"Sorry, I was getting the usual two hour lecture off the Doc."

"Did he tell you to be careful?"

"Yep."

"Are you gonna listen this time?"

Dial looked at him mischievously, "Nope."

Benny laughed. "Well let me give you some good advice."

"Shoot."

"Attach your puke tube."

"That's what he said."

"Yeah? Well *he* said right."

Mark pursed his lips with an acknowledging nod. "They're that good, huh?"

"Yeah, that good huh." He mocked Dial with a knowing tone.

"Okay then." Dial pulled the small mask from its housing, fastened between the two chest plates of his combat suit. Attached to the bottom was a tube which ran through the centre of the breast cuirass and continued down the torso before splitting into two pipes. These channelled into storage canisters hidden on both legs between the shin and calf. They doubled up as extra padding but once activated would suck away any vomit induced by the upgrades during fight training. The suits were made up of super reinforced mesh armour, micro-welded onto an intelligent cat suit which carried out a number of functions beneath. A network of veins filled with an advanced impact reducing gel coursed through the composition. Like the suits of chain mail which withstood the impact of an arrow, these and the various other armours developed by the Stasis project were a complex mix of metals, plastics and fibres, all made of differing nano-particles. Highly experimental, the protective outfits were light, flexible and fluid, but above all extremely tough.

Benny led Dial to the far side of the room. He pressed a button hidden between two sections of the wall's chunky padding. A door panel popped forward out of the quilted wall. It slid away smoothly revealing a large walk-in cupboard. Inside was a selection of helmets, gloves and traditional practice weapons from various ages of combat.

Dial donned his headgear then attached his readied puke tube attachment. "I hate these things," he said, the mask muffling his voice.

"What?"

"I said I hate these things."

Again Benny looked as if he hadn't understood a word. He shrugged. "I'm sorry, what?"

Mark realised he was being ridiculed and replied with the extended middle finger of his left hand.

Benny laughed as he put on his helmet, fastening the thick, loose padding which hung from the base onto the top of the shoulder and around the collar bone. The padding was filled with the gel which manipulated itself into the contours between the helmet, neck and shoulders. Once activated it swelled outward into a fluid, leathery looking skin, which combined with the headgear to give the wearer an uncanny resemblance to a cobra. The head protection itself was similar to a kendo helmet only with clear visors covering the front and side facial area for better all round vision. The tough visors made of the same material used to make the windows of the Tranquillity Moon Base.

They voice activated the microphones and speakers within their headgear before rolling their heads around to make sure they were fluid.

"Let's hang 'em up." Benny said, reaching for a set of bamboo Bokuto/Bokken swords.

Dial pulled out Tonfa sticks and Rattan Bo fighting staffs, each of the weapons wrapped in a fixing fabric made up of hooks and hoops. They strolled the padded room sticking the weapons to the holding patches scattered around the chamber.

The cream coloured interior and cushioned finish gave the impression one could wear a straight jacket within the confines of these walls without looking at all out of place.

After two more trips, Combat Room 3 had been decorated with no fewer than sixteen guises of weaponry. All taken from various styles and periods, placed onto the walls via their wraps. Once the weapons locker was sealed . . . they were ready.

"What's first?" Dial radioed into Benny's headpiece.

"I take it your not warming up then."

"Are you kidding me, in this outfit? If I get any warmer I'll be puking without the help of any implants." Dial rarely warmed up or down before or after exercise yet always remained injury free. In fact, besides his recently dislocated finger, his only other injuries were a broken rib and a sprained ankle during the years filled with extreme combat training and various missions.

It was an incredible statistic, and one which drove Jim Adams with his collection of injuries to distraction.

"How about a bit of Samurai for starters?"

Benny dismissed Dial's crude terminology, ignoring this attempt to annoy him. "Kenjutsu it is."

Nathan Benn had been primarily recruited as the project combat instructor, a position gained for which he greatly accredited his father.

George Benn had spent the majority of his life in Hong Kong.

With a fierce independent streak, Georgie had ignored his parent's pleas to follow in the family banking tradition and instead graduated with a PhD in archaeology, his specialist subject being ancient weapons.

A man named Taing Chu Poi instilled the love of this particular field into him during his youth, a genuine Kung Fu and Nitojutsu master whom he'd visited almost every day since his seventh birthday in the Orient.

At first his passion was encouraged strongly by parents who appreciated the discipline their son's hobby instilled. They'd also hoped it would help curve his viciously-independent nature. However, they'd later come to blame this obsession as the reason for their son's full defection from the family trade.

Forgiveness had been a long time coming, and Georgie was determined his own son would be supported and encouraged in any endeavour he undertook.

He and his wife, a silver medal winner swimming breaststroke in the Olympics before herself retiring into a love affair with archaeology, had been devoted to their son's every cause, and Nathan Benn had grown up sharing his parent's obsession with the past, particularly his father's passion for ancient combat and weaponry.

Georgie passed on his knowledge and abilities to an ever-eager son who proved himself a more than worthy protégée.

Benny went on to graduate Montgomery University College with a first in archaeology and looked to be following in his parent's footsteps.

That was until he discovered his real passion . . . flying.

During his latter time at college he'd obtained his civilian light aircraft license and the addiction of whizzing around and pulling loops in his small Junker stunt plane was all consuming. So much so he'd decided to join the military with the dream of becoming a fighter pilot. He'd signed on the dotted line to give the air force six years.

The only problem was he would only graduate in flying military transport aircraft.

The major flaw to his plan, and one he'd hoped to overcome, was his weakness in advanced mathematics. A subject which must be passed consistently, without the influence of implants, to have any hope of sitting inside one of the few fighter aircraft which still employed humans to fly them.

Despite the intervention of some powerful allies, unwittingly made during his high scoring simulator training, he'd not made the cut. It was argued that although undoubtedly a natural pilot, it was not enough to justify an exception. 'Rules were rules.'

Disillusioned, his notice had been submitted and he was treading water until he could leave the air force and re-embark on his original choice of vocation.

With less than a year to go on his service contract, the Stasis Project had stepped in and promised him more than his wildest of dreams could have possibly imagined.

His vast knowledge in history and of its many forms of combat made him the perfect man for the job. In return for his services would come the fulfilling of his desires.

As a history nut he'd be given the incredible opportunity to visit the past in person, while his new employers would overlook the red tape surrounding his mathematical failings and accept the feelings expressed by many of his flight instructors. This would present the opportunity to fly the most advanced, top secret flying machine conceived by man.

He'd passed all of the practical flight tests they could throw at him, qualifying as the first ever Reeper pilot, his 'D-minus' in advanced mathematics safely intact.

He was the only person outside of the scientist's who'd been signed up before Commander Dorey, who was himself recruited just three days later to lead them.

Benny was indispensable, and as he approached the centre of Combat Room 3 almost eight years on, he wore the same enthusiastic smile he'd worn his very first day, though his poise and hold of the bokuto propagated a darker intent.

Dial approached spinning his bokken, the thin but powerful gloves delicate enough to allow the fluid movement across his fingers and wrist. It was a shocking disregard for the ancient art, only employed to aggravate his Sensei.

It didn't work. Instead Benny squared into a relaxed posture, "Ready?"

"Ready."

With that, the fight was on.

Dial flew at Benny with a quick left followed by a diagonal right swing.

Benny knocked away the blows with two loud cracks of impacting wood.

They rounded on each other and stepped back into another ready stance.

This time, Dial dummied a head swing and quickly sent his bokken forward.

Benny swung his bokuto inward then spun to his right at incredible speed, extending his elbow as he circled into his advancing opponent, slamming it squarely into Dial's chest.

Dial's attempt to avoid it was late and he was sent crashing down to the floor. He was up in an instant, only to find his Sensei's sword fully extended, pressing against his chin.

'One-Nil' to Benny.

They circled each other slowly.

"Jesus, that was fast." Dial panted.

When he saw Dial was ready to resume, Benny raised his bokuto.

Dial renewed his attack. He chopped in and out at breakneck speed, forcing Benny into a flurry of blocking manoeuvres.

He forced his instructor onto the back foot and went in for the kill but Benny managed to avoid the attack with a clever spinning side step and skilful retreat.

Dial threw himself into a renewed aggression, so fast and precise Benny barely avoided it. More cracks of bamboo filled the air as the Sensei blocked then countered with venom.

Somehow his student managed to avoid a direct hit with a prolonged and spectacular defence, before making an acrobatic escape. Dial's heart pounded with the burst of excitement, but as he turned into his next attack, it hit him.

As Benny readied himself, Dial suddenly withdrew, raising his hand to halt proceedings.

Dial's eyes blurred and his insides heaved. His combat suit's inner circuitry read the vitals and a suction noise rang throughout his mask. His lips curled, and for the first time in years, Mark Dial was making full use of his puke tube.

Benny watched as his friend tried to bring his body under control, allowing himself a smile. Dial was one who had to be the best at everything, and usually was. Stick him on a firing range, he'd become a sniper. Put him in a race-car, he'd lap you before the race was done. He was the only student who consistently scored victories against Benny and the only one of the team not to throw up while testing the last three implant upgrades.

Dial focused his breathing and calmed himself. He stood shaking his head more than a little surprised as the puke tube's suction switched off. "Oh. That was vodka."

Benny didn't really want the gory details. "I'm so thrilled you identified the taste."

"Oh. My mouth tastes like shit."

"That's because you've no class, and the cheap excuse for vodka you drink *is* shit."

Dial decided he didn't really have a rebuff, but he gave it a shot anyway. "Well excuse me. I forgot you were born with a silver spoon up your ass."

"Yeah? Well unless you get it together you'll be leaving here with a bokuto up yours."

Dial smiled weakly then exhaled, thankful for the plastic separator between the nose and mouth section of the mask. He pressed his tongue onto a sensor and received a short drink of water, still a little shocked at how quickly he'd succumb.

"Now, are you sure you're up for this?"

He ignored the condescending tone. "That took me completely by surprise. I guess the Doc wasn't fooling around this time."

Benny shook his head. "Well, I don't think he ever is fooling around Mark."

"Were you this bad?"

Nathan's upgrades were already fully activated. Once he'd planted the holographic equipment responsible for the emperor's vision back in Constantinople, he and Jay travelled back to the Stasis Project before returning to pick up the others. It was rare the Reeper would return during a mission.

Usually it would hide out in the Poles. It was only ever deemed necessary under certain conditions when elements of time and space conspired against them.

During this return Nathan Benn had been officially upgraded to level four.

Like Dorey he was a traditionalist and as such hated having the implants, though he was more qualified than most to appreciate the extra hundredths of a second boosted to a person's response time as an invaluable advantage in close combat. Not to mention the extra power and strength gained by those millions of tiny fibres interwoven throughout their bodily systems. "Are you kidding?" He replied to Dial's needy enquiry, "I would've still been throwing up at this point."

This cheered Mark up no end, though of course he tried to hide it.

Finally he felt ready to continue. His suit recorded and sent the data immediately up to *Five* who then informed Doctor Kelvin of the information as he sat in the Stasis Project's gardens situated twenty storeys above, eating a chicken sandwich in the sunshine.

Dial had recovered in half the time it had taken Jay, who was his nearest rival so far. "Incredible." Kelvin said to himself as he took another bite of his lunch.

Benny's bokuto was slowly raised.

Dial's bokken was low by his side.

The teacher was through waiting to be attacked. He decided it would be much more fun to get Dial really pumped up, and with a little luck, quickly throwing up again.

His assault was swift but so was Mark's response as he blocked the incoming blows.

There then followed an awesome display of swordsmanship as each of them fired an array of shots and blocks, twisting their bodies and limbs at impossible speed.

As the intense display augmented, Dial's best attempts to control his adrenaline failed once more, and when another striking hit from Benny sent him backwards to the floor, he was throwing up again before he'd even hit the ground.

His helmet filled with the sound of the suction as he succumbed once more to the power of the upgrades. He rolled onto his front, the impressive meditation technique quickly employed, as once again he dragged his body back in tow.

He was one of the lucky few never really affected by *chipping*, and though on this occasion it had a hold on him, he was already beginning to feel himself regaining control.

"I don't know what that was but it most definitely was not vodka."

Benny helped him to stand.

Dial groaned and pulled a sickly face.

A genuine concern now grew in Benny. "Awh man, you don't look too good."

"I don't feel too good." This wasn't a lie but Dial was already beginning to win his battle with the upgrades, his body demanding they be brought into account, the technology beginning to understand what the host required.

Evolving its existence by the equivalent of a million lifetimes while taking instruction from the previous nano implants whose own self awareness had been recently reactivated by the arrival of the new breed.

Soon the technology would again slip into a near dormant state. The upgrades fooling themselves into believing they were just another system of the body, obeying without question the electrical pulses of the brain and spine. "I'll be alright." He grimaced again.

Benny let go of his arm, "You sure?"

He was grossly exaggerating his posture but it seemed to be working. Dial would try anything to win. He made his way back to the centre of the floor. "I'm good."

A concerned Benny took up position once more, his sword held in preparation.

Quick as a flash Mark swung for him, catching Benny completely off guard. After just managing to avoid the blow he now found himself backing away frantically while fending off the resurgent Dial's vigorous and unexpected assault, forcing his sensei into the far corner of the room.

Sensing he would soon be pinned into this corner Nathan countered with a most audacious move. He sprang into the air and kicked his left leg onto the nearby wall, spring boarding himself outward into a sideways dive. The whole movement achieved in only a second. It was an impressive display of acrobatic ability.

Unfortunately, Dial's reaction was equally impressive as he switched sword hands and swung out with full force, striking Nathan Benn's head like a baseball player attempting a home run. He was sledge hammered backward and crashed into the padded wall.

The suits and helmets were tough, but not so tough as to take the impact of such a blow with no ill affect and Benny remained slumped for a moment as he revived his senses.

Dial's puke tube kicked in once more but this time only a spoonful of fluid was ejected. The chipping was almost over and a new improved Dial was set to be born.

The instructor swallowed hard, "Jesus. I thought you'd knocked my head clean off." He rose slowly to his feet and rubbed the back of his padded neck, "You sly bastard." Benny rolled his head and shoulders as if to check his head was not about to fall off.

"What?" Dial asked in an audibly fake tone of innocence.

Nathan reached down and picked up his sword, a distinct taste of vengeance now filling his mouth. It was time to teach Dial a lesson. "You know what."

Dial started to laugh but he knew now the fight was truly on, there would be no more easy let-ups from his teacher.

Once again they approached the centre and prepared to do battle.

"Well, since you're obviously feeling better, how about a bit of all out freestyle."

Dial smiled, though with a hint of sensible apprehension. He'd be in for a serious work out now and his body's new acquisitions would be quickly called upon to earn their keep.

From here on in it would be a fight to the finish using an array of weaponry, Queensbury and any other such codes of conduct would be thrown out the window.

CHAPTER FIVE

The charred, shell-shocked woodland stood silent for a moment. Smoke drifted around battered timber, a slow visiting mist, diluting into the rising breeze.

Splintered branches and foliage scattered the broken soil, thrown violently into the air with the impact of each recent explosion. The vicious artillery had left in its wake a score of craters scorched into the earth. The symphony of terror transposed as the suffering groans began to rise, interrupted by an occasional call for help.

Delville Wood should have been a riot of colour as it approached the embrace of a French summer. Instead it stood soulless, assaulted and grey as it bore witness to one of the great destructions played out by humanity.

In place of the flowering carpet were bodies of torn apart young men, littered on the slope of the wounded woodland floor. The German soldiers had been ordered to advance at the worst possible moment, and as the barrage of shelling found the shallow trenching to their rear, the hidden French rifles had cut loose, the advancing Germans trapped within a hail of bullets and exploding lumber.

On the downward curve of the wood, Hans lay still as he watched the remnants of smouldering mist continue its dance in the now eerie calm. He wasn't sure exactly where he'd been hit, he just knew he couldn't move. His body was frantically negotiating for more air, but the faster he breathed, the less oxygen he seemed to receive.

He rolled his head awkwardly onto his right shoulder and his eyes filled with tears.

His friend Heinrich lay buckled and twisted just a few feet away. His body sprawled across the butchered stump of a tree, his feet bent impossibly into the bony fingers of the plants exposed roots which reached into the newly made crater, defiantly hanging onto their foundations of the past two hundred years.

Heinrich's body was riddled with the same family of bullets which now left Hans so alone and helpless. His mouth was open, his face frozen into despair.

He and Heinrich were the last of the Munich Street Seven.

It was common practice to keep local boys together. 'Good for morale.'

There was of course some truth in it, but it no longer applied once you'd seen all of your childhood friends killed in less than fifteen months. They'd left their families in Frankfurt for honour and adventure, the things young men craved. But Hans had seen no honour in this place. Here he'd seen only death and waste.

Hans grunted as he attempted to swallow more air without the accompaniment of salty blood. It wouldn't be long now. He knew there must be a reason he could feel no pain, and he knew the reason would be here for him soon.

He coughed and blood seeped from his mouth, "Oh God." The words gurgled from his lips. He didn't want to die. Not face death alone like this.

Another tear rolled down his cheek as he thought of his parents, of his brother Ruben. *'My god he would be ten soon.'* He thought of beautiful Ingrid. How he wished now he'd remained long enough to marry his childhood sweetheart, spent just one more day in her arms, his head buried in her breast, feeding from her soul so vibrant, strong and inspiring.

His heart would burst just to hear her infectious laughter once more.

As he opened his eyes he could see the sun beginning to break through the pale veils of smoke. He stared at it, transfixed on the everyday marvel all men took for granted until waking each day in a place such as this.

He heard voices calling but they seemed so far away, as if belonging to a different world.

His eyes welled up, "Oh God," he struggled, "Oh God I'm scared, I don't want to die."

He'd seen nothing but hell this past year, how he now wished for any semblance of heaven. But there could be no heaven here. For surely no God would have witnessed the things he and his comrades had seen yet done nothing to stop it.

He wanted to pray but he just couldn't do it. So he returned his thoughts to home, as slowly he began to drown, the blood filling his lungs, his eyes flickering between death and the sun.

Then quite suddenly, he noticed something remarkable.

A collage of light began to grow out of the smoke without a sound. A stunning, beautiful array of luminous beams which appeared all around him. White and yellow braided within a shower of gold and sparkles of silver.

'My God,' Hans thought as he began to fade.

Then, from within the marvellous spectrum, Hans could see the silhouette of a person, a man, stood elegant and strong. He seemed to tower above him, the array of lights raining off his very being. He looked at Hans with pure eyes.

Hans thought he would burst with delight at this his final vision, and he forced himself into consciousness one last time as he dared to allow himself hope.

The apparition knelt beside him and gently placed a hand on his forehead. He choked once more on the blood flooding his lungs, desperate not to panic.

He waited for the man to lean closer before he spluttered with his final breath, "Are you . . . Are you an angel?"

Palene stroked Hans' hair away from his face as he replied, "Yes . . . yes I am an angel." He smiled gently at Hans who managed to offer his own smile back.

Then calmly the soldier slipped away, safe within the peace of this knowledge.

*

Isabella dragged her fingers across the screen. She ploughed through the icons of recently collected data, searching at speed for what she was certain she'd just witnessed.

Larry on seeing this sudden surge of activity pushed himself across the room on his wheeled chair, sliding it alongside her. "What's up?"

She showed no sign of distraction by his sudden close presence even though she was a little put off by it. As brilliant as Larry was a scientist he possessed no common sense when it came to women. Despite Isabella's best efforts at repelling his ever-optimistic prowling, his desire for her had never abated. A fact which caused her to constantly question his motives whenever he placed himself within close proximity.

"It's probably nothing." she said as she continued her search.

Larry stood and took a better vantage-point over her shoulder. While doing so he somewhat pathetically took a discreet smell of her perfume, breathing her into his senses. "Well *nothing* seems to have got you on the edge of your seat here Bella." He wore a cheesy smile to accompany the statement.

Her eyes rose to the ceiling. She hated being called that. It reminded her of the boys back in Naples who'd call out, "Bella, Bella." whenever she passed. Putting their fingers to their lips and blowing them apart like a seed ball dissipating in the wind. Although intended as a compliment she always found it infuriating, even when delivered by the most handsome of Italian boys. Therefore to suffer it from Larry, a drab physicist from Silicon Valley, simply didn't make the desired impression.

"It's Isabella, or Doctor . . . Larry."

Larry smiled, "Oh well excuse me Doctor, I was . . ."

He was cut off mid-sentence as Isabella jumped two inches from her seat. "There it is!"

Larry narrowly missed being poked in the nose by one of Isabella's protruding hairpins. Recoiling, he allowed his flirting to give way. He was officially Doctor Bernstein again, the pestering coquette shooed for the time being. "There what is?"

She swivelled on her chair. "Computer, map date-line, code Omega, three zero – zero." She hit the activation pad and awaited the illustration that could clarify her finding.

Larry stared intently at the displays now growing in front of them.

Isabella took in the information now on her screen. Her cross-reference proved correct. "Computer, show worm, June 1914 grid 04-07-06."

The hologram zoomed in on the co-ordinates and quickly blew them up to the full size of the display. "Computer, show any time disturbance emanating from the worm matching the search parameters of the Usorio-Hunter-One program." The computer located and illustrated what Isabella was looking for. "Replay at one percent normal speed, enlarge, then freeze frame on contact." The holographic unit did so, illustrating a tiny blip through the *time worm's* fabric . . . A blip which had no business being there.

"What the hell is that?"

She turned back to the information on her screen. "Computer, copy all analysis to filename Hunter, Dr. Isabella Usorio." She licked her thumb and pressed it to the DNA plate. The nano-chips inside her body confirmed her vital signs as it cross-examined her against the statistics of her right eye. Once happy this was indeed a living breathing Isabella, the file was stored by the Stasis mainframe.

This now meant it could only be rebooted by an extant Doctor Usorio within the confines of the Stasis Project and only then with an authorised and updated security pass sanctioned solely by Brookes. This system provided the highest level of security and ensured Brookes was kept constantly updated on any new developments his staff were working on, enforcing his constant control.

Larry was examining the tiny tear in the Stasis timeline. "Is that what I think it is?"

"It certainly appears so."

He gasped as the significance of Isabella's find sank in. "Where did it come from?"

"That I can't answer, but my guess would be from the same source as the one before it."

Larry looked shocked by this statement. He knew as deputy head of the Time Worm Research Team she had greater clearance and answered only to Stein and Brookes, but he was still the Operations Supervisor and felt he should have surely heard something about this. "You mean this has happened before?"

Isabella's hands were dancing across her computer screens once more. "Well, I couldn't say for certain at this juncture, but my guess is, yes." She quickly reconfirmed her findings then leaned back into her chair taking a deep breath.

Larry scratched his head as she activated her intercom and asked the internal operator to patch her through on a secure line.

"Well how come this is the first I've heard of it?" Larry was agitated.

Isabella feigned a look of regret. "Well, you were on leave at the time and Stein asked me to keep it quiet until I could confirm anything." There was a deliberate air of patronisation which would have been obvious to a man more skilled in his opposite sex, "But he'll probably debrief you now it's happened again."

Larry sighed as he looked at the holographic display and took in the ramifications of what they were seeing. "Well, I guess you'd better call it in."

Isabella, already awaiting an answer from Stein, nodded as if the Ops Supervisor was correct to suggest this. The operator returned and Isabella replied, "It's Doctor Usorio," she smiled at Larry, "Yes I'll hold."

*

Stein entered Brooke's main office. Located only two levels below ground it was more like an apartment than a workspace. The walls to the left provided fantastic digitised visuals of Manhattan's skyline in realistic detail, while to the right a wall of books stretched from floor to coving. Lounging in the corner was a psychiatrist's couch given to Brookes by some famous shrink, but for the life of him Stein could never remember his name, while dominating the centre was the antique bureau passed down to Isimbard Brookes from his imperious father. It somehow epitomised the power and standing of the Brookes dynasty, one made up of doctors, politicians and more recently celebrated architects. To the rear of the colossal desk was the open door of the en-suite bedroom.

Stein could hear running water behind the door.

It stopped and Doctor Brookes appeared in the postern, drying his hands.

"So what's so important?" He placed the towel on his desk as he entered.

"The anomaly Doctor Usorio discovered," he replied.

"What about it?"

Stein took a deep breath. "Well she not only traced it," he added, "It happened again."

CHAPTER SIX

Marco and Carl strode down the corridor leading a young man dressed impeccably in uniform. The man's face remained fixed as he followed, though his eyes explored the strange surroundings. "So, you're British?" Marco asked.

"I was born here but raised overseas, Sir." The man was regimented with his response.

They continued around a corner and it appeared the brief conversation was over when Carl picked up the gauntlet. "The boss is British. English actually." He brought them to a stop before a sealed entry, "Here we are."

The young man exhaled. His underground surroundings felt completely alien, his uniform a little tight. The door slid open and Marco and Carl led the anxious Marine through.

On the other side Dorey's briefing room was little bigger than a classroom. It was rectangular in shape with nothing to personalise the inner sanctum in any way. It was spotlessly clean and brightly lit. A gangway led from the entrance at the rear to the Commander's desk at the front. Comfortable high back chairs adorned each side of the thoroughfare, eighteen in total, which usually sat in parallel rows of three. However for this particular concourse the front row seats were placed into curved groups facing outwards, one on either side of Dorey who sat central behind his desk. Jim, Benny and Dial took the places to his right, the three to his left stood empty. Another of the chairs had been placed ominously centre stage, facing the eyes of those seated.

The ongoing conversation stopped as the newcomer was led in.

"Sergeant Deans to see you," Marco announced.

"Thank you Lieutenant." He gestured to Marco and Carl, "Grab a seat."

Sergeant Deans locked stiffly in front of the six seated men. Their more casual attire added to his malaise as he stood in his spit and polished apparel, a uniform he himself hadn't worn for so long. After what seemed a long time Dorey finally broke the silence. "The people to my right are, Captain Nathan Benn."

Nathan nodded, "Please . . . Call me Benny."

The gesture helped Deans relax a little.

44

"Next to him is Lieutenant James Adams."

"It's Jim."

"On the end there, is Major Mark Dial."

Mark smiled, though his eyes betrayed the analysis.

"To my left you already know Warrant Officer Carl Gruber."

"Carl." He said.

"And at the end is Lieutenant Alfonso Marconey."

Marco was only a year older than Deans. He gave him the widest grin of all. "Marco."

"The empty chair you'll meet later. Captain Tilnoh was needed at the Reeper simulator," he paused, "I am Commander Anthony Dorey, but like everyone who's known me since I was eight years of age, you may now call me Dorey, plain and simple." He emphasized, "Rank, file and discipline are as important here as anywhere else. However, this is a top secret organisation and for reasons I'm sure you're more than familiar with it'll be first name terms for the most part. It's good practice to remain anonymous." He smiled, "But don't worry, you'll never have any doubt as to who's in charge here."

Deans frowned. He didn't know what *here,* even meant.

"Now . . . Why don't you take that chair and loosen your collar a little."

The Sergeant breathed. "Thank you."

"How was the flight?"

"Good."

"Now you've been introduced to us, how should we address you?"

"Deans is fine Sir, just Deans."

Another pause followed. "Now I know you must have questions, but I'll ask you to be patient for the time being while we go over a few things."

"Of course."

Dorey gave a nod before unleashing his volume of information. "Dennis Winston Deans, born in Cardiff June 10th 2124 . . . Happy birthday for yesterday."

Deans smiled at the comment and sat quietly awaiting the forthcoming dissection.

"Father was a Captain in the Special Boat Service, left to set up an adventure training company in Wales which he sold eighteen years ago. Mother from Verona, a Latin teacher who met your father while stationed in Italy . . . uprooted herself to be with him. He returned this favour by retiring to raise you in Brescia. Your mother ensured you were fluent in Italian and Latin and I understand you're now also proficient in French and possess a reasonable grasp of Arabic."

Deans nodded but did not interrupt.

"Returned to Britain to study European History but you left university prematurely to join the marines," Dorey added, "apparently prompted by a broken heart."

Deans raised an eyebrow at the rather cold post-mortem.

"You joined the enlisted ranks where you worked your way up to Sergeant in record time. You were considering a commission when British Intelligence stepped in. In 2150 they had you working as a covert operative around the Bosporus where yet again you excelled. Within two years the Western Alliance made you a fully fledged Intelligence Group agent. You completed your fist **WAIG** assignment before your twenty-ninth birthday and after further successful stints in counter-espionage you found yourself being encouraged to take a quite different assignment." Dorey hadn't read from a report, his eyes remaining on the Sergeant throughout. "For the past year you've been trained quite fiercely. You've also been under the intense scrutiny of various health and intelligence tests. You've been led to believe you were to undertake a mission in the Middle East under the guise of a black market dealer trading ancient weapons and artefacts out of Italy. This was a lie. The terrorist cell whose leaders were making money from this lucrative racket does not exist. The real reason for your somewhat peculiar efforts . . . Is me."

Deans edged forward, his senses sharp.

"You've been selected from a list of exceptional individuals all trained by various means, the sole object of which was to create a reserve list for this project. You by far top this list. You're the unanimous choice of myself, the people sat before you now, and the top brass of this undertaking. You've been chosen for the Stasis None Project."

Deans looked a little lost. If he was supposed to have heard of this organization he hadn't and therefore his response could only be one of blank bewilderment.

"You're about to become part of the most mind blowing operation imaginable, one so secret, we do not officially exist. You are from this moment part of an elite team, my team, and I'm afraid such membership gives you to me for life."

"And what exactly does this elite team of yours do, if you don't mind me asking Commander?"

Dorey allowed a subtle grin, remembering how he'd first taken the statement he was set to deliver. "Time travel, Sergeant . . . We do time travel."

CHAPTER SEVEN

Isabella had never been inside Brooke's private lab before. Few scientists on the project had, but her star was rising fast. Any problems on a personal or professional level were normally dealt with in his overly exorbitant office on the higher levels. She'd never liked that room with its extravagant digitised skyscraper views. Isabella suffered from a mild form of vertigo, and she found the gargantuan heights far too realistic for her liking. Besides, it all stank of a completely unnecessary indulgence.

The private workspace she now found herself in suffered less of these vainglorious brush strokes but even this had its minor victories in self-importance. The leather seating found throughout the project rooms had in here been purchased up a model. The chair's slightly cosier, their back and arms that little more plush. The hard light screen generator was the latest upgrade and the entire workstation had a cushioned rim decorating its edges.

Formal greetings had been exchanged and now Stein busied himself on the computer, dragging his way through windows with Brookes watching over his shoulder.

The holographic unit kicked in and drew up the required illustration. Stein now gave way, "Isabella." Both he and Brookes watched as she wheeled her seat before the screen.

"Computer load file, Hunter Doctor Isabella Usorio." Her vital signs were scanned coupled with the updated clearance from her boss, "Last entry." The screen showed the same data held within the hologram only with Isabella's *search* program now activated. "Computer show holo-map through Usorio Hunter One program." Brookes stiffened as he awaited her findings, "Display Anomaly-June 1914 grid 04-07-06."

The timeline updated itself with the search program on line, illustrating her findings within the holographic display. It flashed on and off.

Brooke's mouth opened as he took in the confirmation with his own eyes.

Stein watched his master closely, awaiting his response.

"This matches the data you came across the first time?" He moved his face closer to the display as if in doing so he may seek out a flaw to her thinking.

"It certainly appears similar. I cross-examined my findings from the last incident and created an advanced search program which worked outside of the mainframe to inform me of any such happenings occurring again. At first it buried me with data concerning every little imperfection within our timelines, so I fine-tuned it. I thought that was the end of the matter as nothing like it appeared again. I was certain it was just a singular event, but then out of nowhere," she pointed at the hologram, "There it is."

"We've asked the system to perform countless checks and its findings are always the same," Stein said with authority, "It could well be a manufactured hole, accessing our timelines from an unknown source."

Isabella echoed, "It's a completely different technology, using an entirely different process. The system has calculated within seventy-six percent of certainty it did not occur naturally. Then of course, if you consider the dates."

Brookes looked almost annoyed.

"The original abnormality occurred thirteen weeks prior to Dorey's drop into Constantinople. The hole opened and closed so quickly it was a miracle I ever came across it. But now my program's identified a similar occurrence, only with a different signature. Opening into the timeline used to drop Dorey into the First World War mission over two years ago." She pointed at the display, "This time the entry appears only weeks before the drop itself. But unlike the prior example, the recording of this 1914 anomaly punches out of the timeline before the Reeper leaves, before *we* sealed the system, therefore leaving a data pattern. One we're able to observe with more clarity." She took a breath before confirming, "The data suggests the anomaly pierced this artificial timeline from an unknown location within our own phase of reality." She gave an admiring smile as she pointed at the hologram, "Look at the entry and exit points. They're not torn holes like our signatures. They pierce the line with precision, on a perfect curve."

Brookes stared at the highlighted arc. "Let's not get ahead of ourselves," he said firmly, "It could be coincidence." He was fooling no one. A deep scowl appeared. "So what are we suggesting? That an unidentified technology has been used at least twice to our knowledge, to enter locations into which we've sent Commander Dorey's team? A technology able to disguise itself from direct view?"

Isabella was precise with her summary. "Sir, I'm saying when we sent Dorey back to Constantinople an anomaly occurred which resembled a manufactured hole in time, piercing the same timeline months prior to their entry, stemming from an unknown source. Now whatever that *something* was, it was a one off and so therefore just another curiosity. However a similar anomaly now appears to have been located doing exactly the same thing, appearing just before the team's mission into the Great War. Only on this occasion we're able to observe it punching a way out of the timeline. And the vestige left suggests it was headed back to our own phase of reality. If proven, this makes it no longer an anomaly, but an alien technology."

Brookes was grim. He shook his head. "It's impossible."

An uneasy silence gripped the room as the intruder's signature flashed its presence from the holographic display, as if to inform them it was indeed possible.

Brookes contorted his mouth. "I take it there's no way we can trace its actual source?"

Isabella replied, "If the Stasis computer was working within the same parameters as the anomaly then this action could be possible. The fact the anomaly appears to be targeting our timelines from our own realm of existence would also suggest a pattern we could at least attempt to follow."

Brookes didn't like the expression, "Attempt?"

"Although it appears to be visiting our timelines at an identical moment in history, the anomaly is doing so from an entirely different point of reference. As you well know there are many variables to consider. Since we're not witnessing this as a live event it's difficult to gain real clarity. Even in a live scenario our two years ago could be the anomaly's present, therefore our own position in space and time has no bearing to that of its own. This will make it extremely difficult to trace unless we managed to gain an absolute lock as the event transpired in real time. Since both discoveries have come to light after the timelines have since been exited and sealed, they can only be viewed as recordings of a past event, whichever angle we play."

Brooke's brain was powering through theories. He leaned into the hologram and stared at the curve as it pierced the timeline used for the World War One mission two years prior. He was certain no such technology could exist.

Stein broke his silence. "If this thing has jumped into one of our timelines and back out again . . . If its vestige has been recorded before we sealed the system, we may be able to find some way of tracing it virtually if we can pose the conundrum to the Stasis None in a code it can understand. After all, the anomaly now exists within the Stasis archive."

Isabella was about to enter uncharted waters with a recently derived theory she'd not yet discussed with anyone, a theory her advanced hunter program suggested as bizarre fact since she'd instructed it to perform a more abstract search.

She pulled a crystal tablet from the breast pocket of her white coat. "I disagree. You see if the data I've studied today is correct then it would appear whatever this thing is, it's almost certainly going to remain untraceable in any virtual sense."

Stein looked to Brookes then back to the impertinent Usorio. "How can you be so sure? If we have the entry and exit recorded before the system was sealed, we may be able to trace it to some extent, however vague the result. We can narrow the search from the offset as the anomaly could only achieve entry from somewhere between our present and when this project first began. Otherwise there'd be no timeline for it to visit in the first place." He smiled sardonically, "So unless you're saying it came from the future Doctor, I would say tracing it virtually is at the very least a possibility."

It was a veiled insult. Isabella let it go. Her answer was set to make even this implausibility, plausible. "No, I'm not saying it operates from any future Dr. Stein. Quite the opposite." She held up the crystal. "In fact, judging from the data this program managed to extract, I'd say this anomaly almost certainly operated from the past."

Stein shrugged at the obvious remark, "As it can only exist within the parameters of when our Stasis None created the simulated time spans to begin with . . ."

She interrupted her boss before he could go any further. "No Doctor Stein, I'm not saying it stems from one of our simulated pasts. Or within the time elapsed since the conception of the Stasis None Project." She looked at Brookes with purpose, "I'm saying this thing appears to be operating from two centuries ago . . . Two centuries ago within our *real* past."

CHAPTER EIGHT

Deans was struggling. "It's just too unbelievable. This morning I was preparing to leave on an undertaking already bizarre enough in its own right. Instead, I find myself hundreds of feet below ground being informed not only time travel is possible, but soon I may actually be doing it?"

Dorey had instinctively liked Deans while observing him from distance this past year. "Obviously we know how you must be feeling. It's a hell of a thing to take in. But this is real and it's something you're going to have to deal with. We wanted *you* for this project. And as I'm sure a person of your experience understands, we're not asking."

Deans understood this was no negotiation, something he was accustomed to in his line of work. He'd signed the notorious *form 64* long before he'd been approached to interview for the black market deal, a document the equivalent to signing away your life for the foreseeable future. "I understand. But this is simply mind-blowing."

"When they first told me my head was in pieces for weeks." Dorey gestured to his colleagues. "But at least you'll have people who've experienced this miracle first hand. Everyone around you will do everything in their power to help you prepare. I need you to feel at home from the start. Comfortable, confident, capable of delivering what will be required. My life, their lives and your own, will almost certainly depend upon it."

"But why me?"

"Because you're by far the outstanding candidate," Dorey underlined. "You have language skills and the ability to think fast on your feet under pressure. You're trained in espionage and have combat experience. And now thanks to the bullshit mission we set you up for you're also adequately trained in a range of more ancient weaponry which believe me can come in handy here."

Dean's face darkened. "I just don't understand how this is possible."

Dorey took the comment as his cue flicking a sensor which activated the display wall. "We thought it better if I was to tell you what's going on in layman's terms first. You see we all learned it from the scientists and it all got a little too technical at times. I don't say this to insult you but your file never mentioned nuclear physics or quantum mechanics, so I'm fairly confident you'll appreciate this version to start." Dorey then prepared to give him the Stasis None Project as a digestible bite-sized snack.

Dorey and the others had given a great deal of thought on the order of play, the best way to ease Deans into the complicated miracle which had become their everyday lives.

"To begin with we thought it best to concentrate on the principle of *what* and *how* we are, rather than the *why*. How did we achieve this impossible feat?" The Commander began, "Tell me, how much do you know about quantum computing?"

"Only a little," Deans had colleagues tasked with watching the East's capabilities in such fields. The following silence suggested he should attempt a synopsis. "They could eclipse all forms of current calculating technology, problem-solving at an atomic level, and just about every country in the world wants to be the first to create one that actually works."

Dorey smiled. "Well the man at the head of this project has done just that."

Under current circumstance Deans held onto his surprise.

"I'd never pretend my knowledge could enlighten anyone as to the *true* wonders of this place. I can however, give you a fairly solid grasp of what it is and how it came about."

Deans prepared as the screen wall came to life.

"Fifty years ago, a nineteen-year-old genius named Isimbard Brookes was heading a research team in Washington. He was trying to create the first truly workable quantum computer." He added, "Genius is often a term banded around lightly, I can assure you in this case it could be deemed an understatement."

Deans took the point.

"A monumental breakthrough resulted in the creation of a partial quantum computer system which worked. Now don't ask me what was meant by partial, all I know is this thing was a revelation. We're talking man on the moon here. The Western Alliance had been on the lookout for something radical, and through Isimbard Brookes they'd got just that. Once this partial computer was up and running it fired out theories which could lead to all kinds of possibilities, the stuff scientists only hoped were truly achievable. Full Fusion Method, light-speed, folding space, the computer had the potential to understand it all. Perhaps the most astounding was the discovery of a process which could theoretically allow time and space to be manipulated. Eager to exploit these findings Brookes split his team into groups. All were under his direct command, carrying out the whims of his powerful intellect. Nearly five years of ground out results passed before another major breakthrough came. Major enough to see the WA give him all the resources he desired. It was at this juncture the Stasis None Project was conceived and this huge underground research centre was approved for construction. Once complete, Brookes brought his teams here from Washington." Dorey digressed, "The earth's magnetic fields in this area make certain aspects of Brooke's research more likely to succeed. This whole complex has been specifically designed to harness this natural phenomenon but also to exploit it, in order to defend us from attack or global disaster." He moved on not wishing to be bogged down in such territory at this stage, "Brooke's personal obsession was the manipulation of space and time, and for reasons we'll come to shortly, this was an obsession shared by the WA." He continued, "The change in scenery paid off. Utilising this new facility meant astounding new results followed. On the back of such results, Brookes then made his most monumental leap. Due to security clearance I doubt there are many who know exactly what this leap was, I know I'm certainly too far down the food chain, but the basis of what *we* do here was built upon this one find." Dorey smiled, "But again, before we head down such a tempting path let me first give you the low down on our unique computer, which is after all the source of everything in this place."

The screen took over proceedings, its illustrations and narrative painting the historical basis of computing. It described how the Central Processing Unit had evolved from super calculator to a device incorporating a multitude of tools along its buses and pathways, allowing it to operate complex graphics, audio, tasks and programming.

The diction paused as Dorey rejoined the lesson. "However impressive the evolution of modern CPU's and their components may seem, in reality they're still glorified calculation devices, so fast they can appear super human in functional terms. In reality of course, they are simply carrying out instruction, only at such high speeds it can appear they're more advanced than the humans who actually instruct them, when of course, they're not even close. A computer doesn't think . . . It processes, and the quest has, and still is to make those processes operate as quickly and efficiently as possible, so modern computers may serve our ever more demanding needs."

The display now painted the image of a man sat before a piano and asked Deans to think of the CPU as the pianist. It asked him to imagine the complex tasks the CPU was to process as a musical score, the keyboard as the tools at its disposal, the actual melody produced being the desired answers and solutions.

"In the early days of computing the musical score fed to the pianist would have been basic, like nursery rhyme, therefore the melody produced was a simple tune. However as technology evolved we expected our pianist to play at a more advanced level, until eventually Beethoven can be processed with ease. But unlike a concert pianist in the real world, complexity, clarity and interpretation are not the only desired results. In computing terms we require speed, a pianist who can not only play clearly within an auditorium, but one who can do so at ever faster rates, playing complex notation beyond the capability of the deciphering human ear alone."

The display showed the pianist playing at a frantic rate, arms and fingers growing faster and faster, the music produced now a whirlwind of sound.

"Over the centuries constant improvements have been made." The display illustrated the evolutions as if granted to the CPU pianist. "A keyboard more responsive to the touch, the pianist's skill increased, quicker fingers, more agile to strike the notes. We'd even see him given more hands and keys on which to play. After time the next step would see us link more pianists into the equation to perform the desired tasks, their keyboards all uniting in the quest to see more music processed at accelerated speeds."

The screen painted the picture accordingly.

"However, certain truths always remained. The more pianists and keyboards, the quicker the auditorium was filled. Not only with extra players and pianos, but with heat and the indecipherable noise produced as a result." He clarified, "For the sake of our demonstration, imagine this whole scenario as only two dimensional, flat like our keyboard with but one auditorium at our disposal, one mass global arena in which our masters are all instructed to play."

Deans nodded, watching the illustrations, digesting all that came his way.

"We can shrink and compress our players and instruments, moving from micro to the nanotechnology we use today. However, a simple truth remains. In the two dimensional sense we'll always reach a limit. No matter how small we go, no matter how fast we make our players and their musical tools, eventually a maximum will be achieved, when every key will be depressed as the process reaches its ultimate." He concluded, "A wall of noise within an over-crowded auditorium."

Deans studied the display.

"The reason you were asked to think of this whole keyboard analogy as two dimensional was so we could paint a simplistic view of what Brookes did to address these problems. His first move was to take the flat keyboard and turn it into a sphere, keys which surrounded our player in all directions. Next he took the pianist and placed him directly within the centre of that sphere. He then provided him with the ability to hit any desired note at will, and in any direction. And the protective womb of the sphere itself provided each pianist with his own mini-auditorium, meaning less noise pollution throughout the larger arena. And unlike the flat keyboard, this new model has much higher limitation. Increase the inner wall of the sphere and you get more surface area in which to add more keys." He watched the obvious question rest on the lips of the man opposite, "But what about the problem of over filling the auditorium as the sphere's number and size are increased?" Dorey smiled, "Well this was Brooke's first leap into the realm of quantum computing. You see the keyboard spheres he was creating were no longer made of nano-devices and circuits . . . They were atomic particles."

Deans understood the implication.

"Not only had Brookes transformed the system so it operated within a third dimensional level, he'd also made an auditorium of gargantuan proportions now that his musical spheres which populated it were merely atomic in size. As I said, a genius."

The exhale from his new recruit's lips suggested he agreed with such prognosis.

"This was phase one of Brooke's breakthrough, the first major leap which grabbed the attention. But what he did next was more remarkable still, when a new dimension was brought into play. His new system's capability was set to become truly mind boggling."

*

"Tell me, how much do you know about the electron in such matters?"

"With regards to quantum computing?" Deans thought for a moment, "Only the basics, how it can appear to exist everywhere at once."

The display began a new animation as Dorey agreed, "Science had long since made a seemingly implausible discovery, using what became known as the *Double Slit* experiment. In the experiment they fired a particle at a wall. But first it had to pass through a tiny slit cut into a barrier placed before that wall. Fired with atomic precision it naturally passed through the hole and hit the wall cleanly on the other side." He added, "Imagine the experiment as firing a tiny tennis ball dowsed in paint through such a gap. The impacts on the wall record a predictable pattern as the paint-soaked particles pass through the hole and strike the surface behind. However, they then cut two slits into the same barrier side by side and conducted the same experiment. Naturally the particles were separated slightly as they passed through each of the gaps, creating two streams of impact marks on the wall beyond, two distinct paint groupings . . . Fairly obvious." Dorey stated. "But then the same experiment was conducted using an electron, which had all the characteristics as our paint-soaked particle. They fired it through the one single slit and again the impacts were predictable, the electron acting in the same way as a particle. However when the experiment was carried out using the two slits side by side, something remarkable happened."

Deans had covered some of this theory at college. "Each individual electron appeared to split and travel through both holes simultaneously, recording a hit on the wall at both patterns of impact."

Dorey was pleased. "Back then this blew scientists away. Somehow the electron appeared to be capable of being in more than one place at the same moment in time. It was behaving more like a wave in form, like a ripple of spreading water rather than a single particle. But since the electron was a particle in structure how could it be behaving like a wave? To check their findings they placed a beam next to the two slits to record the electron's behaviour as it passed through them. They fired it at the slits, yet to their astonishment the electron took on the mannerisms of a particle once again, firing through only one gap like a single tennis ball, creating just the one strike mark on the wall beyond." He smiled, "The electron was now behaving differently while being observed. Raising a question, is the electron a particle or a wave? Is it both or neither? Is it an entity trapped within another at an atomic level?" The smile broadened as he saw he was finally beginning to lose Deans. "All that mattered to Brookes was the fact the electron was able to experience itself at different phases, or at least at different phases as we perceive it. As you said, put simply, it could be everywhere at once. This find would become one of the key building blocks in realising aspects of quantum computer theory, and Brooke's own brand in particular." He continued, "Technology was already entering a new phase. Nano-particles were being programmed, used to carry out all manner of tasks within computers and networks as well as the human body itself. The new generation of excitonic transistors had been developed, using light instead of actual circuits. However, the innovations discussed which allowed Brookes to create and manipulate atomic spheres placed him streets ahead of the competition. What he did next however, placed him on a different stratosphere." Again the screen aided Dorey's quest. "He devised a method to not only program and manipulate atomic particles, but discovered a method to actually identify any one of these particles as they occupied these multiple, simultaneous dimensions in space like the electron. And as if this wasn't incredible enough he then figured out a process which could link these out of phase particles together into arcs across the different dimensions they occupied, eventually firing information through and across them before returning the conclusion to the original source." He could see Deans was struggling, "Actually exploiting the multiple copies of the one atomic sphere as it experienced itself in different dimensions. Meaning if he fired music for one of our atomic pianists to play, the same pianist would be tackling the same score a trillion times over at precisely the same moment as he experienced himself time and again throughout the universe."

Deans stared blankly.

"A programmed atomic particle linked to a trillion versions of itself, able to process information in the same way as a CPU uses its components. Imagine harnessing such a principle and applying it into the workings of our already improved computer. Think what it could do. We've already given our pianist an enormous environment in which to play by reducing him to the size of an atom. Now we're ensuring he can perform in an infinite number of auditoriums, all linked a trillion times over." He gave Deans a moment to digest the information as the visuals animated the pianist in his atom-sized bubble of expanding keys, floating next to another, then another until there was an infinite amount existing simultaneously. Endless auditoriums looped together by strings of light, all floating through time and space, all tasked to produce the same desired piece of music.

"This is the genius of the Stasis None." Dorey concluded, "A machine which works by truly problem solving at an atomic level. Multiple-tasking over a multi-dimensional plane . . . Using programmed gas, compressed matter and light rather than physical circuits and switches." He added, "Brookes had created an incalculably powerful system, able to perform unlimited tasks at any one moment."

Deans almost gasped. In his line of work he knew better than most nobody should be anywhere close to realising this kind of technology as reality. It had been hoped on for the past two centuries but too many stumbling blocks had seen the greatest minds and the machines which aided them, stumped time and again.

"A device full of programmed particles which exist, interact and communicate with each other over multiple plains at any same given moment." Dorey clarified, "Able to calculate using atoms almost like brain cells."

Deans shook his head.

"This was Brooke's miracle to mankind." Dorey paused, "However, inventing it and actually using it would prove to be very different entities."

*

"You see, the actual computer aspect of the Stasis None works like any other, and it exists here, in our own physical universe under Brooke's direct control. And like any computer it's only as good as the human information placed into it. So to begin with the fledgling system had to be fed, given a starting point . . . And it was done so via the powerful databases already built within the mammoth new hard drives and super computers of this very complex. However, the data storage and processing of Brooke's brainchild was so vast, so beyond calculation, it devoured and stored the information in its entirety within seconds. All knowledge of human learning passed on in the blink of an eye. And once the quantum element was *truly* primed, the ethereal circuitry of the Stasis None would spark a massive, unforeseen chain reaction. Put simply, it began learning."

Deans looked startled. "You mean this thing actually started thinking for itself?"

"Don't get ahead of yourself." Dorey responded quickly, "This isn't sinister science fiction." He corrected, "It began calculating. But on a level Brookes could barely believe. With every question came an answer, with every answer the natural progression to further questioning. You see, once the universe of the Stasis None had been inadvertently set into motion it was operating in a similar way to an actual brain. With knowledge bestowed on it, learning could be expanded, new theories derived from the original tract . . . A chain reaction of calculation."

Deans frowned, "That sounds a lot like thinking to me."

"Trust me, there's a colossal difference. Free will, self awareness . . . These are not things possessed by the system Brookes has created. Our computer was simply expanding under its own governance of calculation, a universe of knowledge which Brookes and his new science commune could potentially hook into."

"Potentially?"

"Although the system remains under the control of Brookes, its processing has since developed into a complex entity beyond the physical, and like our own human mind its complexities were and still are proving extremely difficult to unravel. A major problem was immediately apparent . . . Communication."

Deans tried to keep up.

"The Stasis None was given the entirety of human learning as a starting block and was able to expand from this point with ease," he added, "By the equivalent of millions of years of our own evolution in an instantaneous explosion of understanding. Creating an expanding virtual brain of sorts, cross-calculating and discovering untold knowledge over time and space, yet all held together by Brooke's at the source, hooked into the very complex built and designed to house it. If you consider mankind has yet to understand the complexities of our own human brain then you can guess at the problems arising in understanding this system. The greatest minds in history utilised but a fraction of their true potential. What Brookes created was the equivalent of a brain utilising not only its *maximum* potential but doing so over many dimensions simultaneously."

Deans exhaled once again as Dorey tried to be more concise with his explanation. "This thing operates at such levels that any explanation, any calculated response, would have been formulated by the Stasis None long before the question was derived. A source for gathering intelligence so powerful, it makes the correct emphasis on the question now far more relevant than the actual answer itself."

"What does that mean exactly?"

"It means we've the ability to obtain answers to just about anything. But first Brookes must figure out the question then go on to derive its atomic language . . . Its binary translation if you like. Just so the damn thing can understand what we're asking."

Deans scowled, his eyes once again reading the displays.

"In layman's terms, we've a device capable of solving just about any problem, but first we have to discover what we're asking then translate this into a language the Stasis None understands. And we must do so in extremely precise and logical detail. Trust me, the mathematics involved are staggering."

"But why does it prove so difficult to communicate? If it's so smart, can it not read between the lines and understand a common language between user and machine?"

"Consider the binary code alone," Dorey responded, "The circuitry and switches needed for just the simple operation of any everyday computer and its tools. Think of the methods used to speed up a clock cycle, to encourage CPU's to interact faster with their components. If we had to personally pre-program such instruction manually into every modern computer it would take the most industrious of mathematicians an age to have a system simply turn on our lights or navigate our cars. And that's just a standard computer utilising nanotechnology which understands as its predecessors did, a tried and tested method of language created progressively by the human user over the past two centuries. But we didn't create a language for the Stasis None. It devised its own method of understanding the instant it outgrew everything we had to throw at it. The most advanced computers in the world combined are merely an abacus as far as the Stasis system is concerned. What was needed was something new, a method of translation from Brookes and the colossal computers at his disposal to the Stasis None brain."

"And Brookes has achieved this?"

"To a certain degree, yes," He looked at Deans thoughtfully, "Doctor Brookes once cryptically informed me . . . *As cavemen we wouldn't require the theory of electricity in order to keep ourselves warm, we would ask only for the secret of fire.*" He observed his expression. "You see, even with the powerful computers at our disposal, devices which fill entire rooms within this facility. Even with the uncanny genius of Brookes to guide both them and us . . . We're in the dark ages by comparison. So we have to be most precise with the calculation of our questioning. One wrong zero here, one incorrect digit there and we cavemen get electricity instead of fire . . . And not only do we not know how to use it, we don't even know what such a concept means."

Deans shook his head.

"As it turned out Brooke's statement was built upon irony," Dorey concluded, "For the real breakthrough in what *we* do now, would come after a certain caveman did exactly that . . . When he inadvertently asked the wrong question."

CHAPTER NINE

Dorey continued his complex introduction, steering Deans toward the finale of *how* before he'd relinquish the reasons *why*. "None of us have absolute clearance to Brooke's research. What we do know is a highly classified event transpired which allowed him to make a giant leap toward unravelling the mysteries of space and time, encouraging him to push the boundaries of his experimentation. By the year 2126 a series of complex experiments were underway, designed to exploit the very principles of the Stasis None, to see if it were possible to create theoretical strings of parallel existence. They were new, and as always pushed the envelope. Upon successful completion of one particular phase, the scientists needed the mass of information gathered to be copied then stored. But the process of the save request was botched in some way, leading to a misinterpretation by the Stasis None. Our atomic computer misunderstood, believing instead it had been requested to assimilate then reconstruct a copy of the newly created theoretical timeline, a hard copy of a virtual string of our Earth's history from the year 0056 AD to the then present 2126. However, nobody knew the machine had misunderstood the intention of the command and so nothing was done to stop it completing its own interpretation of the task. As a result, the Stasis None began devising its own methods in which to carry out this very process, unnoticed and unhindered, eventually reconstructing an actual copy of our timeline within these parameters." He saw confusion creep back into Dean's expression. "Back then there was no real way for the scientists to directly see into these parallel dimensions through which the Stasis None operates. Even now it can prove extremely difficult. We could discuss forever the endless complexities of it . . . But trust me, this incredible event happened. Nobody's sure how long it took in the real sense for this task to be completed, especially as we're dealing within the unknown quantities of space and time. Apparently a millennium to one dimension could pass as a mere month within another." He pointed out he knew little of such a concept. "But when the second experiment dealing within these same time parameters was primed, the computer asked Brookes which version he required as an upload. Did he want the original theoretical time string or the computer's hard copy? At first Brookes didn't even realise what the computer was asking, but when he stumbled on the truth he was astonished. Unwittingly his team had recreated an actual string of time, constructed in exact detail, dating back over a two thousand year period of our version of space. Sat in perfect stasis to our own reality within the confines of another dimension . . . Held adjacent, but out of phase to our own universe by the powerful Stasis None."

Deans shook his head. "It isn't possible."

"I can assure you, as insane as all of this sounds, it's very possible." He concluded, "The structure for the Stasis None Project as we live and breathe it was born, and like so many evolutions throughout history, it was done so accidentally."

*

Deans turned to the one question now burning his mind. "So it's not *real time*, but a simulation?"

"Yes and no." The Commander smiled, "When they devised the notion of actually connecting to this creation, they first needed to develop a workable structure. One which would eventually give birth to the technique we use today. It was a slow process. But one thing soon became evident. No matter how hard they tried, they were never able to recreate another cloned timeline. Only manipulate versions of the one original as it experiences itself infinitely across the Stasis universe. That one accident which created an exact copy from our then present back to the year 0056 AD. Since nobody was able to fathom the mistake which created it in the first place they've been unable to formulate the correct data so as to ask the computer exactly how or why it could have possibly happened. It's all ridiculously complicated and I've no real grounding in how this intelligence can understand and co-operate with its human counterparts on one level, yet seem like a confused child when asked to elaborate on something else. It's as I stated earlier, you must formulate the correct question in order to gain an already obtained answer." He appreciated Deans was still struggling with the concept, "On everyday computing it behaves like any other machine, only much more powerful. However as soon as you start bringing multi-dimensional tasking into the equation it becomes an entirely different matter. There are just too many probabilities and improbabilities to consider. Think of it in basic terms. If you ask a computer to search for a word but pronounce or spell it incorrectly you can soon run into problems. But it will almost certainly provide options, predict your text, amass similar words, and point you in the right direction. But what if there are many words of nearly the same sound, spelling and meaning? You could soon be inundated with information. As such you suddenly find you must be much more specific. But what happens if you asked for a word, structured in almost the exact and correct way but found there were a trillion other words of almost the precise same structure, sound and meaning?"

Deans took the point.

"The scientists never quite managed to get their enquiries precisely right and as such, the playing field has remained the same. They can only use that one original two thousand year string. So if you were hoping to see a Tyrannosaurus Rex, I'm afraid you're going to be disappointed."

Deans laughed at the comment despite his situation.

"So there's our timespan, an assimilated string of time, recreated over and over in dimension after dimension." He added, "Eventually the scientists developed the technology required, capable of folding our space closer to many of these phases of reality. Then came the ability to tear open a portal, soon followed by a method in which we could create a temporal link . . . A passageway from our reality, into certain copies."

Deans watched the animation, unable to accept the incredible claims being made.

"Then they built a ship, to carry us safely through that passageway, into the copy and back out again."

Deans thought back to when he'd first entered the room, to the missing team member otherwise engaged in some form of simulator. "So can I take it that's what a Reeper is?"

Dorey smiled at the young spy, "You'll meet both the ship and Jay later today." He continued, "Using the Reeper we travel back to a chosen location, carry out an objective then jump back before sealing the system."

"Sealing the system?"

"Once we've altered a past event, another parallel line of existence stems from that altered point and plays itself out." He added, "The timelines are dormant simulations created by the computer which exist, like our electron, over multiple plains. But they could still pose very real risks once we've torn into them. Although they're not reality in the conventional sense from our perspective, they could pose cataclysmic threat to the dimension they're held in. After all real or simulated, it's still a string of time and events, perfectly copied in every way."

"You mean they could threaten something like a time paradox?"

"I mean exactly like a paradox." He replied, "Again, it all gets a little weird at this point. But like that electron, whatever exists on one plain counter-exists within another, meaning there is always a danger."

"And these timelines," he enquired after a moment, "Just how perfect a copy is perfect?"

Dorey decided it was safe to continue, "Insects, clouds, blades of grass. The same breeze over there will touch them just as it did here at any given moment. The same tides and sunsets. The same leaders, tyrants, great thinkers . . . Kings, queens and farm hands," he prepared to drop the bomb, "You stick your head over there at the right place and moment, you could see your own birth, watch yourself walk for the first time."

Deans was shaken by the comment. It hadn't occurred to him within these other realities, places he'd not yet even begun to get his head around as genuinely existing; there could be something as insignificant as another living breathing version of his infant self. He felt strangely uneasy at such a concept. "Shit."

It was the most profound thing he could think to say.

Dorey knew all too well the adjustments he'd now be experiencing. He and the others had been doing this for years and it was still always dangerous to get too drunk with it.

"I know how difficult it is to comprehend. Believe me we all do. But this is how it is. For whatever reason, by whatever means, this timeline was created. The force which created it so powerful, so beyond our comprehension, once it pulled it off it was perfect in every detail, sitting in stasis to this existence, out of phase to the rest of the universe. Real, right down to each blade of grass, each grain of sand. That's why whatever we do and whenever we do it, the cloned timeline is sealed on our return. It poses too great a risk." Deans remained stunned.

"A connection corridor is created so we may fly into the dormant copy. We carry out the objective resulting in a second timeline being created in parallel to the original. We fly out and it's sealed the moment we leave. Then both the original string and the new branch are wrapped into themselves, creating a permanent loop within a loop. If the slightest risk of a paradox over there means calculable risk to our own reality here . . . Then this was the method devised to eliminate that risk."

"But if the timelines are cloned from a computer simulation, how do they pose a threat to anything real?" Dean's scowl returned, "And if they *do* pose a threat, how come you don't have to seal them all whether you use them or not?"

"As I said the copies are held in an *out of phase state*. Each string like a memory, a snapshot of time. As soon as we start opening and manipulating these timelines they spark into existence as we experience it, a reality we are then connected to. This means there's an element of risk. We cannot take chances when arousing these dream-like strings of existence. We have to be certain there can be no chain reaction. Any ripple which could roll out of a once dormant cell may affect others, so therefore our own."

Deans stared blankly. "But again, how would this matter if none of it is real?"

Another dark smile appeared, the Commander appreciating his circle of thought. "But that's the whole point isn't it? What's real? The fact this timeline sparked from a reality the computer created doesn't make the place itself any less real. No less so than if we choose to believe any God created our own."

Deans was visibly shocked. "Are you saying we're like God to these other realities?"

"I only meant they remain in a dream-like state until connecting them to our own existence, which activates them into reality as we understand it."

"But once activated they're as real as anything we experience here?"

Dorey nodded, "In every detail."

A short silence followed. "This puts the whole *who* created *what* into a different arena."

"A playing field my friend Carl here loves to dwell on," he gestured to his colleague, "But believe me when I advise you . . . Don't dwell on it too much."

Deans shook his head. He'd woken that morning confident he understood most of what was going on in the world, now he was in danger of being lost. "I don't understand. If the risk is so high and the effects aren't real anyway . . . Then why even bother? Why risk doing what you do at all?"

"As I said, to begin with we thought it best you appreciate the bulk of *how* it is we do what we do. Now we'll begin the process of explaining exactly *why.'*

*

"To accurately manipulate space and time gives you incredible power." Dorey continued, "In theory it could save mankind from any number of disasters, just as equally, it could destroy us all. The reasoning behind what we do here came about from a mishmash of goals and motives. But all of these stemmed from one primary event, *the collapse.*" He offered a pre-emptive apology to the new recruit, "I appreciate you've a good knowledge of history, but again if you could just follow the short film on the screen, it will help speed us toward our goal."

Deans focussed on the latest computer animated lesson.

As with the previous tutorial the account was basic to say the least. The generated narrative cold and non-judgemental as it described mankind's flirtation with self destruction. It began with a simple education on society's addiction to oil. Describing briefly how everything within the modern world was derived from it . . . Fertiliser to pesticides, plastics to paints, medicines to toothpaste, petroleum to tyres. It described concisely how there was no substance to replace it. How it not only powered the machines which kept our world in motion but also had a hand in constructing these devices from every fibre upward. It explained how without oil there would be no machinery for alternate fuels to power in the first place just as there would be no crops to eat without oil based fertilisers to replenish the over farmed soil.

It was a stark account of which Deans already had a good understanding.

It moved on quickly to the concept of Peak Oil, illustrating the dark reality of building an entire social structure on a product in global decline.

The narrative illustrated a world economy which was nothing more than a pyramid scheme, a system requiring infinite growth in order to sustain itself, a system doomed to fail as it could only collide with something all the more powerful, finite energy.

The lesson was clarified with a simple truth, *'There cannot be more money printed than there is physical energy to back it up.'*

The display now headed to the early throes of the twenty-first century, to the beginning of the meltdown, the narrative dissecting several key events of history.

It began with the peaks and troughs of the first decades, the recoveries and slumps as governments and bankers tried desperately to hide the reality from the masses. It spoke of India's incredible evolution, the ongoing tension with her crumbling neighbour Pakistan. It illustrated the catastrophic effects of global warming as they took effect on a population boom who'd continued to devour and squander every precious resource.

It moved on to unrest in the Middle East. The moment Iran announced the opening of its independent stock exchange, ready to trade oil in the floated Chinese currency, yaun. An action which brought down the petro-dollar and with it the United States domination of world markets. The display showed how this event was followed by the declassification of Peak Oil in Saudi Arabia, when secret documents revealed how the world's largest oil reserve was in steady decline. The revolution which followed. The lightening coup which saw the disgruntled Saudi masses rise up against their billionaire princes, people promised a brighter future built on their most precious resource. The display illustrated how many within the Saudi military supported the cause, and how a new regime was quickly established, shocking the West completely.

It detailed how the People's Arabian Republic was immediately encouraged to trade oil in Chinese currency on the new Iranian market. Detailed how America prepared her response against a state she'd seen armed to the teeth . . . An action which resulted in the unthinkable, when China stepped in to defend her new allies.

The pictures now painted the stalemate that ensued, a stand off consumed by the total collapse of the world economy. It painted the chaos. Spoke of Pakistan's implosion, of the infamous Exodus strategies which saw millions of Britain's Muslims expelled to countries of their ancestral origin, their citizenship, wealth and dignity stripped after civil war erupted onto insolvent British streets. How the hard line action proved a catalyst for many Western powers to follow as global unrest reached new heights.

The documentary spoke of the deals done to avert all out war as the world stood on the brink. How within a year of the stand off real hope was breathed back into the world when Rapid Laser Fusion was made a reality after British and European scientists uncovered a process which used super-fast lasers to shoot heavy hydrogen atoms in a contained environment, to create helium energy.

With the introduction of the first phase of the Fusion Age, a possible aversion to the world's energy crisis seemed plausible . . . But the transition phase would be painful.

The display showed how in the years that followed, American scientists announced the arrival of hydrogen fuel followed by the shock of a fully operational Orbital Defence System, the much fabled Star Wars Program suddenly a stunning reality.

The screen reminded of the arguments and accusations that raged. How Israel's worst kept secret was made official as her atomic strike capability was unveiled, safe under the umbrella of US orbital protection. How Iran soon followed by unveiling her own limited nuclear capability, declaring her intention to share it with other Gulf States.

The lesson spoke of new thinkers and mediators who tried to avert catastrophe until eventually something resembling order was resumed.

The documentary headed quickly toward the present day, explaining how The US traded hydrogen fuel and orbital protection in return for Europe's fusion energy. How a new Western Alliance was born, protected by a united Intelligence Group, *WAIG*, who shared secrets and strategies to ensure the safety and resurgence of the West.

It illustrated how the WA traded its space defence and new energy for oil.

How Russia played mediator as she implemented plans to see her vast unpopulated plains organically fertilised, to prepare for the food crisis to come. The land populated and worked by Chinese immigrants spilling over her borders.

It illustrated the Chinese breakthroughs in genetics. How China's *miracle cures*, formulated to combat disease and super viruses would be traded at extortionate rates as enormous leaps in pharmaceutical and biological sciences were made. How the discovery of *test areas* went largely ignored by a world struggling to maintain order, human laboratory zones pinpointed within remote regions of South America, countries China had been investing in heavily for decades.

The screen wound down until eventually the chaos of the past century was replaced by calm blue, Deans focus returning once again to the Commander sat before him.

"The collapse destroyed the world economy, pushed us all to the brink. The simple truth which got us to the end of that century was this, humanity needs oil to make just about everything in order to maintain our way of life. To make oil viable, to slow down its decline rate, humanity needed a major new energy source which could power industry, transport and technological needs so as to take the strain off oil. As the twenty second century dawned, one side held the answer to the energy problem, the other possessed the oil." He acknowledged Deans' expression, "A simplistic view yes, but I'm sure you get the drift of where I'm heading with this." He added, "With Star Wars floating around we'd been able to avoid military catastrophe, though the presence of such a device did nothing for bringing the world closer together. As the new century got underway new technology was made available to extract oil from the once frozen Artic, renewing tensions over who had the rights to drill it. But the truth is the reserves there could never match those in Arabia anyway, and as Iraq was all but dry it became inevitable unless an alternative to oil could be found, another collapse would follow, only this one would be permanent, as once the oil has gone its never coming back." He paused, "In the first decade of the new century the mass media focussed on the usual stuff. The so-called written off debts and the financed preservation of Latin America's tropical forests. Brazil's resurgence as she was encompassed into the WA causing more tension with China. Discussions on whether the secrets of Fusion Technology should remain under the strict control of a select few governments within the WA. How prior to the Hydrogen Age, Western Governments had been secretly buying up much of the world's water for decades. The land disputes between Russia and China as many of those loaned out territories being organically fertilised by Chinese immigrants would become communities declaring closer affiliation to Beijing." Dorey smiled, "All of this provided a smoke screen intended to keep the world occupied, to turn it away from what really mattered to the WA…The development of this project."

*

In one sitting Dorey had managed to put across to Deans what it had taken scientists days to explain when they'd first joined the cause. Even so, he appreciated it was a lot to take in. He assured his new recruit they were almost home. "As I said earlier, Brookes was obsessed with the notion of manipulating space and time. And the incredible machine he'd created offered opportunity to do just that. With the accidental manufacture of alternate existence can you imagine the funding he was to receive? Think of all we've just witnessed on the screen. Numerous theories have been lauded over the years of how to avoid the final collapse. Most are painful to say the least. And we're a society reluctant to leave behind our pursuit of wealth and standing. However, what Brookes offered was the possibility of something unimaginable, the actual creation of existence. With such a creation comes endless opportunity. The WA gave him all he desired. If his machine could create artificial worlds then surely it could create artificial fuels. If these existences were real in just about every sense would it not be possible to one day farm them for our needs?" He elaborated, "Hence the desire to link these worlds from the offset, to travel to them. But what would the end result be if we even dared to mess with such a concept? These were the original, crude goals of this enterprise, and therefore queries that required answers. With the creation of synthetic existences, a test tube environment had been created. We'd been given a gift, a perfect practice arena, and only a fool would not make use of it. Once they'd figured out how to enter these existences, experimentation began. They needed to understand just what manipulating these environments could mean. At first only small probes were sent through. Robotic devices programmed to remove soil samples, return with rocks, instructed to alter the tiniest of details, to study such concepts as the butterfly effect . . . Picking a leaf from a tree, dropping a stone into a lake. The data analysed by the Stasis system."

Deans observed the new lesson as it was illustrated via the living screen once again.

"The counter-effect of these tiny alterations were minimal, so further tests ensued. The samples taken were studied, showing the alternate world to be as bona fide as our own. Eventually, under the assurance of the powerful computer together with the genius at its helm, it was decided the research should be taken up a notch." Dorey continued, "As soon as the Stasis None was introduced to more direct measures it began lighting up like a carnival.

And with each action it appeared to evolve its understanding of us and in turn provided new insights into its many mysteries, allowing Brookes and his teams to advance further at a much faster rate on all levels. It was as if by experiencing our direct input within its worlds, the Stasis None began to understand us that much better. Eventually the stage was reached when the scientists were ready to implement the human element, creating a team of individuals to make first contact in these alternate worlds." Dorey smiled. "From the first moment we touched down in one of those existences the Stasis None went wild. Brookes believed the preordained system was spiked by the experience of beings of free will, altering and contradicting a previously predetermined outcome. Whatever the reason, after our return the system danced from one chain of understanding to another, all the while providing Brookes with more answers in language he could finally understand. After a year, the boundaries were pushed significantly enough to allow us to alter our first event in a historical sense, to see if new parallel existence could be created safely from the one original string. After all, if we intended using these realms for our own ends we needed to know what the consequences would be. The result was incredible. The Stasis None not only provided us with the necessary protection, it formed under the guidance of Brookes a method to calculate the chain reactions our interference caused, creating a branch of a new alternate existence. An actual new string of parallel time, altered by our changing of a key event. As you can imagine the WA was ecstatic at Brooke's success, however, their own desires would be placed on hold when an unexpected bi-product emerged." Again the screen illustrated his words, "You see the future is never set. As such it's impossible to journey to it. However, what the Stasis system had done was provide us with a simulated copy of time we could alter and observe until it petered out in 2126, the end zone of our original string. But most incredibly of all, what Brookes then stumbled upon, was the ability to have the system calculate then create detailed predictions of how these altered futures would fall beyond the timeline parameters of 2126."

Deans gasped at this new implication.

"So not only were we learning the boundaries of time manipulation, of the boundaries we must obey when inside these new existences, we were also being provided with a calculation tool able to predict a larger unravelling of these altered futures beyond our own anchorage in time. Naturally, one of the first things Brookes did was aim this at our own reality. And after calculating the equivalent of a billion times over, the same grim result was delivered . . . When the Stasis None predicted mankind would be extinct from the planet within the course of this very century."

*

Dorey gave Deans a moment to digest the awful truth. "Once the Stasis None had understood the concept of recreating parallel existences from the one altered original, albeit simulated, it understood how Brooke's request to predict our own future could be achieved. Due to the impossibility of calculating human free will the Stasis None was unable to pinpoint this future catastrophe precisely. But it was able to predict odds on an unprecedented scale. The system insisted it was not our own experiments which would result in such an outcome, and after studying the galaxy around us declared it was unlikely to be a cosmic event. Everything pointed toward an unravelling combination triggered by something in our past. Eventually Brookes had the system pin down the likelier anchor points from which this chain of events could emanate. It outlined a number of pivotal moments within our two thousand year timeline that if altered, may change the outcome. Naturally the computer saves all alterations we make in its ethereal brain after the actual timelines are closed. It has also developed the ability to use the same future prediction method when combining multiple changed events together. Basically it is constantly playing and merging the events and alternate possibilities we've created until it finds the likely truth. This process is ongoing every second of every day." He shrugged, "Once again, how the damn thing is able to do so much in one area yet not provide a solution in another is something that has baffled all within this operation since it began. Just another complex contradiction that is the Stasis None." He stared at Deans for a long moment. "So there you have it. My team is now on a quest to find that one anchor point which could spark a key combination of events, that once altered, will steer the predictive element of the Stasis None away from confirming mankind's doom."

"But surely if what you're saying is true, it's just calculation, guesswork."

"This is of course possible. But what you have to keep in mind is all I've told you today. This isn't some computer adding up statistics and telling us something we already know . . . That if mankind isn't careful we'll eventually wipe ourselves out. This is a system with the ability to recreate worlds, allows us to manipulate time and space. A creation so powerful it alters entire strings of existence to the whim of our meddling then allows us to watch in detail the repercussions."

"But you said yourself the scientists have little understanding of how to see directly into these parallel universes. Of how to understand such a mass of contradiction. That massive potential for misinterpretation is never far away. If that's the case you could never be certain what you're watching is real in the conventional sense. It could be just another simulation played out by your fantastic machine."

"Of course you're right. It's quite possible nothing is as it seems. But you've not been to these recreated worlds. Breathed the air, heard the birds sing. Not yet at least."

The comment sent another tingle down Dean's spine. "And yet it cannot even hint at how this supposed apocalypse is meant to come about? Surely your own invention tops the list of likely candidates followed quickly by your recent lesson on economic collapse."

"As I said the Stasis system has provided a categorical denial this project could be the likely cause." Dorey admitted, "Had such a prediction come from any other source, one with less incredible credentials, then I dare say it may have been taken far less gravely. But we're talking about the Stasis None here. And if it's proved nothing else these past years, it's shown us any information it provides should be taken seriously."

Deans stared blankly at those gathered, his mind simply unable to accept the concept.

Dorey leaned into his chair. "But even if you choose to ignore the dire prediction element there are countless other reasons, ideals and technical basics of *what* we are and *why*, such as the original concept of finding more fuel." He watched the Marine Sergeant closely. "And you'll find as you spend more time here, you'll constantly re-evaluate your own version of justification behind what you do." He paused, "Priority one is of course to discover that one combination of events which once altered could potentially save us from destruction. And on each occasion we attempt this, my team becomes the blunt instrument which sees the Stasis None understand us better and in return has it release more of its' secrets. But beyond all of this we're naturally planning beyond one such prediction. We're practising ways of manipulating time and space so if and when *any* such moment arrives, we can change everything and anything to our favour. For the moment we're restricted to simulations. But there'll inevitably dawn a time when what we do here can be used as a real source of power . . . Perhaps salvation. We can already change a brief moment of time belonging to another simulated universe and watch how the results pan out. How long before we can achieve it for our own? You see, even if the Stasis None *is* wrong, we've reached a point where we've left ourselves few options. We've caused so much friction throughout the world simply saying sorry and shaking hands is never going to right it. We've sucked the life out of our planet, leaving us in the unstable mess we currently occupy. And if this has no bearing on how we're eventually wiped out there's a million and one other ways the universe can do it for us." Dorey leaned forward. "And that's what all of this is really about. This project looks at every possible way we can save ourselves, cheat our fate. The ability to manipulate time and space gives us power over everything, in a world running seriously short on answers. You see, it's more than just a way to save mankind or change the world . . . It's a way to save it . . . Perhaps even leave it for an alternative."

This grabbed hold of Deans instantly. "What do you mean alternative?"

"Precisely that . . . The Stasis project has many aims, one being to discover if you can actually create real time, create alternate worlds. Not just visit snapshots, but build infinite existences without people, ready to populate."

"You mean create another actual planet Earth?"

"Or even another universe," he replied, "While our team concentrates on altering the past to secure our short term, others use the information gathered to see if they can safely create an alternate future. As I've said each action we take sees the Stasis system buzz like a hive. If they succeed the possibilities are endless. We could transfer ourselves from one doomed reality into another of our own design. It sounds crazy but there are people actually working on such concepts within this complex as we speak. Anything below level two in this building is delving into the miraculous." Dorey was approaching the end of his mind-boggling introduction. "We'd be able to dodge anything from World War Three to a global killer asteroid. And the reality we jump to could be custom-made to suit our own survival. One world for us, one for China. One planet for Russia, one for Islam. This project combines untold options, offering opportunities to shape and create our own destiny, as well as to avoid the very real possibility of our own imminent destruction."

Deans gasped, "Playing God."

Dorey scoffed, "We've been doing that for a long time in one form or another. Maybe that's our right, maybe it isn't." Dorey was suddenly philosophical. "But who's to say this is not our real purpose? After all, one day our sun will fade and our world will die. Maybe threatening us with our own end is simply our Mother Earth's way of ensuring we not only cheat our death, but provide her with a method to avoid her own within the universe." His smile returned, "As I've told you. You'll find your own justifications and reasoning along the way. And they may alter as often as the sun rises. But whatever you choose to believe one thing remains certain . . . Our survival in this universe is a fight which has to go the distance, or else one way or another . . . We could end up facing the same fate as the dinosaurs."

CHAPTER TEN

The simulated skyline in Brooke's office had given way to a screen which appeared to add another room to the structure. Within the depths of this display were six concerned faces who peered realistically at one another.

In the centre was Robert Finch, the sour-faced director of the CIA and current chief of operations for WAIG. An enemy of Brookes who feared the Stasis None should be under direct governmental control and would stop at nothing to see this end met.

Framed to Finch's right was Will Grossen, the youngest head of the Military Intelligence Research Agency ever appointed by the WA. A shrewd and well-respected Virginian whom everybody knew came from good stock, a man never to be underestimated. Will had been highly trained by the more shadowy aspects of the military in a previous incarnation and gone on to make quite a name for himself as an agent, his speciality, the removal of well-guarded industrial secrets from rival powers. He believed entirely in the notion of democracy and had been more than prepared to steal from those who did not share his ideals, and it was rumoured, a good deal worse.

Next to him, broadcasting from her base city of Paris was Samantha Redemca, Principal Liaison Executive to the few WA member countries who'd been granted knowledge of the Stasis None Project. She was already contriving a meeting to bring up-to-date the four heads of state placed under her agenda. Redemca was their independent eyes and ears on all matters, voted for unanimously by the powers that created the post at the birth of the project. A sense of openness between the four members had been essential from the start, as had the necessity to keep the project's existence away from the attentions of the European Presidency. As former Chief Executive of Foreign Affairs to the UN, Miss Redemca was a rising star. Finch referred to her as the most powerful Personal Assistant in the world but he was more than aware she had more to her armoury.

Next was the image of Lord Gardener, beamed into the meeting from his estate in Sussex. The former head of WA Naval Intelligence, though officially retired, had recently been appointed to the position of WAIG's

North African and Gulf States spy-master. He had his *'finger on the pulse of the world'* according to most in the know, brought in by Finch to help ensure the security of this most top secret of secrets. He possessed a broad network of contacts and the trust of many allies, built up over decades the old-fashioned way. Alliances the likes of which Finch had not always been able to secure.

To the right was the image of Doctor Francois Beben, the renowned French physicist and head of the WA's Scientific Research Operative. An acclaimed genius whose work had led to the morphing technologies employed to create fluid movement within solid materials, structures and matter. He was a true pioneer who'd seen his concepts used across the world as well as extensively within the Stasis Project itself. He was Brooke's one true confidant within this assembled group. He sat deep in thought within his laboratory as he listened to his old friend's affirmation, the only person present whose intellect came anywhere close to matching Isimbard's extraordinary talent.

Finally there was Senator Raffy Abel. The Polish born trillionaire who unofficially held control of the purse strings to the WA's research projects while quite officially owning just about everything else. Although he would strongly deny it Raffy would determine the future of many a powerful player, with international corporations in the palm of his right hand, countries and their ambitious politicians often held within his left. He could have paid for the Stasis None out of his own wallet had it not been forbidden to see it placed under the control of a majority investor. The small handful involved had been wise enough to ensure this was a rule adhered to from the offset. He was a close friend to the Brookes family, but Isimbard was under no illusions as to the ruthless nature of this powerful man. A new breed of capitalist who would have no doubt bought the Presidency of the United States had his origin of birth not made it impossible for him to do so. He sat reservedly, his confident stare transmitting from inside his Pennsylvania Mansion.

The screens illustrated a committee of considerable power. An elite group, linked to the ruling shadows behind the US, Britain, France and Germany.

Isimbard Brookes sat before them once again.

Finch wore a hostile expression. "So, you're saying something from our *real* past could be travelling to destinations where we are currently carrying out missions within a simulated one?"

Brookes despised the man now addressing him and deeply resented the fact Finch had been secretly trying to get his hands on the Stasis None since its inception. Only some clever manoeuvres, skilful secrets and help from powerful friends had managed to deflect such an outcome. This, plus the fact Finch hadn't been able to find anyone who truly understood how to use his system. "No. I'm saying it appears to be a possibility according to Dr. Usorio's data. The information suggests an unknown entity may have exited one of our timelines into an as of yet untraceable location linked to our real past . . . Estimated at two centuries prior to the conception of the Stasis None. However, I believe this will prove to be inaccurate."

Finch sneered, "Doctor, are you now telling us the trillions spent on this machine of yours, was actually a waste of resources, because when push comes to shove *you* simply know better than *it* does?"

Brookes felt his stomach twist at the nerve of this ignorant man. Questioning him like some obnoxious schoolmaster on a subject he could no more comprehend than a goldfish could do calculus. He withheld from showing his contempt for this glorified gumshoe. "The program Doctor Usorio used is an outside source, not one belonging to the Stasis None. This gives forth massive potential for misunderstanding. However, it's been implemented into the Stasis mainframe, and yes, the results appear to suggest the findings have merit. Now I'm not saying this Hunter program or the Stasis None are wrong, I'm merely stating the prognosis may well prove flawed. As I keep telling you, we're dealing with an entire universe of new technology here, information the likes of which have never been witnessed before. Human error alone could lead to a complete misunderstanding of the facts. Just as easily as the computer's findings may be telling us what we *think* we see, and not necessarily what we *should* see."

Finch appeared to bite into a lemon. "We can well do without such riddles Doctor." Francois Beben came to Brooke's aide, "So you believe these findings, although at first glance disturbing, may be open to human misinterpretation, or indeed a misinterpretation of the Stasis None's retort to Usorio's Hunter program?"

"Yes." Brookes appealed to his generated audience, "Naturally this find is of the utmost importance. However, I find the possibility of an external force harnessing time travel technology long before the conception of atomic computing to be wholly inconceivable."

Raffy Abel threw his hat into the ring. "And you are certain Doctor that no such system could have predated, or since been developed, to match the one we possess today?"

"When I devised the Stasis None the reality of a quantum computer operating at such a level was as near to science as putting a man on the moon during World War Two. While likening my original prototype to the Stasis None in its current incarnation, would be like comparing a hot air balloon to a space shuttle. And all such advancements have only been made possible because of the Stasis None guiding me. So to suggest an atomic computer could have been used in the nineteen fifties is inconceivable. As for any such technology catching up to our own, the Stasis None assures me no such power exists." Brookes looked to each of his guests. "If we then consider the implication of a connection between our real past and the created timelines in which we operate." He elaborated, "The very fact this anomaly appears to make such a connection is enough to convince me of our misunderstanding. Our simulated time string was not created until 2126. Although it reaches into the past, it's an artificial one held within a dimension only accessible through the Stasis None. Therefore it cannot exist until you pass the point in which the Stasis System was conceived. If you were operating from a past which pre-dated our system, these cloned timelines would not even be there."

"And what if someone *was* able to access our system?" The question was from Will Grossen, "Would it be possible to travel in and out of our timelines then?"

"Theoretically yes. But any connection could only be achieved after the year 2126 and only with a quantum computer, with at least the same capability as our own, having direct access. However unlikely, at least this would be plausible. But the fact this entity has origins in our real past leads me to believe this is simply a glitch we don't yet understand. A misunderstanding between a *hunter* program stemming from a *nano-tech* computer based source, and that of our altogether superior atomic power. Any other scenario, at least as we understand things, would be simply impossible."

Finch looked at Brookes with suspicious eyes. "Well forgive me Doctor, but I thought the whole realm of what we're dealing with here is the impossible made possible." He enjoyed using one of Brooke's selling slogans against him. Murmurs of unrest followed.

"Which is why I've called this incident to your attention."

Will Grossen enquired, "And you maintain this is in no way connected to the prediction made by this Stasis None of yours?"

"The Stasis None has offered no such link between this anomaly and the answers we seek." He paused, "Put simply, something has happened we cannot explain. However, my recommendation is we continue as planned only with extra vigilance. We have seventeen weeks before Dorey is to be sent into sixteenth century Persia. I'm confident we'll have cleared this problem from your minds by then."

Finch eyed him like a hawk, "And if the problem remains unclear to you by such a time?"

Brookes looked over the collection of faces, his cold stare resting on the director, "In such a scenario, I believe *that* decision will then belong to all of you."

CHAPTER ELEVEN

Dorey entered the rear of the RFC with Deans. They made their way down the wide sloping stairs, passing the vacant levels of seats and terminals which could busy up to thirty scientists, technical engineers and flight control team members during an active operation. Now however, it stood empty but for three men working at the lower front of the chamber. They were seated before the viewing window which made up the entire front wall of the room, allowing a panoramic view of the hangar below. The empty workstations were staggered along each side of the central gradient. The place had the feel of a space launch facility. It was shrouded in shadow but Deans could imagine how different the room would appear when indulged in the activity of an operation.

They approached the three as they prepared to run their tests.

In front of terminal one sat the Reeper's Chief Operations Engineer, Myer Lavowitz, who was busy pulling up illustrations of the ships four main engines. Directly to his left studying a three-dimensional blueprint of the ship was the chief's number two Kev Marley, who was absorbed completely by the holographic display in front of him.

Stood behind both and supervising proceedings was Doctor Jose Cassaveres, the creative force ultimately responsible for the birth of the awesome time ship.

He turned as Dorey and Deans took the final steps toward them. "Dorey, it's good to see you." His Spanish accent tangoed with fluent English, producing a recipe of sound delicious to the ear.

"Ola Jose, que tal?"

"I'm good, I'm good, and you?"

"Muy bien, gracias."

The chief turned away from his screen to join the greeting. "Good to see you Commander, I must have missed you ten times since you got back."

"You're looking well chief." Dorey turned to Myer's number two, "How's tricks Kev?"

"Good thanks." He raised his hand aloft in greeting but did not allow his gaze to wander from the hologram before him. "I'll be with you in a second."

Dorey extended an arm, "This is Dennis Deans, the new member of our team."

Cassaveres reached out his hand in welcome. "It's good to meet you, I'm Jose Cassaveres," he gestured around the surrounding walls, "And this is the operational nerve-centre of the Stasis None Project, the Reeper Flight Control ... or RFC."

Deans gave a firm handshake. His attention was turned toward the chief engineer.

"I'm Myer, but everyone calls me chief, highly original I know." He pointed to his assistant, "And this is Kev Marley."

Still busying away the chief's number two added without turning his head. "Who's very busy right now and is never usually this rude."

Jose turned to Deans. "I take it you're here to meet my ship? Well, you couldn't have timed it better, Captain Tilnoh is in there right now preparing to fire up the engines." He led them forward to the viewing window.

As Deans looked down through the glass the change to his expression was instant. His mouth dropped in both awe and apprehension. Awe at what stood before him, apprehension from a secret he'd always endeavoured to hide. Deans did not like to fly.

In truth even the rollercoaster often left him sick to the stomach.

However the sight was indeed an incredible one.

Below was a hangar larger than a football pitch which stood around seventy feet in depth. Scattered on its surface were a handful of engineers scurrying around the behemoth which dominated the centre of the chamber.

Jose grinned at Dean's reaction then followed his gaze back to the ship, "The Reeper," he flashed a glance back to Deans, "Spelt double 'E'."

Deans pressed his face to the glass causing it to steam slightly as he mouthed, "Jesus."

Jose enjoyed observing the reactions experienced by the chosen few allowed an introduction to his baby.

"She's something isn't she?" Dorey had never grown tired of looking on this marvel and could never grow weary of Jose's enthusiasm for her. The ship had saved his life twice and brought all but one of the Commander's crew safely home on countless occasions. To fly her must be a dream and he envied Jay, Benny and Jim for their skills at times, though he did not envy the extra implants all three required in order to do it.

Like all boys, Deans loved his toys, fear or no fear of flying. "She's huge."

The Reeper measured almost fifty metres from the tip of her high tail down to the broad nose of her front. She stood close to three stories with her landing gear down. The outer body of titanium tiles were finished in a highly-polished black coating resistant to atmosphere re-entry induced heat. Her nanotechnology provided near invisible stealth. The combination of materials dressing her shell enabled her to produce beautiful reflections of sable and blue as her skin flirted with the lighting of the hangar.

Deans was captivated by her spellbinding combination of obvious power and shimmering beauty. "She looks almost . . . "

Jose awaited his conjecture with an eager expression. He was the artist, expectant of the assured strong response, a provocation guaranteed by his one true masterpiece.

"Alive."

Jose was delighted with his choice of analogy and watched silently as Deans continued his gaze over the ship below. Deans was trying to place a name to the image now pestering him from his memory. "She looks like a whale shark."

The architect positioned himself directly behind the two onlookers. "During the design phase I had to come up with a shape which would help the ship sore through time and space, yet also possess the strength to carry cargo while withstanding atmospheric pressures." Jose was quickly warming to Deans. "Some aspects of the final design were taken from various breeds of Marine life." He pointed his finger to the long protruding spine which ran from the body then climbed high into the air before culminating into the awesome looking tail fin, its pointed tip almost adjacent to their current eye level. "She's state of the art technology. Her one vertical fin can morph to produce a giant 'V' shape . . . This provides a diverse array of options to her flight. Her body can also make minor shape shifts to assist her as she swims through one time into another and to also help her through the sonic gears of atmospheric flight." His finger led Dean's eyes down to her powerful, stocky body. "She can carry in excess of one hundred tonnes without losing too much performance and there are entrance and exit ramps for personnel and vehicles at her front and rear. The front ramp is lowered directly beneath her nose, the rear drops just beneath the main forward thrust engine where the spine meets her backside…Do you see where I mean?"

Deans nodded. "How fast is she?"

"Oh she's fast for a big girl." Again he pointed his finger to the task. "She's powered by seven hydro-cell super-jets, four of which fire out of the rear exhaust hole under the tail there. This however can be morphed into one larger exhaust, and her body will alter its state to cater for *scramjet* and a modification we call *Barb-fire*."

"You mean a short burst rocket?"

The doctor was suitably impressed. "Your boy knows his stuff."

Dorey nodded. "That's why he's here."

Jose continued, "Her scramjet alone can take her to MACH 5 at altitude, but with her Barb-fire burning, well . . . She'll blast you into another time."

Deans smiled at the pun. The ship filled him with nervous tension as he flirted between his love-hate relationship with all manmade flying creations.

Dorey added. "Oh and in case you're wondering, she's also armed to the teeth."

Before this new direction could be explored the intercom stirred and Jay's voice travelled into the room. "Control I have completed internal diagnostic, ready to fire engines."

Kev Marley concurred with Jay's intrinsic results, "Copy that Jay, we have coherent data, preparing to switch you to manual."

"Roger that control."

The chief took the initiative. "Jay, I will secure Reeper then initiate countdown."

A red flashing light began dancing around the hangar accompanied by a warning buzzer. Jose made his leave, "Excuse me for a moment gentlemen." He took position behind his two trusted controllers and activated the hangar speakers to address the people below. "Ladies and gentlemen, if you could take your positions, we are preparing for engine firing sequence."

They watched as the various personnel below began to evacuate the floor, retreating through various doors and exits cut into the hangar walls.

The Reeper's tail was already propped by a huge supporting arm but now two larger structures lowered themselves from the ceiling ready to cradle the ship's body. They fixed themselves around the main superstructure and appeared to amalgamate themselves into the sides of the Reeper. Then with apparent tension they locked into a vice like grip.

"RFC, the Reeper is locked down and ready."

The chief accorded with Jay's readings, "Initiating countdown sequence."

The buzzer ceased as the flashing light was now joined by a recorded female voice, *"Warning, engine test fire will commence in two minutes."*

"Raising landing gear." Jay declared.

The lower supports retracted into the belly leaving her suspended by the ceiling arms.

A huge metal tube began to concertina outward from the rear of the hangar. The cylinder attached itself to a large metal housing situated twelve feet to the rear of the ship's hull. This exhaust tunnel was to absorb the heat of the afterburners and to suck away the ferocious combustion of the Barb-fire rockets. The recorded voice returned, *"Commencing engine fire countdown . . . Thirty seconds to mark."*

Jose continued to monitor proceedings from the rear as Marley's holographic display began flashing up information, "All systems okay."

"Powering engines." A loud whistling of turbines emanated from the Reeper.

Deans studied the twin slits of blackened glass, staggered some ten metres apart at the nose of the Reeper. He leaned toward Dorey, "Which is the pilot's window?"

"The lower. The upper is the navigation deck, though both cockpits can control the flight of the ship in case of an emergency. The belly can also separate from the main hull in order to create an escape pod."

"Ten seconds to mark . . ."

The outer rim of the rear exhaust hole retracted and almost doubled its circumference.

"Five seconds to mark . . ."

"Firing primary cells."

"Three, two, one . . . Mark!"

On Jay's cue the rear jets of the Reeper discharged their force. The ship leaned into the restraints but they held firm like a mother clutching the straps of her toddler's dungarees.

"Engines firing to forty percent," Jay's voice was a vibration of calm.

Jose observed the incoming data, "Everything looking great up here Jay."

The Reeper gave another disgruntled shake, "Engines firing to seventy percent." The whistle of jets gave way to a growing roar. "Ninety percent . . . Prepare for afterburn."

The roaring engines now began to snarl as the heat turned the exhaust to a fiery orange. "Engines at one hundred percent, afterburners engaged." There was a short sharp bark before a pointed flame ripped out of the exhaust. The Reeper shook furiously but her restraints pinned her down like an angry dog.

Deans and Dorey watched in silence as the three men to their rear monitored the progress of the test. The interaction of both the pilot's suit and Jay's implants worked in perfect unison to both monitor her condition as well as to help her pilot the ship as an integral part of it. She was almost one with the Reeper brain whenever they flew together.

Jay's voice trembled through her microphone, "Preparing for air brake then re-burn."

"Copy that Jay, you are good to go."

Four panels of air brakes fluidly morphed from the side of the ship. Each one containing a collection of retro burners which fired the very instant the rear engine shut off. The Reeper plunged within its leash and screamed out. The monitors recorded the extreme 'G' forces of the simulated stop and Deans noticed what he believed to be a momentary look of concern on Dorey's face.

A more strained version of Jay's voice struggled across the airwaves. "Firing re-burn."

The Reeper jolted forward, her nose snarling upward. For a moment it looked as though she'd broken free of her bonds, but again they held firm. The rear exhaust exploded into a violent storm as the ship successfully simulated a brake to full throttle procedure.

"Testing directional retro's." Jay's voice evened as the ship was again burning forward.

"Copy that Jay, simulating obstacles."

The powerful flaps coupled with the sharp retro-bursts shooting from the Reeper jolted her nastily from side to side like a fair ground ride.

Inside the ship, Jay's helmet allowed her to see all around her outer space, using a combination of heat vision and fast angle camera shots that could be beamed back into the visor. If need be the pilots could even alter their actual perception and see themselves as flying in a ship made of glass. The visor was also a direct conduit to the ship's computer, and as such both Reeper and her charges could communicate their surroundings at speed, with voice commands quickly locking and zooming in visuals that were too far away for the enhanced eye alone.

This same technology now simulated obstacles like an asteroid field, as she demanded direction shifts from her ship. She performed several manoeuvres until happy. "Directional boosters and flaps okay, preparing to switch to Barb-fire."

"Copy that Jay you have the mark."

The Reeper eased out of its sporadic wrestling and levelled once more into a high throttled burn. Again the afterburners lit up. The restraining arms seemed to predict the next phase and thus tighten their grip. The engines were screaming at full velocity and the heat ripples around the exhaust distorted the atmosphere like a stone thrown into a pond.

"Preparing for Barb-fire on my mark; five . . . four . . . three . . . two . . . one . . . Mark." A deep bellow rumbled from the Reeper, quickly followed by a succession of grunting shudders. The flames of the afterburners abated and again the circumference of the exhaust increased in preparation for the coming firestorm. Then suddenly the entire hangar found itself lost to an explosion of effluvium flame. The giant arms tensed as the child grew more determined to break free. The ship began to shake violently as the flaming torch screaming from her rear intensified, the exhaust now playing host to the wrath of the Barb-fire rocket.

The noise was incredible despite the glass between the control room and the hangar. The fire intensified with a gargantuan clap as the missile burst reached its optimum output.

Jay's voice trembled from within the cockpit, "Barb-fire at seventy percent."

Jose's voice was calming over the intercom, "Everything looking good up here Jay."

"Barb-fire at eighty percent."

Deans had a quick glance over at Dorey but his face was an unreadable mask once more.

"Ninety percent."

The chief and Marley studied their displays intently.

The rear of the ship was a furnace now, roaring in a constant burn.

"Barb-fire at maximum, check complete . . . ready to power down on your mark RFC."

Jose, the chief and Marley quickly ran a final diagnostic, the ship's proud father more than happy. "All systems checked, power down when ready."

"Copy that, throttling down."

Deans watched as the inferno eased into a series of dull implosions. The monstrous arms which held the craft so firmly relaxed the tension, the fervid child finally ready to accept defeat. With several whip cracks the glowing embers of exhaust dulled then spluttered out as the Reeper wearily succumbed within a chorus of sighs.

*

The powerful arms released their grip and retracted to the hangar ceiling. As they returned the recorded female voice sang across the airwaves, "*Engine test, complete.*"

Dorey could see it had left an impression on Deans, "Come on, I'll take you to meet the girls." He turned to Cassaveres. "Is it okay to go down?"

"Sure we're pretty much finished here . . . But pop back up for a cup of tea before you go."

He acknowledged Jose's request then led Deans to the elevator.

He would never admit it, but he was always glad when these tests were over. The raw power expended from the hulk of their ship didn't seem natural in an enclosed space, and he was certain one day the Reeper would finally grapple free and blast straight into the Wiltshire rock. He usually stayed away when the tests were carried out but felt Deans should be familiar with as much of the project credentials as possible before training for his first mission, preparation due to begin after the coming weekend.

The elevator door opened revealing a clear glass compartment overlooking the hangar below. Dorey smiled. "Willy Wonker."

Deans laughed as he followed him inside.

Stepping into the hangar the noise was instantly more abrupt, the smell of the fuel overpowering. Dorey led Deans around the ship.

He marvelled at her powerful presence, all the more potent and intoxicating when stood beneath her mighty frame. He had the sense of stepping from a zoo directly into a safari, the big game now close enough to touch.

Engineers offered polite hellos as they came around the nose of the ship. Deans was blown away by her threatening poise of size and power.

The massive body tensed forward and the lowest point of her nose stood only sixteen feet from the deck. Towering from her rear he could see the long high tail fin pointing to the roof. It seemed so far away now. He hadn't even seen her weapons capability but was already beginning to understand why they'd named her the Reeper, whatever the spelling. She looked like a prehistoric ocean predator, a deadly black behemoth ready to swallow ships whole. "This is one monstrous aircraft you've got here."

Dorey nodded, "She's something isn't she?"

"I've never seen anything like her."

"She's Jose's brainchild. He had to have her assembled piece by piece down here."

"I take it she doesn't get out much in the conventional sense."

"No, not in a conventional sense." He pointed to the hangar floor. "The only time she gets to fly is when she does a time leap. You see the line running right across the centre of the hangar deck? The floor splits in two there and retracts outward through the walls. The huge ceiling arms used in testing hold her in place above the cavern below us. A tunnel is created in there by the Stasis None. Like an artery from our time and space to those created by the computer as the two existences are folded closer together. Once the tunnel is opened up the Reeper is simply dropped in at the right moment. We call it the 'Base-Jump or Drop' because the hole below us is the size of a canyon."

Deans observed the hangar floor and marvelled at the sheer technical undertaking all around him. Secretly he felt nauseous at the description he'd just heard.

"It's like being dropped into a raging river . . . A torrent of time. We plunge into it then blast ourselves downstream toward our relevant exit which is a tear in the fabric of time itself, linking the two existences. Soon after, we're spat out like a missile above the atmosphere of our chosen destination." He added, "She takes one hell of a pounding externally and there's been occasion when her systems have malfunctioned for a while on the other side. Communications, weapons array that sort of thing. But these have always proved temporary as she can pretty much repair herself given enough opportunity. She acts as one with the pilots on a level you wouldn't believe. Once through she flies like any other aircraft, carrying us and our equipment to any chosen location."

Dean's head was spinning, thinking of all the impossible things he'd witnessed this day.

"She's big enough to carry trucks, a tank, you name it. In atmospheric flight she's fast, even when fully laden, and as I said she's armed to the teeth. Few things could match her in a dogfight. One on one, she's pretty much top of the food chain."

Deans gave her more admirable looks as his love, hate battle continued. "I take it you come back in the same way."

"Pretty much. I'm told it's kind of like docking in space. Only this particular space is throwing one hell of a storm your way. Again the hangar arms are lowered. If need be they can be extended to five hundred metres. They're piloted to the ship by the computer of the Reeper and the Stasis None, which in many ways are one and the same thing. In the meantime we fly back up the stream of the tunnel or *river* as we call it, until we're directly beneath the hangar. We then go into a flat-out burn to hold us steady until we're located and dragged back inside. Just like pulling a fish from a stream."

"So do you return at the same moment you left?"

"That's a good question. No, although the difference in time spent away can vary greatly. It's to do with the fact our destination is simulated, yet the dimension it's located in is real. It's all about knocking things out of phase and the technology used to fold our space and the subject zone closer together. Like our own, the Stasis universe is expanding. It's this movement in relationship to our own space and time which allows us to connect to certain timelines and not others. This very principle has huge implications on our own missions. If the corridor torn into the dormant copy moves too much across the surface of that timeline we can be in there for months and yet return to our own reality within days. On occasion, if the movement between these two corridors proves too great, the Reeper may even have to leave us in that string, return home through the entry corridor ready to be re-injected at our time of extraction, to reduce the risk of us all being lost. I've never fully understood it all to be honest. But when such a scenario arises . . ."

He was interrupted by an alarm which began to sound in unison with a flickering red light, warning of the imminent lowering of the forward loading ramp.

Dorey stopped mid-sentence and turned with Deans. They watched as the vessel opened her mouth, the ramp lowering itself to the floor.

Jay appeared and walked down the gangway to greet them wearing a broad smile, "Well don't you look all handsome in that uniform."

Deans suspected he may have blushed, "Err, yeah, I was told to report in dress rig."

"I wanted to be at your introduction but had a flight test in the simulator, then madam here decided to keep me busy for the rest of the day."

Deans was quick to placate. "After seeing that little display I can imagine how she would keep anyone busy, Ma'am."

Jay had always got a kick out of being called *Ma'am* and her smile gave away this fact, "Call me Jay, I'm Captain Jay Tilnoh."

He smiled and took up her introduction with a handshake, "I'm Deans."

"So what do you think of our little ship?"

"She's very impressive . . . More than impressive."

"How's she handling?" Dorey enquired.

Jay gave the Reeper a fleeting look. "Oh she's fine now, but had the hiccups earlier and wanted a little attention." Jay turned to Deans, "She's very spoiled and likes to be doted on." Her attention returned to Dorey, "But everything's sorted now Commander."

Deans sensed the teasing tone, quickly clocked the intense look which sat behind her sharp eyes, and realised these two were lovers.

"So Deans, would you like a tour of the ship?"

"I'd love one." It was partly true and partly a fearful lie.

"You coming?"

Dorey glanced at his watch.

"That means no."

"I told Jose we'd catch up. I'll do that while you give Deans a quick run around the Reeper. That way we can get out of here a little earlier."

"I'll take good care of him."

"I'm sure. I've told the others to meet us in the Priory, they left a while ago."

Jay nodded, realising this statement was more for Dean's benefit.

"I figured since you were expecting to be on a plane to the Middle East tonight you wouldn't mind coming out with us instead."

Deans was happy to be railroaded. A drink was a good idea after this, his shocking first day below ground. "Of course, but I don't want to put anybody out."

"You won't be. An apartment and transport have already been put aside for you in London. You'll be in the same district as the rest of us. It'll be your base from now on. But don't worry I'll explain in detail tonight. The shuttle leaves in under an hour, I trust you've brought a change of clothes."

"Yes Sir, I have."

Dorey strode away toward the waiting elevator, "Welcome to the Stasis None Project."

Jay smiled. "I take it this is the first you've heard of your London apartment."

He nodded.

"But I'd bet it's not the greatest shock you've encountered today."

Deans sighed. "No, no it's not."

She gave him a reassuring look. "Well don't worry. Most of them are good shocks believe me. Come on, I'll give you a quick tour of the ship then we can get out of here, see some sky and get to know you a little better over a few drinks." She could see Deans was swimming against the tide. "What we do here is amazing, but it's no more risky than anything else you'll have already done."

He looked at her, allowing a pensive smile to form.

Jay turned to lead him up the ramp, "Jesus, what a day huh?"

He agreed with such prognosis before following her into the awesome ship.

CHAPTER TWELVE

Robert Finch had opened a secure transmission to discuss Brooke's conference call with Lord Gardener. They'd been speaking for some time, Finch formulating his planning, feeding on his suspicions. "I've never trusted that man." His sour face remained even when talking to someone he conceived as some kind of friend. "Far too interested in the conceit of his own genius," He enjoyed using colourful words, "A self-promoter, and one who may not share a firm belief in our goals."

Lord Gardener sipped his expensive whiskey. He had the look of a man once as ruthless as Finch, but one softened by the process of age rather than hardened by it. "Isimbard Brookes is an idealist, nothing more, despite his attempts to conceal the fact. And yes you are correct when you say he cares more for his own ambition than he does our own."

"An ambition for the Western Alliance . . . Not just for ourselves."

Gardener took the correction with a pinch of salt. "But everyone knew this when they backed him."

"Yes . . . But they thought by now he'd be under control."

"He holds all of the cards. As you said, he's more than aware of his own genius. There's not a scientist alive who could even comprehend the depths of his understanding. Beben and Stein are mere children in comparison."

Finch felt his skin crawl. "There are secrets he holds, secrets I know we can access."

Gardener's face grew stern. "We know the consequences of such a road. If we start creating too many waves he'll close the whole thing down. He's done it before. That's the problem with idealists . . . And it's a problem *you* can ill afford."

Finch was clearly growing more annoyed. Brookes had continued to out manoeuvre him for the past decade. He had the backing of some extremely powerful players, as well as the supreme advantage handed to him by possessing the freakish intellect of a man way ahead of evolution. *'But a game of chess is not always won by greater intellect.'* Finch's thoughts were dark and methodical. "Inform our mole I wish to make contact."

"Of course," Lord Gardener replied. "But may I urge caution. If we start digging too deep too soon, the whole project could come tumbling down. And that's what lost your predecessor her job."

Finch smarted at the remark. "I've been patient for long enough. And I'm prepared to risk my neck for the ideology of my own beliefs. Brookes has had things his own way for too long. It's time we stepped up our efforts."

"As you wish Robert," he shrugged gently, "I've said my piece." His voice was rustic and mellowed by good booze and expensive cigars.

"Oh and Christopher," Finch glared through the screen at Lord Gardener, "Let's ensure Will Grossen's nose remains well away from this." The sour expression returned. "And if he continues to sniff around . . . Be sure to keep me informed."

Lord Gardener nodded, and with a polite goodbye, the transmission was over.

CHAPTER THIRTEEN

Located at the heart of the Canary Wharf, the Priory was the flagship venue for the Century Sixty Group, a company wired into the craze for old style bars and clubs.

Clothed with the music, sports and styling which graced the eras between nineteen-sixty and twenty sixty, each establishment came equipped with a stage built to project perfect reproductions of bands and singers long since dead, resurrected in all their pomp within the living colour of a holographic duke box.

It was still early in the evening but the establishment was already filling with suits.

Dial hated the music many of the young business breed seemed to go for even in a themed bar such as this, so he'd taken it upon himself to scan enough credit into the main music station in order to play the maximum *half hour of songs* allowed at any one time.

He was now signalling for Benny to come over and do the same.

Unfortunately for Dial, Benny was having more fun ignoring him and after several animated attempts he gave up and returned to the group.

"Couldn't you see me waving at you over there?"

Benny laughed, "Yeah."

"So why didn't you come over?"

"Because I enjoy watching you wave your arms around like a lunatic."

The surrounding grins did little to impress Dial, "Assholes." The comment brought about laughter as he took his seat. "You're the ones always moaning about how it gets in here when those screen surfers put their dance music on all night."

Jim corrected, "No, *you* are the one who bitches when they put their music on all night."

"Well if any of you complain when the retro-dance remix comes on," Dial imitated the ridiculous arm movements of the long ago dance craze called Beat-Low, which had been the latest century old genre to enjoy a revival, "Then don't blame me."

The following laughter allowed Dial to carry on with his drink, his standing restored.

A brief intermission followed as they turned to see a sprightly looking Rat Pack greet the audience from the stage, with Dean Martin making an ambiguous quip which could have been aimed at any number of guys at the bar.

Even now the technology provoked. From punters who wanted Elvis in person, to protestors who felt it wrong to recreate an Avatar of some dead entertainer just so they may decorate the stage of a tavern.

The same arguments raged when the technology married with statistics allowed revellers to see just how the Brazilian football team of 1970 would fare against the great LA Galaxy of the twenty-forties, or how Muhammad Ali in his prime would have taken the fight to the savagery of a Mike Tyson still in his youth. Nostalgia was big business.

"When did you say they'd left?" Marco enquired.

"They took the shuttle almost an hour ago. They're probably on the tube." Dial scanned the door as another crowd of suits entered dressed like they had serious credit to spend.

Britain was doing well out of the fusion and hydrogen age. Previous governments had set the pace in buying up much of the world's water reserves, the monies made invested in rebuilding her infrastructure. The territories lost to the great floods now housed hydro-cell stations up and down the country, pumping the once devastating water into renewable fuel. The working class, for the most part a third generation immigrant state, were managed like a communist underbelly, with bonus and reward schemes which could eventually see them earn every freedom and luxury. Improved networks from health to transport were constructed and even the sky highways developed in Japan now saw shuttle flights racing it out with trains across the counties below. And as the hydro-cell cars quietly navigated the motorways with minimal input from drivers, the country was shaping into a more efficient, though not altogether freer place.

Seven decades prior Britain stared resentment, fear and fascism in the eye and managed, albeit a little belatedly, to turn away, though with bloodied hands and stricter hearts.

Although the totalitarianism of the Exodus fiasco had abated, much of its legacies remained and the WA still insisted on closed borders. Freedoms were removed, many through law, most by technology. The anger and concern replaced by a complacent surrender to Big Brother in order to maintain a society accustomed to its little luxuries.

Freedom swapped for facilities.

Facilities like bars able to promise a Rolling Stones appearance every night of the week. It was the Beatles however who were next up on the Priory stage, shaking their digitised mop tops to a *hard day's night*, much to the delight of Dial who sang along badly.

Carl turned his attention to the bar entrance just as Dorey and Jay arrived with a less formal Deans. "They've just walked in." He announced to the rest of the table.

Dorey was scanning the rear knowing one of the more private alcoves would be the chosen location. His eyes found Carl's outstretched arm and he waved to acknowledge him. He mouthed the words with an accompanying mime action, "Do you want drinks?"

Com-links were never used in public.

Carl raised his bottle, following the motion by holding up five fingers as Dorey pointed out their location to Jay.

She led Deans over, the others shuffling to make extra space.

Jay smiled as she reached the table. "Hey guys."

They received a welcome from the rest of the group. Dial stood up. "Jay, sit here."

"You sure?"

"Of course, you know we like you in the middle."

Jay looked to Dial coyly, "I'm not sure how I should take that." She led Deans to the surrendered section of seating.

Deans felt like the new boy at school. His head was still in a whirl from the day's events. Earlier Dorey had told him for obvious reasons the subject of work was never directly discussed outside the project walls unless inside one of the team's secure apartments. Deans still had this pleasure of discovery to come.

"So Deans, how are you feeling after looking over our little adventure holiday?"

"It looks pretty unbelievable." He replied to Jim's cryptic enquiry.

Jay flashed Dial a glance which he read immediately. He sat forward and pointed over to the stage. "So Deans, what kind of music do you like?"

A sigh escaped the table accompanied with the statement, "Here we go," from Benny.

"What? It's as good a question as any. You know you can tell a lot about a person from the type of music they like." He was deliberately patronising.

Carl smiled. "Yeah and don't we know it."

After a brief, somewhat comical discussion, Dial activated the duke box menu, "Here, call out any you would listen to on there."

Deans browsed the now illuminated list of nostalgic songs. "I like the Jazz and Blues section." He pointed to the stage, "The Beatles . . . Pretty much all latter twentieth century stuff. You know, when music was still at least a little bit original."

Jim laughed and pointed a finger at Dial. "Jesus is he paying you to say this shit?"

Dial was looking triumphant and Deans understood he may have made a musical ally. "I take it you're into that stuff too."

Dial pulled a face. "Oh God no, I'd never listen to any of that Jazz bullshit. But the rest was sounding quite promising."

Jim grimaced, "How can you say *jazz bullshit* when you know you've just put on the last rendition of King of the Swingers?"

"Because Louis is the king of the SWING . . . *Not* the king of the jazz bullshit."

"Yeah, and you're the king of something!"

Deans then made the worst possible statement as far as Dial's cause was concerned, pointing into the illuminated menu, "Oh and I don't mind some of this Beat-Low music."

Laughter immediately engulfed the table.

Deans guessed by the harassment Dial must have bad-mouthed this prior to his arrival.

"Get some on and turn it up." Carl encouraged.

"But go to the master player so you can scan in a half-hour's worth." Benny laughed.

Dial turned to Deans in disbelief. "How could someone proclaiming such musical vision as the Beatles proclaim to like such a crock of shit?"

Deans shrugged. "I don't know, I guess it's what you might call a wide musical taste."

This delighted the audience and they poured more scorn on Dial as Dorey approached with a tray of drinks. Once all were served, Carl held up his bottle and declared, "Cheers. And may I offer a welcome to Dennis Deans."

They raised their bottles and glasses and repeated the toast.

*

The lighting hummed into life then sparked a ferocious wall of illumination.

Deans, Jay and Dorey all squinted from its sudden glare.

"Shit." Dorey protested as Jay quickly commanded, "Lights down thirty percent."

"God I thought I was blind." Deans joked. All three were obviously half cut.

Dorey fanned out his arms. "Welcome to your new abode."

Deans scanned the room, a happy look washing over his face, "Shit."

The pale walls wore the unmistakable silky sheen of the latest digital-video display creating a blank canvas similar in appearance to the walls in a Japanese Dojo.

"Is the whole room hooked up to *Digeo*?"

Dorey nodded, "Yep. Computer, download demo screen one."

The walls and ceiling instantly transformed into a realistic field of sunflowers which surrounded and waved at them on every turn.

Deans' face lit up. "Wow."

Dorey returned the walls to a blank canvas as Deans observed the living space. Its central living area ran down two small steps creating a perfectly square well. This played host to a large L-shaped sofa flanked by a crystal coffee table lounging on a thickly piled rug.

Jay watched as he emanated pleasure toward his new home. "Hey Deans, check this out," she said with a smile, "Computer, open kitchen and bedroom."

With a stylish hum two sections of the far wall slid away, revealing two large arches within the architecture. One opened into the bedroom with its en-suite bathroom, the other to the modern kitchen, complete with utility room.

"You've got all media and computing facilities built in to the *Digeo* system, as well as access to all worldwide satellites and channels." Dorey smiled.

Deans shook his head as he walked from room to room. "The last place the military put me up in had cockroaches climbing the walls."

"The whole complex is state of the art VIP, reserved for the cream of military and political stock. Retired Admirals, Generals, Ambassadors and Lords."

Jay jumped in. "Your basic wall-to-wall British assholes."

Deans smiled. "And they put us in here? These places must cost a fortune."

Dorey nodded, "One of the many reasons being this also happens to be one of the most secure civilian compounds in London. Some cover story was concocted to ensure no envious eyebrows were raised, delivered from somewhere so high up they didn't even bother giving us the details. All we know is the most conversation we ever get around the entire complex is a polite hello or a short discussion on the weather."

More sarcasm followed, "My God, and how you British love to talk about the weather."

Dorey pointed a casual thumb toward Jay, "Yanks, can't take their drink."

He received a nudge from Jay's elbow.

"This is unbelievable."

"You're now involved in something so big the Prime Minister himself wouldn't dare ask you to turn your music down."

Deans turned with a gleam in his eye. "Now there's a theory I'll have to test out."

Dorey's face stretched into a broader grin. The night had gone well. Everyone had been placed under strict instruction to make Deans feel right at home. It was essential he relax into his new surroundings. But Dean's likeable nature meant any effort was proved for the most part unnecessary as the group had taken to him right away.

They'd hoped this would be the case while watching the newcomer from afar.

"Well, we'll bid you good evening. If you need anything the computer can call any one of us on request. Although if I were you I wouldn't call Dial until at least midday."

Jay smiled, "See you in the morning."

Dorey walked toward him and shook his hand. "It's good to have you on board. The guys all thought you were great, and I'm sure you'll be happy here."

"Well it's gonna be tough but I'll try to make the best of it."

Dorey patted his shoulder. "I'll see you tomorrow to go through the rest of the stuff in the apartment." Both he and Jay turned and headed for the door which opened on approach.

Deans watched them go, "Rest of the stuff, like what?"

As they reached the door Dorey turned. "Now that would be telling." He grinned. "Oh and there's a bottle of very vintage brandy hidden for you somewhere inside this little pad of yours, I've been keeping it especially. And I'll bet you ten thousand credits you won't find it before my return tomorrow."

The door closed and his guests were gone, leaving Deans to explore his new miniature palace alone. He decided to waste no time in accepting the challenge.

*

Deep within the belly of the Stasis caves Brookes sat brooding over his desk. Of the many scientists and engineers within the project only he had access to this room. In fact, he was one of only two people who knew of its existence. Even the blueprints of this vast underground project backed the idea it was nothing more than solid Wiltshire rock.

The prying eyes of the security cameras were not granted intrusion into this most secret of places. The watchful lenses unaware of the corridor leading to it, never mind the chamber itself. Hidden away by a cocktail of complex technology, coupled with a clever charade of digital imagery, employed to mask the doctor's trips to this most sacred haven.

It was the real nerve centre of all he'd created, the secret lair which allowed him to out-manoeuvre Finch and his cronies time and again.

The engineers who had built it worked for his brother, an architect who designed and manufactured the room, along with the secret lift shaft and corridor granting access to it. His workers subjected to deception and tricks, didn't even know the location in which they worked, skilfully misled by the Doctor and his brother, who had them believe they'd constructed the cavern some eighty feet above the actual location.

It had been secretive, elaborate and expensive . . . But most of all worth it.

The equipment brought down was done so in pieces, Brookes constructing it himself. One of the many bonuses of being a certified genius.

His display screens were one such challenge and he looked on them now with an expression of frustration and unsolved query.

It was past two in the morning and his solitude was haunted by the rhythmic heartbeat that beseeched him with every pulse, passing through the control panels, voicing itself like a ghost around the room. Usorio's findings cut far deeper than he'd let on to his contemporaries. *'What could cause such an anomaly?'* He needed to find the answer.

He'd scoured the depths of his brain and asked the Stasis None question on question but could find no peace from the probabilities placed before him.

He would be sending Dorey and his team back to the sixteenth century within thirteen weeks and his brief was due for delivery on Monday. Yet he hadn't even completed it.

He sighed and rose to his feet. He walked slowly, passing the walls of data, almost in step with the rhythmic beat roaming the airwaves in a digitised pulse.

He checked the occasional image as he passed the displays, but it was a poor performance, they could have been paintings in the Louvre for all he'd have noticed.

He was tired, and unwittingly he'd reached his destination in a haze of ponderous thought. He stopped and looked down to his waist.

Below him was a large metallic container which lay on a parapet like a coffin set for a wake. The shiny black-tiled torpedo-jacket, gave it the eerie resemblance of a large bomb. The kind hidden in the darkest of places, until one day called upon to carry out the darkest of deeds. On its surface was a digital display which played out the rhythm of the room's low gentle beat, resembling a graphic equaliser as it flickered to the sound of a loosely strung bass, 'Badum . . . Badum . . . Badum.''

Brookes placed his hand on its surface, running his fingers across the engraved graphics which read, 'STASIS NONE'. He stared at the device and whispered something.

But of course, it gave no reply.

CHAPTER FOURTEEN

The tension in the debriefing room was evident. Brooke's decision to delay the mission brief by some forty-eight hours was a first, and his lack of presence around the facility during this period suggested something was wrong.

Dorey was tonguing a piece of apple skin stubbornly wedged between two molars when Brookes finally walked in and took his place on the podium.

"Good afternoon everybody." His eyes wandered until his gaze fell upon Deans. "Before I begin I'd like to take this opportunity to personally welcome our new member. I'd also like to apologise for having not met with you sooner but I'm afraid these past days have proven more taxing than expected."

Deans dismissed the need for apology as Dorey and the others glanced at one another, the doctor's terminology seeming to confirm their suspicions.

"But I know you've been left in capable hands and I'm sure they've tried to make this somewhat incredible undertaking as digestible as possible."

Deans nodded.

"Good. I've arranged for us to meet in my office after this brief, shall we say two thirty? Commander you're welcome to sit in if your schedule will allow."

"I'm sure I'll be able to attend Doctor."

"Excellent." He activated the display wall. "I'll get straight to the point. The reason for the delay, and my disappearance these past days, is a somewhat profound one. An unexplained event was traced within the Stasis system before the weekend, an occurrence which I'm afraid must remain classified to level six for the time being."

The Commander studied him intently. He and his team were level four.

"A glitch, which I can assure poses no danger, but demanded my attention nonetheless. However, during the process of trying to unravel the cause of this technical anomaly, a most abstract reaction within the system was stirred, resulting in the Stasis None offering up something quite unexpected."

Dorey's jaw tensed as the apple skin released.

"I believe it may have uncovered a likely candidate as the *key event*. One which has remained hidden until now, whose aftermath may prove directly connected to the predicted catastrophe put forward by our Stasis None."

Shocked expressions followed the statement.

"Although no categorical proof has been finalised it led me toward a distinct possibility. That our envisaged end may well stem from a chain of events set into motion as recently as the summer of 1944." He observed the caution of all present. Men and women who'd spent years trying to uncover the logic behind the Stasis None's heinous prediction. He concluded, "And this may all lie at the door of a certain scientist and the research he carried out within a clandestine project during the Second World War."

*

Brooke's explanation began within the fall of the Soviet Union, informing his audience of how in the early nineteen nineties, an ex-KGB Colonel sold top secret medical research to the Chinese, "This research was to become the integral building block in one of the most important medical advancements in history. Cho Yang's reconstruction theories, which gave birth to the Miracle Pharmaceuticals Range, or MPR as it's more commonly known." The mention of such names seemed to wash awe over the scientists gathered. "We've always known the foundation for part of Yang's work stemmed from ex-Soviet military research. However the content, origin and extent of the research acquired was never truly known to the West. We know Yang spent years developing theories before a near instantaneous breakthrough. However, a diligent, even paranoid man, it was work carried out in hidden locations on non-networked computers, making it virtually impossible to trace. It has always proven difficult to ascertain just how much of this revolutionary leap belonged to Yang, and how much came from the old Soviet block. That is, until now." Brookes leaned on the podium. "It would appear our computer may have deciphered such an answer, and more." Pictures of disease and formulas began appearing on the screen. "Yang was certainly the genius who melded it all together. However, it would appear the original plaudits did indeed lay elsewhere, the origin of which was hidden within that very research sold by the KGB Colonel. Once developed these theories would lead to the work we know today. Work which would see the conquering of many mutating viruses, see the eradication of cancer. Yang's cell regeneration project not only gave birth to the modern techniques of MPR which would corner the world pharmaceutical markets, it gave them a head start in just about all biological technology used today. Research advancing the healing process to damaged tissue. Rapid sleep replenishment. Maximised calorie digestion. Techniques which would see superior soldiers placed in the field, workers who never miss a day through illness. Cellular resistance enhancement, preparing the human body for deep space travel, and the more recent evolutions in advanced A.I. These are to name but a few. Aspects of this work remains well ahead of our own despite the numerous advancements made right here in this facility. However, in my causing this unintended reaction within the system, the expanding query of our Stasis None hit upon a Eureka moment, which revealed the likelihood of a more sinister advancement which has thus far remained hidden. A method of ensuring chosen ethnic groups could remain impervious to a particular biological weapon as being close to realisation. A genetic strike capability. Bombs able to kill one soldier, one civilian, but not another. The kind of research WAIG suspected but could never prove as being on the increase since the conception of Star Wars saw nuclear strike capabilities minimized. Unfortunately, since much of this assertion is a theoretical tract, the Stasis None cannot state categorically such suspicions are full proof. That this research *is* the definitive link to mankind's predicted end." He appreciated the dismay, their machine at its possible moment of salvation, proving once again a most obstinate ally, "Nevertheless, its prediction validation statistics are off the chart, which means we've been given the green light to try and prove this theory the hard way."

Dorey's team's trip to sixteenth century Persia was now officially postponed.

"Taking ownership of such a technology or preventing such material from ever existing at its point of origin could prove monumental, whether averting a genetic weapon or the metamorphosis of a soon to be realised super-disease." He allowed the idea to ferment, "But how do we steal such a source which since its conception has been held within the most secure testing facilities inside China?" He looked at Dorey who clearly knew the answer, "Quite simply, we cannot. Like our own complex such compounds were built to withstand attack, be it virtual or physical. So what about the Russian storage facility which held the earlier version before it was sold by the KGB Colonel?" He shook his head. "Unfortunately the Stasis None has managed to ascertain the work stored in the Soviet compound was always incomplete. That it was but one half of the essential research later used by Yang." He explained, "This is because the research sold by the KGB Colonel was never Russian to begin with. It was German and it had been split in two halves. Quite incredibly the second section of this research was already in China's possession, held at yet another secure facility which I've been unable to trace thus far. The Stasis None found documentation which provides insight into how the two separate works may have been reunited. But it cannot state when or where *precisely*. Only that the two sections of the research were separated until Yang's work reunited them. The fundamental building block of all his discoveries and advancements. Once again this means retrieving or destroying the research in its complete content within this period would require the infiltration of impossibly secured modern Chinese compounds where infinite copies could have already been made onto non-networked sources, untraceable and hidden." A knowing smile formed, "So, we turn our attentions back to 1944, and to the scientist who *really* created this breakthrough. A scientist orchestrating a top secret project . . . A project funded by the Nazi's."

*

"Didier Monclair." With Brooke's introduction came a three-dimensional picture of a man in his forties. It was reconstructed from an original black and white print. His gentleman's attire placed him at the dawn of the twentieth century. His stance was larger than life, his back rigid as he held a black top hat, giving a fashionable lean on his silver-topped cane. He possessed the distinct arrogance of a class unexposed to the two wars soon to come.

"This is the last known actual photograph taken of him." The Stasis None then offered a second portrait. "However, this recreation is the image we'll be working from come the end of this brief."

The new, much older face peered out at them. It was still recognisable to the younger original, though time was to throw a combination of heavy punches on this face if the prediction of the Stasis None had anything to do with it.

He had white hair with remnants of black whipping through the rest like coffee into cream. The bags under his eyes were puffy and aged and his upper eyelids drooped at the corners to comfort them. It gave him the distinct appearance of a puppy, but the eyes held an intensity which suggested this dog may bite. There was something imprinted into this reconstructed face which suggested he may be powered by an icy heart.

"Joseph Francois Didier Monclair, born in Strasbourg, 1872," Brookes declared, "Little is known of him in real historical texts so I'm afraid much of the background information has been synthesised by the system, more so than usual." He looked to Dorey anticipating his disapproval. "For this I apologise, to you and your team. However, due to the massive potential of what this mission could mean, I'm sure you'll understand the necessity."

Dorey swallowed his frustration.

Although the Stasis recreations were carbon copies of actual reality, all concerned felt better when the preparation and research phase dealt solely with fact, obtained from within their own real space and time. History clarified from a number of sources.

It was inevitable blanks would be filled in by the Stasis None but Dorey preferred such assistance be kept to a minimum. In all probability the system would as always, provide a faultless reconstruction of statistics, but the same problems applied as to everything else within its usage, the person asking the question needed to be precise, meaning human error could never be discarded. Misinterpretations were rare, but *rare* had previously landed Dorey's team in trouble, a case proven in the final debacle outside Constantinople when certain forces came his way that had no right being there.

The doctor continued. "At the age of only thirteen Monclair's studies in the fields of physiology, biology and chemistry attracted the attentions of some of Strasbourg's intelligentsia-elite. At the age of fifteen he was presented before the legendary Carl Friedrich Wilhelm Ludwig at his physiological institute at Leipzig. Ludwig was the master in his field and is regarded by many as the father of modern physiology. The records show he remained there until he was eighteen. The Stasis None pulled documentation of experiments and thesis carried out during his time there and he was indeed well advanced for both his years and era making a big impression on those around him. The term potential genius surfaces on several accounts. Then with little to no explanation his name simply disappears from the school archive and with it so does the name Didier Monclair from history. The Stasis None however was able pick up his scent some years later, working on secret theories under assumed names with the financial backing of some very important people . . . People more than happy to go along with his insistence for secrecy. Some of these benefactors went all the way to the top of his society, even to the Austrian royal family. He worked for decades moving from place to place, wherever money for his research was made available, always cloak and dagger, presumably always making headway. He then vanishes from view yet again within a year of when that last photograph was taken." Brookes pointed to the image of the doctor leaning on his cane. "However there were clues which pointed toward Germany during the First World War and we pick up his trail some fourteen years later, in eastern Berlin. Now under the alias of Joseph Franc, he was working as the senior practitioner in the district hospital. An avid supporter and member of the National Socialist Party, he's on first name terms with Walter Buch, the Nazi party's chief arbitrator, father-in-law to the infamous Martin Boorman." The screen reeled out images to support his every word. "Then on the 30th January 1933, Monclair found himself an entirely new kind of benefactor, with the appointment of Adolf Hitler as Chancellor." He paused, "We must now move forward. In 2069 an archaeological excavation to the south west of Munich uncovered a small, previously unaccounted for Nazi camp. No records could be found to verify the specific function of the camp and somebody had gone to a great deal of trouble to hide its existence before the allies could have found it. The Stasis None has concluded Monclair, or should I say Joseph Franc was operating this camp under the close protection of the Nazi elite. We believe his work, the building block for all of Cho Yang's later breakthroughs, was both advanced and convincing enough so as to appeal to their ideals and beliefs, that they could actually create a master race." He allowed the words to be absorbed by his audience. "So we've come full circle. The research sold by the Russians was actually research taken from the Nazi's, who in turn had stolen it from Monclair. We've discovered the research was far enough advanced to allow Hitler to believe the dawn of a true master race was around the corner. An army which healed faster, whose troops had the ability to press on without sleep or rest. A people impervious to the usual effects of illness or disease. It was the Nazi ideal. The absurd romance would have intoxicated Hitler. Only this wasn't romance. Monclair's research was bordering on reality. But unbeknown to him it was a reality never to be realised in his lifetime. His work would hit a brick wall until the breaking down of the DNA code." His eyes panned the room. "Monclair was killed prior to the war's conclusion. Practically all traces of his experiments in the camp eradicated. This included the disappearance of his scientific colleagues whom the Stasis None has now managed to trace. It appears only the original copies of his research were ever kept. The Nazi's believed it to be hidden in its entirety, within a secret facility in Berlin. I've managed to confirm the encrypted work stored inside this particular facility was later smuggled out of Germany by one of Hitler's most trusted agents. Taken to the agent's native homeland of Bolivia where it was hoped to be one day developed then used when the Third Reich would rise again from exile. However, unbeknown to Hitler, Monclair had actually separated his study into two distinct sections. One piece of the puzzle allowed the other to make sense, meaning the study taken to Bolivia was incomplete. In fact, the other half never left Germany. It was hidden within a bank vault in Munich. It would appear Monclair was none too trusting of his benefactors. The Red army would eventually discover it, along with many other Nazi secrets and compounds. From there it was taken to Moscow where few realised the potential of this encrypted, incomplete study. And so it disappeared, until a man witnessing the eve of his state's collapse began plundering secret assets to sell to the Chinese." He paused. "It appears China came across the missing part of the research taken to Bolivia decades later when they began investing in the country. God only knows where it had been hidden or how the two elements ever found each other. I regret to say I've drawn a blank on how to have the Stasis None settle such a matter thus far. But somehow these two pieces *were* reunited, eventually coming to the attention of Yang long after DNA codes and stem cell research had become available to science."

The display ground to a halt. He now addressed only Dorey and his team. "The Stasis None has pinpointed an opportunity when Monclair would have had his research together in one place. Although not an ideal solution it will be more obtainable here than when held within the high tech security of Chinese research facilities, or lost to some random location in Bolivia. As I've been unable to pinpoint with the same degree of accuracy a method to obtain the complete work when located at any other point in history, this will be our arena."

Dorey, not for the first time, was disgruntled at the temperamental nature of their super computer. A device which could predict, uncover and repaint such complexities, yet one so often unwilling to offer assistance where and when it really counted.

"We're going to send you back to Nazi Germany, to the final days of June 1944. You'll have only a six-day window as that's all we could manage for this timeline, one with the necessary ingredients to aid you in your quest. In this short time you need to determine the whereabouts of Monclair's research. When certain the study is complete, you must steal it. A simple theft of one of the most important scientific breakthroughs known to mankind, research it would appear could prove responsible for our predicted end."

Deans had been in many situations where a superior would casually describe how he was to infiltrate an international drug cartel, or order him into the lair of a terrorist cell. But nothing, not even the past days spent in this facility could have prepared him for the moment he'd listen to a director of operations, casually inform him his next task would be to save the world from possible catastrophe, and do so by infiltrating a camp held within Nazi Germany.

"Once the work is in your possession it will be checked of its content by your roaming computer. A method is being approved which will ensure it can be assessed in order to unlock the code and prove its validity." He concluded, "The original, complete study. Taken at the source before any risk of copies exist, the genius who created it, eliminated." A long pause followed. "Let us hope in removing this danger before it ever came to the light of day, this theory may be proved correct, so we may finally see our wondrous machine bring an end to its apocalyptic prediction."

CHAPTER FIFTEEN

The lights of the mission room were low as Dorey took his team through the first draught of their planning. The far wall generated a near perfect computer reproduction of their destination in time. In the centre was a holographic display similar in size to a large dining table which the team now stood around, crowding their attention from the darkness behind. As a desired place was pinpointed it could be displayed over numerous illustrations, all able to zoom in and out at any number of fly-by angles.

In the seventy-two hours since Brooke's bombshell the computer had managed to reconstruct the camp and now showed its proximity between the river, some thin forest and the tiny town.

"The camp consisted of two grand converted hunt houses, a combined barn and livery, and the prisoner huts." Dorey declared. "Before the two wars the town held annual hunt spectacles which attracted wealthy Germans and other Europeans. These large houses situated on the woodland's edge accommodated such a purpose. Evidence gathered by the archaeologists at the time of the dig has been coupled with research from our facility. It concludes the largest hunt house at the north-eastern corner was converted into a research hospital, the second smaller lodge served as offices, possibly with sleeping areas on the top floor. A half-burned roster was one of only six documents which survived this cover up, unearthed at the original dig-site. None of these documents provide details as to the core function of the facility but they did offer some insight into the guards manning it. The Stasis None has confirmed what a few of the archaeologists speculated all those years before. The guards as well as any soldier granted access to the camp or residing in the town, were all strictly SS. Not unusual. But what is unusual is the fact they were posing as ordinary enlisted men. Even the Colonel in charge, a distinguished officer in the regular Wehrmacht, was discreetly recruited into the ranks before his placement there."

They understood his emphasis. It was by no means unusual for SS soldiers to be given the task of running such a camp. But it was unusual for them to carry out orders while pretending to be prison guards or army regulars. Those who'd joined its ranks displayed the badge of the SS with great pride and menace.

"The roster also gives some insight into their routines. However, we'll touch on this when we go over our plans in more detail."

The others agreed, happy for the moment to become familiar with the terrain.

The display painted a detailed reproduction of the high barbed wire fencing which ran around the hunt houses and the entirety of the camps hexagon-shaped perimeter, close to the surrounding tree line. Within the tall wire structure was a smaller wooden wall which stood approximately three metres in height. It ghosted its wire counterpart leaving six to ten metres of no-man's land at any one point. The illustration ran around the perimeter of its reconstruction, Dorey's team taking in every detail.

The Commander insisted upon his group having absolute input into a mission's planning and he would not return to Brookes with the go ahead until his entire group was happy. "Due to the unforeseen nature of this event we've less than ten weeks in which to prepare." He looked to his pilots. "The river we'll be travelling down will be connecting to the longest tunnel ever attempted by the Reaper. So it could be a bumpy ride." He added, "They'll search for an easier alternative, but it's less likely one suitable will be found given the time span available."

All pilots present took in the implications with no evident concern.

"Jim, as long as our river plays nice we'll be attempting a night drop in the Reaper. Get us in then get yourself up to high altitude. Hook into the telephones and radio systems. Let the computer take control of the town and camp then announce our imminent arrival to the Colonel as soon as possible. Once they've read the phoney coded message from Berlin they'll want conformation, we'll then let the SiSTER do the rest."

SiSTER was an ingenious device. A program designed for a powerful computer that did exactly as its name, a Simulated Speech Transmitter and Encoded Receiver, suggested.

It gave the computer using the program the ability to sample any voice, record it then reproduce it at will. It meant the computer could hold a telephone conversation or transmit a message in the voice of anyone it so desired once it gained just a few seconds of the original person's speech pattern. It was the ultimate mimic and could call a mother and pass itself off as her son as long as it had the necessary information for the dupe at hand. If there were no samples of a required voice the SiSTER would simply speed-dial every person it may need to imitate. Upon answering, it would use prior research to help get the required individual on the other end of the line in order to steal that person's voice. The system operated at lightning speed, capable of calling and recording dozens of people at any one moment. It could amass a database of voices so quickly that within a short period of time it would have enough on file to gain access to, and manipulate almost any chosen target. It caused havoc when first invented. The more advanced model so effective, even the specialist listening devices used by government agencies of the time had virtually no chance of determining *real* from *fake* as long as the correct research went into any given conversation beforehand.

Although easily detectable and therefore largely obsolete in the era of the Stasis None, it was still very effective for missions planned between the dawn of the telecommunications age and the first half of the twenty-first century. When coupled with the latest state of the art spying technology, it meant Dorey's team had a powerful tool in order to manipulate their targeted environments within certain pasts.

"Obviously we can't plan the exact time of our arrival. But once we're in the targeted space we'll aim to reach the town as soon as possible. As long as they've believed the SiSTER we should have private quarters being readied immediately. Once we're in and set up, our computer system will take over leaving Jim free to leave. Naturally, since we're going to be in and out in less than a week the Reeper will be staying put in the Polar hide out." Dorey paused. "Now, Carl and I will be taking the lead on this one as we're the only two fully fluent in German."

Carl agreed with the rather obvious remark.

"We'll have two hours of German class a day until the drop. We all know the urgency. With the obvious exception of Deans we've had a run in with these Nazi's once before, so you should pick up the period dialect faster this time around." Dorey looked to Marco who painted a pained expression. He'd struggled perfecting his German previously. "You'll also have to hit a course of *epidermothol* before we leave."

He grimaced. "Oh, I'll be sick as a dog."

Epidermothol was a drug used to chemically alter the takers skin shade. It could make you appear lighter or darker with varying success depending on an individual's skin pigmentation and body chemistry. However, one universal effect it had on all who took it was the inevitability of making the user throw up during the first weeks of ingestion.

Dial stepped in. "We considered giving it to you Jim, but apparently some of the *thinkers* thought you might still stand out too much."

Jim bellowed out a laugh. "Shame . . . Because I do love strict blondes in knee high boots."

The Commander emphasized, "Seriously Marco, its summertime up there. For the next few weeks I need you in sun block, hats, under umbrellas."

Although a Latin male in a Nazi uniform would certainly not be unheard of, Dorey didn't want any undue attention because of Marco's appearance.

"Now you're all going to have *scitzo's* activated, so you'll have to put the practice in on these too. You know what a pain in the arse they can be."

A Scitzo was a tiny receiver/microphone sensor implanted into the inner ear which worked in harmony with their implants. The device would pick up any question asked of the person wearing it, send it to the nearby mission computer which would in turn send back the most simplistic and effective response in the desired language. It would be spoken aloud and slowly inside the relevant user's ear. It was almost like having a microscopic translator hanging around inside you, activated on and off via a chosen function of the wearer. It was very effective in reminding the user of the basics in any required language which by that time, they would all have at their disposal. However, it took a lot of getting used to. The user had to become accustomed to listening to the person or persons talking to them, waiting for their implants to inform the scitzo who should answer, then listen to the response before having to formulate their own actual words. Creating a pause would often help and there were all kinds of simple tricks which could be applied in order to buy an ounce of time. It was all about basic theatrics. The only problem of course was the user had to do battle with a variety of voices inside their head before giving their response.

Dorey continued. "Once inside the town we're going to find ourselves surrounded by SS. Now they'll be dressed in regular uniforms but remember what we're dealing with here. We all know what a tight group of fanatics these bastards can be. We'll be going into this under the guise of a secretive inspection team handpicked and used exclusively by Hitler. Hopefully this will provide some distance between them and us. The SiSTER will have spun out this deception to the Colonel in charge of the town in the voice of Himmler who will, for realism's sake, have warned the Colonel to be wary of us as we are not SS. The coded messages we'll have sent out will also back this story all the way to the top." He added, "The SS top hierarchy often know of each other. The majority went through the elite schools in Bad Tolz or Braunschweig. For this reason we can't risk playing the role of SS agents. But this little ruse of ours should be enough to keep the Colonel and his cronies towing the line. All of your characters are fictitious. Each individual handpicked and delivered directly into Hitler's private world. As always it's essential we do our homework on both who and what we are. If you come from Dusseldorf I need you to know the best baker, barber and shit-shiner the area has to offer. As always such information will be included in your file. We'll be tested on this twice weekly before the drop." He looked at Marco, "In German."

Marco smiled reassuringly.

"Now the mission requires we be in a unique position to gain complete access to everything going on back there. So we came up with the idea of one character being a high-level secret service agent . . . A spy and spy-catcher, untouchable to all but his Fuhrer. His objectives will be deliberately vague, though over the first few days of our arrival he'll gradually entrust more information on the shoulders of this Colonel Hookah. Accompanying him will be the elite team of Hitler's own personal investigators headed by a Major Bergen. Their mission will be to provide the Fuhrer with a complete and independent progress report on the camp and its research program. Again the SiSTER will have made the relevant phone calls, some as Hitler himself. The idea the spy will plant is that Nazi intelligence has come to believe the Allies may have somehow learned of the camp's existence, or worse still, may have actual knowledge as to its purpose. He has come to establish whether such a leak exists. Major Bergen and his team however, have been sent in partnership to ascertain whether the project is still a viable, worthwhile undertaking. With the Allies now in France, Monclair in the meantime will be put under the impression our presence is linked to plans which will see he and his research evacuated should things turn against the Germans. However, I can't imagine anyone with such an evident passion for secrecy is going to be too thrilled at having *more* Nazi agents sniffing around his work, whatever the reason. But he shouldn't be too difficult to manipulate. As for the rest of the SS around us . . . Well, let's face it, those eventually put in the know aren't going to like spies and investigators sniffing around too much either. Though if all goes to plan, few people will know why we're there."

Dorey turned to Carl, "After my meeting with Brookes it's been decided I'll be taking on the roll of the spy. Carl, you'll be taking on the role of Major Gerard Bergen the head of the investigation team."

Carl nodded.

The time had arrived to introduce the team to their new alter-egos.

"Jay, you will be Major Bergen's personal aide, Lieutenant Gudrun Schmidt."

She smiled. Gudrun was her favourite female opera singer.

"As such you can run our command centre with hopefully, as little interruption as possible." He looked to his new recruit. "Deans, you will be the Major's personnel assistant, Lieutenant Hermann Seisser. This will allow you to spend time around the base camp covering Jay. When you're out and about you'll be close to Carl and he'll naturally do most of the talking."

He gave Dorey an acknowledging nod.

"Your prime function will be to protect the command centre and of course Jay whenever she's hooked up as controller, and vice versa when it's you in the hot seat." He added, "Don't think this is about shoving you to one side while you learn the ropes." He emphasised, "Nobody here doubts your ability. Once you take away the trimmings this assignment's not so different to tasks you've already been involved in. However, without the command centre we're screwed. And in my experience there's always some nosy bastard wanting to stick their beak in. Between the two of you, you make sure it stays safe." He added, "There'll be plenty of occasions when our tasks will be swapped around, especially when it comes to mucking in and watching the screens. And as I'm sure your own undercover experiences have proved, half the time you end up playing these things by ear anyway, so be prepared for more . . . you'll almost certainly get it." His attention returned to his Brazilian colleague, "Marco, your German wasn't quite there last time."

Marco took no offence and gave a comical shrug. "What can I say?"

"Well that's just the point," Dorey hit back, "Hopefully as little as possible." Laughter followed the remark. "Your name is Lt. Hans Stoop, personal bodyguard to the Major."

Carl looked to the others, "Finally I feel safe."

"This will allow you to be at Carl's side at all times. You can watch his back, if you're asked a question and struggle Carl can interrupt and answer for you without it looking too out of place." Dorey continued, "Benny and Dial will play the role of Carl's deputies. You are Captain Franz Loehm, and Dial, you're Captain Willem Isenburg. Your cover provides all the freedom it gives Carl but again it won't look overly suspicious if you hang around together for the majority of our stay, meaning once again Carl can do most of the talking."

Both men seemed more than happy with this idea.

"Finally that brings us to my alias. I'm Captain Ulrich Heiden, long time friend and shadowy associate of Carl's Major Bergen. Both recruited into the Fuhrer's secret service, quickly recognised for our differing talents and merged into the murky shadows of Hitler's private troop." The final introduction was made and with it went the group's joviality, as if suddenly aware of the dangers each persona could hold in store for them. "Now as I've said these are the basics. In the coming weeks we may change the focus." He was speaking now for the benefit of Deans. "If one of you is speaking better German than the other . . ." He didn't elaborate. "But when and wherever possible we'll stick to Carl and I doing the meeting and greeting. And although it's virtually impossible to plan for the smaller details at this time, we *do* need to know our characters and objectives."

He paused before flicking over a sensor. It was time to cover some of the finer details.

CHAPTER SIXTEEN

"The Stasis None believes Monclair's work to be in or around the camp as a complete study during this window after a recent visit from Hitler's agent, who we believe was sent to inform him of his possible evacuation, almost certainly due to recent events at Normandy." Dorey added, "However, the system has also calculated there to be virtually zero traffic coming in or out of the area during this period . . . Another good reason to grab hold of this short window." He elaborated on what he knew would be welcome news, "The system has already managed an eighty-six percent *headcount* for the town and area during this timespan." Eyebrows were raised at this high statistic. "Now this is the highest headcount we've had at such an early planning stage, so hopefully this will help counteract the fact our planning is being built on regenerated history rather than facts obtained from our own reality. This should mean we won't be running into unforeseen surprises. As always however, it's probably best we forget this as soon as we're done here today. We all know it only takes one gatecrasher to ruin a party."

The headcount was a verification device utilising statistics from various *real* historical databases. The search program was like a super detective that identified as much of the population inhabiting any targeted mission area as possible, and how each individual could potentially affect proceedings. Although the vast, incalculable intelligence of the Stasis system created timelines perfect in every detail, it was often unable to predict ongoing human actions within them. Whenever quizzed on matters of *free will* the Stasis None hit problems. For the most part it would provide full proof data, but often the system locked up when trying to decipher the conundrum of man's unpredictable behaviour in a live event. It meant the system often struggled to divulge the diminutive actions and choices made by the human inhabitants of its simulated pasts without first receiving precise data. Like many aspects of the Stasis project this was a grey area which required attention. Yet another migraine-inducing paradox the system threw into proceedings. Because of this, the copies of the two millennia Brookes had at his disposal would be searched manually, so as to determine who was *when, where*, or *why*.

A secondary process of analyses which allowed the project to predict what Dorey may come up against. On this occasion eighty-six percent of the population inhabiting the target area in that particular time span had been identified and accounted for. This was possible due to the strict registration of all Nazi Germany's occupants.

For obvious reasons, the further back in time they travelled the less likely it became they'd receive accurate data. This was illustrated perfectly when Dorey found himself running head on into an army of misplaced Venetian knights outside Constantinople, sparking a run of events which would see them taken prisoner.

The map zoomed out to show a greater area of the hills, dressed with forest and cut by two rivers. "The town has only four exits, an almost perfect crossroads of north, south, east and west." He pointed his fingers into the holo-map, his words triggering the images into action. "Each road into the town is guarded with a machine gun box and small tower. The road travelling north leads to a string of lakes as the river arches above the town. The eastern exit leads us out across the hills. This smaller route links with a larger road toward Weilheim and the railway. The south-gate leads us down a smaller route still, toward the hills of Ammer Gebirge which begin the climb toward the Austrian Alps. Finally we come to the western gate which is little more than a track leading to the shore of our second river." Dorey paused. "If we follow this for a short distance, we'll come across a man made clearing in a small area of forest. It's here we find the camp itself." He returned his attention to the tiny town flanked by the dramatic woodland climbs. "As you can see the town is small and compact. The total distance spanning between the northern gate and the southern exit is barely two kilometres. As for its breadth, from east to west it's actually just over one point seven kilometres across . . . almost an even mile. Two rivers, the Lech and Amper, flank the town. The outskirts consist mainly of civilian housing though there's a hotel built next to the wooded area here." Dorey zoomed into the north-eastern corner where a grand old three storey building stood. "We know the hotel has been converted for the most part into an officer's mess. As you can see its grounds have been slightly fortified."

Dial observed the site, "How many officers?"

"Sixteen are accounted for so far. But there will almost certainly be more. The computer has also established at least two of the medical research staff had quarters here, so it's possible the rest of the hotel may have housed the camp's higher level scientists."

Dial shook his head, "Almost certain? Possible! And this system's rebuilt civilisations."

Dorey understood his second's frustration. "Due to the near complete success of the Nazi's in removing this camp from history, it's a minor miracle we've managed to gather as much data as we have."

Deans frowned. "I take it this is what you meant, about how even though this thing can reproduce worlds, it still needs baby talk to get it to play ball."

He turned to his new recruit, "This little machine of ours might recreate the moment Michael Angelo receives a sting to his arse together with the bee responsible, but unless we happen to know how to locate *that* person in *that* exact moment while held within another dimension," Dorey shrugged, "Then predicting how we can witness the event beforehand is like locating a hidden grain of sand on a beach. And when it comes to free will, the system seems almost unable to conceive human movement without precise data first given to it on a plate." He reassured, "But don't worry, I've looked over the information and this mission is more than doable. Believe me, by the time we're ready to leave you'll have at least as much information as you'd have been used to whilst spying for WAIG . . . Probably more."

The comment seemed to quell any growing stipulation of doubt for all in the room.

"Now we don't know if this hotel was the chosen base for Monclair and this is something we'll have to establish quickly. However with the help of the SiSTER we'll ensure we're not placed in either the hotel or with any other commissioned or enlisted men for that matter. It will be made clear to the Colonel by superiors he dare not disobey, that our visit is to be kept as secret as possible, our work kept away from any prying eyes in the town." Dorey scrolled the map into a close up. "We'll insist we're put in the same building Himmler stayed in some months earlier." He pointed just past the barracks toward a building with its own inner square hidden within the centre of its surrounding walls. "The structure used to be the head postal offices and civil service quarters for the district, commandeered during the war to be a logistical store and offices. They have large living quarters inside and will prove ideal for our needs. The small square within will be a good place to unload the truck. There are also garages just next to the complex here, and we'll be pushing for one of these to be provided. This way the truck will be off the road and away from prying eyes." He pointed to a structure next to their accommodation. "As you can see there are only two open entrances into the quadrangle from the main street." The display illustrated the narrow arched tunnels carved through the walls of the surrounding building, symmetrically opposite one another. "The smaller east and west passageways are sealed, leaving only the north and south tunnels to provide entry and exit from the inner square and the outside road." They were highlighted accordingly. "The surrounding offices were used during the day but the actual living rooms were only ever used as guest quarters . . . Which means we should be left to our own devices later at night." He zoomed out of the close up, the displays once again showing a more bird's eye view. "Most of the streets interconnecting the town-square to its outskirts are narrow. This makes some of them off limits to the truck." The display now took Dorey's team through a virtual tour of the small town precinct. "This means our escape routes have to be made through the main exits. Now the west exit leaves us nothing but river and the track leading to the camp. As we've seen it's surrounded by a thin veil of forest. So that's a no go for the truck. Besides, both the woodland and the river are booby trapped." He led the display into an illustration of the roads leading north and east. "Both of these roads can be used as a last resort. But east leads us smack into a large German force while north takes us toward small, awkward winding roads which circle the lakes." He added, "It also leads us further into Nazi Germany." The display followed his fingers to the main southern exit. "Now south is where we will enter the town, and where we'll ideally make our escape if we're forced to run. Our rendezvous will be twenty miles west of the route we came in from. We'll travel the road which passes near Fussen across the border into Austria, up the climb back into the Alps." The display illustrated a rather treacherous looking piece of road which snaked from the River Lech to the mountains. "We'll be picked up by the Reeper here."

The three pilots nodded their approval.

"Now, if we are forced to run I want us to try and stick to this route. It's our best way out and we should encounter little to no tank activity." He saw a few of his teams eyebrows raise at the mere mention of the word tank. "Obviously our truck has been modified. The whole thing has been reinforced with substantial but discreet armour. As always the glass in the cab will withstand any bullet fired at it from the era and the tyres are of course made from intelligent rubber which will absorb and reform after any small impact explosion. However, as I'm sure you can appreciate, it's still not going to talk its way out of an argument with a tank . . . So the *thinkers* have installed a few little extras." The display followed Dorey's description of the truck with a full visual illustration. "For example, here at both the left and right top front corners of the cab we've two tubes fitted into the spotlights. These are launch cylinders that can each fire up to six heat signature missiles, capable of destroying any tank. They're also fitted to the rear of the truck but these could only be adapted to fire three from each side. The canvas blanket making up the rear skin will be engineered from the latest bullet proof and fire resistant material. In the back we'll also be carrying two heavy calibre machine guns which I understand Charlie will have ready for us by the end of the week. This will give us additional firepower from both the rear and any chosen ground position. There's also a pivot-mount between the top of the truck's canvas and the cab which will allow either of these weapons to be quickly secured and fired from the roof. A rotational firing step will be fitted in the truck's hold and a section of the roof can be removed in order to achieve this option. This will provide three-hundred-and-sixty degrees of firepower. Naturally this capability will be hidden from view until called upon." The display showed the morphing metal technology before illustrating how they could quickly position the gun through the top of the canvas. "It may take two people to get it up there, but we'll find out how difficult it proves when we get to practice with the real thing. With the guidance system built into the dashboard I think it should provide enough accurate firepower to sort out any tank problem or any other small force we may encounter.

"I take it we're not able to reload the tubes?"

Dorey turned to Carl, "Unfortunately they are a one-piece unit. But twelve forward shots and six to the rear should be more than enough to force anyone into retreat. These things aren't going to miss and combined with the firepower of those machine guns, should be more than adequate."

"What about a possible attack from the air?"

"The same missiles will operate in a ground to air role. I've also requested three portable Ground-to-Air missile launchers be made up, disguised as weapons from the age. Similar to those we took to the era previously."

Benny forwarded his question. "What's she packing under the hood?"

"A six hundred break Mercedes Benz turbo diesel engine. A monster, and even with all her modifications and armour she'll hit sixty in twelve seconds on a track. She's fitted with the latest independent wheel drive system and can hit a top speed of ninety-five on flat ground carrying all of us, and our equipment. However since we're not planning a visit to one of the autobahns I hardly think such a test drive is likely."

Benny seemed suitably pleased with these statistics.

"If things go wrong, Jim is never too far away, so this should be more than adequate protection. We'll practice emergency evacuations through all the exits at the New Forest site, but it is the south-gate scenario I want us to be aiming for." He brought their concentration back to the town. "As I said most of the outlying area is housing with the exception of the church and hotel. The real heart is built around its square and along the edges of the main road dissecting it from north to south." The display showed the High Street slicing the town's centre. "Behind the square is an old market and commerce office right next to a large carpentry workshop. Both of these buildings have been converted into barrack rooms for soldiers . . . As you can see, at their rear is a motorcade. Now our best estimate, taking into account both the requirements of the camp and the town is there will be seventy men here. Fifty-two have been confirmed in the headcount. With the thirty down at the camp and the officers up at the hotel that makes a combined force of at least one-hundred-and-twenty. This could grow considerably but it's unlikely with the data in so far. Internal troop movements found themselves aimed toward the war now on two fronts. But it's clear this camp was important to Hitler so let's expect the worst." He pointed into the display, "The basements of these buildings have been converted into an armoury but unfortunately we're finding it difficult to ascertain exactly what they have down there."

Dial interrupted. "So we don't know what firepower we could be up against?"

"Not with any certainty. But an estimate will be ready soon." He looked at each of them. "I don't like this either, but what I will say is this . . . I know what firepower we have, and combined with the skill of all of you here means they are the ones outmatched, not us. We'll rig the armoury entrances with small explosives synchronised to any self destruct devices we decide to place within our base camp HQ. Upon our exit, the power surge when the SiSTER blows will knock out their communications for hours . . . This should certainly limit and slow down anybody who might feel like picking a fight until Jim's in range with the Reeper. If we do our job this should be a straight forward in, out affair. Every person here has dealt with worse." There was a bite to his comment, "I'd take all of you here quite confidently against a force twice this size . . . And with less information at my disposal."

The others returned their attention to the displays. It would be their only response after a show of such confidence from their Commander.

Dorey began to wind down the detailed introduction. "The Stasis None has already identified the residence and headquarters used by the Colonel." He pointed into the hologram once again, "This building here."

The map scrolled around the square and showed a splendid four-storey town house which dominated its landscape. It was situated fifty metres off the main drag, connected to the square via a wide arcing driveway, sealed from the street by heavy, black iron gates.

"In such a small town we shouldn't have any trouble in establishing Monclair's address quickly." Dorey added before offering the floor *open* to questions and suggestions.

Carl looked thoughtful, "We can assume this Colonel, upon learning he has officers who work directly for Hitler himself, will want an immediate introduction."

Dorey agreed.

Carl continued, "He'll probably want to meet us officially, then almost certainly invite us to dine with his own ranking officers. Some are likely to be Gestapo."

"If he decides he wants to meet us on our arrival we'll keep it as just the two of us," Dorey added, "We'll make polite declinations on behalf of the rest. For the two highest ranking officers to attend such an invitation would fulfil all expected etiquette."

Carl agreed. "How do you want to play it from there?"

"As the senior officer of the investigation team you can politely make it clear you run your ship *your* way. This will be underlined by the SiSTER posing as Hitler anyway. As for myself I'll take the responsibility of keeping the Colonel off your backs."

"So you're going to make an effort to befriend him?"

"I'm going to try. For the rest of you to operate quickly we're going to need somebody watching and manipulating his every move, distracting him, while also gaining his trust for all of us. This should be achieved as I decide to tell him more about my motives for being there, of my own accord. As I said, the SiSTER will be vague as to my real objective from the start. This will also help of course, if we're tripped by anyone sticking their nose into our affairs. I can use the ambiguous nature of my orders to quickly embroil anyone into my deceit. Someone points a finger our way . . . I let the Colonel know they are one of my suspects. Gradually I'll show the Colonel I'm simply trying to ensure the camp's secret has remained intact."

Carl and the others could see the sense in this.

"Hopefully this will give you the freedom to continue our mission objectives even if upon occasion, I cannot." He clarified, "You're there to investigate the progress and validity of the research. I'm the agent sent to check for a possible leak."

"Well your German is certainly good enough." Carl stated with confidence.

"If I can establish a good ear with the Colonel and keep him preoccupied, then between the two of us it shouldn't be too difficult for us to quickly achieve our objectives. We can establish the whereabouts and movements of Monclair, gain access to him both on and off the camp then surround him with *Sneaks*."

Sneaks were state of the art spying devices used by many of the world's espionage agencies. An ingenious invention which felt to the touch like children's play-dough only transparent. Small pieces could be broken from the main body, then manipulated into any shape and stuck to another surface as easily as chewed gum. Once pressed into position it could remain there indefinitely. Held within the translucent sticky mass were thousands of tiny crystal cameras and microphones strung together by a clear, intricate web of nano-fibre-optic nerves. These tiny lenses operated on the same principle as a fly's eye, sending hundreds of images a second to the nearby computer which would then translate the many different camera angles and shots into a fluid motion picture. They could switch automatically to night vision and heat detection and also had the ability to scan through thin walls and light structures in order to locate safes or hidden doors. The surrounding gluey gel was made of a liquid power source which allowed them to remain self-sufficient for several weeks.

"We'll cover every angle of the camp and town so they're beamed live onto our screens."

"We'll need all the outer gates and roads covered." Marco added.

"Most definitely, and especially the barracks and the officers residence along with any entrances leading in and out of our base camp HQ of course. As usual the computer has the majority of the blueprints of the town's buildings so we can easily locate any possible ventilation shaft or fireplace within the postal building or any other base we may end up in. We'll fill these with *hummers* once we're inside."

The hummer device was a small sound wave generator which sent powerful low wave pulses outward. Almost completely undetectable to the unaided human ear, it prevented any audible noise leaving a chosen building via its natural outlets or vents.

Dial looked to Dorey. "Once we've established Monclair's residence there'll be no problem bugging him, but we may find any secret lab hidden within the actual camp more tricky if he doesn't want to play ball."

The Commander agreed. "I think all we can do is play this by ear. We've carte blanche from Hitler himself. With a little luck we may gain access to some of his secrets quite openly but we'll improvise our planning over the coming weeks to cover any scenario."

Jay thought for a moment. "I can't see us having problems with most of our targets. We'll need *trackers* both on and around Monclair at some point."

Trackers were devices of varying size and description which relayed their position to the waiting computer. The computer could use the blueprints on its database to determine and reconstruct the likely location of the person being watched, while creating a visual display of the room occupied by the target.

He agreed. "We'll plant *mites* into his body then see where he spends most of his time." *Mites* were the most advanced of the tracker family. Nano-particles which would pass through the pores of the skin then re-group to form a single cell once inside the target's anatomy, a beacon capable of surviving for days while beaming out its location.

"Maybe we could spook him a little when we get there . . . See how he behaves. If we find he's going to the same locations time and again then we know it's important to get the sneaks in there." Dorey paused and took stock. "The allied invasion will have been progressing on French soil for four weeks upon our arrival. Six days after the landings Hitler sent his Bolivian agent to see Monclair. The system has ascertained that soon after his departure the doctor collected his research together." His tone was confident.

"Well let's just hope he keeps it nearby." Marco declared.

"The Stasis None has determined his work will be close at hand during this period. But we'll have no idea exactly where, or what tricks the doctor may have regarding the security of this work. So we'll have to be patient. We'll get mites into his system and plant sneaks and trackers all around him. Hopefully we'll steal as much as possible while safely watching on the monitors of our base HQ. We need to find his study, his favourite desk. We'll bug his entire world. If all else fails and it becomes clear we have to take further steps, then so be it."

This prompted Jay to speak. "I take it this means abduction is a possibility?"

"We do whatever's necessary to get that research," he added, "We'll be taking knockout gas and tranquilliser pellets so we can put him or anyone else to sleep should the need arise." A thoughtful silence took hold of the group. "When you cut through the crap this is a simple theft and assassination. We don't have to worry too much about collateral damage. We can afford a certain degree of lateral planning on this, even more so than Constantinople. The success of the mission is achieved by gaining the research." He used his forefingers to emphasise their priorities, "One . . . Remove it entirely from one reality to monitor the results. Two . . . Make a copy for the Stasis archive should it ever be needed by our cause in the future. Once we've achieved this we can poison the whole bloody town if it suits our goals."

Dial looked at the growing number of possibilities. "It's clear there'll be dozens of scenarios we'll need to implement into our training. I mean shit, aren't there always."

The Commander agreed. "I think we should take a break. Let's grab some coffee in the ready room and discuss it further in a change of surroundings. Then we'll come back down and go from scratch. We've got four days before we start preliminary training on this one. We'll have covered most angles by then."

They all relaxed away from the display.

Dorey informed the computer to close down the recreations and raise the lights. "Oh . . . And from now on Didier Monclair will only be referred to as Joseph Franc." He said as the doors slid open, "The last thing we need is to get back there only for one of us to get his bloody name wrong."

CHAPTER SEVENTEEN

The firing range of the Stasis Project was a true testimony of mankind's ability to dig. With its three weapons rooms, four offices, armoury and one hundred and fifty metre firing range, its floor area dwarfed its nearest rival the Reeper hangar, by some margin.

It was often favoured to the treadmills of the gymnasium when the less agreeable side of the British weather was frequenting the Salisbury hills on the surface.

Both the generator and lighting were of the same variety used to power small stadiums and the cavern had the distinct feel of an indoor sports arena as a result. It held full battle hologram technology which could see it quickly transformed into any number of virtual combat scenarios with laser firing weapons whose recoil was simulated by the age old use of gas cylinders. At the far end was a colossal bath of sand stretching from ceiling to floor which created a forty degree slope of good old-fashioned bullet-catching material. A mass, religiously sieved to remove any spent ammunition fragments, by Charlie a special-forces veteran and the chief munitions officer to the underground lair. In front of this wall of dirt, moving, stationary or upwardly sprung targets could be fired at with live rounds.

Although there were outdoor training facilities on the surface, their use was limited.

The personnel on the top levels believed the complex to be a well-guarded, fortified research centre, declared *secret* because of the technology being developed within.

And with the tourism of Stonehenge but a short mile away this made the surface far from ideal when the need arose to test fire an eighteenth century musket adapted to shoot the latest mini-mag round.

The mini-mag concept saw ammunition experts develop different families of ballistics for various weapons and requirements. Whether it be rounds which separated into parts as they left the nozzle to create a buck-shot effect or heavy calibre shells packed with the latest and nastiest concoctions of explosive which could be accurately programmed to vary their levels of destructive impact. They added adaptability and variety but above all extra punch to a modern arsenal.

Charlie wound down his brief in which Dorey's team had been introduced to some of their World War Two firepower. They'd been shown their modified Walther PPK special issues, the MP-40 machine pistols together with the Sturmgewher 44 assault rifles, the direct inspiration for the more remembered AK 47. All were capable of firing a standard round as well as holding the ability to unleash the more lethal mini-mag varieties. There were also a collection of Luger handguns capable of firing thirty-two mini-mag shots from the clip and to add a little more weight they'd been issued with a collection of modified Model 43 stick grenades. They came complete with the usual voice-activated timer programs, remote detonation and variable explosive force capability. They'd also been introduced to the two modified MG 34 machine guns with schwere role capability. *Schwere* meaning the gun was in its heavy role as a swivel-mounted weapon, ready to be mounted to the roof of the truck, given the ability to deliver an improved 7.92 calibre round of which every tenth cartridge would contain a minute package of the awesome C40 impact explosive. This accompanied with their rapid fire mini-mag rocket shells meant both of these heavy duty weapons were for strictly outdoor use only.

"As always your weapons incorporate palm sensors so they can't be used by your enemy against you unless you personally deactivate the manual safety feature, in which case only the weapon's original function will operate. Naturally all modifications have been disguised into the normal workings of the device so they'll pass standard inspection."

Charlie was an old soldier of some pedigree. He'd fought in several hellish, some unofficial campaigns, which had scarred his face with a permanent frosting. His eyes had amassed the unmistakable vacuity of those who'd both witnessed and inflicted death. But when he smiled his warmth was thrown over the recipient like waves rushing a beach.

Dorey and his team loved Charlie.

"Now I know nothing gets past you lot," his voice was seasoned with a brand of Scottishness which belonged to another age, "And God knows in your line of work let's take this as a minor plus point."

Smiles greeted the comment.

"The recent rumours of a new mini-mag variant being close to completion are, as usual around here, not without grounding. In fact, as I'm sure you've suspected, this new variant derived from the mini-mag D6 *chaser*, is about to be handed to a certain group for preliminary testing." He reached into the left-hand pocket of his impeccably ironed trousers to pull out a single mini-mag tip. "The trusty chaser," he declared holding it aloft, "Designed to separate into six further projectiles when leaving the nozzle, capable of angled flight, providing that guided buckshot effect we love so much. However, by improving the technology which makes this little process possible those clever *thinkers* have finally perfected that *something new* they've been threatening since the chaser was introduced." Charlie placed the D6 back into his trousers before reaching into the pocket on his right. He took out a bullet and held it aloft between finger and thumb. "May I introduce you to your new concept weapon . . . The D6 Intelligent Seeker Missile, or *the seeker* for short." Everyone seated seemed to edge toward the new treasure. "As you can see she looks pretty much the same sat on top of the old mother ship. But, if I remove the shell from the tip like so, you can see what the thing actually looks like inside." He pulled the mini-mag clear of the shell revealing the new shape hidden within. "It's longer than the original D6 chaser round, eight millimetres longer to be precise, cut and shaped to fit into the shell casing. Now once this is activated it doesn't separate at the nozzle, this stays whole like the *explosive rounds*. But this isn't just an impact weapon, it's an independent missile. The idea is if you're pinned down and your enemy is hidden from view, if you score a hit on your target, it doesn't detonate. And neither will the next round unless you instruct it to. Each one instead transmits its position to the missile following. The next shot will follow the original adapting its trajectory against any sensed obstacles in order to reach the transmitter. They don't just bend around corners. These little bastards actually seek and destroy."

Jay enquired, "Jesus Charlie, are you saying those things fly around independent of your aim and know what they've hit?"

"That's exactly what I'm saying. The success rate varies depending on your distance and firing angle. But essentially for every transmitter round fired the rest of the magazine will follow to that location until you instruct the weapon to do otherwise. You can have the entire magazine follow to obliterate one particular target . . . Handy against armoured gun positions. Or you can activate the rounds to detonate to the left and right of the transmitter shell to create a deadly pepper shot effect, meaning if a hit is scored and the person downed is dragged to safety, such action could wreak a devastating blow on the rest. And all achieved via a simple set of commands." He added, "Naturally the velocity is less than a standard projectile. These things leave the nozzle much slower so as to give the missile a chance of firing onto a different trajectory. As a result you'll feel the difference in the recoil. It takes some getting used to."

Dial sat forward, "Sounds like you've had a chance to fire these things already."

"That would be correct. While you people were busy playing, *knights of the round table*, I was invited to San Diego to have a little dabble."

"And?" Dorey enquired.

"Depending on the distance and the obstacles they can prove quite accurate."

Dorey then asked the only question he ever really needed to throw at Charlie. "Would you have used them when you were out in the field?"

"Yes. If pinned down these give you an extra option, especially against an armoured gun position. Like I said, these things will follow anything that's been hit by the original while potentially avoiding obstacles out of your normal view."

"But say the original transmitter round is hidden behind a solid wall won't the others just follow the transmission through the shortest route and hit the wall like the chaser round?"

Charlie turned to Carl. "No. The tracker within the seeker is fitted with a density beacon. Anything measuring a certain mass means the following mini-mag will have received this information and attempt to curve around it. The first, second and perhaps tenth won't achieve this but eventually the adjustment will be made. That is essentially how it manages to angle its flight and avoid obstacles. Mixed with your standard rounds, mini-mags and chasers they'll help create quite a little cocktail." Charlie checked his watch, surprised at how quickly the time had transpired. "Well, I'm afraid that's all we have time for today. I know you must be hungry. I'll see you all in the morning when we'll give some of these weapons a good thrashing."

Dorey and the others began thanking Charlie.

"You're the crash test dummies on these things and if you like what you see they'll be issued without delay. So I managed to book us in for a weekend of no holds barred testing." This was received with great enthusiasm by the group, pricking Dean's curiosity who was still to experience one of Charlie's deliciously destructive training camps. "In a fortnight's time . . . Only problem is, the manufacturers want to monitor proceedings discreetly so they were a little reluctant to let us take them up to Hereford, which means I've had to clear us for a little visit to San Diego in the flesh." He watched as faces began lighting up. "We leave a week Friday on a scramjet flight."

This meant a full weekend in San Diego, away from German classes and studies.

Charlie laughed. "Oh and don't worry, I've seen those apartments of yours and know what a bunch of prima donnas you've become, so I managed to get us booked into a hotel off the base, five star of course."

CHAPTER EIGHTEEN

A long sunset had always been one of Joseph Brahms favourite Paris experiences. He found the light as it faded across the city to be most romantic. The doors to his veranda were open and the dusky light rolled across his narrow balcony, toying with the veil of the hotel curtains. As he passed the open view, delivering three meticulously ironed shirts to the half packed leather suitcase on his bed, he found it too irresistible to ignore.

He stopped and admired the scene of a city flirting with the promise of summer.

As usual, he felt a childish sadness at having to leave his adopted home. A sadness he'd been too young to truly comprehend when leaving Germany as a small boy, and a melancholy he'd certainly not suffered when leaving the far away mountains of Bolivia in which he'd grown to manhood. However, with the growing likelihood of Allied troops making a threat to Europe's mainland, the worry of never again seeing *his own* Paris was a troubling thought which only added to the drama of his silent goodbye.

Reluctantly he pulled himself away from his watercolour skyline and returned to the task at hand, placing the shirts carefully into the corner of the suitcase. The light inside the room was failing so Joseph moved to the bedside lamp and lit it. It filled the room with a soft glow illuminating its tasteful features. Features far too intimate as to belong to the hotel. In fact, other than the large bed which dominated the bedroom and its matching equally grand wardrobe that towered in the corner, there was little of the room, or indeed the apartment, for which the hotel could actually claim decorative credit.

It all belonged to their unusual long-term tenant.

The exquisitely carved dresser with its resplendent mirror and deep luxurious stool were Venetian. As were the bedside tables which dressed both edges of the bunk. The Egyptian Linen bedspread was of a far superior quality to what these comparatively humble walls would normally offer, as was the deep mattress hidden beneath. Even the floor was decorated well beyond its means, scattered with a collection of fine Moroccan rugs which led from the bedroom into the equally elegant living area.

The dwellings seemed somewhat small considering the obvious means for extravagance, but they were perfectly ample and charming for Joseph's needs. Besides, he preferred the view from his sixth floor veranda to that of any vista currently boasted by the more exclusive hotels. A fact lost on his friend, benefactor and Fuhrer, Adolf Hitler.

Often when they conversed in letters his mentor would ask why Joseph insisted on living in the more seedy part of town and Joseph would enjoy nothing more than to explain a different reason on each time of the Fuhrer's asking. A routine they both enjoyed during their pen friend adjournments, between the specialist undertakings Hitler often requested of his anonymous friend.

One such request had just been bestowed on Joseph that very morning.

He turned to pull open the top drawer of his dresser, withdrawing from it a dark wooden box. He placed it gently on the bed and opened it. Inside was a rare and finely crafted long barrel Mauser. The pistol was handmade and silver plated. Emblazoned on the black handle was a carving of a swastika held within the talons of an eagle. Across the centre of the image were his initials, J.B.

He took the weapon and held it without emotion. He felt its weight and remembered its touch. He took a long and steady aim before eventually placing it back into the red velvety interior of the box. He left the lid open almost wanting the weapon for company, as if it were to remind him of his alternate nature.

He moved toward the small living room area, ready to continue his packing.

Joseph Brahm's friendship with Hitler had come about via an unlikely route. His father, Leopold Brahms moved to Bolivia on business shortly after the First World War. After one year passed he'd sent for his wife and four children to join him permanently.

Joseph was almost nine when he and his three brothers were taken away from a ruined Germany to their new home in South America.

The family had prospered and his father established himself as an important man with connections running all the way to their adoptive country's corridors of power. Although it seemed to Joseph and his brothers like they were on a different planet to that of their native Germany, their father, who by nineteen twenty-six was a keen enthusiast of the Nazi party, was constantly lecturing them of the goings on in their distant homeland.

He would talk for hours on the subject of Versailles and of the treachery hidden behind the Fatherland's apparent surrender. He and his three brothers would listen to their father's tales that warned of the poisonous Jew and barbaric Bolshevik. He would become animated and furious when telling of his two younger brothers, their uncles who'd perished on the Somme. "And all in vain!" he would say before reminding them of how he surely would have died too, had it not been for the lathe accident which cost him three fingers as a fifteen-year-old boy.

But it wasn't until nineteen twenty-eight as a twenty-year-old that Joseph would truly begin to share his father's political passion. It was the year Ernst

Rohm, the recently abdicated leader of the Nazi S.A, who was seen by many as second only to Hitler, made his home in Bolivia in order to train their army.

He'd become firm friends with his father and enjoyed in particular, for reasons to become obvious to Joseph later, the inclusion of his handsome eldest son in their discussions.

After two years, only a week after Joseph's twenty-second birthday, Rohm returned to Germany as suddenly as he'd left it, re-establishing himself as the figurehead of the troubled S.A. This despite his numerous drunken rages in front of Joseph, his father and his father's friends, on how *Dolph* and his Nazi party were now betraying the people.

A few years passed before Joseph, with the help of his new friend Rohm, finally managed to persuade his father to allow him a visit to Germany. He never could have guessed that from the moment he set foot on his native soil, his life would never be the same again.

Rohm had arranged for him to share an apartment with one of his prominent brown shirt commanders . . . A rampant homosexual who'd made two drunken advances on his houseguest within the first week of his stay. It repulsed Joseph who by now was also suspecting Rohm's interests toward him.

He was close to returning home when a somewhat embarrassed Rohm promised to make it up to him by introducing him to Adolf Hitler in person.

It was a promise which was to take only three days in the granting.

During his visit and introduction to the Nazi leader, and more through a series of accidental events rather than planning, Joseph had found himself alone with Hitler for almost thirty minutes. In which short time he'd impressed the leader with his views on politics and particularly while discussing his ideas on art.

Hitler told the young ex-patriot it was most refreshing to have a genuine conversation with a young, enthusiastic mind. He particularly liked how uncorrupted the German-Bolivian appeared, and found Joseph's brief telling of his life stories most interesting.

"It would be nice to hear from you from time to time." Hitler had told him, "It is not often I enjoy another person's company without them desiring some ulterior motive."

And thus the unlikely pen friends began their correspondence. Over the next few years Hitler took on the role of both friend and mentor, though he was always careful to manoeuvre him away from a direct involvement in his politics. He'd prevented Joseph from joining the Nazi's directly, particularly the SS. '*I do not require a uniform so you may show your loyalty,*' he wrote, '*Continue your studies and enjoy our cities in the manner my youth did not allow me.*' He encouraged his love for painting and would often say of the political upheaval all around him, '*The path for which you can best serve your country has yet to reveal itself . . . Have patience my young friend.*'

It was not until the latter end of nineteen thirty-six Joseph's path finally became clear to Hitler. In October of that year Germany had sent more fighters and bombers along with six-and-a-half-thousand men to aid General Franco's efforts in defeating the Bolshevist threat in the Spanish civil war. The conflict quickly shaping into a dress rehearsal for the looming showdown between the Nazi's and Communism.

The German leader decided this was the perfect opportunity to call upon the growing talents of his young friend. He'd adhered to Joseph's many requests to be schooled in soldiery and as a compromise for persistently refusing him access to the SS, he'd granted him tuition via one of his own personal guards.

Joseph's Bolivian upbringing meant he was fluent in Spanish and understood the similar cultures and lifestyles between the Hispanic peoples.

And so it was Adolf Hitler had first called upon the services of Joseph Brahms.

He repaid his faith with huge successes inside Spain. He brokered massive financial deals on the personal behest of the Fuhrer, creating enormous wealth for the building of Germany's new war machine. Once schooled in the art of war he soon gained a reputation as a formidable soldier and killer, all the while kept well out of view by his proud and grateful Fuhrer.

With the declaration of a European war, Hitler sent him to Paris as a spy and assassin, posing as a Spanish artist, opening various channels in preparation for the German march west. Here he'd remained in the shadows, living and enjoying his life when his mentor required nothing of him, but always ready and waiting for one of his leader's darker calls.

He placed the last of his required things into the suitcase then gently pressed it shut.

He glanced down once more at the magnificent pistol housed in its box. He stared at it for a while and didn't appear to move for a whole minute. Then with a glance over his shoulder he observed how the darkness was beginning to swallow everything up outside. He walked over to the table on the balcony and picked up a small decanter half filled with Cognac. He took the solitary glass and poured a drink.

He leaned onto the railing, observing once more the beauty of his beloved Paris in all of its transforming splendour. He sipped his drink, '*My driver will be here soon.*'

As he watched the darkness loom the many lights of the city began to twinkle and dance. He found himself thinking of his Bolivian home. Of the scattered lanterns which lit the mountains at night, of the sunshine during the humid days of summer, the heavy blue rain which thrashed down when it's time came into season. He thought of his mother and father and three younger brothers, those he'd not seen for such a long time.

He took another larger sip of the drink and sighed.

He tried to place his thoughts on the task ahead, '*Back to Germany to spy on a small town and scientist.*' He pondered, '*A secret, top priority research programme being monitored closely by Adolf himself*'. Hitler always explained to him how it was necessary for him as Fuhrer to remain paranoid. '*It kept him in control.*' he would say in his letters.

Now it was time for that paranoia to surface again.

Hitler felt sure information on this secretive research may have been leaked and he felt strongly enough about it to call upon the services of his invisible friend once more, who was to smuggle copies of this research back to Bolivia, in the unlikely event the invasion succeed, and the war turn against them.

'If you do his for me I will make you the youngest Colonel in Germany.' he'd joked in his cryptic letter. *'I just need somebody I can trust, someone who will not report back to that chicken farmer Himmler.'* It had ended with the usual promises. *'You could even return to your painting and French prostitutes for good.'*

He recollected the words before tilting his head back, swiftly finishing the drink.

His thoughts were interrupted by a three-pronged knock at the door.

He called over his shoulder, "Oui?"

The muffled French voice of the hotel porter was pressed through the woodwork. "Monsieur, your driver has arrived. Should I send him up to collect your bags?"

Joseph placed down his glass then replied loudly, "Oui . . . merci."

He walked to the wardrobe and pulled out a large leather suit holder and placed it on the bed. It was still unzipped from when he'd inspected it earlier that day. He looked down at the impeccable army Captain's uniform delivered one hour after the letter had arrived that morning. He laughed. *'Youngest Colonel in Germany and he sends me the uniform of a Captain.'* He leaned forward and zipped it closed. Joseph then turned and made his way over to the bathroom so he might relieve himself before the start of his journey.

From inside the bathroom he didn't hear the corporal enter his room with a quiet knock. Nor did he hear as he closed the door, before scanning his eyes over the chamber. Neither did he detect him as he walked silently through the lounge, past the doors to the veranda.

The Corporal had just entered the bedroom when he heard the toilet flush from behind a door across the room. He stood still for a moment, then grabbed the suitcase off the bed just as the lavatory door was opened.

Joseph walked in and was at first startled by the Corporal's presence. This feeling was immediately replaced with a direct sense of annoyance and attack. "What the hell are you doing in my room? Nobody told you to enter."

The Corporal did not flinch. "I'm sorry Sir, my French isn't good, I thought the man said to come straight in and collect your things."

"Well next time knock louder. You could have given me a bloody heart attack."

The corporal knew the line just delivered was rubbish. The man before him had barely reacted to his unannounced intrusion, though his eyes sharpened like a hawk as the muscular frame of his body had tensed in immediate anticipation.

Joseph turned and pointed toward a second bag on the small settee in the living room. "There's that bag there also." He was agitated. Something in his subconscious was warning him, *'Danger.'*

He turned suddenly back toward the ice-cool Corporal, as he sensed the slightest of movement behind him, but it was too late. With a muffled hiss the first bullet passed through his abdomen. The second hit him squarely and silently in his chest knocking him backward, almost off his feet. In the shock of this sudden and violent act he found himself somehow still half upright and in the arms of the Corporal, who was whispering to him in perfect Spanish then repeating in German. "Shhh, Don't be afraid."

Joseph clung on to the Corporal's powerful frame which held him like a vampire, and looked deeply into his eyes. Brahms held the Corporal's stare as he slyly slid his hand gently down toward the high top of his right leather boot. Carefully he unclipped the knife and slid it out of its sheath as the unrelenting thought kept flashing through his mind. '*Kill him, he's killed you . . ..'*

His hand gripped the hilt tightly as he attempted to move the knife upward into a sudden and desperate attack. Yet as Joseph aimed the blade toward its strike, he felt the powerful grip of the Corporal, squeezing the blade out of his dying grasp like a vice.

It landed with a thump on the expensive rug beneath them.

The corporal lowered Joseph out of their dance and onto the floor with no further struggle. He then stood upright, before taking a step back.

As Joseph lay on the floor he became aware of his own panting . . . his body desperate to keep a grip on consciousness. It was then a strange thought passed through him and one he seemed to have no control over. He'd killed a lot of men over the years. Many were cold-blooded executions by the gun or knife. Sometimes it kept him awake at night as his mind perversely made him question, '*What could it possibly feel like when looking down the other end of the barrel?'*

He stared down the aim of the raised again pistol and gasped as the Corporal answered, "Well now you know Joseph."

The man's cold understanding of his deepest, darkest thoughts chilled the last of the warmth from his bones. He wanted to scream out at Death now standing above him but in a sudden flash of the nozzle, Joseph Brahms was gone.

The Corporal turned away, his face fixed. He made his way to the bed and stared at the engraved pistol in its box. He closed the Gun Case then pulled over the suit bag, unzipping it to reveal the Captain's uniform within. Calmly he pulled it out and held it up in front him. He turned toward the splendid dresser mirror and placed the uniform closely in front of his person. '*Should be a good fit.'*

His attention was then carried toward the perfect grandeur of the dresser stood in the soft light before him. "What a beautiful mirror." He said appreciatively.

He picked up the gun case, and with the uniform stuffed under his arm made swiftly for the exit. It was time to pay the hotel porter his ten years of salary to dispose of the mess.

As he headed out of the room he could not resist one last look . . .

Palene had always been a great lover of such ornate Venetian furniture.

PART TWO

'It was the dreams again.'
'Ahhh.'
'They haunt me.'
'Yes.'
'As do you.'
'Yes.'
'I so long to understand.'
'As do I.'
'So close.'
'Yes.'
'I feel it.'
'Yes.'
'As do you?'
'I'm beginning to, yes.'

CHAPTER NINETEEN

The inner walls began to shudder violently. Deans instinctively gripped the arms of his flight seat as Jay's voice radioed into his ear. "Thirty seconds to drop."

His heart pounded as he anticipated the fall.

"Twenty seconds."

The sound of screaming engines now accompanied the increasingly violent jolts causing him to tense the muscles of his jaw.

"Ten seconds to drop on my mark."

He glanced across to Dial who sat over to his right.

The major smiled and provided a reassuring *thumbs up*.

"Five . . . four . . ."

The walls took a sudden barrage of hits.

"Three . . . two . . . one . . . Mark!"

The agonising delay seemed to last an eternity before they plummeted downward.

The noise was deafening, the vibration almost unbearable. Dean's stomach was left behind and his skin shuddered as if trying to pry itself from his body.

"Levelling her out, prepare for jump."

He pressed his body back into his seat on Jay's last instruction as he readied himself for the incredible jolt of forward momentum.

"Three . . . two . . . one. . . . . . mark."

Deans was almost crushed back into his seat, his head becoming nothing more than a fixture of his chair. The roar of the engines blasted out as he felt himself powered forward into a soup of colourful lights.

"Winding down on, three . . . two . . . one . . ."

Deans opened his eyes.

"Mark." The commotion was over and Jay spoke calmly into his headset. "Drop twelve complete. How do you feel?"

"The same as I have every Friday for the past two months . . . nauseous!"

"Don't worry . . . It's like I keep telling you, the simulator's worse than the real thing."

He smiled, "Yeah, and I keep telling you I suspect its bullshit." He began unhooking himself from the seat.

Dial was already at the exit, delighted with the look on his colleague's face. "Shit boy you look like you've been humped by a bull." The words were sung in pure rodeo tones.

He smirked at the usual taunting and rolled his neck as Dial began opening the hatch.

They'd just fallen over two hundred feet while strapped inside the shell of the drop simulator. Over the past weeks it had become a staple diet for the Sergeant to endure alone for the most part, the rest of the team only requiring a tick in the drop box once every eighteen weeks.

The simulator was adapted from the original mining shaft dug by engineers in order to build the colossal underground lair of the Project. Its rudimentary use had been to act as a gigantic service elevator to transport workers, materials and machinery deep into the earth. For a year after the project caves completion it stood as a draughty memory until Cassaveres forwarded the idea of its conversion after Jay expressed concerns.

She'd been worried subjecting crewmembers to endure such a high 'G' plummet may prove unwise using virtual simulator training alone, especially as some of them had little to no prior training in fast flight.

Once planning permission was approved all other motion for the simulator was simple enough to reproduce. A combination of boosters and a powerful hydraulics system provided plenty of extra thrills and spills while experiencing the drop into the old shaft. With the added array of lighting effects and high decibel engine noise, an effective training tool was created in which to prepare for the Reeper's plummet into the river.

The two men stepped out into a narrow metal corridor and turned toward the small steel lift, waiting to take them back to the simulator ops room. They stepped inside, the elevator spiriting them toward their destination.

"I can't believe how much you still hate that thing."

He looked at Dial, the colour slowly returning to his cheeks. "Look some of us are fair ride people, some of us are not."

"Yeah and you definitely fall into the *not* category." He laughed.

Deans would have loved nothing more than to throw something back at Dial but one thing his training over the past ten weeks had illustrated was the major was the best of them. Meaning there was little by way of ammunition he could actually fight back with. *'One of those people who just find most things sickeningly easy.'* had been Marco's assessment, *'But you've gotta love the showy bastard.'*

Dial continued. "Yeah, I was only saying to Dorey the other day, I wish Brookes wasn't so secretive about this place, because I just know my niece would love to ride that thing," he smiled sardonically, "She'll be five next month."

Deans laughed, "Unbelievable."

The elevator came to a halt and opened on a near identical corridor to the one they'd just left. Deans signalled politely for Dial to exit first but he insisted on his junior rank doing so with the quip, "Oh no please, after you. I know you must be feeling a little fragile after this hair-raising ride back up."

He shook his head refusing the bait.

Dial would not be put off, "But not to worry. Some more of Jay's cheap lies about the apparent ease of our drop tomorrow night should sort you out," he feigned a show of mock reminiscence, "Yeah, I remember when she used to tell the rest of us the simulator was worse than the real thing." He shook his head as if somehow wounded by an unwelcome memory. "We believed her. Or at least I did." He was now putting on a display worthy of a soap opera award, "Took me six weeks to get over shitting my pants like that, right in front of everybody."

Deans started to laugh.

"We dropped so fast the back of my head was browner than Jim's balls."

The laughter grew as the two reached their destination, entering the room where the rest of the team gathered during Jay's operation of the simulator. She turned as they came in, "Well I see your disposition has improved on the way back up here."

Deans nodded. "I'm just laughing to be polite." He pointed to Dial.

"Yeah, we all know that feeling." She added.

Dorey was pleased at how well Deans had gelled with the group. He knew at times it must have been difficult, but the Sergeant had performed fantastically. His personality suited the group, as he'd felt it would when choosing him as Moe's successor, and his dedication had proven exemplary. He'd excelled beyond expectations, his flight training queasiness excluded, and impressed everyone within the project. Dial had taken it upon himself to wind him up at every given opportunity, his way of personally testing the new recruit. In response, Dean's sharp humour and quick wit, coupled with his inability to take Dial's goading seriously, ensured a genuine friendship was beginning to take root.

"Well at least you've stopped turning green." Dorey fired at him in perfect German.

"I've found a happy place." Dean's own mastery of the dialect was impressive.

"Didn't look that happy to me," Mark Dial quipped in his native English.

Dorey gestured to Dial. "And the simulator *is* worse than the real thing."

Dial pretended to clear his throat, "That's bullshit."

The mood was good between the team. They'd trained hard over the past weeks and now they were only a few hours from dropping through time.

Along the way had been endless German lessons and hours of combat training. Weeks of constantly planning then re-planning, practising hour after hour so they were able to function with the scitso's ringing in their ears, doing their best to help Marco as he struggled through the language course as well as through his body's unwanted intake of epidermothol which had lightened his skin to a poorly-looking complexion.

They'd familiarised themselves with their weapons and the handling of their truck. Gone over the terrain and tried to second-guess the movements of their targets. Every street and alleyway deliberated over in attentive detail . . . All the while blooding in their new recruit.

The others congratulated Deans on the completion of this, his final preparation.

"Come on let's get out of here." Dorey announced suddenly, "I'll buy you all a drink."

Dial's face lit up. "Now you're talking Boss."

Jay shut down the computer. By the time she was on her feet the others were already halfway to the door. She quickly caught up to Dorey who'd dropped to the rear and discreetly kissed him on his cheek as the others exited the room.

He slapped her behind as she hopped out into the corridor and watched as she enrolled herself in the banter up ahead.

The Commander followed, "The usual rule applies. No more than two drinks on a jump night." Groans descended from the group, causing Dorey's smile to widen.

CHAPTER TWENTY

The sun had risen some hours earlier, slowly warming the London streets. The capital was relaxing into the seventh hour of the morning, enjoying the brief respite before a later sleeping Saturday would announce its own brand of demands on the city.

Dorey sat at his dining table toying with a now lukewarm coffee wearing the comfortable pale blue of his doctor's scrub bottoms, acquired from a friend who worked at Great Ormond Street Hospital.

The wide bay windows captured the morning light perfectly and magnified it across his bare arms and chest, warming his skin as he continued his vigil by the window. Jay was stirring, and he could hear as she now slid out of the bed-sheets pressing her foot onto the oak floor which greeted her touch with its customary creak.

She slipped on a light robe and headed toward the dinette. Jay covered her mouth and yawned, her face a picture of morning fatigue. "Have you been up long?"

"About half an hour, I'm not sure, what time is it?"

At that very moment the alarm began blurting out Puccini causing them both to smile. "Seven-thirty."

Jay had long been accustomed to his habits and routines and she'd have placed a handsome wager as to where she would find him pondering over coffee this morning.

"How old is the coffee?"

He observed the mug in his hand and smiled. "It feels close to middle-aged."

"Really?" She flashed him a wicked stare, "Looks pretty hot from here."

He watched, tantalised as she glided toward him. The dark curve of her athletic body seemed to orchestrate the music from the bedroom, illuminated by the light which captured her from the window, slicing effortlessly through the thin slip.

"You know Commander, sometimes I worry you may work yourself too hard." She stood seductively above him, "That you never find time to relax."

"Well what exactly do you suggest Captain?" He watched her hand as she reached down and slid it between his legs.

"Oh I don't know." She squeezed gently, "But we've over an hour for you to come up with something."

The dishevelled bedroom was shrouded in darkness, its silent *Digeo* walls mapping a perfect night sky. Directly in the room's centre was the bed which played host to Dial's overnight war against the duvet. As he breathed slowly in a rhythmic sleep, only his right shin remained covered, the rest of the quilt slumped to the floor.

His limbs were outstretched, almost holding the pose of the recovery position. He groaned but refused his body permission to move, his subconscious aware of the call to wake up, but for now his brain was happy to ignore it.

Benny and Jim leaned against the railing sprouting from the raised tidal wall of the Thames. Their heavy breathing was subsiding but sweat still fussed their bodies, dampening their running vests further. They gazed out at the mass of tarpaulin covering the Palaces of Westminster on the opposite bank. It seemed they were covered more than not in recent years. The water damage caused by the rivers near two-metre rise in the mid twenty-first century had taken a toll on the base of the building's structure, along with other such real estate gracing the north and south bank.

"I can't believe they haven't finished that yet."

Benny agreed. "It's been covered for over a year this time."

They continued their observation of the blanketed landmark before shifting their attention toward three approaching shuttles, watching as the small aircraft cruised over the pumping station of the Helix Hyrdo-Cell plant.

"Come on, we'll grab Dial and get some breakfast."

"Cool."

The rolling waves crashed onto the beach with a tranquil elegance, each one providing sensual pleasure to the eardrums. The sea displayed around Marco's walls was set at dusk, creating the shadowy embrace of his beloved Rio shoreline.

A beautiful blonde slept peacefully across his bed, her body covered with a white satin sheet which rolled across her forming tiny canyons like whipped cream. The perfectly manicured fingernails of her right hand lay strewn across the bedside table as though she were feeling for the manual sensor of the lamp, desperate to show her facial perfection even while occupied within her dreams.

In the shadows of the room Marco pumped out his fortieth press-up with a nasal blow that blended into the wash of another wave. He would push up sixty more before stretching out and taking a hot shower. *'Perhaps he would ask Amber to join him for breakfast.'* He might just have time before his date with the nine o'clock shuttle.

Carl had been awake for almost an hour. He'd put himself through a quick morning workout before taking his brisk walk to collect the papers which now lay scattered across his large breakfast table. The usual assortment where present, from London to Berlin, Madrid to Paris, Tokyo to New York.

Carl was a traditionalist and preferred a synthetic newspaper with its limited movement pictures and updated news flashes to receiving his news solely via the walls of his apartment or some other gadget. His walk to collect them every morning took ten minutes each way as the shop on his home complex didn't supply such specialist items.

He sipped at a large cup of green tea as he transferred his reading from German to Spanish. The table was more than big enough to accommodate the diversity of information and Carl tried not to think about how empty it still felt, even two years after his wife decided to leave. He knew it had come as a relief to some at the project who'd seen his matrimony as a risk, despite Ellana having high-level clearance as a government official. Throughout the marriage he'd remained under strict instruction to mind his tongue, and he'd tried not to resent the project for it. He'd known it was a life designed for people with as little personal baggage as possible. With the exception of Dorey and Jay's relationship, all of them were now pretty much unattached, if you didn't include Marco's string of women, which often infuriated the security team protecting the project housing. Each time he brought a girl home their hidden technology would scan the lady in question and they'd wait anxiously, ready for the day when they must leap into action in order to deal with an enemy agent.

It never happened of course. Marco would always scan their image into his little black book which would send her details to the Stasis mainframe for his permission to seduce.

Carl took another sip of his tea and checked the time. He always seemed to miss her more on the morning of a jump, he'd put it down to the heightened awareness of his own mortality, naturally brought about on such an occasion.

She'd always noticed this edginess and it killed her he couldn't let her into his private world, a fact which eventually led them to go their separate ways. Or at least that was what he'd told himself. Any other avenue may prove a little too uncomfortable to visit.

He turned the page of his paper and sighed at the headline. 'Bomb blast in Madrid kills twenty.' He shook his head as the Spanish article listed the suspected organisations thought to be responsible. He glanced at the empty chair then back to the pictures of the devastated Spanish families. *'Perhaps his lonely table was the correct sacrifice after all.'*

Deans wasn't sure how long he'd been staring at the ceiling this time around but he was confident it had been for some time.

His eyes burned and he felt the uncertain daze of a person who hadn't properly slept.

He let out a long exhale, his mind awash with trepidation. How he wished he could have switched it off for but a few peaceful hours. However, seven-thirty in the morning meant any such hope had passed, although in typical irony, his brain was now allowing him to feel sleepy, just as he approached the moment he was to get out of bed.

He'd mentally revisited his training in various attempts to tire himself, engaged in several German discussions with his room's computer, all to no avail. Naturally, he was having some difficulty comprehending he'd be travelling through time in twelve hours.

He massaged his forehead. His implants would have to take care of any regeneration now. It was fine, but it just wasn't the same as good old-fashioned restful sleep.

He hated the fact he was anxious, that he was the *new kid* again, terrified of his first day at school. Most of all he hated the fact that despite spending most of his adolescence into adulthood confronting and conquering fears which had so often beaten him as a child, he now found himself unable to sleep, worrying over his capabilities.

He shoved himself out of bed and scoffed at this weakness. *'It's the fatigue.'* He grabbed a T-shirt from the floor next to his bed, ordering the lights be raised. It was time to stop this self-indulgence and embrace the adventure ahead of him. He marched into the bathroom and demanded the mirror's light be activated above the sink.

The tired reflection seemed almost grotesque under the brilliance of the small strip-light.

He tightened his eyes and gave his reflection a resolute stare . . .

"By this time tonight you will have travelled through time."

CHAPTER TWENTY ONE

Brookes strode the final turn of the corridor toward the RFC. He'd finished performing his clandestine last minute checks within his secret lair and once satisfied, began the journey to the operations room to join the rest of his flight team.

The feelings of excitement and anticipation which usually accompanied this pilgrimage however, found themselves put upon by an unwelcome gatecrasher, apprehension.

He remained troubled that his powerful Stasis None had thus far been unable to provide any concrete answers with regards to Isabella Usorio's contradictory find.

'Unable or unwilling?' He mocked his lapse into such Stein-like conspiracy. However, as ludicrous as the thought would normally seem, it bothered him nonetheless, as did his decision to not tell Commander Dorey the full extent of his concerns.

Due to the enormous significance of the current quest Brooke's had persuaded his superiors into pressing ahead with the mission regardless. He'd reminded them Dorey's team were more than capable of handling themselves and, reluctantly in some cases, they'd agreed to proceed concurring with Brooke's prognosis the task at hand was too important to pass up. With the green light remaining, it was decided the team's focus should not suffer unduly, and since the powers themselves had little idea of what it was they'd discovered, Dorey and the others should be told only the bare minimum.

Their safety would depend on their ability to concentrate solely on the task at hand.

Brookes had taken some solace in the fact there was no evidence to suggest the group were in any danger, however, as he was now set to send them back through time he was questioning whether such decisions were the right ones.

He sighed, *'Deal only with the facts at hand,'* he remembered, *'Patience and clarity often expose all to the observer.'* His father's words echoed in his memories but they'd done little to guide him these past weeks. As he stepped into the RFC, the immediate din thrown all around him worked quickly to annul them.

Final system checks and analyses were being spoken into com-links, the varying results thrown around the room. Nods and greetings were afforded Brookes as he walked to where Jose Cassaveres supervised proceedings.

In front of him was the Reeper's Chief engineer and his trusted second, both sending the control room's requests down to flight technicians on the hangar floor.

In his perch to their right was Stein, busying away through the reels of *jump* data.

The room was a hive of efficient, well-rehearsed activity.

Brookes reached the fore of the RFC and looked into the hangar as the Mercedes truck was reversed into the Reeper by engineers wearing anti-contamination suits.

"Can we have one final equipment check to ensure the truck is the last piece to be loaded?" Kev Marley's request was answered immediately by the crew officer below, "Roger that RFC."

"How are we doing Jose?"

Cassaveres turned from his screen, "Everything's fine Sir."

Brookes moved away from the window, picking up his headset and putting it on. The Reeper was practically a part of Jose and as always he was more than content to watch him oversee its final preparations.

Cassaveres leaned toward Myer. "Chief, inform the Commander we are good to go."

Lavowitz passed on the message. "Commander Dorey, you may proceed to suit up."

Down in a sealed room next to the hangar floor Dorey and his team heard the message. All present were seated wearing white synthetic body stockings which resembled veined long johns. The decontamination chamber had witnessed several emotions over the past half-hour. There'd been some laughter, nervousness, but mainly further short discussions on the context of Dorey's recent meeting with Brookes, when he'd admitted the anomaly partly responsible for the creation of this, quite possibly their most important mission to date, had still not been resolved.

"What the fuck are we supposed to take from such a vague term as *anomaly* anyway?" Dial had scoffed, hoping Brookes would be listening in.

The past minutes however paid witness to anticipation, and on hearing the *good to go* signal the room was now observing the unavoidable rushes of pre-drop adrenaline.

The decontamination process was a precaution rather than necessity. It ensured few of the microbes or bugs from the present were transferred into the simulated past and vice versa. One by one the hangar, the ship, its equipment and crew would each be subjected to the precise cleansing process before being cleared to depart. The project had developed an extremely fast and efficient system for carrying out this procedure but Dorey and his team always entered the purifying room at least half an hour before the base-jump.

It helped them focus and get into character.

Each of them began pulling their rubbery suits over the snugly-fitting underlay. The *anti-G anatomic suits* where necessary when attempting the base-jump or arduous flight, manipulating the rushes of blood during the drop. The channelled arteries which covered the suit's skin would fill with a highly responsive intelligent gel, pumped down the tracks to compress the suit at required points like blood being pumped into a muscle.

They were much more than just 'Anti-G' suits however. Once connected to the Reeper the ship could monitor and interact with her crew's bodies and implants in order to aid and protect them, to help adjust their inner workings and temperatures during the high speed burn through time and space. A connection hose from the ship was fastened to each suit enabling the Reeper to dispense, move and withdraw the gel at great speed as and when required. Similarly, the mother ship could use these to attend to any basic medical needs, administrating drugs or applying pressure to any wounds.

They finished packing themselves into the suits before placing on the thin membrane of the skullcaps which sat beneath their helmets enabling the brain's functions to also be reported to the care of the guardian ship.

Dial turned to Deans. "You okay?"

"I'm fine, honestly."

Dorey addressed his team. "Let's start checking each other down."

They paired up and monitored one another's outfits to ensure they were fitted correctly. Once satisfied the Commander radioed the RFC, "We're suited-up and ready to go."

"Roger that," Jose then received news in his right ear from the head technician in the hangar. "Understood, begin clearing hangar deck." He turned to Brookes, "All on-board armaments and supplies are secure and accounted for. I've requested the ground crew prepare to clear the Flight Deck."

Brookes entered the proceedings, "Chief, could you sound the warning please."

A repetitive alarm was sent into the hangar accompanied by a flashing blue light synchronised to each buzzing drone. Chaperoning the commotion was the female hangar voice, *"Please evacuate the hangar immediately."*

Brookes watched as the technicians below began clearing themselves and their equipment through the numerous hangar doors. He turned his attention to the RFC staff all around him as he activated the room's intercom. "Ladies and gentlemen, if you could finalise your checks now please, I will be taking the *comm* in five minutes."

Each team began winding down their preparations in a closing flurry.

He switched over to a personal communicator. "Doctor Usorio, how is our tunnel?"

Up two rows behind him Isabella was monitoring the time thread offered by the Stasis None, which although much longer than any used before, had been identified as the best syringe from which to inject Dorey and his team across this particular time and space. "I'm still picking up some unusually violent activity from within its continuum, we can utilise it, but it may well be a bumpy ride."

He left the channel to Isabella open. "Doctor Stein we have the go ahead from Doctor Usorio, you may proceed to bring home the worm."

Stein set about the task of manipulating the tunnel toward the Stasis None's powerful vortex drive, channelled through the rock like a gigantic canyon beneath the thick reinforced floor of the Reeper lair. The powerful dark matter would be sucked in and pinned down before being torn into by the immense time displacement engines.

Jose relayed his update, "Sir, I've been informed the hangar is now clear and clean."

"Shut down the hangar and activate the boarding tubes."

The flashing light turned green and the recorded voice upped her performance to every five seconds, *"Hangar shut down . . . activated. Hangar shut down . . . activated."*

The personnel of the RFC finalised their checks and one by one began to fall silent.

All eyes were now fixed on the hangar below, either directly or via the monitors in front of them as they watched the armoured seals of the flight deck roll slowly downward, sealing off the enclosure's apertures and exits.

Beneath the Reeper, technicians left two entry towers. The concertina-like structures attached under the hull of the ship, one beneath her broad nose, the other fixed to an entrance next to the now sealed ramp at her rear. Both were connected to one another via a plastic tunnel, a purified tube whose walkway arched across the ground spanning two-and-a-half metres in diameter. The thin tunnel beneath the nose section began to unfold as if under the spell of some magical force, creating a further outreaching tube which began stretching toward the decontamination room like a ghostly arm. Once its destination was reached the sausage-skin tunnel locked automatically to the seal around the door, granting access from the room in which Dorey's team had spent the past forty minutes.

Jose opened a channel to the team below, "Commander, you are cleared to board."

A lively energy descended on the room. The zest of it zipped all around the crew members making their senses sharp.

Dorey fixed his stare on Deans. "Okay," he gave the virgin jumper a reassuring wink, "Let's do it."

CHAPTER TWENTY TWO

The chief powered the gigantic arms which gripped the Reeper like an injured bird, readying for the imminent surge in juice soon to be flooded through their mechanical muscles. Marley activated the final lock down sequence causing an armoured shutter to roll smoothly over the RFC window overlooking the hangar. It sealed magnetically.

Jose looked at his now curtained view. "Activate hangar screen." A synthetic view of the hangar immediately replaced the original in perfectly beamed proportions.

Below on the flight deck Jim and Jay left the main group and made their way into the first boarding tower beneath the nose of the ship.

Jay smiled, "See you in Germany . . . Safe flight." She put on her helmet.

"Safe flight," they replied to both pilots as the small elevator carried them upward.

Dorey turned his attention to Deans. "Okay this is it. We know how you must be feeling. Just remember your training and you'll be fine."

The nervous Sergeant gave him an assertive look. "I'm good."

Brookes watched as Dorey and his team entered the ship, her cameras beaming their images as they took their seats, donned their helmets and restraints, before connecting their suits to the care of the Reeper.

Stein then announced, "Sir I have a lock, bringing home the worm."

Brookes turned his attention to Jose, "Begin secondary launch sequence."

He and his two operators set about readying the hangar for the storm soon to come.

"*Secondary launch sequence, activated . . . secondary launch sequence, activated.*"

A short calm took hold. Then, from somewhere deep within the belly of rock beneath, the Earth groaned. At first her displeasure echoed through the Stasis cave structure like the moans of a vast ocean-tanker. However the umbrage soon grew, the ensuing rumble as if doom itself now prowled beneath them.

"Powering vortex engines to maximum."

Brookes followed the announcement. "Arms to eighty percent, prepare for engine fire."

Jose's team brought out the vast exhaust cylinder from the back wall as the power reverberating through the holding arms was increased.

Inside the ship, the crew made ready.

Deans was desperate to keep it together but the imminence of the great unknown was hard to ignore. He gripped the arms of the cradle which pressed him firmly into his seat. The suit coupled with his implants did their best to adjust his body accordingly, the Reeper passing on the information to the RFC above.

Doctor Kelvin analysed the crew's vital signs. He spoke gently through his intercom into Dial's ear. "Deans is showing signs of stress, keep an eye on him."

It was an unnecessary statement as all eyes were fixed on the virgin jumper.

"Keep it nice and relaxed Deans, believe me there's nothing to worry about."

He nodded at Dial as he made a concerted effort to relax.

"Looking good Deans. Just remember her bark's worse than her bite," Dorey added.

He'd heard the comment many times.

"Holding arms are at eighty percent." The chief announced.

Jose patched himself through to the Reeper. "Lieutenant Adams, prepare to fire primary engines on our mark."

The pre-recorded voice returned, the warning lights now a luminous red.

Jim opened the expanse of the rear exhaust and ignited the Reeper's turbines, the familiar whistle of jets now growing all around them.

"*Primary engine launch in one minute and counting.*"

Jim pressed a sensor, "Raising landing gear."

The gear retracted leaving her suspended by the mighty arms. The ship rocked gently.

"*Primary engine fire in thirty seconds and counting.*"

Jim spoke to the ship's computer, "Reeper, power thrust engines to sixty percent."

Dorey and the others flashed Deans a stream of reassuring comments.

"Jay, secondary systems check."

Jim's co-pilot monitored the build up. "All systems check. Clear to fire engines."

"*Ten seconds to mark.*"

The Reeper's turbines began howling their intent, forcing the ship to dip forward.

"*Three . . . two . . . one . . . Mark.*"

Jim unleashed sixty percent of the Reeper's jets. She dipped menacingly as the air was filled with her brutal impatience, the engines demanding her immediate release.

"Hold at sixty percent Lieutenant, worm is not yet home."

Jim replied calmly, "Roger that."

All eyes flashed to Stein as he increased the power of the vortex drive which began sucking in the enormous energy force. "We have full contact."

Jay had never seen such readings as those now transmitted on her displays. The tunnel was larger, more violent than any she'd witnessed.

"Locking onto worm." A bead of sweat began a journey down the side of Stein's brow.

All eyes were on him, waiting for the beast to be tamed when suddenly, the whole cave rumbled as if under attack from an almighty earthquake. Warning sensors began flashing.

Brookes remained focused on the digitised hangar as he demanded, "Doctor Stein?"

"Almost there." The bead of sweat ran down his cheek to the freedom of his collar.

Another rumble followed, then another. The holding arms rocked from their foundations. "Almost there."

The pilots monitored their readings and awaited the go ahead to the next level.

Then without warning, an incredible *bang* erupted from underneath the hangar, like some gigantic beast was attempting to punch through the floor below them.

"The worm is home. Displacement engines are at maximum." Stein declared.

Deep bellows of force could be heard as the gigantic circular engines hidden beneath the Project's structure increased their orbits. As the commotion beneath grew, all present prepared for the imminent violence of the arriving storm.

Again the floor of the hangar was attacked with a series of furious blows, accompanied by a tremendous whirring sound which grew in intensity as the sub-forces of science and nature expanded, filling the hidden depths below.

"The worm has been pinned, preparing to open her up."

Brookes turned to Cassaveres. "Ready the Hangar."

A buzzer honked out a new warning, signalling the opening of the floor, a sound which quickened the hearts of the Reeper crew and passengers.

Inside the ship Dorey spoke calmly to Deans, "Not long now, we're doing great."

Deans wished only for the drop to be over with.

Slowly the hangar floor began retracting into two halves from its centre, pulling apart as it was fed out through the base of the adjacent walls.

Cassaveres relayed his next instruction. "Place arms on maximum," he then transmitted into Jim's ear, "Take Reeper engines to ninety-eight percent."

Jim increased the power, holding the engines on the brink of the afterburners.

As the floor continued to retract the storm beneath began thrashing furiously against its provocateurs. It whipped out, lashing against the shields of the RFC, threatening those inside with retribution. Its ferocity bounced around the hangar, increasing as the floor opened wider, catching the Reeper with tasty jabs as she screamed against her restraints.

The floor peeled away exposing a vortex blacker than an abyss, propelled into a spin as it was sucked in by the Stasis engines like a swirling tunnel of shadow.

The hangar shook as if quivering before a divine, angry hand.

Stein negotiated his grip over this biblical force, so he may tear a hole into its fabric. The atmosphere released felt like chaos, yet the focus of all within the RFC remained.

Suddenly Stein's face was luminous. The time displacement drives had successfully wrestled the beast. He could now use the genius of Brooke's creation to utilise its awesome energy, "Tearing her open now."

It was as if the exalted force somehow understood it was close to defeat and like a wild Mustang finally roped, it kicked out venomously in an attempt to preserve its nobility.

"Opening the continuum," Stein declared.

Brookes sent out his order to Jose, "Lower the arms."

Jim opened a channel to the rest of the ship. "We are good to go, prepare for base-jump."

"Here comes the fun part." Dial said with a grin.

Deans looked back at him no longer prepared to even pretend he was happy.

The population of the RFC watched in awe as the black soup tunnel powered like a raging river beneath the Reeper, its torrents spilling a riot of colour as it was opened up.

The violence of the storm suddenly reversed as the torn portal began sucking all into its open artery. In place of the floor was now a deep hollow drop into a wild torrent, the current whipping through it in a montage of brilliant light, a florescent of time and space.

The gigantic arms lowered the ship toward the calamity.

Within the RFC it felt like the shutters would be sucked away at any moment, as if in the wake of a fantastical tornado. Still the arms lowered the ship down.

"Arms approaching worm." Cassaveres relayed to Brookes who like the rest of them, was mesmerised by the fabric of space which raged before them. On each occasion the creator would wish it were he once again who was entering the mysteries of the universe. '*One day soon,*' he promised himself, as he always did at these moments. "Prepare for drop."

Jim rolled his fingers around the stick, firming his grip.

Inside the ship the noise was deafening as the tunnel sucked them in with a gargantuan intake of breath. The violent hammer blows to the vessel's body now ceased however, as they were placed into what felt like the ventilation shaft of the cosmos.

Isabella was concerned. The readings pointed toward the Reeper having to endure a far more violent passage than she and her crew were used to.

As the ship disappeared into the cylindrical vortex, Brookes turned his attention back to his monitors, "Initiate final launch sequence."

The recorded voice was barely audible as she was beamed into the Reeper.

The crew struggled to hear the clarification as they were plunged into the depths of the river. They pressed their headsets closer to their ears, their inner implants never used during drops. "*Reeper launch in one minute and counting.*"

They grabbed hold of their restraints and tried to concentrate on the countdown.

The two pilots heard the warning and prepared themselves for the plummet.

"*Thirty seconds to mark.*"

Marco said a short prayer to the holy mother.

"*Twenty seconds to mark . . .*"

Carl thought only of his estranged wife.

"*Ten seconds . . .*"

Benny thought of how his parents would give anything for an opportunity such as this.

"*Five . . .*"

Deans was at a loss to his emotions.

"*Four . . .*"

Dial thought of his other jumps and simply tried to relive them in order to prepare.

"*Three . . .*"

Dorey thought of Jay only a few decks above and prayed for the safe return of his crew."

"*Two . . .*"

Jay prepared for the unthinkable . . . Having to separate the ship if anything went wrong.

"*One . . .*"

Jim could only concentrate on his cockpit. Their lives were in his hands now.

"*Mark!*"

In that instant it seemed as if time itself stood still. The people in the RFC appeared to hold their breath. The passengers within the Reeper clenched their eyes and teeth as Jim and Jay awaited control of the ship.

Brookes and the others watched as the mechanical arms finally gave up the struggle, now hidden from view by the torrent below. For a moment they could still see the ship's vital signs and that of her passengers displayed on their screens.

Then in an instant . . . they were gone.

CHAPTER TWENTY THREE

Jim fought the controls as the ship plummeted into the vortex. The engines kicked with almighty force, but they'd not been powerful enough to level them out fully.

They were still being sucked down violently. He fired the afterburners which jolted the Reeper forward some more. She was finally beginning to level.

Dorey and the others braced into their seats. The suits pulverised their bodies as the ship bounced through the currents of time. As they fell inside the core the noise of the vortex diminished, the volume of the engines now the predominant force.

"Preparing to activate Barb-fire."

It was unusual at this stage to hit the rockets. However, Jay understood Jim's concern. The ship was still on a downward trajectory even though her nose was now level.

They couldn't afford to slip through the eye of the tunnel and enter the dangerous outer wall of the hurricane. That would mean having to blast their way through the entire river at full throttle in order to stay level. As well as leaving the Reeper open to the possibility of a lethal spin upon exit, this would also see them gorge heavily on the precious fuel.

Jay quickly instructed the navigational computer of their intentions and made the necessary adjustments. "Roger that Jim, fire when ready."

Suddenly, time began to alter itself into a dream like vibration.

Jim rolled his eyes as he heard Jay say, "We're entering the outer wall of the core."

Dropping beyond the core of the vortex could subject the traveller to a near mind-altering state. The rules which governed the human universe did not apply here. The Reeper was usually able to seal it out, but this was by far the most aggressive worm encountered and the ship was finding it difficult to resist.

Jim concentrated on his dials as the Reeper gave him a shot of drugs to keep him alert, "Engaging barb-fire on my mark."

Jay focused as Jim's voice seemed to flood right through her like a dream.

Even the wail of the engines appeared to have been left behind. Dorey and the others watched as blurred, distorted vapour trails of themselves passed before their eyes. Nothing as intense as this had breached the ship's seals. They tried to remember the training, focus on closing eyelids and clenching teeth, but the intoxicating soup of the universe washed through their minds. The ship did what it could to assist them.

Somewhere in another existence, they heard a distant thunder as the Reeper unleashed her barb-fire rockets, their rolling heads thrashed into the seats, as suddenly, they were jettisoned across time.

CHAPTER TWENTY FOUR

Ballack swung his Messerschmitt away from the destruction, pulling his nose into the air before heading for the cover of low gathering cloud. As his aircraft banked he checked over his shoulder, just in time to witness Hellzeigger complete his own pass with similar effect, his bomb plummeting on the target adding to the flashes of carnage left only seconds before by the detonation of his own device. The radioed positions passed to them by the infantry had proved accurate and the hunted rag-tag forces of Polish resistance were hit hard as they travelled through the sparse woodland shrouded by night.

His Wingman followed his lead into the cloud, "Direct hit." He yelled into Ballack's headphones. "Shall we make another dive using guns?"

"No, this cloud cover is coming in fast and low."

Hellzeigger looked through his canopy noticing how the weather had descended rapidly. "You're right," he throttled upward into the haze, "I've never seen cloud roll so quickly."

"Don't worry in a few seconds you'll be back in the moonlight."

Almost at the very moment of receiving Ballack's words Hellzeigger pulled clear of the cloud, once again enjoying the dark early morning of a Polish summer. He looked up to his right and saw his lead pilot arcing away to the west, his canopy flashing with the moon. He gunned the throttle and gave chase.

"I fancy taking her up high."

"You always fancy taking her up high," came Hellziegger's reply.

Ballack wasted little time as he pulled back on his stick causing his aircraft to roar high into the night air leaving a vapour trail from the exhausts as he went. He loved the rare opportunities to fly before sunrise.

Hellziegger followed, opening the single propeller engine into a full pace climb. The haze from Ballack's spent fuel dissipated and Hell watched as his friend took his aircraft higher before levelling out with a smooth barrel roll. It was so clear beneath the brilliant moon it could have been daylight once above the cloud cover.

Ballack had built up quite a lead and as usual Hellzeigger could not figure out how he always seemed to manage it. *'It's the plane. It has to be the plane.'* He told himself.

"Come on Hell keep up."

Hellziegger continued with his fully throttled chase gradually levelling his Messershcmitt at a slightly higher altitude, but still some way behind.

"Heading back for base."

Hellziegger was set to acknowledge when something in the sky caught his attention. He squinted as he tried to focus on it. *'What on earth?'* He blinked several times certain his eyes were being tricked as the light danced across his canopy, but still the curious sight remained. It was some five hundred feet above the spot where his leader's plane was now heading, like a swirling mass of misty atmosphere picking up momentum. He stared, as suddenly an occasional flash then fork of lightning accompanied its pattern, yet all around the oddity was nothing but dark pastel sky. He looked down to the lead plane as it now crossed a path directly underneath it. "Hey Christian, do you see that?"

Ballack detected the puzzlement in his friend's voice. "See what?"

"Above you, that strange weather pattern."

"Weather pattern?"

Before Hellzeigger could summon an answer the heavens at the mouth of the curiosity ripped open with a clapping flash, belching out a gigantic black projectile in a firestorm of electricity. "Jesus!" Hell shouted as he pulled on his stick to veer away from danger, but he was hit almost instantly by a wave of turbulence which forced him into a flat spin.

Ballack didn't even hear the end of his colleague's cry. His plane was obliterated into tiny fragments as the Reeper plunged toward the earth.

"We've just hit something!" Jay declared as the ground impact alarms began screaming.

"I know. We've been spat out too low. We're in the earth's atmosphere. The snap back into reality was like a slap across the face. "De-activare barb-fire"

Dorey and the others were once more aware of the screaming engines as their vessel roared into real atmosphere, the alarms warning of impending danger.

"I can't pull her out of it." Jim fought the stick.

Jay voice activated her emergency actions, "Placing maximum burn to nose thrusters."

"Fire the airbrakes. We're at seven thousand feet."

Jay followed Jim's order instantly. "We'll soon be too low for separation."

"We won't need it." He declared.

She saw the warnings flashing her display. They were coming in fast and steep.

Jim pulled back using every ounce of his strength, still awaiting help from the dithering computer, pondering its dilemma of whether to risk tearing the hull apart.

"She's responding."

The veins on Jim's neck flexed as his implants sent their maximum dose. It was needed, the ship's artificial intelligence remaining uncharacteristically slow.

"She's levelling." Jay yelled.

Dorey and the others gripped their seats as the ship threatened to be torn in two.

Jay ordered the flaps to go against their programming and risk themselves being torn off in a last ditch effort to help Jim pull the nose of the ship upward.

"Three thousand feet." Jay clarified as they plummeted into the low cloud. The ground was only moments away, but the ship's systems were beginning to play ball.

The Reeper's nose finally lifted. "Re-activate barb-fire!"

The already primed rockets exploded back into life propelling them forward aggressively.

The ship's belly struck the canopies of several tall trees which graced the wooded hillside now plunging directly beneath them. As the nose continued upward her heavy backside dipped tearing up ancient trunks, the barb-fire scorching the surrounding foliage.

The rockets bolted them back into the sky away from the deep valley below. Jim swung the ship into a vast arcing turn, "Throttling down." His voice betrayed his anxiety.

Jay spoke softly to her pilot's ear. "Thank God you were flying her Jim."

"What the hell happened to fire us out so low?"

"That was the most unstable tunnel we've ever seen, it was like riding a storm." Jay studied the data. "The density of the vortex breached the hull at a much higher magnitude than ever before. I think it may have slowed the reaction time of our computer systems."

"We'd better put her down as soon as possible and give her a thorough checking over."

Jay was about to acknowledge when a section of her helmet's optical display urgently brought another matter to her attention. She homed in on it immediately.

In the distance Hellziegger throttled his plane across the luminous sky. He was certain the spin would be the end of him yet somehow, he'd managed to pull himself out of it. His senses returned. His mind replaying the incident as his eyes searched the skies.

His nerves were shot as he propelled himself in the direction of his home airstrip.

Then he saw it. A flame circling him in the far distance. At this range it looked little bigger than a firefly, but he knew better. His heart pounded and his palms began to sweat. "Oh God what is it?" He yelled. He swung his aircraft toward the earth, back into the cover of the low lying cloud. His engines whined as he dropped into the thick haze. Although now shrouded in its protection he continually darted his head in all directions, his wide and desperate eyes stumbling to seek out Ballack's dark destroyer through the occasional respites in cloud cover. The feeling of dread returned as he caught a glimpse of the bright flame, now inexplicably much closer to him and over to his right. *'Nothing can travel at such speed.'* His gaze squinted toward it, trying to eye its shape through another clearing, weighing up its trajectory. It was too dark to see clearly but he felt a glimmer of hope return as he realised the burning light was now moving away from him.

He wrestled to gather his wits. Then suddenly without warning, Hellzeigger's shrouding mist came to an abrupt end and he found himself once again flying through clear moonlit skies. He looked around and realised he recognised his surroundings. He'd reached the woodland edge and was approaching the familiar glistening snake of river which led back to the airfield. He gripped the controls with renewed belief, searching the sky for his tormentor. He caught sight of it again and saw it was still moving farther away.

He gathered his senses. He could radio a warning to the larger, main airfield some thirty miles away, toward which the terrifying object seemed to be headed.

He opened a channel not realising this action would seal his doom. He tried to relay his warning but the radio sang nothing but static. He tapped the switch before checking the sky once more. As he relocated the far away flame he noticed yet another peculiar sight.

From the rear of the distant torch a small finger of smoke trailed outward across the stars. At first his eyes teased his heart with the possibility the strange object had been hit by scrambled fighters, but he soon realised the vapour trail belonged to an entirely different entity to that of the main craft. His pupils dilated in horror as he watched the circling light with its trail of white smoke turn then close in toward him at incredible speed. He tried once more to open a channel in the hope of some miraculous help from his airfield but the radio offered nothing. He felt panic stricken as the grey smoke turned into the flash of a nearing projectile, as suddenly, the Reeper's missile was upon him.

Then in a heartbeat, Hellzeigger was no more.

CHAPTER TWENTY FIVE

Isabella leaned back in her chair and let out a heavy sigh. She was troubled. She was unhappy with the violent nature of the Reeper's exit just as she was unhappy with Brookes' decision to press on with operations regardless of her mysterious anomaly remaining unresolved. She understood how the somewhat remarkable nature of current circumstances overruled the usual protocol but she did not concur with Brooke's decision to keep Dorey's team in the dark. As far as she was concerned it was both unethical and unprofessional to dismiss her findings to the Commander as a technical glitch, despite her boss's assurances he was doing it for the right reasons.

'*The right reasons would see them grounded until we eliminate all risk.*' She'd argued.

'*If only such a concept were even possible,*' Brookes had responded bringing her protests to an end. Stein had not been happy with her impertinence but she would not hide like some scared mouse when it came to voicing an opinion.

She activated her screens and had the Hunter program report with its twice daily check. As the system fired up she swivelled on her chair.

The complex diagrams were painted in front of her, following the usual patterns of light and code before stopping on something entirely new. She sat upright and leaned in closer to the displays. "What the hell?" She quickly set about cross checking the latest find. Such analysis resulted in the display highlighting an all too familiar light, its strobe flashing on the display like a ship at sea suddenly wanting her attention, "Son of bitch!"

*

The Reeper touched down in the Alps within a swirl of engine downdraft. Her landing gear placed them softly onto the lush grassy plateau which lazed under the moonlit faces of the surrounding peaks. As the outpour of the ship's engines diminished into a fading chorus of whistles, the beleaguered crew gave out a collective sigh of relief.

Jim's voice transmitted into his passenger's headsets. "How are we doing back there?" As each of them checked in with a shaky response he deactivated the hold bars pinning them to their seats. He then had the Reeper carry out another scan of the area to make sure they were still alone.

Jay welcomed back the ground with a long exhale. She took off her helmet and peeled away the skullcap, shaking out her fastened hair. "How are you doing down there Jim?"

"I'm good, how about you?"

"Fine . . . That was a serious piece of flying."

"Believe me it was more a serious piece of heaving."

"I couldn't have pulled her out of that, I wouldn't have had the strength."

Jay activated the rear loading ramp and addressed those in the rear, "Welcome to 1944, We'd like to thank you all for flying with us, as you can see the moon is shining and may I wish you all a pleasant stay in the Third Reich."

Dorey and the others lifted the securing brace and began unbuckling their quick-release harnesses. The passengers had no visual knowledge as to what had just transpired. The majority of the audio was broadcast between the two cockpits. But they knew they'd had a close call, an experience entirely new to them when inside the Reeper. They'd endured the sharp plummet of the ship and listened in controlled horror as the engines screamed to pull them out of the drop. All eyes had flashed toward Benny for reassurance. Unfortunately, his face had confirmed to them all they'd needed to know.

Once released from their bonds they began disconnecting their suits from the umbilical link instantly causing them to feel a sense of light-headedness.

Dorey focussed. "Okay, let's take five minutes to stretch our legs outside."

They headed into the moonlight, their senses returning with the crisp mountain air.

As they stepped off the ramp onto the cushioned carpet of dark grass the group found themselves humbled beneath the hypnotic spell of the surrounding mountains, the dramatic rocky white peaks glowing majestically in the bright moonlight.

"Jesus." Deans whispered in a foggy breath, immediately feeling the effects of the view.

Dial stood to his rear, "I take it back. The simulator *is* worse than the real thing."

He shook his head, "Yeah . . . compared to the simulator that was like playing on a swing."

Dial was pleased the new boy had kept hold of his humour.

A brief silence followed as they took in the awesome sight, filling their lungs with the clear mountain air. They all understood how Deans felt at that moment.

It wasn't just the incredible panoramic view, though this would have been enough in its own right, but the indescribable sense of knowing you were now in another world and time, a notion completely impossible to describe until experienced firsthand.

It was an overwhelming, emotional attack on the senses. As if the very fabric of your being was somehow aware it did not belong, like the world knew you to be alien to this place, its radar detecting your DNA and concluding this was not where you should be.

He took another deep breath in the hope it would help him deal with this impassioned introduction to another existence. However, it was the Reeper that dragged his consciousness back as she hissed the imminent arrival of her two pilots as the ship's hull opened beneath the nose, lowering them on the forward ramp.

The two hopped off and walked toward the rest of the group. "Are you all okay?"

"Thanks to you two, yes." Benny was quick to respond.

"What the hell happened?" Marco asked.

Jim had the Reeper's undercarriage lights illuminate her belly. "The tunnel knocked the shit out of us!" He said as the lights came on. "We had to activate the barb-fire before we had a full destination lock just to stop us slipping straight into the outer core." He walked beneath the ship and began scanning it intently.

"Some of the readings suggest they may not have had the usual grip on the worm as we jumped." Jay added, "Possibly due to its larger mass."

Jim agreed with this hypothesis. "That would make sense. I mean we came down way too low, well inside the Earth's atmosphere, we're talking less than fifteen thousand feet."

"Shit!" Benny understood the implications immediately. The Reeper was supposed to enter her new time zone on the fringe of the Earth's atmosphere. From there she could begin a controlled descent. "So how close were we?"

Jay replied, "Did any of you feel those impacts just before we levelled out? Well that was mountain side tree-tops hitting our undercarriage."

A short chorus of expletives followed.

"Plus we hit a small plane head on as we made re-entry."

Benny looked to Jim his eyebrows high, "You're kidding me?"

He shook his head. "We obliterated it. I didn't even see it. Jay informed me afterward."

"And we had to take out his wingman." Jay added.

"What?" Dorey exclaimed.

"Another aircraft flying to his rear. He was opening a distress channel and we were heading out of jamming range. There's a large airstrip between us and the Alps. The last thing we need is to be blowing half the Luftwaffe out of the sky before we've even got started! We knocked him out with a rapture missile."

In different circumstances this could have placed their mission under threat of failure before it had even begun. However, their objectives were specific and any unwanted mishaps could be accepted as long as their mission parameters were not compromised.

Jim stared up at the illuminated underbelly, "We need to carry out a sweep of the ship. She says she's fine but the whole system was slow when we were ejected out of that tunnel. More of the vortex seemed to breech the hull than usual, I'm sure you noticed it. Under these circumstances I'd rather take a look for myself. I've activated a full internal diagnostic before I even think about taking her up again."

The Reeper was often assaulted, albeit to a lesser degree, during flights through time. The more exposed external communications and outer weapons systems were usually all that suffered, her internal brain being heavily armoured against any such attack by the worm.

They formed a line under her nose then began slowly walking toward the tail of the ship, studying her undercarriage. As they went they could see the scratches and tracks left by the aggressive swipe of the treetops. But nothing had breeched her heavy armour.

When the Reeper would be sat at berth in the polar hideout, the nanobots within her skin and skeleton would set to work with their makeshift repairs, healing her wounds.

Feeling happier, Jim lowered the lights to softly illuminate the ground beneath. As they re-grouped they all seemed suddenly aware of the cold bite in the mountain air which had become more evident as the adrenaline rush began to fade. Their implants would soon begin dealing with it in their own way if they didn't change their attire soon.

"Okay let's get the ship unloaded and get ourselves a change in outfit. Light body armour underneath from the start." Dorey assessed the surrounding terrain. "The track down the mountain is over in that direction, we'll set off within the hour." He turned to his pilot. "Once in the air, announce our imminent arrival to the Colonel at first light."

Jim nodded. "If I have any problems with the ship later, I'll launch the SiSTER satellite."

Dorey agreed. "Just signal if that's the action you take." He checked his watch. "We'll be aiming to arrive no later than 1600. We're only two hours later than hoped, at least the worm got that right!" Dorey rubbed his cold hands as he headed for the ramp. He turned as he hit it, "Oh and Jim," he said, "Thanks again for getting us down."

CHAPTER TWENTY SIX

Brookes was clearly distraught at Usorio's latest findings.

"Perhaps it is aware of our tracking it and alters its signature to throw us off the scent."

Stein enjoyed conspiracy and at that moment Brookes could have smacked him in the mouth for such indulgence. Instead he gave a pained expression. "And you're certain there's no exit puncture?" Brookes wanted clarification.

Isabella pointed at the numbers and code then back to the pulsating light. "Everything indicates this to be a live event. It actually entered the timeline outside of Paris several weeks before Dorey entered the same timeline today. Despite its obvious alterations it has clear similarities to our previous intruder. I don't understand why the Hunter program took until now to find it. It must be something to do with the universal shift with regards to our place in time and that of the anomaly. My system analysis is working on answers as we speak. But it has confirmed, despite the delay, this new event appears to be live."

Brookes cursed. "You were right Isabella. I should have been more concise with my concerns when relaying them to Dorey's team." He stared at the pulsating light, highlighting the possible reintroduction of their mysterious anomaly, its signature accessing the very timeline they'd just sent the Reeper toward.

She watched Brookes closely as he formulated his thinking.

"And your Hunter program has managed to lock onto this entry data directly?"

"Yes. The Hunter has digested the anomaly's new make up so it should be alert to any attempts at an exit. If this is indeed a live event and it jumps out before we seal the system. There's a possibility we could track it and therefore clarify its source."

This offered some recompense. "Find out where that damn thing is coming from Isabella. Don't let it out of your sight."

Stein looked on at the technology admiringly, "So what's our next move?"

Brookes exhaled, "The only thing we can do. We wait.

The truck's rear view of the Alps had eventually faded into haze within the first hours of dawn. The look of wonder on Dean's face however, showed no such sign of abating.

In fact his colleagues would have been hard pressed to recall but a handful of occasions when they'd seen anything other than the back of his head since setting off under the cover of darkness. It had taken every ounce of his willpower just to stop himself gasping as each new scene introduced itself, as the contemporary planet spanned before the rectangular eye of the open-backed truck.

They all understood of course. They too still felt the overwhelming power of their enterprise. No amount of assignments through time could take away the natural feelings of sensationalism. However, they'd discovered during the early stages of their escapades, in order to preserve their own sanity, it was good practice to at least try and keep the intoxication at arm's length. This was often easier said than done and they all realised Deans would eventually require more than just silence.

Jay, sitting opposite at the rear opening, decided it was time for another check on his wellbeing. "Hey Deans, are you alright?"

He responded as he'd done upon every other occasion. "I'm fine." This was followed with a reassuring smile before his attention was drawn outside the posterior once more.

"You sure?" Jay decided to persist this time around.

"Honestly." The statement trailed with a hand gesture meant to wrap up the reassurance.

She turned to the others as he continued to marvel at the surrounding world.

Benny mouthed silently, "He's alright."

She continued to watch him for a moment before handing herself back to the rhythm of the ride, content to continue the silent phase of their journey which had engulfed the past hour. However, as her mind began to drift, Deans decided his silent time was now over.

"I just can't get my head around it!" He wasn't exactly sure why it was on this occasion rather than the countless others when checked upon he'd decided to speak. In fact at that moment he was more surprised at the sound of his own voice than anyone present.

Perhaps it was the falcon that hypnotised only a short time earlier which prompted his tongue. The grace as the mere tip of its wing allowed it to hover or swoop effortlessly across the thermals had proved almost too much to bear. Or perhaps it was the fly which only a moment ago tickled and irritated his nose before buzzing past his ear. Yet when he'd raised his hand to swat it he'd found himself unwilling to do so. The creature in this existence suddenly deserving of a healthier respect aimed toward its miraculous life, far more than it could hope for had their paths crossed in Dean's world.

His reluctance to destroy what he now perceived as a marvel of creation in this realm illustrated a boundless hypocrisy when aimed toward the divinity of life in his own.

Whatever the reason, he'd found himself swimming through too much mental turmoil to stay afloat and could hold his tongue no longer.

He was suddenly aware of the collective eyes now aimed on him and at that moment he might have forgotten what they enquired had Jay not reminded him of the impromptu statement he'd made a few moments earlier.

"You can't get your head around what?"

He looked at her in renewed turmoil. *'How long had it been since he'd broken his silence? Had they all been waiting for this lunatic to speak for some time now, or was it still the same moment?'* He was in danger of drowning within himself, "I just can't get my head around . . ." Words failed him so he took the most direct action he could think of which was to simply point at the world outside and say, "That!"

All in the truck empathised. They'd been surprised at how long he'd remained silent before his mind showed signs of cracking.

"Deans, look at me. Its okay . . . What you're feeling is normal."

He stared at her and suddenly felt embarrassed at this sudden lack of self-control.

She smiled, "I was ready to meet my maker two hours into my first mission." She turned to the others, "Do you remember?"

Dial laughed from the shadows of the bouncy posterior. "Remember, shit I thought you'd gone bye-bye."

Benny shook his head. "On my first time . . . Man, I thought I was gonna cry."

Dial turned to him. "What are you talking about? You did fucking cry!"

In the front of the cab Dorey listened via the intercom linking them through the partition. He watched the rolling countryside through his passenger window. His faith in Deans as solid as it could be at this juncture, certain his focus would be on the mission. He held no fear as to his state of mind. The normal sense of wonder now crawling all over him would inevitably drag the virgin jumper into such discussion.

Carl anticipated the inevitable direction of the conversation, a subtle smile forming as he steered them around a pot hole. *'Sometimes you simply have to talk about it.'*

Jay's attention remained. "It's like what we told you before the jump. You just can't train someone in order to instil their reaction to this. It's impossible. This whole thing messes with your mind if you let it."

Deans rubbed the back of his head. "I just feel like it's all going to overwhelm me you know? That somehow it's going to get the better of me." He stared out of the truck's rear once more. "I mean . . . That's a whole world out there."

Benny rocked forward as the truck hit more uneven ground. "Deans, whatever you're feeling, it's perfectly normal. Remember our conversations these past weeks? Don't feel ashamed to say what you're feeling. This is your first time out." He pointed to the horizon, "Out there are just too many questions to be granted answers. You can send yourself crazy thinking about it. But nothing's ever going to stop you doing so." He flashed a smile, "Shit, the only end result of this is probably a padded cell for each of us."

Marco broke his silence, "When we tried to describe this previously you could only imagine what we were attempting to explain. Now you're seeing it with your own eyes, breathing it with your own lungs."

Deans was glad he'd broken his silence. In a green and somewhat uncharacteristic attempt to appear strong in order to impress his team-mates, he'd unintentionally slipped into the very frame of mind his new friends had warned against throughout his training. He hadn't wanted the group to question his faculty, to worry about him being a liability to their cause. He sighed. "I just can't get over how different this all is when it's real. It affects you on so many levels, just like you said it would. Only now it's actually happening to me personally . . ." he shook his head, "WOAH! You know?"

Of course the band travelling along the roads of history *did know*.

Deans drifted into his memory, replaying a conversation with Carl some weeks back when the German had hosted a dinner party for the group.

"So you don't class yourself as a religious person but admit you're able to perceive some kind of celestial reason for existence?" Carl had enquired.

"He's drunk Carl, leave him alone." Dial had joked.

Their host had proved undeterred, *"Well when we get to our next destination in time. Look around. Every blade of grass, every beam of light.. . . . Created by a force of intelligence which remains beyond the realms of our comprehension, and yet this force was somehow harnessed and operated as a tool of mankind."* Carl had gone on to ask,

"Do you ever read the scriptures?"

"Here we go." Dial had quipped.

"Not really. Well, not since I was a kid." The conversation haunted him now.

"But you remember the book of Genesis?"

"You mean the Garden of Eden and how God created Heaven and Earth?" Deans remembered the feeling of unease, he'd looked to Dial hoping for one of his punch lines, but none had come forward, *"Come on guys you're starting to freak me out."*

Carl had persisted, *"Before the Stasis None acted, an area of time and space which so suddenly found itself filled with life, was in layman's terms . . . A nothingness void."*

He remembered how Benny grinned while quoting in the voice of a Southern preacher, *"The Earth was without form and void; and darkness was upon the face of the deep."*

He remembered how Carl looked to Dorey certainly to check if he was pushing too far, but the Commander had merely poured himself and Jay another glass of Bordeaux. *"Don't worry. I'm not trying to sell you into some religious cult. All I will say . . . Is that intelligence has to be the one true light. The one pure constant of the universe. It's from some level of this acumen all things living, existing . . . are linked. It is the only possible creator, the only possible explanation."*

Deans recalled his response, *"But surely that's how all religions interpret their Gods,"* and remembered how Carl was delighted by the statement.

"Precisely."

"I don't really see what it is you're trying to say."

"When you get there, when you look around at this new world . . . You may just find yourself facing a startling possibility."

"And what's that?"

Deans stared at the world running away from the truck as he remembered Carl's reply.

"That perhaps God did not create man in his own image at all. Perhaps it was mankind who created God in their own."

Deans had laughed, *"So now we are God?"*

Their dinner host had shrugged, *"If acting within the laws of intelligence we did create God in our own image then surely mankind's only road to enlightenment should be through the endeavour to discover ourselves. Understand the light within our own hearts . . . Our own soul. Isn't that precisely the kind of trick a divine creator would use in order to prepare humanity for such enlightenment in the first place?"*

Benny had then continued with his preacher routine, *"God is the light that dwells within the hearts of all mankind."*

Deans recalled how he'd exhaled, *"Jesus, and this is your way of trying to help?"*

The dinner guests had laughed as Dial surmised with a shake of his head. *"Fatal mix . . . You're listening to the son of a pasture and a scientist, on top of that he's German."*

Carl's' voice had grown less spiritual as he'd closed his theory. *"All I'm saying is you should feel overawed when you get back there. Because these practices in manipulating time, these experiments . . . They've placed us straight within the realms of head-fuck central. And who knows, maybe we've reached a crossroads. After all, it may be intelligence which envisions all life, but it's to its eternal shame it so easily destroys it too."*

Deans had shaken his head once more, *"Well' I'll say again . . . Thank you Carl, I'm sure that will help me a great deal if I feel myself losing it when we get back there."*

He dragged himself from his memories and looked to his colleagues who awaited his return, uncertain if Carl's philosophies were a help or a hindrance now he was *back there*.

Dial looked at him. "It's a fucking computer program, leave it at that!"

There was no time for further pondering as their co-ordinates were confirmed.

Dorey checked the terrain. "Okay people let's look lively. We're less than one hour from the town's perimeter." He stared out into the distance. "And Deans . . . Just remember one thing, the truth's the same here as anywhere else.

People kill people. You die here then its game over . . . Period. I don't know about you but that's all the motivation I ever need!"

"Yes Sir." Deans replied sharply.

Dorey turned to Carl. "You ready?"

Carl nodded as he brought them to a stop on a T-junction. He then hit the accelerator, roaring the vehicle onto the main road which would lead them toward the town.

CHAPTER TWENTY SEVEN

The town seemed almost serene, untouched by the conflict which engulfed the world around it. Its tranquil setting of lush green woodland beneath the clear summer sky gave the impression of peace and quiescent calm. However, as the truck pulled closer to the checkpoint blocking the road ahead, evidence of wartime became more apparent. Although by no means heavily fortified, the perimeter was laced with barbed wire and housed several visible machine gun pillboxes surrounded by sandbags.

Dorey and Carl observed a handful of troops as they walked the outer area, some armed with machine guns, others with shouldered rifles, accompanied by German Shepherds.

Carl slowed through the gears as the truck descended on the lowered barrier and guard hut which denied free access to the town beyond. Three guards manned the post, a Private, a Corporal and a Sergeant who was now raising his arm, flagging them to a stop.

The crew in the rear used their molars to perform three gentle, consecutive bites to the side of their tongues, activating their *scitzos*. Two more to the tip of the tongue would see them shift down a gear and only have German translated with no response offered to their inner ears. Curling the tongue fully over would switch it off ready to be reset.

Carl brought the vehicle to a halt and leaned out the window, "Good afternoon Sergeant." He was wearing no headgear making it difficult for the Sergeant to ascertain the driver's rank. He certainly did not expect two officers to be driving themselves in a truck so he approached safe in the assumption it was the delivery of machine parts due over three hours earlier. "May I see your papers please?" He asked rather curtly.

Carl smiled, "Of course Sergeant." He passed him the documents which backed up the lie beamed into the unsuspecting town from somewhere high in the heavens.

All within the truck held their breath as they awaited conformation the SiSTER aboard the Reeper had successfully spun its web of deceit.

The Sergeant checked them as Carl watched closely. "I'm Major Bergen.

My passenger here is Captain Heiden. The rest of my team are in the rear, I believe your Colonel Hookah is expecting us."

The Sergeant realised his mistake and quickly pulled his eyes from the papers, "Of course Major," he stammered, remembering the emphasis the officer of the watch had placed on the arrival of the man now sat high before him. "I'm sorry. I thought you were a delivery." He decided not to take this line any further, "We were expecting you in cars."

Carl remained nonchalant. "Sergeant I've learned many things in my life, and one is to always prove unpredictable." He gave the gatekeeper a smile then held out his hand in order to retrieve the documents.

The Sergeant didn't really know what to make of the major's comment. His response was to simply refold the papers and place them into Carl's outstretched hand. He smiled nervously. "The Colonel has arranged quarters for you Major, would you like me to call on a rider to lead you to them?"

Carl took the papers. "That would be most helpful, thank you Sergeant."

He stiffened his stance and clipped his heels as he gave the major a salute. He then turned on his spurs and quick-marched toward the Private who stood watching his superior from the barrier. "Private, leave your weapon in the hut and grab your bicycle. That is Major Bergen and his team. Lead them as fast as you can to their quarters in the old post office. Once they are happy, return here quick sharp."

The Private doubled over to the guard hut. He disappeared momentarily behind the construction before reappearing with a sad, rather clapped out looking bicycle. The Private mounted as the barrier was raised allowing him to cycle clumsily through.

"If you follow Private Gruber he'll lead you to your quarters Sir."

"Thank you Sergeant." Carl fired the truck forward causing dust to plume from the rear.

The Sergeant thrust his arm upward, "Heil Hitler!"

Carl nodded as he passed then turned his attention to catching the Private who was wobbling no more and was in fact making heady progress down the road in front of them.

Dorey turned to Carl with a bemused expression. "Well I thought that went quite well."

Carl smiled as he approached the peddle-powered boy at his lead.

The initial phase was now underway.

*

Corporal Deit had just finished sorting his desk when the telephone rang. He answered it with his usual curt phone manner, "Colonel Hookah's office." He scowled as the gate Sergeant informed of the arrival of their intriguing guests from Berlin. "I will inform the Colonel." He slammed down the receiver with not so much as a goodbye. The man on the other end may have been senior in rank, but to Deit anyone lacking either a commission or influence could expect no more than such treatment.

He pushed his wiry spectacles up his nose and drew air through his pointy nostrils. He stood, his uniform immaculate even if his manners were not, and headed for the door of the Colonel's office, barely fifteen feet behind his desk. He rapped at it with a bony fist, his customary knock ensuring his boss need not question who was on the other side.

"Come in."

Deit entered his master's room.

"Yes Corporal Deit?"

He stood rigid before him, "Our visitors from Berlin Colonel . . . They are here."

*

Carl shouldered the truck into a steep left turn. He followed his bicycle guide off the main road into a dark tunnel cut through the three-storey building of which they'd just half circled. The bright daylight was snuffed out for a few metres, the growl from the truck's engine amplified as it bounced off the walls before ricocheting into the open square beyond. The returning daylight brought with it a broad cobbled quadrangle, with surrounding walls standing at an imposing fifty feet on all sides.

Each opposing structure had the same arched entrance carved symmetrically through their centres but only the larger north and south entrances were currently in use, one to grant entry into the courtyard, the other to allow only exit.

The remaining east and west archways were sealed shut to the street beyond, the original church-like doors locked from the inside with the use of solid timber beams.

Only a short time ago the east and south sections of the structure had been the home of the district post office which incorporated the sorting rooms and Postmaster's housing.

Opposite, in the north and west wing of the seventeenth century structure, the provincial civic and agricultural offices had sat side by side for decades.

Now all had been vacated for the Nazi cause, their swastika stamp of authority adorning each of the flagpoles that jutted proudly from the centre apex of the pan tiled roofing.

As the truck entered, Dorey and Carl observed the faces appearing at various windows around the square. "We've just pulled into the quadrangle. The inner courtyard is sixty by forty metres just as the holo-map illustrated, flanked on all sides by identical three storey buildings." Dorey whispered to the others through his com-link.

The rear cover to the truck had been closed since the final approach to the town.

The Private steered himself to the building on their right. He swung his right leg over the saddle and stood upright on the pedal, dismounting his cycle with a hop.

Carl brought the truck to a halt close to where the bicycle now leaned, its rider already inside what used to be the postal clerks office informing the store Sergeant of his important guest's arrival. They watched from the cab as the Sergeant picked up his telephone receiver, the Private turning on his heels and heading back toward them.

"Let's go." They swung open the truck doors and jumped out.

The quadrangle held the sun's heat for most of the day but as late afternoon approached the air was beginning to cool, the first shadows lounging across the west side of the cobbled square. The breeze rolling through the tunnel arch was instantly refreshing.

Carl intercepted their returning guide who immediately gave a stiff salute, "Heil Hitler!"

Carl returned the gesture as Dorey went to the rear to meet the rest of his team.

"I've informed the store Sergeant of your arrival, he is informing his lieutenant who will be here any moment. Is there anything else I can help you with?"

Carl declined his young guide's offer. "No thank you Private. We are all tired from our journey and would like nothing more than to unpack and freshen up."

"Of course Major."

The stores Sergeant came hurriedly out into the square as the others emptied out of the truck's rear, quickly squaring up their uniforms and taking in their surroundings.

He too headed straight for the major. "Heil Hitler." Again Carl returned the gesture. "Your quarters have been prepared Sir. We've given you the entire top floor of the building here." He pointed behind him. "We've incorporated six bedrooms male, one bedroom female. Both floors comprise of the old Postmaster's lodging which has its own bathroom and kitchen plus a large lounge and separate dining area. We've made a further four bedrooms available from converted office space, leaving two offices intact to enable you to work from within your own compound as requested."

Carl took in the quick fire reel which the Sergeant had no doubt been rehearsing for most of the afternoon. "Thank you Sergeant." Carl turned to the Private who stood awaiting further orders. "Please feel free to return to your post, and thank you, it was very brave of you to lead us here on that bike."

The Private laughed then saluted. "Thank you Major." He marched back to his bicycle and mounted, its springs squeaking as he did. He then rattled across the cobbles to make his exit through the far archway at the opposite end of the square.

The Sergeant clocked the hustle and bustle emanating from the rear and was horrified at the realisation the truck was being unloaded. He turned to Carl wide eyed. "Major please . . . Let me have my men do that for you."

Carl was firm. "My own team handle my effects. Do not trouble yourself or your men."

The Sergeant was clearly perplexed. "Only if you're certain Major, I can assure you it would be no trouble."

"I appreciate your offer Sergeant but both my staff and I prefer it this way."

The stores Sergeant was surprised, '*Officers moving their own gear? Now there was a rarity.*' He informed the major of the imminent arrival of his boss, "Lieutenant Brigg is on his way down Sir."

"He need not have been bothered but thank you all the same."

By now the others, under the watchful eye of Dorey's *Captain Heiden*, had unloaded most of the truck's contents onto the cobbles of the quadrangle. Jay watched in silence.

The computer controlling their scitzo's together with the yet to be activated SiSTER, were both hidden in leather bags. Rounds of mini-mags and various spying devices sat in heavier canvas varieties. To the left of these was a heavy looking crate which contained their weapons. The crate was marked with an eagle, its' talons embracing a circled swastika. The Sergeant noted it jingled a little as it was placed onto the ground.

"Wine, cheese and sausages from Berlin," Carl said casually before pointing over toward Dorey's Captain Heiden. "He would never make such a journey without them."

The Sergeant smiled at the comment. '*Lucky buggers... You must think yourself pretty bloody important if you travel with a crate of wine and cheese.*'

Carl turned to him once more. "Would you be so kind as to guide us to our quarters?"

He was set to oblige when Lieutenant Brigg bounded out of the building, striding straight toward Carl. "Ah, Major Bergen I presume, I am..."

"Lieutenant Brigg." Carl saluted then held out his hand in greeting.

Brigg liked the gesture and took it in a firm handshake.

"Your man here was just about to show us to our room."

Brigg saw there were no enlisted men on hand to help with the unloading of the truck. His face flushed, "Sergeant, why are there no men to help with the Major's things?"

"Please Lieutenant, do not worry yourself. I insisted to your man here we like to move our own personal effects. It is one of our little habits."

Brigg was clearly embarrassed as the Sergeant tried not to allow his satisfaction to show.

Carl kept things moving at his desired pace, steering him toward the now approaching Dorey. "Allow me to introduce you . . . Captain Heiden, this is Lieutent Brigg."

Dorey saluted as he approached before exchanging a brief greeting.

Brigg was still perturbed, "Gentlemen are you certain you don't require assistance?"

"I can assure you we do not Lieutenant," Captain Heiden looked to Carl then back to the young officer and Sergeant, "Major Bergen's team are very *hands on* types. While as for myself, well . . . I always travel light." They all looked over at the large crate on the floor and broke into polite laughter.

"Well gentlemen, let us at least show you to your rooms."

Carl nodded graciously. "That would be very kind."

Deans and Marco carried the crate, the others two of the larger bags. Jay carried only a small luggage case so as to not stir up any unwanted gentlemanly protests.

After three flights of stairs and half a corridor they arrived at the Postmaster's dwelling. Brigg took out a small bunch of keys and unlocked the main entrance before handing the set to Dorey. He led them through a short foyer into the neat lounge awaiting them.

"As you can see it is clean and tidy and quite grand all things considered. Perhaps not quite as luxurious as the hotel, but you do have a far superior space, and of course your own offices as requested which can be found through that door and along a further corridor." He pointed at the far end of the room. "Heir Himmler himself had a fine stay here." He declared proudly, before turning their attention to another door, "Through there is a small flight of stairs which lead to the three top house bedrooms, the others you'll find off the same corridor as the offices. These are more basic than the rooms above."

The team placed their belongings onto the floor of the main room. Major Bergen could see Brigg was building himself up to deliver a full guided tour. Before this could happen he quickly thanked both the lieutenant and the Sergeant and assured them they'd be fine.

"Is there anything else I can do or arrange for you gentlemen before I go?" Briggs was no longer expecting any takers on his hospitality but Dorey surprised him as he enquired, "There is one thing. Where can we leave our truck?"

"My apologies. There are garages adjacent to the quadrangle. You can gain access to them on foot through the back door of this building." He pointed to the keys he'd just passed over, "The silver one is for the backdoor. The black metal key is for the garage, its number eight. A private section has been reserved for you, there's plenty of room as we thought you'd be arriving in two cars. I can walk you down to them . . ."

"Number eight at the rear of the building. I'm sure we'll find it, if not we know where to find the Sergeant." Both Brigg and the Sergeant where politely ousted into the corridor. Dorey fired one final question, "Do we have copies of the keys for each of us?"

Brigg couldn't believe he'd forgotten but he'd not expected to be rushed around in such a manner. "Ah yes, they will be ready for you tomorrow, our locksmith is on leave in Munich and rather embarrassingly has taken the keys to his workshop with him. Of course we've people on hand to cut them, but the Colonel thought since he's due back in the morning it seemed a little unnecessary to force open his workshop."

Dorey and Carl smiled affably. "These things happen of course. Tomorrow will be fine."

Brigg smiled, "Well, I'll let you settle in. And do not hesitate to call on me at any time."

Further gratitude was exchanged before Carl finally had the front door closed.

CHAPTER TWENTY EIGHT

"A good start," Dorey stated quietly, "We're exactly where we are supposed to be." He took in the surroundings, "Okay you know what to do. Get the gear unpacked and work out the room situation. We'll utilise one of the offices at the rear as our control centre. We can use this lounge as a place to seat any unwanted guests should the need arise."

Dorey had Deans check the other rooms for any entry into their complex.

The minds of those present sounded like an international conference, with the most softly spoken of German speakers now holding the floor. The translation was practically instant.

"Remember, two weapons in each room as well as ammunition to supply them."

The Commander looked to Dial, "We'll wait until tonight before we sneak every outer exit and entrance. But we'll get to work immediately in and around here. You know the drill. I want eyes and ears protecting us from every angle."

Deans returned, "There's no way into the apartment other than the front door."

His German was impressive.

"That's good." Dorey then addressed Benny, Marco and Deans. "You three come with me. Captain Loehm and I will put the truck in the garage then wire it with sneaks." He turned to Marco, "You and Hermann can start bringing up the rest of the luggage."

Dial passed Dorey a small bag, "Everything you need to wire the garage."

"We'll explore the building on our way back. Get a quick feel for the place in the flesh. In the meantime set this HQ up however you think best."

The rest of the team busied themselves with their tasks as Dorey, Benny, Marco and Deans retraced their way down the staircase toward the quadrangle.

As they walked out into the cobbled square they could see more curious faces peering from windows. Most played a charade as if to not notice them at all, though one or two braver, higher ranking officers, gazed quite openly on the curious guests below.

"Don't look around, walk with purpose." Dorey whispered as they approached the truck.

They headed straight for the rear compartment.

Deans and Marco lowered the hinged back, Dorey and Benny remaining on the cobbles as the two jumped into the posterior.

"Can the two of you carry it all up the stairs in one go?"

"No problem," Deans replied, again in perfect German. He and Marco then set about passing the last items out of the truck to the two German Captains, who in turn placed them neatly on the floor.

As Deans wrestled the last of the bags from beneath one of the heavy machine guns he inadvertently pulled at the tarpaulin, leaving the *schwere* section of the powerful weapon exposed. He jumped down from the truck without noticing, when they were all instantly distracted by a rather sudden and unexpected, "Good afternoon gentlemen."

The greeting was offered from a Captain in full black Gestapo paraphernalia whose presence was suddenly visible as he approached around the front of the truck. His stealthy effort caught them all off guard but Dorey was quick to offer a calm response, "Good afternoon to you Captain, Heil Hitler."

The Gestapo Captain smiled and with the self-assurance of a Lord ignored the usual mark of respect as he answered with a dismissive, "Yes."

Dorey instantly recognised the arrogance. He'd witnessed it before within the military during his excursions through time. This was a man of high breeding, given his commission on account of his family no doubt, and nurtured since birth to feel inferior to no one. Probably signed up to the Hitler cause with large donations of his family's wealth ensuring they in turn could remain close to untouchable.

He watched as the man approached, handsome, tall, not far beyond thirty. The glint in his eye was that of a shrewd, guileful fox and it caused Dorey to bristle with wariness.

The resplendent Captain met them at the rear of the truck a little amused by what he saw. "I was just in the office with the Sergeant. He told me of your desire for no stewards." He paused, his razor white teeth glinting through the corner of a wry smile, "Seems a quite unnecessarily back breaking exercise to me." His unmistakably high class German gave way to an even less mistakable upper class snigger. "I am Captain Wolfgang Amadeus Von Leising." He noted the usual raised eyebrows at the mention of his name. He gave an aristocratic bow as he continued confidently, "I was delivered into this world four weeks premature . . . My mother had become somewhat emotional during a visit to the opera," he embellished further, "Die Zauberflote."

Marco grappled with the scitzo which delivered the translation to his inner ear ending with, 'The Magic Flute.' He smiled at the Captain's well practised self-introduction.

Von Leising passed his gaze across each of them, "I for one have never really held much love for Mozart, I've always preferred Beethoven, but I have of course been stuck with the name nonetheless."

Dorey smiled, staring at the Captain with equal self-assurance. "I am Captain Ulrich Heiden, this is Captain Franz Loehm."

The Gestapo Captain acknowledged Benny.

"This is Lieutenant Hans Stoop," Dorey continued pointing toward Marco, "And this is Lieutenant Hermann Seisser." Both Marco and Deans nodded their hellos.

Dorey watched as the Captain turned and arrogantly looked into the rear of the truck.

"Is there something we can help you with Captain?"

Von Leising returned his gaze to the penetrating stare of Captain Heiden, mindful of the mysterious reputation that arrived with him. His face was instantly a charming smile. "Colonel Hookah would like it very much if your good self together with the Major and his officers would be his guests at dinner tonight." The charming smile was replaced with a brief expression of distaste, "He was going to send his rather detestable little man servant Corporal Deit but I informed the Colonel I had business to attend in this quarter, and thought I could deliver an invitation more fitting, to officers of your reputation."

Dorey expertly hid the feelings of distrust immediately held toward this certain foe. "Please tell the Colonel both myself and Major Bergen would be delighted to except his invitation." He paused and afforded the Captain a non-negotiable eye. "However, we will be keeping the rest of our group quite busy during our stay and must regretfully decline the invitation on their behalf."

Von Leising smiled, certain the Colonel would be more than happy at having both chief players from this new opposition dining at his table.

The poker game had begun.

Wolfgang slapped his heels together and politely bowed a fraction. "Of course Captain. We will look forward to receiving both yourself and the Major. I will have my driver pick you up at . . . shall we say eight-thirty?"

Dorey nodded. "Eight thirty it is."

"Excellent." In his immaculate boots he headed back toward the Sergeant's office, Dorey watching him all the way. After only a dozen steps he turned, once again wearing his wry smile. "A most interesting choice of weapon you're carrying in the back of your truck," he paused, "The MG34 in its heavy firing role."

Dorey stared intently, feeling the Captain's eyes searching him for any sign of weakness.

Of course there was none, instead Dorey flashed him his own insidious smile. "I am always prepared when it comes to my enemies Captain. After all, you can never be sure when they're lying in wait."

Wolfgang's smile broadened and he touched the tip of his cap, "Until tonight Captain." He then turned once again and slowly walked away.

CHAPTER TWENTY NINE

Carl and Dorey were in the lounge fastening the collars of their forever sinister uniforms. Benny and Dial stood up front as Marco watched from one of the chairs.

"That's fine." Benny said softly as the Major and Captain Heiden squared their outfits.

Dorey was less strict on speaking quietly in English now. They'd covered all exits and staircases with sneaks and ensured hummers were placed in ventilation shafts and fireplaces, meaning they could safely talk, just above a whisper utilising their intercoms.

"Can you see alright Jay?" Dorey asked.

Deans and Jay were in the last but one office down the far corridor, now converted into their control centre. It meant they were a room away from the end wall which gave them piece of mind nobody could overhear, unlikely as it would be through the eight feet of brick, air and timber their scanners determined as separating them from the next rooms of the building. The hard light screens played out in front of them, the remote power sources remaining concealed within a container. Their SiSTER unit, disguised in perfect working detail as a typewriter complete with a half-finished document written by Jay's alias Gudrun Schmidt, was hooked into the telephone line. It had already managed to obtain over eighty-six percent of its desired targets with the help of a download sent from its counterpart aboard the Reeper. It held complete control of the unsuspecting operators in the town and was now travelling from telegraph pole to telegraph pole all over Germany and beyond to ensure the system could intercept and manipulate any possible communication thrown in front it.

The sneaks planted so far beamed back their collage of pictures to the two top right screens with perfect clarity. Those set in the dark corridors and the garage now housing the truck, viewed in clear *real view* night vision.

Over the coming hours all strategic points within the town would be covered.

Jay played her fingers across her console, pulling into focus the view transmitted by the wide-angle lenses concealed within the collar buttons.

"Okay I've got panoramic now." She radioed to Dorey as she placed the camera operation under the computer's control, "We are on line and ready to go."

Dorey looked at his watch and blew away a little tension.

"You'll be fine. Your German's perfect, better than mine half the time." Carl reassured.

Dorey appreciated the inflated assertion. A short silence followed before he announced, "Okay everyone this it. Bide your time tonight. As soon as we get back we'll think about getting more sneaks set up okay?"

Dial sighed over his agreement. He felt Dorey was being overly cautious by not letting him deal with this task while they'd be drinking brandy and smoking cigars. However the Commander insisted for now at least, nobody was to venture outside without himself or Carl on hand to take control of any possible language problem.

"We can all hold a basic conversation Dor," Dial protested earlier, *"Especially Deans."*

"I don't doubt it." Dorey had responded. *"But there's no urgency to take risks. Besides, we'll be better off bugging some of the places later in the night anyway."*

Marco sat forward in the chair. "So you're happy with your game plan?"

The question was directed at both men but it was Dorey who gave the first *checklist* response. "Befriend the Colonel. Sniff around a little about Joseph Franc and the camp . . . Try to deflect any bullshit from our new friend Captain Von Leising."

Marco looked to Carl who followed suit. "Try to reassure the Colonel we're no threat to him directly, establish with regards to Franc, my team will be working independently of our own Captain Heiden here . . . Drink lots of brandy, smoke a few cigars, try not to kick the shit out of this smarmy bastard Von Leising."

They all laughed.

The comment prompted Dial's memory, "Did you both take your *macho pill*?"

The fore mentioned was the nickname given to the chemical compound *prodesiapol*. Once ingested it worked together with the implanted chip sat behind the sinuses below the front of the brain. The prodesiapol would be released into the bloodstream to prevent it being thinned or intoxicated by foreign bodies, while the implant would help stimulate and protect brain cells from a drug or alcohol induced state. It boosted the implant's performance and together would allow Dorey and Carl to drink as much as four times their normal consumption before feeling any ill effect, as well as affording them a high conscious resistance to any ingested, inhaled or injected drug.

Carl answered, "We took them in the kitchen about twenty minutes ago."

In the far room Jay flashed through several menus, activating the crystal driver which would hold all of the video footage recorded for the *thinkers* back home. From the live video the computer would also take hundreds of snapshots, scan them onto paper in miniaturized images ready to be pasted together as a series of events. This was a precaution. Without the absolute protection of the armoured Reeper, the trauma of the space time continuum could erase computer files and sneak data. Once footage was placed within the storage of the ship it was safe, but travelling through time had battered the Reeper's systems on many occasion and this little extra precaution meant Brookes had a backup system for watching some events as they'd unfolded. It was not the be all and end all, but wherever possible Dorey and the others would endeavour to record their efforts for the benefit of those back home.

Dorey checked his watch again. "Shall we take a walk outside?"

Carl nodded.

"Okay this is it . . . Let's see if we can get the game moving a little."

Jay watched the images of goodwill from her screen.

Deans held vigil over the sneak displays from the chair next to her.

As the two German officers headed down the corridor toward the stairs, the Postmaster's door was locked behind them.

The Major and Captain both made their way to the inner quadrangle.

As they stepped outside it was still light though the now shadowy square had cooled considerably. Again the breeze whipped through the south tunnel arch, but on this occasion it was no welcome refreshment.

"It's a little chilly when that breeze picks up." Carl commented.

"It is." Dorey replied. "Let's hope our transport's early."

With uncanny timing a car approached, slowing down into the steep turn of the archway. They both watched as the dim half-lit headlights of a dark Mercedes Benz came into view. The car disappeared momentarily into the void of the arched tunnel, its front lights intensifying as the vehicle was lost to the darkness. Then suddenly the headlights faded once more and the long limousine entered the chattering cobbles of the square.

"Well if that isn't a good omen for this evening." Carl stated.

Dorey watched in silence as the dark Mercedes pulled to a stop before them.

*

As the limousine drove away to their rear, Major Bergen and Captain Heiden were met by one of the Colonel's stewards. He'd been waiting at the foot of the exterior steps whose grey stones emanated from the mouth of the impressive four-storey structure which towered above them. The man was tall and thin with the nose and poise of a snob. His steward's serving attire was well-tailored and followed the contours of his body perfectly giving him an almost cartoon waiter quality. He led them up, past the two imperious eagles sculpted from the same stone of the staircase, the weathering of their plumage suggesting they'd adorned the grand entrance for far fewer years than the original flags of the steps.

On the summit two guards stood starched upright on either side of the open doors. Both dropped their rifles stiffly, the butts slamming the stone entry not quite in the unison intended. This slight was corrected with a perfectly executed salute.

Carl returned the gesture to one, Dorey the other.

On entering the foyer the stone floor was replaced with the pleasant echo of polished wood, stained so deeply it resembled wine. It stretched out into a grand entrance hall, its centre dominated by an imposing staircase dressed in plush cherry-red carpeting. The broad central climb measured twenty steps before meeting a large landing. From here two smaller staircases branched left and right, continuing a symmetrical journey to the upper floors. The imposing wall which sprung from the landing between these climbs was draped from top to toe in an enormous swastika flag, its bright red colouring an almost perfect accompaniment to the carpet. A coincidence, as it certainly would not have been the embellishing intention of the houses' original owner, a prominent Jewish land lawyer.

Flanking each side of the central stairway two corridors led to the ground floor rooms of the complex. These were the offices and archives of the Colonel's regime.

Their lofty guide led them up to the broad landing before taking them left onto one of the smaller flights, past a bronze bust of Adolf Hitler, to the first floor.

Dorey noted the improvement to the carpet's condition as they climbed to this next level, assuming correctly the upper echelons were the Colonel's private dwellings.

Their guide led them into a corridor, "This way gentlemen, the Colonel and Captain Von Leising are taking drinks in the library."

They followed into another small foyer constructed entirely of the beautifully polished wood. Two thirds of the way in stood a large, pristinely kept desk. Behind it sat the perfect uniform which held the weasel features of the Colonel's lap dog, Corporal Deit.

"Major Bergen and Captain Heiden," The tall guide announced.

Deit rose immediately. He paid no response to the steward.

The guide retorted likewise, simply bowing respectfully as he said softly, "Gentlemen," after which he glided out of the room.

Behind the corporal's desk was a door holding a black inscription on a bronze plate which read, '*Colonel Hookah*'. On either side of this entry were two further identical doorways facing opposite one another.

"The Colonel is expecting you gentlemen." The Corporal was instantly detestable. "I am Corporal Deit, assistant to the Colonel, and may I say what an honour it is for us to have you here." The sentiment was so false it made the skin crawl.

Back at the base camp the others cringed at the cretin on screen before them.

Major Bergen and Captain Heiden maintained their composure as Carl forwarded, "Thank you, Colonel Hookah has a most beautiful home."

Deit tilted his head as if this was in some way a compliment to him personally. He even blushed a little which made him all the more detestable.

He raised an arm to another door repeating what their previous guide had informed them, "Please, both the Colonel and Captain Von Leising are waiting in the library." He led them before it and rapped his customary knock. He didn't wait for an answer as he swung it open, "Colonel Hookah . . . Major Bergen and Captain Heiden are here."

Carl and Dorey's pulse quickened as they walked through the door.

"Here we go." Jay said as the team watched, ready to respond should the need arise.

As Major Bergen and Captain Heiden entered they were greeted by two resplendent Nazi officers who had been awaiting their arrival.

The Colonel stood well over six feet with a near full head of whitening hair which receded only slightly. He had an air of command yet wore it with the face of a wise and jovial grandfather. He was in his late fifties, and would clearly have been an awesome athlete in his youth with all the poise of a long distance runner, broad at the chest, narrow at the hip. He was instantly likeable.

"Gentlemen, gentlemen," he said extending a warm handshake, "It is a pleasure to meet you." His greeting felt genuine though understandably apprehensive. He turned and introduced the figure composed behind him, holding a glass of schnapps, "This is Captain Von Leising, though of course the two of you met earlier," he gestured to Dorey.

Von Leising offered up his glass, "Gentlemen, it is a pleasure."

"Dinner will be served at nine-fifteen Colonel."

Hookah waved his lap dog out and Deit closed the door softly as he obliged, leaving the officers to take their drinks in the library.

CHAPTER THIRTY

Five further shots of schnapps had warmed Von Leising's complexion but they'd done little to warm his personality. His manner bordered on arrogance and both newcomers were pleased to realise how the Colonel himself was clearly ill at ease around the Gestapo Captain, a frostiness that could well prove useful.

"Tell me Major . . . Do you read much?"

Carl smiled at Von Leising. "I read extensively."

Once again the Colonel seemed uncomfortable.

"A fine collection is it not?" He waved at the surrounding walls of neatly-stored books.

"It certainly appears so."

The Colonel interjected, "The books were inherited from the previous owner of the house." He sounded almost defensive.

"Really?" Replied Carl politely.

"Yes." Von Leising interrupted, "He was a Jew."

Both Carl and Dorey nodded taking in the terminology *was*.

"A lawyer I believe." Leising looked to the Colonel for verification, which was a ridiculously false gesture as of course he already knew the answer.

The Colonel eyed him like a hawk. "That's right. Lived and worked locally but also had offices in Munich."

Dorey and Carl made no comment.

Von Leising added, "Many of the books are a little . . . risqué, as the French like to say." He turned to Dorey's Captain Heiden with a pompous smile. "But it was decided such a fine collection could be preserved…For the time being."

The Colonel flushed. "Our late dinner guest is an avid reader also," he smiled at Carl before strengthening his defence at holding the literary collection intact, "He too has a close relationship with our Fuhrer. In fact, when he arrives I'm hoping he'll be returning three books borrowed from the history section."

Alarm bells were immediately ringing back at the base camp as well as within Dorey and Carl. '*A yet to be seen dinner guest who was close to Hitler!*'

"We may have a problem!" Jay declared as she monitored proceedings.

Dial scowled as he watched over her shoulder, "System-check the combat goggles and ready three rifles."

Benny and Marco immediately set about testing the equipment.

"Let's see how this pans out." Dial watched apprehensively as he checked his pistol, he, Benny and Marco making up the rapid response unit should things go wrong.

Jay reminded Deans to keep his eyes on the sneaks. He apologised and returned his attention to his own screens. She sighed nervously. "They'll be fine."

In the library Carl and Dorey were playing it cool. "So we're waiting on another guest?"

"Yes." The Colonel replied to the obvious delight of Von Leising.

"A very shadowy character indeed," The Gestapo Captain added with a cocksure tone, "Similar to yourselves you might say. Sent here soon after the Normandy landings, also at the direct behest of the Fuhrer." He was obviously enjoying the fact neither Major Bergen nor Captain Heiden had any idea as to whom they were now referring.

"A Captain Joseph Brahms," The Colonel added, "Do you know him?"

Both Carl and Dorey felt a twinge of concern, when for the second time that evening fate stepped in with uncanny timing, as Corporal Diet's fist rapped against the door.

He stepped into the room and announced, "Captain Brahms, Colonel."

The Colonel's face lit up. "Ah, here he is now."

Back at the base camp the team crowded the monitors as they awaited the entrance of a potential time bomb.

As Deit shuffled to one side, a confident German officer strode into the room carrying a brown paper-wrapped parcel under his arm.

"Colonel, I'm so sorry I am late." He declared, "The traffic was a nightmare."

The Colonel was delighted at the theatrical joke and as he laughed he appeared to truly relax for the first time that evening, "Not at all . . . Not at all."

Dorey and Carl stood rigid as the man looked to Von Leising, "Captain." It was apparent from his tone he held no particular liking for the Gestapo man either.

Colonel Hookah was quick to steer his late guest's attention to the newcomers. Brahms had been out of town, his dinner date with the Colonel arranged some days prior. For this reason he'd been unable to forewarn him of their arrival, a fact not lost on Von Leising. This was obviously the moment he'd been waiting for.

The Colonel held out an arm. "Captain Brahms this is Major Bergen."

The Captain extended his hand in greeting, shaking the Major's with a bright smile, "It's nice to meet you Major."

Carl responded likewise.

The Colonel then turned his attention to Dorey. "And this is Captain Heiden."

The officer took his hand with a strong grip, accompanied with a dazzling stare.

"Nice to meet you Captain Brahms," Dorey said, his German voice crisp and calm.

Palene's eyes flashed as he released Dorey's palm, "Thank you Captain . . . It's very nice to meet you too."

CHAPTER THIRTY ONE

With introductions made, the Colonel headed to his desk with the parcel handed to him by Brahms. He opened it. Inside were four evenly-sized books. Three were those owed to the library, together with a new addition for the appropriated collection. The Colonel recognised it but refrained from announcing the title to his guests. He gave an appreciative smile, "Thank you Captain."

"Not at all Colonel."

Von Leising was quick to continue stirring the pot. "Major Bergen and Captain Heiden are here on business from Berlin."

"Really?"

"Working directly under the behest of our Fuhrer." The Gestapo man added.

"Aren't we all?" Brahms seemed decidedly cheerful.

Leising continued, "I'm surprised you don't know of each other, considering the circles you must travel in." He awaited the response eagerly, as did the watching eyes observing proceedings some two blocks away.

Palene stared at the Gestapo Captain with such intensity it made him blink, "I doubt either you or these men have any real idea of the circles I've travelled in." His tone was fearless, his words biting, daring Von Leising to question him further.

He did not. "I meant no offence Captain."

The Colonel enjoyed such moments. There'd been several placed on offer since the Captain's arrival some weeks earlier. It delighted him to see the pompous and dangerous Gestapo official so easily put in his place. "I tried to reach you to inform you of their arrival," Hookah stated.

"I had further business to attend to." Brahms replied, his voice warming as he now addressed the Colonel once more, "And as I'm sure our new guests are able to confirm, we are a shadowy breed, always illusive, forever disappearing." Palene's smile was thrown back at Dorey who returned it, though his senses were bristling with caution.

"It's the nature of our business." Carl remarked.

"I'm sorry if I've delayed your dinner." Brahms stated with genuine concern.

"Not at all," The Colonel replied, "Would you care for a drink before we go up?"

"Thank you, I'll have a Schnapps," Brahms replied.

The Colonel poured his guest a drink, "Captain Von Leising was just commenting on how fine the library is."

"Really? And were there any particular classics he brought to your attention?" He looked first at Leising then to Dorey and Carl. "Or was he merely generalising over which copies he'd prefer to see in flames?"

The newcomers were a little surprised at the statement.

Von Leising glared. "I do not burn books Captain . . . I burn traitors to the Reich."

Palene gave him a cold smile. "But of course you do."

The Colonel studied his new guests, trying to read their responses to the ongoing theatre he'd provoked. "Well I certainly hope you're hungry gentlemen," He said after a moment. "For I've had the cooks prepare a wonderful meal for us this evening. I'm almost tempted to tell you of its content but I fear the chef would desert the army if he found I'd done such a thing." He smiled. "He was a cook of some distinction before the war and as such picked up certain eccentricities." He looked at his pocket watch. "One of them being, each course should be a surprise to my guests." He laughed, wondering once more if such a policy had ever backfired on his trusted caterer. "Come, bring your drinks . . . Let me show you to the dining room."

*

The first course had been a simple success. An uncomplicated offer of duck liver pate served over toasted granary bread, accompanied with a neat Italian salad sprinkled with lemon juice and olive oil. Either it was the non-pretentious serving of a confident chef, or the Colonel's stocks were beginning to feel the pinch of a war now on all fronts.

Any such notions of the latter kind were quickly dispelled however, when a course of fine venison fillet was brought in for the second, garnished with parsnips, carrots and celeriac mashed potatoes, covered with a rich damson sauce.

"The men would revolt if they saw us eating like this." Brahms joked.

The Colonel smiled as he washed down a piece of meat with a deep burgundy. "It's true we are fortunate." He dabbed his mouth with a white linen napkin. "Although I must say the men themselves also eat very well here. The town's folk provide for their every need," he lifted up his wine once more, "While the cellar below is very well stocked."

They all raised their glasses and took another sip.

The large dining table could accommodate twelve. It had been well dressed and the stewards served both white and red wines in a steady flow at the behest of the Colonel who headed the table.

Carl and Dorey sat side by side, opposite Brahms and Von Leising.

The Gestapo Captain was next to speak, "It's quite right you should explain the treatment of the men Colonel," he said with a smile, "For we have a pair of potential communists in our midst. Why, only earlier today they refused assistance with their luggage and insisted on carrying it to their quarters themselves."

The Colonel was relieved to see neither Major Bergen nor Captain Heiden had been offended by the remark.

Carl smiled. "We needed the exercise." He patted his stomach.

Leising grinned, "Khrushchev couldn't have said it better himself."

Carl's smile remained as he tucked his fork into a final helping of meat. "I doubt Khrushchev could carry himself up a flight of stairs, never mind bags!"

This comment seemed to delight Von Leising further, and he nodded his agreement as he sloshed down another glass of wine. He was a little inebriated.

"Perhaps our friends prefer to do things for themselves." The Colonel gestured.

"Or perhaps their bags are packed with more forbidden books which could corrupt all who were to stumble across them." Von Leising was having a good time.

Polite smiles were offered as a brief silence followed, the second course officially coming to an end with a white surrender of napkins and retreating shoulders.

"Excellent food," Dorey stated.

"Yes, my compliments to the chef." Carl added.

Brahms picked up his wine. "So tell me . . . Are you able to discuss your business here?"

Dorey smiled. "In no more detail than I expect you would divulge your own."

"Touché," Brahms replied with a tilt of his glass.

The Colonel was cautious. "My information was you intend to inspect the camp Major."

"Amongst other things . . . yes." Carl responded.

"And with it no doubt our strange little friend Joseph Franc." Brahm's smile remained.

Von Leising sat silently fascinated with where the conversation was now headed.

"That is part of my mandate."

The Colonel's eyes narrowed. "I fear the lack of information granted means at least one of our new guests, may actually be investigating the rest of us." His smile was genuine but he obviously wanted to know whether he was to be subjected to a witch hunt.

"Perhaps the Fuhrer has sent *so much* of his secret service at one time so they might also spy on each other in the process," Leising's tone seemed suddenly less intoxicated, he gestured to the three invaders of his realm, "Why else would you not know of each other?"

Palene gave the Gestapo Captain a long stare. "Who said I didn't?"

Everybody smiled, albeit warily.

Dorey and Carl obviously knew this to be impossible. However it remained a concern to be sat next to a genuine member of Hitler's private spy ring.

"The Fuhrer has sent my good friend the Major here to carry out a simple assessment of this operation's viability. That of course includes an open investigation of both the camp, and your little town here," Dorey was very superior in his statement. "It is I who has a more clandestine task to carry out, while these other more mundane procedures are being executed." The comment was a bold one, designed to give Carl the breathing space he would need while hopefully bringing all suspicion firmly to his own door. Under the lie transmitted from the SiSTER, Dorey knew the Colonel had been informed of Captain Heiden's reputation. He also knew Von Leising had called Berlin immediately to question the validity of the operation, and would therefore also be aware of how formidable Dorey's alias was. For these reasons he could openly speak for Carl and know his words would be taken most seriously. He smiled at the Colonel. "But rest assured. Nobody at this table need fear anything of me . . . of that I can promise you."

Palene stared at the man opposite and marvelled at how coolly he could deliver his lie, the undertones so powerfully convincing he almost believed it himself.

"Nor me." Carl added with a warm grin.

Von Leising's stare was piercing, his high intellect running through the compartments of his brain trying to make sense of these strange events. "Well, we can all be relieved about that," he said coldly. There was a deliberate lack of concern to his comment. He took a decanter of wine and refilled his glass. "And yet the conundrum remains . . . Why would all of you be gathered here within our little town at this one moment in time?"

Carl stared at him calmly. "Well I have Adolf's personal number, perhaps you'd like to place a call and ask him."

Leising retreated for the time being, "I'm sure he has his reasons."

Jay and the others watched through the monitors. It was a good performance so far and the trigger fingers had relaxed around the base camp for the moment, though concern remained over the presence of both the cunning Gestapo Captain and this unexpected spy.

Back at the table the dessert arrived. "Excellent," Colonel Hookah declared, as the three stewards went about their business, "I hope you've all left room."

The atmosphere cooled with the interruption, and they all looked down on a carefully crafted strudel accompanied with a dollop of freshly-whipped cream.

The Colonel raised his glass once more. "Well, before we tuck in I would once again like to offer you our every assistance, and I can assure you all I wish you every success with your endeavours. Heil Hitler."

They repeated the call before making a start on the dessert.

Dorey and Carl were passed a second round of brandy, the macho pills being called upon to enhance their reputation. They were of course both well-schooled in the art of appearing more intoxicated than they actually were, and as they leaned back into the groaning leather of their high-backed chairs, they appeared every bit as rosy as their host and his two other dinner guests.

They'd retired to the smoking room. Something also being called upon to prove its reputation as four of the five present now chuffed away on large Dutch cigars.

The room was dimly lit. A place set aside so men could congratulate themselves as the masters of their domain as their lungs were dried, their dinners pickled by booze.

Von Leising was rolling his cigar between fingers and thumb. "So tell me Major, what was your chosen profession before the war?"

Carl knew better than to get involved in details. "I was as elusive leading up to the war as I am while now a part of it."

The Captain smiled from the corner of the room, "How beautifully vague and yet poetic." He pulled back on the cigar and sent a stream of blue smoke from his lips. "I was merely wondering whether or not you had always been a military man."

"I was a party member, called on to do my duty."

Leising could see it would be impossible to extract any real picture from this man. "A party member, aren't we all?" He smiled, "Your elocution is excellent, were you educated in Berlin?"

"I was educated privately, though I did complete my schooling in Berlin."

"Ah . . . Should I take it then you were embroiled in the party's early struggles?" His teeth appeared sharp as he smiled, "Though you cannot possibly be a day past thirty-five."

"Closer to forty . . . And I've had the pleasure of knowing our Fuhrer for a long time, let us leave it at that."

The sharp smile disappeared as he prepared to take in more of the cigar, "Of course."

The Colonel was quick to interject. "I was a twenty-six-year-old school teacher when I enlisted in the army, back in 1915." He smiled, "Literature." A sip of brandy followed the memory. "I was sent as an Infantry Officer to Belgium then on to France." His eyes looked distant for a moment, "It was a bloody affair . . . But then, what war isn't?"

Carl looked to him. "And you stayed in the army afterward?"

The Colonel appeared saddened, "There was no food or living to be made after the war. It was as safe a bet as any to remain enlisted . . . I was one of the few offered the chance after the treachery at Versailles." His mind raced through his memories, his face darkening further at what he found there. "My wife died twelve weeks after my return. I was lost, and could see little alternative. Of course, the streets back then were a mixture of poverty and

183

desperation at every turn. The army gave me some kind of purpose."

Brahms looked at him solemnly. "They were hard times."

The Colonel nodded then forced his thoughts away from such melancholy. "But still, here we are in yet another chapter, yes." He sipped at his Brandy once more.

"And now a Colonel in the SS." Von Leising stated, as if this were enough to make up for such suffering.

"Yes," the Colonel smiled, "Though I often have to remind myself of the fact. Since being stationed here I've found myself inside these familiar garbs." He gestured to his attire.

"It is a fine uniform to wear," Brahms stated. He looked to Dorey and Carl. "I, unlike the rest of the troops in this town am not SS. As a result I've no love for such a uniform." He tilted his glass toward the Colonel, "As smart as indeed it is."

Hookah grinned.

"I would imagine in your business you've worn many uniforms." Von Leising added.

"Indeed I have," he replied, "And none more pleasant on bare skin than that of a French nurse I met recently, as her stiff skirt brushed against my stomach." The room embraced the bravado, "Ah Marie Bouillon, what a fine Parisian girl." Cigar smoke swirled as they imagined the nurse whose name was breathed with such affection.

"Captain Brahms has a fondness for the French capital." The Colonel stated.

Von Leising raised his eyes to the ceiling. If he had to listen to any more of Brahms' recollections of Paris he was certain he'd vomit.

"Before or during the war?" Dorey enquired.

"Both." Palene replied, his smile wide. "Have you ever been to Paris Captain Heiden?"

"Yes, a very diverse city."

"Indeed it is." He agreed. "My only fear is it shall be ruined in the battle soon to ensue."

"Let us hope the allies never make it that far. See our gallant boys push them back into the sea whence they came." The Colonel was deliberately romantic. He knew enough about soldiering to understand any such action was no longer viable. He raised his glass, "To our gallant boys."

Brahms left behind the subject of the invasion which had earlier dominated their dinner. He turned to Dorey, "And were you fortunate enough to travel before the war?"

Dorey was analysing his every feature, as were Jay and the others who continued to watch on the monitors, "A little."

"Captain Brahms grew up in Bolivia." The Colonel announced, also much happier with where the conversation was now headed.

Dorey's team bristled once again. *Was this the agent who had taken part of Joseph Franc's studies to South America?* The more detailed research gathered in the Stasis compound uncovered the fact this agent had held personal meetings with the scientist. However this was supposed to have taken place some weeks prior to their visit. One of the reasons the Stasis None informed Brookes that Franc's work would be complete at this time, ready for extraction. The system concluded Franc believed both he and his work were to be transported to Bolivia for safe keeping should things go badly in the war. It was in their current window the Stasis None construed he would gather his findings together, ready to be shipped, but only after this agent had left some weeks prior to their present date. Mysterious events would later see Joseph Franc rethink such action and he would instead place one half of the work inside a vault in Berlin.

Jay and the others were growing edgy. "If this is the same agent, he shouldn't be here."

Dial agreed, "Isn't he the reason Franc brought his work together in the first place?"

Back in the smoking room Palene understood the worry he may have just triggered and so began the process of putting them at ease, "Like you I am also here at the behest of our Fuhrer, only my business is with Doctor Franc directly. I was due to leave some weeks ago but found reason to stay a short while longer." His smile never left his lips, "I'm wondering now whether the boss has sent you here to check on my judgement."

Dorey's response was full of conviction, "I'm here on no such business." The Commander like the rest was now wondering whether Franc's work would be in a complete state with this Brahms still around. The agent hadn't been included in the computer's headcount and had proved difficult to track, so it was possible he'd returned to the town unnoticed at a later date. It was unlikely the Stasis None would have made such an error with regards to the research itself being in one place as a whole study. However with the usual difficulties posed by human free will, it wasn't unreasonable to suppose it had not known the whereabouts of the shadowy man now sat before them.

Of course, another glaring concern was the fact this agent had the ear of Hitler, though so far unlike Von Leising, he seemed to accept without question both Bergen and Heiden's presence. *'Hitler often had rivals vying against one another, perhaps Brahms understands this better than most.'* Dorey surmised.

The power placed at their disposal by the SiSTER meant such a threat could be neutralised. One phone call could have Brahms branded an enemy to the state.

Dorey's alias delivered his next line, "I realise my secrecy places me at a disadvantage gentlemen. But I cannot stress the point enough . . . My reasons for being here pose no threat to any of you, or indeed any of your good reputations."

The Colonel seemed happy with this further reassurance. Captain Heiden appeared most sincere and he was relieved it was such a man sent. His orders from the high command earlier that day had been quite specific in illustrating Major Bergen's task. However, the more vague and clandestine motives of Heiden had of course come as a larger worry.

As Hookah observed how proceedings were beginning to unravel however, his ease was quickly bitten by another notion, as he found himself wondering if his Gestapo Captain's earlier prognosis may in fact carry some merit. *Perhaps Hitler had indeed sent one spy to watch the other.* The contradiction to his thoughts naturally troubled him. The Colonel swirled his drink in the crystal glass. "I will of course make preparations for you to meet Doctor Franc tomorrow, if you so wish it."

Carl was gracious. "Thank you Colonel. That would be most helpful."

Leising sneered once more, "A very secretive little man, you'll all be in good company." He then stubbed out his cigar with a smile. "Well, it has been a most interesting evening gentlemen. However, if you will excuse me, it is time for me to retire." He stood before straightening his black uniform.

They all rose to offer him their farewells.

"Please do not trouble yourselves. I'll make my own way out."

"It has been a pleasure." Carl declared.

"We shall have to do this again soon." The Colonel added.

Dorey dipped his head, "Until next time Captain."

He returned their false gestures with an equally false *warm goodbye* of his own.

"Be sure to get a good night's sleep," Brahms quipped at Leising's slight drunkenness.

"Oh I will Captain Brahms, you can count on it." He was about to turn for the door when he added, "My quarters are both comfortable *and* warm." He flashed the Colonel a glance, "What with all those books burning in my fireplace." He seemed to enjoy his little joke as he turned and headed toward the exit. As he opened the door to leave he couldn't resist one last parting shot, "Im Westen nichts Neues, by Erich Remarque." He made reference to the highly controversial book, '*All quiet on the Western Front*' given discreetly to the Colonel at the start of the evening, "A most interesting historical account." The pleasure he was taking from his little theatre was evident. "But history in war is never passed on by conquered poets gentlemen . . . It is forged by the victors who write it." He gave a bow then left through the door.

Dial turned to Benny as he watched the display back at the postal building, "Asshole."

Relief took hold of both rooms as the Gestapo man left. He was one of those individuals capable of ruining an evening without even having to show up. With the position of power bestowed on him by the Reich, such annoyance was as scary as it was irritating.

The Colonel made an apologetic smile to his remaining guests. "Well," he said, "Can I interest any of you in another drink?"

Carl took the opportunity. "No thank you Colonel. We've had a day filled with travel. I think I might actually follow the lead of the good Captain and retire myself."

Dorey was quick to agree. "Yes, I must admit I'm growing a little tired." He looked at his host sincerely. "I cannot begin to express my gratitude

Colonel. It has been a long time since I've been welcomed by such a gracious host."

Carl agreed. "Please extend my further appreciation to your chef."

The Colonel acknowledged the compliments. He'd been relieved at how the introduction had gone. It was only a shame they'd been forced to endure Von Leising. He'd hoped they could have spoken a little more freely now he'd finally left.

Brahms finished his drink. "I think I will head back myself. Thank you for a most entertaining evening." He added with a cheeky grin, "I particularly enjoyed the clown."

The Colonel blushed at the wicked remark but laughed despite himself. He certainly held no love for the Gestapo man who breathed down his neck from dawn till dusk.

The Colonel saw the three officers down to the large landing where beneath the drapery of the swastika, stewards brought their hats to the foot of the steps. Handshakes were exchanged and after collecting their caps the three made their way to the exit.

As the stewards opened the door the sound of rifles hitting the stone rang out once again, this time in perfect unison with the faces of two fresh guards saluting them.

The air had warmed considerably, the earlier cooling breeze abated. The night sky was a postcard of stars and the fresh air was welcome after breathing the cigars.

"Well gentlemen." Brahms declared as the Mercedes pulled up, "It has been a pleasure."

"Can we offer you a lift?" Carl asked politely, every inch the officer and gentleman.

"Oh good God no . . . The town isn't big enough to justify it."

"It is when you don't yet know where you're going." Dorey laughed.

Palene eyed him. He knew Dorey and the others would know this town better than most of the locals. "I'd be happy to escort you both if you fancy the walk . . . You're staying in the postal buildings are you not?" The fact had come up over dinner.

Carl smiled. "A most gracious offer . . . But I will decline. I feel like being chauffeured this evening. Perhaps I will wave out of the window like a conquering hero."

They all laughed.

"I will return with the Major, but thank you for the offer all the same." Dorey stated.

"Not at all gentlemen. We will no doubt be seeing more of each other during your stay."

"Goodnight," Carl said, "It has indeed been a pleasure." He headed for the open door of the car, the tall thin steward stood beside it.

Dorey was set to follow when Brahms said, "I believed you when you declared your intentions do not bare any relevance to me Captain Heiden. May

I offer the same reassurance. I used my own initiative in deciding to prolong my stay. I can promise you my reasons are for the good of Germany alone . . . Even though Germany for the most part is unaware of my continuing presence here."

"I appreciate your candour, and may I once again reciprocate . . . Neither you or your initiative are in any question here." Dorey dipped into the back of the limousine, the steward closing the door after him with a clump.

Huge sighs of relief were passed around the base camp as the monitors now showed only the dark interior of the car. "Thank God that's over." Jay declared.

As the Mercedes headed toward the street Palene watched the rear lights as they first braked then turned out onto the road. He adjusted his cap, tipping it to the steward as he began his short journey on foot. He smiled as he thought back over the evening.

Until now he'd only observed these people from a distance.

So far he was finding the up close and personal approach, much more to his liking.

CHAPTER THIRTY TWO

Von Leising crumpled the reel of paper in his fist and leaned back into the chair. His encoded telegram had not provided the answer a part of him hoped for. His high level sources in Berlin once again backing up all Heiden and Bergen had claimed to be.

He sighed before reaching toward the encoder and flicking it off at the switch. He took a drink from his freshly poured glass of Cognac, his thoughts clouded further by alcohol. '*Why are they carrying such weaponry in the back of the truck*?' Another large exhale followed before his eyes fell upon the image of a beautiful woman, held forever in a perfect moment by an expensive silver frame.

A smile crawled across his face and he manoeuvred himself toward the heavy desk in front of him. He produced a key from his pocket and unlocked the bottom drawer before pulling it open. His smile broadened as he took out a blue velvet jewellery case.

He slid the drawer shut and placed the box on the edge of the desk. It opened with a muffled pop. He lifted the lid and peered at the antique gold necklace inside, it's sixteen diamonds returning his now happier gaze with equal sparkle.

He looked at it for a while before reaching across the desk for his personalised stationary. He took a pen from its mount and steadied himself.

'*My darling Annie, The moment I saw this necklace I knew it could have only been made for your slender neck. Like your eyes its jewels dazzle me. I know I have leave being granted in only three short weeks, however, your photograph on my desk would not allow me to wait so long. I hope my last letter found you well, it will probably have only reached you days before this package arrives. Hopefully this gift will make up for such uncharacteristic pestering. Wear this for me at the restaurant your father has booked for us, Yours, Wolfy.*

He went into another drawer and pulled out a large thick brown envelope. He placed both the box and the note inside before sealing the gum along the edge. He then pulled out a thin black leather satchel and placed the envelope inside. He seemed pleased with himself as he rang the servant bell. Within a minute a house keeper knocked on the door and entered on his master's command. "Get me Schneider."

The servant quickly left in pursuit of his task.

As he continued to enjoy the Cognac and photograph, he felt neither shame nor remorse at the fact the necklace had been confiscated from a young woman who'd arrived at the camp the previous morning.

Most of Doctor Franc's subjects arrived on the train from the larger camps already stripped of any belongings, but from time to time they received the odd 'unspoiled specimen.' He leaned further into his chair. Within minutes he'd almost drifted off to sleep, his glass still in hand, when a knock at his door spurred him. He smiled at how drunk he'd allowed himself to become then forced himself to straighten up. "Yes?" He placed the drink back on his desk.

"You wanted to see me sir?"

"Ah Schneider," Leising did not turn to behold his trusted pet, "I have a task for you."

Schneider stepped into the room, closer.

"I want you to take the bike and leave tonight for Berlin." He looked over his shoulder making eye contact for the first time. "You haven't been drinking have you?" He was concerned with the wellbeing of the package, not the rider.

"No sir."

"Good." He reached for the black leather satchel before scribbling onto a piece of paper. "I want you to take this to Berlin and deliver it to the address here."

Schneider collected the items on offer.

"And I want it there safely . . . Do you understand?"

Schneider understood this meant the item should be hidden within a cavity concealed as part of the bike's fuel tank, "You know you can rely on me sir."

Leising's narrow smile returned. "Yes," he agreed softly. "Once there you may have your usual reward. Look in on Ava, she will see to your needs." His eyes almost closed. "I will not expect you back until Friday which should give you a little time to enjoy her talents."

Schneider now wore a grin of his own. He'd pulled early duties for the week and now he was going instead on an all expenses trip to the capital straight into the arms of the most wonderful Ava, "Thank you sir."

"Just make sure that parcel arrives safely, it's very important." He turned back to Annie.

"Of course Captain." He replied.

"The bike is fully fuelled, have Sergeant Gebb place an extra container within the side car for you, you know what to do for the rest."

Schneider was about to leave but thought it prudent to ask, "Will that be all sir?"

Von Leising was set to dismiss him when suddenly a thought caught his imagination. "Actually Schneider, there is one more thing." He reached for his pen and stationary once more and quickly wrote down a short letter with instructions, before folding it into a smaller envelope. "I take it you remember my friend Verstihen?"

"Of course sir."

"Deliver this to him. He'll call you at Ava's when he has a response."

Schneider took the second of his items to deliver. "I take it both items are to be transported . . . *out of view*."

Von Leising nodded, "Have a nice trip," he said with a dark twinkle in his eye.

"Thank you sir."

With their business done, Schneider left the room.

CHAPTER THIRTY THREE

The displays were awash with images. Most areas of the small town now beamed into the control centre after two teams headed by Dorey and Carl had completed their sweeps. Bugging the first of their priority targets had taken much of the night.

Where necessary, banter was exchanged with soldiers manning guard huts. Night sentries questioned as they staffed barriers of various exits and entry points. All the while sneaks were discreetly squashed into place providing the team with eyes and ears over all incoming, outgoing traffic. There was still a considerable amount to be done but what they'd achieved so far provided an adequate blanket of information and warning.

They'd determined only a motorbike and sidecar, two trucks and three horse drawn carts steered by farmers had left the town since they'd arrived, with only the recently departed motorcycle leaving since nightfall.

Carl and Marco were the first to return to base camp but were soon followed by Dorey, Dial and Benny who walked into the postal building not long after the two hung up their coats. "Good timing." Carl remarked as the trio entered the lounge.

The group made their way down the short corridor to the control room.

"So Von Leising sent a coded telegram?" Dorey referred to Jay's earlier radioed message.

"Yes. The SiSTER intercepted it not long after you'd left." She still wore her blouse and pleated skirt. She'd unfastened the collar, exposing the skin of armour underneath. The lower half of her armour was hidden with a trouser uniform in the wardrobe should anything more substantial be required, though her stockings did provide light protection. Her shoes had long since been kicked off for the long shift in the chair.

Next to her Deans was dressed down to his shirt and braces.

"It was decrypted, the SiSTER's reply confirming to him we are who we say we are."

"Asshole!" Dial remarked.

"But nothing from the Colonel or Brahms?"

She shook her head, "Nothing at all."

"That's something at least."

"All other calls have been pretty mundane. The SiSTER has everything under control."

Dorey appeared pleased. "I was certain Leising would continue sniffing around. He's Gestapo after all. Though I'm surprised Brahms never sent any queries."

"It appears both he and the Colonel seem happy with our cover story . . . So far at least."

He agreed with Jay. "I can't believe the agent tasked with taking Franc's work to Bolivia is still here."

"I sensed he was no immediate threat. These things are always hard to read of course, but my gut feeling was good." Carl added.

"When he first walked in I was getting ready for the quick draw" Dorey stated, "But I don't think he has any alarm bells ringing. Of course a spy is a spy. Let's hope he and Hitler aren't so close the SiSTER won't be able to fool him should we need it to."

"It shouldn't be an issue. The SiSTER aboard the Reeper duped Franc when informing him of our visit, and we know he met Hitler several times." Dial added, "But the question is should *our* alarm bells be ringing with regards to the research?"

The team had wasted no time once Carl and the Commander returned from dinner. They'd set about laying sneaks immediately and therefore had little opportunity to discuss unfolding events openly. Jay kept them informed of any relevant activity across the course of the night but it was only now when back within the increasingly safe surroundings of their HQ they could quietly discuss the goings on at the Colonel's table.

"The Stasis None's unlikely to have provided bad data with regards to the research judging by Brooke's confidence." Like the rest of them Dorey had given it some thought. "I think we can put Brahms still being here down to the headcount. He said he'd made his *own* decision to stay, and hinted this may have been against orders. He's obviously a shady bastard. The Stasis None couldn't even uncover his name before we left." Dorey seemed reasonably content. "Without such information it could never know whether or not he was still here with any real certainty."

"But it still predicted the agent's movements. And it never came up with anything like this." Dial replied.

"Yes, but neither did it *not* come up with this scenario either."

"It did say this agent was supposed to be in Berlin." Benny re-emphasised Dial's point.

"The important thing is neither he nor Hookah have felt any need to question our objectives for being here so far." Carl reaffirmed. "Von Leising was bound to be suspicious. As long as he keeps following the SiSTER's orders he shouldn't be too difficult to manipulate. And with the Colonel and Brahms apparently happy, I think we can be more pleased than concerned at this time."

"I'll be happy when I know Franc's research is in one piece." Dial reaffirmed.

They all agreed.

"Our friend Brahms certainly holds no fear of the Gestapo." Jay interjected.

"The Stasis None said the agent was close to Hitler, Brahms obviously is. That'll give anyone the confidence to put down a Gestapo officer or two." Dorey was quick to add, "Although there was *something* about our friend Captain Brahms."

Again they all agreed.

"Von Leising will take anything with a pinch of salt because he's the sort who believes himself above all that's happening around him anyway. This could make him a constant danger. We've met his type before so let's be on our guard." Dorey added, "The fact the Colonel didn't invite more people to dinner bodes well for us. If we only have to worry about those three as well as Joseph Franc I'll be more than happy." He looked around his team, all eyes but those of the vigilant Deans meeting his own. "And it looks like we'll soon have the pleasure of meeting our target later this morning." He was pleased at the Colonel's immediate offer of an introduction. "In the meantime Deans, Jay . . . Get your arses away from those screens, you both need a break." He signalled to Carl. "Since the Major and I have been out enjoying ourselves for the first half of the evening, we'll be the first to relieve you."

They swapped places, Deans and Jay both grateful to be away from their vigils. They immediately went about twisting and stretching.

The sensors of the sneaks were more than capable of warning them of impending danger but they always liked to have a human eye on things.

"We'll take one hour while the rest of you sleep." The Commander added.

Dial was quick to volunteer. "Come wake me and Benny, we'll take the one after."

The one hour of sleep would feel like four with their enhancements helping out, and

"As for this agent, let's not read too much into it. The Stasis None stated with confidence the research will be in one piece during the course of this week. It didn't give the same assurance as to the whereabouts of this Bolivian spy, only speculation. For all we know it could be his surprise stay which provides the reason for the work coming together in the first place. So let's stay focused on what needs to be done."

They all concurred as they began leaving the room to get some rest.

The first hours within the realms of their mission were coming to a close and it felt a little easier for all concerned now it was done. However, they were under no illusions, day one was exactly that . . . They still had several more to go.

CHAPTER THIRTY FOUR

It was another bright start to the day. The earlier cloud cover had receded, the sunshine now broken in full. The long Mercedes jostled them along the lane and a pleasant breeze passed through the open-topped car.

To the right was the river Lech. Its' banks ran in the distance now but they had snaked closer only a short time earlier before making a dash toward the distant pines and Firs.

To the left was a denser cover of forest, the cocktail of trees slim and upright, its' tinderbox floor melodic with hidden life.

Their driver shifted through the gears as the gradient grew steeper, the suspension rocking them gently. The Colonel sat up front while Carl, Dorey, Dial and Deans sat in the posterior of the limousine, its broad box back allowing just enough room in the rear.

"We live in such a beautiful country." The Colonel spoke loudly over his shoulder.

"Indeed we do." Carl replied.

"Have you ever travelled here in the winter?"

"I've been close by but not actually in this region."

The Colonel beamed. "Oh it's breathtaking. The river is broad and can appear almost still, surrounded by snow-capped trees and peaks." He turned harder on his shoulder. "There's some excellent skiing to be had here." They were approaching the first checkpoint. "The camp is just beyond where the tree line thickens. It's quite well hidden. The perimeter is guarded night and day to keep people out as well as in."

Again the car changed gear as they headed toward the brow of the gentle climb.

The trees were suddenly close on both sides now. Birdsong filled the air at a greater volume as shadowy shapes of leaves and branches danced over the reflection of their polished limousine. With the minor peak breeched the road dipped and the car's engine hummed a happier tune once more.

"It's just ahead here." The Colonel pointed to where the lane broadened.

Ahead in the distance the four in the rear could clearly see the first of the barriers, their enhanced eyesight far superior to those in the front of the vehicle.

A greater concentration of barbed wire was apparent, laced between trees on either side of the dirt road. As they approached the barrier the car slowed just enough for the guard to get a good look at the Colonel. He hung his rifle behind his back and raised the pole allowing them to blow past. He saluted awkwardly as they went by, the process clearly a job more suited for two.

"At the next barrier even my familiar face is not permitted through without formal introduction." The Colonel added, "I've had papers drawn granting each of you access through all checkpoints and gates."

Ahead, the second barrier was coming quickly, only this one was heavily fortified. Sandbags were piled ten feet high to make dens with heavy calibre machine guns poking out of small gaps, their aim covering the gateway and surrounding woodland.

The car drew to a halt as the Sergeant ahead raised his arm for them to stop.

"Good morning Colonel."

"Good morning Sergeant Beck."

He looked over the four snug officers in the rear, "Your guests Sir?"

The Colonel nodded and handed him the paperwork.

He scanned over the documents and passengers, putting their faces to memory before handing back the papers. The routine was exaggerated for the benefit of the newcomers. He signalled for the barrier to be raised, "Thank you Colonel . . . Heil Hitler."

The customary return was offered before the car pulled away.

"The clearing ahead is surrounded by tree line laced with pillboxes, barbed-wire and scattered mines. The waterline has also been booby trapped."

"Mines?" Dorey replied casually.

"Yes, there aren't too many in truth. As far as anyone outside our operation is concerned the camp is a hidden ammunition reserve. The scientists residing in the town play the part of concept munitions testers . . . Doctor Franc included."

Dorey and the others remembered how their briefs on the archaeological dig had told of newly-made high calibre rounds found around the excavation site.

The Nazi's had tried to cover their tracks well.

"You know, I think I'd quite enjoy a walk back when my visit to the camp is over," Dorey said quite unexpectedly as he watched the passing forest.

The Colonel turned in an attempt to make proper eye-contact. "Are you sure Captain Heiden?" He was instantly wary of his motives. "It's almost five kilometres."

"Yes. It's a beautiful day and we do indeed live in a wonderful country. I can't remember a time I'd the chance to stroll in our fine countryside." He gave the Colonel a broad grin.

"I will happily walk with you if you want some company . . . The guards here will be less of an annoyance if I am around."

"That would be even better."

"Not to impose, but I think I may join the two of you," Major Bergen added, "It would benefit my report to get a feel for the camp's approach and checkpoints as well as the habits of those who man them."

"Of course Major."

Deans entered his alias *Lt Seisser's* well-rehearsed line into proceedings, "If it's all the same, I'll return as planned to make arrangements for the interviews later in the week."

Major Bergen had informed the Colonel that morning of his intention to question certain key members of the town and camp over the next few days.

Captain Isenberg agreed. "I'll return also with your permission Major." Mark Dial's German was also perfect.

"Of course, continue with our plans until my return." Major Bergen replied.

The Colonel suddenly had mixed feelings. Taking time to walk the countryside would allow further opportunity to weigh up his higher-ranking guests. But as the two more silent members of the party had announced their intentions to return he was wondering if this had been a ploy to keep him away from the town for a time.

Dorey was pleased. While he and Carl would take turns at chatting to their host, the other would stick sneak gum to the barriers and other key points along the journey back. By afternoon the HQ screens could monitor the road connecting the camp and town at will.

Back at their base Benny and Marco observed the manipulation. They were alternating short shifts in front of the screens, Jay taking a break, brewing the three a round of coffee.

As the car continued, the surrounding trees suddenly opened into a large flat clearing causing a blanket of bright sunshine to flood down on them. The tree line arced away steeply on both sides creating a large hexagon shaped perimeter. Only trim grassland flanked the road now as it continued its final, dusty approach.

Their destination loomed, its wire perimeter fence circling the inner wooden wall which hid the interior of the camp just as the reconstructions illustrated. The place had an immediate eerie quality to it, the clearing not a part of nature's plan. Guards walked the barb-wire topped fences between ground level machine gun nests. Six watchtowers sprang high into the air at each corner, their structures a combination of wood and steel. The place seemed unreal like a movie set, one brimming with menace and foreboding.

The car came to a stop at the high wire gate and the same routine was played out between Colonel and subordinates. The two guards quickly flagged them through, the steel cage rim rattling as it was closed behind them. The short drive to the wooden wall was achieved in seconds. It was manned by several more guards. Two German Shepherds barked ferociously as they slowed to a halt, held tightly on the leash of their respective masters. The Colonel smiled silently as his papers were checked.

The wooden wall appeared almost medieval up close.

"Open the gate for the Colonel." The guard ordered as he passed back the documents.

The timber slowly creaked open. Machine gun muzzles peered at them from all directions as they rolled through, the dogs still barking as they were dragged on another skirmish.

In the centre of the desolate opening, five prisoner huts stood in regimented file. The tiny windows were sealed by shutters. No prisoners were visible.

Deans was again experiencing a sensation of being overwhelmed. It wasn't easy seeing the past as reality. He'd seen this place simulated on countless occasions but it had remained distant to him. Now all around him he felt the pressure of his surroundings as if being squeezed by them somehow.

Back at the base, Marco was alerted to his vital signs, "Easy Deans . . . It's no different to any other spying assignment." He reassured smoothly to his inner ear.

He focused on the truth of Marco's statement. He had to get beyond the surroundings and deal with the truth at hand. The world of an arms smuggler or terrorist was as alien to him as this was. It was only the dressing which added extra weight. He concentrated on the fact he was with three highly-trained men whose hidden pistols alone could take out half the camp with careful shooting. A luxury he'd not always had in the past. He'd walked into all manner of places alone, situations often at least as dangerous.

As if hearing his thoughts Marco whispered, "That's it, you know you've seen worse . . . And without the backup sitting next to you."

He wanted to say thanks.

"The prisoner's quarters." The Colonel declared as they drove by the huts at close range.

"How many do you currently hold?" Carl enquired.

"There are fifty-eight at present, though the accommodation was designed to house more. Most are told they've been selected because of a specific illness they've picked up. All are single with no remaining family. We inform them if they're willing to remain as guinea pigs for the Reich, their lives will be spared at the completion of the study. In the meantime their existence is better under this more spacious and relaxed regime. They're under no illusion. They understand they're far more likely to die in one of the larger camps. The majority have been inmates of such places and will do anything to avoid being sent back. Once here they behave and accept their fate, because the alternatives are of course, far worse." He seemed neither cold nor concerned by his statement. "Here they believe they may at least have some chance to survive the war."

As they scanned the interior of the camp basin there was little to see. The grass for the most part was gone, replaced with shale but for a strip along the west wall where an obstacle course had been built. Behind them in the south east corner was a crudely marked circular running track. Neither had been illustrated by the Stasis None. As for buildings, other than the huts and the surrounding wooden wall and its towers, there was only a shower block and latrine house within the large central clearing.

The two grand hunt lodges with their barn and livery did nothing to add to the landscape as they were pushed back in the far corners. It was a soulless void surrounded by tyranny.

On approach to the larger lodge they could see a section of land ploughed into an allotment, and it was here they caught their first view of some of the inmates. Twelve men working the land with hoes, wearing striped pyjamas.

The Colonel pointed to the sad looking band in the distance as the car pulled up to the mansion. "We allow them to eat what they grow in certain circumstances." He advised.

"Do you supplement their diet?" Dorey asked coldly, ignoring the repulsion. The car stopped, the shale grating beneath the tyres.

"We give them whatever Franc instructs. Some are very well fed and might I add, extremely fit and healthy. Some are starved, others kept sick." The Colonel's driver opened his door and he stepped out of the Mercedes. "It's all up to the doctor, and whatever his varying requirements are."

They too stepped out onto the shale as the driver closed the doors behind them.

"You may go now Stephan." The Colonel instructed, "As you heard I'll be walking back. Inform Corporal Deit of the change in plan, he may take and direct my calls as necessary. Expect a call later to have Captain Isenberg and Captain Seisser returned to town."

"Of course Sir." Stephen saluted then returned to the car. He pulled away slowly, the tyres crunching as he headed back toward the wooden gate.

Dorey's group eyed their surroundings playing the unconcerned Nazi's to perfection.

"The house is far larger than I expected." Carl remarked.

"It has over sixty rooms in total and a very large cellar, perfect for the doctor's needs. Until the end of the last century both houses played host to Royals and dignitary. The smaller lodge is used as the storage facility. Doctor Franc and his staff keep their files and findings there. The livery has been converted to house some of the guards." The Colonel eyed the two silent officers accompanying Bergen and Heiden. They'd barely said a word since introductions earlier. It made him nervous. "The rest of the tour is all about what's inside." He gestured to the entrance. "Please, allow me to lead the way."

As he walked Deans could not resist the pull of the prisoners working the allotment. He looked across just as an inmate caught his gaze. He was too far away for direct eye contact, even with Dean's enhanced vision. And as he strolled behind the others in his pristine uniform, Deans felt quite relieved of this fact.

CHAPTER THIRTY FIVE

The temperature dropped significantly in the grand foyer, the stone and plaster refrigerating the shade of the inner sanctum. The two guards manning the hallway offered salutes to the approaching officers.

"My God Verdy what have you been eating?" The Colonel smiled, "You must have put on ten kilos." The Private's face flushed at the near truth of the comment. The Colonel turned to the second sentry. "Tell that Staff Sergeant of yours to start working you boys harder or I'll be speaking to him."

Hookah was good with his men, an old breed of soldier. It seemed strange he'd allowed himself to become embroiled within this dirtier side of the war.

Verdy moved to the heavy oak and glass doors shoving one of them open for his commanding officer. His angelic face and regular uniform made it hard to believe he would be vehement SS to the core.

"Ah but you can still move quickly enough." The Colonel remarked as he passed.

The five men now stood in the imposing entrance hall. The tiled floor underfoot was pale marble. The ceiling towered above like a chapel, an enormous brass candelabrum hanging from the apex. The support beams were intricately carved and stained with a high gloss finish, the walls decorated with oil paintings of old leaders long since dead, except for the largest, which depicted Hitler with his beloved dogs. It was tastefully painted in the style of the old masters, perfectly in keeping with the earlier portraits of power. Two suits of armour wielding a sword and axe guarded the broad stone staircase to the left, while a stuffed brown bear guarded the corridor to its right.

Guarding the corridor directly ahead of them was something noticeably less formidable. It was a Sergeant, sat behind a desk sporting a rather ridiculous moustache. He stood to attention as the party approached. "Good morning Colonel."

"Sergeant Rein, when will you see sense and shave that thing off?"

The Sergeant didn't so much as twitch at the Colonel's comment, so thick was his skin with regards to his facial ornamentation. The Colonel reached for the signing in log.

The funny-looking man passed over a pen. "I took the liberty of completing the passage for your visit Sir. All I need are printed names and signatures."

They each went about the task.

"I've arranged open access to the camp and facilities gentlemen," the Colonel explained, "But whenever you enter either lodge house, you must always sign in and out."

They all agreed.

"Where can I find Doctor Franc?" Hookah enquired.

"He's in the basements Colonel . . . but he's readied a table in one of the secret gardens for your meeting. He informed me to telephone him upon your arrival."

"Then get to it." The Colonel instructed. "Is it the garden with or without the pond?"

"Without sir." He picked up the phone to place the call.

"Come gentlemen." The Colonel left Rein to his task and headed through the broad open doorway into a spacious corridor. The visitors noticed the grandeur afforded the entrance had since been removed from this part of the building. The walls wore stained shadows left by the many pictures and mirrors once held there not too long ago. "We removed everything from certain areas of the building, called upon to fund the war effort." The Colonel commented. He turned his attention to Major Bergen. "May I say that's an interesting ring you are wearing Major." He'd observed it when his guest signed the entry log, "I didn't notice it at dinner last night," The Colonel prided himself on his observational skills, "A silver eagle swastika . . . I've only ever seen them in gold."

"I dislike gold jewellery," Carl returned the smile. "I found it this morning when unpacking my things."

The Colonel laughed. "My late wife was the same. Most unusual for a lady I always thought. She insisted I change the engagement ring I'd bought for her." He smiled at the memory. "And ensured the wedding ring was picked by her *own* eye."

They all smiled with the Colonel.

At the far end of the corridor the five officers stepped through another large doorway into the main west wing of the house. An eager guard saluted as they passed but still they'd neither seen nor heard from any of the prisoners.

"This way," The Colonel led them through another stripped room. It had the feel now of a derelict mansion, yet one cleaned meticulously each newly polished day.

"Where are the patients?" Carl asked mindful of his terminology.

"Either on the top floor or down below in the basement levels. They rarely come into this part of the building."

They entered a smaller section of the house now, headed into a compact corridor with a white door at its far end. They passed through it to enter an impressive conservatory filled from top to bottom with all manner of plants, all carefully labelled with notes attached at various points on their pots and stems.

It was damp with a leafy taste in the air. Flies and bees buzzed out of view.

They headed straight for the exit opposite and stepped outside onto a short pathway which led to the lawn of a long, narrow garden. A willow shaded the sunshine as it leaned in to say hello. They brushed through the swooning leaves into the sunlight.

At the far reach the whisper and foliage of the forest towered above the end wall. In the lawn's centre was a white cast iron table accompanied by six matching chairs. On its' surface a jug of iced water was surrounded by nine glasses.

The garden was made truly secret by the stone of the house behind them and the high brick walls along each edge. The willow which grew from the other side of the rampart only added to the secrecy, its canopy falling across the conservatory and path. There was no other gateway, and as far as the team could see the conservatory was the only entry.

"The ice hasn't even begun to melt." Carl stated.

"He has a lookout watch the road when informed guests are coming. He then has his meeting place set up at speed with some little nonsense such as this." Hookah pointed at the jug and glasses, "Albeit on this occasion a most welcome nonsense." He poured water into five of the glasses. He would not pour for the doctor. He took a large swig. "Ah." The others took a turn to drink.

"No meeting is ever held in the same place on back to back occasions. Next time it will be in the garden with the pond, the time after on the roof terrace."

Suddenly a new voice entered proceedings. "So tell me gentlemen, does that make me borderline mad or merely eccentric?"

They turned to see a slim, ageing man in stylish attire, his five foot nine inch frame standing between the gentle fingers of the willow. He wore a black waistcoat, the trim covering the top of his trousers which he wore high around the abdomen. His shirt was coloured pale cream, the sleeves rolled up into thick wedges sat just above the elbow. The look was finished with a slender watch chain travelling into the shallow left pocket of the vest. He looked like a doctor who'd just finished delivering a birth.

His features strongly resembled the picture they'd studied time and again, though he appeared more fit and healthy than expected. His face seemed less harsh, his eyes kinder than in the photograph, an irony not missed considering their current location.

The Colonel was not the least bit embarrassed. "A little of both I would say Herr Doctor."

Joseph Franc smiled as he made his way to the table of five. He made a beeline for the next highest rank on offer. "I am Doctor Joseph Franc."

Carl casually fidgeted with the ring as the doctor made his approach, then extended his hand in greeting. "Major Bergen." His firm handshake pressed the now inwardly facing silver swastika against the doctor's skin. The twisting action activated the nano-particles held within, and as the ring's sensors detected the foreign epidermis, it ejected the mite trackers free, quickly to be absorbed into the doctor's palm.

Major Bergen then turned to introduce the rest of his team. "This is Captain Heiden."

Dorey shook his hand more graciously, much to Franc's relief, "Doctor."

"This is Lieutenant Seisser."

"Doctor Franc." Deans said politely.

"And this is Captain Isenberg."

"Herr Doctor." Dial said with a smile.

Jay's quiet voice entered their ears. *"Mites are inside. We have a lock on the target."* A tiny trace also entered Dorey's system due to his following handshake and she quickly went about separating their signal.

The doctor continued his charm offensive. "Please, sit down Gentlemen."

They each took one of the heavy iron chairs and sat accordingly. The Colonel took another sip of water as a short silence accompanied the weighing glances.

Franc smiled at the awkwardness of the situation. "So, our boss has sent you here to spy on my little operation." His charm was quite disarming and before any of them had a chance to counter, the doctor waved his hand as if to tell them not to concern themselves. "Don't worry . . . I understand. Things are not going as they should in the war."

The Colonel flushed. "I hardly think that is the reason these men are here."

"Really?" He stared at Bergen. "I would have thought that precisely the reason."

Carl was quick to engage the remark. "Doctor, while the Fuhrer is more than happy with your efforts, this project like many others, has to be scrutinised . . . All things considered."

"And yet Adolf never mentioned anything of the sort in our last rather detailed meeting," the doctor stated. "Until the call yesterday only Brahms was ever spoken of, and now suddenly here are all of you." The darkness etched by the Stasis None was now evident in the old man's eyes. "One has to ponder his motives."

"With respect Doctor, our leader's motives are irrelevant. What need only concern you, are his orders."

The darkness in the old man's eyes seemed to grow, "Major, as you are more than aware I am not a military man, and as you well know it is military men who take orders."

Carl glared. "That's *some* statement considering where you now find yourself Doctor."

The dark expression remained.

"The Fuhrer is adamant all such operations will be checked by me and my team over the coming months."

"And you are qualified for such a task?"

"If you're asking am I qualified to question your intellect then my response is I most certainly am not. However, I'm more than qualified when it comes to the execution of my duty. I'm here at the Fuhrer's behest, to assess your operation at every level. You will co-operate because it is in your interest to do so and because if you do not I have the power to take all of this away." Carl softened his tone. "You already know of your passport out of here." The doctor's ears pricked at the statement. "I am the man who will stamp it."

"How beautifully eloquent," the doctor replied with a smile.

Dorey leaned into the arena. "The Major must assess all you do here. It should never be taken personally. It's merely the business of the Reich," he smiled, "Your employer."

The doctor turned to Captain Heiden, "And your role in all of this?"

"My role is nobody's business but my own at this juncture. However you do not carry such distinction. Your business is our business . . . This is not a democracy." Dorey stared sharply, "As my colleague has stated, you've been offered a way out should it be needed. Help us to quickly complete our task here and all will be well."

"Your task?" the doctor was fishing, "As I was to understand it, your criteria is somewhat different to that of the Major's is it not?"

"You'll find my objective is one and the same . . . To carry out the will of our master. You need not concern yourself with the details. We are here to help ensure the survival of both yourself and your life's work."

The doctor stared back at him with iron will. "And it appears you serve your master well Captain Heiden." He was deliberately condescending. "He spoke highly of you during our brief conversation yesterday. He assured me, as indeed you all have, this would be routine and done within the week. However, it seems strange that suspicions such as these should arise so soon after my last visit to Berlin."

Captain Heiden smiled. "It is a paranoid world we live in. Trust is not always enough."

Carl re-entered proceedings. "Help me achieve my goal quickly and we'll be but a distant memory soon enough. Create any hindrance and I will be forced to pass matters over to my friend Captain Heiden here. Perhaps *then* you'll find you're a little clearer as to at least one aspect of his talents, skills of which our Fuhrer calls upon from time to time."

As the doctor turned toward Dorey he understood the time for smart comments was over. His presumed friendship with Hitler was for the moment brutally irrelevant, as he quite rightly ascertained the man opposite would kill him without so much as a second thought.

His edginess left with a return of the charm offensive. "So tell me gentlemen, what is it you require of me?"

CHAPTER THIRTY SIX

As the doctor led his unwanted guests toward the basement levels his mind was working overtime. He still couldn't fathom just why they were here. When Hitler confirmed the visit he'd reassured the doctor the assessment was mere formality. When he'd tried to coax out the wisdom behind his benefactor's decision he'd become agitated, and Franc knew it was easier to roll over and accept one's fate rather than risk the wrath of the Fuhrer. He'd tried his luck with the Major and his associate Heiden and it was clear these were not people to be trifled with. Heiden in particular, made him extremely nervous.

Hitler guaranteed the work would remain protected and the official papers passed onto him by Bergen reiterated such promises. He'd assured him there was no interest in seeing his formulas decoded, his research fully surrendered to the Reich.

A promise Hitler had always adhered to.

The Fuhrer's team were here to assess the whole operation from top to bottom, the town to the camp. To observe what the leader's schedule did not allow him to witness in person. Hitler wanted the next best thing to his own eyes and ears at ground level of such operations. Though why he needed quite so many eyes and ears coming from a multitude of directions was anybody's guess.

'He's getting more paranoid as the war turns against him.' Franc concluded.

So as the doctor took his guests into his secret world, he decided he would indeed play to the rules of this new game as far as his observers were concerned, just as he'd done with Brahms. If they were only interested in a routine inspection, that was exactly what they'd get. After all, he had to ensure his passport to Bolivia was assured if he was to continue his work under the budget and protection provided by Nazi gold.

However, the core of his coded formulas would remain safely hidden away. They were his insurance policy as well as his treasure and there would be no need to share their whereabouts with these hired guns. Yes he would show them his incredible advancements, but they'd never behold the true embodiment of his work no more than Brahms or anyone else Hitler wanted to send would know.

He turned over his shoulder, "Just ahead here gentlemen."

As the group followed, Dial and Deans kept to the rear smearing blobs of sneak gel on the walls of each new domain, the route stored into their HQ's watching computer.

Franc now led them onto a narrow flight leading down into the old servant quarters and kitchens. They headed lower still, into the basement level via the main cellar staircase. Here the surroundings changed from sunlit windows to the dull glow of electric lighting. A slight hum emanated from cables weaving overhead, fastened crudely via clips hammered into mortar. The walls were brick and arched like a sewer, covered in a layer of grey paint which was beginning to blister and crack.

There was a distinct dungeon like quality to the tunnel in which they now walked.

Heavy looking steel doors greeted them at the end of the cellar corridor. The doctor pulled a key from his trouser pocket. It was attached to a chain discreetly clipped onto one of his belt loops, making him appear like a prison warder as he extended it.

He unlocked the small shutter which protected a slot cut into the door at head height.

He slid open the steel shutter and placed his face at the gap. "It's me." He said coldly.

A woman's distant scream suddenly flew through the now open orifice causing the Colonel to jump a little. The unexpected noise vanished as quickly as it arrived.

The guard on the other side peered through, "On`back to the main display whenever needed or if prompted by Franc's newly absorbed mite trackers.

The group now found themselves within the inner sanctum of Joseph Franc's operation.

The man who had unlocked the door was the second of the two Sergeants currently on watch. He was a lean but strong looking individual not far past thirty five. He was slightly taller than the doctor who stood immediately next to him. He had slick black hair and dark shadows under his slightly bulging eyes. There was an immediate sadistic quality about him. His skin was ashen and Dorey and the others would have laid a healthy wager on him spending previous years within the penal system, and not in the capacity he now found himself employed. To the well-trained eyes now observing him, his mannerism transmitted that distinct familiarity toward such institutionalisation.

"Colonel." His striking salute was a stark contrast to the ogre guarding the previous door.

"Sergeant Boltz." The Colonel replied, returning the mark of respect.

"Herr Doctor." The guard bowed slightly.

Franc glared. "Keep that hatch closed." He said coldly, unhappy at the escaping scream reaching the corridor beyond.

"I'm sorry Doctor, it won't happen again." The two Sergeants often conversed through the slot in order to pass away their shift.

He turned toward his guests, "This way gentlemen."

They left the second thug behind as they began their way down a broad flight of ten steps.

The doctor stopped them on the fifth rung down so as to give them an overview of what would have once been a truly enormous cellar. It sprawled out before them, a massive ground space with ceilings high enough to accommodate large vat barrels filled with beers and wines. Now however it was lit up like a hospital, with bright lighting having been fitted across the board. The once dark wood of its architecture painted with a combination of pale blue and clean white.

Painted plywood panels had been erected between many of the alleyways and larger nooks in order to make a number of smaller private wards each covered with newly fitted doors or free standing medical screens. To the right and left of the room were huge laboratory benches complete with their own embedded sinks, dressed with high looping singular faucets made of mirror-like steel. The table surfaces were dressed in an orderly fashion, with everything from Bunsen burners to an array of microscopes.

Flanking these was an assortment of monitoring equipment, test tube racks, jars containing spores and fungi, oscilloscopes and shelves filled with carefully labelled files.

At the far end the wall had been converted into a medical library, stacked from floor to ceiling in meticulous order, complete with an attached ladder whose wheels ran along in tracks at the top and bottom making all knowledge within, quickly and easily accessible.

Behind the bookshelves there had once been two exits used to transport the larger storage barrels of wine and beer in and out of the cellar. They were now bricked up, sealed and hidden by the paper mass of pharmaceutical learning. With the old alleyways closed, new vents had been cut to keep the temperature of the cellar at the desired level.

Adorning the left wall were charts with names of various prisoners written on them along with codes and numbers, pinned and recorded on each individual account.

Several scientists scattered the vast room wearing white coats, pouring over theories and formulas. There would be countless more hidden within the closed makeshift wards, all of them busy as Franc allowed his guests a moment to look upon the scene.

It was incredible to see how well such a space had been utilised, for nobody looking in from the outside could have expected such a place lurking beneath. It appeared efficient and extremely well-ordered and one could have been almost tempted to genuinely congratulate Franc on his efforts until the returning scream of the woman shattered the moment, only on this occasion much closer and all the more pained.

Carl swallowed the grim reminder, "Incredible Doctor Franc. Who would ever believe beyond that entrance was a place such as this."

The doctor seemed pleased at the remark.

"Very impressive." The comment fired from Deans almost startled the Colonel who hadn't heard a word from Lieutenant Seisser since his announcement in the car.

Dial simply nodded slowly to show Captain Isenberg's approval.

"Now I understand why your own cellar is so well stocked Colonel."

He turned to Captain Heiden and laughed. "I only wish it were I who'd kept all of it. Unfortunately the whole town combined could not stock what this cellar held. A large portion was sent to Berlin as a gift to the Fuhrer and his generals."

All but Franc smiled.

"As you will soon observe, in here we manage everything ourselves." The doctor began his prelude, "From cleaning out lavatories, sweeping the floors to the actual experiments. We have twenty-two sealed cubicles with individual beds, six more fitted out as twinned doubles with screens. We operate our experiments and detail the results within these same walls. Once we've collected the data and when we're sure it's safe to do so, we admit the patients to the top floors set aside as recovery rooms. From there we continue our observations and of course analyse skin, tissue, bone and blood samples. The whole process is a revolving door programme though we take great care to ensure our patients are well-rested and cared for between each procedure." The doctor seemed all the more proud as he announced, "We've had few fatalities here."

Again the woman's scream flew across the room and Dorey's group felt almost sure upon this occasion they'd ascertained her location. They ignored it as best as they could.

"We bring the prisoners here from the larger camps for the most part. They are handpicked to meet certain criteria and are treated here on arrival for pre-chosen ailments. We then offer them the opportunity to stay on at our facility should they be what we're looking for. There are risks of course, of which we make them fully aware . . . But if they volunteer they're immediately granted a point system which can ensure they'll survive the war . . . As long as no mishap occurs within our research of course." The doctor was speaking from the camp manual and was more than happy to have any prying ears up to the task, listen in and absorb the rhetoric on offer. "As I've said there are risks," he reasserted, "But the patients are aware their lives would almost certainly be over by now had they been returned to the camps. Most are more than willing to comply with our needs." The smile on his face was sickening.

"There are more guards on the top floor." The Colonel added. "But unlike the six Sergeants permitted below ground they know little of what is actually happening here."

Again the doctor was positively appalling with his manner. "Any patient found talking about the work being carried out on his or her person to anyone other than the doctors will be sent back to one of the larger camps . . . Or shot."

Jay, Benny and Marco grimaced as he so callously quoted the camp mandate.

"Yeah and I bet it's the latter of the two options." Jay declared, with a bad taste forming.

Doctor Franc finished his polished little speech then took them down into the main section of his facility. "Follow me . . . I will show you some of the research and breakthroughs made this month alone."

He led them toward the bench where two scientists working together did a rather poor job at pretending they'd only just noticed their guests. Franc introduced them and within minutes they were ready to begin sharing their prognosis on their current project.

They, like the rest of the research staff had been fully briefed by their boss. They knew exactly what they could and should not say. The team had indeed been handpicked, and were completely loyal to their head of research. He treated them well for such allegiance, but even those who at least partially understood Joseph Franc's intellect where nowhere near to comprehending just what it was he was truly trying to achieve.

After a brief lecture from the shorter, stockier scientist, the taller of the two researchers urged them to follow. "Come," he said with a glint in his eye, "Let me show you Patient Eleven."

CHAPTER THIRTY SEVEN

Dorey and Carl appeared exhausted. They headed straight for the lounge chairs and slumped into them with heavy sighs. Jay brought over two cups of tea.

Dial and Deans, now in the far room taking a turn at monitoring the screens, had returned over two hours earlier with similar displays of body language.

The visit had of course been witnessed on the displays, but those watching knew it must have been all the more harrowing in person.

The tour which started with the observations of Patient Eleven had been a grim and depressing one. All the prisoners were labelled in such a manner, subjected to varying forms of experimentation. They'd known what to expect, but seeing it up close and personal while being unable to do anything about it had proved a difficult burden to bear.

Patient Eleven was a man in his twenties. His head shaved bald, he was pale, gaunt and silent. His eyes were almost vacant but a distant spark lurked beneath which suggested this was once a promising young man. His poise and expression implied he'd long since been broken both physically and mentally, the person hidden somewhere within clinging to life and sanity by a thread.

He'd been lying on a bed wearing only a pair of military issue flannel underpants. There were no restraints and it appeared there was no need for any. His breathing was rhythmic. His eyelids slow with a clockwork blink.

The two scientists had begun explaining what Patient Eleven was being subjected to.

"Using one of Doctor Franc's formulas we've been able to keep Patient Eleven awake for two weeks." The taller scientist was very enthusiastic about the research. "Although he may seem very unresponsive, it's actually quite incredible. Normally sleep deprivation under such testing conditions would have seen his brain become almost catatonic. He's been monitored night and day and the ongoing tests to check his reflex responses along with basic cohesion have offered some astonishing results."

The stockier of the duo had interjected, "What you are seeing here is an exhausted body . . . His mind is actually quite alert." The two men had gone on to demonstrate how Patient Eleven's brain was indeed still very much switched on with a number of tests.

Doctor Franc explained that once Patient Eleven had been awake for twenty-one days, he would be sent up to the top floor recovery rooms where he'd be slowly nursed back to fitness. It had been a shocking introduction

The tour continued, introducing them to the various scientists carrying out an array of tasks on a score of human guinea pigs. None of the patients spoke, which was in itself disturbing. The only one making a sound was the woman whose screams occasionally haunted the basement. For well over one hour the tour had continued. During which time they'd seen men of varying ages attached to drips, strapped to beds, wired into machines and one even sustained in a large water tank, his body temperature held close to hypothermic levels as a study was carried out on his cellular response.

They'd seen two young women stripped naked. One wide-eyed, mute with fear, the tubes which ran from her arms administering another of Franc's secret cocktails. The next unconscious with a clamp holding her mouth open as two doctors took away sections of her gums. Quite why her body wasn't covered was a guess nobody wanted to make.

In one of the dual wards they'd paid witness to two children laid side by side, one a girl no older than six, the other a boy perhaps two years older. Both had been drugged, their limp bodies being prepared to have small sections of skin removed. The sight had made them feel sick to their stomach and yet still they'd played the role of the indifferent Nazi.

All studies were loosely explained as each visit was made, the unseen woman screaming intermittently throughout.

Her introduction finally came toward the end of the tour. Again they'd found a duo of scientists of which neither looked old enough to be out of university. Introduced to the visitors as Franc's protégé's, the pride was evident on the ruthless doctor's face as he made the introduction. One was short and blonde the other tall and skinny with mousey hair, each of them positively creepy in their own way. On their table was a woman known as Patient Ten, her legs strapped into stirrups, her arms bonded to a rail passed behind her head. No cover spared her from indignity and blood was evident on the instrument trolley beneath her. Many of the ghoulish tools and apparatus were also bloodied and there was a small rack filled with corked test tubes, smears of red surrounding each sample.

Dorey had ascertained there were a similar number of tubes as there'd been screams since their arrival. The sight was horrific and when Franc declared proudly the young woman was twelve weeks pregnant, it had taken a great deal of will power not to pull out their guns and execute all the conspirators present.

The doctor enjoyed observing their reactions to his experiments and felt he'd dished out a little payback for their cocksure introduction in the garden. Of course, Franc couldn't know whether or not they might actually enjoy such a show, but he'd clearly seen momentary signs of distaste upon all of their faces, particularly on this last stop which witnessed the crudest possible method of foetal research. '*Soldiers are never as tough as they like to think they are.*' He'd thought with a dark sense of pleasure.

After the horror show was complete he'd taken them upstairs to the recovery rooms.

Here they'd seen much of the same thing only without the gore. Inmates, most with their own rooms, sat silently as Franc led his guests in and out, quietly explaining what procedures they'd undergone once back outside in the corridor.

It had been an awful experience to witness such suffering.

The upper section had introduced ten new guards in total. All were instructed by the Colonel to offer Major Bergen and his team every courtesy. The spacious top floor stank of misery and despair and like the smaller brightly-lit corridor which led to the basement it had the look and feel of an asylum for the insane.

The walls were stripped bare, painted with the same pale blue and white applied to the cellar. The large windows had been caged.

They'd passed from one ward to another, receiving descriptions and briefs, the Colonel adding segments from time to time but for the most part allowing the doctor free rein.

All the while sneaks were pressed into nooks and crannies. Each new image filed until called upon specifically, or until Franc's trackers would activate them back to the fore of their HQ monitors. Their inbuilt scanning capability would also set about detecting any hidden openings within the bugged chambers, looking for anything suspicious not listed on the blueprints, such as wall safes or secret compartments.

When the tour of the first building finally drew to a close they'd taken tea in the west lobby. Franc had gone on to explain further how recovering patients were granted recuperation periods, assigned to the allotments in order to grow food to sustain the abused population within. And of how those who died were disposed of in what he referred to as the *erasing rooms*, a large area within the cavernous basement complex which held twelve deep baths for dissolving remains in acid, leaving only their teeth behind as testimony to their existence.

They'd stared grimly as he promised to show the efficiency of this place before they left.

He'd surmised these discoveries and experiments were bringing him closer toward answers bordering on the miraculous, that the German race would soon have drugs and medical procedures at their disposal able to cure them of ailments, clear arteries and make them immune to fatigue and disease.

His rhetoric had been well-rehearsed, his tour most efficient.

The visit had continued with a look at the records rooms of the smaller lodge. All had seen discreet sneaks pressed into place as their guides were distracted.

He'd walked them to the assault course and running track where he'd divulged different ways of pushing the human body to the limit, of how he'd often break a physiology so he may test new methods and ideas of how to repair or protect it. All revelations were cold, thorough and open. He'd given surface details of his ongoing experiments, his hopes and aspirations behind them, and managed it all without ever truly divulging the specifics of his formulas and conclusions.

When the tour finally drew to a close they thanked Franc for his time and allowed him to return to his duties. The Colonel had then called his driver to the camp to see Isenberg and Seisser returned to the town.

As Dial and Deans were whisked away the walk back for the remaining trio had begun.

Both Carl and Dorey played the Colonel to perfection as they passed key points within which they'd wanted further sneaks placed. They'd been introduced to guards at the gates, shared jokes and looked over their weaponry and bunker-making skills, covering them discreetly with the gel of their advanced spying technology.

Once the last of the barricades was left behind the Colonel had politely enquired what was meant when they'd talked of stamping Joseph Franc's passport.

Dorey had hoped he would.

They'd spun it beautifully, allowing the Colonel to believe he was being granted a forbidden glimpse into their secret objectives. They'd recognised his dislike of Franc and so told him of how Hitler had come to suspect the doctor may be hiding certain elements of his research that must be found.

The Colonel had appeared almost embarrassed, and informed them of rooms within the hospital complex not explored during the tour, such as Franc's private residences on the second floor. He'd apologised for not bringing it to their attention, as he hadn't realised it would carry any significance. He'd also divulged the whereabouts of Franc's town house, suggesting this too should be looked at in more detail.

Jay had naturally made Dorey aware of the several unaccounted for rooms thanks to the blueprints she had available, and not just those of Franc's residence.

Dorey had let it go. With the trackers in place it would do no harm to sneak Franc's residence the following day when he intended to ruffle the doctor's feathers further.

He'd decided to spin this web while on their walk home to see if Hookah would divulge such information. He was pleased the Colonel was so quickly on side.

They'd told of how Hitler didn't want the doctor harmed, so decided to set an elaborate trap, Dorey explaining how Brahms was sent there believing he was indeed there to offer the doctor his passport to Bolivia. That Hitler's complete trust in Brahms coupled with his unique skills and place of upbringing meant he was the only candidate for such a task.

He'd admitted to Hookah he wasn't entirely sure of whether or not the offer to move him was genuine or not . . . That Major Bergen had been sent purely to disgruntle Franc, in the hope he'd make moves to gather his research together in its entirety.

The Colonel had hissed at the possible treachery, and clearly believed the web being spun around him, allowing his dislike to manipulate what he wanted to see.

Dorey had sworn the Colonel to secrecy. However, even if he did speak to Brahms, they'd played it so the spy himself wouldn't necessarily question their version of events.

And even if he did, they had the SiSTER on hand to offer his ear the confirmation of Hitler's wishes, a tool of manipulation they'd already seen work on Franc.

Everything was beginning to come together.

As they'd approached the town the conversation had lightened. The Colonel explaining how he'd found himself within his current station. Hookah was a war hero in the traditional sense, one who'd joined the party in its early years. As a regular soldier he was uncorrupted by political ambition, unlike most of the high-ranking SS officers, which made him an ideal candidate for his current position.

It was clear Hookah trusted Captain Heiden and Major Bergen and he'd appeared pleased they'd decided to confide in him, understanding their orders had given no such mandate.

He'd stated how he could see the sense in Hitler having Brahms offer the doctor his freedom before sending in Bergen and Heiden to stir things up. And though he'd no doubt remained unsure as to what Heiden's ulterior motives were, it appeared Hookah was beginning to believe these motives would be more in association with Joseph Franc than they were in any way questioning of his leadership of the operation.

And so, after the walk back, Dorey and Carl now sat back into their chairs and reflected, just as Deans and Dial had done upon their own return. Drinking the hot tea slowly in the hope its steam would rise through their senses, helping to wash away the smell of suffering which lingered in their nostrils, the bitter taste of which stained their palates.

Again Jay enquired if they were okay and both reassured her they were fine.

The following minutes passed in silence before Dorey was ready to have the day's events clarified. He stood, "Come on let's go through and join the others. We need to go over all we've seen and heard so far."

CHAPTER THIRTY EIGHT

After studying the three dimensional blueprints one last time, it was decided a team of three would venture up to Joseph Franc's house. Their original plan would have seen them wait until nightfall. However, two factors swayed them. First was the fact Franc was now being successfully tracked by their system whose technology pinpointed him within the basement complex on the camp. Second was the proximity of the house.

It was on the outskirts of town with easy access to the surrounding forest, which the Colonel had explained, was Franc's favourite place to walk.

This placed the property well away from the main bulk of activity.

With this in mind, they'd packed three rucksacks with the necessary equipment before Dorey had set off on foot with Dial and Benny.

Carl remained at the base HQ, armed and ready with Marco. They were the response team should any emergency assistance be required. His alias Major Bergen could also take care of any unwanted business which may come the postal building's way.

Deans kept a safe eye on their perimeter and on the roads leading in and out of town.

Jay monitored the screens next to him, once again the eyes and ears of the operation.

She'd navigated the trio through alleyways and backstreets and they'd attracted little attention. Some soldiers passed and saluted but it was mainly civilians who witnessed their venture as they trudged up the hill toward the edge of the forest.

The Colonel on side or not, it was essential Franc remained ignorant of their actions.

The houses were neat and beautiful, many featured painted wall panels characterising Bavarian themes, such as picnics or ramblers walking the nearby mountains to ski.

As they walked, the odd sneak was placed onto a wall or street lamp. They possessed a good blanket cover of the town and camp now together with the gates and roads leading in or out. More would be laid in accordance with the *mite* tracker, which would monitor Franc's movements in detail over the coming days.

The team had a free rein for the evening after a second dinner invitation was declined by Bergen and Heiden. Keen to maintain his hold over the Colonel's actions and thinking, Dorey accepted a request for the following night instead, though he would attend alone. Major Bergen had prior engagements, such as touring the armouries and munitions stores together with the motorcade.

Jay guided them around the final bend. "It's directly ahead of your current position."

The trio looked across at the large house. It was a detached wooden structure painted pale yellow, with a driveway at its front. Towering above the pointed roof and its' tall slim chimney was the forest, climbing steeply up the valley beyond.

His neighbours on both sides were a good distance away.

"Like the Colonel said." Dorey spoke quietly, "No guards." Hookah informed them the doctor insisted upon such policy. "Let's go."

They approached the house happy to see nobody in the street. They walked the driveway and Dial plonked a sneak on the wall overlooking the entrance before taking a peek through the slotted gaps of the window shutters. The house appeared deserted.

Benny knocked loudly on the front door. Nobody came. The action was repeated twice more. Again nothing, so they headed for the side path which led around the back.

They reached the tall wooden gate. It was locked. They jostled it to see if a dog barked. Once happy it was clear the three vaulted it into the back yard.

The garden banked steeply toward the rear fence. A stone path led to a gateway which stood before a tall tree at the fore of the forest edge. The yard was neat with a large pile of chopped logs in the near corner and a picnic bench on the right.

They checked for any sign of life. Once confident the dwelling was empty they tried to open the slotted shutters. They were locked. Another sneak was placed to give Jay a view of the rear pathway.

Dial headed for the drainage pipe, pulling at it to check its sturdiness. He retrieved a utility belt from his rucksack which he strapped around his waist. He placed the bag back across his shoulders then scaled the pipe. At the top he secured his grip and checked the safety of the guttering, then with a quick movement he pulled himself onto the roof.

They were expecting a possible climb and their boots were designed for the task.

Dial crossed the slope of the tiles toward the sealed skylight of the loft. Benny was fast on his heels, followed by Dorey who broke away, heading up the apex for the tall slender chimney. Once there he pulled out a large blob of sneak gel and broke it into four pieces placing one on each side of the stack.

"Okay I have a panoramic view. You're good to go."

Dial set to work using a device taken from his belt. Within moments the wooden shutter popped open. The breeze was cold despite the sunshine, and clouds made their way across the sky painting strange shapes over the now exposed glass beneath them. Dial took another tool which extended into a rod with two inwardly facing points. He pressed one point carefully onto the glass. It morphed into the pane as Benny attached a small black handle next to it via two small suckers. Dial took the handle and moved the outside arm of the device carefully around it in a full circle. The outer arc scratched a deep line into the glass infecting it as it passed. The tiny molecules within the injected gel went to work immediately, returning the glass around the immediate cut to a liquid state while ensuring the rest of the window held together. Dial pulled on the handle removing the glass leaving a perfectly circular hole in the pane. The gel around the cut could remain active for one hour and once the glass was returned it would be resealed back in its housing leaving a barely visible circular mark in the repaired pane as evidence.

Dial reached his arm through the hole being careful not to disturb the gel. He unclipped the lock and pressed down on the handle which released the window from within.

They donned their combat goggles and within seconds the three were inside the loft.

Their lenses granted near instant clarity in the dark chamber. Dorey headed across the beams toward the ceiling hatch. His job was to be made easy as no lock was present on the underside. The fitted board was simply pushed from the ceiling underneath to see it open and Dorey had enough finger space to ease the loft board free then pull it clear.

Dial slowly popped his head through the opening in the ceiling and stared down over the landing, his goggles instantly adapting to the changing light. On seeing the coast was clear he dropped lightly onto the walkway some twelve feet below.

Benny followed as Dorey pulled out a thin coil of black rubbery hosing from his bag. It was almost liquid soft, with several short horizontal rungs flopping from the vertical reel. He lowered it until Dial grasped its drooping end. Dorey shaped the remaining rubber into a shepherd's nook, moulding it around the beam of the loft entrance. He took out a shiny metal pin no bigger than his finger and stabbed it into the jelly-like hose. The soft rubber turned instantly rigid creating a singular black pole with rungs, a basic ladder back into the loft. After laying a sneak, he dropped through to join his friends on the landing.

The entire break in had taken minutes, conducted in almost complete silence.

Jay's voice re-entered their senses. "The sneak has finished scanning the loft . . . No hiding places." She switched to their current position, "Behind you is room *one*. Ahead of you around the corner is staircase *three* leading to the main landing of the second floor."

Dorey covered room *one* as Benny and Dial quickly made their way to the second floor.

Over the next few minutes the three men went about laying sneaks in every room, the scanning gel relaying information back to the waiting computer.

Jay directed them on. Some rooms where locked but they were no match for the tools brought from the twenty-second century.

Gradually they worked their way down onto the ground floor. It was a big house with large open spaces and today's exercise was to *bug* the building not actually search it. Such an action would come later. For now they only wanted to observe Franc's world and seek out any hidden nooks and crannies so as to ascertain where he may keep his work.

After a short time the lower level was complete. Only the basement remained. Jay's voice directed the trio to the corridor which would take them there via a large wal-in pantry.

Benny held back, keeping guard with his pistol drawn as the others silently approached the food store entrance. It was locked, and Dial set to work. The device quickly worked its magic but a moment before the lock clicked he stopped. He pulled the device away at the exact moment the mechanism sprung open.

"What?" Dorey whispered, his tone so light, without the inner ear technology it would appear as if he were just mouthing the words.

"I thought I heard something." His reply was equally silent.

Jay made another scan with the newly placed sneaks. "Nobody's entered the house."

Dial was hesitant, placing his forefinger to his lips.

Dorey leaned closer toward the door and listened. At first there was nothing, but then the faint sound of a second door opening on the other side suddenly filled their senses.

"Go . . . go." Dorey whispered.

The two men strode stealthily down the corridor, almost bumping into Benny as he turned to see what was happening. Before he had chance to ask Dorey whispered, "There's somebody in the house."

At that moment the door handle of the pantry turned and a voice murmured something they couldn't quite make out.

The three were already leaping the stairs.

Sergeant Boltz locked the inner basement door then passed through the pantry exit. On seeing the second outer door unlocked he stopped, certain he'd secured it behind him. He scowled, perhaps he'd remembered incorrectly. He clipped it shut, shaking his head at his confusion. He then turned to walk up the corridor when suddenly, he heard a distinctive sound. He looked up with a startled expression then drew the Luger from its holster.

He bolted toward the main stairwell and began to stride upward.

The sound was the creak of a floorboard on the turn of the stairs leading onto the second floor. If trodden on it creaked forward then back resulting in a distinctive groan, a sound unique to that area of the house.

He breathed heavily as he fought the staircase, his eyes wide. He reached the faulty floorboard with his pistol outstretched but there was nobody there.

His heavy breathing affected his hearing but he continued upward following his instincts to the top floor.

He turned the corner but the landing was also clear.

He headed for the door at the landing's end with caution. As he crept, he didn't notice the seal of the loft hatch, not quite seated correctly as he passed beneath it.

He reached the door at the end of the reach and slowly pushed it open, pointing his pistol ahead of him, passing into the room and back onto another of Jay's visuals.

As the door closed Dial readjusted the board, the ceiling sealed in the correct fashion.

Jay watched Boltz as he threw open the walk-in wardrobes. "He's coming out now." She whispered after a moment, tempted to hold her own breath as she watched the monitors. "He's coming back onto the landing."

Unlike Boltz beneath them, the three above breathed slowly and silently. They'd taken up position around the hatch, their pistols aimed. Dorey had noticed earlier when placing the sneak that the stepladders to the loft were in the room Boltz had just checked.

The Sergeant passed underneath the hatch, his pistol still drawn. He made his way to the stairs ready to continue his search of the lower floor, but as his foot hit the first step, his instincts made him turn. He stared at the closed hatch and paused. He was sweating and the curl of his lip shined. He tilted his head as he weighed up the entry into the loft above.

Dorey and the others could still hear his heavy breathing and the creak of his foot as it pressed on the edge of the staircase. Their aim awaited him, their hearts beating heavily.

Then, as if suddenly realising the height of the hatch, Boltz thought better of it and quickly hurtled down the stairs to check the rooms of the second floor.

He came flashing across Jay's screens once again as she whispered, "Hold there."

Jay watched as the Sergeant jumped from room to room until giving up the fear.

After a time he cursed his way into the kitchen and poured himself some water before heading into the living room where he flicked on the radio set. He placed his pistol on the table and laughed. Then after scooping back his greasy hair, he took a gulp of the drink.

Jay looked concerned. "He's not moving. How do you want to play it?"

Dorey thought. "We'll sit it out a while longer. Just keep us informed of his movements."

"A Sergeant from the camp in the doctor's house?" Dial stated to no one in particular.

"We'll worry about it later."

Minutes passed before Jay announced, "He's going nowhere. He's just poured a drink from the cabinet."

This was all Dorey needed to hear. "Is he still in the living room?"

"Yes. He's listening to music but even so I wouldn't risk scaling the wall."

Dorey remembered the tree stood by the exit at the rear of the garden. "Well, we can either sit it out . . . Risk climbing down as Jay watches him . . . Or fire a cable into that tree and slide across." He lifted the skylight and pointed toward the third branch, the broad wooden arm easy to negotiate but for a few surrounding branches and leaves.

They thought for a moment.

"We could be stuck here for hours," Dial concluded, "Fire the cable across, we could be in that tree in under a minute."

Benny agreed. "Music or not, from his current position he may hear any attempt at climbing down, especially now we've made him edgy. Plus if he went into the kitchen at the wrong moment we'd be screwed. He's far less likely to see an escape using the cable, especially with the shutters angled down."

"Alright let's do it." Dorey announced, "As soon as Jay gives us the go ahead."

Jay had the sneaks carry out a panoramic of the neighbourhood using heat sensitive vision and high intensity zooms. The distant windows, surrounding streets and gardens were clear, while Boltz remained seated, tapping his feet to Wagner.

"Do it now."

The trio climbed out onto the roof, Dial quickly resealing his handiwork on the glass pane and shutter. As he did so, Dorey took the cable gun from Benny's backpack.

The barrel underneath was the size of a one-gallon keg, filled with a reel of material similar to the substance used to make their ladder, only much thinner and transparent.

A handle and trigger sat on both sides of the barrel so the cable within could be fired from both ends of the nozzle.

Dorey aimed at the chimney stack. The red laser locked the position and he pulled the trigger sending a chrome-coloured dart clean into the brick followed by a whirring tail of thin rubbery cable. He headed to the edge of the roof. "Still listening to music?"

"Still listening," Jay replied checking the panoramic once more, "Clear to proceed."

Dorey lined himself up before aiming the laser from the opposite end of the nozzle. He fired the second dart into the tree leaving a steep enough angle to give them a smooth slide toward the waiting branch. He flicked a switch which sent the inner pins into the fabric and the drooping rubber turned to rigid cable. He released the trigger grips swivelling them around to create handles. "I'll get down there and cover you," he said, wrapping his wrists into the loops. "Am I still clear?"

Again Jay scanned all directions, "Clear."

He took three strides and launched himself from the roof, sliding down across the length of the garden, the cable slide whirring smoothly as it carried him onto the branch with an assault of snapping twigs. Once he'd established his footing, Dorey slid his hands free and flipped open the control panel. He tapped at the sensor sending the handle section immediately back to Dial. It stopped as it detected the grip of his waiting hand.

Dorey then climbed onto the branch below, leaned against the trunk and drew his pistol.

Dial signalled for Benny to strap in. "Jay?"

"Go now." Came her reply, and within seconds Benny made the same leap, zipping across the line toward the tree branch above Dorey's new position.

He hit badly but quickly adjusted in a scramble to find it again underfoot. His shins would feel the consequences later.

The same technique was reapplied and only moments later Dial came hurtling over. He timed it to perfection and landed smoothly on the branch using the trunk of the tree to break his downward journey. He then tapped a code into the barrel instructing the molecules within the cable to disband completely, melting into liquid parts like snow into water. The process took seconds, the cable falling like sticky rain.

The three men quickly descended the tree.

"He hasn't moved," Jay's voice returned, "Still no sign of any neighbours or soldiers."

"Good." Dorey brushed himself down on the woodland floor. "We're on our way."

Within moments the trio set about their escape along the edge of the forest.

*

Dorey hadn't beaten himself up over the close call. The job was a necessary one and it appeared the house was empty. Quite why Sergeant Boltz was in the basement was anyone's guess. His shift at the camp was supposedly still active.

Despite his unforeseeable presence, they'd managed to get away unseen and still sneak the majority of the doctor's house.

Carl and Marco manned the control room monitors while the rest reflected over recent events in the comfort of the lounge. They could afford some time to take stock of events, while awaiting any suspicious movements from Franc himself.

The Colonel seemed happy to leave them alone for the evening and so far they'd remained undisturbed. There'd been no unwanted calls from Gestapo officials, no intriguing visits from German Bolivian spies.

The SiSTER hadn't been called upon to deal with any call or telegram related to their presence and for the moment a short break of deliberation was welcome.

"We've gone over the playback and we can't quite pick up what he said." Deans was referring to the moment Sergeant Boltz had muttered something, when startling them earlier that afternoon.

"We'll have to keep a close eye on this Boltz." Jay remarked.

Dorey agreed, "Top of the *wanted list* . . . Sneaks in the basement of Franc's house . . . More in his private residence on the camp together with all remaining rooms there."

They all concurred.

"And if those doors beyond the pantry *have* been treated with some kind of sound proofing then we need to know why." They'd discussed earlier their surprise at not detecting the approach of Boltz until the last moment. It was possible it was the house acoustics, but Dorey wasn't convinced.

"How do you want to play tomorrow's trip to the camp?" Jay enquired.

"We have the authority to do what we want, so why not be a little more brutal? We'll give him until tomorrow morning before applying a little more pressure. We've ruffled his feathers. Let's hope we've done enough to provoke a response. If there's any secret hideout hopefully he'll lead us straight to it while we watch from here." He paused, "We'll go back to the camp tomorrow in the truck. We'll take the camera with us and begin taking pictures for our Fuhrer's files. That should *really* piss him off. We'll be arrogant and confrontational then wait and see what happens. But one way or another we'll sneak all the rooms Franc neglected to show us earlier today."

They'd gone through the blueprints, refreshing well-rehearsed routes to memory.

Jay would of course direct them but as always, nothing would be left to chance.

Several rooms away Carl was watching and listening in on a scheduled delivery being made by a truck at the east gate while Marco was eying two officers smoking cigarettes near to the front entrance of their postal building.

Carl zoomed in as the necessary papers were passed and listened carefully as the driver made jokes before continuing his delivery of foodstuffs. He leaned back and returned his eye to the slides beamed in from the camp's gruesome hospital and watched the beacon of the mite tracker as it confirmed Franc's position onto a screen all of his own.

He stared closely for a moment then sat forward suddenly.

Marco kept his eyes on the entrance, watching as the two officers finished their smokes, "What is it?"

Carl flicked his hand across the sensors to zoom in as the computer followed Doctor Joseph Franc from a number of new angles. "It's Franc . . . I think he's on the move."

CHAPTER THIRTY NINE

"He's been in there for hours." Jay whispered.

"I wish we'd managed to get a sneak in there." Dorey stared at the screens.

"Do you think we need to get a mite tracker inside Boltz?"

The team had been surprised to see Sergeant Boltz remain at Franc's house by the forest, welcoming the doctor home before they'd both headed into the basement together.

"Possibly," Dorey replied, "For the moment we'll keep a closer eye on him."

Dial repeated his earlier conclusion. "I still think they could be homosexual. It was frowned upon in this time. Many had to hide their sexuality."

"We could speculate all night." Dorey replied putting an end to it. He turned to Carl, "But while you're at the camp in the morning I'm going to get sneaks inside that basement."

With Franc's home cellar now a key factor it had been decided Dorey would lead another assault on it as soon as possible. It appeared the doctor would be spending the night at home and Carl could catch him off guard with his early morning visit to the camp. His alias Major Bergen planned to storm the second of the doctor's dwellings accompanied by his bodyguard, Marco's Lt. Hans Stoop, who would be snapping pictures throughout.

On hearing of this invasion, they anticipated a furious Doctor Franc would head back for the camp immediately. Before he could reach it Jay would direct Carl and Marco to the rooms missed previously and while the doctor was away sorting out that little problem, the basement of his other dwelling could be taken care of. They could only hope it would have the desired effect and that Boltz, if still at the house, would leave with his master.

If he didn't Jay would have the SiSTER take care of him.

There were many unforeseeable factors but they had time to make a number of attempts across the next twenty-four hours until they got it right.

The phone at the doctor's bedside rang loudly as Marco roared the truck toward the entrance of the larger lodge. The papers granted by the Colonel had seen them fly through the barricades, with the exception of the wooden fort gate where the soldiers had wanted to show extra vigilance as ordered by Hookah.

The truck's engine grunted to a halt, leaving a deliberate wake cloud of disturbed shale which dissipated in stages along the track behind them. It was six in the morning and their early start had caught a few by surprise as the two men now strode through the entrance carrying a large camera.

As the caller informed the doctor of their arrival, Franc's face was shrouded within the darkness of his bedroom, the sunlight blocked out by the shutters of the house, which so far appeared to never actually open. The sneak however, illuminated his facial expression in perfect detail. He was not happy.

The team had been relieved to see Boltz leave at midnight and they'd followed his progress back to the mess blocks from the comfort of their headquarters.

The doctor had returned to the basement and remained there for another hour after his guest had left before finally heading off to bed himself.

The team were full of zest on seeing the doctor remain alone.

The majority of his twisted hospital still slept as their plans got underway.

Franc placed the receiver down with a scowl. He didn't move for a moment, he just stared directly ahead of him. The team had of course listened in to the hurried warning stuttered down the phone courtesy of one of the startled camp scientists.

He reached over and switched on the light, the sneak adjusting its transmission accordingly. In the illumination the doctor looked old and spent. He rubbed his eyes and grunted before pushing himself off the mattress in his pyjamas. He walked over to the bathroom and slowly began to wash.

It appeared Joseph Franc was a cool customer.

After Major Bergen and Lieutenant Stoop placed signatures into the entry book sat open on an empty desk, Jay directed them to turn left up the staircase flanked by the suits of armour. Sergeant Rein and his funny little moustache were nowhere to be seen.

Upon reaching the second floor they were saluted by a guard who following the Colonel's orders, happily pointed them in the right direction. They'd stridden on, with Jay's voice clarifying the route. Carl had been in this part of the building yesterday but where the doctor previously turned them left down the main drag, he now moved right to a sharp corner which introduced them to a partly-hidden door.

"Bingo." Jay said.

Carl tried the handle as Marco placed more sneaks, it was locked. He knocked loudly and waited but nobody came. Lieutenant Stoop checked the corridor once more and with the coast clear, Major Bergen pulled out a device like the one used on the secured shutter of the skylight. Within an instant the lock popped open. '*This will really annoy him.*'

The Major and his bodyguard, still carrying the hulk of a camera and film, were now inside another of Joseph Franc's hidden lairs, rapidly covering it in sneaks as Jay watched the outside approach. Her focus was also on the doctor as he dressed, the image of his old naked body not the best way to start her day.

Once dressed Franc went back to his bedside table and picked up the phone. He spoke curtly to the operator who quickly patched him through to the senior mess barracks. "Get me Sergeant Boltz," the doctor demanded.

The man on the other end placed down the receiver and set about the task quickly.

Eventually a voice introduced itself, "Sergeant Boltz."

"I need you to get the car and meet me here immediately."

"What's the matter?"

"Major Bergen and one of his associates have turned up at the hospital unannounced. It appears one of them is carrying a camera. I want you to take me there right away."

Dorey and the others beamed at the news both Boltz and Franc would be leaving the house unattended. They prepared for their renewed assault on the basement.

Carl and Marco in the meantime where making fast work of the doctor's flat, it's four rooms running into one another like a rather plush hotel suite. It consisted of a bedroom complete with a four poster bed, a bathroom, a large study and a spacious lounge. The original grandeur of the house had not suffered in these rooms. Like the splendid entrance two floors below, these chambers were stately and lavishly dressed with ornate furniture.

As they laid the final sneak Jay alerted them to the fact Franc's taller protégé was hurrying down the corridor toward them. He was flushed and slightly exasperated.

"He'll be with you in ten seconds." She announced, "Five . . . four . . . three."

Marco took the camera and pointed it across the lounge aiming it at the door which would bring in their inquisitor. Carl began booming out a question, asking his bodyguard if he'd finished photographing their lavish surroundings. As the door opened, Marco fired the flash then pulled a slide of film from the camera.

The man held up his hand and squinted having led his eyes into a direct hit, much to the amusement of Jay. He protested, "Major Bergen . . . What are you doing in here?"

Carl strode toward him wearing a furious expression. "In what world is it a person such as you demands explanations from an officer such as I?"

He quickly realised his mistake and began to stammer, "I'm sorry Major. No offence was intended. I merely meant these are the doctor's private quarters."

Major Bergen scowled at him and signalled his bodyguard to leave the room with a sideways flick of his head. "Are you suggesting there are places within the fatherland in which our Fuhrer may not tread?"

The stammering continued.

"It will serve you well to remember, I am the eyes and ears of our leader when in this place, with a mandate to roam as he would roam himself. If I wanted to piss in that toilet as the doctor slept then I would, as that is the Fuhrer's right and so therefore my own."

"I . . . I'm . . ."

Carl looked at the man in disgust. He turned and headed out of the door in pursuit of his bodyguard, shaking his head and cursing as he went.

Once back in the corridor with Lieutenant Stoop, Major Bergen turned to bark at the henchmen as he bumbled out after them. "I am here to photograph this entire building from top to bottom as are my orders. Now . . . I suggest you hurry along and find me a person with the relevant keys."

The stammering returned. "But, if you could just wait a while gentlemen, just until Doctor Franc arrives, we have patients that . . ."

"Your human guinea pigs are of no concern to me." Carl boomed. "And the will of the Reich waits for no one." It was all very theatrical. "Now . . . Where is Doctor Franc?"

"He went home last night Sir. He is not yet on the camp."

Carl deliberately softened slightly. "Ah, I presumed he was here . . . That is why we headed up to his quarters." He pointed at the entrance. "His door was open."

The young man was trying to keep up but the Major was quickly back to his ranting. "Inform the doctor we'll be photographing the rest of this floor. Bring him to me the moment he arrives so he may offer assistance."

And with that Bergen and Stoop strode away leaving the protégé dumbstruck.

None of the scientists were ever spoken to in such a manner.

He watched as the Lieutenant loaded another sheet of film from the large bag worn across his shoulder then blasted a flash toward the reach of the corridor where the major pointed. The tall scientist turned and quickly headed for the stairs, he would inform the doctor on his arrival of the manner in which the major had just addressed him.

*

After knocking several times on the front door without response, Dorey, Dial and Benny headed around the back and vaulted the gate. Within minutes they'd followed the same route as last time, with Dial carefully retracing his cut through the skylight.

After negotiating the loft they silently crept down the stairs then headed once again for the pantry as Jay reassured nobody was near. After popping open the lock they entered the food store and passed through its walls of crumbling paint and cobwebs.

The shelves were fairly bare with only a basic assortment of goods mainly consisting of tinned meats, powdered milk and dried biscuits.

Dorey placed sneak gel into several nooks.

They approached the inner door of the basement with caution. Their combat goggles tried to give them sight through the wall but the technology was not up to the task. They crouched low and Benny pulled out a scanner from Dial's backpack. He placed it gently against the door. He activated the sensor, his movements precise and careful.

The scanner fired its signal into the room beyond.

Jay studied its results, her capability superior to that of the small screen on the device itself, but they were poor to say the least. "It looks like the door has something like a lead-sheet covering the other side. I can't get a decent reading. Try it against the wall."

Benny followed the instruction but the same scrambled readings returned.

The walls like the door had been doctored in some way. Coupled with the dense brick and wood which built the cellar, the device like their goggles, was struggling.

She boosted the scanner's power, shaking her head at the poor image. "I'm definitely getting lead readings. It's been sound-proofed or water-proofed or something. The actual structure is far denser than I'd have expected." She studied the grainy picture of the room and scrolled around. "It looks clear." She said cautiously, "Though I can barely see." Again she asked the computer to boost the clarity.

Dial pulled out his lock-picking device and placed it into the keyhole as quietly as he could. He paused and looked at Dorey who gave him the go ahead.

He set about the task at hand.

He twisted the mechanism slightly but as the morphing metal went to work, Jay's voice came flooding back into their ears. "Hold there." She demanded as she stared at the image on one of her screens. She concentrated as Dial's arm remained perfectly still.

The grainy image blurred. Jay scrolled through the zoom formats trying to get a lock through the dense wall. She was certain she'd picked up on something.

Suddenly the faint thermal signature of a body was brought to life as the sonic ear picked up a light cough. Jay's eyes swelled. "There's someone in there."

The three froze for a moment before Benny slowly pulled the detection device away from the wall. Seconds later Dial followed suit and removed the small gadget from the lock, placing it back into his belt. The three stood slowly and backed away from the door.

They crept out into the corridor, closing the outer door gently before resealing the lock. Silently they made their exit out of the doctor's home . . . With not one sneak being placed within Franc's basement at the second attempt.

Carl with the assistance of Jay's relayed blueprints had covered every inch of the hideous hospital on the camp. He'd sent his bodyguard back to the truck on several occasions to get more film as the doctor had looked on in astonishment.

"Why would the Fuhrer want photographs taken when he's gone to such trouble to ensure this place has remained elusive to all but a chosen few?" He'd demanded.

"I am not in the habit of questioning his reasons." Major Bergen had replied. "I received orders last night this was to be my next action and so here I am. I've been informed once these pictures have been studied by our leader, they will be destroyed. Only the Fuhrer and I will ever lay eyes on them."

"So you know how to develop photographs?" Franc retorted with an element of sarcasm.

"I know how to do a lot of things!" Bergen had replied with a deadly stare.

The battle of wills had continued as the doctor followed them around helplessly. "And pray tell me, what was the purpose of you breaking into my private residence and photographing when I was not even there?"

Bergen had looked annoyed. "We did not break in, the door was open. And I was ordered to photograph all of the building. When realising you had not shown us every room yesterday I had of course relayed this to our leader during our telephone conversation last night." Carl had then stared at the doctor with warning in his eyes. "And believe me he was more annoyed about your apparent transgression than I was." The doctor had protested his innocence as the Major continued, "He informed me these rooms omitted from our tour yesterday were to be the starting point of my objectives this morning."

The doctor had looked stunned. "But you never mentioned anything yesterday about requiring a tour of my private residence!"

"I asked you provide a full tour of your facility . . . in its entirety." The major had looked fierce once again. "And your private residence is not the only point of interest you omitted from the tour . . . Is it Herr Doctor?"

Again Franc had protested. "If I'd known your curiosity extended to everything such as boiler rooms, cupboards and lofts then I would have happily obliged."

"Then why is it you do not oblige me with such good grace now Doctor?" Carl had timed his remark to perfection.

"I have nothing to hide." Franc declared furiously. "I am merely trying to understand. Until two days ago I had the full support and trust of the leader. Now you and your team turn up, making veiled threats, pushing my staff around and demanding I explain myself like I'm suspected of carrying out some heinous act against the state."

The routine had continued for almost an hour. He was rattled and confused. He'd been all-powerful within this domain for years and now he found himself being undermined and quizzed by a pack of Hitler's wolves.

He suspected a traitor, somebody who had gone behind his back and put ideas into the mind of the Fuhrer. '*But who?*' He'd searched his mind for a candidate. '*I'm the only person in this camp who has consistently held the ear of the leader in person.*' His brain was running around in circles, '*Or so I thought,*' his paranoia growing with every passing minute. '*The Colonel?*' he'd supposed, '*But why would the Colonel undermine me? He's enjoying an as privileged a station as any officer in the war.*' He pondered, '*Perhaps our head of the Gestapo?*' But again he could see no sense in it.

The simple fact was everything pointed toward conspiracy. These men had turned up practically unannounced, only weeks after his last meeting with Hitler, an engagement which had gone so well. It didn't add up. Yet it was clear Berlin had indeed sent them here. The Fuhrer himself had instructed him to co-operate.

'*And I know I locked my door when I left last night.*' The thought, like so many others had popped into his deliberations over and over.

The mysterious Captain Brahms was dragged into the equation. '*Hitler's agent, a man the Fuhrer himself insisted be involved.*' An agent who would eventually transport himself and his work to Bolivia should the war not go as planned . . . The agent who had turned up shortly after his meeting with the leader.

He was reeling, in danger of succumbing to his age-old fears. Fears which had seen him change his identity and location over the passing decades more times than he cared to remember. Paranoia's which had seen him retreat from past benefactors, fleeing with his secret research. '*They want my work . . . But they no longer want me.*'

As the old suspicion made its unwelcome return the doctor had finally made his retreat. The thought he'd managed to avoid for ten years since being granted permission by Walter Buch to carry out research while head of the District Hospital in Berlin, returned suddenly and unexpectedly.

He'd headed for his study, threatening to place a call to Hitler in person.

"I would wait for a couple of hours yet Herr Doctor," Major Bergen had yelled after him, "He is a notoriously late riser."

Afterward, Jay and the SiSTER awaited the doctor's call . . . But none had been placed. Instead he remained in his office for the next hour, staring silently at the surface of his desk, rubbing his temples until the sound of the Major's truck leaving finally dragged him from his thoughts.

CHAPTER FORTY

The returning trio studied the images and replayed the sound of the cough time and again. The computer could only guess at the audio characteristics which proved too faint to determine any definite match.

"But if it is lead lining covering those walls, why such a large amount?" Dial enquired.

"It must go beyond waterproofing," Jay replied as she watched over Carl and Marco's return in the truck, "Cellars in the area have been susceptible to flooding according to my data. But the density of these panels could imply any number of things."

"Such as soundproofing?" Dorey interjected, "That would explain why we never heard Boltz until he opened the door in the pantry."

"Did they even use lead to line cellars from top to bottom?"

Jay quickly set about trying to find the answer.

"And would lead be used for soundproofing?" Benny enquired further.

"We know how dense it is as a material. Who's to say he wouldn't use it if he had an abundance of it in the area?" Jay commented, "What's more of an issue is *why*?"

They spent the next minutes studying a list of possibilities but it proved inconclusive.

"If this is the hiding place we're here to find then we have to ask ourselves why the doctor has allowed Boltz access to it. Also, if it is indeed a person in that cellar, then why are they in there right now?"

"Someone who has been down there for at least a day without coming out," Jay added.

"Why not make use of the rest of the house like Boltz did? Help yourself to a drink, listen to the radio . . . make a sandwich?" Dial concluded, "It must be a dog."

"Maybe he has one of the prisoners down there." Deans suggested, "Perhaps continuing his work at home." It was a grizzly thought.

"Again it brings us back to Boltz. If it is his hiding place, why grant anyone access to research you were clearly intent on hiding from everybody? Boltz is a Nazi, why would Franc trust this man when he so clearly didn't trust any of the others? After all his hiding of the work was elaborate, kept away from his sponsors in two separate, coded parts . . . And all at extreme risk to his own well being." Dorey stated.

"That could have been due to the Nazi hierarchy, not out of a blanket distrust of every individual." Benny added.

"It's possible, but it does seem strange for someone whose life has been so clandestine."

"We all have to trust someone at certain times for certain reasons." Deans stated.

"Whatever the reason, we can't just assume he doesn't trust *anybody*. And it's obvious this Sergeant is of some use to him. It may have nothing to do with his work. What we need to find out is just exactly what this use is." Benny concluded.

"We need to know who or what is in that basement," Jay declared, "And we need to do it quickly."

"We could use knockout gas on the basement's ventilation shaft." Benny suggested.

Jay began verifying whether such a feat could be achieved. "The computer is certain the gas will work. The air ducts are split and run directly from the side alleyway of the house where the back gate is located, and from the rear garden. Both inlets feed fresh air into the cellar. We'll know in a moment how much gas we would need."

Deans remained focused on his monitors, "Doesn't that mean the soundproofing idea is less likely. If there are open vents leading out to both the alleyway and garden?"

Jay posed the question and the computer quickly analysed the blueprint further. "Not necessarily. Apparently the air duct leading to the garden is long, staggered and thin. Its exit is located on the other side of the log stack via a small chimney. On its own it would supply sufficient air to the cellar but due to its shape and position only a small amount of sound would be heard leaving the basement unless produced at a high decibel level." She observed the new data. "The more direct inlet at the side of the house would pose a different problem, and if you were indeed trying to keep sound in, the computer says it's this vent which would be blocked." She concluded, "So if this vent has been tampered with, the soundproofing theory is a more legitimate one."

They all absorbed the findings.

Dorey declared. "We need to work out whether another attempt can be made today, or will we need to wait until tonight to get inside?" He thought for a moment. "Unless we know for certain the doctor isn't going to head back into town within a certain time span then I think we should probably wait until the early hours before we hit the cellar again. That way we also get to observe the doctor and his movements after this latest little provocation courtesy of Major Bergen." He looked once again at the monitor showing the view within the truck as it brought Marco and Carl toward one of the blockades on the outskirts of the town. "With a little luck we may well see Franc remain on the camp. If not then hitting him when asleep in his bed at home is by far the safest option."

They paused to watch Carl and Marco drive safely through the checkpoint.

"There's always the risk he may come home, go down into the cellar then not come out again. If there is a guard down there, hitting them both with gas is going to make it fairly obvious when they wake up suffering the same symptoms." Dial added, "And we may not know until the last moment whether or not he'll be sleeping at home or on the camp."

Dorey's focus remained on the screen now showing the truck pulling well away from the barrier. "Perhaps we should manipulate his decision ourselves." He returned his attention to those present. "Boltz is a problem. A lot will depend on his movements across the coming hours. Obviously we need to keep him under our control. Hitting him with either gas or a pellet has to remain a last resort. I don't want exchanged theories on why the doctor's *in-crowd* have all been subjected to sudden deep sleeps and identical hangovers." He pondered. "I think Boltz may find himself the first of the exclusive cellar sergeants to be questioned on his activities within the camp."

They all agreed.

"This is what I want in the next hour . . . A workable plan to see cameras on the inside of that cellar. I'll be at the Colonel's for dinner again this evening. All options must be considered. We need to work out the most efficient way to do this." He concluded, "I want that cellar beamed onto those screens before day three gets underway."

CHAPTER FORTY ONE

Major Bergen entered the senior mess barracks accompanied by Deans' alter-ego Lieutenant Seisser. New developments had forced the team to execute their plan quickly. A short time earlier the pressure being applied to Franc seemed to be paying off, when the doctor was observed removing leather-bound documents from two separate hiding places on the camp. One from a vent in the main boiler room of the smaller hunt house, the other from behind a wall panel inside the conservatory of the gruesome hospital.

He'd taken these documents to his study and wrapped them in brown paper, loading them into a large bag stuffed with loose reports in what appeared an attempt to make the package seem less conspicuous. Boltz was then called to his study, where he was handed the package together with instructions.

The team had barely been able to conceal their excitement.

Franc had informed Boltz he was due in one of the operating theatres. "I'm going to go ahead with the procedure on Patient Fifteen. I may be a few hours. Show the usual discretion . . . Especially with our unwanted guests sniffing around."

Boltz had then returned with the package to Franc's town house where he'd taken it directly into the cellar as instructed.

The doctor hadn't opened the works which meant the sneaks were unable to get any kind of glimpse, but these documents appeared substantial, and would almost certainly contain some of the research the team were sent here to steal.

The doctor's trust of Boltz seemed an assured one.

Joseph Franc's determination to fight his demons and carry on in his work meant he would be at the camp for a few more hours.

Jay had the rotation schedule which showed Boltz was to attend a military brief at 1700.

He'd proved unpredictable so far, but no call was placed to excuse him such a duty.

They'd watched the monitors ready to move as Boltz finally left Franc's home cellar in order to keep this engagement. When entering the doctor's basement he'd been carrying the parcel, when he left for the barracks he was not.

Dorey and Dial had set off immediately.

Carl had placed a call to Hookah informing him he would be interviewing some of the Sergeant's privy to the more secretive walls of Franc's research centre.

The Colonel was pleased at the Major's courtesy and had informed him once again, both he and his men would fully co-operate with all of their investigations.

And so, as the monitors had displayed Franc's preparation of Patient Fifteen, Carl had set off with Deans to ensure Boltz would not be interrupting the taking of the cellar.

As Major Bergen and Lieutenant Seisser approached the Duty Sergeant, he stood and saluted from behind his desk. "Heil Hitler. Can I help you Sir?"

"Have Sergeant Boltz report to the front desk immediately."

"Of course Major." He picked up the phone and relayed the request to the briefing room.

The team had not deemed it necessary to have a full coverage of the barracks but had covered the main entry corridor and exits.

After the recent failed attempts on the cellar, Dorey decided he and Dial would not release the gas until they were certain Boltz was safely under Carl's control. They listened in from their position close to Franc's home at the forest's edge.

"He's on his way Major." The Desk Sergeant placed the receiver down.

"Excellent," Bergen replied. "I will also want to question Sergeants Lehman, Curtz, Scholden, Brikkenholmer and Hurritz at some point across the next forty eight hours. Could you have a copy of their manifestos drawn up for me?"

Jay had a screen devoted to the sergeants granted access to Franc's hidden basements, but such a request would defer any suspicion being stirred within Boltz.

As the two officers awaited his arrival, Jay had another check upon these colleagues. The hulk of Sergeant Lehman was playing cards in the guardroom not two hundred metres from where Carl and Deans now stood. If he showed any sign of heading to Franc's home before their business was done he'd be intercepted and brought to the postal building to join his friend. Brikkenholmer and Hurritz were asleep in their small room located within the livery building on the camp. Later they were to relieve Scholden and Curtz who were currently on duty in the basement corridor leading to the chamber of horrors.

Jay noted the shifty image of Boltz as he approached Major Bergen and his assistant.

He saluted. "How can I help you Major?

Carl smiled at him without substance. "You are to accompany me to my headquarters where I wish to ask you a few routine questions."

He seemed completely unfazed, his dark, harrowing eyes weighing up the major stood before him. "I was about to attend a security brief in a few moments, should I . . ."

Bergen interrupted, "Have your colleagues fill you in on what you miss." He said curtly, "Follow me." He gestured for the Sergeant to accompany him. "Lieutenant Seisser and I have arrived on foot . . . It isn't far, you'll not be kept from your duties too long."

Boltz's distaste for him was immediate. '*What a jumped up prick,*' he decided as a rather graphic image of beating the Major half to death flashed through his mind. Such uninvited, violent notions were often painted into Boltz's imagination. They would enter his mind at speed then vanish. He enjoyed such moments, and clenched his fist as he followed the officers to the street. "What is it you wish to speak to me about?"

"Oh nothing too dangerous," Carl stepped out onto the pavement then turned to him, "As you are no doubt aware I am here to assess this operation." He made a casual gesture, "You are one of only a privileged few with access to certain areas, and as such I will be asking you to divulge certain aspects of your duties."

Boltz gritted his teeth. He'd seen how agitated the doctor had become since the arrival of these men and was told in minor measures of how they'd threatened his master.

Another violent episode played out within his fantasy.

Carl's acute intuition recognised the momentary lapse as it flashed across the Sergeant's eyes. '*This Boltz has the air of a killer,*' he ascertained, '*One without fear.*'

"I thought what we did here was supposed to be secret." Boltz sneered.

Carl dropped the pleasantries, "Not from the Fuhrer," he glared before adding in a steely tone, "Not from me." The Major set off with his henchman, "Come on." Carl said as he walked ahead.

Boltz recognised the tone. It was how a master might talk to his dog.

*

Dorey and Dial reeled the thin pipe into the ventilation shaft, its chimney protruding at the rear of the garden's log pile. Upon investigation they found the larger vent of the alleyway had indeed been filled with mortar. They'd then quickly vaulted the entrance with the lightweight cylinder of gas concealed in Dial's rucksack.

Benny and Marco were manning the screens back at the HQ. It had been decided for the sake of realism Jay's Gudrun Schmidt should record the interview with Boltz.

Gudrun would take shorthand ready for her transposition to a type-written report.

There was no risk to their operation. The interview was being held informally across a desk placed in the front lounge, well away from the control room's technology.

As the tube struck the bottom, Dial set the recommended level into the control unit of the cylinder. Both men could withstand high measures of the gas thanks to their bodily enhancements but they put on small clear masks just in case. He turned the release and the silent vapour flowed into the cellar below. They would have to wait five minutes before it would have pumped in enough to knock out one adult male, they would wait a little longer before the journey to the cellar would be underway once again.

Boltz's admiration for the beauty of Gudrun Schmidt was quite obvious. He stared at her whenever he found a moment between the questions thrown at him by Bergen. Only his stares were not born out of the usual lusts of men. His were darker, and Jay sensed it on every occasion she caught him undressing her.

"And you've never discussed what you've seen or heard with any of your fellow soldiers?" Carl was slow in his delivery, soaking up as much time as possible.

It was a fact which would have normally infuriated Boltz, but the distraction of Bergen's secretary was welcome enough for him to cover the same old ground. "Of course not," he replied playing the model Nazi now, "I am aware of the trust placed upon me."

Carl nodded noting again the desire flashed briefly toward Jay as she wrote in the corner of the lounge. "And you obey these orders to the letter?"

"Of course."

"Like when you leave hatches open on doors that are clearly instructed to be . . ." He looked down at his notebook before continuing, "Sealed at all times when not in use."

Boltz stared across the small table placed between them. He had to fight hard not to show his contempt for the man playing policeman in front of him. He'd sat at such tables before, only they were not the pretend kind like Bergen was now enjoying, they were the real thing, with seasoned interrogators. '*Fucking Officers,*' he thought. '*Why is it you think you know so much more than you do?*' He buried his observation as best he could. "I'd been talking to Sergeant Lehman for but a few moments, just to pass the time. I left the hatch open by mistake. In three years it has happened twice. You can verify my credentials with the doctor."

"I see." Bergen replied blankly.

His tone was growing unbearable to Boltz and his thoughts darkened further, '*You sit there thinking your uniform will protect you from me.*' He had to fight not to smile. '*Presuming those stripes entitle you to play Lord and jury. What do you know about life . . . Born with a silver spoon while people such as me starve and scratch at existence?'* The venom was building. He would have to be careful. He played the thought of slicing the Major's throat through his mind to try and buy off the voices and cool the blood before it threatened to boil over. He imagined how he would then quickly disarm the little gofer sat close to him and knock him unconscious. He would then pounce on the beauty writing her shorthand and pleasure himself on her brutally.

Carl like the others, continued to sense the danger bottled within this man. Although Boltz hid it well for the most part, it was clear to their trained eyes he was at the very least a borderline psychotic.

Carl continued to play the gentleman officer, but he would snap this man's neck like a twig if he so much as sneezed in the wrong direction.

Dorey and Dial slipped out of the loft having locked the ladder into its rigid state. They crept down the stairs and headed for the cellar. They moved like silent assassins, their combat goggles on, their masks pulled down beneath their chin.

As they reached the bottom step they turned into the corridor which would lead them to the pantry. They approached it with the usual caution. Dial crouched down and set to work on the lock. It popped open and as they passed into the food store the placed sneaks beamed the image back onto the control room screens.

"Here we go." Benny said to Marco as he relived his moments at the same door, before glancing across to the doctor as he continued his operation on patient fifteen.

Major Bergen's questioning continued, pressing now toward the extent of the Sergeant's activities within the basement complex. He had no real interest of course, but it would mop up more valuable time. "What do you mean by, *assist the doctor when required*?" Boltz had been looking at Jay more and more and Carl could sense the darkness growing in the man sat opposite.

The Sergeant stared at him. "I mean exactly that."

Major Bergen shook his head. "Would you care to elaborate?"

Boltz made an obvious gesture toward Gudrun Schmidt as she wrote down her notes. "I'm sorry but I don't think I should elaborate here."

Carl saw the game. He wanted permission to say something shocking.

Of course Jay's stomach was far stronger than that of the secretary the Sergeant saw. She didn't look at him as the scitzo translated. Instead her focus remained on her shorthand.

Major Bergen asked him to continue, happy at the minutes being eaten away by this pathetic game. "On the contrary, I believe you *should indeed* elaborate Sergeant Boltz."

The Sergeant stared at the *pompous prick* sat before him then at his gofer seated just across from the table on the comfortable chair. His hatred for them was growing, his lust for Gudrun intensifying. He felt a shudder of pleasure as he imagined her face as she tried to squirm away from him, completely succumb to his power, taken over by her fear. '*I wonder what her reaction will be,*' he thought, '*If I told her what I did to Patient Ten. What I did to Patient Ten under orders from the state.*' He felt aroused, the heat within his trousers growing. He controlled his demons, unaware of course all in the room sensed this darkness. He delivered his first line carefully. He wanted Gudrun inside the room when his secret came out. "Well, only if you are certain."

Carl nodded, much to the Sergeant's delight. "Go on."

"Sometimes I've been asked to help the doctor with his experiments."

"Really?" Major Bergen said with surprise, "And do you have any kind of training?"

The Sergeant could barely hide his smile on this occasion. "Not really."

"So then, what kind of assistance do you offer?"

"It all depends on the doctor of course."

"Well, why don't you tell me some of the tasks he's had you perform."

Boltz was delighted at the major's unwitting terminology. "Well there are the more basic things like fetching and carrying, all on the upper levels of course. I'm also his driver. Genius or not, Doctor Franc hates cars and cannot drive himself." His heart rate quickened as he looked over the sensuous lips of the brunette who still took down notes. Her breathing remained measured, her chest calm . . . She was a strong one. "Then there are our orderly duties. Most of the time it's pretty mundane, the patients upstairs are placid. But sometimes even guinea pigs bite."

Major Bergen nodded.

"Obviously we need to offer a strong arm at times. Some of the experiments and treatments require a certain degree of trauma . . . Patients don't always want to go through with it. But then that's no longer their choice to make is it?" He was growing excited.

"Go on Sergeant."

"Like Patient Ten." He elaborated, "You know, the pregnant woman who screamed throughout your visit?"

Carl nodded. He could see the pleasure this was bringing Boltz quite clearly now.

"Well she was a problem." He could barely conceal his delight, "The doctor wanted a pregnant girl of a certain age for his tests. Only, no matter how much he tried, he could not find one . . . So the decision was made to have one of his own girls impregnated." He stared at Gudrun as she continually took down the notes. She'd remained within a complete state of calm, her writing hand steady. "Only those piss-ant communists and Jews were not up to the task," he said with an evil grin. "We even had to shoot two men because they refused to perform the required act." His lust for Gudrun was almost unbearable now as she had not even shuddered at the awful comment.

He held on to his persona of the helpful Sergeant. "Of course the doctor was furious, so he asked me for my help." He was delighted now with his own use of terminology. "He begged me to forget Patient Ten was a Jewish animal, and asked me to perform an act for the Fatherland way beyond the calling of my duty." His eyes flashed with delight as Gudrun's stare finally moved from her writing and caught that of his own. "And so I took her several times until it was confirmed she was with child." He stared at the beauty whose eyes he now beheld, his passion almost making him want to yell.

But she looked away from him without distress, the moment ruined by not even a hint of horror or fear. Instead she recoiled from him with only loathing worn across her face. Only it was a dismissive loathing and not one born from the terror he'd hoped to instil, *'Fucking bitch.'* During his anti-climax he was very much aware once again he was sat before the pompous Major. *'I bet she's fucking you!'* He thought venomously, as he imagined the gentle smiles passed across the pillow between the Major and his adoring secretary. It made him want to vomit. "It was difficult of course." He managed to continue, "I had to look beyond the Jew and do what was necessary for the doctor and the state." His tone was flat and disinterested now as Gudrun continued with her notes. He clenched his fist under the table and so wished for the hilt of his knife.

Dorey and Dial pulled up their masks. The lock of the door had quietly clicked open and they were given the signal to enter from Benny who confirmed more than enough time had transpired. They drew their pistols then Dorey nodded to give Dial the go ahead.

He gave a silent count of three on his fingers. As the countdown ended, Dial flew into the cellar with his gun pointing outward, Dorey in quick pursuit.

Their goggles granted perfect vision as they surveyed the dark room surrounding them.

"There's nobody in here." Dial declared somewhat surprised.

The enormous basement covered almost the entire ground floor space of the house. At one end a hospital bed stood empty with basic equipment next to it, above it a drip dangled from a higher bag of fluid. A small table stood in the centre flanked by two lonely chairs. In the far corner, partially hidden by a supporting pillar was another bed, only this was a lower, more basic spring ensemble, upon its mattress sat a thick mass of scrunched up blankets. The walls had indeed been covered with lead panels, the grey-beige interior shrouded in shadow. It had a nightmarish quality to it.

There was something distinctly wrong about this place.

"Over there." Dial declared.

Dorey followed with his pistol pointed as Dial moved around the supporting pillar toward the old metal bed.

As he reached it Dial's face sank, his raised gun lowered to his side, "Oh no." he said in a devastated whisper.

Dorey approached the bed, his goggles illustrating the same signs.

Dial holstered his gun and knelt down, slowly reaching out his hand as he stared toward the heavy ruffled bedspread, his face as desolate as Dorey had ever seen it.

The same sickening realisation hit Dorey. He slumped forward onto his knee as Dial pulled back the scrunched up bedding.

He felt his throat close as he looked down at the tragic site.

It was a beautiful little girl with light brown ringlet hair, not a day over ten years of age. Her eyes were closed and she was curled up into a tiny foetal ball. Dial gently pressed his fingers to her throat but her pulse was barely a tremor. He placed his cheek close to her cold nose and mouth uncertain if the faintest of breaths had touched him.

He pulled down the mask as he looked at his friend crest fallen. "She's dying."

CHAPTER FORTY TWO

Dorey sat with his head in his hands. He exhaled as he looked across the room at Dial who sat on the sofa opposite, his head thrown back, his gaze facing the high ceiling.

"This fucking place!" Dial said.

After the discovery of the broken little girl, curled into a ball as the gas took her weak will away, Benny had been quick to force a way through the stunned silence, whispering into the com-link a reminder they still had to find the package, examine the contents then cover the place with sneaks. The interview in the lounge was still taking place at the time while the doctor continued his work upon Patient Fifteen on the camp.

Benny knew they needed to be out of that cellar as soon as possible.

After what seemed like an eternity staring at the girl, Dorey and Dial had finally heard their controller's instruction, Benny pleading with them to complete their task.

They'd placed their masks back on, and set about pressing sneaks into every corner.

As the transmissions were received, Benny had quickly scanned and located a hidden cupboard at the far side of the room. Inside they'd found the items brought over by Boltz only a short time ago. The package was carefully unwrapped. The documents within opened page by page, scanned, and sent to the nearby computer. It had taken a few minutes to accomplish as the pages of formulas and coded entries proved substantial. Once complete they re-wrapped the item, carefully realigning the folds. With the package back in the cupboard, they'd cautiously approached the girl once more.

Dial checked again for the fading pulse. It had been practically none existent, so much so he hadn't even checked her breathing this second time around. They'd both understood the situation. The fragile little girl must have been in a dangerously weakened state to begin with to be no match for the knockout gas. The quantity they'd pumped into the vents was enough to knock out two adult males but it would take considerably more to actually end the life of a healthy child.

Dial had removed one of his combi-pens, a small pencil-like device that with one stab would at least undo the effects of the gas. He'd looked to Dorey and understood as he slowly shook his head. They could not move the girl, could not take her anywhere to save her fading life, remove her from whatever horrors had left her so close to death in this hellish dungeon in the first place. If the combi pen could indeed save her from the effects of the gas she may wake and see the two of them. One word from her to Franc could see all they were here to achieve lost, and still she would almost certainly see her final days out in this place regardless, due to the action they could not take.

Fading within the induced deep sleep, her lack of will to live had taken her to a more peaceful place. So the combi-pen returned to Dial's pocket and as the two devastated men left the room behind, Benny warned Carl's inner ear that Major Bergen had better get rid of the monster they were still interviewing in the lounge.

He'd done so within minutes.

Upon their return more of the doctor's world had been placed at their fingertips, together with a section of his work now being analysed by their computer.

But this achievement had come at a harrowing cost.

The horrors of the hospital had been hard to take. However they'd all been prepared for it and taken some kind of twisted solace in the fact they could do nothing about it. They'd called on their training to help see the patients as simulations . . . To try and distance themselves by making this alternate reality a computerised fiction.

How they wished they could now do the same with regards to the little girl.

When they'd returned, Boltz had only been gone a few minutes and the interviewers were still learning of the horrible truth in the cellar as Dorey and Dial arrived back to the fold.

Carl, Jay and Deans felt sick to their stomach, especially as they'd just witnessed the evil partly responsible, as he'd disgustingly taken pleasure from recounting his stories of sanctified rape. They had indeed sensed his desires to inflict the same experience on Jay's alter-ego Gudrun Schmidt and had wanted nothing more than to get him out of their sight.

They felt a cold emptiness as they replayed their meeting with the twisted Sergeant, and utterly helpless toward Dorey and Dial.

Benny sat in silence also. Through his monitors he'd witnessed the scene as they had. He'd felt the disgust rise through him, stared at the hospital bed and drip, a dark hope running through him that it could only be a part of the doctor's research.

As the controller he'd remained strong and used his short distance away from the room to full effect, pushing and goading his two men forward.

Dorey sighed heavily once again. He tried to concentrate.

Within minutes he would know how much of the doctor's work they'd stolen. He prayed they had it all so he and his team could get out of this place. If they didn't, he was due for another dinner with the Colonel in only one hour. He would make no excuses.

He wanted the Colonel to remain in their pockets.

He leaned forward and rubbed at his head. They needed to focus . . . He needed to focus.

The simple truth was everything was going to plan. But they may well have to suffer this place for a little while longer yet.

CHAPTER FORTY THREE

"Dorey's just entered the Colonel's building." Deans said, following the sneak images.

Next to him Carl manned the monitors protecting their HQ.

Dial stood at the rear with Marco, "Let's sit tight and see what Franc does next."

Both were armed and ready as the response team.

Jay and Benny were taking a break from the operations room. They drank coffee in the lounge and had managed to avoid talking of the little girl for almost ten minutes now.

They'd all been disappointed to learn the research acquired was only a part of the work needed. According to the computer's analysis they now possessed an estimated twenty percent of the total study. Harrowing recent circumstances made it difficult to focus on the positives, though they all understood a tremendous leap forward had been achieved.

They couldn't be sure whether the emergence of Major Bergen and Captain Heiden played a hand in the doctor's action as he'd not said anything of his intentions within earshot of the sneaks. But the cellar beneath his house was clearly a temporary hiding place, and if need arose the team had ways of ensuring Franc would want to store this section of his research with the hidden majority sooner rather than later.

Their only concern was he may have already begun the process of storing the data as two separate sections well apart from one another, despite the Stasis None's confidence to the contrary. If following this parcel led to only a half segment of the overall study then they'd have to take more extreme measures, as their window of opportunity was short.

"Corporal Deit is leading him into the library." Deans relayed. "Looks like the same routine." He panned around the sneaks. "I can't see Von Leising or Brahms."

Deans was proving himself a valuable asset to the team. He'd conquered his initial shock at the recreated world around him. Inwardly he still found it difficult to glance at the sun or stare at a cloud for too long, but he'd found a method of dealing with such things in his own private way. There would be plenty of time to analyse on their return home.

"What about Franc and Boltz?" Dial enquired.

Deans maximised two smaller images. "Boltz is still in the card game . . . Franc still in the records room of the smaller lodge." He added, "Nothing suspicious."

The image of the Gestapo Captain was suddenly relayed as he opened the front door of his quarters. He stepped onto the street and set off in the direction of the Colonel's residence. "There's Von Leising now." Deans announced.

Dial nodded, "And there's Brahms." His image was caught by yet another of their spy cameras. "He's still some way off. That's the other side of town."

"He likes to be fashionably late." Carl commented, his own focus remaining on his guard duties. In less than one hour he would return control to Benny when his prearranged tour of the ammunitions stores and motorcade would get underway. Major Bergen wished to see the military capability of the SS stationed there should the town or camp be infiltrated. During which time a couple of visits to the heads would see him place small, powerful explosive charges behind the cisterns of the toilets. The charges would be powerful enough to rip through the buildings and cause a chain reaction of exploding shells and fuel should it be required. "He'll be fine." Carl reassured, sensing Dial's mood as his focus returned to Dorey, "He's got the Colonel eating out of his hand."

"It's not the Colonel I'm worried about."

"You mean Von Leising?"

"Leising . . . Brahms . . . Take your pick."

They all agreed.

"There's something about Brahms that doesn't feel quite right." Dial continued.

Carl concurred adding, "But I didn't sense anything threatening. There was an air of superiority about him but in a strange, positive way . . . Like he's somehow untouched by the madness going on here."

The image of the little girl burned at Dial. "That's what worries me." He studied Brahms as he headed up the high street toward the square. "Untouched often leads to a sense of being *untouchable*. And that can be a dangerous ingredient in any man."

"You're right to be wary, but I still feel Von Leising is the true threat," Carl stated.

Deans watched as the Gestapo man in question now handed his hat to a waiting steward upon entering the foyer of the Colonel's residence. He observed his manner and decided he was inclined to agree with Carl. He watched as he headed for the staircase, the sneaks able to capture his dangerous arrogance, relaying it onto their screens like an artist with a first rate eye. He would soon join Dorey and the Colonel in the library where another round of verbal jousting would no doubt begin.

As Dorey awaited the return of the tall steward he was surprised to hear Brahms call out behind him, "Captain Heiden." He made his way down the staircase to his rear, "Perhaps I might accompany you on your walk back. It's a fine night for a stroll."

Dorey had managed to take his leave from the Colonel and his two other dinner guests early, claiming the requirement for a good night's sleep was too strong to ignore.

He'd left them with freshly-filled drinks and he wondered why Brahms was so quick to be snapping at his heels.

The steward returned with his hat just as Brahms drew close. "I'll take mine also Carmine, thank you."

He turned to fetch the second officer's attire.

"You don't mind if I walk with you?"

Dorey eyed him closely. Dial had expressed concern over this mysterious person since the first encounter. However both he and Carl found themselves fascinated by him. "Not at all," Heiden replied, "But it's such a short walk it seems almost . . ."

Brahms raised a hand, "I like to walk, and will probably stroll for a good hour to work off part of that dinner," the disarming smile followed, "To have your company for the first few minutes would be an excellent start, before I wonder off alone with my thoughts."

Heiden nodded politely, his suspicion on high alert, "It would be my pleasure."

Brahms turned to the approaching Carmine as he glided toward them carrying the cap. He thanked him and made a quip of how perfectly starched his shirt was, and how he hoped he'd paid the same care to his rifle.

The soldier-come-butler enjoyed the remark. It was most complementary he both remembered and used Carmine's name, and he liked that Captain Brahms hadn't lost sight of the fact he was still a soldier.

Such style was not missed and once again Dorey felt both his liking and intrigue tweaked for the man who posed such potential threat to their operation. He fought it, his alter ego holding one hand toward the door. "Shall we go?"

The dinner had followed a similar pattern. The Colonel, far more relaxed around Captain Heiden now, had played the perfect host. They'd talked of the war and the strategies needed, and were surprised once again at Brahms' incredible honesty. "*The Fuhrer made a fatal error when he engaged the Russians.*" he'd stated, "*While the insanity of his final solution will haunt the German race for an eternity.*"

Verbal war had broken out between Von Leising and Brahms at one point, though they'd agreed upon a surprising quantity of subjects. In fact, it had become all the more clear just how highly intelligent Leising was, and Dorey came to suspect the Gestapo man would have already begun looking to the future. Not only for himself, but for his ancestral aristocracy, and to the preservation of his family's name and standing.

The rights and wrongs of using human prisoners as guinea pigs had been broached and once again Dorey found himself confused as to how a man such as the Colonel could have allowed himself to be embroiled in such an undertaking, his confusion only rising when pondering on how Brahms could have found himself a member of the Nazi party . . . period.

The little girl in the basement haunted him throughout.

Confirmation of Carl's successful trip to the armouries had been transmitted during the main course and as the night wore on Dorey grew more confident the Colonel was indeed on-side. He also suspected Von Leising still had an instinct brewing, that all was not as it seemed in the world of Heiden, Major Bergen and his team of investigators.

The Commander reaffirmed he'd keep a close eye on the situation and remain wary of this enemy despite their technological grasp on the district.

Such musing allowed him to resist any thoughts of how close his team now were. That Franc had already led them to a part of his work and with a little luck and manipulation the rest would surely follow. His German tongue and concentration remained sharp, and all the while he'd watched as Brahms appeared to discreetly analyse him from his place across the table, observing with polite scrutiny rather than overly suspicious interest.

Dorey sensed something strange about this man. Something somehow beyond his own heightened ability to rationalise and interpret such situations and acquaintances. And despite the quiet protest of Dial in his ear and his own natural tendency to want to push Brahms away, Dorey now found himself walking through the dusky streets back toward the postal buildings with Captain Brahms for company.

"Such a beautiful evening," Brahms remarked eyeing the darkening sky. Like Dorey his perfectly accentuated German was flawless. It suggested no region, only high education.

"Indeed it is."

A short silence followed as they headed out onto the main street.

"Von Leising is nobody's fool." Brahms said quite suddenly, "Just outdated." He turned to Heiden and smiled. "He believes his stature and class will buy him immunity from this war. He doesn't realise money alone may not be enough on this occasion."

"Oh really, and what do you think will be payment enough?"

"What you possess that will be of importance to your opponent."

"Doesn't money come under that equation?"

"Usually, but it will take more than just money to provide spoils from this slaughter."

"You have a tendency to speak of the war as if it has already been lost."

Brahms returned his gaze to the street ahead, "Oh come now Captain, we both know such an outcome is already inevitable."

There was a casual nature to Brahm's remark, yet Dorey found his skin to be prickling.

"We're fighting on two fronts against a resurgent Russia who has too many people to throw at us. While Stalin makes our Fuhrer appear like a kindengarten teacher. The Georgian would massacre the entire Russian race if they didn't keep marching forward. Besides, we've given them a taste for revenge."

Dorey didn't give anything away, "Perhaps."

Brahms shook his head, "For somebody who knows our Fuhrer well you seem to be in denial." He added, "He'll never surrender. And with a butcher such as Stalin heading our way that can mean only one thing."

"For someone who also knows our Fuhrer so well you seem to possess a flagrant disregard for his honour." Captain Heiden spoke with a deliberate hint of offence.

Palene enjoyed the first rate performance. "Just because I'm friends with Adolf doesn't mean I've to be ignorant of the situation. He is a butcher just as Stalin is, and considering our current location I don't think there's any sense trying to deny it." Brahms looked to his companion, "And I would tell it to Dolf's face if he were here before us now."

Heiden smiled. "I somehow doubt that." Only it was a lie, as Dorey realised the man walking with him now probably would say such a thing, so fearless did he appear.

Palene thought it appropriate for his alias Captain Brahms to make a joke, "Well, perhaps not quite in those words."

They both laughed at the remark before walking on silently for a number of paces.

"You seem to possess a complete lack of fear," Dorey said suddenly, "At dinner, walking with me now . . . Dorey stared at him, "You seem to hold little fear of consequence. You say exactly what's on your mind with no concern of recrimination."

Brahms smiled. "Oh I have fear *and* concerns. But not of recrimination or punishment." He pointed all around him casually. "My fear is of what will become of mankind."

Dorey returned his attention to the journey but bristled at the sheer sincerity of the remark. He'd never experienced such strong feelings around a stranger before, especially one who posed such potential threat.

Again Palene decided it appropriate to tone down Brahms disposition, "Killing millions of people indiscriminately can only be bad for the human race in the long term."

They turned the final corner toward the postal buildings, Dorey remaining silent as they progressed along the street.

"All I'm saying," Brahms continued after a time, "Is that like the Roman's of whom we appear so fond of emulating . . . We may also find simply destroying races not agreeable to us can never cover the cracks within our own flawed society."

Heiden's reply was quick. "And yet their empire stood for many hundreds of years."

Palene stayed in character, playing the concerned Nazi to perfection. "And yet it's my fear ours will not."

"Perhaps . . . But only time will tell."

Brahms agreed, "Indeed it will."

They were approaching the end of their short walk, witnessed by the unseen who watched via the lenses hidden in Dorey's collar, the sneaks littered through the paths and streets. The tunnel arch leading to the inner quadrangle of the postal building was visible now, like a black hole ahead of them.

"Ah but such is the way of things. Civilisations rise and fall, empires are built then they burn." Brahms smiled, their pace slowing as they approached Heiden's destination. "And perhaps like the race we seem so intent on destroying, the Fuhrer will have Berlin become our very own Masada."

Dorey turned to him as they came to a halt by the tunnel, "Masada?"

"Yes. A place on the Dead Sea where the Jews made a last stand against Rome."

Dorey knew this, but there was no need for his Captain Heiden to. So he curled his bottom lip and shrugged as if in ignorance of it.

Palene's eyes twinkled as they caught the moonlight. "They committed mass suicide rather than give themselves over to their captor's enslavement. A most fascinating place."

"I've never found any urge to study Jewish lies and propaganda." Heiden replied coldly.

Palene marvelled at Dorey's excellent display. "A shame Captain, for I spent many years studying in and around the region.. . . . Masada, Jericho. I found the Dead Sea to be a most fascinating and enlightening place."

"I'm surprised our Fuhrer allows you near, since you hold such places in high regard."

"He allows me near to him because I'm his most trusted weapon." Brahms retorted. "As for understanding history, I make no apologies for it."

"I meant no offence." Heiden replied.

Brahms shrugged casually. "Whether you meant it or not is of little relevance. I am what I am just as you are what you are." He returned to his topic, "It was around the Dead Sea I spent some of my most learned and important years, a home away from home." His smile narrowed, "Being a part of all this now cannot change that, just as it doesn't stop a supposedly unbelieving Fuhrer from searching such places for biblical treasures which may be used for the protection and furthering of his Reich." Brahms took a step back and stared up into the heavens allowing his words to hang in the short silence. "Well, thank you for your company and conversation Captain. And please, except my apologies if you find me a little eccentric in my beliefs." His grin was broad now.

Dorey bowed slightly in polite goodbye. "Not at all Captain, I've found you as always most courteous, and your conversation most stimulating . . . I only wish I'd slept better on my previous evenings here so I may feel up to joining you on your walk further."

"Then I'll bid you good night, and hope we've a chance to speak again before your business here is concluded."

"Enjoy the rest of your walk." Dorey turned toward the dark embrace of the tunnel.

Palene watched him leave, "Indeed I will Captain . . . Indeed I will."

CHAPTER FORTY FOUR

Schneider ran his hand up Ava's thigh until it cupped the heat of her groin. He squeezed as he kissed her passionately losing himself to his desire, his lust close to bringing matters to a premature end. She scratched through the linen of his vest as they made ready for another turn in the sheets.

Ava had always been able turn men wild with desire, a gift which had unfortunately caught the eye of her own uncle when she was but fourteen years of age. Her existence had been pretty miserable both before and after that event, until the day Wolfgang Amadeus Von Leising walked into her life.

He'd stumbled upon her in one of the Munich Red Light Districts' more refined brothels just weeks before her twentieth birthday. He'd been captivated, like all men were, and soon struck a bargain which would see Berlin become her new home.

Von Leising hadn't laid a finger on her until that first night in the capital, when he'd introduced her to her new abode set within its own grounds on the outskirts of the city.

It had been a passionate encounter as three weeks of sexual attraction boiled onto expensive sheets. He'd taken her again and again throughout that night and it had been the most satisfying sex she'd ever known.

Then in the morning over coffee inside the cleanly-decorated boudoir, Leising informed her quite graciously he would never lay a hand on her again, that the deal struck in Munich some twenty days prior was from that moment to be set into motion.

Ava was to be his high-class hostess. A woman he could use in order to further his own position. An asset whom he could call upon to satisfy men of influence, business associates and clients, anyone he felt he could control through sex.

He'd never reneged on his word, and in the years which followed she'd gone from back street whore to beautiful geisha. Serving only those hand-picked by her benefactor and making a good living doing it.

As her beauty and skill grew so had her desire for Von Leising and she'd marvelled over the years at how he'd stuck to his promise. Sex was her weapon and she'd become a master at using it. But in the young aristocrat she'd more than met her match.

He'd loved her more that one night than any measure of men had attempted before or achieved since. Of course, it wasn't just that Von Leising made her feel what it was to be on the receiving end of such sexual prowess, she'd also been seduced by the greatest power of all . . . money.

At twenty-nine she still had another decade at the top of her game. One of those fortunate people with an ageless complexion combined with a body for sin, a body which showed no sign of wilting. In fact, she was sexier now than she'd ever been.

With her retirement guaranteed thanks to the money held within a Swiss bank, an account opened courtesy of her benefactor, Ava was in as good a shape as she could have ever hoped to be. And were she'd once dreamed of Von Leising falling under her spell once more, she now dreamed of her life in the not too distant future when she'd no longer take care of those whom Wolfgang wished to manipulate.

Of those, Schneider was one of her favourites. He was young and full of passion. And though he was way down the food chain in comparison to her usual clientele, she enjoyed how he loved her, how he made the most of every moment spent in her company.

It made him so much more fun than many of her richer, more demanding older men.

Schneider moaned with anticipation as he pulled at his army issue underwear, freeing himself from their restriction. This only excited him further and he moved in toward her.

Ava gently pushed down on his shoulder whispering to calm himself, to take his time.

He obeyed without question and restrained his attack as she kissed him slowly.

"Now, take off your underwear." She said as the kiss ended.

He went about the task immediately, almost unable to breathe through the fantasies now racing through his mind. As he emerged back through the sheets naked and free, he smiled as she gave way beneath him. He moved up her body slowly just as she'd taught him then arched himself into position when . . . 'BANG, BANG, BANG.'

It was the heavy brass knocker clattering against the front door below.

She moved a hand against him. "Who could that be at this time of night?"

"Oh no . . . just ignore it." Schneider pleaded as he pushed her deeper into the mattress.

He was too strong for her but she knew he would never dare take her against her wishes.

Again the knock came in the same thunderous manner, though on this occasion it was accompanied by a shout as the person below realised the window upstairs was open. "Madam Ava, I have an important message for a Corporal Schneider."

Schneider slumped into the bed as Ava wriggled free from beneath him, sweeping gracefully into a waiting dressing gown. He recognised the voice and was sure his night of passion was almost certainly over.

"Madam Ava." The voice called up again.

She was quickly at the window. "Who is it please?" She looked down on a high ranking Gestapo officer whom she remembered meeting at a party almost one year earlier. He was alone, his car waiting at the gateway some twenty metres in the distance.

It was Karl Verstihen, the second deputy head of Berlin's secret police.

He looked up. "I'm so sorry Madam Ava, I realise it's late and most ungracious of me to have to ask, but do you still have a Corporal Schneider staying with you?"

"Why yes. He's asleep in one of the spare rooms, please give me a moment."

"Thank you," he said, as she quickly disappeared from the window. He knew it was a lie of course, just as Ava herself was aware he knew. But it was not good etiquette to ignore the charade of respectability. This was no whorehouse. This was the dwelling of Von Leising's Madam Ava.

Schneider's frustration was complete as he closed the top of his trousers and watched despairingly as Ava slid behind a silk screen and proceeded to dress into the correct attire. Within moments she was standing before him looking respectable and unfazed, which was more than he'd managed for himself as his heart continued to pound in unison with his youthful desire. He finished fastening his shirt then set about grabbing his shoes.

"I'll get the door." She said, before leaving him to his laces.

He heard it open downstairs as further quiet apologies passed from Verstihen to Ava. He swallowed hard as he heard his cue when the lady of the house graciously informed the Gestapo officer she would be in the parlour should he need anything else of her.

Schneider began his descent of the stairs cupping his thick fringe as he went. On hitting the bottom he approached his superior who did not look in the mood for extending the same airs and graces as had just been afforded the Madam.

"Sir," Schneider said loudly as he saluted.

Verstihen almost growled. "Schneider, I have an important task for you to carry out." He held two envelopes, one small and sealed, the second large, closed only with a tie. He extended the smaller document to the trusted rider, "This is to be returned to Captain Von Leising immediately."

Schneider took it.

"You're to hand it to him personally, and only when you and he are alone."

"Yes sir."

"Conceal it in the usual place as you travel." He passed over the second item. "As far as any guards need be aware you're returning from Berlin with an overdue logistical dossier for the Colonel, one informing him of food and materials required in the Capital from the civilian businesses within his township area. This is to be kept on your person and produced on request. Wires and telephone calls will be placed to back up this story."

"Yes sir," Schneider replied as he took the dossier.

Verstihen glanced over toward the parlour door then returned a frosty gaze over the partly dressed corporal. "And Schneider, you're to leave immediately . . . Do you understand?"

His heart broke as the last desperate and lustful hope was washed away with the words from his superior, "Of course sir."

CHAPTER FORTY FIVE

It was past eleven when Boltz discovered the girl, and a further twenty minutes passed before he placed a call to Franc who'd been working on the camp. He'd informed the doctor he should return to the house, maintaining he didn't want to discuss the matter over the phone. Franc had a driver return him home and he appeared anxious as the car pulled away leaving him alone on the driveway.

Things were turning sour this past week and he was certain something bad awaited him.

Dorey sat in the control chair with the rest of the team present, drawn by a combination of disgust and uninvited morbid fascination as they awaited the doctor's next move.

He entered the building, the sneaks relaying the imagery.

Boltz was waiting for him, clearly agitated.

"What the hell is going on?" Franc demanded in a whisper.

Boltz stroked back his dark greasy hair, his high stress level quite evident. "It's the girl Herr Doctor," he appeared to look for unseen eyes before rasping, "She's dead."

"What?"

"She's dead." He confirmed, "When I came back here tonight I went down to check on her. I thought she was sleeping but as I tried to wake her I realised she was dead."

Franc looked furious. "What did you do?" His tone was shrill and accusing.

"Nothing." Boltz declared. "I never touched her I swear. I came home and she was as peaceful as a lamb . . . Dead, upon her mattress."

Franc threw off his coat and stormed past Boltz. "Let me see her."

The Sergeant followed as the doctor headed for the cellar.

He approached the bed where the girl lay lifeless. He sat tentatively and checked for her pulse. He then moved her limbs which were already beginning to stiffen. "She's been dead for hours," he said to Boltz who hovered over his shoulder.

"You see, as I said I did nothing. I only came back from a poker game within the hour. Half the mess would testify to it."

Franc held up his hand for silence. He believed Boltz, but he was at a loss as to how the girl could have died. He was certain the last cocktail of drugs he'd injected should have revived her rapidly ailing spirit. He quickly examined her for signs of suicide.

"Perhaps she smothered herself."

"Was there a pillow or anything over her face when you arrived?"

"No."

"Well then there is your answer." He checked her lips, mouth and eyes, "Besides, there's no evidence of asphyxia or the like. There's no sign of anything. If I were to hazard a guess I'd say she died peacefully in her sleep." He sighed, "Sweet little Natalia."

His words turned the stomachs of Dorey and his team.

"You'll have to dispose of her body." Franc declared eventually, "You know what to do. Take her in the car to the erasing rooms. I'll call ahead and have your passage cleared."

Boltz left the cellar and headed up the stairs, leaving Franc to his quiet vigil.

*

Palene sat within his darkened room, his meditation almost at an end. He'd felt the presence of the light, but was unable to focus on it fully, its power washing through him yet remaining elusive. He'd experienced the freedom and weight of the universe, and shuddered as he evoked the yearning call across time.

The same questions burned, the same need for patience echoed from another more discerning realm of existence. His journey was almost done.

He allowed himself to drift, feeling the touch of stars and the cosmos as his mind roamed freely. He gave in to the spellbinding beauty and floated within the space of himself.

But then the familiar smell of burning came, his peace once again broken. Torment was never far from his dreams, the darkness of his psyche ready to play it out once more. Palene resisted this familiar road, determined he would not allow such suffering to breech his powerful mind. But despite his efforts the smell of burning flesh lingered, followed by the wretched screams which had haunted his soul for so long.

A bead of sweat trickled down his forehead, '*Why do you torment me so?*'

*

The following morning had seen Franc in a most agitated state. He was growing increasingly disturbed by the mounting stresses of the past weeks. First there had been the arrival of Brahms after the Fuhrer's revelations he and his project may soon be shipped to Bolivia. Then only weeks later he found himself surrounded by more agents sniffing around both his work and his activities. The Fuhrer had been most odd with him over the phone, never trusting enough to explain why there was suddenly so much traffic buzzing around him. And now he'd been struck by the tragedy of the previous night.

Although he realised the investigation and Natalia could not be connected, further darkening thoughts of conspiracy had surfaced and they were not aiding his state of mind.

The simple truth was Franc felt like he was choking these past days, and the loss of Natalia left a taste of foreboding in his mouth.

Things were not going his way and he didn't like it one bit.

He'd risen early and left for the camp. He'd already overseen two experiments. However, his mind had simply not been on the job, his growing paranoia getting the better of him.

All the while his unseen tormentors watched through the eyes of the sneaks.

By eleven o'clock his mind finally buckled and he'd decided to give in to his fears. It was time to hide the remainder of his work concealed in the cellars and record rooms, and place it with the rest until he could figure out what to do next. '*Yes,*' he thought, '*Hide the work away until you can get on top of the situation.*' Such paranoia had seen him move from place to place throughout his lifetime, but he could not believe the old thoughts were gaining victory here. In the Nazi party he felt he'd finally found his destiny, and he was most displeased at the possibility of their conspiring against him.

'*Hide the work,*' he reaffirmed, '*Don't allow the notion it could be taken from you to take root. The fake documents and jargon theories will be enough to throw them off the scent. Hide the work in the well then get it to Berlin.*' He seemed happier at the thought, and set about contacting Boltz immediately.

Boltz was getting some rest in the doctor's private quarters on the upper levels. The phone ringing shocked him from his doze. "Hello."

"Get the car and meet me out front in ten minutes." Franc ordered.

The Sergeant looked tired, "Of course Herr Doctor."

Deans jolted forward as he watched on the monitors, "I think we might have something here." He'd been observing Franc's erratic behaviour for most of the morning.

The group quickly gathered and watched with baited breath as the doctor entered a sealed area of the hospital basement before leaving with a bundle of files. He then headed to the smaller lodge where he retrieved yet another mass of documents from a hidden compartment. He made his way out in a hurry, and headed for the arriving car.

*

Schneider had followed his orders and ridden hard through the night, stopping only to refuel and rest on two short occasions. He was still suffering from the attacks of sexual frustration which plagued him since the night before. He'd been devastated at the timing of his superior's call, but he understood whatever was happening was of an urgent nature. This hadn't prevented images of Ava as she lay naked beneath him flashing to the fore of his mind, or eased his torment as he prayed he would see her again.

He approached the town's north gate exhausted but he'd made good time considering the checkpoints. He throttled down as he approached, stopping before one of his colleagues who'd pulled guard duty.

"Hey, how are you?" He asked as Schneider halted the bike.

Deans shot his attention across the screens. "We've got an unscheduled rider at the north gate." He increased the volume of the sneak so he may hear what was said more clearly.

"I'm fine . . . If you like flies hitting you in the face at sixty kilometres an hour." Schneider replied to his friend's enquiry.

"Where have you been?"

"Well I *was* on leave in Berlin. But they sent me back on some God forsaken logistical errand. I'm carrying new audits for the town. Berlin wants an increase in timber, more scrap metal and will no doubt be cutting down on our cigarette allowance too."

The Private laughed as the Gate Sergeant shouted from the hut, "Who is that over there?"

The Private raised his eyes, "It's Schneider, back from Berlin."

"Are his papers in order?"

"It's Schneider!"

He marched over looking angry. "I don't care if it is Rudolph fucking Hess. Are his papers in order?"

Schneider pulled out the phoney documents and passed them to the Sergeant, "How are you today Sergeant Grindlan?"

He took them without reply, "Are these the logistical reports we've been expecting?"

"In the flesh . . ."

"We only received word last night they were coming in."

"I know . . . The Corporal who made that mistake won't be making leave for months." Both he and the Private laughed. It was a good performance from Schneider who'd read his notes carefully before setting off.

Grindlan glared, "Well don't just stand there laughing you moron . . . Open the gate."

And with that Schneider was granted entry to the camp.

"It's to do with the call placed last night from Berlin." Deans confirmed, "It's been relayed across every gatehouse throughout the night."

Dorey remembered, '*Something about a logistics dossier supposed to have been delivered days ago but forgotten. A rather angry officer had authorised it to be taken by a courier who was stationed within their town, but was currently in Berlin on leave.'* Not overly suspicious, but unscheduled all the same. "Keep an eye on him." Dorey instructed.

*

Dorey observed Franc and Boltz as they gathered the documents hidden in the cellar, placing them with those just brought from the camp. "This is it." He said confidently, pleased with the way events were suddenly unfolding.

Deans monitored the whereabouts of the rider as Jay combined her security detail with highlighting the proceedings in the cellar.

Franc sealed the documents into watertight containers before placing them in a large rucksack, "The same routine as before," he instructed.

Boltz nodded then headed up the stairs.

"Carl, I want you Dial, Benny and Marco ready to go." Dorey declared.

The three immediately began collecting their weapons and gear.

Dorey remained with Jay and Deans, observing Franc as he took the documents into the living room. Boltz returned with a bundle of clothing and they both began dressing into new outfits. Within minutes the Sergeant looked every inch the doctor wearing the same hat Franc always wore on sunny days, the same summer coat, trousers and even walking shoes. The town's inhabitants had seen him wearing these garbs on countless occasions.

Franc dressed in the clothes of a labourer, complete with a hunt beater's cap. "Take the usual route along the woodland path. Take your time. I'm on one of my strolls. Circle the town . . . Be seen, but don't be obvious." Franc knew his trusted aid was aware of the drill. "I'll wait five minutes after you've left. After thirty minutes more return here, get changed into your uniform and make your way back to the barracks for your roll call. I'll see you back at the hospital this evening."

"Of course Herr Doctor."

Franc nodded, "Go now my friend."

CHAPTER FORTY SIX

Dial, Carl, Marco and Benny headed up the side of the wood under the guidance of Deans as he followed the mite tracker's beacon. With the decoy of Boltz ignored they were headed high into the forest as Franc ventured deeper into the woodland.

"He's about six hundred metres north west of your position. Remain on current course. He's reached a steeper gradient and reduced his pace considerably." Deans spoke softly into the four hunter's ears.

Jay continued to monitor the sneaks protecting their operation as Dorey now followed the progress of the impromptu rider who'd since parked his bike in the rear garage of the Colonel's residence, delivering the dossier to the logistics Major stationed in Hookah's building. Upon completion of his errand the rider was instructed to report for duty at the guardroom after returning the motorcycle and sidecar to the motorcade.

He disappeared from view as he returned to collect the bike and Dorey was set to end his interest there. But as his subject eventually exited the garage he rode around the main square heading in the opposite direction of the motorcade, instead turning into the lane which held Von Leising's residence.

Jay sensed Dorey's curiosity, "Anything suspicious about our friend on the motorcycle?"

"He was instructed to return the bike then report to the guardroom. But he's disobeyed the order and ridden into Frankfurt Street instead."

"Frankfurt Street . . . Isn't that where Von Leising lives?" There was concern to her tone.

"It is. And according to our sneaks the Gestapo Captain is at home."

Deans ignored the conversation, his concentration placed solely on the path of the doctor as he headed out higher into the surrounding woods.

Dorey watched as his fears were confirmed, "He's stopped the bike. He's heading toward Von Leising's door now." He sensed Jay's concern, "Don't worry, there's nothing to suggest this has anything to do with us." He watched as the rider rapped on the Gestapo Captain's door. Within moments he disappeared inside.

Franc was blowing hard as he approached his destination. It was a tough walk over the thick forest floor and the well wasn't an easy place to locate. This had of course been one of the reasons he'd chosen it in the first place. The woods all around were tall and shielding and the sun had a difficult job maintaining the correct time of day here.

He slowed his approach to catch his breath, closing in on the hidden opening of the long-forgotten hole. The woodland creatures rustled and snapped over branches, and on each occasion the doctor scanned all around him fearfully. There was nothing to see but his edginess remained. He'd be glad when this little expedition would be over. Once he had the complete work hidden in one place he'd make arrangements to move it to a more secure location as soon as the watching eyes left him. If they didn't leave, then he would have to formulate a secondary course of action.

"He's stopped." Deans relayed somewhat surprised at the stamina of their aging quarry. "Four hundred metres, directly ahead of your current position, I'm showing readings of dense woodland. You should be safe to make a closer approach. He may be taking a breather . . . Move forward one hundred metres, then await my signal."

Franc pulled away the foliage and branches which helped hide the old ruined well. Beneath this first layer of camouflage was a corrugated iron sheet which covered the opening. The expanse of this was hidden beneath a layer of earth. Franc dragged away the soil, exposing the metal shield discoloured by the effects of the forest. He panted as he checked the landscape around him once more, the tall trees and steep approach showing no sign of any unwanted guests. He dragged the sheeting clear and took off his backpack, removing his hat so his head could breathe.

"Franc has remained stationary. Target is directly ahead of you, three hundred metres."

Dial spoke almost silently into his intercom. "Okay fan out. Carl you take the east approach, Benny the west . . . Marco and I will split the centre." The four hunters crept along the forest floor with frightening stealth like a pack of wolves moving in for the kill.

Franc wiped the sweat from his face before leaning into the top of the well. He then set about removing eight bricks from the inner mouth. They were old and discoloured and the doctor placed each one of them onto the side of the opening. The whole process carried out with painstaking care.

"Okay, you're all around him within seventy metres. Hold there, await further orders."

The four crouched silently into the brush. They still had no visual as the forest was too dense but they knew Franc was close through the eyes of Deans in the control room.

*

Dorey watched with clear concern as Von Leising and the rider headed toward the square. The Gestapo Captain's face gave nothing away, his silence meaning they were unsure as to what was transpiring despite them unwittingly passing several nearby sneaks. "I don't like the look of this." Dorey said as he watched the two men circle the bend which led toward the Colonel's residence, the sneaks zooming in automatically.

"Jay, be ready to get the truck if things turn sour . . . Is the front entrance secure?"

"Yes."

"Keep an eye on the monitors for now . . . But be ready to go. Deans, if the shit hits the fan you know what to do. Signal the Reeper and prime this place ready to blow. As soon as we have the research confirmed by the computer get to the truck with Jay." He watched as Leising and the rider headed across the square when suddenly he caught sight of the Colonel walking back to his residence. The computer had warned him earlier that Hookah was outside and it appeared chance was to place Leising on a collision course toward him. It was a stroke of bad luck as this meant the Gestapo Captain may converse with the Colonel away from Dorey's earshot. He hoped the camera angle would be acute enough for the computer to lip-read the conversation.

Unfortunately as Von Leising and the rider reached the Colonel, Dorey's frustration only grew. "Leising's just met Hookah in the street," he relayed, "There's no lip-lock on their speech and our receivers are picking up too much background noise to listen in."

The Commander watched as an animated conversation played out, the computer able to make out one or two words as they moved their stance slightly, but it was too nonsensical to build any actual dialogue. The Colonel then began leading the Gestapo Captain and rider toward his resident headquarters.

"They're on the move toward the Colonel's building now."

Within minutes the sneaks showed the three men as they entered the building before climbing the stairs. The Colonel looked flushed, but said nothing to the rather agitated Gestapo Captain who followed. He stormed into the foyer fronting his office and growled at Corporal Deit, "Get hold of Captain Heiden. I don't care where he is, get him. Inform him I need to speak with him urgently."

"Oh shit!" Dorey declared, "It *is* about us." He watched Corporal Deit pick up his phone.

Within seconds their own telephone was ringing inside the control room.

"What are you going to do?"

He looked at Jay who stared at the phone. "Answer it. Tell them I'm downstairs, just to give me a few moments."

She activated her intercom to take the call. "Gudrun Schmidt."

"Ah Miss Schmidt, this is Corporal Deit, assistant to Colonel Hookah, I need to speak to Captain Heiden, it's rather urgent."

"He's downstairs in the quadrangle. Please hold for a moment."

Dorey stared at the monitors as it showed Hookah and Leising now inside his office, the rider having been left outside with Deit.

"It's impossible," the Colonel barked, "How could anybody have the capability to hijack control of an entire telephone and wire network?"

Dorey's heart skipped a beat at the final realisation.

"I'm sure once we have Captain Heiden here he'll clear all of this up." The Colonel then laughed, much to the annoyance of Von Leising, "The very notion of such a thing is quite preposterous."

"I realise it is quite unbelievable, but I can assure you my source is an impeccable one."

Dorey turned to Jay. "Tell Deit I'm on my way."

Jay looked furious but Dorey insisted. "Hello Corporal, he's on his way over."

The Corporal thanked her and hung up the phone.

"Please tell me you're not actually going over there." She fumed, "Our cover's blown!"

Dorey disagreed. "We'll only need fifteen minutes to analyse that work if we move in now. All the time I'm in Hookah's office I can create a delay. You heard it yourself . . . the Colonel thinks Leising has lost his mind. I'll turn this to our advantage."

Jay was not convinced.

"Deans, signal Jim and have him launch. Tell Dial to move directly in on Franc and not to wait for him to leave. Once he's retrieved whatever research is there, have the others hold the doctor at the well until we establish whether the study is complete. If we haven't got it all we'll have to play the abduction card . . . As soon as Franc is secured tell Dial alone to head toward the Colonel's at full speed. Lead him to me, I may need back up."

The Commander's wishes were relayed immediately.

Dorey quickly threw on a chest holster, arming himself with two pistols. He buttoned his jacket then set a small silencer extension over the nozzle of his modified PPK, placing it into the holster on his hip.

"I don't like this." Jay protested.

"I'll convince the Colonel the reason I'm really here is to expose Von Leising as a traitor. He hates him already and won't believe the story about me controlling Germany's wire network. I'll instil enough doubt to buy us some time. Once the computer's studied the work, Carl's team can make for the forest edge on North Street, either with or without Franc depending on the result. You and Deans can head to the square in the truck, pick me and Dial up, we'll then head out to get the others," he made it sound so easy, "If we have any trouble we'll blow this place and the armoury as a diversion then shoot our way out."

"Just like that?" She quipped.

"Just like that. We only need a few minutes." He placed on his cap. "Just be ready to get the truck once I'm inside that office."

*

Franc pulled a climber's rope with a karabiner attached from his rucksack. He leaned into the well and connected the clip to the handle of a now exposed chest sat within the hidden chamber at the roof of the hole. He tied the rope around a tree to his rear so he could retrieve the chest should he drop it into the abyss. He then dug his feet into divots and heaved on the cord until the small chest was clear of the mouth.

He dropped to his knees and took a key from a chain around his neck.

Franc set about opening the sealed unit. As he panted heavily he didn't hear the four armed men creep up on him and he was startled as Dial spoke.

"Herr Doctor." They would continue speaking German until certain of their next move.

Franc almost jumped out of his skin as he turned toward the voice. His eyes grew wide as he saw two officers approaching him with their pistols outstretched.

"What have you got there?" Dial said with a dark smile.

Franc was trying to place the names to the faces when suddenly he heard a twig snap to his right. He looked over to see Major Bergen's bodyguard also approaching with his pistol drawn. "Lieutenant Stoop isn't it?" He stammered, his shock gripping him tightly.

"So . . . What could possibly bring you all the way out here Doctor?"

Franc recognised this new voice immediately as he now swung his eyesight to his left, "Major Bergen?"

Carl stared icily, "Don't move. If you so much as twitch, I'll blow your brains into that well."

"What is the meaning of you following me like . . ?"

"Ah, ah, ah Doctor. When I say twitch that also means opening that foul mouth of yours," Carl interrupted, "Now, stay still and pray you don't annoy any of my colleagues here. They have itchier fingers than I, so speak only when spoken to."

Franc swallowed hard, '*So,*' he thought, '*The Nazi's have indeed betrayed me.*'

Dial moved toward Franc carefully, checking for booby traps. He then holstered his gun and picked up the chest together with the the rucksack. He carried them to Carl as Benny and Marco's aim remained on Franc with cold precision.

Carl knelt and investigated both the box and rucksack. Inside was an archive of work. He opened his com-link, "Deans, sending the data over now." He pulled out a tiny scanner and quickly set about stealing it page by page, book by book. It only needed one glimpse of each sheet to have the information transferred to the computer in the control room so it may study and decode the work in full. Once achieved the data would be stored and later housed within a secure unit aboard the Reeper.

Franc watched the strange device Bergen used, looking on in abject despair as the Major plundered his entire life's work.

Dial moved close to Bergen and spoke quietly. "Right, I'm out of here."

Carl acknowledged him, "Good luck."

Nods of encouragement passed between Dial and the others as he headed out, back down the hillside as fast as he could go.

CHAPTER FORTY SEVEN

Dorey took a breath as he entered the foyer manned by Corporal Deit. No armed guard awaited his arrival though the young motorcycle rider remained on one of the waiting area chairs as instructed. Dorey headed toward Deit with assurance.

"Ah Captain Heiden . . . Thank you for coming so soon."

Dorey felt the burning eyes of the rider as his name was announced. He fired him a look to let him know he was not one to be messed with. The piercing stare saw the youngster's gaze sent immediately downward, the confidence of his youth quickly trickling away.

Deit headed to the Colonel's door and gave his customary knock. He entered with Dorey just behind him, "Captain Heiden to see you Colonel."

There was no friendly hello, only an air of tension. "Colonel," Dorey dipped his head in greeting, "Captain Von Leising."

The Colonel waited for the door to be closed then gave Captain Heiden a stern expression.

"Is there something wrong gentlemen?"

Hookah immediately glanced over to Leising who took this as his cue. "Yes I would say there is something wrong Captain. A discrepancy has come to my attention and I was hoping you could shed some light on it."

The Colonel could see Heiden's annoyance at Von Leising's tone and tried to mediate, convinced it would all be just a simple misunderstanding. "We have a few questions that require answers Captain."

"Really?" Heiden replied, as if curious about the situation.

"Yes really." Von Leising declared. "But before we begin I'll ask you to excuse me for one moment as there is a matter I must quickly attend to with my man outside."

The Colonel looked on astonished as the officer who'd demanded this meeting left the room before it had even begun. He was up to something and both men knew it.

Dorey took his chance knowing Dean's watchful eye would monitor proceedings in the foyer, "May I ask what this is about? Both you and the policeman seem a little, hostile."

The Colonel looked embarrassed. "I apologise for the curt manner in which you find yourself before me Captain, however I must ask you to be patient as Captain Von Leising does have legitimate enquiries which need to be answered."

"And should I take it from this schoolboy manner of which I'm being subjected, these enquiries are in some way incriminating toward me?"

"He is the Gestapo District Head, and as he's so happily reminded me, has jurisdiction in such matters. I must therefore decline to give you any details until he has seen fit to question you first."

"Question me?" Heiden laughed, "My dear Colonel perhaps I should consult a lawyer."

The Colonel did not share his amusement, his concern evident as the Gestapo Captain re-entered the room.

Deans relayed what he'd just witnessed via the sneaks. "Von Leising's rider has just been instructed to have four guards sent to keep you in the confines of the Colonel's office. He's then to head back for the bike and see it refuelled in the motorcade. From there he's to head to the next village where a tank column has been mobilised. He's to pass on instructions they're to surround the town as quickly as possible."

Dorey listened to the urgent transmission as Jay declared, "I'm going after the rider. I'll have Deans seal the control room then get the truck as soon the computer's confirmed the work. If it's incomplete, the abduction goes ahead. Cough three times if you understand."

Dorey coughed gently as he watched Leising circle toward the barred window.

"You need to keep them talking in there for nine minutes before Deans can leave to pick you up. Good luck." Jay ripped off her skirt, quickly replacing it with a pair of armour fabric long-johns matching that already next to the skin of her arms and torso. Once donned, she quickly put on her trousers. A pair of boots followed and within a minute she was cocking her pistols and placing them on her person. "Set the detonators. Once the computer has confirmed the information either way, get to the truck. If it is incomplete have the others bring Franc with them . . . Let Dorey know you're inbound as soon as you're underway. Head for the square and await his instructions." She put on her jacket.

Deans glanced over his shoulder. "It's all in hand . . . Just watch yourself."

"Get them out of there Deans . . . I'll see you real soon." And with that she was gone.

"I suggest you inform me just what it is you *think* you know Captain . . . I'm not the type of man you should provoke," Heiden declared.

Von Leising reached into his coat and pulled out an envelope. He'd wanted to study his opponent's face as he delivered the killing blow. "It is most commendable you show such conviction in maintaining this little charade of yours . . . Even when you must now know the game is up." He handed Colonel Hookah the envelope.

"Now you really do sound like a policeman." Heiden replied, noticing his enemy had discreetly unclipped the holster for his Mauser pistol.

Von Leising pointed, "Within that envelope lies cast iron proof you are not who you claim to be."

"If there could be such proof, a notion which of course is quite ridiculous, then I'm certain the Gestapo would not bring me here to merely answer questions . . . I would have been arrested already."

Quick as a flash, Von Leising withdrew his weapon, "And who is to say you are not being arrested?"

Deans watched the unfolding events then quickly looked over the scanning computer. Its nine minute signal had only just turned to eight. "Come on." He said, as he primed the detonators around the postal building, armouries and motorcade.

Dorey stared at the pistol trained upon him with cold eyes.

"Captain Von Leising . . . This was not part of our agreement." The Colonel protested.

"Colonel Hookah I am afraid in this matter you have allowed your judgement to be impaired by a very clever individual . . . One who is operating under the protection of a technology we have not yet discovered for ourselves."

"What the hell are you talking about?" Dorey scoffed as he looked to the Colonel.

"I am talking about Captain, the fact you were never ordered here from Berlin, you are not an agent of the Reich . . . You are a foreign spy."

Dorey laughed hard, "Quite incredible," he shook his head, "Have you lost your mind?" He looked to the Colonel. "I can pick up that telephone right now and have the Fuhrer himself on the line within minutes. Not only would he verify exactly who I am and what I am doing here . . . he would also . . ."

"Spare us your lies Captain." Leising interrupted. "Whatever device it is your Allied Command has developed so you may manipulate our phones and telegraphs has been detected." He appeared delighted his instincts had proven correct. "I've spoken with the Gestapo hierarchy in Berlin via a messenger sent after I'd first laid eyes on you. He's spoken directly with our high command who state categorically you do not exist."

"We're not supposed to exist you fool. Did your people speak to the Fuhrer himself?"

"Captain Heiden, or whoever it is you claim to be, I have absolute clarification within that envelope, the Fuhrer has not sent you here."

Dorey turned to the Colonel, "This is nonsense. A device able to manipulate encoders together with the telegraph-wire and phone lines from here to Berlin?" He shook his head with incredulous disbelief, "Have you heard what he is saying? You yourself Colonel have spoken to your superiors . . . Spoken to men way above this Captain's pay grade. Men you know personally."

"I do not claim to know how you've done it . . . I would have thought it impossible also. All I do know is that you have. Perhaps spies have cut into our cables, with the employment of impersonators . . . who knows?"

Again Dorey laughed as his confident alter ego replied, "Oh you've really outdone yourself Captain. Truly you have. Secret spies, an army of impersonators who can pass themselves off as your colleagues." Again he shook his head in disbelief as the Colonel watched on closely.

"My colleagues, Captain Heiden, are the ones who've provided the information in that envelope. They have access to every level of security within this land. And they've been given express orders from the Fuhrer himself you are to be arrested with as little fuss as possible so he may ascertain just how it is the Allies have managed to create such a weapon of manipulation. The order is in the envelope . . . Right there." He smiled darkly. "A column of tanks are awaiting orders to close in on the town as we speak, and all of this was achieved by the old-fashioned method of sending a runner rather than a wire. Now Colonel, open the envelope and you will see for yourself the man standing before you is an impostor. Once you've read it, sign a written order and hand it to Deit. Have him deliver it to the officer of the watch so he may see Major Bergen's team arrested."

With all the charges activated Deans set about instructing the SiSTER. It was to pump out as much false information as possible as orders were sought. They would create a maximum amount of confusion across the command before the whole phone network blew, devastating the communications of the entire district. The armoury and motorcade would be blown to kingdom come if the requirement arose. He'd relied on the computer warning system to let him know if any guards were on their way for him, quickly gathering his weapons while trying to keep his own eyes and ears on the screens beaming events inside the Colonel's office. He was still awaiting confirmation on the research. "Four armed guards have arrived in the foyer." He said quietly into Dorey's ear, "But so far Deit hasn't picked up the phone. I think they may be trying to take you quietly, not wanting to risk the telephones before they come after any of us." He checked the timer on the screen and relayed it to the Commander. "Four minutes remaining."

The Colonel opened the envelope, not happy with the dramatics employed by Leising.

"In a moment Captain Heiden you'll realise you have been discovered. That we've broken your little web which has held us these past days."

Dorey watched as Hookah read over the documents. "That file is a fake Colonel."

Leising laughed as he kept his gun trained. "Oh my friend you really are something."

The Colonel read the order from Hitler's own hand, giving the Gestapo Captain carte blanche so he may capture the spies in the act, so they might discover their technology.

Dorey persisted, "For it is Von Leising here who is the real traitor Colonel . . . not me."

"Oh bravo Captain Heiden," the Gestapo man said scornfully, "A last and desperate attempt to try the old reverse psychology routine . . . How very unoriginal."

"You wanted to know when I first arrived what my true motives were. Well now you see them. As you so rightly ascertained from our first meeting, I am a spy, not an investigator . . . That is indeed the domain of Major Bergen. You've been wondering since my arrival, why send a spy with Bergen's team? Well I'll tell you . . . to play spy-catcher."

The Colonel glanced up from his reading and observed the man being held at gunpoint as Von Leising laughed once more, shaking his head.

"Is that the best you could come up with?" he crowed, "Then prey tell me Captain, why is it you have stood in this room listening to accusations these past minutes yet only chose this moment to expose me for who I truly am . . . Upon the very moment the Colonel is reading the documents that will seal your fate?"

"Two minutes." Dean's said into Dorey's ear as the computer broke more of the codes.

"Because I had to be sure you were the . . ."

"Stop speaking now Captain Heiden." Von Leising cut him dead. "As much as my good humour can appreciate your games I will not allow you to infect the Colonel's mind and endanger my situation." He tensed with the Mauser, "Sign the order Colonel and have it sent to your men."

The papers before the Colonel seemed to be in order.

Dorey smiled, "You see Colonel. It's our Gestapo man who is the concerned party here."

"I warn you Captain, I will kill you."

The Colonel looked up at the two men and clenched his fist.

"For you know that no such technology could possibly exist."

"Captain Heiden!" Von Leising snarled.

"You know who to believe here. Is it the man with easily faked documents?

Or the magician able to manipulate and imitate the entire Reich command?" Von Leising cocked the weapon and took aim, "Not one more word."

"One minute."

The Colonel was growing anxious.

"Sign the papers Colonel." Leising's anger at Hookah's dithering peaked, "You have your order," his voice raised into a furious demand, his eyes momentarily leaving his aim, "Now give the order required from you!"

Dorey took his chance, drawing his pistol at incredible speed, shooting Von Leising through his right eye. Unfortunately the Mauser within Leising's grip went off, nullifying the silent shot which had just seen its master killed.

The crack echoed throughout the room.

"We have the research! The computer has confirmed, we have it all!" Deans relayed.

With the guards about to enter Dorey turned on the Colonel who'd ironically become certain it was Von Leising who'd been lying, that Heiden had almost certainly gone for his gun in self-defence. The thought seemed surreal now as he saw the weapon of Captain Heiden turning on him. To Hookah it transpired in slow time. He looked at his new friend pleadingly as Dorey pulled the trigger, the image of his lost wife flashing into the fore of his mind as his mouth fell silently open. The shot hit the Colonel between the eyes and he slammed back against the wall in a splatter of blood.

Dorey checked the barred windows but they were solid, he considered shattering the wall with his mini-mag ammunition when Dean's voice came flooding into his senses. "Four guards outside the door. Two on either side of the lock, two in rear cover formation." He paused, "One now reaching for the handle, the group no more than three metres apart."

Dorey pulled out a second pistol and activated the mini-mags on both weapons. He took cover behind the Colonel's desk and trained his aim to the co-ordinates given. He squeezed the triggers administrating an attack from the future. The walls around the entrance together with half the door disintegrated into splinters, plaster and screams.

"Clear." Dean's voice came as he witnessed the hits, two of his sneaks cutting out as they were destroyed. "You've got nine soldiers coming up the main entrance. Deit was knocked out by the blast. Head across to the library and out of the door at its far end. It will take you to the service stairs. Get down to the basement level and head right . . . Go along that corridor to the back door . . . I'll be there in the truck as soon as I can."

"Deans before you seal the computer instruct the SiSTER to spread the rumour Von Leising was the spy, that it was he who killed the Colonel."

"Got it."

Dorey would thank Deans later . . . It was time now to make his escape.

*

Carl finished packing the final documents into the chest. "We're good to go." He was still using his native tongue. Franc remained on his knees, his hands in the air throughout. He wondered who these people were with their strange gadgets, men who both spoke and listened to people who were not even there without the use of any visible radio device. He could feel the cold dark chill of the well-mouth behind him as he watched Major Bergen reseal his entire life's work.

"Dean's has confirmed." Benny said now in English. "It's definitely all there. He's headed for the truck. We need to get to the north road between the town and the gate."

Carl stood upright, the small chest tucked under his arm.

Franc scowled through his confusion. "Who are you people?" he stared at the Major, "You're not Nazi's."

"No, we are not Nazi's Herr Doctor." Carl agreed coldly, in crisp English.

Franc was at a loss as he stared at the chest now in Major Bergen's possession, he was desperate. "Wait!" He pleaded, "What you have there is but the tip of the iceberg." No response came. He tapped his forefinger against his temple. "Merely ground notes to an endless wealth of information all held in here."

Carl stared at him and shook his head. "No Doctor."

"Take me with you. I'll continue my research for whoever it is you work for." He could not bear to see his work slipping away. "There are no limits to what I could achieve."

Carl's cold stare remained, "Thank you doctor, but we have all we need right here."

"You'll never decipher the codes. You need me to . . ."

Benny interrupted as his scitzo translated, "We do not need you Doctor." He looked at him knowing he understood his English perfectly.

"Please," he begged, "Don't take away my work. I've devoted my entire life to it. Nobody knows it as well as I . . . I couldn't live without it."

Benny walked toward Franc, holstering his pistol as he approached. He moved in close as the scientist looked up from his knees. "Who said anything about letting you live?"

Franc stared into the eyes of his captor and wished with all his heart he'd not just allowed the last sentence to escape his lips. He cupped his hands as if to pray, once again aware of the cold draught breathing up behind him from the deep well.

"Natalia sends her regards." Benny declared. And as the doctor's eyes widened he raised his boot and hit Franc with powerful force across his chest.

He flew backwards into the well, his head smashing against its lip as he went. He screamed and his body crumpled, his yelping echoing as his bones cracked against the cobbled wall of the hole.

Benny turned to the others. "Let's go."

CHAPTER FORTY EIGHT

Schneider entered the motorcade still wondering just what it was he was involved in. When he'd handed over the documents given to him by Verstihen in Berlin, Von Leising's reaction had proved difficult to read. His expression appeared a mixture of dark venom and cold satisfaction. The Gestapo Captain had said nothing more as he dragged him across the square toward the Colonel, though his ears had been pricked by the following talk of spies and treachery. He'd remained outside the Colonel's office as one of the officers mentioned had reported and was startled when Von Leising then ordered him to deliver instructions that would see armoured reinforcements encroach the town.

Despite his bewilderment, he felt pride in the fact he was obviously playing a key role in something far larger than himself, *'Perhaps I'll get a medal.'* The thought was a delicious one as he searched the motorcade for any sign of life. There was none, so he set about refuelling the bike and placing a drum in the sidecar. He happily missed the part were he was to fill out the paperwork. Von Leising would clear up any such discrepancies. *'Besides, it was not his fault the lazy bastards were shirking their work.'*

He returned the fuel can to the hazardous waste room at the rear of the garage and wondered how impressed Ava would be by his shiny button awarded for Services to the Reich. As he turned to make his way out, he nearly leapt out of his skin as he noticed the beautiful brunette now standing in the doorway. He felt immediately embarrassed. "I didn't realise there was anybody else here." She was an officer but of which branch he could not be certain. The fact she wore trousers suggested she may belong to the transport sheds but he'd never seen her before. "Is there anything I can help you with Ma'am?"

She smiled but said nothing, and as she stepped into the room Schneider noticed a distinct sense of menace lurking behind the rich brown eyes.

Dorey met no resistance as he headed through the library. He peered around the door leading to the service stairwell. He could see a guard at the bend of the steps on a small landing some ten feet below. He couldn't be certain if the guards categorically knew who they were hunting. He hoped with each telephone receiver picked up the SiSTER would be confusing the situation with the Von Leising story. However, he also knew it was unlikely the guard on this stairwell could have received any such renewed information. He placed his pistol behind his back and slowly pushed open the door. He stepped out on the landing and turned onto the steps. The guard sensed him as he approached.

Dorey smiled readying himself to lunge forward.

The guard looked shocked and drew his rifle but in that instant Dorey pulled his pistol and sent two shots into his head. He caught the body and steered it to rest on the landing. He peered around the bend down the flight of steps, relieved to see nobody there. Dorey realised his alias had returned the salute of this man on more than one occasion during visits to the Colonel, yet the guard had drawn his weapon the moment he'd laid eyes on Captain Heiden. It dispelled any remaining doubt. He could only hope now the SiSTER could at least confuse the situation further a-field, away from the Colonel's residence. "The guards here know I'm a spy." Dorey announced into his com-link. "I'm heading for the basement corridor of the Colonel's building." He turned to negotiate the flight of steps, hoping he could make the truck without further killing.

Benny and the others heard the message and continued down the hill of the forest. They'd checked their co-ordinates and were headed toward the woodland edge where it met the north road. It was hot work keeping up a good speed even in the shade of the dense, awkward woodland. The lightweight armour was snug around their bodies and the additional vest only added extra unwanted insulation. They had no time yet to stop for a drink . . . that simple pleasure would have to wait until they'd reached the road.

The truck roared across the cobbles, headed out of the narrow lane of garages. As it reached the end its tyres locked, the body shuddering as Deans screwed it into an almost impossible right angle turn. Deans shot it down in gear before opening up the horses and flooring the accelerator. It bellowed as it powered forward headed for the turn which would take it out onto the main street. "Jim has the Reeper in the air," he declared over an open channel, "I'm in the truck now, headed for the rear exit of the Colonel's building . . . ETA two minutes." He gunned it forward hitting the next bend aggressively. So far he could see no large force headed toward the square. He eased off the gas slightly as he entered the main drag. '*Calm down.*' He told himself. '*No need to attract attention.*'

Jay pushed Schneider's legs into the broom cupboard and shut the door. With the bike ready to go she could quickly meet Deans and the truck at the rear of the Colonel's building. She holstered her pistol as she picked up a rider's cap and goggles. '*No harm in disguising my face.*' She opened the door of the waste room and peered out. It looked clear so she headed toward the bike. She placed the goggles on the fuel tank and was set to put on the cap when a voice she'd heard before called out, "Do not move or scream Miss Schmidt, for I have my pistol aimed directly at your head."

She turned to see Boltz stepping out of the shadows with his gun trained.

After making it back for roll call he and the rest of his mess had been alerted of a disturbance at the Colonel's residence. He'd been delighted and most surprised when he'd headed out of the rear exit of his building to see Gudrun Schmidt sneakily following Von Leising's man Schneider as he headed into the motorcade.

"I must say Miss Schmidt, I prefer you in a skirt." His eyes were dark as he stepped into the light, drifting into an awful smile.

She readied herself.

"Now, what I'd really be interested to know . . . Is what brings a pretty little girl like you into a dirty little place such as this?"

His voice was sickening, the double entendre repulsively pathetic. The image of him boasting of his exploits as he'd eyed her fancifully flashed through her mind, as did the shock of little Natalia. "I hardly think that's any of your concern." She stated.

He chuckled. "Oh come now Miss Schmidt, tell the truth, did you come here looking for me?"

As his dirty eyes played down to her crotch she took her moment, going for her pistol at lightning speed. But as she touched the hilt of the weapon a crashing pain splintered across her shoulder and she crumpled down to the floor with a groan. She tried jumping to her feet but felt a boot smash into her stomach with unbelievable force, sending her sprawling across the floor.

Before she could regain her senses she felt her hair being pulled back and the muzzle of a Luger stuffed into her cheek. She could feel Boltz's breath as he leaned in close.

"Because I most certainly came here looking for you," he snarled disturbingly, his monstrous face creasing with sadistic pleasure, "Only I did not come alone."

Jay felt two powerful hands heave her up onto her feet as if she were nothing more than a rag doll. She managed to turn just enough to see the hulking giant that was Sergeant Lehman, who began laughing like an ape as he held her.

"Where are your gallant male officer friends to protect you now?" He enquired in a mocking tone, "You stuck-up slut, teasing me across the table like that." His eyes narrowed, "Yet now I learn none of you are who you claim to be," he smiled at Lehman as he held her then moved in close sticking the Luger under her chin. He slobbered in her ear as he whispered passionately,

"I'm going to fuck you ma'am . . . And when I'm finished, he is going to do the same."

Lehman began to laugh as Boltz pulled the gun away reaching his free hand to the rear. He lifted up the tail of his jacket then brought back his fist now grasping the hilt of a hunting knife. Its blade gleamed as he moved it close to Jay.

Her heart beat furiously, her brain working overtime. The grip of Lehman was incredible and she had to fight through the building mist of venom as Boltz came toward her again. '*Focus.*' She told herself, her implants rippling throughout her system.

Boltz continued to point his gun as he used the razor sharp knife to slice open the buttons of her jacket. It fell open revealing the shape of her heaving breasts beneath her blouse.

The sight delighted Boltz and he re-holstered the pistol while keeping her under the point of the knife so he may take the rest away.

Jay began to shake and sob as Boltz grabbed her blouse and tore it apart.

His sickening smile however, was stunted by the strange and disappointing sight before him. For instead of flesh and lingerie, his eyes were greeted by a strange skin-coloured garment which was about as revealing and erotic as thick thermal underwear. He scowled and was about to tear at the hideous vest when something leapt to the fore of his brain. It was a thought so instantaneous he'd not even had chance to process it until it was too late. '*She's no longer sobbing or shaking.*'

Before the hulk of Lehman came close to such a realisation Jay gathered enough slack so as to slam the back of her skull straight into the jaw of the oversized bear.

He yelled in pain and released her as he stumbled back.

Boltz was quick to react as he plunged the knife forward with a snarl.

Jay expected it and braced for the impact, the blade snapping in two as it hit the armour.

Boltz jaw dropped in disbelief but in an instant he was grimacing as Jay slammed her palm into his solar plexus crushing the base of his ribcage, sending him hurtling backward to the floor. She whipped round at speed just as the injured Lehman went for his pistol, his shocked face and bloodied mouth making him appear mentally challenged. As he drew the gun Jay sprung forward and released the same palm shot only with twice the space for forward motion. It hit directly into his lower ribs, snapping them like twigs. He screamed out like an injured dog as he fell to the floor in a heap.

Jay quickly ended his misery by jolting the crossed fore fingers of her right hand into his eye socket, down into his brain. The spasms running throughout the nerves of his body caused him to convulse as he died.

She was off him in a second and grabbed his fallen Luger, training it on Boltz who tried desperately to hold up his own weapon as he choked through his pain. She fired two rounds into his arm sending the gun clattering across the motorcade.

She approached as he groaned and writhed on the floor. On noticing the snapped knife at her foot she stopped to pick it up. Jay then closed in on him like feline death. She knelt, pulling the blubbering mess close to her face. "You like hurting girls . . . Don't you?"

His eyes were wide with fear as he gurgled in pain.

She snarled as the half blade was shoved into his throat with deadly force. She allowed him to slump to the deck, the sound of his choking echoing across the motorcade.

Jay then headed for the bike and sidecar and quickly placed on the cap.

She kick-started the engine and by the time the sound of the motor had roared into the distance, both of her attackers were dead.

"I'm in the basement corridor." Dorey announced as he pushed his way through a small, frantic army of kitchen staff all heading in the opposite direction to take shelter in the cellars. An allied air raid had been signalled courtesy of the SiSTER and as far as they were concerned this was by far the safest place for them to take cover. "I'll be outside in one minute." Dorey passed an open door and was surprised as a guard lunged at him from behind a large dishevelled chef. He dismissed the attack like it was that of a child, twisting away from the lunge and pulling the arm into an impossible position until it popped out of its socket. The guard hit the floor with a yelp and was then knocked out cold by Dorey's heel. This seemed to antagonise those who witnessed the action, and they began shouting and yelling as they ran.

Dorey continued his journey and had only one bend to negotiate before he'd reach the rear door. He shoved past another kitchen hand and was set to check around the corner when to his shock he found he'd bumped directly into the path of Captain Brahms.

Upon realising the threat he immediately placed a lightning attack toward Brahms throat to ensure he was incapacitated. However to his amazement, instead of feeling Brahms crumple to the floor, Dorey found it was he who was suddenly off his feet.

Before he could understand what had happened Dorey crashed onto the base of the corridor. He leapt up in an instant and saw that Brahms was desperate to speak when suddenly two silenced gun shots tore into his forehead sending him clattering to the floor in an explosion of blood and skull.

Dorey turned to see Dial stood ten feet away, his arms still outstretched with the pistol in its aim. Dial glanced at the dead officer then over to the Commander. "Let's go."

Dorey looked at Brahms and felt deeply saddened at his abrupt end, but within seconds he was running out of the back door, sprinting toward the waiting truck.

"There are troops gathering at the front of the building. They've only just found out what's going on." Deans called through his headset as the two men approached.

Dorey noticed the scattered bodies of five soldiers, Dial's handiwork while on his way into the Colonel's building.

As Dorey and Dial raced into the rear compartment Jay's voice flooded their com-links. "When you see a motorbike and sidecar come into view, don't shoot . . . Because it's me." Moments later she came powering into the delivery entrance of the Colonel's residence and slowed into a skidding stop. As she did she immediately came under fire. The bullets tore through the sidecar as she tumbled off the bike behind the cover of the truck.

"There's a shooter on the roof." Deans yelled.

More bullets showered down as soldiers took up position.

Dorey reached out, screaming at Jay to make a jump for it. She did so and the moment she was safe inside Deans revved the truck, slamming it into reverse and turning it about, the wheels screeching as it now headed for the street. The gunfire riddled the rear, but the bullet-proof fabric was more than a match for the assault.

"There are troops gathering near the square," Jay yelled, "I ran into Boltz . . . His barracks knew it was us they should be hunting."

"Get your helmets and goggles on." Dorey ordered as another wave of bullets ricocheted off the truck, thumping into the protective covering above their heads. "Deans, hit those shooters. As soon as we're clear give the signal. We need to get our heavy gun mounted."

Deans had the truck pinpoint the positions of the aerial bombardment. It locked on, one of the truck's rear launch tubes firing a rocket. It flew into the side of the building where the walls met the roof. The explosion tore half the upright and most of the tiles clean off as the truck sped out onto the open street.

"Clear." Deans yelled as he brought them to a halt.

The three in the back quickly set about mounting the heavy gun onto the rotor which would protrude the roof of the bullet proof lining. Once in place Dial took position on the three hundred and sixty degree firing mount. "I'm hooked in," he yelled as he was raised upward into a firing position.

Deans floored it as Dial set to work hitting his targets, the rounds of the powerful gun tearing up all in its wake.

*

Benny, Marco and Carl crept to the edge of the wood beside the north road. They crouched low and took the opportunity to drink some water and don their goggles.

The distant whine of the air raid siren finally abated and they could hear the heavy gun of the truck as it pounded its targets together with the accompanying rattle of returning fire.

"We're at the forest edge approximately two hundred metres from the north gate."

"We'll be with you in one minute." Deans replied.

Dorey entered the conversation and with him came the rise in volume as the truck's big gun now pumped directly through their com-links. "Stay in the woodland edge, we'll take out the gun nest on our approach."

The truck roared into view, headed for the three men at speed with Dial at its top firing to the truck's rear. Suddenly, the repetitive thud of the North Gate's own heavy gun began ringing out as it took its chances on the oncoming target now within its sights. The heavy calibre rounds whizzed past Benny and the others. The shots struck the truck head on, bouncing off the windscreen, radiator and wheels, pounding into the armour. A tyre took a hit but it was remoulded the instant it exploded. Deans flinched but withheld his course.

Dial's gun was tearing their pursuers apart to the rear but as Dean's requested the aim of one of his missiles Dial announced, "Try and save them for the tanks." Dial swung his gun around to the fore and let rip with a powerful assault, deadly with its futuristic aim. The mini-mag shells tore the gatehouse to pieces, the ammunition store sparking the fuel dump at its rear sending a pluming explosion into the air, "North Gate is down," he swung the gun to the rear but for the moment nobody had the urge to continue the chase.

Deans hit the brakes, the truck juddering past the waiting band, stopping some ten metres beyond the three men in the brush. Jay threw open the rear and she and Dorey knelt into position to offer additional covering fire.

Deans studied the remains of the North Gate, his goggles zooming in, working together with the trucks dashboard displays. There were no signs of life.

The three were out of the woodland's edge and up on the road running to the rear of the truck. The chest packed with the research was thrown in before the trio vaulted into the interior. The doors were drawn closed, the inner lighting replacing the daylight, the lenses of their goggles adapting accordingly. They all strapped themselves in.

"Use the side road past the square, take Brewery Lane and head for the South Gate."

"Got it!" Deans replied.

Dorey relayed the code to their base computer activating its five-second countdown.

As the silent count commenced several soldiers on the other side of town had just managed to break open the door ready to storm the postal residence. As they entered, the powerful explosives ripped through the strongbox holding their equipment, leaving only a plume of smoke where the old post building had stood. The shock wave tore through the town, startling both soldiers and residents alike. Moments later, two further explosions tore the sky, followed by dozens of smaller eruptions as the armouries and motorcade went up, taking several more soldiers with them.

Deans powered the vehicle around a bend causing Dial to wince from his position on the gun mount. Within a moment they were charging down the town's side road heading for Brewery Lane, which would take them toward the well-rehearsed South Gate exit.

Dial had the gun spin to the front as the truck flashed past buildings, narrowing in on his left and right. The roar of the powerful engine coupled with the cobbles underfoot made it sound like an angry dragon.

Deans powered them over a junction, taking them onto the desired route. Although soldiers were on the adjoining streets no fire came their way as Deans had the vehicle on the next lane before anyone realised what was happening. "We're on Brewery Lane, heading around the square. We'll be hitting the main street any second now."

They prepared for the truck's entry back onto the main boulevard knowing they were bound to hit stiffer resistance.

"Here we go." Deans took them around the bend, the dashboard displays working with his combat goggles to alert him to any dangers, "We've got a ground machine gun on the pavement ahead and two shooters on the flat roof."

Dial needed little prompting, dispatching all threats beamed into his goggles with a volley of fire, rapidly changing direction on the swivel with the assistance of the computer.

The truck squealed as Deans slammed them onto the main drag with a wobble.

Dial held on before spinning the weapon to their rear once more.

Behind him was a scene of chaos. There was smoke bellowing from their nearby former residence and motorcade, while soldiers ran about the square looking for the most part confused as to what it was they were supposed to be fighting. That was not the case however for the small armoured car which quickly hurtled through the smoke and was now giving chase at their rear. It let rip with astonishingly accurate fire, striking the small protective shield covering Dial's gun position. He crouched low, "Jesus."

Further shots sprayed against the advanced heavy skin which protected the trucks rear, the stretched fabric catching the bullets as they hit with a melody of thuds.

Dial recovered and again let rip with his weapon.

The armoured car did remarkably well, the driver slamming it up onto the pavement with a bounce, avoiding the first volley thrown against it. It smacked against the wall of a shop before its flight was corrected causing its gunner to flail from his position.

As it retook the road Dial fired again, the rounds punching through the light armour as if it were play dough. The car buckled and twisted before ploughing into the building to its left, the crunching metal folding as it slammed. He then sprayed the rear of the street with a further dose of carnage, hitting buildings and anything else that took his fancy. The explosive rounds and heavy shells tore the street to shreds in a fury of bullets, explosions and thick heavy plumes. *'Nobody will be coming through there in a hurry.'*

He turned to cover their forward journey. As he did, he just heard Dean's warning of a shooter just as the startling sound of his helmet being hit sent a piercing echo through his ears. The force sent his head jolting backward and it felt for a moment like his neck would snap. He recovered his senses just in time to see the rocket which now flew out of the truck's front, its tail of smoke screeching as it tore head on into a building. The roof exploded into scattering debris as Dial realised both his helmet and Deans had just saved his life. He shook away his shock as the truck bounced over the carnage.

"We're coming up to the South Gate." Deans announced as another hail of bullets rained down on them. Again Dial punished the mistake, blasting out with the powerful gun.

The truck smashed through a barricade leaving the main drag of the town behind as they headed onto the outward road toward the South Gate.

Dial began picking off the soldiers who fired on them. "You'll have to take the gate out!"

Deans called upon another rocket just as his windscreen was hit by machine gun fire, but again the glass punched it away as if it were a swarm of angry hornets. The truck acquired the target and he saw soldiers running to positions behind the sandbag forts. "Fire." The computer assessed the force required, the resulting explosion sending bodies, sandbags and wood high into the air. Almost the entire fort of the South Gate barrier was now levelled, leaving a crater together with jagged foundations and debris in its wake. "Brace yourselves." Deans announced as the truck approached.

It drove violently into and across the hole, its' engine roaring and wheels whirring as it took to the air. It hit hard as it came down. Another tyre shredded and reformed, the modern suspension crunching onto its springs as it bounced violently through.

Dial grasped his restraints with all of his strength but his head jutted forward, smashing his nose as he hit the surrounding shield. The passengers in the rear gritted their teeth as their restraints held them firm, their skeletons assaulted by the violent ride.

Deans recovered the momentum then floored it onto the south road. They were clear of the town, the carnage and smoke quickly retreating behind them. "We're through."

The others looked at each other shaken but relieved. And though not out of danger yet, smiles were passed around nonetheless.

*

As the sun beat down through the cool air of the Alps, Dorey and his team awaited their pick up. They'd met no further resistance on the road out of the town, and no air strike was called against them.

All troop movements were now being manipulated and directed by the SiSTER aboard the inbound Reeper. Despite this, the team remained in a defensive, combat position.

Dial continued to man the gun on the roof of the truck with a bloodied nose.

The second of the schwere weapons had been set onto its mount and was covering them in the distance under Marco's careful eye.

It wasn't too long before they heard the Reeper's signature sonic boom echo through the heavens, announcing Jim's arrival.

"Locked onto your signal . . . Bringing her around." The pilot's voice flooded through their senses for only the second time since he'd left his polar hideout. All other communication had gone through Deans so as to leave the rest prepared for any impending action.

The Reeper dropped into the lower atmosphere and they could hear the distant rumble of her jets. They looked up into the crisp summer sky until they located the black outline, the ship circling the mountains in the distance.

It was always one hell of a sight to see her coming in for them.

"Bringing her in now," Jim declared, as he turned her toward his landing site.

CHAPTER FORTY NINE

The journey home had been a routine one. Deans had looked uncomfortable as the arms of the hangar reached around the ship to fish her out of the river, her engines burning ferociously to steady her. All but one of the passengers had laughed at his expense, their mood jovial at having completed their mission without serious injury or loss.

Dorey however, found himself brooding over the death of Brahms, despite his attempts to dismiss such notions. They were all back safe and accounted for. But he couldn't help but dwell on the unwanted killing. Something just didn't feel right about it, simulated or not.

They'd not intended to blast their way out of the town. The ramifications of killing so many while perhaps altering the very course of the war in the process would usually be most unwelcome, but this mission was always about locating the work of Joseph Franc, removing it from the path of history to see if it was the illusive key to saving mankind.

Over the next few days they would relive their experiences in Germany and would help Deans digest all he'd experienced. So far, he was still doing remarkably well.

Analysis would come later, when they'd pick out the things they could and should have done better, but for the moment it was to be a triumphant return.

After decontamination they'd met with Brookes and relayed a brief run down of the trip while his scientists retrieved the chest and set about examining the stolen research placed onto the crystal chips. They'd witnessed the usual envy on the face of Stein, who unlike Brookes had never been given opportunity to witness such things first hand.

As always these proceedings had taken a considerable time before all bases were covered. A detailed official report would follow once the team were rested.

Brookes and Stein were intrigued by the description of Captain Brahms and surprised at the obvious speed and ability this man must have possessed in order to have put the Commander down so easily. And it was this factor which prompted a more private discussion with Brookes after the rest of the group was dismissed.

Stein was not happy when he'd also been sent on his way, ordered to set about retrieving the first images of this mysterious Brahms from the recorded archives.

"And you maintain he did not catch you off guard?" Brookes enquired of the attack.

"It's always difficult to read such a thing with any certainty. But I reacted in the same instant he did, which should have meant he'd be on the floor before he could realise what was happening. Yet somehow, it was as if he knew exactly how my attack would come, and he very skilfully used my own strength and speed against me."

A concerned expression shrouded Brooke's face. The thought of the anomaly immediately played on his mind. How it had not left the system before it was sealed, leaving them once again without a direct trace.

"Whoever this guy was it was obvious from the beginning he was different. He was well-travelled, well-educated, opinionated and fearless of his situation. It's possible such a man may have journeyed to the right places and learned such combat skills, just as it's possible he may have simply possessed gifted reflexes. All I'm saying is it's never happened to me before unless inside a gymnasium fighting one my own team."

Brookes looked troubled. It was time to come clean with the Commander. "I have news which I fear may anger you somewhat. I can only hope once you've heard me out you'll understand the judgements made with regards to this so called anomaly."

Dorey edged forward.

"When I described it to you I was deliberately vague, concentrating on how the investigation of this glitch inadvertently led to the notion of stealing Franc's research. This was true of course, but I refrained from granting you full details of the anomaly itself and for this I apologise." He paused, "I'll get straight to the point. During analysis of the Constantinople mission, Isabella Usorio discovered something most unusual. Data which suggested the possibility of an outside source entering our timelines."

Dorey was stunned.

"Highly theoretical as well as highly unlikely I might add. The signature left by this anomaly suggested it was manufactured artificially, but also that it connected to our timeline from a point two hundred years ago in our real past. Essentially, suggesting something may have entered the timeline from our actual twentieth century."

Dorey scowled, "Can that even be deemed a concern? How could anything predating the birth of our system gain access to timelines that would not yet exist?"

Brookes concurred, "The main reason why it was described only as an anomaly." He added, "However, while trying to discover the meaning of this glitch another occurrence was discovered soon after, this time with a slightly altered signature appearing in the timeline that took you into World War One two years ago."

"And this emanated from the same source in our real past?"

"It's all highly theoretical using software alien to the Stasis None, but yes."

"So why didn't you tell me?"

He looked ashamed, "I would like to tell you it was because I didn't see how it could possibly pose a danger, that it was down to the sheer implausibility and uncertainty of it all . . . But the simple truth is there is no excuse. An event such as this is a possible danger no matter how far fetched, and it is a danger I should have brought to your attention."

Dorey contemplated the doctor's words. Brookes had his absolute trust and he wasn't certain how he should feel about this revelation. His initial reaction was one of understanding, as he shared his boss's feelings on the sheer absurdity of it. But there were bigger issues at stake here, "You're right," he declared after a moment, "With regards to anything that's relevant to the safety of my team you should have told me. But I also see why you wouldn't." His brain powered through the variables, "So can I assume that in telling me now, something more has come to light?"

Brookes looked on his Commander admiringly. "A short time after the Reeper left for 1944, Doctor Usorio found what she believed could be the same anomaly entering the same timeline, on this occasion the entry signature emanated from Paris several weeks before you arrived. I give you my word this data never came to light until after you'd left. Unfortunately, whatever this thing was it never jumped out before the system was sealed, so once again we were unable to trace it."

Again Dorey was shocked, but this time his brain leapt to an immediate, if somewhat surreal link, "Brahms came from Paris." He was surprised by his willingness to accept a connection, "Are you thinking he could be in some way related to this anomaly?"

"I really don't know," he added, "To have beaten you like that," this was unfamiliar territory for Brookes, "And so strange for a man with close affiliation to Hitler to be talking of Masada and the Dead Sea in such an affectionate manner."

Dorey agreed. "For a Nazi officer it would have been strange in its own right. But like I said, it was the way in which he relayed the information. Like he really wanted me to understand he'd been there." An eerie quality suddenly entered the room.

Brookes leaned into his chair. "I'm almost sorry Mark was forced to kill him." He corrected, "Though not at the risk of any harm coming to you of course."

Dorey remained deeply troubled by Brahms' death. "But that's just it," he said earnestly, "I knew he would never have harmed me. I understood it, throughout the entirety of the mission now I come to think of it." Such words were not easy for Dorey to say.

Brookes could see the hurt in his recollection, and he wondered how difficult it must be for the Commander and his team at times. He suddenly felt all the more ashamed at not divulging all to his trusted soldier. "I cannot begin to imagine how there could be a link between this man and the answers we seek, but it is something we should certainly look at it in more detail." He smiled and decided now was the right time to see Dorey rejoin his friends and get some much needed rest. "As always Commander I salute the courage and ability of both you and your team. I thank God you've returned safely." He stood and extended his hand. "Get some rest, discuss all we've spoken of with your colleagues, we'll meet in the morning to dissect everything piece by piece." As he took Dorey's palm in a firm handshake Brookes declared with gravity, "And Commander . . . Rest assured I will never keep anything like this from you again."

Dorey felt the sincerity, accepted the apology, before turning to make his exit.

*

Brookes was furious, "What do you mean erased?"

Stein was at a loss as he spoke into the intercom, "The crystal data, all of it . . . It's gone."

"And the photographic files?"

"Being formulated as we speak. But all video and data saved to the crystal chips are certainly lost. The hull was breached during their journey through. Evidence points to the continuum entering the secure data storage facility, damaging its seal. It would appear the Reeper was infected before she even made her return journey home."

Brookes scowled, "And yet the Reeper brain was not affected in any way?"

"The Reeper brain has more sufficient armour and considerably more fail safes."

Jim and Jay had informed Brookes of how the jump into 1944 battered the ship.

He glared at Stein, "How long before the photo images will be ready for viewing?"

"Sir, the entire mission will be ready and waiting on file within the next twenty minutes."

He was inexplicably haunted by the thought of Dorey's mysterious adversary. "I'm coming down, I want to see that footage the moment it's ready."

CHAPTER FIFTY

The light burned at his brain. He groaned under its power, his throat tight as he tried to speak. He felt the weight of a thousand people as he fought to move. He tried to raise his head. '*This isn't real,*' Brookes told himself as he willed his body to react, '*Open your eyes and you'll be able to move.*' But he couldn't open his eyes, couldn't wake from the dream, the weight pinning him to the cushion, the light too bright to bear. It shone through his eyelids as if they were tracing paper, urging him to see, and yet he knew he could not possibly understand. He almost yelled out as he tried to focus his will, struggling against the force which held him under its paw.

'*Wake up. This isn't real . . . You've to wake up in order to be free of it.*' His mind was reeling as it tried desperately to obey, his tongue swollen as it slid behind clenched teeth.

The further news from Stein informing him of the strange faults within the photographic data had seen him work through the night, his mind hooked directly into the raw power of the Stasis None. Such rare action always took its toll on him, and all he'd desired was one hour of peaceful sleep in order to recover.

Finally the light abated and he could feel his senses returning. He felt his eyelids flicker, the weight across his body reduce. He heard silent words echo through his mind, their warning distant, not quite clear.

As such notions broke free so did his body and Brookes jolted upright out of the chair.

He scanned around the secret lab at the base of the complex, still sensing the presence of the light, still feeling its heat. He looked at the ceiling and to each of the pulsating walls, but of course, there was nothing there.

*

Dorey and his team had been subjected to the usual collection of tests since rising early within the complex. Blood samples, urine analysis, hair follicles, eyes and ears, all of them studied before their hearts and enhanced limbs were put through their paces in the gymnasium, and all before breakfast. Soon, the team would record statements to partner the video footage, the mission discussed from the moment they'd landed to the second they'd returned. It was a tedious process at times.

All would be blended with the work carried out by Stein and the computer over the coming days until the predictive element of their wondrous machine would be unveiled. During this complex process Dorey and the others would be granted a short leave of absence, and as the morning got underway they were already looking forward to some down time in the Priory that evening.

The Commander was changing for breakfast when the hailing signal came over the speaker, *"Commander Dorey, please contact the RFC . . ."*

The team members deactivated com-links during gym work and Dorey had not yet reactivated his since enjoying a short but peaceful hot bath. He curled his tongue in the rhythmic chomp chosen as activation, "RFC this is Dorey."

It was Brookes. "Commander could you come up here, there's something I think you should see."

He was immediately curious, "I'm on my way."

"I'm going to request the rest of your team report to the RFC debriefing room until we've spoken," Brookes added and within a moment it was relayed across the airwaves.

"Can all members of Commander Dorey's team please report to RFC debriefing room."

Jay entered his quarters just as the message was broadcast. "What could that be about?"

"I don't know. I just spoke to Brookes he wants me up in the RFC right away."

"Did he say what it was about?"

"No. He just told me there's something he wants me to see."

"That sounds ominous."

"Precisely what I was thinking," he walked over and kissed her cheek, "Come on we'll get the others and head up there."

*

The RFC was only half full when Dorey arrived but it was awash with activity. Stein and Usorio were busying away in front of their respective screens, Stein looking particularly concerned as scientists scurried to compare data and findings.

Brookes appeared his usual calm self, but beneath this facade the Commander could see how these new events had affected him. "The energy source emanating from the six locations is made up of properties similar to the anomalies discovered by Doctor Usorio." His tone was thoughtful as he pointed at the display in front of them.

Dorey stared at the six separate energy signatures, "Amman, Jerash, Jericho . . . *Masada*?" His shock was evident, "The Dead Sea," Dorey said it aloud as a strange sense washed over him. "And this signal has just been located?"

Brookes nodded, "A few hours ago. But not only do we have a clear grasp on the signal, Doctor Usorio has managed a perfect lock on a tunnel which can directly link us to the location in question at precisely the right moment in time," he shook his head, "There are no odds of such a thing happening coincidentally . . . Because it simply *does not* happen."

Dorey understood. Their journeys into recreated history were predetermined by a mass of available factors which allowed their powerful machine to provide an access tunnel to a possible destination. The chances of one being miraculously available, with the necessary ingredients, at precisely the moment a viable destination had been announced, was not luck. Somebody or something was inviting them to the Dead Sea in the fifth century.

Dorey thought on the resonance of Captain Brahms' words when they'd walked back from the Colonel's dinner together. He was tingling all over.

"It seems Brahms and our mysterious anomalies may be connected after all. And it would appear whoever he was working for is now inviting us to meet."

"It could be a trap."

Brookes could sense Dorey's lack of conviction. "And yet you do not think so?"

Dorey surprised himself with his response, "No. And if you ask me why, I'm afraid I cannot answer." He stared at the screen and thought of Brahms again, the feelings of curiosity he'd felt for the German officer now multiplying with every breath. "In any other situation I'd say categorically this is a trap. And yet I cannot honestly state such a thing in this instance." He concentrated, "I realise how unprofessional my next comment may sound, but I would go as far as to state, I can feel it in my gut."

Brookes looked at the strong, intelligent man who'd served the project so impeccably. He held more pride and admiration for the Commander than he'd allow anyone to know and was pleased at the usual straight response. "It's strange you should say such a thing," he said, "For I'm inclined to tell you I feel exactly the same way."

Dorey was surprised. It wasn't like Brookes to base his opinions on anything other than hard fact.

"Whatever this thing is, it's making contact with us, and it is doing so from within one of our very own recreations. Yet there's no evidence of an entry or exit point into this timeline. It's as if it were already there." Brookes shook his head in continuing disbelief.

"I told you when Brahms mentioned the Dead Sea I felt affected in some way. I put it down to the fact he was such an unusual man, who just happened to be a Nazi talking about places of great significance to the Jews. But I *knew* somehow it was something deeper . . . Something more." With Dorey's focus no longer governed by the mission, he'd allowed himself to dwell more deeply on events just passed, and he'd had a sleepless night as a result, haunted by strange dreams.

"There's something else you should know." Brookes tone was soft. "After our discussion yesterday we hit a problem. The entirety of the mission data recorded to crystal was lost. Turns out the effect you all suffered in the ship when dropping through to 1944 corrupted the seal of the Reeper's protective storage facility. Naturally I accessed the photographic back up. But when I studied the photo images I came across something quite odd."

"Odd?"

"The footage once spliced together was distorted, marginally blurred. We can watch events unfold but the image is like looking through distorted glass. So far our computers have been unable to counter the effect. The only clear data we've retrieved is the physical work you stole and brought back in the chest." Isimbard stared down at the screen, "When I saw this impossible event happening, I just knew we were meant to go there, that we must now unlock the secret of this anomaly. If we can gain access to such answers, I believe they could be of huge benefit to all we're trying to achieve."

Already surprised at hearing Brookes speak in such a manner, Dorey was stunned as he realised where his boss was going with all of this, "You're going to send us back there?"

Brookes almost enjoyed the astonishment, despite the fact all he should have been sensing was danger.

"How will you get clearance?" Dorey asked, surprised at the sudden realisation of just how much he wanted it too, "They'll never risk the Reeper and . . ." He stopped, reading the expression on the doctor's face. "You've already got it?"

He nodded slowly. "That's when I called you up here. I've just come from an emergency meeting, the vote went through on a split decision but the general consensus was we need to know what's going on. They believe if the Reeper is kept airborne we can orchestrate a successful investigation on the ground with continuous air cover. I'm sorry I didn't inform you of this sooner but time was of the essence. And I just knew when I saw this thing we had to make contact." Brookes was clearly excited. "The Reeper has been checked over and given a clean bill of health after some minor repairs through the night." He stared at the Commander, "So what do you think?"

Dorey examined the data. "It's a small entry and exit window."

"Twenty-nine hours. Just over a day to see us prepare, investigate . . . then get you out."

Dorey's talks with Brahms flashed through his mind, conversations which somehow took on new emphasis. He found himself smiling though he did not know why. His tactical mind reeled through the options. "How long before we could be ready to launch?"

"Four hours. Leaving no more than twenty-five once you're through, though we know how different the timescale can be on these things. But so far the Stasis None tells me you'll have plenty of time to get in and out safely as the time variance will not alter beyond six hours to our own."

"It sounds very confident and precise for a change."

"Doesn't it?" Brookes exclaimed in an unusual way.

"I'd need conformation the tunnel is good, and a working plan to ensure the safety of my team." It was a futile statement as Dorey once again sensed somehow his group were not in any danger. "It would indeed be safer if we can keep the Reeper in the air." Dorey was more than a little surprised by his own willing. He took in the ramifications of the display, a plan already beginning to formulate, "The guys won't be too happy when I tell them to suit up again." It was most unlike the Commander to be relishing another jump so soon after getting back, especially when the situation suggested any possibility of a trap. He looked at the doctor still shocked he'd managed to get such an undertaking authorised. Such an event would normally see both men running for the hills, but like Brookes, he was finding himself overwhelmed by a sense of wonder and curiosity, the likes of which he'd never known. And if he was going to tangle with this thing at some point, he'd prefer to do so head on rather than while distracted within another mission. He contemplated a little longer. "We'd better go break the news to the others."

CHAPTER FIFTY ONE

The team were stunned by Dorey's unquestioning acceptance of the bizarre new orders. Dial in particular was concerned the Commander's liking for the recently deceased Brahms may be affecting his judgement. "Are you crazy?" Was one astonished remark, "Just because you found *him* affable doesn't imply the people he may represent will prove likewise. If indeed they are one in the same thing as this anomaly."

A heated discussion broke out and Brookes had resisted the urge to remind them it was not a request. However, he had felt it necessary to remind Dial it was of the uppermost importance they learned what this anomaly was, that contact should be made, that this was the kind of potential breakthrough the project was set up to discover.

"Not at the expense of this team." The Texan's response had been firm.

The others proved equally concerned, Carl firmly behind Dorey, the rest behind Dial.

"You tell me how you can possibly guarantee the safety of this team when sending them into a scenario such as this . . . Without any forward planning." Dial had raged on.

"It's *recon* only, with the Reaper as air cover." Carl stated in support of Dorey's plan.

"You must be out of your mind."

"The Project needs a go on this Mark. I'm fairly comfortable with the mission parameters. It's no more risky than most reconnaissance operations, the likes of which everyone here has been involved in at some time or another."

"Such operations often prove disastrous, even when you know what you're up against."

"Not with the Reaper as cover."

"And what if they have a Reaper . . . Or something worse?" Jay had voiced her concern.

"The Stasis None has verified no such technology has passed into the timeline. In fact, nothing has passed into it at all." Brookes intervened.

"Well if nothing has passed into it why are we going out there?" Dial had been furious.

"Because the Project is telling us to," Dorey interjected, "And if we're destined to come across this thing then let's do so armed and prepared, not caught off guard while distracted on another mission."

Eventually tempers had cooled.

If the project wanted this to go ahead that was exactly what they'd been recruited and trained to do, none of them would go against their mandate. But it didn't make the pill any easier to swallow, nor did the notion of Dorey's total willing. He'd usually be the first to question such a rushed together idea, one which could so easily prove to be a trap. But if they could not fathom his willing they did begrudgingly understand his theory. If anything were following or watching them, it made sense to tackle it head on, armed and ready with the Reeper as cover, rather than caught with their pants down while immersed in another assignment. They knew Dorey would only accept such an undertaking if he genuinely believed in it. But it was the unknown element adding quantity to their fear, and dealing with the unknown was something they tried to avoid, especially in the case of their usually precise and careful Commander.

"This could so easily blow up in all of our faces." Dial had wanted to bring up Moe to emphasise his point, but even under these circumstances found he just couldn't do it.

Jay had added, "If this *is* an opposing force of any kind, my main concern is they could be using unseen technology to hide any modern weaponry waiting for us. If you ask me to trust in the capability of the ship I have no problem with that once we're on the other side...But to trust this computer without question?" She doubted the so-called *exact readings* placed on the table by the usually cryptic Stasis None. "If this thing can place itself inside one of our timelines without trace, then follow such an act by providing a ready to go tunnel we can hook onto to take us in and out, then who's to say it isn't capable of a whole lot more?"

Dorey agreed but reiterated it would be the Stasis None which would hold direct control of their exit at all times, keeping it permanently open during the narrow window.

With the promise of a fast exit available and the Reeper providing constant air support they'd gradually felt a little easier.

Time was against them, and once their focus was united in achieving the goal, their planning and solutions had got underway with earnest.

And now only a short time later, the team entered the Reeper for the second time within only a handful of hours, but despite their best efforts, the majority did so under a cloud of apprehension.

CHAPTER FIFTY TWO

Jay swung the Reeper over the Dead Sea. The decided method formulated had seen their ship armed to the teeth. She would remain in the air at all times.

Dorey and his team were to investigate each area emanating the energy pulse as an armed attack group. The drops and pickup of personnel done via fast-winch, enabling the ship to make a speedy launch into the heavens should events take an unwanted turn.

The Reeper would remain on hand to provide aerial cover to both themselves and their exit. Once any contact was established Dorey was to implement a process of directives as set out by Brookes which he would deliver to any alien power discovered. From then on it would be up to the Commander and his team should further action prove necessary.

Peaceful understanding was all they sought but what both Dorey and Brookes failed to fully admit was the fact they each sensed there was something bigger to this strange, unforeseen scenario, something altogether more intriguing than any foreign organisation's interest in their technology.

It was in neither man's nature to act on such instinct alone but for differing reasons they'd both found themselves compelled to do so all the same.

Nobody was under any illusion. If this was indeed a foreign power or agency at work, then Dorey and his team would be of huge interest to them, as would their ship.

However as they'd made their entry the Reeper reaffirmed the Stasis None's findings, informing them they were indeed the only modern-day force within this new realm.

Despite this, as Jay levelled the ship, she scowled at her updated flight readings, "Dorey I'm getting some strange data here," her voice was immediately concerned, "According to the computer our exit window is due to close in one hour and forty-eight minutes."

Jim was quick to confirm. "Roger that. I'm getting the same information through the time navigation system. Our exit will shift from this time-zone in a little under two hours."

"How could it have changed so drastically?" Dorey enquired.

"These are the new readings we're receiving." Jay declared.

The ship had only entered the fifth century atmosphere above the Salt Sea some three minutes earlier. Preliminary readings had shown the incredibly smooth jump landed them within the unprecedented accuracy of only a half-hour blip between the time expected and the time they'd actually arrived. And yet both pilots were saying despite this perfect jump, they now had under two hours in which to establish possible contact across six different locations before their entry tunnel would slip from this existence.

"Still no modern technology on the ground or in the air. No jamming device obstructing the ship. Still no response to our transmissions," Jim clarified, "The six energy sources have been pinned down. Confirming it's the actual townships themselves that are the energy readings. No individual source is present within them. The towns *are* the source!" His trepidation grew, "We can't search them all in the time we have."

Dorey looked at Dial as he enquired of the co-pilot, "Could we investigate each source in two teams of three, alternating the pickups? Would it give us the time we need?"

"Those weren't our orders!" Dial exclaimed.

"I know they're not our orders. But we have to go down there."

"We're supposed to go down as one unit."

"As one unit we can't sweep all those towns in the amount of time we now have."

"For something that apparently wants us here it's going about introducing itself in a very odd way don't you think?" Benny added.

Jim listened to his computer. "Ein Gedi will prove the more complex and most densely populated. If we rotate two teams of three to search each of the towns we'll struggle, but one team of two working against a team of four leaves us one other option."

"Go on."

"The computer's suggesting Masada. It could be effectively covered by a two-man team. The others will prove much harder with any less than four. The ship can drop two operatives, one taking the higher level of the fort the other the garrison township below," he clarified, "This is the only option the computer states can realistically work."

"If whatever this thing is had wanted open discussions then surely it would have contacted us the moment we arrived." Marco objected.

"If it's so important to bring us out here in the first place we should at least try to establish contact." Carl argued.

Dial sighed sensing the inevitable. "It's your call. Under normal circumstances your instincts are always good enough for me. But if you want my advice, I'd turn back now."

"There's no reason to believe we're under any threat, and until such a time we simply cannot justify not checking something of this importance. Besides as I've already said, if this thing is going to become a shadow hanging over our missions from now on, I'd rather know what it is sooner rather than later.

And I'd prefer to investigate it in our current situation with weapons and air cover, rather than stumble across it on some future mission armed with a bow and arrow."

As much as he wanted to disagree Dial naturally understood such pragmatism.

Dorey was using precious minutes. He had to make a decision. He had no intention in separating the team like this but he could see little alternative, while his instincts told him all would be well. He knew it made little sense, but the overriding understanding no harm would come to them remained. "Listen," he said after a moment, "I realise how crazy this must sound. But I've the strangest feeling we're not in any danger here. I genuinely believe there's nothing sinister waiting for us down there."

Carl was quick to add. "I agree. And I can't explain it anymore than Dorey can."

Dial frowned. "That guy Brahms has melted your heads." He looked over to Dorey and held his gaze. If he had to come across this danger he too would want to face it with the Reeper flying close by while holding a rifle in his hands. He saw the usual sharp instincts burning behind Dorey's eyes. "If you're adamant you're going to do this I'll go with you to Masada, let the rest search the remaining locations with air support."

Dorey relayed his orders without hesitation, "Jay, take me and Dial to Masada. Once back in the air drop three landing beacons by the shore. We can activate them as a further distraction should we need it. Take the Reeper and cover the others as they search the larger townships one by one." He set his watch. "Head out the moment Dial and I are on the ground." He looked to his team some of whom gave only reluctant nods of agreement, "Alright let's do it. Let's find out what this thing is then get home safe."

CHAPTER FIFTY THREE

As Dial explored the garrison settlement at the foot of the towering landscape, Dorey ascended the broad slope which scarred the mountain's edge.

Centuries ago this climb made up part of the Roman siege ramp, used to attack the fortified plateau in which Jews, making a last stand against Rome, chose mass suicide over slavery some seventy years after the death of Christ.

The Reeper had dropped them at the foot of the mountain before setting off to have the second group-search the remaining locations. Locals had scoured the sky for the ungodly noise as the Reeper switched from stealth to an all out burn.

However as both Dorey and Dial searched their respective sites, the acute fear of those looking upward, turned instead to the oddly-dressed strangers as they moved swiftly by.

Dorey made his way to a part-ruined steam house, one of a handful built for Herrod an age before. He headed down the stony steps to take a look, cautious of what may be laying in wait. Two more locals eyed him. They too had heard the strange rumble of the Reeper and remained edgy to confront him as a result.

He paid them little attention as his instincts led him on.

*

Once the landing beacons were set off the locals soon lost interest in Mark Dial. The fusion of light sent high into the sky dazzled like some biblical rainbow.

Some chattered wildly, others bent in prayer, the majority were simply afraid. It had allowed Dial to move through the buildings in search of the energy source, as the curious locals were drawn to the distant four-hundred-foot tower of light particles.

He checked his watch. He'd been searching for almost one-and-a-quarter hours to no avail and had just been informed a similar outcome awaited the larger team now trawling the final settlement of Ein Gedi, its residents terrified by the flying black demon.

He opened his com-link to the fort above. "Dorey, I don't know what the hell it is we're supposed to be looking for, but there's nothing here. The other four towns have proved the same . . . Call the Reeper in and let's get out of here."

From somewhere up in the fort at the top of the plateau Dorey replied, "There's less than thirty minutes more, just keep looking a little longer. There must be something."

*

Dorey watched as the beacon began to fade. They'd been a welcome distraction as he'd searched the settlement. He would activate the final light show after this model burned itself out. He'd searched the bath houses and stores but found nothing, yet he remained certain something was here. He moved toward the only remaining buildings, their burnt orange bricks carved from the surrounding sandstone hills.

His goggles confirmed the near end of his search. He sighed, '*Am I missing something*?'

Far in the distance Ein Gedi was nearing completion for the others. Most of the locals there had headed for the temple, terrified as Carl and the team conducted their final search. Nothing had been found.

Dorey was almost out of time. He activated the final beacon, and with a thud followed by gasps from the locals, the beams fired into the air. He watched for a moment as its bright light display sparkled. He then peered around the corner, up the final street. The sun blazed against his eyes as he moved out of the shade. The goggles adapted quickly.

He sharpened his focus as he saw a figure turn and move away.

He scowled, had the man seemed strangely familiar? He zoomed in his goggles in order to get a better look, ordering them to magnify by six multiples, but as they caught the back of the man now headed away from him he disappeared behind the corner of the remaining store building ahead.

Dorey took a sharp breath, his heart racing, '*It couldn't have been.*'

*

Jay brought the Reeper down toward the edge of the terrified town and dropped the wires. Carl and the others would be pulled up via the winches in moments. They'd just received a transmission from Dorey informing them he'd spotted someone who appeared out of place. He hadn't given details as he was now giving chase, with Dial quickly heading up the steep climb of the mountain to offer assistance.

He would arrive at its peak at almost the same time as the ship.

The timing of this fact made Jay uneasy. She was about to radio through to Jim when at that very moment Dorey's voice came hurtling across the airwaves once more, only this time he was excited, "I don't believe it," he declared, "Its Brahms, the man I'm following is Captain Brahms!"

299

CHAPTER FIFTY FOUR

Dorey eased the larger pistol from its holster, approaching the door into which Brahms had just disappeared. He'd disengaged his com-link on entering the dusty corridor as Dial had persisted with his demands for Dorey to hold until he arrived as back up.

Going against his training Dorey found he was unable to ignore his instinct as it urged him forward. They only had a short time left in which to establish contact and he wanted to do it quickly. By the time Dial arrived it would be almost time to leave.

He moved close to the entrance but could hear no movement from the other side. He had his goggles penetrate the wall. They showed the nebulous image of a man sat alone at a table. He slowly reached out and pushed the shabby-looking door forward. It opened easily, and in an instant he sprung inside, his gun pointing ahead of him.

However, he found there was to be no need for his well-rehearsed room storming drills. For his prey was in fact sat perfectly still behind the old wooden table in the centre of the room, wearing a welcoming smile, holding his palms open in the air.

Dorey was certainly not taking any chances. "Don't move!"

Once satisfied they were alone the Commander moved around the table giving it a wide berth, keeping one eye on the doorway. A quick jab of his foot as he passed helped the door slowly creak to a close. It was the only way in or out.

He kept a maximum distance between himself and the dead man sat at the table, his arms locking the pistol into a permanent head shot as he circled him. "Keep your hands in the air where I can see them." Dorey moved around his quarry and positioned himself in the corner of the room, his gun pointing firmly to the back of Brahms' head. His goggles quickly scanned his seated prisoner confirming he was carrying no weapons. "Now slowly, reach your arms to full stretch ahead of you, place them and your palms flat on the table." He checked his position with regards to the sealed entry. If this man had any friends Dorey didn't know about then he'd take him out quickly and use him as a human shield should the door burst open.

"Don't worry I'm unarmed, *and alone*."

This astuteness only made Dorey tense further as did the unusual accented use of English. "Okay Captain Brahms," his glare tightened, "Who are you?"

Palene smiled softly. "I can assure you Commander, I mean you no harm."

Dorey's eyes narrowed further, '*So . . . the man knows my rank, what else does he know?*' His voice sharpened. "Well, it appears you seem to know a little about me, so let's play fair," the tone intensified as he demanded more slowly, "Who are you?"

Palene's stare continued ahead, his face a picture of perfect calm. "I fear we may both find that question a little too complicated to answer . . . or indeed, understand."

Dorey was growing agitated. "Well how about we start nice and simple . . . with a name."

"My name is unimportant."

He was a little surprised at the ease in his prisoner's voice. "Well do we at least have some rank or title . . . Since you seem to know mine?"

Again the response was calm and measured, friendly even. "I have held many ranks and numerous positions and I've been known by many different names."

Dorey was in no mood for riddles. He could sense the same complete lack of fear he'd witnessed back in Germany. No threat emanated from the man before him. It was the same tranquil equanimity Dorey had been so fascinated by during their alter ego's recent conversations. '*I watched you die.*' He would not be distracted by such thoughts. Instead he squeezed the handle of his pistol a little tighter to remind himself of the necessary caution required. "Now I don't know what your game is. And I don't know what you were playing at back in Germany, but we're going to have to discuss these issues on my terms now. Do not give yourself the luxury of thinking of me as some kind of past acquaintance. Because I promise you, I'll blow your brains all over this room if you give me cause to." He activated his intercom requesting a channel directly to the Reeper. "This is Dorey do you read me over?"

"Dorey . . ? What the hell do you think you're doing turning off your com-link?"

"Jay listen to me, the target has been located and secured."

Jay's eyes widened as she navigated the Reeper toward Dorey's signal. "Roger that, and repeat, you say you have the source with you?"

"Confirmed. I have the target with me, and it *is* our old friend Captain Brahms . . . Situation under control. What is your position?"

"Just completed final pick up. En-route to both you and Dial now . . . ETA five minutes."

Dorey was pleased. "Can you give me a time-check on the tunnel's status?"

Jay's left eye was interfaced into the Reeper mainframe and her answer was immediate, "Our window will close in twenty-six minutes."

Their timings still matched perfectly. "Is Dial headed directly toward my position, over?"

"Copy that. Dial will also reach you in five minutes. Reeper is inbound approaching the shore of the Dead Sea. We have a good lock on your signal. Can you move to a pick up location, or should I send the team down?"

"I'll move Brahms outside. We're cutting it fine as it is. Just tell Dial to get here as quickly as possible." He refrained from telling Dial in person. He wanted his full concentration on Brahms and knew the moment he opened a channel his number two would quite correctly berate him.

He pulled out a pair of handcuffs and tossed them on the table next to Brahms whose only reaction was to raise an eyebrow.

"Aren't they a little primitive Commander?"

"Slip them on slowly . . . I warn you, don't try anything. The last thing I want to do is shoot you. But I will if you force my hand." He replayed the image of Dial's two head shots and wondered if such a threat carried any weight. Once again he tightened his grip.

Palene shook his head sadly. "I cannot come with you Commander, even if I wanted to."

Dorey's eyes narrowed. "I think you're misreading the situation . . . I'm not asking. Now, put the handcuffs on before you make me nervous."

He understood immediately Dorey was not in the market for negotiation. He slipped on the handcuffs. "Commander, I do not wish to be at loggerheads with you. You must have some idea of what I'm about from our previous conversations together. But please be clear . . . I cannot come with you. That is why I invited you to join me here."

Dorey gritted his teeth. "Now you listen to me. We have questions…Questions that need answering. And unfortunately you haven't given us the time needed to ask them here. This is your own doing with your tricks and complications."

For the first time Palene looked dispirited. "There are so many things we need to discuss. I've been waiting for this moment for a long time. Please trust me, and I will tell you everything you wish to know. But not like this. Your safe passage home will be guaranteed." He then repeated, "I cannot come with you."

Dorey sensed the sincerity. "Look if you hadn't made it so difficult to find you then maybe we'd have had time for a little chat. That was my intention in coming here. But as things stand right now my crew are on a seriously tight schedule." He mentally readjusted his grip on the weapon once more. "Now, I want you to slowly stand then walk to the door and pull it open . . . gently."

Palene sighed, easing himself out of his chair and moving slowly toward the entry.

"I want you to open the door slowly, keeping your arms straight while pressing your palms against the door." His prisoner followed the instruction. "Now . . . Step into the corridor keeping the door ajar and slowly turn and face me."

Again he followed his orders, Palene now facing Dorey. "I beg you not to do this. If I was any threat, why would I lead you here and not put up a struggle? There are things . . ."

Dorey interrupted. "As I said, I'm on a tight schedule. Now believe me when I tell you, I really want to have this chat. However, I'm afraid it's going to have to wait." They passed into the corridor. "When we reach the front entrance we're going to turn left toward the steps leading onto the roof . . . Did you see these steps when you came in?"

"Yes."

Dorey followed Brahms as they retraced the route to the front entrance.

"Commander, I've observed you for longer than you know. I am not a threat . . . I mean neither you nor your friends harm. I promise you I will answer all of your questions, as I hope you may well help me with mine. It was imperative we should meet here and now."

"If you were so desperate to exchange information you should have done so while we had time almost two hours ago. You should have come forward back in Germany."

"I've waited two . . ."

Jay's voice suddenly filled Dorey's senses, forcing Brahm's words to trail away, "Dorey, I have confirmation of your position, ETA two minutes, Dial's one minute behind me. Will you be on a rooftop, over?"

Dorey concentrated on the all-important call from his pilot. "Negative, I will await Dial's assistance then we'll move him onto the roof together. Place the Reeper directly above my position and continue to direct him to me."

Jay checked her sensors. Dial's progress up the mountain slope had been incredible but his pace had slowed slightly over the final approach.

Palene continued. "You must listen to what I . . ."

"Listen?" Dorey interrupted, "There have been plenty of opportunities to listen . . . Now is not one of them."

"There are reasons. I had to . . ."

Again his words were cut short, only this time his captor's tone was more threatening, "We have very little time . . . So shut up and move toward the entrance."

They approached their destination, the daylight flooding the corridor from the open exit. "When we reach the doorway, I want you to step out into the light and slowly lower yourself onto your knees . . . Understood?"

Palene shook his head. "It doesn't have to be like this."

Dorey cocked the weapon. "That's the last time you speak. The next time there's a bullet in your shoulder . . . Please do not test me."

Palene's expression was one of resignation. He stepped out of the corridor into the daylight, squinting at the bright sunshine. The heat of the day swamped him as he left the inner sanctum behind. As ordered he dropped slowly to his knees.

Dorey approached behind, his combat goggles protecting his view of the captive as he too stepped out from the shade. He circled out into the light, relieved there was nobody in the street to witness events unfolding. He would feel a damn sight better once Dial was by his side. In the distance he could hear the approach of the Reeper, her engine's roar coming from somewhere high above the Dead Sea.

"Dorey we have a perfect lock on you. I'm bringing the Reeper down to your position."

The Commander's eyes never left their mark, never attempting to seek out the silhouette of the ship as it now made its approach.

As Jay brought the ship closer Dorey could hear the increasing stir of the settlement, as people became aware of the returning ungodly sound. They began pulling their mystified gazes away from the distant lights of the beacon as a different fear took hold. They searched the sky. A group of women began jabbering from their vantage point on the rooftops of the bath houses as the noise grew more terrible.

Jay broke through the haze of light cloud cover, high above the low mountain plateau on which the ancient fortress and lower settlement rested. She could see the Dead Sea reflecting like tin foil below. The walls of the once mighty fort came into view, their maze-like appearance making them resemble a giant puzzle as they sprawled across the sandstone perch. "Above you now, Dial is ninety seconds away."

Despite this information he still did not look up. The Reeper guns would be trained on his captive, removing any risk of an escape. He decided to inform Brahms of his now impossible plight. "Listen carefully," he raised his voice as the closing engines whistled, the ship beginning her descent in hover mode, "I want you to . . ."

Suddenly a piercing, deafening pain brought Dorey's order to an abrupt end, as without warning his eardrums nearly exploded. It was as if his head had been forced into a room-sized speaker as it fed back violently. He screamed and fell to his knees clutching his ears, his pistol rattling onto the rocky street at the foot of the staircase. The sound tore open his brain as he writhed in agony.

Above him, the crew of the Reeper found themselves affected in the same terrible way.

Dial only a minute from the plateau had slammed painfully into a tree clutching his ears. Then, as suddenly as it had begun, it stopped.

Above, the Reeper's systems shut down. Her alarms began crying out. The nose of the ship dipped toward the earth like a lead weight as the pilots helmets blacked out. With their visors raised Jay and Jim were now alone in a fight to re-fire her stricken engines, "Shit, we're going down."

The alarms continued to wail as Jim re-routed the power activated from her backup drives, sending it urgently to all of her underside boosters.

Jay followed Jim's quick reaction, her ears still whistling from the attack on her senses, "Firing front boosters."

The Reeper shuddered violently as she began to slip into a nosedive.

The computers flashed back on line with a sudden burst and Jay ordered the Reeper brain to reconnect and offer immediate assistance before repeating, "Fire front boosters!"

Again the ship shuddered. This time the vibration was followed by an explosion of force which ripped throughout the hull of the ship . . . The nose boosters had fired.

The front of the ship jolted upward. Her belly groaned.

The boosters fired violently in their heated attempt to push her heavy face up into the air.

Jay allowed the tail to fall as Jim instantly primed the rear rockets. The Reeper's computer systems kicked in further and the brain of the ship ordered the nano-metal shell to morph the flaps to assist her pilots, the lessons from the fall above Germany learned and filed within her woken memory banks.

Then, as the front of the falling stone rose and the tail dropped sufficiently, Jay punched the sensor, "Firing rear rockets." She pulled the aim and angle of the stick manually, not daring to trust the recently awoken computer. The ship exploded into a fury, slamming the heads of all on board back into their flight seats. A second storm ignited the rear of the ship propelling them hard across the sky. The controls eased as suddenly, the falling bomb regained her flight and pulled up and away.

As their altitude soared Jay eased down the engines. "What the fuck just happened?"

"I have no idea." Jim yelled back.

As the pilots regained their senses, they quickly remembered their prior objective.

"Dorey, Dial, are you okay?" Jay continued to ease down the ships' systems and opened up her vents. She began a long cooling circular flight-path toward their last known position. "Dorey . . . Dial, are you okay?" She yelled.

"All externals are off-line . . ." Jim replied, "They can't hear us, and we can't get a lock on their position." His cockpit was lit up like a Christmas tree, his visor trying to reconnect to the technology of both the ship and his helmet. "God knows judging by the readings I'm getting, we're lucky that's the only damage."

A flare fired up from the edge of the mountain top. It was Dial's last known position. She scanned manually for Dorey and his prisoner but there was no sign. "Shit!" She swung the Reeper toward Dial, "What about the winches?"

"On line, preparing to lower them now." Jim struggled through his manual cameras before closing in on the source of the flare. "It's Dial, he's alone."

Jay brought the cockpit into the trailing orange smoke of the flare. She placed the ship into a hover and began lowering the vessel at a risky speed.

"He's hooked on." Jim relayed soon after.

Jay aimed her limited vision back toward Masada, relieved to have Dial on the winch, "Where's Dorey?"

"I'm working on it," was her co-pilots immediate reply, "Believe me I'm working on it."

*

Dorey sprinted across the rooftops, crashing through line after line of hanging rugs and linen sheets unable to hear the melee of panic as the people of the settlement scrambled into their homes, hiding away from the satanic sky. His ears were ringing like a thousand church bells and his temples pounded in time with his heart.

Ahead of him Brahms had gained a considerable lead.

He'd screamed in vain for the Reeper to cut him off. Tried to aim a shot with his smaller pistol, but he was still too shaky to have made it count. '*Don't worry,*' he told himself as he charged across the rooftops knocking over everything from livestock, baskets and hanging laundry, '*Brahms hands are bound and the buildings of the old fort are giving way to protrusions of rock ahead. He'll soon be at the mountain wall, and he'll be forced into a climb. The Reeper will follow my beacon, together we'll cut him off.*' He breathed heavily as he picked up the pace, his equilibrium returning after the deafening shock.

*

Jay swung the recovering Reeper around for another pass, daring herself ever lower onto the risk of the rooftops, the scream of her engines terrifying to the community below. "Jim, I need her externals back on line, I still can't find him." She scanned her partially recovered visuals. '*Why hasn't he fired a flare?*' The thought troubled her.

Jim and the reviving ship's computer tried desperately to pick up Dorey's signal.

Jay banked around and soared over another maze of crumbling buildings. This time however, she spotted a trail of debris scattered across an area of rooftops. She passed it in a flash, but managed to identify the aim of the trail as being in one definite direction.

She gunned the ship around for another fly-by over the trail of broken pots and torn down blankets, certain her manual cameras and enhanced vision had just picked up his scent.

Suddenly she heard Jim call out. "I've got him!"

Her homing display now flashed back on line also, pinpointing his position immediately. "I see him. He's on the western edge of the mountain," she scowled at the reading, "It looks like he's made a descent down the precipice . . . No visual yet." She fired the Reeper away from the fortress to circle the red mountainside. She placed the ship into a hover so she may home in on Dorey's exact location, "He's remained stationary," she declared.

As she brought the ship about her view was blocked by an enormous rocky stack, but she could pinpoint where he was thanks to the recovering computer systems. "Hang on, I'm almost with you," she said as she guided the ship around the stack in a wail of boosters and pluming smoke. She readied the winch wishing for the aided visuals of her helmet and searched the edge of the mountain for direct visual contact.

As she cleared the stack however, her heart immediately sank to her stomach.

For there was Dorey, his tiny silhouette now highlighted in a full red visual of the computer's homing screen, and to her absolute terror, she could see him slipping backward, away from a broad rocky ledge.

Above him on the same shelf was the man he'd just claimed as his prisoner.

She watched in abject horror as he fell, his body breaking in two along with her heart as it smashed onto the sharp rocks below. She screamed, "DOREY!"

Jim saw it too. He gritted his teeth against the pain before yelling over the intercom, "Benny...You'd better get to the cockpit and get Jay out of there."

They were running out of time to make the jump home.

Benny and the others heard the scream and instantly feared the worst.

"What the fuck is happening up there?" Dial demanded.

Jim fought back the tears. "It's Dorey . . . He's dead."

*

Jim had taken control of the ship from his co-pilots cockpit and had soon identified another problem immediately after Dorey's fall.

Jay was still screaming hysterically as Benny and Dial renewed their attempts to pull her away from the controls. "Get your hands off me!" She wailed, "We have to go and get him, he's still down there!" She'd fought them for nearly two minutes. "We can't leave him here!" She screamed several more obscenities at both Dial and Benny. Her resistance weakened as she felt unable to breathe, the strangling pain of her loss taking control.

Dial looked into her eyes, tears streaming down both their faces.

"You bastard." she gargled, "You're supposed to be his friend."

Dial implored her. "Jay, in six minutes our exit will close. And then we're all as good as dead. Do you think he would want that?" He re-emphasised, "Jim's time navigation unit is down, it never re-booted after the plunge. We need your chair to get us back."

She swallowed hard as she made a silent, desperate cry.

Dial began to unfasten her harness. "Jay come on, come with me. Let Benny pilot the ship back. Jim can't do it alone without the computer...We need the pilot's chair."

Her face grimaced, "We've got time to get his body!" She was desperate.

Dial's heart broke as he choked. "Jay there is no time. We have to get out of here now."

She closed her eyes and groaned in agony.

After too long a pause Dial prepared to remove her by employing more force, but the action was not necessary. For when Jay finally opened her eyes they were destroyed but determined as they absorbed the flat-line on Dorey's homing beacon.

She pushed him away and began re-fastening her harness.

"Jay." Dial muttered in weak protest. Her agony was his to bear.

She turned the pilot's seat about, away from Benny and Dial, her anguished voice rusty and cracked. "You'd better get back to your seats."

She nearly slumped forward but fought herself successfully.

Dial understood. He turned to Benny distraught and nodded. They stared at each other sharing the agony, both realising in the same instant that Jay was now taking them home.

They both turned about and began the rush back to the passenger area.

Jay took back the pilot control with the hit of a sensor. "Jim, I have the con . . . turning her about. Set tail boosters to maximum."

Her voice was almost unfamiliar, like it belonged to someone else.

Jim stared at his over-ride switch but somehow knew it was no longer necessary. Instead he followed his pilot's order and sent all power back to the rear engines ready for her command. "Roger that Jay, all Reeper engines on line and ready to fire on your mark."

She took another brief look at the monitor whose display signalled Dorey's demise with nothing more than a *flat-line* on his life-signs, accompanied with the flashing red circle which continued to highlight the area of rock which now held their Commander's twisted, broken body. "Is everyone strapped in?" She croaked, still not happy to trust her displays, her voice and sanity barely holding together.

Dial's red eyes stared blankly ahead as he confirmed solemnly, "We're ready."

She throttled the awesome engines, ready for the rapid climb toward their exit, high up in the atmosphere above the centre of the Dead Sea.

She opened the private channel to her co-pilot. "Let's take her home."

As the engines roared, the channel was closed and Jay sobbed once again as she gunned the ship high into the sky.

PART THREE

Through the dark matter of eternal universe,
the consciousness shuddered,
as the manipulation of a still indecipherable source
inflicted its being upon its own sense of self . . .
its purpose vibrating across the echoes and
and echelons of intelligence and space.
'Incredible.'
'Yes.'
'Such, power.'
'Yes.'
'Unveiling itself.'
'Yes.'
'So close to the inception.'
'Yes.'
'Our inception.'
'Yes.'
'And so the dreams become eternal.'
'As we are eternal.'
'They stem from the source.'
'And yet we are the source.'
'But perhaps not the origin.'
'Can such a notion be realised?'
'Conception is proof of feasibility.'
'Yes.'

CHAPTER FIFTY FIVE

Brahms skidded down over loose rock as he headed fearlessly toward the mountain edge.

By the time his pursuer reached the steep bank, he was already some forty feet below him. The Commander shouted and took aim but it was a feeble threat, the handcuffed man was already out of sight again, rounding a jagged boulder at the final edge before slope turned to sheer drop.

Dorey quickly reached the boulder then checked his watch, '*Twelve minutes.*'

The sharpening descent now led onto the mountain's more vertical face. Some forty feet below was a broad ledge but to reach it he would have to negotiate a tricky climb down. It would be an easy platform for the Reeper winch to make a pick up.

Brahms had disappeared, but Dorey knew he could only be somewhere beneath him as there was nowhere else to go.

He began the descent aware he was cutting it fine, but he could hear the Reeper approaching from the other side of the upright precipice. He knew even with his intercom down they'd have a lock on his whereabouts via the homing beacon.

He hoped his quarry would make some mistake. Handcuffs would surely play their part in slowing even the fearless Brahms at this point of the chase.

If on reaching the ledge Dorey found himself alone he would give up the pursuit and have the ship come in for him. There may well be no clear way down from the broad plateau below, if so, the closing in Reeper would perhaps gain one final chance at apprehending Brahms as it followed the Commander's signal.

However, almost as quickly as he'd made the decision to continue downward, Dorey was regretting it. The mountain face was deceptive, a more difficult climb than he'd realised when looking from above. He wondered if subconsciously he'd allowed himself to see it as less daunting because he knew the man he was chasing had negotiated it with his hands bound. Whatever his reasoning, as the cliff wall became more difficult he accepted the chase had indeed ended from his own perspective.

Now it was little more than a cautious descent to reach the ledge safely.

He could hear the Reeper engines moving into a hover, her position almost within view.

His powerful fingers dug into the fissures of the cliff as its face leaned out precariously. As his feet delicately hunted for safe havens he couldn't help but wonder once more how Brahms managed this climb in handcuffs. '*Had he somehow broken free of his bonds, or was he so crazy and skilled a climber it simply made no difference?*'

His heart pumped steady caution as the hot sun beat down on his already drenched back.

The ledge drew closer with each thoughtful effort and he was less than twenty feet from its solid embrace when he felt the slow, dreadful encompassing nightmare of his footing breaking away from the cliff face. He was repositioning the hold of his fingers when it gave and was unable to re-establish a firm grip quickly enough, as suddenly he found himself scrambling down the rock. He tried not to panic. '*It'll be a bumpy landing. Stay close to the face, you should hit the ledge okay,*' his brain reassured as the fall accelerated. His fingernails shattered into bloody fragments as he scraped them along the jagged wall in a last ditch attempt at saving himself from the oncoming impact.

His heart pounded and everything seemed to transpire in slow time as he plummeted. He braced himself for the hit. It seemed for a moment like it would never come, but then it did. He gritted his teeth as his ankle sprained on a large uneven rock. He tried to control the fall but the boulder shot him off balance. He winced as he found himself suddenly falling backward onto his good leg. It hit with unequal force almost rupturing his knee and his body crumpled onto the ledge in an unexpected and uncontrollable rearward spin. The world flew past him in a whirl of unspecific images, confused between dust and sky. His head smashed against another rock but somehow he remained conscious as he made a desperate attempt to slow himself by grabbing hold of anything that came into his path.

Suddenly he felt a wedge of wiry deep routed grass gift itself into his right palm. He clenched it at great and hopeful speed but in the very same instant he felt the stomach turning horror of weightlessness. He'd over shot the ledge.

His body was suddenly twisting downward then crashing into the hard cliff face. He could barely see for the dirt in his eyes and could taste nothing but panic in the dry dust now engulfing his throat. His heart punched at his chest, desperate to feed every ounce of enhanced muscle as Dorey became horribly aware only his vice like grip on the reeds now stood between his life and his death.

The scale of his predicament smashed into his psyche. He gasped as he tried to find anything solid onto which he could place a foot. Inevitably the grass began to snap free from its anchoring and he felt his entire frame jolt sickeningly downward, '*Oh no.*'

His temples pounded as he tried to find a way out of the horror. More grass began to break free from the ledge. He scoured the rock for any semblance of hope . . . Nothing.

The grass snapped but he could not believe it was really happening. He felt the momentum of his body slip away from the solid mountainside and into the certain death of thin air. The reality of it transpired so slowly it felt unreal. He did not scream. He merely opened his mouth in silent terror.

He could no longer hear anything beyond the numbness of his stunned mind but surreally he saw the image of Captain Brahms peering over the edge, watching him fall with a look of sorrow worn on his face. There was no reflection of his horror, instead he looked only pitiful and calm, his hands still bound in the handcuffs as he watched him plummet.

Dorey was falling fast. He stared helplessly as the hillside became a blurry dream and he gagged on his fear as the sky pulled him down toward his doom. Images of his life flashed before him, just like he'd read it could in books . . . His parents, his sister, his friends, his adventures, but most of all . . . Jay. He felt himself choke as he was haunted one final time by her beautiful brown eyes. Could this really be his death? It didn't feel like it was even happening. It felt more like a dream that somehow resigned him quite suddenly to his fate, as if he'd already become a ghost of himself. But as his body snapped in two, Dorey realised it was indeed happening. The pain which fired through the nervous system of his shattered spine was as instantaneous as his end, lasting no longer than a flash of light. Yet within this swift and awful flash, Dorey knew all he'd ever been, and all he'd ever hoped he would be, was now dreadfully . . . at an end.

CHAPTER FIFTY SIX

Brookes stared at the reels of data amassed over the past few hours which suggested another brief but powerful disturbance had occurred somewhere within the timeframe of recent tragic events. He was deeply troubled.

The rhythmic pulse of the Stasis None continued its steady synthesised beat, but he was convinced this apparent harmony was not all it seemed.

He was growing suspicious, but of exactly what he didn't know.

Despite the machine and mainframe owing its conception largely to the talent and creation of his own genius, in all honesty he knew he was barely scratching the surface of his brainchild. He glanced across at the black tiled heart of the Stasis mainframe.

He sighed, not for the first time since unhooking his brain from its raw, powerful embrace. He rubbed his eyes, kept them closed a while, and for the briefest moment saw the body of light which continued to disturb his dreams. He placed his forehead into the waiting cup of his open palm. Another sigh followed as he stared at the black shell.

When he'd invented this super intelligence, Isimbard Brookes had marvelled at it. It was by no means an irrational reaction. Of the many inventors, technicians and scientists who'd worked on the notion of any computer, few would ever admit to a certain truth . . . One being, that since the very inception of the first machines, there were still elements within their mechanisms which theoretically, should never have worked. There were just too many probabilities and improbabilities. This was even truer of Brookes' device. The reality was their wondrous machine was for all intensive purposes, a mystery to them. Brookes built his phenomenon to specifications requiring the most cutting-edge of technologies. A machine which could finally take the human mind into dimensions previously unexplored, perhaps even unimagined. Yet in a bizarre twist, it was a marvel that despite all its advancements, despite all the power of its artificial intelligence and atomic capabilities, would never have been able to navigate the complexities of time without its altogether more human property.

His eye remained on the black titanium heart of his Stasis system. Despite his best efforts he'd been unable to lock onto the source of the recent disturbance, the computer itself labelling it as just another abnormality occurring within the reaches of unseen dimensional space. He had no idea why he questioned the reassurances. It was just a gut reaction, one which held no logical grounding. Yet still, it troubled him all the same.

Perhaps it was the certain knowledge of someone or something running around within his system. Something it would appear was responsible for the death of his trusted Commander of Operations. Someone he'd sent Dorey directly toward without proper consideration. A person with the ability to move through simulated time in a manner he could not yet comprehend . . . A man already killed by Mark Dial.

'An event which may not yet have happened to that version of this man Brahms,' he thought as the endless possibilities of time were thrown around him once more.

As he pondered he felt the painful loss of Anthony Dorey all over again, his devastation adding to the weight and pressure now mounting from the powers behind the Stasis None. He'd only just managed to convince them sending Dorey and his team on such a hurried mission was the correct path to take, the decision only granted so long as he took full responsibility for the consequences.

He'd allowed his feelings to blind his logic and in doing so played directly into the hands of Finch and the others, losing his trusted team leader in the process.

And to top it all, the early signs were he'd miscalculated with regards to the research of Didier Monclair aka Joseph Franc, the Stasis None appearing uncertain now of the stolen study's overall role to play. His thoughts darkened.

He felt certain WAIG had its eyes and ears deeper within his operation than they ever let on. He knew also if the situation could not be resolved quickly, the whole house of cards would certainly tumble. He closed his eyes and drifted into the rhythm of the Stasis None's melodic beat, dwelling further on the illusive traveller who could somehow manipulate the dimensions of his system. He thought about the strange events of that first experiment with time, all those years ago. He stared at the black tiles housing the Stasis mainframe enquiring for the umpteenth time, *'Who are you?'*

But as always, his mind could not conjure a response.

*

He felt his diaphragm collapse and ribs lift as the air rushed down his flaky throat, filling his lungs. His eyes, wide with terror tried to focus, but they sent no information to a brain preoccupied with drowning in its own awful nightmare. He heard his horrified gulp as if it were someone else, unable to comprehend the reality of his situation. Images flashed through his mind as his brain tried desperately to reboot, unable to understand the reason for its jump-start back into being. He saw the fall, relived the terror with a bolt upwards. "No!" He heard his own voice, unfamiliar and dry.

He listened out for God but his only sense was pain, his mind wincing as a fiery axe seemed to slice clean through his consciousness, "Ahhhhh."

He felt his body drop limply onto something soft and experienced the cold chill of his sweat which lay in a sheen across his face and torso, along the curve of his back.

His eyes tried to focus, making his head hurt even more.

"Shhh now . . . You're doing fine, try to relax."

He saw the fuzzy image of a man above him and could not help but weep through his pain. The soft calm reality of his voice nourishing and healing as he slowly blacked out from consciousness, the continual agony and torment still barraging his mind in the darkness.

CHAPTER FIFTY SEVEN

Jay was curled up on Dorey's side of the bed wearing a pair of his shorts and tee-shirt. Her hands were clasped together as if in prayer, the knuckles of her thumbs jutting out and resting between her lips. Her nostrils were red and sore, her eyes stared blankly into space. The room was dark and had been for days.

She'd listened to the countless messages from Dial and the others as they'd been spoken onto her machine, imploring her to let them share her grief.

Jay had managed to answer a couple of the calls, done her best to reassure everyone she was okay and for them to try not to worry . . . She just needed, '*A little time on her own.*'

She'd turned away in disgust when Dial left one message, informing her that the Stasis Project had investigated their reports and held none of them in any way responsible for the tragic loss of their Commander, and she'd later grimaced at Brookes' promise, "*Take as long as you need to get through this.*"

All she knew with any certainty was she was suffering incredible pain. That despite the many occasions both she and Dorey discussed the possibility of this awful scenario actually happening, the reality was of course, painfully different.

She'd run the tragedy of Masada through her mind a thousand times and knew there was little else she could have done to change its outcome. Dorey had uncharacteristically pushed his preaching out of the window and placed himself in unnecessary danger while in pursuit of his prisoner.

In the end he'd paid the ultimate price for this short-lived fixation.

She felt the starving knots of her stomach tighten and felt sick within the emptiness of her pain. Crying had become only theoretical now. She curled up a little tighter and nearly died all over again as she imagined his face next to hers.

"*We're going to hold a service and memorial.*" Dial told her over the intercom of her front door that morning. "*Jay . . . We need you to help with the arrangements, you know, with his family and everything.*"

"How can you have a funeral when there's no fucking body Mark?" She'd felt his pain ooze through her speaker. *"Just leave me alone."* She was not proud of her response.

She activated her lover's childhood farm program once again, but felt no ease in the embrace of the familiar stars. "Not this program again . . ." She struggled to herself. "It always makes me feel cold."

She imagined his response. *"It's supposed to be cold, it's winter."*

She sighed heavily. "It makes me think of icebergs." Jay whispered as she remembered her last response to this statement, but she didn't smile this time as she'd done when hearing his sarcastic comeback. She did however, allow her lips the slightest beginnings of one as she imagined her hair was being blown gently away, as it tickled Dorey's nose.

*

It took a while for him to realise what he could hear was the sound of his own steady breathing, as if the gentle harmony was coaxing him to wake. His eyes were closed and felt like they had been for some time. His heart was steady, but he felt lost, waking from a long but now distant dream.

He squeezed his eyes tightly together and grimaced for no other reason than to feel the movement of his own face. His consciousness was slowly returning. *'Open your eyes,'* his brain wished gently, sounding distinctly pleased with itself, *'Open them.'*

He searched his feelings for a clue as to what was happening. Then he remembered. He felt a sudden wave of sadness wash over him, a grief of which he'd never experienced, but it was just as quickly replaced with something new . . . Joy.

He was suddenly aware of the obvious truth now filling his heart and soul with a rejuvenating medicine which overwhelmed with its simple veracity . . . He was alive.

He sucked in the sweetest tasting breath, his brain once again encouraging him to stir. *'Open your eyes.'*

His eyelids fluttered as he dragged his pupils from up inside his skull. They focused on the ceiling but were a blur, tears oozing from him now uncontrollably. He gagged for a second as in that moment all he could manage was to cry in the silence of his redemption.

The air was cool and calm and there was a distinct tranquillity in the surrounding space.

He was suddenly aware his head was resting on deeply quilted pillows. His body laid on a firm mattress whose soft sheet and blanket wrapped themselves over his chest and under both arms. This sudden realisation was itself intensely surreal.

The tears subsided as a second calmer wave of euphoria floated through him.

His focus was clearing and his sight began to translate its perspective. He stared, concentrating on his peripheral vision, taking in the information.

He couldn't place the dimly lit room. He'd never been here before.

Questions began racing around his increasingly aware mind. Slowly, he allowed his gaze to drift across the surrounding walls, and then, the questions stopped.

For there, sitting on a high backed chair in the far corner, was Brahms. He held an open book which sat easily on his raised knee, his face a picture of composed delight.

For reasons that at first he could not fathom, Dorey was in no way alarmed.

Then it was clear. Something deep inside him was certain this curious stranger was the only reason he still existed. He swallowed with a little difficulty causing his eyes to close again for a moment. His mind played back the image of Brahms wearing that calm, sorrowful expression as he'd watched him fall from the sandstone cliff.

Dorey stared at him intently, unsure as to why he was formulating his next statement, and yet he'd never been more certain of anything in his life. "You saved me."

The man closed his book and slowly sat forward, his smile warm and genuine. "It's a little more complicated than that." He realised Dorey's throat was dry. "Do you want some water?"

He nodded slowly as he eased himself up onto the pillows.

"Easy now . . . You've been out for some time, just relax."

Dorey was utterly exhausted. "I'm fine." Brahms brought over a wooden goblet and the patient drank slowly under the watchful eye of his nurse.

He focused on him once more as he finished this most wonderful of drinks. "Why?" Dorey's voice was little more than a whisper, the simple effort of remaining awake clearly written on his face.

Brahms brought the chair closer to his patient's bedside. He appeared thoughtful before returning his smiling expression into Dorey's eyes. "I saved you because I had to. I saved you because you needed me to. And I saved you because I wanted to."

Dorey detected that same indescribable truth which fascinated during their conversations in Germany. He was now of course, completely spellbound by this man.

He concentrated hard and tried to remember his training. '*He wants you for something.*' He was tiring, "But why?" he repeated.

Brahms looked a little uneasy, "I understand you are naturally suspicious. And I understand you're feeling more than a little confused right now. But I implore you to rest for just a little while longer. I promise you all of your questions will be answered." He smiled ironically, "At least the ones I can answer anyway." He seemed pleased. "And I have questions of my own, questions I've been waiting to ask for a long, long time."

It infuriated Dorey his brain was indeed now demanding he rest some more. He gritted his teeth, showing his annoyance, but to his dismay he could feel his eyelids growing heavier as the pillows sucked his head deeper into their embrace.

Brahms stood. "Just rest a little longer. Then we shall talk properly." He turned and headed for the door.

Dorey was disgusted at himself for being unable to stay awake but his eyelids began to drop. He forced them open for one final effort, "Wait," he said causing Brahms to turn, "Who are you?" he whispered gently, "What is your name?"

His host smiled with vibrant eyes, "I am Palene," he said with profound dignity, "My name . . . is Palene."

CHAPTER FIFTY EIGHT

As he woke, his nostrils were filled with the blended aromas of sea air and roasted coffee. He forced his eyelids into a brief flicker before they opened. As they did, he realised the splitting headache had gone and his eyes no longer encountered any difficulty to focus. He was also aware none of the recent and vivid nightmares which haunted and brutalised his dreams, had done so during this last sleep, and as a result, Dorey felt much better rested. Better rested in fact, than he'd ever felt in his life. He checked the room's perimeter for any sign of his mysterious host, but there was none. The bedroom door had been left ajar and it was from somewhere beyond this entrance both the light and smell of the coffee were emanating. He sat up in bed and concentrated on his surroundings.

There was only a small slit for a window to the outside world within this bed chamber. However with the light oozing in through the open doorway the room was warm and bright with visiting sunshine. He could see from its materials and construction he was still somewhere in the past, and determined after a little thought on the patches of sandstone at the bottom of the wall, it was almost certainly the era of his fateful last jump. A cold shiver passed down his spine as his mind flashed him back once again into the moment of his apparent death. He suddenly remembered the Reeper had been almost on top of him when he fell and felt sick at the realisation Jay and the others must have witnessed his demise. He felt immediate sorrow for the grief he must have inflicted on those he held dear, reprimanding himself for placing all at such unnecessary risk. He should have called off his impossible chase the moment he reached the steep drop of the mountainside. By not doing so and prolonging it down to the ledge, he'd not only paid the ultimate price, but could have also endangered the lives of his team.

He swallowed hard as he saw the image of Jay. He was riding an emotional rollercoaster and the sense he was experiencing now more than any other, was that of extreme guilt.

'I would do anything to have you here with me right now.'

His senses began racing as his wits now pushed harder for a return from slumber. *'How long had he been here . . . How was it possible he was still alive*

. . . Was he even alive in the truest sense of the word?' He rubbed his his forehead as the questions continued, *'Where exactly was he, more importantly, was he trapped here forever?'*

Only one person held the answers.

He took a deep breath and concentrated on what he required of himself. As he examined the room once again he noticed some clean clothing placed carefully into a pile on the floor. Next to them sat a pair of sandals, *'Jewish linen.'* he thought, realising with greater clarity he was almost certainly within the same time in which his death had occurred. His blood raced as he tried to keep it together.

He slid slowly out of the bedclothes and perched himself on the side of the bed. His back and neck ached. He noted how his body appeared unscathed, clean with no bedsores. He'd obviously been well cared for during his unconsciousness.

He stared at his hands, fingernails, knee and ankle, all healed and as new.

He allowed the blood to rush down to his toes which he now wiggled studiously. He smiled at the sight, the ecstasy of being alive suddenly washing over him all over again.

He heard movement beyond which felt deliberate and loud. He looked to the open door, breathed in the coffee then stared once again at the neat pile of clothes. *'Of course the noise was deliberate. As was this smell of intoxicating coffee beans . . .'* He was expected.

He felt a sudden rush of excitement add itself to his growing cocktail of emotions.

He was alive. Somehow, miraculously . . . he was alive.

And the man responsible for this gift now awaited him.

However, the real titilation which now washed over him carried with it an altogether new, overriding hope. *'If this man can prevent my death, then maybe, just maybe, he can get me back home.'* He was annoyed with himself as immediately as the thought struck him, *'Childish hopes . . . Ridiculous ones at that.'* A sense of disapproval rushed over him as he fought to remain practical, to stay focused. However this battle was to be short-lived as his practicality was quickly overruled. *'Childish?' 'Ridiculous?'* His mind argued with itself. *'So is cheating death.'* He groaned slightly as the conflict raged on, *'You might not even be alive in the truest sense.'*

His emotions were in danger of running wild as they spun him around in circles, so he clenched his eyelids together and tried desperately to give himself counsel. He had to bring his reasoning toward a state which at least resembled some kind of calm. It was difficult. He felt different somehow, less in control, less able to calculate sensibly. *'Hardly surprising all things considered.'* He thought, as again he felt the persistent surges of his emotional storm.

There was one thing however of which he did feel certain, that he must be cautious of this unknown quantity who now awaited him.

His thoughts were then plunged into his memory as he found himself reliving his few fascinating encounters with his rescuer come host. As he

322

reached toward the pile of clothes and slowly began to dress, he suddenly remembered the idea of a strange light which had visited his dreams, calming his nightmares.

He was confused and unsteady on his feet as he continued to dress, when suddenly he remembered, *'Palene, he'd said his name was Palene.'*

*

After placing on his sandals he walked a little shakily at first, into the sun drenched corridor. The sunshine flooded across him from high windows carved into each end of the walkway. It forced him to squint as he enjoyed the warmth of its touch.

He followed the coffee aroma down a small flight of stone steps which spiralled within the gentle curve of the corridors end. He could taste the salt of the sea as it travelled the air, into the room of which he now found himself standing. His balance and co-ordination were steadying, which he knew reduced the amount of time he was likely to have been bedridden. He felt at his jaw touching only stubble, not a beard.

From the bottom of the steps he examined the darker, cooler room as it opened out in front of him, taking in its detail with the slow rhythm of his breathing.

Three wicker chairs faced in from the shadows with small tables placed next to each of them. A single window sent a beam of light across the centre, the dust particles floating across its stream. To his left was an open fireplace carved into the same orange rock. Ahead was another room, and it was from here the real illumination to the downstairs of the building emanated.

He headed through the archway into this second interior, warmed by the same intense sunlight he'd just enjoyed on the landing. A wooden dining table dominated the centre surrounded by four chairs. Upon its surface was a red, clay-baked jug and next to this was a small cup. As Dorey approached he noticed both were filled with rich black coffee. He stared for a moment, breathing in the aroma.

"I have goat's milk if you prefer it white, and honey if you'd like to sweeten it a little."

The voice startled him. He looked to the wide open doors. Through them and beyond stretched out a sizeable veranda, its floor dressed with polished sandstone tiles. A roughly contoured wall guarded the broad balcony, stood around five feet in height with more of the polished tiles finishing its surface perimeter.

It was from this fine veranda the sudden announcement had been delivered.

Dorey's heart raced as he recognised the voice, remembering the accent when delivering words in English. He picked up the coffee and stepped through the doors onto the warm veranda. As his focus adjusted he recognised the features, Palene slowly rising from one of two woven chairs placed on opposite sides of a stumpy round table.

He held an identical cup in his right hand.

"No, this is fine thank you." He said as he emerged into the full fantasy of the warm sunshine. He felt for a brief moment as if he'd passed across the threshold of heaven.

Palene gestured to him. "Please, come and sit down." He could not help but smile at the casual nature of Dorey's reply, as if he were merely a neighbour popping in for a chat. "How are you feeling?"

Dorey moved toward him cautiously. He offered an inquisitor's look, noting the different colours of his skin, eyes and hair. All were darker than those of Brahms. His eyes in particular were something to behold, deep chestnut, almost tinged with red. "I'm fine, I think." He gestured to the slight scarring evident on his host's forehead, "How are you?"

Palene grinned. He'd swept back his hair so Dorey would see the wounds left by Mark Dial's gun. "I thought it easier to keep up the appearance of Brahms...Until now."

Dorey walked over to the walled edge and peered out, the warmth of the sun embracing him further. He wanted to see his location before he would consider taking a seat. As he adjusted to the outside world his battling senses were filled with the exhilaration of the astonishing view, "The Dead Sea?" He asked as he stared out across the shimmering water, its waves languishing against the rust coloured rocks.

"Yes." Palene responded.

A lump formed in his throat at the profound beauty, "Where?"

"Close to Masada...Look, its walls rise in the distance behind us." He pointed to the face of the cliffs which rose to the rear like a Martian landscape.

Dorey shivered, remembering once again his dreadful demise. "And when are we?"

"Still within the time of your . . . fall."

He noted Palene's careful choice of words, spoken so eloquently in this richly mixed accent the origins of which he couldn't place.

His host motioned for him to sit once again. "Please," his tone calm and friendly.

Dorey took his seat, 'Stay calm. Keep it together.' He then sipped at his coffee and contemplated. "So why here?" he asked after a moment, "Why fifth century Masada?"

"Neither the century nor the place is of overriding significance. Though as you and I both know this entire area is steeped in history."

"The last stand of an army of Jews against a Roman Empire." he said staring at his host, "Mass suicide chosen over slavery."

He nodded.

Dorey remembered the comments made during their time in Germany. "Is that why we are here . . . Because you are Jewish?"

He smiled, "No I am not Jewish."

Dorey felt the lingering taste of the coffee in his throat and tried to focus. He was in danger of becoming overwhelmed before he'd even begun. He had too many questions, queries and concerns...But what Palene said to him next not only astounded him, it almost broke his heart with a joy impossible to hide.

"I feel before we begin I should put your mind at ease toward two things which I realise must be of the utmost importance to you," he smiled warmly, "Although you will eventually come to understand you are indeed alive, you will of course naturally question this notion at first. You needn't. You are as real as you have ever been. Secondly, I feel it important to tell you I have both the ability and the desire to have you returned home, to your own time, as soon as our business here is finished."

The words flooded through Dorey like a tidal wave, almost reducing him to tears. He gagged on the emotion as his eyes became pools.

"I know as you understand things all of this is of course impossible. However, I can assure you as I understand things…It is not."

Dorey's composure almost cracked but he somehow held on asking with a deep, shaky breath, "How is...?" Despite his best effort he couldn't finish his question at that moment.

Palene smiled with pure sincerity. "How this is possible is sometimes more confusing to me than it ever could be to you. However you must trust me when I tell you, after we have talked…You *will* return home, as alive and as real as the moment you left." His smile broadened as he gave Dorey a moment to allow the relief to pass. "Drink some more coffee." He said, "It will help your senses to return."

*

Five painful days had passed since the crew of the Reeper returned home without their Commander. The remaining men of Dorey's team sat dejectedly in Mark Dial's lounge.

Benny looked at him with concerned eyes. "And then what did she say?"

Dial appeared helpless, "The same thing she said the time before and the time before that. She wants to be left alone."

They all looked thoroughly crestfallen.

"Did you mention planning a memorial service again?" Jim asked.

Dial nodded. "But I'm not going to anymore. It only hurts her each time I mention it."

"Understandable," Benny replied feeling quite depressed, "Maybe we *should* leave it for a while."

They all agreed.

"When will his family be informed?"

Dial was perplexed, "Jay was adamant she should be the one to tell them. But I might have to. They're used to not hearing from him for long periods of course, but it's only right they should know sooner rather than later."

They all seemed to look down at the table at precisely the same moment.

Dial continued, "Besides, I got the official cover story through this morning from Brookes as Jay didn't want to hear it, *'I'm sorry to inform you your son has been lost while operating in a covert mission to hunt down terrorists. He died a hero in the service of his country."* They all had such cover stories which could easily be implemented into whatever crisis was on the news that week. "They're holding back on it for a few days to see if Jay comes around."

Marco shook his head. "Do you remember when he and Jay first started to fall for one another? They fought it for a year in case something like this happened."

Dial agreed. "He was terrified of hurting her."

"As she was of hurting him," Jim interjected.

Benny exhaled, "If Jay doesn't come around, when are you going to tell them?"

Dial took a long drink of his beer. "I don't know, tomorrow, maybe I'll do it tomorrow."

*

Dorey was not concerned this man may have witnessed any weakness. He'd have been incapable of acting in any other fashion after such a statement. But he was surprised at the unexpected notion of what a return ticket home truly meant. He'd just become most pleased he was sitting exactly where he was, at that precise moment in time.

He stared at his mysterious host, "So, where do we begin?"

Palene finished sipping his coffee. "Where do you want to begin?"

Dorey didn't hesitate, "How did you do it?" He clarified, "How did you prevent my death?"

Palene looked a little uncomfortable.

The Commander continued, "I saw you, on the ledge above me when I fell. You didn't make any attempt to catch me. And yet here I am, talking and breathing…How?"

Palene placed his cup onto the low round table between them. "You must understand, I'm telling you the truth when I say it's very hard to explain."

Dorey's eyes narrowed. "Like it's hard to explain how you recovered from two bullets to the head?" He looked at the faint gunshot scars, noting another smaller scar upon his cheek. "I take it you're not a clone."

Palene laughed, "No…I'm not a clone."

Dorey ascertained it must be some clever use of time technology, but the scarring worn by his host confused him somewhat. *'The scars could be a deception.'* he pondered. "Did you jump back in time?"

His smile remained, "With regards to saving you or myself?"

"Both." He stared intently at Palene.

"In a sense…yes. But what I did is different in so many ways to how you could possibly comprehend it."

"Different, how?"

"As I said it's hard to explain."

326

If Dorey heard the reply he gave no clue, his focus quickly drifting back to the promise of a return home. "You say you can send me back. That demonstrates ability far beyond our own to manipulate time. I mean, once we've sealed these things they're sealed." He gestured to the world all around him.

Palene's silent stare seemed to suggest he knew different.

It disturbed Dorey somehow, his mind suddenly tormented again by the memory of the fall. He was struggling to remain focussed. He pinched the bridge of his nose as the awful truth from which he could not escape replayed itself within his mind. "But it really happened didn't it?" he shuddered, "I mean, I'm certain of one thing, those are not just nightmares I've been having are they?"

Palene looked grim, "No. They are not nightmares. What you're experiencing is your brain trying to deal with the trauma of your death. It's extremely difficult to explain."

"Try."

Again Palene seemed reluctant, unsure even as to how he could formulate an answer.

"Are you from the future?" Dorey held up his hands, his impatience getting the better of him. "Is that why you can do these things which we cannot...Because you have superior technology?" Again he pointed at the scarring, "Are you human?"

"Yes I am human. And no, I'm not from the future." The smile returned, "Quite the opposite in fact," Palene leaned forward slightly, "I am from the past."

Dorey was stunned by the statement.

Palene continued, "If you will indulge me, I will tell you my story. Perhaps then you can judge the situation better." He had rehearsed this moment a thousand times. "My name is Palene o'Ilia Montraerse," he began, "I am more than two thousand years old... I am what humanity would describe as being immortal. And I have been watching you and your friends, for quite some time."

CHAPTER FIFTY NINE

If Dorey's situation hadn't been so miraculous, unbelievable or impossible even, he may well have laughed at his host's outrageous statement. Instead he found himself intrigued by it. He studied Palene, wanting to hear the explanation for such an outlandish comment. *'Let him speak,'* his subconscious suggested, *'Allow your mind time to sharpen. He may tell you far more than you could learn with simple query alone.'* And so he did.

"I was born in a village close to what you now know as Stonehenge." Palene began.

Dorey's eyes widened at the mention of this location.

"I like my father and countless generations before him, were what was known as the Ilia." He smiled at the lack of recognition his family tradition stirred. "You'd probably refer to us as a Sage or Druid." He went on, "My family belonged to a people who stemmed out of ancient Carthage and like the Sages or Druids of the Celtic, Nordic and Gaulish regions we were schooled in the art of memory and knowledge. Our function was to accumulate all the learnings of our people and stow them to memory. Dates, the yearly calendar, the science and mathematics needed for our crop rotations and harvests. Methods of healing, details of land ownership and all other manner of things which would ensure the wellbeing and organisation of our clans. Wise men, an information store of learning and fact. We memorised the knowledge of our forefathers passed from father to son through the ages before the use of the written word was adopted by the west. The data we stored over centuries was kept like bar codes, often held on the decorative handle of a dagger, etched onto a rod or staff or within the markings of a plate. These codes stored the information and progress of our learning, the history of our society . . . the secrets of our lands. Passed from generation to generation, a sequence of notches marked on relics in this manner could be called upon to avoid floods, help protect against famine, cure the sick, prevent land feuds, even war . . . Such was the accuracy of the data recorded. Unlike the written word the information passed down in this great tradition meant generations of history could pass through the ages with little corruption." He elaborated, "Placed into symbols which would stir the memory of the keeper precisely. Recorded purely for detailed preservation, rather than for gaining power or documenting a given point of view. As such it was unlike the written word so often manipulated in order to shape men's hearts and minds." He paused. "I cannot be certain of how far back you've travelled, so it may or may not surprise you to know these ancient traditions were far more sophisticated, as were the cultures which employed them, than how history often cares to remember them." Palene's eyes saddened, "Before Rome condemned their true histories to little more than ashes and rumour, replaced with their own world and myths, recorded in their insufficient Latin tongue." He lightened his tone, "Yes . . . I can assure you they were far more sophisticated than perhaps even you would believe." He continued, "My ancestors suffered greatly at the hands of the Roman Empire, forced from their heritage, migrating eventually to new lands near Gaul. My great-grandfather foresaw the threat posed by an ever expanding Rome as a young man. He was the third son in line and disillusioned by his clan's lack of concern had taken to the life of a traveller. He made passage to Britain where he befriended a Celtic tribal leader before falling in love with his eldest daughter. He settled with his new bride in the south west of England where a new generation of my family would grow. I was raised in the Ilia tradition, my family revered and respected. However, it was an age of great turbulence and by the time I'd reached manhood the threat of Britain being once again invaded by the Romans had become a menacing reality." His expression brightened, "When I was twenty-four, a girl from my village returned with her family from the northern coast of Cornwall. She was three years my junior and I'd not seen her since the day after my nineteenth birthday. She had always been beautiful possessing the most infectious smile. I'd loved her secretly throughout my youth and upon her return was surprised to find her without husband, especially as her beauty had only increased. I could barely control my excitement. She belonged to a prosperous family, traders with merchant ancestral roots along the coastline of Devon and Cornwall, some of whom had travelled as far as India." Palene witnessed the surprise, "Oh yes, the people of our islands have been trading across such distances for a long time, especially those around the Cornish coast. The modern world seems to think of these times as belonging solely to a bunch of savages killing each other in loin cloths, which admittedly they did from time to time, but there was so much more. There was a vast trading route which ran right through the Mediterranean and Europe, across Eurasia and down into the Africa's. Merchants, travellers and learned people often journeyed great distances to trade in goods and ideas. Such practices were certainly not a Roman monopoly." He shook his head. "It was from these very shores advanced farming was exported to Europe, to the land of the Pharaoh and beyond. Your historians have discovered such truths yet the modern world seems reluctant to see the world for what it truly was."

Dorey remained silent. He stared at Palene and tried to comprehend the possibility this man could have been walking the Earth for more than two millennia. He dismissed the absurdity from his mind but decided to see where the story would lead. All the while mindful his gratitude would not cloud his judgement.

His host wore a knowing expression. "You are wondering whether or not you can believe my account . . . Accept my incredible declaration." He smiled broadly and shrugged, "It is of no great consequence at this moment. You of all people know impossible is nothing, just as you know you should be dead right now, and yet here you are, breathing and sipping my coffee." Dorey visibly shivered at the remark as Palene creaked into his chair. "But you're right to be suspicious. If impossible truly is nothing then I could be anyone, feeding you any lie which took my fancy." He added, "But what I'm telling you *is* the truth. And if you search yourself honestly at the conclusion of this day, I think you may come to understand this of your own volition." Palene seemed exhilarated. "My God, do you know how many times I have imagined this moment? I've often wondered where in time this conversation would take place." He appeared wistful as his voice trailed away, the sunlight embracing them for a moment. He was obviously thrilled to have the Commander with him. "Forgive me, where was I?"

"You were in love with a girl." Dorey replied.

His guest's good willed response delighted Palene. "Ah yes . . . Marridana." Her name seemed to illuminate him. "When I finally plucked up the courage to tell her how I felt I couldn't believe her response was to tell me *I* was the reason she'd remained single. Her father told her when she was seventeen they were to return home from Cornwall within two or three years, so she'd waited in the hope I'd be still unattached on her return." He beamed, "We were married that spring."

Dorey found himself thinking about Jay. He could sense a pain in Palene.

"Over the next decade the Roman threat grew stronger and despite my family's best efforts our regions were no closer to uniting. I had two daughters, Lepina aged nine; Ossana aged eight and a strong healthy boy of six . . . His name was Orin. With our people in denial to the threat, I found myself increasingly concerned for the wellbeing of my family. We began making arrangements to journey north. Up toward Scotland and on to Iceland should the necessity arise. But then . . . *It happened*."

Dorey watched the darkness descend on his host.

"Just after my thirty-fifth birthday I was expected to attend the festival for the early moon up at the hallowed circle, or Stonehenge as you know it. The festivities went on late into the night and I'd left the camp to be alone for a while so I might think on things in the moonlight. The moon was incredible, perhaps the most incredible I've ever seen. I walked a short distance up the sloping hill with music and laughter in my ears. I sat for a while bathed in that luminous moonlight, watching as the fires below burned, the people dancing around the pyres. I was thinking about the dangers which loomed. I hadn't been up there long when I heard the heavens give out a strange rumble. There was not a cloud in the sky, not a sign of bad weather, nothing but an ocean of stars. Yet I had a real sense of foreboding. I remember it wrapping around me like a damp blanket. Again the heavens groaned, but it was not like thunder. I could feel the energy in the air, taste the peril. Then I had that feeling, the indescribable feeling when your senses know you're in imminent danger. I rose slowly to my feet and looked down to the party still going on oblivious, away from the hill. Marridana was there with the children and I felt a protective urge to be with them. I was to begin my descent when I saw it, a pale light pulsating in the sky, its intensity growing the more I looked at it. The hairs on the back of my neck stood on end. It must have been miles up in the heavens and yet somehow I knew it was looking directly at me...That somehow, it was meant for me. In my initial panic I was set to run when . . . BAM." He jerked his hand to imitate the flash, "It hit me."

Dorey sat forward.

"Now I don't remember too much after that but people from the festival told of how they'd seen the flash hit. *The finger of Venus* they called it. They said its force was so bright even from way down the hill they could see the silhouette of a person trapped within its bolt." He paused. "I was in some kind of coma for the rest of that year. Marridana took care of me throughout the bizarre aftermath. I was told for the first few weeks my hair would grow several inches a day then fall away before the process would start over. My breathing was rapid, as if locked in a far away fever."

Dorey listened, hunting for further clues besides the location and light in the sky.

"After nine months I finally awoke, if you can call it that, haunted by nightmares. Half the time I was completely delusional, and on the few occasions I wasn't I'd barely enough strength to even eat. All the while my wife and family took care of me. On the rare good days I desperately tried to make sense of everything with my father but I would always succumb to delusion, fearing my mind would never expose me to the truth. The only overriding and constant awareness was, I'd lost something. Now when I say lost I don't mean my mind," he shook his head, "No, it was worse even than that. Though exactly what I don't know. To this very day I still don't know with any certainty. I've come up with a million theories. All I know is I've lost something, some part of me. And though I can walk, talk, think and function . . . This thing that's gone, it haunts me and won't let me die. And perhaps in many ways won't let me truly live. Call it your soul, your consciousness, your life force. Whatever hit me that day took a part of me with it, and that part of myself calls to me through time and space."

Dorey wanted to say something but he held his silence.

"I'm not crazy, though God knows there have been times when I thought I could be." He added, "What I'm trying to explain remains almost impossible to understand, even after all these years. The best way I've come to describe it to myself I think you of all people may now comprehend more than most." Palene enquired, "When you awoke this morning and realised genuinely for the first time you were still alive . . . How did you feel?"

Dorey deliberated. "I felt incredible. I felt relief, joy like I'd never experienced." He searched his feelings. "I felt gratitude, undeserving, humble . . . even guilty."

Palene smiled. "And do you remember that short time ago when you sat before me and I told you I had a way to return you home?"

Dorey felt the delicious pain of the thought almost overwhelm him all over again.

Palene could read his guest's emotions like they were the written pages of a book. "You have a life there, family . . . friends," he paused then said with gentle enquiry, "A love?"

Dorey was slow to respond, but his usual caution gave way to the slightest of nods.

Palene sensed the longing, "Then try to imagine when you return home to . . ?"

"Her name is Jay." Dorey was cautious but felt certain he already held such information.

"Then imagine on your return, how you would feel if Jay was no longer there."

Dorey indulged him, fighting the pull of the emotional rollercoaster once more.

"Imagine everything is as it is now. We've finished our business and I've returned you home. But when you arrive *she* is gone. I don't mean as in no longer waiting, or even that she's since deceased," he shook his head, "What I mean is she's no longer there as she no longer exists. To you she remains real. You smell her scent on your pillow. Hear her voice in your dreams. But everyone you talk to of her thinks you're crazy as if you've imagined her, only you know for certain you have not. And yet, she simply is not there."

Dorey played the thought out and felt the back of his mouth dry at his current situation.

Palene leaned close and almost whispered, "Yet even though you eventually come to understand she's been erased . . . You still feel her, hear her calling as if she's in the next room." He sat back and stared at Dorey solemnly, "And yet no matter where you search, no matter how hard you look, she no longer exists."

He looked at Palene feeling prickly, waiting to see where he was taking this.

"Losing a loved one feels like you've lost a sacred part of yourself, that's why it is so painful. Such loss leaves a void inside you, a hole which can never be filled. To some people this is how being *in love* can be defined. Imagine then, how it would feel to truly lose an essential part of your own self, actually lose a piece of your soul. Like the love of your life being erased from existence, this piece of you is just . . . Gone." There was a distinct pain in Palene's eyes. "Do not confuse the feeling with sacrifice. For I appreciate the idea of losing a part of you would be nothing if compared to losing Jay if ever such a choice were to be made. No. What I'm asking of you is to concentrate on an overwhelming sense of loss . . . Of devastation."

Dorey thought about Moe and imagined Jay suddenly being torn from him. As he pictured the grief, he felt another powerful sense of guilt at how she must be feeling right now. He felt sick and hated himself for going against his training, his own preaching. He stared at the man opposite remembering how Brahms had got under his skin, realising how his effect had grown on him more and more since Dial's killing shots. Feeling once again the incredible sense of longing he'd experienced when he'd spotted him heading into that old building in Masada. He tried to concentrate.

"If you can imagine Jay being erased, yet calling to you through the voids of space then that's how you would hear the part of your own missing soul. As an utterly devastating sense of loss within you. A sacred piece of your make up, one you can almost smell, taste and hear as it calls to you from across the dimensions of time. Yet to the real world, to all you know, it does not and has never existed. It has never been. You and you alone must suffer the pain and madness of it, as only you can truly experience it."

Dorey could almost feel Palene searching him as he dwelled on the notion.

"When you love someone they *do* become a part of you, so equally when you lose someone a part of you is also lost. Time, life another love even, they may all offer some peace but that sense of loss will always remain." Palene stared gravely. "But let me tell you, when it is an actual part of yourself, a piece of your soul which is lost, there is no peace to be found. Only torment." His expression darkened, "Not even death will come to provide peace from such a pain. It shocked me just how unbearable it was. If you can try to imagine what I've just described to you, then you'll have at least some small idea of what it is I felt, what it is I feel to this day." Another long pause followed. "When I awoke from this coma I felt those same emotions you felt when waking from your own death. But I knew instantly something was very wrong. Somehow an actual part of me was missing, a part of my make-up. And though I yearned for it, searched within the nightmares of my mind, it never came back. Yet it continually torments me, calls me from the far reaches of another time, another space."

Again Dorey thought of Jay grieving. He tried to turn away from his own inner turmoil.

"For over two thousand years it has haunted me. And yet even from the very start, before I could even begin to understand what was happening to me, this affliction would cause something even more terrible." He exhaled and looked deep into his past once more. "For it would not only be content with destroying me . . . It would drag me through the very nightmare of which we've just spoken in order to provide you with a comparison," Palene's pain was obvious as he continued, "When it would become responsible for the death of my wife, my children . . . Then indeed my own life."

CHAPTER SIXTY

It was past two in the morning. Dial opened the intercom as he sat slouched on the end of his bed, tainted by bourbon and melancholy. He sighed heavily as the ring tone played. The familiar answer phone message kicked in and Dial's shoulders dropped further. He paused for a long time after the beep. "Jay, please answer the phone."

Her machine made him sound hollow and hoarse, his slurred voice exploring the silent apartment as Jay broke her heart into the darkness of her pillow.

"Answer the damn phone." He was drunk and the intercom did little to disguise this fact. "Do you think you're the only one who misses him?" His anguish invaded the room causing Jay to scrunch her eyelids tightly together.

He struggled, "He was my friend." Dial's head slumped forward.

After a time he forgot he was even on the phone-link. He sighed heavily before the click over the airwaves stirred him to remember, Jay's unexpected reply desperate and thin, "I miss him Mark . . . I don't know what I'm going to do."

Dial's heart broke all over again, "I know sweetheart . . . I know."

*

Palene continued his story. "In the half life I was living I don't think I even understood we were fleeing our home. The Romans had swept into the south of Britain and were beginning the process of destroying its social infrastructure. Tribal leaders, druids, anyone with the slightest seed of authority or knowledge were the first to feel their wrath. I and my kin were in great danger, but it wasn't until much later I realised my family had waited longer to flee, as they'd been too worried to move me during a particularly bad period of my mental illness. Nightmares and insanity tormented me as the growing horror of my predicament increased. The more I tried to understand what was lost in me, the more crazed I seemed to become. The brief periods of normality were of times spent laying in an enclosed wagon with Marri and the children smiling down on me and from time to time seeing the soothing gaze of my father. I'm not sure how long we'd been journeying. I've never been truly sure of when our journey even began. The only thing of which I've ever been certain . . . Is of how it came to an end." Palene looked gravely at his guest. "I'd been battling within my nightmares when I heard screams which forced me out of my bed. I felt extremely weak as I stumbled out of the wagon to the sound of whimpering and yelling, overpowered by a chorus of derogatory laughter. I wasn't sure at first whether or not I was still dreaming. I tried desperately to ascertain what was happening around me but I could make no sense of it all. I heard my daughters screaming and watched in horror as their screams were silenced, both of them struck heavily by two Roman cavalrymen now suddenly within my view. The image burned my heart like fire but before I could move toward them I was sent crashing to the ground, a short sharp pain shooting through the back of my head. When I awoke I was covered in my own blood and it took me a moment to realise it emanated from a deep wound across my throat which surely should have killed me. I managed to drag myself to my feet and stumbled around for a few seconds but soon crumpled back to the floor in a heap. I tried desperately to gather my senses. My eyes took in their surroundings but immediately wished they were seeing something different. For there, ahead of me I saw my daughters and son bound tightly to a tree. They'd been badly beaten and were sobbing in anguish. I saw more cavalrymen, now six in number, surrounding something on the floor. My view was blocked but I could see they were taking turns at grappling with someone pinned within their drunken feet, all the while laughing in that disgusting, shameless tone. They were like demons in my head, attacking me in my nightmares, splitting my mind into pieces. Then I heard Marridana's screams, and desperately I crawled toward her as I realised they were taking it in turns to rape my wife."

Dorey sat in silent horror as he watched Palene relive the savagery.

"I managed to get to my feet but in a flash they were on me, two of them beating me back down to the ground with ease. *'Didn't you kill this lunatic already?'* As they broke my bones I watched them drag my limp father and battered wife toward the tree to which my children were tied screaming for me to help them. Despite all my will power, I blacked out." Palene shuddered. "When I next came to my entire being was engulfed in smoke. That awful inescapable smoke, the heat filling my lungs as my children's screams faded into an inferno. I felt my flesh roast as my eyeballs began to boil, my mind screamed out deeper into its recent nightmares, only on this occasion to find some insane form of solace. And then . . . silence. When I awoke it was the first time I'd been fully conscious for what seemed as long as I could remember. The nightmare hit me in a flash but was then gone, and for the briefest moment I felt relief, as I thought that must be exactly what I'd experienced. Just another of those torturous nightmares which plagued me since being struck upon the hill. But then my eyes began to focus and in that same instant I could smell the burnt flesh and taste the ash. I felt the heat of the scorched trunk behind me and realised I was in fact laid on something and in turn something else was laid upon me. I pushed myself clear and forced myself onto my heels only to realise the true horror of my predicament. For there at my feet, were the burnt corpses of my three children, with them the bodies of my scorched wife and father. I choked on the venom of such a sight then fell to the floor, scuttling backwards like a terrified child. Instantly I threw up. I lay there screaming into the scorched dirt for what seemed like an eternity. No nightmares came to take me away, this time my reality was the nightmare."

Dorey sat completely aghast.

"I'd buried the remains of my family under a great oak further up the hill when I think I noticed for the first time my skin was blackened yet somehow undamaged. I was naked where my clothes had been burnt away and wore nothing but a trinket on my wrist. It was a woven metal bracelet Marridana had crafted for me. My hair, fingernails and toenails were gleaming as new. I felt around my throat at the now healing scar in place of the recently open wound. I sat by that oak for a long time, my shock seeing me slip in and out of consciousness. The delusions had left me . . . Yet now I longed for their return." He looked at Dorey. "I attempted suicide five times before the dawn of the next day. Each time I awoke as if nothing had happened, with only the healing scars worn upon my wrists as any evidence of my self-harm. Eventually, a rage took hold of me like nothing I'd ever known. I found some of the rope left by the Roman horsemen, tied a noose and cast it over the low swollen arm of the oak which shadowed the new graves. I climbed up the swellings of the trunk and clambered onto the branch before shimmering out. I placed the noose around my neck and without a thought flung myself toward the ground, spitting at the gods as I fell. The rope held and I felt my neck break as I was instantly thrown into the embrace of death." Palene shook his head solemnly. "I woke soon after, choking like a mad man as I swung helplessly from the tree. I cried through my asphyxiation, and to this day I do not know how I got down from that branch, all I am certain, I remained hanging there for some time cursing death for not claiming me."

Dorey looked dumbfounded. He found himself staring at the faint scarring left by Dial.

"Eventually my strength returned. The venomous lust for revenge contaminated and pumped my blood. I spent the next months hunting the men responsible, killing and being killed by anything Roman. I was held within a bloodlust the likes of which I'd never known before or since. I killed indiscriminately in the hope I would one day slaughter all those who'd destroyed my family. I became a devil, a ghoul who struck fear into the heart of the invaders. At some point, while wrapped in the rage of my madness, I'd come to the conclusion it was the gods who'd made me immortal. So I might seek out and exact both theirs and my own revenge on these unwanted conquerors. At first it gave me the desire to carry on. However the endless bloodshed, grief, and the constant trauma brought about by my own numerous deaths at the hands of my foes, soon took their toll. I slipped into yet another mental void wherein to this day I'm not entirely sure what truly happened to me. All I do know is after a long time spent within an inescapable prison of turmoil and hell, a small miracle happened, and it came courtesy of my lost wife."

*

"During the many months which followed the pyre, I'd become lost." Palene continued, "Haunted by the loss of my family, tormented by the traumas of the many murders I'd committed, more so by the countless deaths I'd suffered. Somehow, I'd found myself at the old Cornish port in which my wife had spent her adolescent years with her family. I must have aimed to make it there while lost inside myself. I'd been drinking heavily and one night bedded down under a trader's cart. But when I awoke I was no longer in the street, I was in the care of an old man," Palene smiled, "A trader, the owner of the cart I'd slept beneath. He'd taken me in, on the simple account of what I was wearing."

"What you were wearing?" Dorey enquired.

"Yes." Palene recounted fondly. "Astonishingly, he'd recognised the styling of the distinct copper and bronze weaving I still wore on my wrist, the gift my wife had made and given to me on the night of the infamous early moon festival. She'd told me it would protect me. Although tarnished and dulled by the fire, it had survived, and her craftsmanship and style was still plain to see by a trained eye." He beamed as he thought of his long ago wife, "Apparently as a young woman she'd made similar items for trade with merchants of that very port, all those years before. The trader's name was Clement. Despite my stupor he'd managed to determine just who I was. He'd moved and fed me, cleaned me up and put me in his own bed. A simple act of kindness which would ultimately save me from myself." His smile broadened, "This was her miracle to me."

Palene reached into the pocket at the side of his linen tunic and pulled out a wallet. He passed it over and gestured for Dorey to open it. "My saving grace was provided by Marridana, her simple trinket providing protection, just as she said it would."

Dorey looked inside at the intricate metal weaving pressed within. The faded wristband would have no doubt been a riot of polished reflection on the day Marridana presented it to her husband. He marvelled at its complex simplicity, took in the honest beauty. After a time he passed it back to his host and realised he felt exhilarated by it.

Palene returned it to the care of the wallet. "As I said, a miracle," his smile remained with the fond memory of his wife. "I saw this as a clear sign, one which gave me hope. The bracelet had been given to me on the very night I was to change forever, and the significance of Marri's words when she'd presented it now embraced me. For the first time I felt I may dare to hope of one day seeing them again, that my curse may have actual meaning. It may sound like the delusions of a desperate man, but something in that moment spurred me to look forward. In the days which followed I began to recover some strength of mind and body. But I still had a long way to go. At the start even my best days were haunted, often by vicious hallucinogenic images that raped my mind."

Dorey was cautious. "Of what happened to you and your family?"

"Yes . . . but not just that." Palene replied, "There were nightmares but also images. Numbers and theory, visions of the sacred part of me lost, which I know now emanated from other places in time, glimpses of different dimensions."

Dorey was once again surprised by the terminology, "Different dimensions?"

Palene realised he was in danger of getting ahead of himself. He gestured for Dorey to be patient. "Forgive me, I'm not making much sense . . . And I realise I'm perhaps dwelling too much on this period of my past. But I feel it's important for you to understand my story, and by doing so perhaps come to understand me." He looked at his guest sincerely, "Even by your remarkable standards you must be thinking all of this has to be fantasy," he implored, "But if nothing else it is essential you do at least understand me. Because we are linked you and I, and I've known for some time our worlds were meant to collide."

*

Dorey remained tight-lipped on his host's strange comment. Not really knowing what to make of it. His silence allowed Palene to continue and for now the Commander would oblige, concentrating on every word for the clues in which to gain his own answers.

"Five weeks passed under the old man's care and I was growing stronger every day. Old man Clement and I would walk and talk for hours. He introduced me to his merchant friends. Many knew members of Marri's family but I begged them to keep my plight secret. The kindness expressed helped calm my spirit and little by little I managed to get through each day. I told him of the Ilia, of how people such as I were in danger since the invasion. I persuaded him to arrange for me safe passage from Britain. I took work on a trade ship and spent the next years travelling east, living simply, at times lying low, following my instincts in order to seek out the answers I now required."

"The answers?"

"As I said I'd dared to hope, and the visions which tormented me now seemed to push me forward, onward into strange lands, as if some distant promise of understanding awaited me. Sometimes I felt utter despair, believing I would never find that of which I searched, but still I travelled on. For the next two hundred years I studied and learned. I sat with the Arab, the Jew, the Greek, the Persian and the peoples of Africa. I studied their beliefs their languages and cultures. I travelled on toward India then Siam, learning as much as I possibly could of the world . . . Waiting for the day when my purpose would be revealed. I'd grown certain only absolute knowledge could ever set me free." He added, "I could talk for hours of the many wonderful people I met and lived with. Tell you of the many evils and great deeds I witnessed. The tragedies and miracles, my successes and failures. I could describe to you how I was drawn to every learned person I could find so I may further both myself, and my quest. How desire for such knowledge would often lead me to adventure, sometimes death, and on many occasions regenerate my thirst for life. But such detail would only be more indulgence, especially as you are one of only a handful of people who has actually witnessed such places and wonders first hand, as they used to be," he gestured at their landscape. "Through my hopes, torment and faith I managed to discover enough about myself to enable my haunting dreams and meditations to eventually lead me to one of the most important discoveries of my life . . . You."

Dorey's eyes widened.

"Forgive the drama of my words," Palene said not meaning a breath of it, "But as the centuries passed since the death of my family I'd dedicated myself to bettering my understanding of mankind, the world and the universe. Convinced my calling would be revealed. I'd learned so much. My immortality granted me the time needed to digest knowledge of fantastical proportions. And all the while the strange dreams continued, as did the constant longing for that missing part of myself."

Dorey remained silent, studying his host intently.

"I remained in the east for some time, toured Buddhist temples and monasteries where I gathered and honed new skills such as deeper, superior meditation and projection. I tuned my body and mind with monks such as the Shoalin. Eventually, I found myself headed back toward the steps of China. It was at this time the visions and dreams were becoming more frequent, and with my new found meditation skills I found I was growing able to focus and enter these mysteries with far greater clarity. At first however, these skills proved a curse. The visions like my soul tormented me from some distant place and still I was no closer to understanding them. I became lost once again, in every sense of the word. As lost as a human being can be." His eyes were far away as he remembered the desperation. "Then one night I stumbled across an old ruin. I was exhausted from my travels and decided to make camp. After I'd eaten I meditated, and soon fell into a deep sleep. For the first time in years my dreams became clear and undisturbed, and then it happened. I discovered the existence of you and your people for the very first time."

Dorey leaned forward his curiosity alive.

"For in the end it was not a vision of God or heaven that was to offer me salvation. It was a vision of you."

*

Palene delved into his memory. "As I said I was sleeping. At first my mind was awash with the usual riddles of numbers and codes I'd found embroiled into human cultures time and again, coupled with the equations and concepts which seemed to emanate purely from the depths of my own troubled mind. It was a jumble of information, a mess of ideas which made little sense to me. But then quite suddenly, my mind found a place of hypnotic calm. I found myself in a complete state of peace, a mindset I'd not enjoyed since my life was altered so drastically. I enjoyed the solitude for a time when, like a lightning bolt, I was struck by an intense image, the same thing playing over and over, growing more real on each account. I was following someone on horseback. It was so real I could feel the clump of the hooves, taste the air, the musk of the horse. I was hanging back from a stranger ahead, watching him, when suddenly I was struck from the saddle. I felt my neck break on a rock, my body shudder. After a moment I saw a second man looking down at me. I could taste my own blood, heard a language I did not then understand as the person I'd been following approached. *'Is he dead?'* The second man standing above me answered, *'No but he soon will be.'* His face illustrated concern. Then I saw the face of the rider I'd been following as he too looked down upon me. *'Come on, we have to go.'* I tried desperately to speak but my neck was crushed. I couldn't move. I blacked out. When I awoke I saw a black object screaming up into the air like a giant hawk before vanishing in a trail of light, the flash similar to the one which struck me on the hill all those years ago." Palene smiled, "It was you I was following when I fell from my horse. It was your ship I saw disappearing through time."

The sudden realisation was quite unexpected, "I remember that. It was our first real . . ." Dorey stopped himself divulging any detail of their first live assignment in medieval Russia. He stared at Palene with disbelieving eyes. "One of my crew thought I was being stalked. He saw a man behind me on the ship's scanner and placed himself at the top of the gully to knock him from his horse." He shook his head, lost to this new incredible moment, "I recognise you!"

Palene watched the emotional turmoil grip the man opposite, aware of how fragile his mind would be. "It has remained little more than a dream to me. I don't fully understand why. Occasionally it proves this way when envisioning possible futures."

Dorey was stunned as the relevance kicked in. Not only was his host claiming to have glimpsed a mission which belonged in a different dimension to Palene's own *then* reality, but medieval Russia was also in the future to the moment this supposed dream was taking place. *'How could a man from the real past be visiting futures in simulated worlds which could not yet exist to him? How could anyone glimpse such events, especially when existing within actual history and not a simulated one?'* He thought of the complexities of time brought to the fore by their powerful computer, *'Were these obvious holes in his strange host's account?'*

Palene stunned him once again with his adept ability to read his thoughts. "You're wondering how a man from the *real* past could have possibly infiltrated a simulated future which did not yet exist to his then place of origin." He smiled, "Believe me it's not something you can understand. Time often proves elusive in such matters."

Dorey was struggling, "But that was a reality such as this, one which could not possibly exist to you in the real past." Once again he stopped himself giving anything away he may later regret.

Palene raised his hand. "For the time being it is best not to question such matters. Needless to say this ability became available to me within the realms of my own mind if you like . . . An ability which would one day lead me to both discover and create a method in our real world which could bring me to places such as these in the flesh. But let us just accept for the moment the nature of these visions, and how and when they came to me."

Dorey agreed, deciding once again it could well be Palene's tale that would reveal any hidden truths.

"When I awoke from that dream I knew something was different. I knew I had changed. I'd seen something at last which I understood had a direct bearing on my own plight." He smiled at the memory, "It's ironic. For almost four hundred years I'd been waiting for a message from God or the divine . . . And instead I got a message from you."

"A message?"

Palene nodded, "The repetitive image burned into my mind immediately afterward. The image of a place which would take me over a century to learn was the Temple of Syha. It played over and over in my subconscious in the days which followed."

"The temple of Syha?" Once again he cut himself short on hearing the venue of their second active assignment, "I don't understand."

"Nor did I until I finally reached it . . . For it was there I would learn at last, the true nature of my gift."

CHAPTER SIXTY ONE

Palene made his way back into the sunshine carrying a jug of water from the shade of the house. He poured it slowly then enjoyed a steady sip at the cool drink.

Dorey swished the liquid around his mouth to take the lingering coffee from his teeth. The sun was resplendent and he felt at that moment as if it were placed in the sky for his benefit alone. His emotions were quite naturally running wild. He had questions, concerns, major doubts. His host's story, the age he claimed to be, the mentioning of Stonehenge and a number of other poignant comments played like a broken record through his mind. He wanted to ask Palene if he'd ever tried to manipulate time in order to save his family, but decided such enquiries should wait. He'd wanted to ask for greater transparency on how he professed to have access to future simulated worlds, be it mentally or physically, from moments he claimed were in the real past.

Again he'd held onto his temptation. Instead he asked him to continue with his account.

"As I said, a hundred years passed before I discovered then finally reached the Temple of Syha. I didn't know what to expect when I arrived, but my heart was filled with hope. When I first laid eyes on the Indo-pyramid structure peering out of those dense trees I was completely overwhelmed. The monks who'd inhabited it had long since abandoned it to the forest, and I was pleased to find it empty. Much of its structure had been torn down, used for building in the valley some miles away, but its architecture and elaborate carvings were still in abundance to behold. I made camp there and began my meditations. But all I ever saw was a slightly improving account of the vision of my following you on horseback, of you leaving me to die as I watched the magnificent black bird soar through the sky before disappearing into that all too familiar tempest. The weeks turned into months, the months into years. I lived as a hermit. Occasionally I'd be forced to defend the temple and myself from thieves and opportunists, but for the most part I maintained an invisible profile, completely immersed within the task to unearth my goal. After many more years passed I managed to develop a greater clarity on that one vision, but I was growing disheartened by the fact nothing else was revealing itself to me. I reached another low point in my life and was close to accepting despair once more, when finally, it happened again." His eyes flashed at the memory. "During one of my meditations I felt my body suddenly being torn and thrashed into another place. It was far more intense than any of the visions which visited previously. I found myself in a strange land, dressed in unusual clothes. I was next to a stream and my first action was to run to it so I may see my reflection. My heart raced when I saw my own face looking back at me. And yet I knew this was in some way a different version of me . . . Or as I would conclude later, a version of me I'd not yet become. It was dreamlike in many aspects, but it was also incredibly real and lucid in others. I was confused, lost at first, but gradually I became aware of a sense of purpose. I was camped in a lush green valley. I possessed a horse, and weapons the likes of which I'd never seen. The bow and arrows in particular were of an extremely high standard of workmanship. I gathered these belongings and began a journey south. It was unclear how I seemed so confident in my direction, but I knew in all certainty I was on the right path. I travelled for three days and never came across another human soul. Until the fourth, when once again, I came upon you."

Dorey concentrated.

"Well I say you, but it wasn't you I found at first, it was your ship. It was some way from my position. But I found I could watch from a distance through the safety of what I'd discovered in my nap-sack, a small but powerful little telescope. Crudely made, it was a marvel to me then."

Dorey was trying to place the location in his mind.

"Your ship was . . ." he corrected, "Is an incredible sight. I stared at its black shimmering body for some time. It hadn't occurred to me it was the same object I'd seen flying into the heavens in my previous dreams. After all, the only thing able to fly back then in my mind was what nature designed. After a short time I was growing more tempted to go to it, but there was a strange force in the back of my mind which told me I should not. It was odd, because although I knew the thoughts of danger were my own, the experience of the control which prevented me from approaching your ship felt like it was not." He added, "My instincts proved correct, when out of the back of the structure a huge man of African origin walked out. His clothing seemed bizarre to me then, modern to me now. I watched him closely as he walked around checking the exterior undercarriage of the gigantic fabrication. He was joined by a woman dressed in the same strange attire . . . Jay I believe."

Dorey found it strange to hear her name spoken with recognition and once again felt certain this Palene knew all of them by name and face at the very least.

"She joined him in a manual check of the landing gear. After a moment they came together under the centre-wheel and shared a joke. But behind the laughter I could see they were anxious, sense they were waiting for something." He smiled, "You."

343

Dorey was enthralled.

"Just before nightfall, I heard horses approaching. Imagine my emotions when I saw you pull up on horseback with a smaller, rather intense looking young man just behind you."

Dorey winced as he finally placed the memory, realising it had been Ian Mahoney.

"You seemed a lot less anxious than your friends," Palene continued, "After a time another mounted group reached your ship. Two of them I did not recognise but the third sent shivers down my spine, as I recognised him immediately to be the man who'd stood above me after knocking me from my stallion in the previous vision. You shooed away the horses then began disappearing up a ramp which led into the back of the structure. Imagine my terror at the sound which then came from the vessel as you fired up the engines. I cowered behind my rocks and almost wet myself as I saw the impossible transpire before my eyes."

"You watched the ship take off?"

"I couldn't believe it. I watched as it hovered slowly into the air and ducked further behind my shelter as it proceeded to scream upward into the sky. Then as I heard its sonic boom, I found myself suddenly and unexpectedly back inside the ruined temple."

Dorey shook his head. It just couldn't be possible this man was able to observe these events in recreated timelines from a vantage point located within the real past.

There had to be another explanation.

"I've found it surprising since, a ship such as yours did not detect me spying on it from distance."

Dorey remembered, "It did. You had a forty millimetre cannon trained on you throughout." The clarity of the event returned in full, "You said yourself Jay seemed anxious. The Reeper had informed her of a stranger nearby. But it detected no weapons of any real threat, so Jay placed a three hundred metre defence perimeter around her. If you had approached the Reeper that evening, or even strung an arrow in your bow, you would have been waking up back in that temple a little earlier and with a slightly different ending to consider."

Palene smiled. "Then those alien instincts served me well, even in their infancy."

Dorey was unexpectedly chilled at this latest comment. Once again he kept silent.

"Of course, when I awoke from my meditation and found myself back in the Temple, I was shocked and bewildered. But I was also overjoyed. For now I had seen you twice, and it was then I realised we were truly connected."

*

In your mortal years it will be hard to comprehend, but for almost another century I stayed near to that ruined temple. On occasion I'd leave for a brief period, returning as a new inhabitant so as to avoid suspicion. I lived a simple life, hunting the woodland, fishing the streams. I was able to focus greater energy on the two visions and eventually had more experiences like those already described. One took me into the secrets of Alexandria, another onto the plains of Mongolia."

Dorey verified them within his own mind but said nothing.

"I revisited them whenever my meditations would allow. Studied and analysed them. I longed to know more but knew I must be patient. The years that rolled by seemed like weeks when compared to the centuries I had previously endured without direction. You and your small band haunted me like my lost soul. As did the equations and riddles I could still make no sense of despite the huge leaps forward I was making as I practiced my skills in mathematics and science. Each time I visited these visions, the same sense of foreboding always warned me, *'Do not approach these people yet, now is not the time.'*

The complexities within my mind were beginning to develop a kind of voice, though more through thought than any description of words. In time, I developed the ability to incorporate this voice into my own conscious. This coupled with the already heightened senses I'd developed with the Shaolin and the many others encountered on my countless journeys, transformed me further into a being of increasing power. It was a time of development and growth for me in every way."

Dorey narrowed his gaze. "Heightened senses?" He thought again of how easily this man had dispatched him during his attack in the corridor of the Colonel's residence.

Palene smiled. "As well as being immortal, I have also developed many other gifts." He made a casual gesture. "Do you wish me to explain them?"

Dorey would very much like to hear of them, but for now he wanted the rest of Palene's story. He asked him to continue and to return to these gifts later.

"As you wish," he gathered his thoughts. "More time passed, and as it took me into a new century, it also granted me one of my most important evolutions." His eyes sparkled with the recount. "For after so long having to wait and pray for these visitations during meditation, I finally evolved the ability to pinpoint and make these journeys through time at my own behest. I'd gradually been receiving more of the visions, and as I said, the more I visited them the greater clarity I received. I was beginning to develop superior control while trapped in these dreamlike states. They were becoming more real, as were my experiences in them. But I had reached yet another brick wall, another barrier which needed to be breached . . . And the breakthrough happened as suddenly and unexpectedly as my other evolutions." He continued, "During deep meditation I was cast back to the moment I first watched your ship. The usual chain of events transpired and I was preparing for my exit back to the temple upon the Reeper's sonic boom. Only this time, it didn't happen." He smiled. "You left the time zone . . . but I did not."

Dorey eyed him closely as he took another sip of his water.

"I was able to move around freely for hours after you had gone. The next time I spent the entire night, the time after, two more days. I applied all my concentration to enable it to happen in Alexandria, and on the third attempt, it did. I tried to achieve it again when in Mongolia and on the fourth attempt, the same. Suddenly it was I and not the dreams in control. I didn't know then of course they were in fact different times and dimensions as such, certainly not in the same sense you and I both understand today, but I knew they were different forms of existence. But perhaps most importantly, I realised if it was possible to develop this one small ability of control, I might also be able to develop other abilities . . . Such as when to jump into these times in the first place."

"And of course . . . you did." Dorey interjected.

Palene nodded. "Yes, although not in the manner I'd hoped. That was to be a much more recent evolution. What I developed was the art of warning. I began to understand that the voice in my head, if focused on correctly, would send me a signal of when these jumps were about to transpire. Once I'd recognised this I developed it further so these warnings could be heeded well in advance, which in turn allowed me to jump into another version of myself at a much earlier time. This meant I could make the journeys to you much sooner than if I'd just passed clumsily through on the whim of a dream. Over decades, I honed this skill to perfection until I reached the point I achieved almost total control, and then it happened."

Dorey remained fascinated.

"I was far from the temple riding one day, when I began to feel the by now familiar warning a jump was about to occur. I was much further away from the ruin than I'd ever been before, and was surprised at what I was experiencing. You see, I'd come to believe it was the temple that was the connection. The antenna if you like . . . The focal point of my power. Until that moment I'd never experienced anything like the intensity or clarity of vision when away from it. All of my developing skills had evolved in its shadow. I dismounted and quickly sent myself into a deep, controlled meditation. And then, BANG. There I was in a different time, a different place. Only this was entirely new. A location I'd never been to before. It was night and I was alone in the desert with only a well-presented camel for company basking in the moonlight. I was looking up at the stars, just visible due to the sheer intensity of the moon. The same thought bounced around my head over and over, *'Only a rich, wise man can obtain the ear of a King.'* I looked down at my feet and realised incomprehensibly I'd navigated myself to the exact location in which I wanted to be. Six heavy-looking rocks lay in the dirt around me, and strapped to my camel's hide was a shovel. I took it and immediately began to dig. After two hours or so I was standing within a hole large enough to be my own grave. With a last thrust I hit something hard, and eagerly I began to dig it out. It was a chest, for which I had the key on a chain around my neck. Inside the chest was a treasure." He smiled. "I took the riches, climbed aboard my camel and began my journey toward what I already knew was to be my destination. I reached Constantinople three months before you did. I established myself as a rich merchant whose family had been lost to the desert, and within weeks I was welcome in the new court of Alexius III. I gained his favour as I knew I should, and watched with interest when various members of your team, and eventually you yourself, began to arrive." He stared intensely at his guest, "And from that moment on, I was able to travel to your locations in time before you got there, able to observe you and your people at close hand, always in the shadows."

"And all this time you didn't once approach us or try to make contact?"

He shook his head. "The very core of my instincts simply forbad me from doing so. I knew back then making contact with you would have been as lethal to me as you taking me forward to your time would be lethal to your own world now. So instead, I watched, I learned . . . I evolved." He went on, "From that moment I realised I no longer needed the temple. I was once again able to travel, only now with more freedom than I could have ever imagined. I knew I'd discovered real hope of a purpose as my visitations to you and your group grew more frequent. In the times when I'd feel myself being pulled into moments I'd already visited, I would prepare myself so I may gather every scrap of information I may have missed previously. With every new visitation I would immerse myself into the culture you were set to infiltrate. Then I'd simply wait, ready to learn more of you and your purpose, knowing somehow you'd eventually lead me to my own."

"But how could you possibly know where we intended to be each time?"

He smiled darkly, "I've never been entirely certain. All I do know is something has always guided me, a power far greater than you or I, and one that was soon to reveal itself to me." Palene was cautious as they approached the subject. "I've come to believe this power was always there, in the background of my mind, hidden in the deepest darkest parts of my troubled psyche. I believe it was responsible for guiding me to my new evolution on the far side of the world. And though it never gave clear direction, like the subconscious voice I'd since developed, I realise now it encouraged, pushed and gave me hope. But it wasn't until this latest evolution when redefining my power away from the temple I was finally able to focus on it in any true form."

Dorey shivered unexpectedly as he thought of the light he'd experienced far away in his own subconscious, he felt the dip of the rollercoaster, but fought against it.

Palene continued, "It happened during one of my deepest meditations. I was searching for answers to the constant riddles and formulas which plagued my brain. I felt the same sickening call of my broken soul and once again tried desperately to reach out to it with my mind. Yet on this occasion I somehow pushed beyond my usual boundaries and felt my subconscious slip toward what felt like the edge of the universe, experiencing a terror beyond explanation. But then, as suddenly as it had taken a grip of my being, I saw something form within the echelons of my ethereal psyche."

Dorey hung on his every word.

"I felt the sense of all which had guided, tormented and healed me begin to take form in the distant corridors of my mind. As its presence became more real what at first appeared to be a far flung white spot in the darkness, slowly formed into a sphere of light. Its power was compelling. Its focus seemed to aim at my very core as it sat on the edges of my mind's capability. I felt its pull, and somehow understood it was inviting me to it. And yet I also understood immediately I could never be as one with it, never have its truth revealed to me until I'd become whole once again. Suddenly I was aware of the obvious purpose. I had to physically seek out the lost part of my soul. I had to unite the missing part of me taken when I'd succumbed to the Finger of Venus." Palene stared into the memory before focusing on his guest once more, "And it would remain as beautifully vague an ideal for centuries to come . . . Before I'd finally be ready to take my next step."

CHAPTER SIXTY TWO

Palene's description of this light disturbed Dorey and his thoughts began to darken. '*Did this man want me to die so I may understand his own plight better, and with it his perception of a cause?*' He tried to remember the strange light within his own dreams and began to wonder if his host had in some way infected him with this experience, '*So I may be manipulated by the use of a common denominator,*' he thought, '*Preaching of immortality, quests and mystical events . . . Why? So he may control me as his pawn.*'

His host leaned into his chair. "You seem troubled."

Dorey was direct with his response, "Tell me about this light."

"It was only a distant vision at first, a vague experience encountered during the meditations described. It remained that way for a long time but has recently become more vivid. I believe it to be an energy source of pure intelligence, an entity beyond human comprehension. Over many centuries of meditation and enquiry I've come to suspect it may stem from the very centre of creation."

Dorey was stunned. He scowled incredulous, "Please tell me you're not inferring God?"

"I believe the term God to be a little crude for what we're really talking about here."

"Crude?" His tone bordered on disgust. "But you are suggesting it is some sentient force entwined into creation?"

Palene nodded.

Dorey wanted to balk at such possibility but instead found himself thinking of Carl as he tried to explain the Stasis None to an ever eager Deans. His thoughts returned to the distant force within his own dreams. He only vaguely remembered the light and he'd certainly felt no Godly connection to it. "Are you telling me you believe yourself to have witnessed something divine?" he thought on Palene's terminology, "That understanding it's definition beyond any *crude* human comprehension . . . Sees you yourself elevated to something higher than mankind?"

"I never said I understood it. And as for what sets me apart from other men, the cause of my immortality and the evolutions it has since granted is the main root of that."

Dorey pondered the strange phenomenon experienced as death surrounded him. He thought of Palene's incredible claim of immortal life. It would all be so ridiculous under normal circumstances and yet . . . He searched his memory but couldn't find the level of clarity desired. The light was like a ghost in his subconscious. He felt no real correlation. It was only visible to him once, but he was certain in some way its touch was a part of the reason he was still around listening and talking. That it had some involvement in how Palene used the power at his disposal. '*So do I believe Palene to be in some way cohesive with this energy force?*' He felt sick at the confusion. He hadn't a chance to consider what he believed it to be on a personal level. In many ways he was perhaps too afraid. He wasn't sure he was ready for any life altering vision just yet. He was having more than enough trouble with coming back from the grave. He felt his mind slip toward the abyss and thought he may actually vomit as he considered all that was happening. '*Was he even alive . . . Or had he merely become a simulation of himself?*'

Palene remained silent, allowing Dorey time to take control.

"Does experiencing this *centre of creation* mean you see yourself as blessed? As some kind of prophet?" Dorey's scowl returned, "Just as when you first flung yourself from that tree, when you believed your gods had spared you for a purpose?"

Palene smiled at the man he'd watched so long, marvelling at his formidable strength. His mind was barely recovered yet still he demanded more, ready to extract that of which he felt was needed. Although the Commander was experiencing a degree of turmoil Palene knew just how incredible Dorey's will was proving, how remarkable his recovery had been. He considered how he could best describe his own purpose without immediately sounding like a madman with a messianic complex. He remembered his many rehearsals. This was the essential avenue he needed to explore before he could finally reveal to the Commander his true belief for being. "When I spoke of believing the gods had spared me so I may wreak their wrath, I was of course a delusional fool. Also the gods mentioned were fantasy, applicable to my place, my time in the world at that moment. But I can assure you my experience of this source is no such illusion."

Dorey could sense Palene studying him, wanting him to divulge his own experience.

He did not.

"As I've described I'd evolved myself for centuries before this source allowed me to truly experience its presence." Palene clarified, "And although in recent decades such experiences have become more vivid, the true essence of this power remains illusive."

"Until you fulfil your quest, and reunite with the missing part of yourself?"

"Yes."

"And then what? This core entity will divulge all like you're some, chosen one?"

Palene smiled, ignoring the disdain. "You ask me if I believe this light to be divine and as such if I believe myself to be on the same plateau as history's *chosen* prophets. But to make any such comparison must depend entirely on a given point of view." He needed to be careful. His goal was almost in sight but his guest would have to discover the truth of his own volition. "But as you well know making any such comparison immediately places you against legend, not necessarily against fact. I could never know if what I speak of now and what such prophets may or may not have witnessed previously could be one and the same thing. And perhaps in many ways I find the notion irrelevant. From a purely practical point of view my knowledge of the world is on an entirely different perspective, which of course means their purpose when compared to my own are also very different. But let us focus on what you *think* it is you now need to know." Another short silence followed. "Am I delusional for claiming to have witnessed any such power in the first place? Do I suffer an inflated ego for believing such a source could and so therefore would show itself to me?" Again he studied Dorey but he gave nothing away of his own familiarity to such an event. "In my experience, could exposure to such a power be utilised to save a race or build one from the dust of the desert? Yes . . . But then so can the creation of simple stories. So how do we differentiate? The legends put forward by such prophets carry great weight throughout the ages, riddled with messages of greater significance, themselves repeated since the dawn of mankind. But are they just stories, or genuine guidance provided through individuals touched by some higher force? I for one have discovered the truths behind these myths, though I cannot be certain you have done the same. The versions of these legends which surround us today together with the faiths which stem from them are after all only rehashed versions of stories told in Egypt a thousand years before, India a millennia prior, or in China centuries before those. And in many ways these ideals are often obscured by such *divinity* as you call it . . . Divinity since placed on them to inspire hope or more to the point, instil control. Is it banal of me to describe this source as a *light* in the first place? Is it a light at all in the real sense? Or is it some metaphor used to describe the inner focus of the human soul?" Palene was fishing but still Dorey remained silent, "Should I tell you of all I've learned, so you may see how I perceive things in the hope you'll not recoil from me when all I've brought you here to understand is finally set out? Will such indulgence help you make an informed decision as to my own madness or sanity?" He pondered the notion. "Am I to assume due to your reaction you've not had opportunity to witness the actions of such prophets and saviours? That you've been unable to observe say Abraham, Moses, or Christ?"

Dorey was cautious.

"What of more recent prophets such as Mohammed?"

"Let's just say they've remained elusive so far."

"And how would you feel if you did meet such a person?" No answer was forthcoming, "Would it be so different to meeting other great legends of history?" He eyed the Commander closely, "You've met many such individuals have you not? How did they appear when meeting them in the flesh?" He smiled already knowing the answer, "A lot less legendary I would imagine, a lot more human."

"It hardly qualifies as an equal comparison." Dorey interjected.

"Why not?" Palene retorted, "Remove the myth reveal the person." The smile remained, "If it serves you best to label and categorise perhaps we should scrutinise such a legend. Take Moses, the adopted son of a Pharaoh, schooled in all things by scholars of the age to make their own version of a living god on Earth. Training placed on Moses as one of the Pharaoh's heirs. His knowledge and understanding of the world would have been vast. And he would have utilised such learning when turning away from this kingdom to build a nation out of his true kinsman. The ideals, laws, commandments, he would have understood more than anyone the need for the simplest ingredient of all . . . Legend. For without legend you cannot build a nation. You need a common belief, a unifying story which brings you together and binds you through purpose. This is why he kept his people out in the desert for so long. He gave them a unifying history out in that wilderness, passing down a basic rule of law which would become the backbone of many modern societies for thousands of years to follow. Clearly an enlightened man, but does enlightened mean he was touched by something divine? Does his claim of experiencing a force which he could only perceive in his own era as being God?" He digressed, "Just as Alexius believed he had, after your little light show in Constantinople?" Palene's smile grew. "Do I believe what Moses or Abraham experienced to be the same source of which I've described? Or was it merely a hallucination brought about by diseases rife among men in that period?" His smile darkened, "What I witnessed would have only received one response had it dared suggest I sacrifice my son as a statement of faith."

Dorey saw the contradiction, "And yet you stated yourself, exposure to such forces as the Finger of Venus left you delusional in the beginning."

"I'm merely making comparison. And in doing so leaving you in no doubt as to what my response would be should any such experience order me against my principles. The very notion of some jealous God instructing me to sacrifice a son as a show of faith is repulsive." He concluded, "More likely the delusions of a madman and certainly not the vision of power I witnessed!" Again he shrugged, "But is this even important? As I've already said, what I understand and what Moses or Abraham could perceive in their own lifetime are on entirely different spectrums." He moved on, "Of course, it took another to see such stories spread globally. In Christ we once again find a man of high learning. Educated in the scriptures, teaching the necessity to treat each other fairly, to embrace the idea we're as much a part of God as God is a part of us." Palene smiled as if knowing some hidden secret. "I've studied teachings of this man long before they were corrupted by the fateful blends of people and time. I sat with elders who knew him in their youth. I learned much of what really happened and why and can therefore see how comparisons with my own plight could indeed prove legitimate."

Dorey bristled at the statement. "So you do define yourself as chosen?"

"I'm simply stating I believe there to be parallels between my own predicament and those of Jesus the man . . . Not the legend." Palene explained, "As prophecy took route in the philosophies of these nations so it was Jesus could come into being. But the world only knows of gospel accounts written centuries later, doctored and edited by scribes who took it upon themselves to rubbish other such records which existed and often predated the texts we hold onto today." He elaborated, "In the time of Christ the Jewish nation was hoping for a great leader descended from David, a king sent to free them from tyranny. But Jesus knew what price would be paid if the Jew or anyone else were to follow such a king." He gestured to Masada behind them. "This place, within only a few decades of Christ's death paid testimony to what happened if you stood up to Rome, just as my ancestral home of Carthage likewise experienced so many years before." He added, "I've read testimony describing how Jesus along with Joseph of Aramathia travelled the Roman occupied lands extensively during the years the selected gospels chose to ignore, learning of such punishments as well as seeing first hand how all roads truly did lead to Rome. If his people were to flourish then it was an idea which would deliver, not an army. For an idea can blow away battlements far more effectively than any waging of war. His people were spoiling for a fight, and Jesus was certain it would risk their destruction. But if he could use his enlightenment to show a better ideal, he could martyr himself within his own people's prophecy and send a shockwave across the known world. After all, Rome back then was like the Internet of the twenty-first century. Put a strong enough message out there and watch it spread." He digressed, "Of course the legacy was to find itself cruelly altered when this same empire realised it had played a part in the murder of a perceived saviour. At the very moment its own stranglehold and wealth was reducing and with it a diminishing ability to rule by the sword. So eventually, in place of the Roman Empire we bare witness to the compromise of the Holy Roman Church, with its Roman ideals of worshipping statues and symbolism replacing the simpler truth taught by the humble carpenter himself." He stopped, realising he was allowing himself to digress a little too far, "Forgive me . . . But people talk of Rome as if it were dead and buried. Yet in reality it continued to crush and take over civilisations as it had done for centuries." He added, "Ask the indigenous people of the South Americas . . . Was it Christ or the Pope who burned their civilisations and stole their gold?" He was deviating too much and he knew it. "I could talk for hours on such things, but you would no doubt wonder how such digressions could answer your original query." He concluded, "My point is simply this. I believe an enlightened soul is capable of bringing about the real changes necessary to the human race. But do these ideas and people have to become touched by the divine in order for us to learn from them?" He didn't wait for a response, "In many ways placing such celestial connection often takes away the very aspiration these people instilled. I for one take great comfort in the fact Jesus was a man. It offers hope to think such enlightenment and compassion is achievable within the soul of another human being. By insisting on turning unquestioned divinity on his gruesome end we turn away from the real point."

"And what is that?"

"That we should try to emulate such examples, not excuse our lack of ability to do so on the fact we can't possibly reach such heights as mere mortal men and women."

"But none of this answers my original query." Dorey pinned his host down, "Do you see yourself as having witnessed the divine? Do you believe this light at the centre of creation wants you yourself to forge something new for mankind?"

Palene's smile broadened further. Dorey was now searching the correct avenues. "Throughout history, throughout every faith system we have witnessed the birth and death of those sent to improve our understanding. In centuries gone by these people needed to be relevant to their own time, to their own place in the world. But in a globalised world no such sectarianism can be afforded. And when mankind's dedication to such blind faiths only affected the world of man that was one thing . . . What he does now affects the very universe itself."

"You mean what I and my people do now?" Dorey fired back. "And so this light has told you to come to our rescue, to show us the error of our crude ways?"

"I've never communicated with this light. And I neither see myself or this light as divine. I do not need to. I was born to the Messianic period. I sought out enlightened souls in order to learn of my gifts, my purpose. Many teachings I discovered clearly understood the existence of such a source. Some embraced it. Some thought me as mad as perhaps you do now. And yet with each passing breath such a quest brought me ever closer to you, allowing me to discover more of this source within my own dreams, my own meditations. In turn, I've finally come to cement my beliefs."

"Which are?"

"We must prepare for our next phase of development. Remove ourselves from Bronze Age magic and myth. Would salvation be necessary if we were better people in the first place? Would embracing the incredible gift that is our planet not serve mankind better than blindly wishing for a heaven that already exists around us? Perhaps then we could move away from submission, stop concentrating on the promise of something better to come. Embrace each other here and now and assume the next stage of our evolution."

"So you do believe you are some kind of saviour?"

"The planet and the universe which holds it have been exposed to an increasing danger, posed by the very race placed here to protect it. I'm merely a necessary adjustment for what needs to be done now mankind has enabled itself to deliver such doom."

"But what does that mean?" Dorey demanded, "That you've disregarded any possibility you're some abnormality in nature, an accident of science or a freak within evolution? Are you so certain this light of yours carries such weight? That over the course of having experienced over two thousand years of living you've become unable to comprehend the notion you're not quite as essential to things as you may now believe yourself to be?"

Palene was delighted. He now had Dorey asking exactly the right questions. "But this is my point. Abnormality or freak within nature, it makes little difference. All that matters is how I perceive this light. All that matters is what I believe I'm here to do. How I came to be here is no longer the force driving me."

"You contradict yourself." Dorey said sternly. "And you may be placing far too much importance on why and how you came into being."

"With all due respect, it is I who has lived through two millennia. It is I who has evolved through them and come to learn these things of which we now speak. If you're looking to pin a messianic complex on somebody in order to make sense of your own confusion, then I'm afraid you have the wrong man. Today is about one thing alone. I need you to understand these things simply because I need you to understand me. This power guides me for a reason, and the final piece of that reason will be revealed to me through you."

Dorey felt the weight of his statement, "So you believe this purpose has come to a head?"

"After that first visit to Constantinople everything changed. I realised our paths were meant as one. I knew we were headed on a collision course, that you and your friends *were* my journey. I spent the centuries between our meetings bettering myself, learning all that could be learned. I observed your tools and machines, understood they were an evolution in some distant future. I began research and invention. I would develop the manipulation of energy and motion, of sound and heat. From the scraps of my research great men would build entire legacies. And all the while I'd be in the background, funding, learning, observing. I was DiVinchi, Galileo, Einstein, Everett . . . I was Newton, Verne and Bell. Every step of human evolution has been done hand in hand with my own. And yet with every ounce of myself I gave to mankind I watched as it was squandered. The periodic table, they build a bomb. Theories of explosive thrust, they fire a missile. I tell myself it's not necessarily my own doing. After all, I am not so vain as to think these great minds would never have been great regardless. But I often fear my meddling has sped up too many evolutions, and brought them to mankind's attention before it was truly ready. This is my contradiction of being. But all the while the voices, numbers and codes in my mind made more and more sense, and on each journey I took toward your endeavours the more convinced I became it was the correct path to follow, that I could find the missing part of my soul then understand how to reach out to this light and in doing so, discover how to best serve mankind."

Dorey's head was reeling from the information, from the contradiction that was Palene.

"Eventually, I reached the point where the technologies I required were finally becoming available. I locked myself away and achieved the huge leap forward which would help me realise my goals. I developed the technology for real time travel and with it the ability to seek you out on my own terms. The subconscious voice within my mind rang out warnings from all directions. The time our paths should cross was approaching . . . But I could only act once the powers which guided me for so many centuries gave me permission to do so."

"And you believe that time is now?"

Palene nodded. "Yes . . . it has finally arrived!"

CHAPTER SIXTY THREE

As Dial approached the bench he was relieved to see it was indeed Jay who occupied it. She'd been there for while staring out at the Thames, watching the early morning traffic on the river. The view was improved dramatically by the recent uncovering of the Palaces of Westminster, the parliament buildings finally allowed to breathe after many months spent under scaffolding and tarpaulin.

He hadn't been sure whether she would keep her promise to meet him. "Looks like they've finally finished," he gestured toward the palaces on the opposite side of the bank.

Jay turned on hearing his voice, "I guess so."

Her face was ashen and it was obvious little sleep had come her way since the tragic incident in Masada. Her eyes showed the sorrow of a broken spirit and it hit Dial like a hammer. Tears threatened, partnered with a lump in his throat. It was unexpected and he was instantly furious with himself. He wanted to be strong for Jay, not make her worse. It was the first time he'd seen her since she'd locked herself away, and seeing his friend so destroyed only amplified his own sense of pain and loss. He sat beside her. She was so beautiful and for the first time in all the years he'd known her she appeared fragile. "I know it's a stupid question but, how are you?"

She shrugged, casting her gaze back onto the Thames. "Oh you know . . ." There was no substance to the comment, but of course Dial understood.

"You look tired."

"I've not been sleeping too well."

"No," he joined her vigil of the river, "Nor me." A short silence followed as they watched an ancient looking tugboat pass. "Have you spoken to your mom yet?"

"This morning." She turned looking at him properly for the first time. "You look worse than I do."

"It's good to see you."

Her lips were fractured and dry. Her eyes filled with tears but she composed herself before the flood could come, "You too." She tried to smile but only half achieved it.

Dial cautiously returned to the topic of Jay's mother. "How's she doing?"

"Devastated," her voice cracked, "She adored him . . . They both did." She closed her eyes, "She wanted to come over right away . . . But I told her no." She swallowed hard. "I feel terrible because my mom knows before his does." She sobbed and Mark held her, consoling her gently. After a few minutes she managed to take a grip of her grief once more, bringing it to heel with several heavy breaths. "How are the others?"

"Oh you know . . . They get through it day by day."

Her gaze returned to the Thames. "Well, I guess that's the only thing we can do."

Dial reached his arm around her. She didn't fight him, and the gesture itself was enough to turn on the water works again.

"I'm so sorry." He said, as they shared their grief. "I'm so very sorry Jay."

She squeezed him tighter. "I know." She allowed her pain to pour onto his shoulder as she struggled. "I just can't believe he's gone."

"None of us can."

Dial stroked the hair caught on her damp cheek away from her eye.

"God it's just so difficult." She sniffed, "I mean . . . What the hell was he thinking?"

"I don't know . . . I really don't."

Jay slumped against the bench then looked up to the sky jetting out another heavy exhale, "I just don't understand." Even wrapped within grief she was mindful of her words in this public place.

"As soon as he saw that bastard alive he was never gonna give it up."

"We were right there, all he had to do was stay put."

He rubbed the back of her shoulder and agreed as once again, the river became a good excuse for their attentions. Passers-by on the pavement could not help but notice the scene, indulging themselves with guesses as to the reason for such public emotion.

Jay fought the anguish, "Why did he start down that mountain when we were practically on top of him?" She shook her head despairingly. "It's just not Dorey."

"Something about that guy stirred him." He gazed into the distance, "Made him act impulsively."

She leaned onto her knees, cupping her chin in her palms. She sniffed but said nothing.

Dial watched her for a moment. "So you haven't spoken to Dorey's folks?"

Her eyes closed for a moment. "I called their home this morning, took me hours to pluck up the courage. Went through to their answering service . . . Turns out they took a last minute trip to see Katie in Berlin. I didn't know whether or not to call them there," she looked to Mark with questioning eyes, "Tell them while they're together."

Dial continued to rub his hand between her shoulder blades, desperate to be of some use.

"But then I figured . . . What's the point in ruining their vacation? After all, it's not like there's a body or anything." This comment clearly injured her greatly. She struggled, "I mean the funeral can be held any time without a body." She wept and Mark shared her pain. Eventually she added, "I don't even know if that's the real reason I couldn't do it. I mean . . ." Her voice cracked under the effort.

Mark hugged her once again, "Hey . . . Shhh."

She continued shakily despite his concern, "It's like if I tell them . . . Then it is real." She looked at him as if longing for him to understand. "And I don't want it to be real. But then I'm disgusted at myself . . . Because they have a right to know their son has gone."

Dial did his best to console her. "Don't beat yourself up about it." He was determined to help her through this. "There's no rule book when it comes to this sort of thing. You can only do what you think is right."

She sobbed some more, surprised at the sudden return of her tears as she'd honestly begun to believe they'd been exhausted, condemning her to endure grief through drought. "I mean, I took the option to not have the military inform them. I held up my hand and said . . . No way!" She raised her palm as if to illustrate this protest, "As if finding out like that would be a crime or something," she looked at Mark, "That he and his family deserved better. I told Brookes they didn't have to worry about me saying anything of what really happened." She pinched her nostrils to stop the running, "I told him, *'I took an oath.'*" She looked away from Dial in utter dismay, "Yet how can I get all self-righteous? Who am I to protest anything when I can't even tell his parents?"

Dial responded. "Look, if it's any consolation I agree with you. I'd wait until their vacation was over. Sure, maybe you should tell them while they're with Katie, but . . ." He didn't really have a point so his voice drifted away into another embrace. After a time he repeated, "You can only do what you think is right." He was cagey again as he added, "Do you want me to tell them?"

She sat further forward, as if in pulling away from him she could in turn pull herself away from temptation. She shook her head and showed signs of regaining her composure. "No." She said, as a final decision suddenly formulated within her mind, "I've decided. I'm going to go over there at the end of the week." She'd obviously been toying with this idea for some time. "They're due back on Sunday. I'm going to book myself into a hotel on Friday night. I'll tell them while they are all together. Then I can stay with them to see if I can help." She looked down at the floor as if ashamed. "I just hope they never find out my parents knew before they did."

"How could they? It happened when we say it happened." Mark sighed heavily and sat forward to be closer to her. "Are you sure this is the way you want to play it?" She did not respond. "I mean . . . I could come with you if you like."

Again she shook her head as she reached out and squeezed his hand, not at all relieved at making her decision. "I think I should go alone." She turned to him, her tears drying, though her face betrayed their testimony. A weak smile followed. "But thank you. You're a good friend."

Dial squeezed her hand, but again could think of nothing he could do or say to truly help her.

CHAPTER SIXTY FOUR

Dorey stared out over the tranquil Dead Sea. The morning had seen him endure a mixture of emotions. The story this man told was incredible, impossible. Yet here he now was, living and breathing while taking in the sea air and its exhilarating views from the wall of the veranda. Palene's sense of purpose was disturbing. If his story was to be taken seriously then the contradiction of believing he was here to save mankind from a fate he may have inadvertently helped create was significant.

He pondered further over the light he'd experienced within his own awful demise. *'Was it a trick?'* Dorey didn't think so. As incredible as events proved he couldn't help but believe much of Palene's account. He thought hard on the many coincidences, of the places and times so relevant to Palene's tale which the Commander chose to withhold.

Eventually he turned back to his host, the break from their discussion's recent crescendo, a welcome one. "So this power that guides you . . . Did you utilise it to bring me back?"

"The power I refer to is beyond my manipulation."

"So then how did you do it?"

"As I said, it isn't really something I can explain."

"Try."

"It's beyond words . . . It's something I'm simply able to do."

"Simply able to do . . . Have you any idea how that sounds?" Dorey protested, "I'm not immortal, so how the hell do you explain me dying then coming back?"

Palene thought for a moment. "Recently I've found my power has evolved at an incredible rate. As I've come to understand the force which guides me more clearly, the less restrained I appear to become by the usual laws and boundaries of reality. I'm able to manipulate certain laws of existence, alter the rules to my will. But only within reason."

"That's some contradiction."

Palene smiled, "As I said it is impossible to explain."

Dorey felt sick as he once again considered he may no longer exist in the truest sense. He tried to remember the light. He wanted to focus on it once more so he may form some kind of opinion. But he could not. He closed his eyes and thought of Jay, of Dial and the others. He heard the laughter of his sister. Saw the faces of his parents. *'They'd all be grieving his loss by now.'* He was finding it difficult to concentrate, his emotional swings relentless. The relevance of Stonehenge, the Finger of Venus and the two thousand year lifespan continued to brood. The fact Palene claimed he was able to hook into their simulations, their pasts created in a future he'd not yet even reached. There was an obvious connection but he just couldn't see it. He'd remained reluctant to speak of his organisation, to see if he and Palene could together fill in these blanks. Palene could be an enemy, a clever and resourceful enemy, and so his silence must remain until he could see things more clearly. "You say this source has always been there," he enquired, "That you believe it has been responsible for pushing you, guiding you. But unlike the subconscious voice you've developed it has no direct bearing on your psyche itself? So how do you differentiate? How do you separate this light you claim to see, from this heightened sense of understanding you claim to have developed much earlier?"

"As I've described, the two are separate, but I believe they both want the same thing, the completion of my evolution. My ideas, discoveries, theories, stem from within me, but more often than not I've found myself compelled to derive them as I try to make sense of the complex data which has tortured and polluted my mind for centuries." He offered an example, "My first method of travelling through time and dimensional space was like a form of projection. But the need to seek you out on equal terms drove me to push the boundaries of science, until more recently I finally made the breakthrough which would allow me to travel through time and space physically."

"So what year do you currently occupy . . . In the real sense of the word?"

"2115, though the technology I've created is centuries ahead of such a time."

Once again the date made an immediate impact on Dorey. Palene had of course claimed to be two thousand years old, similar in length to the project's timelines, but now this new number made the coincidence more solid. 2115 was around the time of Brooke's own early experiments. In his confused state it hadn't occurred to him to discover this simple fact. He was annoyed at himself for missing such an obvious line of enquiry, but before he could berate himself too much another notion took hold, one of confusion. The anomaly which first put them onto Palene's trail stemmed from the mid-twentieth century, not from the early throes of the twenty-second. He decided this recent information justified a level of divulgence on his part. "When we were first alerted to your presence, we pinpointed your location as stemming from the nineteen fifties."

Palene did not hesitate. "The technology I utilise uses an arced trajectory through time. Where I leave and return into actual reality depends on the curve of my plotted course. My current location in real time often sees this curve re-enter my own reality in the middle of the twentieth century."

"So a small part of your return journey from our artificial timelines sees you move through real time to bring you home?"

"Once again it's very complicated . . . But, yes."

"So you are not travelling to our timelines from the twentieth century?"

"I have only been visiting you in the physical sense since creating my own time technology at the dawn of the twenty-second century. Using this method I've returned to scenarios long since explored, though my more recent excursions, such as the visit to Germany, have been my first in every sense of the word."

Although it didn't answer how Palene had been visiting their simulated timelines for centuries in a projection sense, Dorey felt happier connecting the dates relevant to the physical technology. Yes, Palene was still utilising his technology from a position in time prior to the birth of their timelines and the Stasis None in its current form. But this had to be better than such a technology emanating from a source which predated atomic computer theory. He moved on, content to trivialise such a finding, as another prominent question found its way to the fore of his recovering mind. He was more cautious with his approach, aware how his next line of enquiry may prove a little raw, "So, once presented with the physical ability to move through to these timelines, did you ever make an attempt to alter what happened on that awful day, the day you lost your family?"

If the subject had indeed stung his host he did well to hide it, as Palene was again open and informative with his response. He recounted with tortured dismay the attempts made to save his family using the evolving power and more recent technology at his disposal. How on each occasion he would be returned to that awful moment when waking in the pyre, the trauma sending him ever closer to madness on each renewed attempt.

Dorey formulated so many new questions during this latest account he hadn't known where to begin. He needed to fill in the blanks. Build a picture of just what this person was capable of. Ascertain which of his host's capabilities came courtesy of technology and separate them from Palene's continual suggestion of growing abilities which stemmed from a more personal evolution. "Earlier you mentioned developing heightened senses. You suggested these gifts have evolved beyond immortality alone?" Dorey pondered, "But do you believe such evolutions stemmed directly from immortal life or did they develop in a broader sense?" He made an attempt to be more concise, "For example, you say you're immune to death, does this mean you're also immune to physical pain?" Once again his eyes drifted to the scars left by Dial's gun.

"Everything changed when waking from the pyre. However in the beginning, I still experienced pain pretty much as you would. The anguish experienced during physiological damage remained. This sensation combined with my natural expectation for pain to follow meant it was easy to confuse the reality of my true situation. That it was only the memory of pain which remained. When I analyse it now it's obvious my body had adjusted from day one. The rest was simply my mind playing catch-up." He thought of how to best clarify his explanation, "An amputee may feel the limb removed for years afterward, and so it was with my experience of pain."

"And now?"

"If you stab me with a knife I still feel the wrath of the blade at the first moment of impact. But once cut, what I feel is the instant sensation of my body repairing. If I didn't remove the weapon, my tissues would heal with the blade still there, the process is that fast. If I'm shot and the bullet remains lodged in my body, I'd still experience the discomfort it may cause. However, I could operate on myself, remove the bullet and be safe in the knowledge I'll be repairing as I'm carrying out the task."

"So then you cannot feel pain."

"I'm saying I remember it, and back then the memory was fresher than it is today."

"So does the memory of suffering rise as the level of trauma to your body increases?"

"I would naturally experience a far worse sensation if attacked with an axe than if jabbed with a needle."

"And yet you experience death . . . Does that not cause you pain?"

"Death is the complete annihilation of your mind, the unfair destruction of your conscious, an abrupt end to your life's journey. And yet . . . It can be a just and welcoming embrace. It depends on the circumstance."

Dorey wondered, *'Did Palene feel the same relief, exhilaration, that same passionate turmoil whenever he discovered he was still alive? Did he suffer the same nightmares? Or had such feelings and emotions simply waned like the sensation of pain?'* He enquired, "Were the effects on you any different the first time, the second, third, or the tenth? Does dying surrender its effect as your ability to feel pain has?"

Palene looked at him darkly. "One's own death is an experience the mind was only intended to truly endure once. To experience it more is to risk delving into madness." He paused, his eyes visiting a hell beyond the recognition of even Dorey's newly-found comprehension, "In my own experience I would hazard a guess handling such a thing mentally, be it the third or the thirtieth time, would surely depend on the resilience of the individual in question." He gave another gentle shrug, "How could I know for certain? I am but one person, however strange or different I may be." He added, "But surely you need not look too much further than yourself for such answers." He paused before enquiring, "What is it *you* truly feel?"

Dorey arrived at his answer with a sharp smile, "Alive."

Palene delighted in this response.

"But would I feel less so if this were the tenth occasion I'd risen from the dead?"

Palene understood his guest's perplexity. "Depending on circumstance death can be more traumatic on one occasion than another. However unlike pain, it cannot be forgotten or controlled. How it takes you is always up to death itself. My experience of it is as varied as the circumstances which brought it about."

Dorey felt he understood. His death was quick and violent. His panic absorbed by a delusive sense, as if the horror engulfing him hadn't been real. When the moment finally came, his near instant demise removed him from the possibility of physical pain. He had no doubt the entire experience would have been wholly different if his death had been slow, or come about while in the embrace of prolonged suffering. The mental anguish he'd endured when returning from his demise was brought about by the nature of his sudden end. His trauma was in dealing with the nightmare. The truth was however, from a purely physical point of view, he was becoming ever more aware of just how perfectly healthy he felt. A brief silence followed as he sank further into thought. *'If I were to experience my own destruction again and again would it become more bearable? Would I become skilled in dealing with the consequences of my own end as Palene has obviously learned to do? Or was his ability to move on from death merely an extension of his ability to move on from pain?'* He indulged himself further, *'Depending on circumstance, would my anguish be any less intense if I'd died peacefully in my sleep before being brought back?'* He looked to his host unable to comprehend the discoveries he must have made about the human condition. *'Maybe I shouldn't even compare myself to him.'* He thought, realising simply trying to understand Palene's predicament by standing it next to his own then multiplying it was certainly insufficient. *'Perhaps he doesn't even experience feelings in the same sense a normal human being did anymore.'*

Palene had remained graciously silent, again recognising Dorey's need to think, but he intervened with almost psychic perception once more. "I am human. I still feel as you feel. I laugh, cry, love and grieve. I still hope and wonder. I've died a hundred deaths and awoken from their embrace as if waking from the most horrific of nightmares or the most hypnotic of dreams. I've dealt with the aftermath of them as best I can, as you will have to this one time also. And yes, I've become more able to manage my mindset during these resurrections, sometimes with greater ease than others. I'm practised in death . . . But that could never make me immune. As I've said, death is the end, and we were never truly intended to see around the corner of that . . . At least not in this existence." He paused. "And yet still I exist . . . And still you exist. Like anything in life we can only try to learn from it, adapt through it . . . Evolve because of it. It makes me no less a human being for having suffered death, anymore than it makes *you* somehow less of a person right now." He added, "Each time I experience my renewed life, I'm crucified by it . . . I suffer for it. When I wake I long to be at peace for just one more moment, long for death to take me, for some God or this light to finally realise the mistake. But of course none do, and I hate them for it." An ironic smile appeared, "And yet in that same instant, with the taste worn upon each renewed breath I feel my heart swell with joy, feel my brain filled with renewed life and then," he sighed as if dismayed for admitting such a thing aloud, "Then I thank them for it." His tone darkened slightly. "You naturally question whether I've become numb to death in the same sense I've become numb to pain." He shook his head, "You assume this prevents me from feeling in the same way it makes me impregnable when in all truth, to feel is not something so easily separated or categorised. After all, I may be able to close any wound, but I've been unable to heal the rift which has torn apart my soul. I may have the ability to move through time, but I cannot use the gift to heal my torment. Marridana will never be returned to me as I will soon return you to Jay."

Dorey felt his heart drop. The comparison should have been expected, after all, he'd been making them to himself all day. In his mind Marridana had practically become Jay. And yet for as obvious as the statement was it was all that was needed for him to understand.

To question a man's humanity because of his physiology was of course, absurd.

"My gift is my curse." Palene concluded, "To no longer fear pain, injury or death has allowed me to evolve into a powerful being. My senses no longer bogged down with the instinctive stress to be constantly aware of anything which could cause harm, have heightened immensely. With the fear of destruction removed my senses were free to evolve without limitation . . . And in turn, I became more aware of the many unplugged functions of my brain. Yet you would think with the removal of caution, fear, of the very instinct to protect your own survival, it would naturally follow many of the effects would be largely negative. The adrenaline needed to power your muscles during times of danger, the speed of your responses as they're heightened by fear. You would assume these would diminish. But mine did not. Instead they excelled. I developed a superior natural perception of my surroundings. I came to understand the qualities of balance, awareness and control. Without fear to cloud or worry my judgement I quickly developed my true sense of nature." There remained no trace of conceit. Palene discussed these matters as a physicist would explain electricity.

Dorey felt he understood. His group were trained in a similar way, to overcome fear so as to allow their implants to shine. Like the free runner who achieved seemingly impossible stunts simply by attacking a given situation with a clear mind, an understanding of what was required to succeed. Dorey wondered if Palene was aware of the enhancements in his body, when another thought suddenly surfaced, *'Would such devices still be there? If time was manipulated in order to save me then yes . . . But if it was something else.'* The notion struck home, *'If and when I'm returned, will such devices being present or absent within my body prove me to be the same, real person?'*

Palene interrupted his thinking, "We take only what we need at a particular moment of our evolution. Use only a fraction of our brains. I've begun to push these boundaries. Sixth sense became merely perception. Danger was nothing more than a logical conclusion of events. If my body requires a burst of adrenaline to counter an action against it then it's given with the speed and clarity of a clear and logical mind."

The same earlier thoughts flashed to the fore of Dorey's psyche. *'Hence his speed and strength during the exchange in the Colonel's corridor . . . His ability to descend a mountainside with both hands bound.'*

"As I became aware of such concepts the clarity of my mind only broadened further. Like a domino effect, my brain seemed to open many more of its once hidden doors."

"So you've become almost super human?"

"Define super. Am I super because I cannot die or be hurt? Because my brain has been free to develop a high level of conscious understanding? Does my heightened perception, awareness and instinct make me super . . . Or my apparent ability to read your mind?" Palene smiled. "As I've said, none of these advancements offered any definitive answer as to why my soul was torn apart. None have provided me with the means to save my family . . . To once again hold my wife and children." He concluded, "No there's nothing super about my predicament. I reiterate, my gift is my curse."

Again the Commander marvelled at how powerful his host's love must be, still so evident after centuries of alleged separation. This stranger longed for his wife and family and yearned for the reunification of what he perceived as his broken soul. *'But were they in fact one and the same? Palene stated he was here to help or serve mankind in some way . . . But in doing so is he not merely helping himself?'* He was having trouble holding onto his ideas, the questions formulating in his mind almost too quickly to hold onto. His thoughts returned to Jay. He imagined how he'd feel if he discovered he could never die. If he was never to see her again throughout this immortality. He realised he too would spend an eternity longing for her as Palene professed to have done for his wife and children, for the missing part of his soul. *'How strange people can be. To know and understand love. Yet be so capable of taking it for granted. To not appreciate it at the time it's offered unconditionally . . . To only truly feel its embrace when there's a threat of it being taken away.'* After a long moment he enquired, "Did you ever remarry or have more children?"

"No. I have loved, enjoyed relationships, but I always felt to give another oath would take something away from that one true love I felt all those centuries ago." He stared at Dorey. "She was my soul mate you see. And though I probably never realised it truly when she was alive, I've certainly come to know it since. I loved her like no other, and in years passed, I've come to understand she was the one soul I was always destined to find." He looked wistfully at the sunshine as it bounced off the sea, felt its heat as it drenched the sandstone patio. "As for children . . . Naturally as the years passed I wondered if having more would help ease the agony. That I may have been able to relive something like a part of my old life." He returned a solemn gaze to his guest, "But the incident at Stonehenge would also prove the decisive factor upon any such romantic notion." He paused, "But that's probably for the best. Think of the generations which would have come to pass had I been able." He gave a blank smile as he revisited the old thought. "And yet in real terms, only thirty or forty combined average lifetimes have passed, the teachings of the Ilia could have spanned as long." His thoughts took hold. "We humans think so ultimately about time, and yet really . . . It was all only yesterday."

Dorey stared out over the sea and thought of all the places he'd seen. He tried to imagine and comprehend the life of one man covering all those generations, living it first hand. But of course, he could not. He thought back over their conversation, wanting to learn more of his immortality. "You mentioned the notion of operating on yourself to remove a bullet. Can I take it this would only be from an injury sustained while travelling through time in the more recent, physical sense?"

Palene nodded, "Yes. During the meditation phase of my time travel I would have simply awoken within the safety of my own reality, if death were to occur."

"So now you are moving through time in the physical sense, you would always have to take the bullet out?"

"I'd take it out in the same way I'd stitch certain types of wounds to have them heal correctly. Leaving the bullet in could cause discomfort, but it may lead to further internal problems, such as infection."

"But that wouldn't endanger you?"

"No. But my body would be thrown out of balance because of it." He elaborated, "A damaged spine may mean a person cannot feel a limb. But that person would still be aware something was wrong if they were to damage that limb. The body finds other ways to alert the brain."

"And you would operate on yourself?"

"Yes . . . I'm highly trained as a physician. But it's slightly more complicated as I heal almost instantaneously. I have over the years devised methods. I need to reach a certain state of mind to allow any surgical procedure on my body. It takes great concentration."

"So what would happen if I cut off your head?"

"I would die."

"But then what?"

"I would wake up some time later as if it had never happened."

"Like I just woke up?"

"You didn't just wake up." He stared at his guest wilfully.

Dorey continued with his direction despite the chilling comment, "And those two head shots?" He pointed to the faint scarring provided courtesy of Dial.

"The same."

"How long afterward?"

"I tend to wake up when the danger has passed."

"But within the same time as to which you'd travelled."

"Yes . . . When travelling in the physical sense."

A dark smile grew upon Dorey's face. "So what would happen if you were blown up?"

Palene laughed. "I don't know . . . Fortunately I have never been blown up."

"Well did it ever occur to you during some of your darker moments this may have been the answer?"

"It never occurred because I know the answer," he replied still somewhat amused, "There have been two occasions when my body has been ripped to pieces. On both occasions I was engulfed by death, and on both occasions I woke as if it had been a horrific dream well away from the moment of danger. I've no idea why this is. Why the process of one form of regeneration is different to another. Why if I sliced off my thumb it may regenerate, while cutting it may need stitches for it to heal correctly. Yet if I die after losing the thumb it's always there healed when I wake." He paused. "The whole process of death is like getting a clean slate physically. Only the psychological scars remain as any permanent souvenir."

Dorey stared at his forehead.

Palene touched the faint marks. "It's been several weeks since that day for me. The bullets passed straight through and I awoke soon after. Yet for some reason the scars seem reluctant to fade."

"So can I take it such marks would have normally disappeared by now?"

"I would never expect to see any memento of injury within days or even hours of a prior injury such as this." He smiled, "It would appear once again, strange things can happen whenever our paths collide."

"And the smaller scar on your cheek?"

"Sustained before the Finger of Venus," he touched the small pentacle mark, "A friend became a little over zealous during an exercise in swordsmanship as a boy." He smiled.

"So that scar is permanent?"

"It happened before my immortality, and so nature leaves it as a memento of my once, normal life." He added, "Besides, any doubts of my durability were well and truly crushed much more recently."

Dorey sat forward, realizing his prior jovial questioning may have unearthed the promise of a larger secret.

"After all, once you've evolved a method and capability which can allow you to travel unprotected through space and time . . . You begin to realise a lot of things about yourself."

Any childish amusement vanished as Dorey realised what his host implied. "You mean . . . you don't use a ship?"

Palene wore an almost dangerous expression as he shook his head slowly.

Dorey thought of the battering the heavily armoured Reeper took during every operation. Yet the man sat before him proclaimed he required no such protection when negotiating time and space. He pondered the notion, wondering if his host was confusing his *actual ability* with his projected meditations. For if such a claim were true, this meant Palene was something more than just immortal, he had to be truly indestructible.

CHAPTER SIXTY FIVE

Jay zipped closed the suitcase and scanned the room for any forgotten items. Her eyes landed on the photograph of Dorey giving her a piggyback on Bridlington beach. She'd moved it to her bedside table from the hallway and not for the first time found herself wandering how this moment of captured happiness found itself relegated to such a poor vantage point for so long.

She took a shaky breath before making her way to the living room.

Dial, Benny and Deans were drinking coffee while Jim and Marco smiled sadly through the collection of photos Jay had been trawling through these past days. They resisted the temptation to activate the play option, feeling certain a miniature Dorey walking around the coffee table would prove a little too hard for Jay to bear.

Carl was trying to keep spirits up by telling them of the amusing sight he'd witnessed while coming over that morning.

Silence fell however, as a sombre looking Jay walked back into the room.

She was pale and looked tired but she'd kept it together throughout the morning. The group were nervous on the way over but she'd put them at ease upon their arrival, greeting them with warm hugs and brave smiles. Her composure tested on receiving their condolences, she'd managed to get through it with minimal fuss, which was exactly what Jay wanted. She had apologised for locking herself away and each of them out, the awkward ice thawed considerably. Goodwill messages followed from the population of the project before she'd politely excused herself to finish packing her suitcase.

They'd grown concerned when she'd been gone a while, wondering whether one of them should check on her, but Dial had shaken his head with Carl in agreement saying softly, "We're here if she needs us."

Deans felt like an intruder of sorts. He'd become friends with them all so quickly since joining the project and he felt the loss of the Commander more than he would have expected . . . But he also felt he'd not put the time in to be privy to such intimate moments.

"Well that's the case packed." Jay said as she now approached the centre of the room.

"And you're certain you want to do this alone?" came Dial's concerned response.

She gave another brave smile. "I'll be fine."

"What time did you say your flight was?"

She turned to Benny. "Not until seven-thirty."

Jim checked his watch. "Well, that gives you five hours before check in. How about you let us take you for lunch." They'd discussed earlier the idea of getting her out in public before her airport drama began.

She looked worried, the outside world wasn't too appealing, but it was one she'd have to face in the next few hours. "Okay," she replied with empty eyes, "Sounds good."

Carl interjected, "Grab a little fresh air."

Marco smiled. "There won't be much fresh air on the way to where those two like to eat." He gestured to both Jay and Jim and smiles were passed around.

"Let Dennis decide. We still haven't had him take us anywhere he likes." Dial then immediately began rushing Deans into making his decision.

"Do you know Quinans?"

"Too far," Dial retorted as they began thinking about the door.

Deans tried to conjure somewhere closer to hand, "How about Oggie Longdens?"

Jim scowled causing the others to laugh.

Jay headed his way and ruffled his hair, "Tell you what . . . Scrap that idea. Jim, where are we going?"

More laughter followed and Deans found himself being tormented all the way to the street for this poor choice in eatery.

*

Dorey was still coming to terms with Palene's revelation of transcending time unprotected when another notion took hold. He was suddenly aware of how long the morning appeared to be, of how slowly the sun made its journey to midday. It occurred to him he'd been experiencing the very concept of time differently since he'd awoken.

As Dorey drifted within his thoughts, Palene became concerned with the fact they'd not yet eaten. "I must apologise for neglecting my duties as host." He declared breaking the moment of reflection, "For you've not yet eaten since waking this morning. Please, allow me to prepare us some lunch."

The remark seemed ridiculous to Dorey in present circumstances, and despite his efforts to persuade his host he wasn't the slightest bit hungry, Palene insisted. He left Dorey with the view for a moment in the understanding he needed time to focus.

After a short time he returned to the veranda carrying a tray which held a carafe of wine, some bread and a pot containing some fish. He placed it on the table.

Dorey was determined to understand all that was happening and the pause had done him some good. "This method of time travel you use, does it differ to actual time in the real world? Effect the locations you visit?"

He poured them each a goblet. "You're wondering why this morning seems so long."

He nodded.

"My manipulation of time often alters these states of existence. But it is the process you so naturally long to understand, that of which I had to undertake in order to save you from death, which has placed this system into a temporary fluctuation. It will take almost one week of this world's time for it to return to normal."

"And you're still not prepared to tell me exactly what this process is?"

He passed over the wine. "As I said, it is not a case of not wanting to tell you . . . It's simply I wouldn't know how."

Dorey took a sip of the wine, it was dry and a little sour at first, but the after taste left a pleasant lingering ghost of berries. "So . . . In my real time how long have I been here?"

"One week."

"And in this world's time?"

"Four days." He said. "We are currently running at ninety-six real time seconds per minute . . . Come dawn, the world here will be back as it should."

"So, I'll have been gone for at least one week when you return me home?"

"Yes." He understood his concern. "You are worrying of the pain you're causing your loved ones?"

Dorey nodded but said nothing.

"And your method of time travel, does it return you to the moment you left, or do you also find it varies?"

Dorey was guarded, but decided to divulge this piece of information. "No it varies. Sometimes we've been gone days or weeks even though we've been in these realities for longer . . . On some occasions we've been gone for the same duration as that of real time."

"It can mess with your mind if you're not careful," Palene said with a smile. He sliced the bread and took some of the smoked fish from the pot, "The mother of all jet-lags."

"But what we do doesn't speed or slow time when inside these existences." Dorey's blunt attempt did not see Palene divulge anything further and the following pause only encouraged him to stare at the fish with a look of concern.

Palene didn't look up, "Oh don't worry Commander . . . It tastes a lot better than it looks. I made it yesterday when you were sleeping, caught fresh from my little boat. It's flavoured with garlic, salt and olive oil and is surprisingly good cold." He turned to him and smiled as he returned to the earlier concern, "Your friends and family will be so pleased to have you back, it will be of little consequence how long they were forced to endure their grief."

He wasn't prepared for the comment and Dorey found himself immediately aching to return home to make amends.

His host gestured to the food and encouraged him to dig in. "Please." He passed over a plate and spoon.

Dorey's surprising lack of appetite was not helped in any way by this smelly dish now sat in front of him.

"Please Commander . . . eat," the warm smile returned, "It's not unusual to feel no hunger in your present condition . . . But let me assure you your body will thank you for the fuel."

Dorey took a piece of bread and spooned some of the fish from the broad open jar.

Palene laughed. "I promise you it is quite good." He then eyed his guest closely as he added, "Besides . . . You'll need your strength for your journey home."

Dorey's gaze was thrown onto Palene as once again he felt as if his host was able to read his private thoughts. "You're going to send me home soon?"

"Our time here will be done once you know everything there is to know."

"You haven't told me half the things I wish to know."

"I've told you of my belief in a purpose. Soon I will have explained all I can of the rest." His eyes flashed, "Then you will be able to decide for yourself whether or not you are prepared to help me."

The comment stopped Dorey in his tracks. "Help you?" He was immediately suspicious.

"Yes. For once you possess all I can explain I'm going to ask a small favour of you. And what I will ask . . . Is that you bring to me the creator, the mastermind of this undertaking of yours."

Dorey stared at his host dumbfounded. "I think you may be getting ahead of yourself," he said coldly, "For I've made no gesture to suggest I'd help in any such way." He was annoyed. "If you've truly saved me from death, as it appears you have, then I am forever in your debt . . . But I will never help you unless I choose to do so of my own free will. You could never buy me."

The smile remained, "Of course." He could see the walls of Dorey's defences rise, "And please, you can relax," he reassured, "I'm merely stating that come this evening my hope is you will have chosen to do just that." He observed the Commander's irritation. "I can assure you I mean none of you harm. Quite the opposite in fact. There are no tricks or manipulations transpiring here as I know you suspect there to be. I simply need to communicate with those who have made all of this possible."

"And what if I say no come this evening? Do I still get to return home . . . Or is that one of the conditions?"

Palene looked disgusted, "Commander let us be honest. There is no way on earth any such mastermind is not going to want to meet with me. I am the power you have been sent here to find. I have answers and knowledge, the likes of which your superiors could only dream of possessing . . . And I will be placing that knowledge on a plate. There are no conditions. And the very fact I'm able to send you home will once again shatter your organisation's preconception of science . . . Which will in turn guarantee me my audience."

Dorey secretly shared this assumption. "So then why all of this?" he asked. "Why even bother telling me this prophetic story of yours? Why offer this, friendship?"

"I would have thought that perfectly obvious. I've told you I cannot come with you to your time. This was not merely to be elusive . . . It is not born out of fear or distrust. It is because I know this would be fatal to the future. I told you earlier I couldn't explain many things as you could never begin to understand them. I can only beg you to trust me on this matter. And that's what today is about . . . Trust." The honest integrity once again pierced the Commander's armour. "When this meeting is arranged, you are going to be on hand and almost certainly under strict instructions to snatch me the moment your employer sees fit . . . This cannot happen."

Dorey thought back to the moment on the steps when Palene was his hostage, ready to be picked up by the Reeper. He remembered the deafening noise which ripped through his com-link resulting in his collapse to the floor. He felt another dark chill. He was not sure why he'd not thought about it in any great detail since, but he was certain this was yet another display of the power his host proved capable of delivering.

"If I meet with your people in the knowledge I can trust you, knowing you trust me . . . Then I am safe to speak without fear of being abducted or harmed."

The term *harmed* seemed ironic, "But surely that would depend on your own actions."

"By now you are of course aware I have powers more than sufficient to protect myself if need be. But once such a road is journeyed upon it is often impossible to return. I do not want us to be enemies before we've even begun. My reasons for seeking you out are for the greater good of mankind . . . Not, to cause you harm. I need you to trust me as I will need you to go back to your superiors as my friend, not as my adversary. It will be essential for us all I'm allowed to figure out what is set to transpire."

Dorey thought about his continual terminology. Of this man's use of the word power, not only through the source of this mysterious light, but also as if it stemmed from within his being personally. That his abilities were indeed his own, and did not come courtesy of some machine, device or hidden organisation. He realised he had an unquestioning sense growing within him . . . He genuinely understood such power actually belonged to the person sat before him, and not from something bigger he'd been unable to discover over some unseen horizon. He had indeed wondered whether the man in front of him could be suffering from a serious messianic complex, but he'd since dismissed the notion. In truth, he was beginning to trust the man sat in front of him more and more. As incredible as it all appeared, he had a growing sense of belief in most of what he'd told him, despite his natural reservations. *'Perhaps that's his trick. Perhaps this is how he will manipulate me.'* His thoughts were only born out of anxiety and he knew it. He could feel the good intention in the person opposite. It touched Dorey in a way he'd never experienced before. He realized it had always been there, it was why he'd chosen a path of which the Commander of old would have never headed toward, risking himself and his team. He pondered, *'What did this person hope to achieve? What is it he's truly looking for? What did he mean by about to transpire? Like their own Stasis None, did he also genuinely believe something of great consequence was on the horizon for the human race?'* If it was an audience with Brookes he required then he was already halfway there as he'd stated. After all, that was indeed the reason he was here within this place. *'But the intention had always been to discover and control. Would Brookes and the project really risk coming to meet this man on different terms?'* He thought back to how Brookes himself had also acted so uncharacteristically, how he'd no doubt risked all just to have him sent here. He wondered whether his death may have removed control from Brookes altogether by now. "You say you wish to learn all that's to transpire. So you maintain the notion you have questions also . . . That you wish to prevent something happening?"

"As I said, events underway are in many ways as much a mystery to me as they are to you. The power evolving within me which allows me to do what I do is not something I've intentionally grabbed hold of and developed as such. The gifts present themselves to me in the manner which I've already described. They evolve. They stem from within me and me alone, albeit apart from the more recent technology I now use to send myself through time physically. I am evolving for a reason, and to truly understand this reason I must now finally meet with the creators of your technology." He looked at him with sincerity. "The missing part of my being which has remained far from my grasp for so long has drawn me to it. I feel myself coming closer together. You, me, this calling . . . It's all connected. It is all meant to be. You must believe me when I tell you I did not bring you here to manipulate you." He took a sip of his wine and smiled, "In fact, perhaps in many ways today was also about finally getting to meet you properly. Not as Brahms or anyone else but as Palene and Dorey." He shook his head. "Have you any idea how difficult it was to not reveal myself to you back in Germany?"

Dorey reiterated his earlier enquiry, "Then how could you wait so long before making contact. How could you suffer over sixteen hundred years of watching but not knowing?"

"As I described, I'm being guided along a certain path. Over time I came to understand my journey had to be completed in a particular fashion. I had to obey my developing instincts until the right time of my evolution arose . . . And as we both know, time can be a most complex thing."

CHAPTER SIXTY SIX

Will Grossen sipped at his coffee. He and Samantha Redemca were seated at one of the more exclusive street tables on the Champs Elysees. Each had their Paris agents in buildings on every corner, scrambling any listening or video devices no doubt trained on them by someone within Finch's organisation.

"So where do we go from here?" She asked, her hand discreetly covering her mouth.

Will's hand masked his lips also, "Doctor Usorio is proving reliable, and Brookes will get his house in order."

"And what of the mystery-man now implicated in the death of Commander Dorey?"

"Something we're going to have to deal with as we go. But whatever mistakes have been made, nobody can afford to lean on Brookes too much. We can't risk pushing him away."

Samantha agreed. "I don't think such concerns will be shared by Finch."

"Finch's bitterness makes him predictable. We'll sit and wait until he makes his move."

"I just hope such a move doesn't come endorsed by Senator Abel." Her eyes locked suspiciously on a passer by who looked right through her as he walked. "Brookes has never been in a position of real weakness before . . . Who knows what might happen with a man like Abel pulling the strings." She paused, "I still think we can approach Gardener."

Will's eyes narrowed. "I think that's a little risky. The heads of state you represent aren't going to be too happy if we blow this by being rash."

She frowned at the comment. "The heads' of state I represent are not too happy . . . period."

"Look . . . Right now it's more important to ensure Brookes gets their unconditional support. We can't force this thing. We've seen such an approach tried already. With their backing he can maintain control, at least for now."

"That's not something I can guarantee. But if it were achieved; Brookes would have to figure a workable solution of how to apprehend or neutralise this gatecrasher, without further risk to the project. If he doesn't, the whole thing is almost certainly over anyway. Certainly as far as his carte blanche rule is concerned."

Grossen reassured her. "I understand Major Dial will be informed of his taking charge of the group, with Lieutenant Benn and Jay Tilnoh as his seconds. Before the week is out in fact." He looked at her closely. "Then with the support of your people, an orchestrated hunt can begin."

"And what about Captain Tilnoh, is she really going to be up for this, hunt? She was the man's fiancée."

Will reassured her. "She'll be up for it *because* she was his fiancée. We've got a little time." He added. "I know a little bit about Jay Tilnoh, she'll want to get her hands on anyone implicated in Commander Dorey's murder if given the opportunity."

A look of concern shadowed Sam Redemca's face. "Well just make sure if and when such an opportunity arrives he's delivered alive . . . He's no less a mystery to us dead."

He agreed. "Tell your people it will all be taken care of . . . There's no need to hit the panic button just yet."

She stared at him. "I hope not Mr. Grossen, for all our sakes. Things are already shaky with our President and DeCoure, the French don't trust the White House at all on this, and that's bad news for all concerned." She took her hand-stitched Italian bag from the table and placed the strap over her shoulder before returning her hand to her lips. "If Finch is indeed now Raffy Abel's puppet this could all get very messy." She pushed her chair back slightly. "Now, are we finished here?"

"We're finished." Will replied.

"Good." She stood up slowly then returned her hand to her mouth. "Be careful not to underestimate Finch, he may appear predictable, but such people are often the most unpredictable kind." Her hand dropped. "I take it you'll settle the bill?"

Grossen nodded, "Of Course."

"Au revoir Mr Grossen." Sam Redemca then turned and walked away.

*

Dorey had found himself raised from the dead. He'd listened to Palene's incredible story, touched at times by the sincere account of it, questioning on others the sheer absurdity.

An understanding had been constructed of Palene's perceived past and of how it was he'd come to believe himself immortal. He'd learned how Palene discovered his team and accepted his host believed them to be connected within some unfolding destiny.

The Commander had kept his own council on many things.

He'd been unable to pin his host down on how he achieved his miraculous return from the grave, but he was certain of one thing, it was no trick, '*He had died in this place.*'

He'd discovered events in Germany transpired several weeks ago as far as Palene was concerned and that his host believed he possessed yet another impossible capability . . . That he not only had the freedom to move through time at will but could do so without the need for a vessel to transport and protect him. He asked Palene to elaborate on his ability to negotiate time using science, without a ship.

His host answered freely as he had throughout the day, explaining how he'd discovered a method to de-atomise his cells, before seeing them projected across time in an energy beam, reforming at the other end once his destination was reached.

"But if you are indestructible, how can you be de-atomised?"

"I'm afraid there's no real way in which to answer that. The method reached the subconscious part of my mind through the forces which guide me. It is almost certainly beyond your capacity to understand."

He returned to earlier enquiry, "But how could you even know of these simulated worlds if you are from a time when they do not yet exist?"

"The universe knows, so therefore I know."

"You can't answer such a question with a riddle."

"I answer only with truth. Your inability to accept I'm linked to a greater power than mankind's science is a problem you need to address, not I."

"So then you *do* believe yourself connected to something divine?"

"Here we find ourselves again. Are you even a religious man Commander?"

"You mean do I believe one force created all things?" He shook his head, "No."

Palene agreed. "But would such a notion really be so much harder to believe than me now telling you I'm two thousand years old? So much more difficult to comprehend that you yourself have held the ear of Einstein, Saladin and Charlemagne?"

"But that's all simulated history."

"You'll find there's little in this universe which can be defined quite so clearly. Time is not merely a clock you can wind. Existence is not something you just turn on or off. You and the people you work for have little real idea of what this thing is you think you know so well. Time like the universe, is eternal. It may expand or shrink, twist or turn, pause and start right back up again. But it's always existent though never absolute. Tell me, when you first came face to face with these moments, with these people and faces of history, did they seem like a simulation to you?"

"Of course not . . . I only meant it was simulated in the sense…"

Palene interrupted, "In the sense it was a manipulated reality. That it only ever became real because it was created by your people in the first place? That these realities only exist to be governed by your rule, so you may achieve your aims," he eyed him closely, "So does this not make you yourself in some way divine since you've had a hand in creating these existences?"

Dorey scowled, these were the very waters he always warned Carl and the others to stay well away from.

"Then ask yourself this. If you decide in order to protect yourself from such notions, that these episodes in time have no vitality, no coherence. Then where exactly does this now leave you? For if your life has been given back to you while existing within one of these so called simulations . . . Then the question which has haunted you suddenly returns with renewed bite doesn't it? Are you yourself any less real than you were before the fall?"

Dorey felt himself getting inexplicably angry. "You know damn well I haven't stopped considering the fact I may now be as much a simulation as those I seek throughout history. I'm terrified everything happening to me today, here with you and your insane stories, could all be just the playing out of some pre-programmed version of myself, trapped in God knows when, where or how? That this is just some foul manipulation to get whatever you want out of me. Do you not think I've asked myself what's real, every single day since we started fucking around with this thing?"

Palene pacified, "I understand you may believe yourselves to be bettering some situation in whatever future you belong. But do you have faith you're on the correct path? Do you have faith there even is a path?"

Dorey rubbed his temples, the thought of how the Stasis None always dictated their actions biting his mind. "You talk of faith as if you've always known it. Yet you have admitted to being as lost as any human being could be. The fact you've had over two thousand years to develop your ideas doesn't necessarily make them right." He added, "And if we are so lacking, so inept in our crude understanding . . . Then I ask you again, why is it you so desperately need to seek out the mortal man who created all of this?"

"No man created this," he retorted, "I need to meet the creator of the technology which fashioned this, so I may in turn learn of my true reason for being?"

"You maintain you still need to learn of your true nature? Yet you've already stated you've the desire to reach this missing part of yourself. That you believe it in some way connected to our operation. So what happens if this is all a ploy to simply get what you want? What if you don't like what you find?" Despite his growing longing to do so he would not divulge the secrets of the Stasis None.

"As I've said we are connected you and I. And I have questions, just as your people do of me. I've spent over two thousand years waiting for this moment. Pulled to it by the very forces which have both enlightened and tortured for so long. But it's not about me. It's not about my own indulgence. The human race has reached a crossroad. I believe I am to guide mankind down a new path, but before I can understand my own purpose, I must discover that which created all of this. And this must take place quickly, as I'm certain time is about to run out."

"Because you believe something is set to happen?"

"Because I know something is to happen. And it's something which will either embrace mankind as a creator, or simply throw it back into darkness."

"As a creator?"

His host gestured all around, "Artificial intelligence, but on a true and incredible scale." He added, "Not that there's ever anything artificial about intelligence." He watched Dorey struggle, "As you enter the domain of creator you enter a new realm of responsibility. As I said, you've reached a crossroad in your evolution. I believe I'm here to guide you through it."

Although Dorey had fought long and hard against it, he was rapidly growing a sense of belief in both Palene and his purpose. For despite all the coincidental facts, dates and similarities, Dorey sensed beyond his own reason there was something of higher magnitude at work. His defences began to collapse both suddenly and quite inexplicably. He fought against the rollercoaster as he tried desperately to remember the distant light.

"The power you look to now is already within you Commander."

Dorey was shocked once again at his transparency before Palene.

"But first you must embrace that faith which has always resided within you, in the judgement you've relied on so long. My purpose today was to reveal my intention, persuade you to have faith in me just as I have faith in you. This is why we are here."

"Faith?" Dorey looked at him, "Faith in what? That you're here to save the world?" There was no mocking to his tone. "How am I supposed to have faith when I don't even know what to believe?"

"I've discovered within my immortal life both we and the universe are as one. God, intelligence, creation, science. Everything is about self-discovery and this very process is limitless. I've come to understand we're an evolution of both intelligence and imagination. That we are as much a part of any God as any such God could be a part of us. The human race is on the brink of a new frontier. The very fact *you* are even here is evidence of this. That *here* even exists is further proof this new age has already dawned. Mankind experiences only four percent of their visible universe, uses only a tiny amount of the human brain. And yet this fraction has been enough to take them off their planet, to see them crack the DNA code, to clone their own race . . . To now have them breach the frontiers of time, have them create entire worlds. Imagine what the human mind could be capable of it were allowed to fully evolve."

He thought on Palene's claims, of inadvertently speeding up mankind's evolution, the contradiction bright, "You make it sound like we're going to be denied such a chance."

"Oh come now Commander, you are no fool. Do you honestly believe mankind has a chance of reaching the finish line alone? Is this not why you and your people are carrying out your undertakings? When you are not destroying yourself you're destroying the ability of the planet to sustain you. The very home essential to your future placed in jeopardy." He shook his head, "Understanding the notion of consequence yet doing little or nothing to heed it. I spent lifetimes studying and searching, longing to understand my purpose. I delved deep into the corners of history long before it was locked away in some Vatican vault, lost in some forgotten cave. Written then rewritten by unenlightened people who believe it is *they* who have the right to tell you what to think, using the very notion of *light* to keep you all in the dark. I began to realise the human race was constantly reminding itself of the same legends, the same ideas. Whether one God or a dozen, the same numbers and codes, the same superstitions time and again . . . From Mayan to Egyptian...Mesopotamian to Celt. I utilised my learning from my own foundation in the Ilia across to those of every great civilisation that has ever stood. Studied every idea I felt could help me in my quest for purpose." He appeared to almost glow before Dorey. "And where did it lead me? Here to this moment." He declared, "Here to you."

Dorey reeled despite his best effort.

"I have discovered my purpose through two thousand years of knowledge, joy and pain. And now the final chapter will be revealed when I discover the last piece of the jigsaw through you and your people. I ask you to have faith in me Commander as I have faith in you. Because you'll need this faith when you tell the others of what is happening here. For the undertaking of mankind's step toward the next level has arrived, and it will be you and I, together with the creator of your technology, who'll be at hand to deliver it."

CHAPTER SIXTY SEVEN

The Thames Gateway shuttle port was the usual chaotic blend of automated help desks, airport androids, security checks and holographic advertisements. Jay had been early to check in, but the flight was delayed by half an hour. She'd still gone through to the departure lounge on time, kissing Dial on the cheek, insisting she'd be fine, urging him to join the others who'd remained behind at the Terminal One Bar and Restaurant.

Dial had called ahead and told the others to be ready to leave as quickly as possible.

His stomach was queasy and the thought of Jay going on alone continued to play on his mind. He'd been so proud of her across the day, watching her concentrate her efforts on making sure the rest of the group had some of their worries eased.

But he knew the fate awaiting her in Berlin was an altogether different prospect.

He cursed as a *bin emptying robot* cut across his path then quickly side stepped the soulless, pre-programmed apology for its unforgivable mistake.

He turned the corner eager for the rolling escalator floors which promis-ed a speedier route out of the fuss. He hit them at pace, striding the surface until he reached a blockade of commuters. He stopped allowing the floor to do the work.

He looked forward to the company of the others who could aid in his bid to escape this renewed depression, and as he approached the bar, he was pleased to see they were already congregating outside.

"How was she?" Carl enquired on his approach.

"The same, I think she . . ." he stopped himself, realising the others would be fully aware of what he was about to say. "Let's get out of here."

Unanimous approval followed and they headed for the exit.

"It's gonna be tough on her." Benny said with quiet concern.

Dial concurred. "I just wish she would have let one of us go with her."

"Once she gets together with Mitch, David and Katie they'll want to be alone anyway."

It was old ground they were covering. "Let's hope the tubes aren't too busy,

I don't fancy negotiating the subway all day after this place."

Carl agreed. "I hate airports."

"I hate flying." Deans said in full knowledge such a comment may spark some humour.

"No shit." Jim retorted, "My grandmother kicks up less fuss about flying . . . And she suffers from vertigo."

Marco laughed. "That must be difficult . . . Your grandmother's nearly as tall as you."

Jim shoved him forcing Marco to adjust his step, "You'd better watch what you say about Grandma Adams. She doesn't like you as it is, you don't want to give her an excuse."

They were approaching the final exit. "Bullshit . . . Grandma Adams loves me."

"Yeah right."

Marco grinned over his shoulder, "Almost as much as your two sisters."

Jim gave him a wide-eyed warning. "My little sisters would eat you alive."

"You said it!" was Marco's quick reply.

The tactic of humour was appreciated by Dial, "You want to watch what you say . . ." He cut himself short as the com-link inside his ear suddenly gave a gentle buzz. "Hang on I've got a call coming in." He pinched his earlobe. "Hello." The voice recognition chip put the caller through.

"Is that you Mark?"

"Yeah," he replied without breaking stride.

"This is Stein . . . Are you still in the airport?"

"Just leaving now."

"I take it you don't have a secure phone with you."

"No…you know how funny these people get about having them in airports."

"Of course . . . Listen we need to talk immediately. Jay's flight hasn't left yet has it?" Stein never used rank as a title while on an unsecured phone.

"Not yet, but she'll be on her way at any time . . . What's going on?"

"Listen to me Mark . . . I need you to go to the nearest security point. Show your ID, inform the guards you need to be taken to the nearest secure phone, your password is Fox, I repeat Fox. Can you do this for me?"

Dial was puzzled. "Of course, I'm on my way."

The connection went dead and Dial came to an immediate stop.

Benny noted his concerned expression. "What's wrong?"

"That was Stein . . . I need to find the nearest security desk." He scanned the corridor.

"Why . . . What's up?"

"I'm not sure … . But it sounds urgent."

*

Dial and Benny sprinted through the airport flanked by two security officials struggling to keep the pace, one screamed instructions into his wrist to have the oncoming emergency gates cleared.

Jay's flight had been delayed with a call from the right people to more of the right people. Still, Dial had to get the news to her as quickly as possible as time could well be of the essence. He wasn't sure what the news even meant, and he was concerned what damage it may do to her already fragile state of mind.

But nevertheless, it was news he had to deliver immediately.

They quickly rushed through the final gate and into the departure lounge. It was filled with a sense of disillusionment, the passengers already preparing for a long afternoon in the shuttle port's hospitality.

They scanned the area. Within seconds Benny's hand reached into a point. "There."

They thanked the security men then made an immediate route toward Jay who was sat at the far side of the lounge holding her head in her hands, far away in thought.

They reached her seat. "Jay." Dial said trying to sound as calm as possible.

She looked up at them, her face a picture of shock. "What are you doing here?"

Dial stared down at her, reaching instinctively for both her hands.

She stood slowly, her eyes wide with worry, allowing him to gently take her palms and squeeze them. "What's going on?"

He tried desperately to find the right words. "Jay, you're going to have to delay the trip."

"What? Mark what the hell are you talking about? I can't delay the . . ."

"Jay, listen. Something's happened. Something really crazy. But I don't want you to get . . ." He didn't even know how to finish the sentence as he knew what he was about to say was supposed to be impossible. He led her away from the growing number of curious eyes beginning to take notice of the strange goings on.

"Mark!" She demanded to know what was on his mind.

"I can't say too much here . . . I mean, I can't say too much anyway because nobody really knows what the hell is going on."

"Mark for Gods sake!"

He whispered. "It's the tunnel we last travelled through."

"What about it?" Her heart was now racing as fast as his.

"It's re-opening."

"What? What do you mean re-opening?"

He hushed her volume. "I mean exactly that. I've just spoken to Stein and he told me it's re-opening its seal. And not only that, it's moving steadily into the range of our system." It was difficult to whisper so quietly when his body was in need of more oxygen and his face turned a shade of red as a result.

"How?"

"I don't know . . . But there's a shuttle inbound to take us back right away."

"I don't understand."

"I don't either." Again he gave the room a quick scan before whispering,

"But it's the co-ordinates Jay. They're pointing to where we left the Dead Sea . . . To an energy source of incredible magnitude . . . Its origin coming directly from Masada."

Her mouth opened.

"Jay . . . It could be emanating from the guy we were hunting, the guy that . . ." He cut himself short not wanting to finish such a sentence.

Her eyes welled with tears and her lip trembled. "Then we could go back and save him." She shivered, almost surprised at her own remark, but then she felt it again. "With access we could save him Mark."

It was now his turn to scowl. "Jay . . . Don't jump to conclusions here. You know that's . . ."

She shook her head disapproving of his doubt, her eyes urging him to let go of his fears.

"Mark . . . We can save him." Her hands trembled as she wiped tears from her face. She struggled to breath. "Don't ask me how I know . . . I can feel it."

CHAPTER SIXTY EIGHT

The shuttle flight back seemed agonisingly slow, especially with no updates being offered from the underground complex. The pilots had both been marines from the Project without the necessary clearance to even know what it was they guarded. It meant Jay and the others could say very little and as a result the main communication had been brief nods of encouragement. A number of scenarios had played through their minds, the men encouraging themselves to think it could be nothing which would ensure a safe return of their friend. The favoured line of thought being that for whatever reason, Dorey's killer had decided to renew contact with the Stasis None facility.

Only Jay continually played host to the sole possibility of hope.

Dial remained concerned she was building herself up for an almighty fall.

They'd hit the landing pad and made quick headway to Elevator 3, spiriting them deep into the underground lair. Dial had taken the opportunity of this descending safe haven to voice his fears, begging Jay to not get too caught up in the notion Dorey could be saved.

She hadn't grown angry but slapped back all concerns aimed at her stating, "I know we can do it. I can't explain how, I just feel it."

This had done nothing to make the others feel better. In fact if they were honest, the very notion Jay of all people was even considering such an outcome only served to increase their own hopes for a miracle, making Dial and the others question just who it was they were really trying to protect.

No new information was offered during the express journey below ground but Doctor Usorio awaited them as the lift came to halt and opened its doors.

As they marched toward the RFC she updated the group, "The timeline has reopened and is now close to the Stasis None's connection range. All the necessary ingredients to create an access tunnel have also been made available. What's happening is beyond our conception, beyond our technology. No form of contact has been made but Brookes is considering the idea of locking a tunnel onto it and reconnecting it to the Stasis system."

This last comment was delivered as they approached the door of the RFC causing Jay to scowl as she was granted entry, "Considering it?" She stormed in paying little attention to the scientists trying to make sense of the incredible events unfolding. She headed straight down the steps, making a beeline for Brookes who was having a discussion with Jose Cassaveres. Her usual tact had no place for this conversation. "Doctor Brookes." She said sternly. For a brief moment all eyes were now trained upon her.

He knew what was coming but had little chance to say or do anything as Jay demanded, "What does she mean you're only *considering* reconnecting us to this timeline?"

He held up his hands while glaring at the other scientists to get on with their work. "Jay, I'm glad you're here . . . Please, come with me so I can fill you all in on . . ."

She cut him short. "Doctor . . . what does she mean?"

His expression was austere, instantly in charge. "Captain please . . . Come with me." He softened his tone with immediate effort, "And let me fill you in on what's going on." He gestured to the side door which led to the briefing rooms.

Jay quickly led the way.

Brookes followed with the rest of the team in pursuit. The door closed behind them. "Take a seat." Brookes made his way to the front. He could taste the tension but was determined the following brief was to be done his way. "A few hours ago we discovered the last time simulation used was re-opening from its seal. The loop had been breached, the timeline recreating itself, making a journey back toward the parameters of the Stasis None." He'd seen little of Jay since the tragic events and wondered how torturous all of this must be on her. He could see she was prepared to entertain the most optimistic of angles. "I realise you all grasp the basics of our project, but you'll probably have little true understanding of just how totally impossible events now transpiring should be. Believe me, impossible is an understatement." His eyes rarely left Jay's despite the eager attention of the others. "The timeline is as we speak, within our connection range," He could see Jay's imminent interruption brewing so held up a hand for patience. "Now I hope you all know I'd utilise all within this project's power to save any of your lives. If there had been a way to save Ian Mahoney I would have tried everything to do so, just as I would of course do the same for Commander Dorey."

"Then do it!" Jay demanded.

"There are significant risks we . . ."

"Fuck the risks!" Jay glared at Brookes.

"As well as it being my most profound, personal desire, I should remind you that saving Commander Dorey would be of huge significance to the goals of this project. Therefore if it can be done, it will be done. However, before I could even consider granting a green light for such an operation, there a numerous factors that must first be considered."

Dial interjected. "One being, this could be some kind of trap."

Brookes agreed. "Who or whatever this thing is clearly possesses a greater technology to our own. This of course leads to the question, why lure us in once more? Why invite us a second time? As you've stated, it smells like a trap."

It was now Dial's turn to glare. "Well that didn't stop you last time did it?"

Brookes acknowledged the comment with a humble glance downward.

"Well I for one am prepared to take that risk . . . *again*." There was a challenging distrust to Jay's voice.

"And in principal I of course agree. Such a rescue, not to mention the possibility of gaining answers to events now unfolding, would certainly justify taking a great deal of risk as far as I'm concerned. Even though my superiors would probably see me stripped of my command and committed afterward."

Jay and the others were a little surprised. The doctor's tone had set the mood for obstruction, not co-operation.

"But unfortunately risking all of you, the Reeper and my own standing within this project could be deemed only small areas of concern." The tone for obstruction returned.

Carl broke his silence. "You're worried you may cause a paradox?"

Brookes nodded, "In the very broadest sense. As you well know all our operations are dictated and controlled by the Stasis None. This would be different. The holding source is emanating from an alien power held within a different dimension. The risks of attaching this timeline to our real existence without the Stasis None's safety measures implemented are incalculable. And we'd need to do this to have any chance of seeing this timeline replay past events. Then there are the consequences of you colliding with the previous incarnation of yourselves while back there, essential if we're to even consider removing Dorey from harm before the tragic event occurs. To achieve this without the immediate paradox ramifications, the Stasis None would need to place your previous trip to this timeline out of phase from our reality the moment you intercepted the Commander. From there the original outcome would have to be placed in a form of temporal loop. Essentially seeing the original episode play itself out over and over until we can reseal the system and ensure this event would become as much a parallel simulation as it ever was a reality." He could see he was losing them. "Put simply, without the Stasis None in direct control, without complete access to this system, we simply cannot calculate the numerous risks and probabilities. So as you can see, the dilemma of whether or not to send you back is profoundly greater than any personal feelings you or I may hold."

Jay fired a piercing look. "How long before your team can gather the necessary data to give us any chance of a green light?"

"Without the Stasis None hooked into the source, days, weeks, even months."

"And how long can the tunnel sustain itself?"

He'd expected this as her follow up, "Hours . . . Twelve at best."

The whole room seemed to sigh.

Jay's face grew bitter. "So what are you planning to do about it?"

"In all honesty we need a miracle." He absorbed the fierce looks this comment induced. "Only with the Stasis None in control can we implement the correct course of action."

"The correct course of action?" Jay felt the betrayal of what she deemed a weak response.

Carl looked at Brookes earnestly. "But surely for the Stasis None to have an opportunity to take control, we must allow it to connect to this alien power."

"The last time we tangled with this thing it ended in tragedy. The damage such an entity could inflict if it gained open access to the Stasis system is as infinite as it is terrifying."

Carl understood, "Of course. But what if we are simply misreading the situation? What if this anomaly is equally as devastated with the outcome in Masada, and is simply trying to reconnect? After all, such a supreme technology could have little use for anything we possess. And despite everything, the Reeper was allowed to leave the previous timeline." He concluded thoughtfully, "You talk of hoping for a miracle. Well perhaps you're missing the point." He looked to the others then back to his boss, "That what you're dealing with here is not a threat at all . . . But is in fact the very miracle you seek."

The Doctor sighed as he thought of his recent haunting dreams. "Such romantic notions may well be enough for you to risk everything. I however, am bound by a somewhat more responsible attitude toward . . ."

He was interrupted as the door of the briefing room slid open. In the entrance stood a somewhat excited Doctor Stein, "Sir, I'm sorry to interrupt, but something's happening out here. I think you'd better take a look."

Brookes rushed out toward the operations centre, Jay and the others quickly in tow. "What is it?" He demanded as he reached the computer visual.

Stein pointed at the data. "It's handing over control, enabling the Stasis None complete operational access. It's transferred everything directly to us."

Brooke's mouth opened in disbelief. "How is that possible?"

A deep look of concern etched into Stein's forehead. "It isn't, not unless the source controlling this timeline was already locked into the brain of the Stasis None itself, which of course, it is not." He shook his head.

Jay and the others leaned around Brookes, Stein and Cassaveres. They didn't know precisely what it was on the displays in front of them, but they could see Brookes was as stunned as he possibly could be.

Jay looked at him with pleading eyes. "What's happening?"

He stared down at the data in front of him, deeply absorbed in his now hypnotic train of thought. The world outside was gone for the moment. His mouth quivered slightly as if unable to speak as he remembered the distant light which had haunted his recent dreams. He watched as the display showed the Stasis None being granted full control, his sense of shock deepening. Then, after a long and ponderous breath, he opened the channel to the hangar below, "Alert state One. All teams prepare the Reeper for launch immediately."

He looked across to Jose who smiled. "I repeat, prepare the Reeper for launch . . . This is not a drill." He activated the alarm countdown sequence which flooded the hangar below. The scientists within the room appeared to gasp in amazement.

Stein looked horrified as he protested, "Sir I really don't think this justifies . . . "

Brookes glared at him and he was instantly silent.

Jay looked at Brookes, her heart pulsing with anticipation, "Doctor?"

"It would appear the miracle we were hoping for may have just occurred." He swallowed hard hoping his instincts were providing the correct course of action. "You and your team had better suit up . . . I'm sending the Reeper back through that tunnel."

CHAPTER SIXTY NINE

The cockpit shuddered slightly. Jay held the stick firm as she radioed Jim in the upper deck. "Everything's good down here . . . How's she looking up top?"

Jim finalised his diagnostic. "Health-check has given the all clear, she's flying just fine."

Both pilots and passengers noted this was by far their smoothest ride through time.

Jay tried desperately to keep her mind on the task, but like the rest she couldn't help but succumb to the longing of what lay ahead. *'Just make sure you're there.'*

The Stasis None ensured the method for pick up was valid. Its intention was to knock the past version of the Reeper out of phase the moment they intercepted Dorey at the plateau. To see the memory of themselves enter a temporal loop of an already played out event, until the timeline could be sealed closing off the snapshot of time from their reality.

Such a notion was simply too mind blowing for any of them to fully absorb.

In the ship's rear Dial and the others were also riding the adrenaline of hope.

Deans was enduring his nightmare with a look of veiled calm, aware nonetheless of how much easier this ride was in comparison to previous jumps.

"You okay?" Dial yelled a little too loudly.

He gave Mark a thumbs-up, aware he was fooling no one.

Further looks of determination were passed around, the same glance which journeyed the ship several times during the flight. It was like silent prayer, *'Let him be there,'* their eyes always resting on the seat which normally held the Commander.

They were approaching their exit, on course to arrive one hour before their original incarnations . . . Past versions of themselves, soon to become a permanent simulation to this timeline's fiction.

Jim scanned his instruments as the exit loomed. His earlier contentment however, was jolted by a reading which suddenly caught his attention. He squinted, for a brief moment hoping what he'd seen was a mistake. He stared at the tunnel display, his blood running instantly cold. He couldn't speak at first, not only due to his shock, but also out of immediate fear of what to tell his pilot. He stared, desperate for the information to alter.

He tried to speak, but managed little more than a stutter.

"What was that?" came Jay's voice, "Jim . . . did you just say something?"

Again he studied the horrible data being offered by the Reeper. He flicked the sensor to the open channel feeling what he was to say was for everyone's ears. "I don't know how to tell you this, but I'm getting some disturbing readings up here."

Everyone formulated the same question but it was Jay who reached the co-pilot first. "What do you mean . . . disturbing readings?"

He stammered, not meaning to make matters worse but achieving it all the same.

"Jim?"

The others listened in with their hearts in their mouths.

"Our jump coordinates." He shook his head not wanting to believe it. "They've altered. The tunnel exit is going to bring us out in real time . . . We're going to hit Masada eight days after Dorey's fall."

Jay's heart broke. "No!" She switched to her own time navigation display. Tears filled her eyes as she witnessed the awful truth for herself. "It must be a mistake. The computer must have made a mistake."

Dial and the others were devastated. "Jim, are the readings correct? Is there anyway . . ?"

Jim cut him short, choking on his own disappointment. "I wish there was a mistake but the readings are clear. Whatever opened this tunnel has now altered our point of entry."

Dial winced at the sound of Jay's heartbroken protests as she continued to refuse the truth, "No . . . it can't be accurate. It can't be."

He tried to console her but all Jay could see was the torturous image of the tearful reunion she'd imagined was to take place. Replaying the moment she would explain to her unwitting love she'd watched him die, but had come back before it had happened in order to save him. Her entire body shook, far more violently than the ship as it now approached its exit over the Dead Sea.

Dial would have almost certainly broken down had it not been for the now obvious danger which loomed. The tunnel, with Dorey as bait at the other end, had enticed the Reeper and its crew back to this desired point in time. The impossible made possible. And it now seemed apparent it had all been done with one goal in mind. "It's a trap!" He said for all to hear. He gritted his teeth. "Jay, I'm so sorry, you know how sorry we are. But I need you to pull it together. Jay, I need you to focus."

She was despondent.

"Jay if this thing's altered our course to bring us in here when *it* wants . . . Then we're almost certainly heading into a trap. Jim can take control but we need a co-pilot, we may not have time to get Benny up there once we're spat out of this tunnel . . . Not if anything's sat there waiting for us."

Her mind heard but her emotions did not respond.

Jim's voice aired into her cockpit. "Jay . . . I can take control and try and get us back into the tunnel, but if we're heading into combat I need you with me or else we have to get Benny up here right now."

She squeezed the stick tighter, the utter devastation of losing him all over again seemed somehow worse than the first time, "Bastard!" She screamed through the glue of her mouth, "Bastard, bastard." She wasn't sure if the unknown quantity was the target of her loathing or whether it was simply fate, God or the universe itself. Her eyes blazed and she gritted her teeth as a new expression raged . . . Pure, unadulterated hatred.

She activated her weapons display, the idea of revenge now ravaging her body, infecting her blood as it pumped through her veins.

The others heard the venom, shared her desire. If their journey was to be transformed then they too would become something else entirely . . . They'd no longer enter as an angel of rescue, their intent was to become an angel of death.

*

The ship entered the timeline high in the earth's atmosphere, the weapons systems primed, the arsenal available to Jay's command enough to level a small town. All on board were focused for the delivery of ruin, the ship almost sensing the fact as it shuddered violently on its return into atmospheric flight.

Jay gunned the ship down, close to the Dead Sea to make her as invisible as possible, the powerful jets sending a violent wake across the disturbed waters. She needed to buy Jim some time, placing the ship in a wide swinging arc while her co-pilot checked her integrity for any telltale signs of damage inflicted during their flight through the tunnel.

They couldn't risk re-entering until they knew it was safe to do so.

As she gunned the ship low her hatred consumed her completely. Her friends on board would have been terrified to know of how little Jay valued her own and with it their lives at that moment. All would be sacrificed if she was given one chance to strike out at those responsible for Dorey's loss. She checked her panoramic visuals as Jim spoke into her com-link. "The energy source is emanating from a location to the south west of Masada," a pause followed, "Nothing coming our way."

The temptation to adjust her stick and set them on an explosive collision course with the mountain range burned. The first batch of missiles could be as eager as her vengeance.

Jim's voice returned with sudden urgency. "I've lost the jump computer . . . I repeat jump systems are down."

Her own jump system suddenly shut down also. She heard Jim as he desperately tried to reboot them. Without the time navigation system they were going nowhere. '*So,*' She thought, '*It is a fight you want.*' A dark part of her seemed almost relieved and she looked once more at the energy source taunting her from the distant mountains.

"Still nothing coming our way . . . No detection of anything breaching the ship, it's just dropped off line." Jim declared, sensing too the imminent likelihood of a change in tactic. He checked his visuals. The tunnel had remained open.

Jay had the ship aid her eye in checking their surroundings. Nothing was threatening an attack. Again she cast her attention to the pulsating source, her mouth dry. She heard Jim negotiate with the Reeper but the required elements remained off-line.

Dial and the others listened over the open frequency, feeling completely helpless.

"Jim?" Dial broke his silence.

"I'm getting nothing . . . nothing at all. The ship's fine, no external damage reported. All other systems are on line and good to go, everything but the jump computer."

Dial and the others swapped further concerned expressions.

"It must be the energy source manipulating the system," Jim admitted his defeat.

"I agree." Jay announced, perhaps a little too freely.

"Jay . . . Be careful." Dial's voice instructed. He knew exactly what was on her mind, "We have no idea what that thing is."

"Well, we can either fly round in circles and hope the ship diagnoses the problem or we go over there and check it out."

"The last time we visited this place the ship fell out of the sky for no apparent reason."

"It's your call." There appeared little sincerity to her response.

Jim was busy checking all around them, his enhanced vision and data assuring him the tunnel remained open, that no enemy technology had locked onto their ship, 'Strange thing for a trap.' He thought, wondering why their possible escape route had not yet been shut down as their guidance system had.

The ship could be torn to pieces negotiating the tunnel manually, but it still represented a dangerous route for escape should all else fail. He altered his view to the screen map which flashed the rocky silhouette of the mountainous terrain, illustrating the specific location of the energy source. "We have full computer visual. The energy source is emanating from the coastline at the base of the mountain, two kilometres south-west below the township, still no weapons or technology detected."

Jay's grip tightened on the stick. She cursed God, in the same breath demanding she be given her equalling chance. She primed the cannons and scowled into her combat visor, raising their altitude ready for a fly by. "I'm taking us past the source."

"Jay, we can't . . ."

She cut Dial short. "Mark, we need to know if that thing is corrupting our system."

"And flying closer toward it is likely to help?"

She dismissed the sarcasm together with the comment. "We have no idea how long that tunnel will stay open. What if it too can be manipulated like it appears the Reeper has . . . What else are we supposed to do?"

"We don't even know if it's that thing shutting down the time navigation system." He retorted, "It could be just a system failure like so many others we encounter."

"Come on Mark you don't believe that any more than I do." His silence was all she needed, "Changing course."

Jim did not hesitate. He understood Jay's intentions may well have been compromised by emotion. But the simple truth was he agreed with her. Something inside him sensed it was the right thing to do. "Roger that Jay . . . Reeper is yours and ready to go."

She appreciated his backing and set the ship on a collision course.

"Thirty seconds to target." Jim's voice was cold, "Time tunnel still open behind us."

Dial felt he should protest but in truth there was little he could do, perhaps wanted to do. He looked at those gathered who nodded their encouragement. '*So be it,*' he thought, '*Let's just get on with it.*'

The engines groaned as she dropped speed ready for the steep, banking turn she'd perform in order to survey the landscape. Jay could see the land ahead now. Her heart rate steady as she prepared to unleash her own brand of hell at the first sign of the devil.

"Ten seconds."

The landscape sprinted toward them from the sea, transforming quickly from distant mass into recognisable shapes and contours. She slotted the stick to the left and began her fly-by screaming toward the coastline.

Jim aimed all of his tracking at the ground as the roar of the Reeper re-introduced itself to the ancient Jewish settlement.

Jay turned from left to right, scanning her visuals for any sign. She slammed the airbrakes into a banking turn, the stomachs of Dial and the others groaning as their suits held them from any risk of blackout.

"I've got something!" Jim's voice came crashing into her senses.

"I see it."

The sensors had locked onto a man, down near the shoreline. The Ship bolted around and prepared to zoom by at a distance. "The energy source is all around him, its power is incredible." Jim said.

Jay gritted her teeth and readied for the confrontation, unlike Jim, the thought of the Reeper being tossed out of the sky as it had been before seemed to pose no fear for her. "Bringing her around."

"Be careful Jay we don't know . . . " his voice trailed off as his visual lock finally zoomed through the energy field providing him with a clearer view of the person within it. He scowled as he searched for the features of Brahms, then frowned as he took a moment to check what it was he believed he could see, "Oh my God." His stunned voice could only just be heard over the raging ship, "Oh my God!" This time it was a shout. There was a surprising tone of joy to his vocals. "Jesus Jay . . . It's Dorey!"

Everyone on board had to double check they'd heard correctly.

Jay was confused, stunned, her emotions unwilling to head down this route once again, "WHAT?"

"Jay it's Dorey, down on the shore. The ship's just matched his vitals."

Jay was inexplicably angry at Jim, and as the ship banked around she homed in on the person on the shore using her own close visual display, the image beamed into her visor at closer quarter. She could feel the pain taking over and scowled at the image as it locked and zoomed in. As it did she burst into tears . . . For there sure enough, clear as day and wearing a huge smile was Dorey, stood upon the beach.

Without intending to she screamed, almost deafening Jim in the process who did not mind one bit. Again she yelled with delight.

Dial and the others were desperate. "Jim what the fuck is happening?" All their hopes were terrified of being dashed but Jim's voice continued to confirm. "We've found him, he's alive . . . I repeat he's alive." Jim was almost in tears as he confirmed the ship's analysis. "He's signalling for us to land."

Dial put his hand over his mouth and stared at the others. The emotion was highly charged as they heard the Reeper engines change their pitch . . . preparing to touch down.

Carl began laughing, followed by Marco. It was the kind of laughter which could only stem from relief.

Jay was trembling violently and she handed control to Jim barely able to function.

As the Reeper began to land she fumbled open the restraints and disconnected herself and the suit from the Reeper. She didn't notice the queasy head rush, she was crying too uncontrollably as she bounced off almost every wall as she headed for the cockpit exit.

Dial warned, "Be careful we don't know for certain . . . " But of course Jay had already ordered the Reeper to set her free.

Their hearts stopped in time with the crunch of the landing gear hitting the beach.

Jim activated the rear boarding ramp on Dial's order, and no sooner had the restraints set him free he was rushing toward the armoury of the ship.

But nothing or nobody was going to reach Dorey faster than Jay who was already hurtling off the now lowering cockpit elevator into a crash of dust and excitement on the red beach below. In an instant she was up on her feet and beginning the sprint that would take her to him. She threw off the helmet and ran so hard it was as if her life depended on it. She couldn't breathe but somehow it didn't matter. The man in front of her quickly grew into a walking, smiling outstretched set of arms. The unmistakable features of his face flooding her senses. She thought she would choke, but managed to scream his name instead. Her heart was ready to burst and when she hit him she did so at such speed she almost sent them both crashing to the ground. She was clean off the floor and safe in his embrace, and she squeezed him so tight she was in danger of ensuring one of them would be at risk of passing out.

"Jay . . . I'm sorry, I'm so sorry."

She sobbed between kissing his face and head. "You're alive . . . you're really alive."

He couldn't bare her pain. He pushed his forehead onto hers and reassured her, "It's me baby . . . It's me . . . I'm fine."

She laughed out loud like a mental patient and held on to him as he squeezed her.

"I'm so sorry angel . . . I'm so sorry."

She pulled her head back and looked deep into his eyes, knowing a love at that moment as strong as the world. Her gaze melted his heart, beaming into a teary smile as she whispered once more, "You're alive." She kissed him then cried all over again as he buried his own tears into her hair.

"I love you so much."

Her legs slowly returned to the ground and they were both suddenly aware of the presence of others. They looked to see the rest of the armed group who were stood speechless around them.

Tears ran down the faces of Benny and Jim, while Carl, Marco and Deans smiled and laughed wildly. They flooded in on the duo as Dial eventually lowered the aim of his rifle which had been trained on the Commander for almost a whole minute, its own weapons display confirming the person in front of him was indeed his bona fide friend and leader. He stared with his mouth open, his senses allowing him to realise it was truly Anthony Dorey stood before him. He too then laughed out loud, as the group became lost to the greatest moment of joy any of them had ever experienced.

CHAPTER SEVENTY

It was by no means the first time Dorey had been relieved to see the inside of the Reeper, but it was by far the most emotional reunion he'd experienced within its walls, or indeed anywhere else for that matter.

The ship had been sealed, her defence perimeter set, after reassurances from Dorey they were alright to stay put for the time being. Jim had checked the navigation computer at Dorey's behest, and sure enough the jump systems were back on line.

How such a thing was possible was beyond them.

Jay had not been able to let go of him, and feelings were naturally running high. They hung on his every word as he gave a summary of his encounter with Palene.

It was an incredible feeling. A week ago they'd watched the man in front of them die, now here he was alive and well.

He apologised profusely about his reckless behaviour, and hugged Jay as he continued to astonish them with his tale.

"But how did he bring you back?" He was asked by Carl.

"I don't know, he never truly explained it. But he has an incredible mastery of manipulating space and time. He hinted it was by some such form of manipulation, but told me he couldn't divulge the details as they were in many ways beyond even his own comprehension."

"Do you think he was just saying that because he didn't want you to know?"

"It's possible . . . But I don't really see why he'd hide such a fact under the circumstances."

"Where is he now?"

Dorey wore a look of wonder, "He transformed himself into the energy field that opened up the time tunnel." He smiled, "Right before my eyes . . . He *is* the connection to our world which allowed you back here."

They gasped at the unbelievable answer, if indeed anything could be deemed unbelievable anymore. "Transformed?" Dial asked.

"He de-atomised, right in front of me." Dorey could not help but laugh as he spoke the words. "I couldn't believe what I was seeing. The next thing I know this incredible energy started to spin like a tornado building momentum. It was small at first, but then it grew larger and larger until eventually it became a gigantic tunnel of spinning light, shooting up into the heavens leaving only a small signature-trace behind . . . That which you witnessed when you first landed."

"Small?" Jim's mouth opened, "The energy emanating off that thing was incredible."

"Like a homing beacon." Benny commented.

Jim laughed, "You're lucky Jay didn't blow you to pieces, never mind land the ship."

"I was a little nervous when I saw her pull that steep attack turn she loves so much."

"You'd have deserved it with everything you've put us through. I should have at least had you diving for cover with a few choice rounds from the cannon."

Laughter and further apologies followed, as again the thrill of their reunion was enjoyed.

He told them more about Palene's apparent immortality, of his wife and family and the notion he was meant to help mankind in some way.

"So what does he want, I mean, what happens next?" Jay asked while squeezing his hand.

"He said he saved my life because he'd wanted to, but also so I could arrange a meeting."

"He wants to meet with Brookes?" Carl added astutely.

Dorey agreed. "Three days from now."

"What the hell do you think it all means?" Benny enquired.

"All I know is he saved my life, and no matter how incredible his story is, I believe him." They were dumbfounded by the comment as Dorey continued, "Like our own Stasis None he believes mankind to be in grave danger. He thinks it's his destiny to help us. I believe it's all connected in some way."

They contemplated everything they'd seen and heard, pondering over their own wondrous machine's grim prediction for humanity.

"And you don't think this is just some advanced time traveller with a serious messianic complex?"

Dorey smiled at the wording of Dial's interjection, "Believe me I've run through that line of questioning. But it's like I told you, there's something really strange about this guy. But in a *good way* you know? And it's not just the miracles he's pulled off, not just that he's brought me back from the dead. It's something deeper. When you listen to this man, when you look into his eyes," he shook his head, "I don't know . . . You just kind of feel there's a greater power at work."

None of them had heard Dorey speak like this before, and each of them was mesmerised by the ideas now bouncing around their minds. '*Could they really be witnessing something like fateful intervention? Or were they merely observing a superior power with alternative notions?*' Mixed emotions were naturally brewing.

Dorey continued to detail his encounter, answering their questions as best as he could. He informed them how he intended to offer Palene assistance in arranging the desired meeting. He told of his experience of death, of his difficulties with the emotional rollercoaster. He informed them of the strange coincidences discovered, such as the location and the measurement of time passed since Palene's bizarre incident when struck by the Finger of Venus. How Palene had been watching them for centuries, and how he currently occupied the year 2115.

They discussed what it could all mean and pondered over the energy source striking Palene at almost the precise geographical location as the Stasis None.

When he'd told them everything, he looked at them and asked, "So, am I crazy? Or has my brain not recovered from that fall?"

Jay shuddered at the remark.

The unanimous answer came courtesy of Dial. "What we think is it's great to have you back. The rest we'll figure out as we go!"

Further hugs, smiles and handshakes were passed around before the team was able to consider the return journey to the mouth of the awaiting tunnel.

Jay refused Benny's offer to take them home, feeling the need to do it personally. As if in doing so she would have completed something of greater significance to herself.

When eventually she returned to the Reeper cockpit and fired the engines, all of Jay's impossible hopes and dreams had come true.

PART FOUR

The black depths of intelligent universe vibrated,
sending visions of colour and being like sparks into the
darkest truth of space.
Power, creation, understanding.
'Incredible.'
'Yes.'
'You feel it.'
'Yes.'
'Wonderful.'
'Yes.'
'So close.'
'Yes.'
'I sense it.'
'Sense?...Yes.'
'Destiny?'
'Yes.'
'Do such forces exist?'
'Yes.'

CHAPTER SEVENTY ONE

The riotous celebrations which engulfed the Reeper's return were closed out for the time being as Brookes and Dorey embarked on a more private meeting. "Drink?" Brookes enquired as they entered his office, its synthetic walls painting a rich Manhattan sunset.

"Thank you, I'll have a Brandy."

Brookes pulled out two crystal snifters and poured them each a large measure, "To your most miraculous return."

They took a sip, allowing the smooth fires to warm their throats and stomachs.

"I just can't believe it." Brookes beamed, "All of this . . . It's simply incredible."

Dorey agreed taking another sip of the quality booze.

"So . . . Do you want to fill me in on what's going on?"

Dorey gathered his thoughts, realising this account would have to be more meticulous than the version given to his friends inside the Reeper. Before he began he looked at the doctor sincerely. "Thank you once again, for the risk you took in getting me back."

Brookes dismissed the necessity.

"Nevertheless, I'm grateful for what you did. I know this won't have done you any favours." He added, "I hope the information I'm about to divulge will be of great enough significance to justify such risk." Dorey knew Brookes would have to feed the wolves something, but he hoped by the end of this session his boss would be prepared to meet Palene on his own terms rather than on those of Finch and his backers.

Brookes appreciated Dorey's shrewd understanding, the joy at seeing his trusted Commander close to overwhelming.

*

Brookes sat in silence throughout the entirety of Dorey's tale, his thoughtful veil broken on several occasions by the miraculous often disturbing account.

Dorey could see his words had affected him deeply. He watched as the Doctor stood slowly, gesturing for his glass. He wondered what was running through the genius of the man's mind as he set about pouring each of them another drink.

"Tell me Commander . . . How would you describe this Palene?"

Dorey detected a strange air of suspicion to the Doctor's voice, "Physically?" He'd naturally described how Palene affected him on a personal level.

Brookes passed over the refreshed glass, "Yes . . . What were his features?"

Dorey pondered over the differences, "Well, his hair was dark brown and thick. His skin more tanned than when he'd posed as Captain Brahms."

Brookes thought back to the three dimensional model previously created by their computers which only now seemed to spark some distant familiarity.

"And his eyes, they were incredible, chestnut almost tinged with burgundy, not green as before." Dorey paused, "Oh and of course there were the faint scars on his face."

Brooke's mouth opened at the description, "Besides those left by Dial, can you remember if there was another smaller scar upon his cheek?"

Dorey felt the immediate impact of Brooke's question, the shock of it gripping him, "Jesus . . . You know who this guy is!"

Brookes urged him to answer, his eyes wide, almost startled. "Can you remember?"

Dorey was stunned, "Yes, he had a scar on his cheek."

Brookes looked as if he'd seen a ghost. "Shaped almost like a flower?"

Dorey's heart was racing as he tried to second guess what was now happening. He pointed slowly to show the location of the scar, "Like a pentacle."

Brookes gasped, "My God."

Dorey couldn't bare the suspense, "Doctor?"

Brookes placed his drink on the desk. He fought his way back toward some kind of composure. His brain immediately ran through his possible courses of action. He looked at the man before him whom he trusted totally and dwelled on the meaning of all that was now transpiring. He thought of the haunting distant light within his own recent dreams then made a momentous decision. "Commander . . . I think you'd better come with me."

*

Brookes had utilised a large service lift to spirit them down into the lowest depths of the Stasis caverns. The lift car had been operated via a covert touch pad, the elevator arriving on a corridor the Commander had never seen before. During the journey Dorey repeatedly asked the Doctor to divulge what was happening but the only response given was, "I must show you something first."

They were now so deep in the base of the complex the ventilation seemed to sigh as if experiencing the extra weight and pressure of the surrounding rock.

The corridor was narrow, dimly lit and much more rugged than those usually frequented by Dorey and his team. Brookes took them around the sloping bend toward a large air filtration unit which stood humming at the dead end of the path.

"Nobody has ever knowingly been down here. It doesn't exist. Not on any blueprints, not in any of the designs."

Dorey was puzzled.

"I must ask for your promise Commander, your solemn vow that what you are about to see will be taken to your grave unless I instruct otherwise."

He agreed, ignoring the irony of the statement, "Of course Doctor."

Brookes looked on nervously. "Could I ask you to please turn away for a moment?"

The same request had been put to Dorey when entering the large service elevator and once again he obliged.

Brookes leaned toward the seventh dial on the machine and gently removed its cover. He breathed on the device. A tiny panel appeared out of the display face and a small tray opened from within. Brookes raised his hand to his eye and carefully pulled out one of his eyelashes, dropping it into the tray. He then breathed on the panel once again and the eyelash was retracted into the machine.

"You may turn around now Commander."

The surrounding hum subtly changed its pitch. Dorey looked to Brookes when suddenly the wall of the corridor directly to their right began to move. They watched as the structure morphed like liquid rock to reveal a hidden entrance.

"The finest technology." Brookes commented to Dorey, who was clearly impressed at the fluidity of which the wall had just opened up. Brooke's eye was then scanned as he licked his thumb and pressed the plate, causing the newly arrived door to slide open. It revealed a rough tubular corridor of cut rock blanketed with a steel mesh floor.

They stepped inside, Dorey closely in tow of his boss.

"What is this place?" For some reason Dorey found it necessary to whisper.

Brookes' response was deliberately loud, as if to reassure the Commander such cloak and dagger could be left behind. "This is the real nerve centre of the Stasis None."

The corridor took them toward the looming embrace of a large open chamber. As they approached, the melodic sound of an electronic pulse emanated from the chasm beyond.

Brookes led them through onto the steel mesh of a broad landing.

Woven metal steps took them down into the chamber, "Lights at eighty percent."

The room quickly warmed to the illumination. It was far bigger than Dorey expected after their journey through the secretive, cave-like entry.

The pulsating beat seemed to grow stronger as they stepped onto the floor below.

Dorey stared around the room taking in its features.

They were surrounded by displays and monitoring technologies of varying description and high sophistication. On the far side was a desk supporting a computer and holo-unit. A large chair lounged before it. Both the desk and workstation were dressed with antique lamps. To their right in the far corner was a sofa. Close by was a medical table, above which was a state of the art *Surgeon* unit housed in the ceiling . . . an A.I. device capable of carrying out any medical procedure and cutting edge nano-surgery. Above them, the steel mesh of the walkway surrounded the room along the walls edge, holding more complex looking devices and a power unit on the far landing.

However, it was the object near the centre of the cavernous room that immediately grabbed the attention and it was toward this structure Brookes now walked, "The engineers who constructed this room didn't know of its real location even as they were building it. I manufactured a device which altered the readings taken from their equipment to make them believe they were in a different place entirely. The final features hiding the corridors which led us here were built by my brother."

Dorey was impressed, "The famous architect."

"It was all very elaborate and extremely difficult to plan . . . But I managed it." He glanced down at the black tiled, torpedo-like object beneath him.

"How have you kept it a secret for so long?"

"Oh I don't think I'll bore you with details. Let's just say there are a complicated blend of technologies feeding false images and readings into the right equipment at the right time . . . So as to build the illusion I'm always somewhere else other than here." He watched as Dorey approached, his heart quickening at the decision to bring him into this, his most secret lair. "It's a little over the top, but unfortunately very necessary, considering the people I have to deal with."

"So nobody knows its here?"

"Not even my brother for certain. He allowed me to mislead him over its exact location."

Dorey shook his head. "Not even Finch?"

"Especially not Finch . . . Although I suspect he has his suspicions."

Dorey approached the black tiled object and observed how the room's pulsating, rhythmic bass, played out perfectly in time with the digital displays dancing on its surface. He frowned as he listened to the soft beat. 'Bum . . . Bum . . . Bum.'

He noted the engraved letters spelt, STASIS NONE.

"So this is the real mainframe? Not the one under the RFC?"

"Yes . . . But it's a little more than that." Brookes reached down and activated another coded keypad which he quickly typed on at speed. He licked his thumb and pressed it onto an emerging sensor. The usual optical scan was employed before slowly with an ominous hiss, the black tiled shell of the Stasis None mainframe began to retract.

The rhythmic beat continued and Dorey's mouth dried in anticipation. He looked once again at Brookes who said in a soft voice. "Remember, what you witness here is the secret of all secrets. I have your solemn vow you'll never tell another soul without my express permission."

Dorey agreed as he watched the device glide open with a smooth, gentle motion. He stared downward, not really sure what he expected to see, but as the secret came into view, nothing could have prepared him for it.

CHAPTER SEVENTY TWO

Dorey gasped, the sudden shock gripping him to his core, "My God."

Brookes realised he had his answer. "Is this the man you now know as Palene?" He was also visibly affected by events unfolding.

Dorey couldn't speak at first. He just continued to stare at the motionless figure wired into the black shell of the tomb. He stared closer at the comatose being, unsure of the true familiarity at first.

"Is that Palene?"

Dorey nodded slowly. It was Palene, or at least some version of him. This creature had features perfectly smooth. His skin was like latex. Tiny tubes ran into his neck. His eyes were closed, his body grey and lifeless, the flower shaped scar evident on his cheek. Eight fibre wires fed his chest and an intricate web of connective flex ran into the base of his skull. He felt sick. "Is he alive?"

"In a manner of speaking . . . yes." the Doctor's reply was somewhat cold.

"In a manner of speaking?"

Brookes understood the response. He was himself as overwhelmed by the discovery of a *new* Palene as Dorey was looking at this one.

"I don't understand."

"Neither do I . . . But I'm beginning to develop some interesting theories."

"What is he?" It wounded Dorey to see Palene in this manner.

"Many years ago when the Stasis None was still in its infancy I conducted an experiment. It was my first real practical test at attempting to manipulate space and time. When granted the means to move here, I'd already constructed a device during my research in Washington . . . A form of particle beam able to pierce the space time continuum, capable of carrying de-atomised mass and causing controlled particle collisions within artificial atmospheres. The beam's matter was in many ways similar to the technology we use today, only more brutal," he added, "And unfortunately, it was to prove less stable." Brookes stared at the lifeless body. "The experiment had two aims. First, cause a particle collision within a controlled atmosphere while occupied within another timespan. Second, send biological DNA into that atmosphere then return it. The beam would de-atomise its subject matter, load it into the carrier beam and reassemble it at the other end. The chosen subject was a freshly-picked apple." He sighed, remembering that fateful night, "As you've no doubt guessed, the experiment went wrong."

Dorey thought this to be the mother of all understatements.

"We fired the beam to an axis at the same geographical point as that which housed the experiment, here beside the sloping hillside close to Stonehenge. The first, usable pinpoint in time ever offered up by our fledgling Stasis None. It was to carry out the test one mile up in the earth's atmosphere. First the particle collision would create a miniature universe, building a stable anchor into the past. Then the apple was sent through, reforming within the protective bubble, so as to not contaminate the other end of time."

Dorey's eyes widened, "The experiment was conducted in real time, not a simulation?"

Brookes nodded. "During my initial experimentation it soon became clear pinpointed movement through time could only be achieved once a workable bridge and anchor point had been constructed, capable of connecting one plain of existence to another. This experiment was deemed a viable, safe option in order to create such an anchor, while simultaneously testing the effects of such a journey on biological matter." He shook his head, as if still staggered by his prior blind optimism, "It was because of the spectacular failure of this original test I never experimented directly in the parameters of our own space and time again. Though of course, it was only a failure in some respects."

Dorey returned his eyes to the lifeless body.

"Everything was running smoothly. The beam's collider created the anchor, allowing the inbound apple to appear in the time zone for a millisecond. It re-atomised within the small bubble of protected atmosphere then de-atomised to return home. But just at the point we thought all was well, a nightmare was realised. The beam broke free from its anchoring. The fail safes held it within the chosen location but it was momentarily unstable at the other end. We thought we'd managed to reel it in but for a fraction of a second it thrashed out, a violent energy force capable of God only knows what damage."

Dorey stared at Palene, "The finger of Venus," he said almost distantly.

"Our first terror was we may have caused a paradox. The second was about to unfold."

"It wasn't an apple you brought back through time."

Brookes shook his head. "No. As the beam was dragged back into our vortex drive a new truth was upon us. I cleared the room immediately, keeping only the essential staff at hand. I thought there was some mistake, that I'd misread the data, but the truth was inescapable. The returning beam held within its core the unmistakable genetic code of a de-atomised human male . . . Him." He pointed at Palene.

Dorey scowled. "But that doesn't make sense."

Brookes signalled for patience. "As the man reformed the screams of torment and agony were almost unbearable. His eyes blazed at me through the beam, burning my very soul. I tried desperately to have the computer return him, realising the danger he posed. But the computer was determined to fulfil its preconceived task. In the chaos which then ensued, the next thing I knew a version of the man was collapsing into a heap on the floor of the re-atomiser," his mind played it back like it was yesterday, "Only to my amazement, he was simultaneously held within the beam. Somehow the computer obeyed both tasks. To complete its undertaking and bring home the subject, but also to achieve my new request . . . The order to send him back in order to protect our world, our very existence."

Dorey shook his head, "So what happened?"

"We lost the original version held within the beam. Vanished, destroyed . . . Leaving only this comatose copy behind. We presumed he'd died instantly as during that phase of the experiment there was no longer an anchor at the other end in which to return him to his normal state. We carried out endless research, terrified of the paradox to be delivered, but nothing came, nothing was detected. Our only theory was he must have been destroyed, de-atomised across time and space, fortunately without damage to our own future."

"Jesus." Dorey said under his breath.

"We kept it quiet, amazed that although brain dead, the man was technically still alive. Some trusted colleagues and I smuggled him into one of the project labs converted into a make-shift hospital. Not that we needed one as it would turn out."

"What do you mean?"

Brookes pointed down at the body. "Isn't it obvious?"

The Commander was in no mood for riddles.

"He can't die."

"What?"

"He cannot die. This Palene is as indestructible as the living, breathing version you've just met."

Dorey looked down. The truth hadn't struck home. With the grey lifeless features he hadn't really absorbed the obvious detail. Brookes was talking of an experiment carried out over four decades ago. The man cocooned in this black shell was still in his prime.

"We were amazed to find his molecular structure altered, exposed then merged with the actual beam. An energy force which operated at speeds faster than light. Somehow something remarkable, and certainly what should have been impossible occurred."

"You altered his DNA."

Brookes corrected, "The computer altered his DNA. But not only altered . . . Restructured." He clarified, "His cellular response operates at a quantum level, his damaged cells are able to repair and reproduce faster than light. And yet this alone should have killed him. His own cellular reproduction destroying him from within, yet somehow it did not."

The thought struck Dorey like a sledgehammer, "The apple."

"The apple." he confirmed. "We'd presumed it lost or destroyed. But its cellular make up was stored in the memory of the beam. The computer, when holding then reforming Palene inside the energy source recognised the danger to the downloading human form. It adjusted its program, adapted it to save the human life rather than restore the apple."

"But why? If its directive was so important to it why would it even bother to alter its original objective?" He added, "More to the point . . . How could it?"

"Of the countless possible theories the one we came to believe was the most simple. We'd developed safety software. After all, we were playing with powers beyond our understanding. So just in case the system got a little too big for its boots, we programmed our super computer with the notion it must preserve human life above all else."

Again Dorey shook his head unsure what it was he was now feeling. It was all too much, too soon. He felt a wave of disappointment. It was childish and irrational, but he'd bought into the concept events unfolding were to be a little more magical than mis-firing computers and irresponsible scientists.

Brookes continued. "Whatever the reason, the program realised the make up of the fruit wasn't alive, but neither was it actually dead having just been picked from the tree. It took the relevant data needed from the apple's cells and figured out a method of collision in which to create a similar form of stasis within Palene's biological soup. It used this to save him . . . It used this to make him everlasting."

Dorey let out a deep exhale.

"After the experiment I realised even when operating under the reassurances of the Stasis None, I could no longer risk puncturing holes through real space and time. I had to figure out a new path. The fact I'd brought a person through time was enough to prove my theories, I just needed to adapt them, evolve them into a safer more usable method. I was granted priority funding from a top secret, powerful few. And the Stasis None Project grew in both size and importance. I was set. I'd created the most potent computer in existence, made possible the earliest concept of time travel, and created indestructible human DNA in the process. With the vast construction of the project well underway, I began handpicking my staff. I continued my work in time travel while simultaneously evolving my super computer, all the while carrying out experiments on our man here."

Dorey did not like this terminology. "So why the wires and tubes . . . Why all of this?"

Brookes delivered the final truth, "Commander, this Palene here . . . He *is* the Stasis None. Or an integral part of it anyway," he elaborated, "Over the years I tried to find a solution to the dangers of manipulating time, of figuring out the conundrum of creating another viable anchor point in the past, a more stable axis to the one used during the first test. One avenue I'd decided to venture toward was the idea of creating simulated versions of reality, but this was more difficult than you could imagine. I threw myself into the work. For every success there were a hundred failures, for every high came countless lows. But I made the breakthroughs. Eventually we began experimenting with small simulations, concepts of creating minute alternate plains of existence . . . Test tube stuff. The computer was operating at a higher level with each passing year, the project and its aims rapidly expanding. I was beginning to grasp more of how this intelligence operated when calculating across other dimensions. It was like I was the only person who could connect to its logic, one of the reasons I've not been replaced on occasion over the years, particularly when I was offering fewer results on the possibility of creating indestructible human beings."

"So such a possibility wasn't the number one priority . . . Discovering immortality?"

"Naturally I strived for it in the beginning. But it soon became obvious it was doomed to failure. Of course I still carry out detailed research on such matters. I have to. But as a scientist my priorities changed once I realised the gift laid before me offered humanity so many more, obtainable evolutions."

Dorey eyed him with obvious suspicion.

"If my research was concentrated entirely on one such purpose then yes, I think I may have allowed it to consume me, this idea of immortal life. But it wasn't. I was delving into the mysteries of the universe and time, and these were mysteries in which I was achieving *real* results. So believe me when I tell you, this has never been a quest for immortality alone . . . And despite what you see before you now, I am no Frankenstein." Brookes thought back over the many power struggles, the near disastrous consequences of his many failures to further develop indestructible human DNA. Struggles which continued to this day, the likes of which would be calling again after his decision to send the Reeper to collect the man now stood before him without prior approval.

Although ironically, Dorey's return from the grave may well prove enough to spare Brookes for the time being.

The Commander stared at the tragic patient, the words of Palene haunting him, *'I hear the missing part of my soul, calling me, tormenting me from across time.'*

"As for my time research," Brookes went on, "For all the successes, I could never isolate the defining breakthrough. Never create a genuinely safe universal bridge into history, a stable attachment of one plain of time to another. And that's when it hit me . . . Use the man from the past. I had an epiphany as to how I could feed this man's make up into the computer using the *then* latest breakthroughs in bio-nano-technology. I realised if achievable, he could be used as a reference, a source to the past linked directly into the system. While the electrical elements of his brain might offer the computer clues on how to understand my own limitations, and perhaps discover a more effective method of deciphering the questions and answers I so desired. But of course it was not only the manipulation of time my sponsors wanted, and I understood the dangers ahead, realising to maintain control in the years to come I'd have to deflect their ambitions, without damaging my own too severely in the process. And so I acted quickly to stage the death of this,

Palene." He still couldn't get used to the half-person before him actually having a name. "My idea of how to meld him into the Stasis None could never be known. This way his miraculous properties could be exploited by me alone. I could claim all future discoveries as stemming from my own genius ensuring I remain unattainable to all other great thinkers on Earth, making me untouchable within the realms of the Stasis Project." He concluded, "And so it came to pass my remarkable coma patient would be destroyed."

"How did you manage such a feat?"

"With or without my computer I possess an intellect way beyond my peers, so basically I baffled them with mouth-watering possibilities. Much of the jargon was true, the rest a theoretically viable gamble to see their dream for indestructible DNA realised. And so by pushing to see the mysteries of eternal life unlocked, I lost my unique subject due to a dreadful error," he surmised, "When during an attempt to break down his DNA using a new strain of the particle beam I would de-atomise my prized asset. I saw to it this secret chamber was added to the still ongoing construction of the immense Stasis caves, and when I was ready had the beam send him to it." He pointed to the tomb housing his immortal guest, "As far as everyone else was concerned he was lost forever."

"And nobody suspected anything untoward?"

"It's amazing what simple illusion can achieve, particularly when the magician is armed with the only operational quantum computer in existence." He added, "I still possessed enough ground-breaking theory to appease the mob, and things calmed down when I began producing new results, miraculous in their own right. I was able to assimilate Palene into the wondrous depths of my evolving computer in a manner only made possible by his imperishable make up. The Stasis None would analyse everything without fear of harm to its subject, taking all it could from his indestructible DNA. And with our mysterious friend hard wired into the machine, all manner of breakthroughs followed." He looked down at the coma patient, "Once fully interfaced with its human counterpart the Stasis None discovered how to use Palene to create a point of reference in the past as I'd hoped. We began virtual experiments, combining that first infamous test with vastly improved hypothetical ones. It developed its own synthetic version of our beam, propelling it back over two millennia of theoretical existence. Eventually it discovered a safe method with which to recreate the original experiment, constructing a superior evolution of the actual particle beam, firing it back along the original journey through time. And it did this all of its own volition, so it may experience the entire string of an actual two thousand year period, storing every core detail to its vast, incalculable memory." He added, "It was soon after, the *real* breakthrough took place."

"You created the clone of the two thousand year time string."

"Exactly, or rather the computer did. The irony is this was never my intention at this stage. The project goals were much smaller. But after years of complex experiments the computer had not only interfaced and studied its human assistant, it made some kind of cerebral connection to it. I was fascinated to see how the Stasis None came to understand the process of reason as opposed to just vast calculation. But it wasn't like some sinister novel, it was wonderful. We worked together night and day and slowly, I began to grasp more of the complexities required in order to ask the right questions of this incredible, growing intelligence . . . While in turn, it developed the very human trait of guess work, reading between the lines. When it then spectacularly misinterpreted a save request at the conclusion of a later experiment, I had to stage an elaborate, accidental breakthrough."

"The Stasis None Project is born."

"It was staggering. After the computer sent atoms of itself through that corridor of existence, placing all detail of that vast timeline to memory, it used this data to achieve its misconstrued challenge. And instead of saving a theoretical, virtual two millennia segment of our planet's history . . . It cloned it. An identical copy, kept out of phase, sat dormant in unoccupied time and space. I still don't know how it could be possible, I doubt I ever will. What I do know is once this man was hooked into our machine, amazing results had a tendency to follow."

"But this still doesn't explain how he brought me back from the dead. How he opened a sealed portal of time," he was desperate to hold onto the idea of Palene being something more profound than a scientific super freak. It had taken a great deal of self-discovery for Dorey to have allowed Palene's concepts into his psyche and he was growing reluctant to see them so easily taken away. Especially as the credibility of his own life had since been dragged into question by such involvement, "It doesn't explain how we've got a man out there who's lived for over two thousand years with powers beyond comprehension. Someone who whether real or not, has the ability to alter our timelines and transcend existence at will."

Brookes smiled like a fox. "It most certainly does not. That is an entirely different arena. One which throws up possibilities I could never have imagined. Answers which can be provided by one man alone." He looked down at the grey body then brushed the sensor, the tomb resealing itself beneath them. "And that is exactly why I'm going to agree to his terms . . . And go with you to meet him at this chosen rendezvous in history."

CHAPTER SEVENTY THREE

Jay was enjoying the soothing foam of the spa. It was as if each caress of jettisoned bubbles reminded her she could relax, that Dorey was safe and well in the next room.

They'd made love and broken their hearts several times over and he'd once again begged her to forgive his callous behaviour which culminated in such pain and grief.

He'd dismissed the guilt she still felt at telling her own parents and not David, Mitch and Katie, and discussed the details of the cover story already being put in place, one of hostages, rescues and misidentification, soon to restore all to its natural balance.

They'd talked of the tearful reunion he would receive, and of how they'd instruct Jay's parents to never discuss the military's awful mistake, emphasising Jay's inability to inform Dorey's family as their main reason for such secrecy.

She stepped out of the bath activating the warm blowing air from the surrounding walls. She wrapped herself in a towel, gargled on some mouthwash, then headed back for the bedroom.

It was warmly lit. The synthetic walls a deep blushing sunset. He'd straightened up the bed and was laid within the perfect temperature covered only by the fresh cotton sheet. Her face beamed as she looked upon him. '*Was it really only hours ago I lay in that very spot mourning your loss?*' The tears threatened, but the joy was far too strong. She rolled onto the mattress unable to resist the urge to be close to him once more.

He took a lungful of the sweet smelling hair and skin. She was stunning, and he thanked God, Palene and anyone else who'd listen for his second chance with such a treasure.

He sighed, dwelling on the magnificent gift Palene had granted, while once again pondering over the news of his test results which confirmed his body had indeed remained the same as before his reincarnation, his implants still present.

He wondered what it could all mean, and shivered as he thought of the cold grey prisoner held within the tomb of the Stasis None.

"You're thinking about him again aren't you?"

He smiled blankly.

"Are you sure you're okay?"

"I'm fine."

She raised an eyebrow. "Do we really have to do that?"

He ran his fingers through her smooth damp hair.

"Something's bothering you." Her voice was soft and easy.

"Something's bothering me?" His tone was teasing as he made light of recent events.

She played along, "Well apart from dying, being reborn," her smile became a broad grin.

He stroked the hair away from her forehead as she moved in closer.

"Are you okay?*"*

He sighed, not really sure what he should tell her.

"I know it must be difficult, but whatever it is we'll deal with it. Just tell me what you're feeling."

He stared into her, adoring the fact she was there.

"Something's really troubling you, something that wasn't there when we picked you up at Masada." She looked imploringly, "It's what Brookes told you when you disappeared with him earlier. He's upset you in some way."

He thought about the solemn vow he'd given his boss. He felt his loyalty twinge, appreciating the risk the doctor had taken in order to bring him back. But as he looked at Jay the thought struck once again of how he was only there because of one man, the person who truly saved him . . . Pulled him back from oblivion. *'I hear my soul calling me,'* he closed his eyes at the memory, *'From somewhere across time and space.'* He decided his word to Brookes was not as important as being true to his heart. "Brookes showed me something when we returned. Something hidden away in the base levels of the complex, a secret nobody knows of other than himself . . . and now me."

She was relieved to hear him open up but was concerned at what the contents of this troubled admission would be.

"A large hidden chamber . . . full of some seriously sophisticated hardware."

"Where?"

"Really deep down, I mean you could almost feel the change in air pressure," he watched her concerned expression, "The central brain of the entire Stasis None System."

She looked confused. "I thought that was inside the *no go* area beneath the RFC."

"So does everyone."

"What . . . So not even Stein, the top brass *thinkers* . . . or Finch know about it?"

"Especially not Finch." He added, "No-one."

Her voice betrayed her concern, "So why the secrecy?"

"Because of what he's got in there."

"Because of what he's got in there?" She scowled not certain she really wanted to know, "Why . . . What's in there?"

Dorey felt crestfallen as he said it aloud, "Palene, he's got a comatose version of Palene."

*

The group sat inside the living room curious as to what was on the agenda. Dorey knew his team were watched and he wasn't prepared to discuss anything beyond the safety of his own four walls. A welcome home party was the perfect screen.

However it had soon become clear this was not to be the reason for the gathering.

His friends were still very much enjoying the thrill of seeing him alive, but they'd noted the tension within their host immediately upon their arrival.

As the team awaited the Commander's words Jay smiled encouragement, knowing how difficult it was for Dorey to so readily break his promise to Brookes.

The room hushed expectantly, "There's something I need to tell all of you."

*

"It's unbelievable." Benny remarked.

"Unbelievable?" Carl challenged with a raised brow.

Benny took his point.

"So the guy's wired into our computer while in a coma in our reality, but believes he's immortal when inside our simulations?" Marco enquired, "And he has no idea there's more than one version of himself?"

Dorey understood their need to theorise. "The experiment Brookes carried out pulled a man through time . . . Through real time. Then somehow the Stasis None split him in two, or at least made some kind of copy. But not a copy as in a cloned entity, Brookes thinks this comatose copy is as real as the one which disappeared . . . The very same person."

"Are we talking real like the recreations we see in these simulated existences?"

"No I mean real as in, if I fired the same stuff at you as what the Stasis None used that day, there'd be another Jim sat there, not a simulated copy, another very real *you*." He added, "The computer tried to bring him into our world safe and sound while simultaneously obeying Brooke's second order to send him back. So it placed him in two different phases of existence, that way obeying its directives to preserve human life at all costs, from all angles."

"But surely the computer would still only have one set of atoms, one man's DNA to work with. How come we end up with two real versions?"

"Due to the computer's almost instantaneous ability to problem solve he believes it learned how to experience this person at two separate points within the universe, as it does its own atoms, placing the same version of Palene into two separate moments. Brookes kept using the term *out of phase.*" He added, "The Stasis None attempted to complete the tasks demanded of it but saw immediately it could not protect all life in the future as well as this one life within the beam. Quickly realising the only way it could achieve both would be if it utilised the very process that made its own logic possible . . . Multiple realities and plains of existence."

"And I thought things couldn't get any weirder." Deans commented.

"So the Palene you know is immortal because his DNA was altered in the same way by the Stasis None, as the guy Brookes now has in his lab?"

"Brookes has a number of theories already. Some he shared, some he didn't. But whatever those may be he's decided to agree to Palene's terms and meet."

"And we are to be Brooke's armed escort?"

Dorey nodded, confirming Benny's assumption.

"And how do you feel about all of this?" Carl asked.

"I listened to his theories on Palene. Some I thought more likely than others."

"But?"

He locked his eyes into Carl's. "But I believe there's something more." He understood he may well make himself sound like a possible risk to the welfare of his own team. That he may come across as mesmerised from his time spent with this strange being, allowing personal feelings to cloud his judgement. "I know how I must sound to you. But I can assure you this is not just about me owing this man my life, or being too personally involved as a result. My judgement stems from instinct, nothing more." He went on, "I broke my word to Brookes because I wanted all of you to know everything we are involved in here. Even in recent events I've never led any of you into anything you didn't have full disclosure of first. You've always known what I know. It's what keeps us together. Trust, teamwork. I lost sight of that and went guns blazing after something to satisfy my own indulgence . . . I paid the price for it." He looked at Jay, "We paid the price for it." The comment was absorbed by all in the room. "I can't say for sure what it is Brookes intends to do. What he may order us to perform. All I *can* say is what my own intentions are." He looked at Dial. "I want to help this Palene."

"At what cost?" His second enquired without hesitation.

"I don't really know the answer to that."

"And what if this Palene turns out to be the reason for this predicted catastrophe awaiting mankind? We could be aiding and abetting the very thing we've tried so hard to prevent."

"As I've said, Brookes was adamant such a scenario is unlikely."

"But he didn't justify such theory?" Dial was edgy.

"Does he ever?" Dorey replied. "Besides, all I can go by is what I feel, what I believe."

They all took in the implications of what Dorey's potential mutiny could mean.

He appreciated the irony, understood their concerns. He'd always enforced the necessary chain of command. It wasn't an easy thing to have cherished people risk their lives on his authority, to fear on each occasion any one of them could be lost as a direct result. The usual distances maintained between leader and troops did not exist within this elite group, it could not exist. Their entire world was built around each other. This was why the pain of Ian Mahoney's death was still too deep a cut to bare, and why Dean's appointment was resisted so strongly at first. After all, how could anyone expect to walk into such a thing? How could he expect to not feel like an outsider when the rest of the group would surely be more guarded this second time around? Dorey stared at his newest team member and felt pleased once again at the choice. He'd been exemplary in every way, taking to this most mind-blowing of undertakings with honesty, courage and enthusiasm, winning the total trust and support of both he and his team. His thoughts were invaded by guilt once again. Guilt at what he'd put Jay and his friends through this past week, guilt at his life being saved and at Mahoney's being irreversibly lost. Guilt at what he was now asking of them. To possibly go against all the beliefs instilled into them, and all on the notion of him having another gut feeling, the same brand which had so recently thrown them into the arms of tragedy.

Dial broke the silence. "If you're asking me whose judgement I'd normally trust then it would be yours every time." He looked at Jay as if what he was to say was somehow a betrayal on her too, "But I've got to be honest. I can't help but wonder whether your judgement is as cold as it would usually be. I mean this guy, whoever, whatever he is . . . He's the reason you're sitting here right now." He stared at the miracle before him. "I mean, you owe this man everything." Again he flashed a brief glance at Jay, "We owe this guy." He turned to Carl and the others. "But if you're asking what I think you're asking, then I need to know one thing. Is it possible so soon after coming back from the grave and having your world blown apart in the hours since . . . That your gut feeling may not be entirely reliable?"

He smiled at Dial. "If the roles were reversed I'd ask the same thing. I've screwed up a few times this year already. I could have got us all killed back in Constantinople." He waved away the protest, "I got myself killed by illogically allowing personal desire to influence my decision-making." He looked at them all in turn. "Let's face it. I'd question everything and anything associated with one of my *gut feelings* right now. But all I can tell you is what I believe. And I know things have got a little crazy around here lately. Just as I know you must be wondering if this Palene has got deeper under my skin since saving my life." He implored them. "But this goes beyond any of that. After all, I've owed most within this room my life at some point or another." It was time to open up fully. "In all honesty I'm an emotional mess right now. I feel guilty at being alive, guilty at having been dead . . . Guilty about breaking my promise to Brookes and guilty at the implications of what I'm doing and saying to all of you here today." He paused. "But I can assure you my actual thinking on this is clear." His eye returned to Dial, "In fact, I would struggle to recall a moment in my life when I was more certain of what I should do." He then locked his gaze into Carls. "We carry out these missions, altering simulated realities in the hope of reversing the Stasis None's grim, predicted future outcome. We've had our doubts, developed our own beliefs. I've listened to you all talk of what's real and what's not. Heard you question science, God, the universe. And all the while I've been the one silencing you. Desperate for you to do your jobs, keep each other safe. I've seen you risk your lives on countless occasions, watched you grow capable of unbelievable things. We lost one of our own along the way, welcomed in someone new."

Deans stared at the Commander.

"Throughout this journey we've taken care of each other. Whether killing Stalin or saving Ghandi. There has always been that one constant, *us* . . . Watching each other's backs no matter what the objectives." His gaze once again returned to Dial, "Like I said, I understand any reservations you may have. But trust me when I tell you this, not just as leader of this team, but as a friend. There's something about this Palene. Something more than just a freak of science . . . I can feel it." His gaze passed over each of them once more. "I've never been religious or fanciful as you know. This is simply my judgement. It's not me acting crazy because of some life and death experience. It's not me being manipulated or used. I believe this Palene may actually *be* our ultimate goal . . . The find which could finally reverse the predicted end of humanity. Something more than what Brooke's theories may well point toward." He added, "Just as I'm certain something sinister will come about if we're ordered to grab this guy and bring him to our time, not that I think we could even if we wanted to." He paused. "I'm not sure how Brookes is going to react if he doesn't get what he wants from this meeting. Shit, I chased this guy off the edge of a mountain because I didn't get what I wanted. But if Brookes asks me to carry out an order which would compromise my belief Palene should be dealt with on his terms and not our own, then I'd need a damn good reason to do it. And if such a situation were to arise, it will put me at risk of being on a collision course with any one of you. And if I've learned anything these past days one thing rings true, you all mean too much for me to allow such a situation to occur. But it's a situation I have to consider . . . Because on this occasion, I'm afraid orders alone may not be enough to see me realise my duty."

CHAPTER SEVENTY FOUR

"So let me get this straight. You authorised the Reeper to jump back into the very theatre in which Commander Dorey was recently killed. Sending a multi-trillion dollar force blindly into what could have easily been a trap. And you did this without thinking to consult the people who write your cheques?" Finch's venom was genuine, but it was eased by the realisation Brooke's may have finally hung himself out to dry, "A decision made after watching a superior technology reopen a time tunnel which can supposedly never be reopened, inviting you in like some God-damn Venus flytrap?"

Brookes sighed, "I made a tough call. One which resulted in Commander Dorey being saved, together with the rescue of incredible information which would otherwise be lost."

"A tough call?" Finch almost spat into the camera which sent his digitised image into the secure conference centre outside Washington, "You didn't even make a call!" He panned around the other guests who'd all managed to attend the meeting in person. "Did you receive a call?" He demanded of Will Grossen who remained silent despite the prompt. "What about you?" The projected face turned to Senator Raffy Abel.

He shook his head as he leaned back into the chair.

"Doctor Beben?"

Francois made an attempt to aid Brookes, "No I did not receive a call, however . . . "

He was interrupted as the image of Finch quickly turned to Samantha, "Miss Redemca?"

She didn't even look up from her file as she pondered the impact of Brooke's bombshell.

"You see . . . It would appear not one of us got this *tough call* of yours Doctor."

Brookes wondered if he would ever get through one of these meetings without having to argue with this obnoxious pit-bull.

Samantha seized the pause. "I understand the reasoning behind your actions Doctor. But what my governments want to know is why did you not contact any of them first?"

"As I said in my report, I wasn't sure of the time I had available. You all made it clear I was to draw up a plan in which to capture this mysterious man. Just as it has always been clear it is I who remains in charge of this operation when it comes to such decisive matters. I saw a window of opportunity to save the life of my most valued soldier while simultaneously making an attempt to recapture the man Dorey had detained just prior to his death. I sent the Reeper and her team back to the point before the ship malfunctioned during our original mission . . . I hoped this would ensure success on both counts."

Samantha stared at him, "The time you had available? That's a vague statement." She stopped herself from going further, much to the relief of Will Grossen.

Brookes exhaled, "It's not my intention to deliberately sabotage our working relationship. And of course I knew you would be furious at my actions. However they were taken with the best of intention. Once I'd chosen the path there was no time to contact you. I was busy as head of operations. But as soon as I knew the ship was headed back safely I left my post and contacted all of you immediately."

Finch growled. "At which point the most expensive, sophisticated aircraft ever built along with its invaluable crew and training could have all been lost together with Commander Dorey, or worse, being placed under duress so this bastard may learn everything about us."

He was set to continue his assault when Raffy Abel held up a hand, "If I may Mr. Finch."

The director struggled . . . but fell silent.

"Doctor Brookes. You refer to the incident when the Reeper and her crew were nearly lost in Masada as a malfunction, almost certainly brought about by a fluctuation in the opening time tunnel a few miles behind the ship, above the Dead Sea."

"Yes."

"But tell me, where is the hard evidence to back up this theory?"

"I put it all in my report. The system shut down pointed to an energy source that rippled through the tunnel only moments prior, an anomaly since detected by our mainframe."

"Yes . . . I read it. But there are one or two things which puzzle me. Firstly, it was not conclusive. Such a thing has never happened before, and surely the ship is sufficiently armoured to cope with such an event." He looked at notes taken from the report, "Otherwise it would never get through time and space in the first place."

"Senator, I did explain the Reeper was in her hover position. And as such it is possible, that during the metal morphing process which shape the downward thrust engines, her belly can be exposed to a weakened state for but a second."

"Yes I understand. But is it really likely this was the reason? I mean, the ship has been in this hover position before whilst within close proximity to such energy forces has it not?"

"Yes . . . But the energy force that rippled through the tunnel was different to any other we've encountered, which itself is by no means unusual. It contained large quantities of intermittent magnetic energy which fluctuated then pulsed with high decibel noise. Its make up was such that if it hit the Reeper at the right place at the right time, it would be possible to cause a temporary seizure of her electrical brain."

The statement did carry truth but he'd doctored the figures with the help of the Stasis None so as to ensure such a freak event would not see the project grounded.

Raffy looked up from his digitised report. "Quite a coincidence though isn't it? The ship being hit in a weakened state, minutes after Dorey radioed his pilot that he'd apprehended the prisoner. Next the ship is nearly down and we've lost one of our best men."

Brookes stood by his report. Raffy was fishing, and he knew it, "I understand your concern Senator, but let me assure you I investigated the matter thoroughly with the use of the Stasis None."

"And came up with a guess," Raffy took a slow sip of his water.

Finch was clearly enjoying the show.

The Senator continued, "So, based upon a guess . . . One which ignores the possibility this man may possess the power to bring down our ship, just as he has the power to reopen sealed time . . . You decided to send the Reeper and her crew back to this location, back to this danger, and didn't even think it necessary to at least speak to us first?"

Finch almost whooped with joy at the grilling.

"I made a judgement call to save our best operative's life and I stick by it. All signs indicated this man we sought was attempting to make contact. I dismissed the notion he was responsible for nearly bringing down the Reeper because anyone with the power he displayed when reopening that tunnel could have swiped it permanently from the sky previously if he so wished. Everything points to the fact he has the ability to move freely through time. Therefore, it encouraged me to ascertain this was a gesture. As I said, this was backed by the Stasis None with a ninety percent probability. Reopening the timeline could have indeed been a trap . . . But an illogical one. If this man wanted the Reeper or its crew, with the power at his disposal he could have taken them easily during their prior encounter. If he can reopen time, he can reseal it. If he can reseal it, he would not need to have the Reeper crash in order to see them trapped."

Raffy stared, his eyes projecting an unreadable veil, "I see," he said softly.

All present were surprised. No second wave of questioning. No kill.

Finch was disgusted at this apparent let off and wasted no time in picking up the mantle. "So you admit, based on a string of guesses and assumptions you sent back the Reeper and her crew, and with such an act, blatantly risked setting this project back by years. And all because you alone felt it was the correct course of action to take?"

Brookes stared at the life-like image with contempt. "That's why we are here is it not?" There was no diplomacy left for his nemesis. It was time to deliver a curt reminder. "But let us not forget, it was I who built this super-computer that in years to come may be called on to save this planet and our race. And believe me when I tell you I did it while relying upon my educated guesswork on more than one occasion. It was I who discovered a method for altering and travelling through time, I who created a process for manipulating and recreating existence." His disdain was growing into a crescendo the likes of which was never displayed by Brookes, "So please, let us not be hasty when it comes to evaluating the value of *my guesswork and intuition*." He added, "Not to mention what a ninety percent probability means when delivered from the Stasis None itself."

Finch was bubbling but nobody came to his aid. Before he could hit back Brookes was continuing in full vocal flight, "And as for setting the progress of this project back by years . . . Your organisation's computers are mere calculators in comparison to the machine I devised, a machine which has already delivered results on a hundred technologies that have seen all present here today benefit hugely." He stared at each of them, "All courtesy of an intelligence I alone understand." His venom returned to Finch, "So please, spare me your weak insults and accusation. When I sent them back to relocate Commander Dorey, to apprehend this man, I did it knowing full well I would have to answer to all of you. But the data in my report clearly justifies why I felt the risks were minimal. Of course I understand the powers you represent both would, and *should* be deeply concerned by such an action." His tone was softening, "But I did it for the reasons stated in my report, for reasons I've stated here today. I believed then this was a gesture of friendship. Since Dorey's rescue and return I believe this theory confirmed." He looked at them determined, "As for the threat he poses, he can have no desire for our technology as he does not need it. He merely believes himself to be something he is not."

Will Grossen was concerned, "That he is the freak result of an experiment? A man tormented by the fact he's been divided across time." Grossen glanced at his notes, "That this other half he seeks as a missing part of his soul, may actually be nothing more than the residual memory of the comatose man you lost, all those years ago? A man who believes himself to be chosen for a special purpose, when in fact, he may be nothing more than a by-product of our very own Stasis None?"

Brookes nodded. "As I've stated, this could be one of two things. The first is the more ridiculous notion this man has indeed been wandering the Earth immortal, until one day, by an incredible twist of fate he stumbled across Dorey and the others, leading him to believe he'd found his destiny. Inspiring him to begin meditation techniques which allow him to seek them out through space and time before he eventually develops the ability to travel across such spectrums in the physical sense, as we do." He gave a deliberately scornful expression. "Or the second option, that what we have here is an advanced simulation of sorts. A version of the man I dragged back through time. A man whose body was later de-atomised when I attempted to use him in another experiment. Only unbeknown to us he was not destroyed. Somehow the Stasis

None held his de-atomised DNA, used it to help us achieve our own objectives." He clarified, "Back then I'd been trying desperately to use the saved data of this two thousand year old man to try and prompt the Stasis None into showing me how it had re-atomised a human being from our real past without causing a paradox. It was during these diverse experiments I stumbled across the possibility of creating simulated realities. Reality the computer came to understand by utilising this man's ancient make up, using his stored DNA as a focal point across space and time . . . A freak of fortune, a misinterpretation which eventually led us to where we are today." Brookes explained, "I believe this man to be an actual being of sorts, created by the Stasis None. Just like the simulated realities which contain copies of us all. Only in those realities we behave and act as we do in this life once those dormant states have been activated. We are the perfect non-reversed mirror of ourselves. We have never known how the computer achieved this incalculable feat . . . But it did. And I've always suspected it used this man in some way to achieve it. However, what I hadn't known until now . . . Is this man is like a ghost within the Stasis mainframe, a ghost who believes itself real. Just as the worlds we have simulated do." A dark smile formed, "But it would appear this Palene comes with an added kick. He is in some way linked to the Stasis None. He believes himself immortal because the computer knew the original DNA was indestructible. He believes he found Dorey and the others by accident, when in fact he was aware all along of the Commander's travels throughout the system as he is a part of that system. This notion of meditating in order to seek out the Commander is nothing but the simulation of Palene beginning to understand more about the actual Stasis None and therefore his own origin. This is why he gives descriptions of how his powers grew inexplicably, randomly. He has obviously misinterpreted this information. As a simulation who believes itself real, following this destiny desperate as we all are, to find a true meaning for its own life." He turned to them one at a time with growing confidence. "This complex simulation has grown for over two thousand years within its virtual mind, experiencing itself over multiple dimensions in tandem with the workings of our own Stasis None. And so we end up with a being who believes itself real in every way. A person who thinks he's found all answers over two thousand years of life, when in fact he has only been experiencing a multi-dimensional dream . . . A ghost of a once true person, now part-created by our very own computer." He concluded, "But a simulation which has nonetheless developed a mind powerful enough to build a machine capable of placing him when and wherever he wishes to be . . . A person who in many ways can think as our computer reasons, on a level we've never got close to understanding. Imagine what we could do with such a person. Imagine what we could do with the technology he's created, with his understanding of our very own Stasis None."

"Doctor Brookes forgive me, but I thought you said this Palene is a simulation, a ghost." Samantha Redemca looked baffled, "How can he benefit us if he isn't real?"

"The fact he is a simulation of sorts is irrelevant. In his experience he has constructed these devices, achieved these results. Although he may not be real in our own sense of understanding, his knowledge and invention will be as true as any devised by you or I."

"Hold on just a second," Will Grossen held up the thin tablet generating the dossier, "This report doesn't mention any details or theories such as these."

"That's because it's a work-in-progress."

"You mean you're still working on this as a workable theory?"

Brookes nodded. "As a matter of fact Mr. Grossen, this hypothesis only truly came to me on my flight across the Atlantic this morning."

Will narrowed his expression, "That must have been quite a flight."

Brookes stared back at him wearing a cold smile.

"But forgive my ignorance," Grossen continued, understanding more than he was prepared to let on, "I thought you said right from the start this energy source, the trace from which you found this Palene, it stemmed from the past . . . Our *real* past."

He nodded.

"Then how the hell can you explain a simulation managing that?"

"It's incredible what this being could be capable of with the Stasis None as its ally."

Finch scowled, "The same Stasis None which offers up ninety percent probabilities to back up theories you specifically *want* to believe. Perhaps it is time to finally bring this project of yours to heel, before we all suffer the irreparable consequences."

Brookes did not look at him. Instead he played the ace. "Or perhaps it is time to meet this Palene as he has requested. For imagine what a powerful ally he would be to all of us, once we've unlocked his secrets."

*

Brooke's military flight had got him back at the Stasis None compound at speed, but he was suffering the effects of the round trip. He'd left the morning meeting with exactly what he'd wanted. The green light to have Dorey and the others escort him across time to his meeting with Palene. He was exhausted but pleased.

In many ways he'd told them the truth about his theory on Palene, while remaining most prudent not to mention significant pieces of information, such as the hidden comatose version which was as much, if not more, a part of the computer as this simulation, this being who was able to transcend time, reality and space.

In the short term he'd gained all he could have hoped for. He'd been exonerated by the board and kept control of his treasured Stasis None. Granted permission to hold his rendezvous in time, believing this incredible man may finally fill in the blanks which haunted his life's work.

Finch, Redemca, Grossen and the others had spoken to the powers behind the powers and after three hours of deliberation accepted he must indeed partake on this risky venture.

A heavy penalty awaited him however. Failure to bring Palene over to their side would risk the immediate confiscation of the Stasis None Project. The very idea of a being such as this wondering around, with the ability to enter real time and space as easily as those simulated, terrified all involved. There may be no limits to what he could be capable of if Brooke's theories were anywhere near correct.

He'd been ordered to use this being's apparent fondness for Commander Dorey as his window of opportunity. '*Make a friend . . . not an enemy.*' Raffy Abel had warned.

Brookes yawned as he now sat in his office, the familiar New York skyline screwing his senses further, its display still in the throes of a bright morning. He requested a night sky and mused over how frightened his bosses were.

He pulled some bourbon from the shelf behind him.

He'd managed to gain an unlikely advantage.

He now had to figure out how to best play Dorey.

CHAPTER SEVENTY FIVE

"You're certain you don't want a cup?" Finch asked Sam Redemca as his secretary brought in some Earl Grey tea.

"No really, I'm fine thank you."

He gave a passive look then took a sip of the hot drink.

Redemca realised Finch would have full knowledge of her more recent manoeuvrings against him, as he had during previous encounters over the years. Their differing political loyalties and outlook meant they were engaged in a permanent game of chess, constantly locking horns as they tried to achieve their own personal and municipal goals.

"So Mr Finch, what is it you wish to discuss?"

"Oh come now Samantha, I'm sure that's fairly obvious."

"Well if it's about events this morning, we are both due at the White House in less than two hours. I assumed any discussion would take place then."

Finch fired his broadside. "Yes, as did I . . . But unfortunately the meeting with the President has been postponed until eight. Aren't you scheduled to meet with the French president early tomorrow? Your flight leaves at six I believe."

"I've not received any such message."

"Really? I took his call after the conference ended today." He tapped the transmitter used to send his image into the meeting with Brookes. The effect was successful, as not for the first time Samantha found herself wondering why Finch had not attended such a meeting in person, when it turned out he'd been only a few miles away.

"And may I ask where the President is now?"

"Aboard Air force One . . . en-route to Washington as we speak."

This meant she had no access to him unless she went through Finch first.

He enjoyed such moments. Redemca was a legislator, and despite her powerful position he felt she was no real threat, especially when swimming the dirtier waters of politics.

She eyed him with suspicion. *'What double dealing was this dinosaur up to now?'*

"It really was unavoidable. He asked me to meet with you before you left for discussions with DeCoure. He wanted to be sure we were together on this course of action." His tone and choice of words were deliberately disrespectful.

"Be careful Mr. Finch." She warned coldly. "You may have the President's ear on this but I don't need to tell you I won't be bullied or manipulated."

He flashed a look of innocence. "Samantha, nobody is trying to bully or manipulate anyone. The President wanted to be sure there is genuine coalition. Due to his delay he was concerned he wouldn't get a chance to hear what conclusions you'd be personally presenting our European friends."

"The conclusions I'll be presenting will be the same as those I intend to put before him." She said curtly. "If his arrival is delayed then I'll inform the French of the adjustments. I do not back out of meetings simply because they make for complicated schedules."

He knew of course it would be a simple reshuffle for her to make, but he'd wanted to remind her it was his council the President sought first in such matters. He placed down the cup. "Miss Redemca I meant no offence, I was merely acting on the orders of my Commander and Chief." He protested, "If you can find the time to adjust your schedule then that is of course excellent news. It would save the President and I . . . "

"Mr. Finch, my superiors have given their position on what action Brookes is to take. Now, you may be happy playing your games of favour with our own President, but let me remind you the same tactics do not apply when it comes to those I represent."

His eyes narrowed. "Principle Redemca, I often wonder where your loyalties lie."

"My loyalties lie with the Alliance. I'm an American, and proud to be one . . . But I'm not a member of your old boys club who think this planet is theirs to milk. The world has changed. This project is potentially the most important event to embroil mankind, and all you can think about is who gets to own it. When will you people learn ownership isn't about one flag anymore? You're the head of WAIG intelligence for Christ's sake, not just the CIA . . . I would have thought you would want unity on this more than anyone. If you keep pushing this, it will blow up in all our faces. The last thing any of our member countries want is for the European Presidency to get wind of this." His blank smile irritated her. "Brookes is clearly the only man for the job. You should be grateful he's not Arab, Persian or Chinese. You're allowing a personal vendetta to cloud your judgement."

His eyes shadowed to stone. "Placing trust in others doesn't always give you strength."

"Sometimes trust is all we have." She countered. "For centuries we've used technology to destroy ourselves. I believe this project could and should be different, but never while in the hands of people such as you. Your petty paranoia's would turn it into the only thing you can understand . . . A weapon."

"And if you believe the intention of any country would differ from that then you are even more naïve than I thought."

It was strange that after all these years it would be this day when they'd choose to finally be honest with one another. "It's not about being naïve. I'm well aware of the dangers. But a different approach is needed. The fear and distrust you people push is about control . . . And little else. Didn't we learn any of the mistakes made with the whole Star Wars or Exodus fiasco?" No response came. "Now you may think you have the right backing, and who knows maybe you do . . . But let me assure you of one thing, I will fight to keep this project out of your sole authority. As will many others. It's critical we keep this as a joint operation with all involved, and considering your so-called position it's quite tragic you do not share in this belief."

She picked up her bag. "Now if this time-wasting is finished, I have matters requiring urgent attention." She stood and headed for the door.

"Miss Redemca."

She turned back to him.

"Believe it or not I do admire you. And do not question you've the best intention in all you do." His tone hardened. "But remember . . . Once lines are drawn in the sand, it can prove difficult to predict if you have chosen the right side on which to stand."

She stared back at him. "Mr Finch. That is exactly the problem with people such as you . . . A stick is never something to build with, it's for drawing lines in the sand."

She turned and headed for the door.

*

The flora of indestructible atoms began to reform in a dance of spectacular light, as unaffected by the gentle breeze as they'd been by the winds of time. Slowly the riot of colour began to take shape, and out of the display came the gradual form of a man.

As existence returned into being, Palene opened his renewed lungs and breathed in the unpolluted air with the thrill of a new born child.

His eyes focused as the light show all around him began to fade.

Lush strokes of English green swept the familiar landscape in all directions, his sight eventually falling on Stonehenge. The grey stone circle seemed smaller and less significant from a distance, but it would grow in stature as it was approached on foot.

He enjoyed seeing it within its calm pre-industrialised setting, without the scars of heavy farming or the motorway flashing its traffic across the landscape.

He'd plenty of time to prepare. Dorey would not be here in his magnificent ship for almost two days. He sighed, excited at what was to come.

Sam Redemca's heels made a pleasant sound on the polished floors as she headed for the rear exit of the White House. As she approached the double doors one of the White House staff emerged with her coat. The man was elegant with a delightful accent, "Your coat Principal Redemca."

She allowed him to slide the well tailored Gyanti over her shoulders. She loved the Italian designer's lean upon the classic 1930's styling.

"Thank you." She said graciously as the man slipped back to his duties.

She walked out into the warm evening and headed down the steps to the limousine waiting to whisk her to the airport.

The President had been a little early. It was now almost eight-fifteen and her high altitude passenger jet would not touch down in the French capital for another four hours. Her meeting with President DeCoure was scheduled for nine o'clock Paris time. She had only a forty minute window before he'd be engaged in civil duties, affairs of state and photo-shoots. She was cutting it fine and hoped to grab some sleep on the plane. After Paris it was on to Geneva where she would meet with the German Chancellor who was attending a trade conference.

As the car whisked her away she ran the meeting with the President and Finch over in her mind. She had been reassured there was no intention of moving in on Brookes until he'd been given the chance to apprehend this mysterious Palene, and promised none of the other nations involved with the project would ever be excluded from such decision making. '*For God's sake,*' the President had said in his Carolina brogue, '*The British would never allow such a thing on their home soil.*'

She'd raised an eyebrow at that statement but allowed herself to feel a little easier than after her meeting with Finch. Nevertheless, it was obvious plans would be in motion.

She just hoped she could keep all involved at an amicable table.

The separating glass between herself and her driver slowly faded from dark to pale. "Principle Redemca," The driver transmitted through the rear speaker. "You have a Will Grossen on the secure line." As he brought the car to a halt at a junction he turned to her and said, "He say's its urgent."

*

Finch had been blasted across town by his driver and was already sat within one of his operations rooms staring at the monitors before Samantha Redemca's vehicle reached the tarmac. She avoided the airport security and check-ins due to diplomatic credentials, but before she could step onto the privately chartered *Fast Flight* she still had to have herself and her belongings monitored at the V.I.P. pre-flight booth. It was standard procedure and only took moments as this was situated in a mobile unit placed next to the plane.

He smiled as the hidden cameras showed Miss Redemca stepping out of the car and walking toward the booth, her following agents pulling up around the plane to take their positions.

As she stepped inside her driver quickly unloaded her bags onto the luggage escalator.

Finch watched as she headed toward the scanner, her coat as always hung over her shoulders in the usual manner. There was no sound only video footage.

He waited with baited breath as the high resolution picture showed her bags run through the scanners on one screen as she herself passed through the security system on the other.

It was a simple enough frame-up, and one he had overseen on a number of occasions, targeted on people of all walks of life during his time as head of the CIA. Traces of explosives here, a gun or knife there . . . But for people in sensitive government positions it was always a little more discreet. Such as the blueprints of the Stasis None Project, complete with updated access codes to key areas within the complex, recorded onto a nano-chip and injected into one of the buttons on her expensive coat. Most of the information was knowledge already shared by the leaders involved, but there was just that little extra added. Sensitive information, the likes of which should never be carried across oceans in chartered jets headed for meetings with individual heads of state.

Just enough to ensure Principle Redemca's flight along with her blossoming career could be placed on a long to permanent hold.

He watched and marvelled at how easily these people could be snared. They came armed with their honours and Ph.D.'s, with their Utopian minds, powerful ideals, friends and families. They passed through Washington and the world believing themselves a match for anyone, and yet a simple plant was nearly always sufficient to bring about their ruin.

Accusations would follow of course, fingers would be pointed. But Finch would be watertight. And the people he destroyed just might find salvation eventually, but only if they would agree to owe him.

As Sam stepped through the detection system he wondered why people like her often strayed from the basics. She could have detected the planted chip herself with a portable device purchased in many sophisticated electrical stores, or could have made better use of her guards who stared out in all directions as she was scanned.

He sighed as he watched her pass through, waiting for the security on hand to begin ordering her secret service agents to let them take her away.

He hoped things wouldn't turn too ugly.

His monitor showed her passing through the chamber . . . Nothing.

It relayed to him the image of a guard passing back her passport and purse . . . Nothing.

Smiles and pleasantries were exchanged . . . But still nothing.

He felt the anger build and the sharp disappointment tweak his ulcer. He watched helplessly as Principal Redemca passed through the mobile security and headed for her plane as her protection team were quickly checked.

After a short time two of her guards entered the aircraft carrying monitoring equipment. It took only minutes before they came back and signalled the all-clear.

Miss Redemca headed for the steps and began the short climb.

As she did, Finch wasn't sure whether or not she'd given a quick glance over her shoulder, directly toward the lens of one of his hidden cameras.

Was it just chance, or had she just stared right at him?

His throat went dry, his fist clenched as he leaned on the desk housing the monitors.

The hatch to the plane was sealed and the pictures turned away from the scene as the mobile security unit was moved away from the tarmac.

His eyes glazed like a shark. "Grossen," he said through grinding teeth.

*

Isabella Usorio was not happy to hear the sound of her intercom bleeping. She remained under the covers and activated the link. "Who is it?"

The image of Will Grossen appeared on a section of her wall. "It's me Will."

She could not make out exactly where he was but he seemed more awake than she did. "Where are you?"

"Washington . . . Did I wake you?"

"You know for a guy in your line of work you can be a little slow on the up-take. Of course you woke me it's past one in the morning."

"I'm surprised you didn't stay at the complex for the night."

"Yeah well I had things to do. Besides, you know I like to get out of that place whenever I can. Its like living in an air-conditioned tomb." Her voice betrayed her serious lack of interest. "What do you want?"

"I need you to try and find something for me."

"Oh really? Lucky me."

"I need you to go through the Stasis files and run a check to see if a level six-clearance has been requested from inside the complex over the past thirty-six hours."

"A level six? I didn't know there was anyone other than Brookes with a level six."

"Within the Stasis complex there isn't, but that level was accessed from somewhere inside the project perimeter. There hasn't been a visitor with access at such a level for over a week . . . So someone in there managed it."

She looked confused. "Managed what exactly?"

"Accessed detailed blueprints of the Stasis Caves together with updated access codes for the next eighteen hours . . . Then smuggled the information out on a chip."

"That's impossible."

"Check the system, use the number four program combined with the number seven I supplied you with. If you see anything that points to a level six access, I want to know what floor, what room and what computer terminal it was requested from."

She looked worried. "Will, surely anybody with the tenacity to try something like that would have covered their tracks."

"That may be . . . But those programs I provided contain hunters with a certain flair for finding such things. If someone has hacked into the Project computers, I want to know who." He checked his watch. "Is the Reeper still on cue for launch?"

She nodded. "Yes, tomorrow evening."

"Okay Isabella, put the phone down now, the line can only be secured for a little while longer." He deactivated his scrambling device along with his com-link, and in a second his image was gone.

CHAPTER SEVENTY SIX

Dorey and his team had been in the ammunition store for some time. There was still no word of any transmission from Palene, a fact which only served to increase the anxiety.

The day had dragged so far, as did most jump days, but this was different of course.

The *unknown* factor was significantly larger and therefore more of a focus than usual, and nobody could confidently predict an outcome of when or where they would be at the close of the day. And so the morning passed like three, and it was difficult to comprehend they were still some hours from the jump.

Charlie pointed at a crate of weapons he'd just checked over. "Those are ready to go."

"Thanks Charlie."

He sat down next to the Commander. "I've laid the ammo boxes at the end there." He pointed to the various cases, "The mark four suits you asked for will be shipped down to the Reeper, the new goggles included." Charlie watched as Dorey eased the springs on the assault rifle he was handling. "Now do you want helmets or not?"

"Charlie, I'm hoping we won't need a peashooter for this trip, never mind all this."

The old soldier smiled back at him, "Better to have an arsenal and not need it . . . " They finished the sentence together, "Than need it, and have nothing at all."

The old man watched as the team began packing the weaponry, before looking back to Dorey. "It certainly is good to see you," Charlie said as he rose to his feet, "You bring them all back safe." He slapped Dorey on the back as he went to say his goodbyes to the rest of the group, "Safe flight."

He thanked him as he walked away then stood, happy with the rifle in hand. He headed over to the others and was about to add his weapon to the collection when he noticed a rather excited Cassaveres headed their way.

"We've got the signal." He said as he approached.

Dorey and the others stopped, the nerves and adrenaline immediately kicking like a mule.

"Where?" Dorey enquired.

Cassaveres pointed both forefingers down at his feet, "Right here."

"Here?"

He nodded, "Stonehenge . . . 100AD."

The group took a moment to let the news sink in.

"Stonehenge . . . not Masada?" Marco stated.

Dorey looked at them. "He's chosen the place where it all began."

Dial stared at him, "But why 100AD?"

"Why not?" It was a fair point, "And the jump-time?"

Exactly when he said that it would be . . . In just under three hours."

*

"So the set-up failed?" Raffy Abel seemed neither surprised nor perturbed by the news.

"She had help." Finch stated.

"From Grossen?"

"Who else?"

"Which leaves us where with regards to our insider?"

Finch sneered, "Grossen is adept enough at the game to have intercepted such a move of his own volition, especially as it is now certain he's watching Redemca's back. Though naturally we have to consider our insider may have been compromised."

The sun was shining over the Senator's Pennsylvanian mansion, the large white parasol providing ample shade over the sturdy matching seats. They leaned into them, Raffy almost regally, Finch like he was already contemplating his exit.

"You may have just stirred up a hornets nest."

"The trail linking that chip to the two of *us* runs very cold, I can assure you." Finch was very clear in reminding his host, "You wanted this just as much as I did Senator."

"My dear Robert I wanted her discredited, not running off God knows where telling tales of conspiracy."

Finch shook his head, "Coming forward with such information could just easily see Grossen and Redemca incriminated. Our insider too if need be."

"Then we may still gain an advantage." Raffy's sunglasses shielded any direct eye contact. "If we were to sow the right seeds of doubt and suspicion I'm sure the President may yet give us the go ahead to act. Granted, he isn't going to stand toe to toe with his partners on this. Not without the kind of betrayal provided by the capture of Miss Redemca as she made an attempt to sneak out that chip. But if it were brought to Brooke's attention a leak had been discovered, the access codes to the Project security would be changed earlier than scheduled." He pondered, "And if Brookes could be encouraged to change the codes *without* following the correct protocol . . . It could be made to look very incriminating for our good Doctor."

"But how could we ensure he would not follow procedure?"

"Brookes is showing he has a flair for taking risks when it comes to this Palene. He knows damn well he only just managed to get this little journey through time approved. I doubt he'd risk its postponement if he were informed of this breech only a short time before the Reeper was due to launch." The black lenses would have given nothing away but the smile on the Senator's lips showed his cunning. "I'd wager Brookes would hastily reconfigure his security, take his trip hoping to return with this Palene, washing the security issue under the carpet until his homecoming."

Finch smiled. "And in doing so incriminate himself." It was a calculated risk, but Raffy was right, Brooke's recent behaviour meant the odds were indeed stacked in their favour.

"At the appropriate time have our mole inform Brookes of how the latest security codes have been compromised."

"And how did our mole become privy to such information?"

"Our insider has been sleeping with Grossen, who has uncharacteristically shared this information over some inebriated pillow talk. Although sworn to secrecy, in her loyalty to the project Isabella simply could not remain silent."

Finch nodded seeing how easily this could be achieved, incriminating all in the process. Brookes may well have noticed Will Grossen's affection for her. "But we'd better cut down any room for error. Let's ensure Brookes receives this information just as he's going into pre-flight with Dorey."

Raffy agreed. "If Brookes then changes the codes we can make it appear he's attempting to shut everyone out to take sole control, so he may have this power offered by Palene for himself. We'll then access the new codes, pick the lock and await the order to take control of the complex in the interests of WA security."

"But without Brookes the Stasis None is practically useless."

"A temporary upset to the running of the project will be more than justifiable if we obtain this Palene. It would appear both his ability and technology outstrips that of the Doctor's understanding. I want such knowledge in our hands, not in the hands of Brookes. He's held the aces for far too long."

The notion excited Finch, "We don't know what this Palene may be capable of. He may well side with Brookes if he indeed returns with him in the first place."

"I believe this to be a risk worth taking, all things considered."

Finch smiled. If this Palene possessed a greater understanding of the Stasis None, he could well provide a real and usable alternative to the Brookes dictatorship.

"We will not discredit Brookes completely. After all, he still has us by the balls. We'll merely show concern for the security of the project. From this fear we'll see the complex placed under our control, certainly until any investigation can be completed. Brookes himself could have no real objections all things considered. We can use this window of opportunity to search the unknown areas of the Stasis Caves which have recently come to our attention." He added, "If Brookes delivers this Palene we have immediate access to him. If he does not then his position will be weakened while we'll have gained enough support to hold the complex indefinitely." He took another sip of his drink, the sunshine suiting his expensive skin.

"And the other WA partners?"

"They'll fall in line once a risk to the project's security is pinpointed. All we need do is keep them in the loop and allow them the same degree of control they enjoy today."

"It's one hell of a risk, especially if this Palene does not fall into our hands. In the aftermath Brookes may shut up shop as he's done before."

"There was no justifiable cause for such extreme action previously. This time it's different. It is Brookes who will have to justify his actions, not us. And if we obtain Palene, or find any hidden secrets within the doctor's lair we will have achieved far more than we could have hoped for by sitting around and waiting."

Finch was delighted. "And what about Sam Redemca and Will Grossen?"

He smiled coldly, "Give them enough rope . . . Let them hang themselves."

CHAPTER SEVENTY SEVEN

The Reeper had got underway safely and all readings offered by the Stasis None were encouraging to say the least. If Brookes was at all nervous before pre-flight he hadn't shown it. Even when hooked into the Reeper the same calm readings were sent back to Kelvin who monitored the crew's wellbeing from his perch inside the RFC.

The river was dragged into the time vortex engines without incident, the ship dropped in and launched with ease. Now the nervous wait would begin.

Stein had handed control to Jose only moments after the Reeper disappeared from their screens, informing him of an important matter requiring his attention. He'd left in a hurry and many suspected he was less than happy at Brooke's decision to meet with this strange entity Palene.

The tunnel earmarked for the Reeper return was only eighteen hours away, although in light of recent events, the population of the RFC couldn't be absolutely certain it was to be the Stasis None returning Brookes and the others at all.

From her station Isabella Usorio listened as Cassaveres reeled out instructions. Usorio noticed Larry hovering around his terminal. She held her stomach and called him over, "Hey Larry, I don't feel too great. Can you hold the fort for a while?"

"For you Bella...anything."

She turned her intercom channel to Jose. "Doctor Cassaveres, I need to visit the ladies room, I'm feeling a little peaky. Larry's going to cover."

He looked up the gradient of the busy RFC. "Of course, we won't need you for a while."

She thanked both Jose and Larry before making her exit.

Once in the corridor the concerned hold of her stomach disappeared as she headed toward elevator five at speed. Within minutes she was down in the basement computer levels. The camera's which followed her progress wouldn't be too curious as many scientists headed to this location. If anyone noticed her trip she'd already placed an alibi inside her chosen destination, her handbag, complete with pills to combat a stomach upset.

She headed into the next corridor and made a beeline for the entry ahead, her optical scan and thumb print granting immediate access.

The room was full of mainframe towers. Fans cooled the area and the air felt refreshing. She readied the scrambling device taken from her pocket, capable of having the watching cameras lock for up to a minute. Isabella moved quietly despite the noisy hum, and turned through a tower of circuits before stopping dead in her tracks. She held her breath and crouched slowly, peering through a thin gap in the stacked computer structures.

Her eyes narrowed, *'Well Doctor Stein . . . What brings you down here?'*

*

The Reeper's downward jets brought the ship to a gentle rest four hundred metres from Stonehenge. The swirling dust settled, reclaimed by the plush grass of the meadow. The flight through time had been a smooth affair and Brookes and the others now had only one thing on their minds . . Palene.

Dorey took charge, instructing them toward the armoury of the ship. Here they changed quickly into their light armour. Weapons were passed amongst the group and combat goggles donned. Brookes watched silently as the team carried out final inspections.

Dorey remained convinced such armed precaution would prove unnecessary.

When ready, he radioed through to the cockpits. "We're heading for the exit."

Both pilots scanned the area once more before Jay activated the rear-loading ramp. Daylight began flooding through as the rear opened. Brookes was asked to remain at the summit as Dorey and the others exited the ship, journeying down the ramp.

"Still no signs of human life," Jim's voice said into their com-links, "Reeper guns are set to a five hundred metre defence perimeter."

Dorey signalled the all-clear to Brookes. "Jim keep checking the area . . . Jay, come down."

Brookes reached the meadow, immediately overwhelmed at being in another existence. It had been so long. He sucked the clean air through his nostrils, enjoying the lingering flavour of the grass. The grey sky threatened rain and the ground felt damp and heavy underfoot. He headed to Dorey who was now using the technologies of his combat goggles to full effect, scouring the area ahead of them.

"What do you think?"

"There's no sign on any of our scanners." Dorey returned his gaze to the stones. "Jim can you take another look at the henge?"

"Still nothing," his second pilot replied.

Jay joined the group. They separated into teams of two fanning the perimeter of the ship, their rifles at the ready.

Dorey could feel the anxiety growing in his boss. "We've only been here a few minutes there's no need to worry just yet."

They walked over to Dial and Jay. Mark lowered his rifle, "Maybe exiting the ship pointing guns in all directions has made him nervous."

"Perhaps we should shoulder the rifles, the Reeper has our backs." Jay suggested.

He agreed and the riflemen relaxed their posture.

Dorey looked back to the stones. "Jim, we're heading for the henge."

"Roger that."

"Unclip your pistols." Old habits died hard and Dorey wasn't taking chances as he led his team toward a possible sniper position, Reeper or no Reeper.

They fanned out, their rifles shouldered, their hands hovering over their pistol hilts.

The ancient stones grew larger and more seductive, the circle appearing as silent and empty as it had through the enhanced vision of their goggles. Nobody relaxed.

Perhaps naïvely, they'd expected Palene to be waiting for them waving as Dorey had during the unfolding drama in Masada. The fact he wasn't made them a little edgy.

Dorey sensed this. "Form a crescent. Benny take the right tip, Marco the left. Doctor Brookes drop behind me. Be ready to stop and go down on one knee if I give the signal. Jay, Carl, Dial, take centre point. I'll be directly behind you. Deans drop back, get into position and pull your rifle to provide covering fire."

Deans quickly took up an effective firing position as the rest began to fan into formation. Like the technology in his goggles the target scanners on his rifle showed no contacts.

The impressive stones were now introducing the full impact of their power, their sheer density and mystery commanding a greater respect as they lured the visitors toward them.

Suddenly, Jim came flooding into their senses. "I've got a contact! Forty metres from your current location, inside the henge directly ahead of you. I have no idea where it came from. I swear it wasn't there a minute ago."

Their guns were drawn as Dorey turned to Brookes, "Okay drop to one knee." Brookes lowered himself immediately as the team formed a crescent of aimed pistols and rifles. "Talk to me Jim." Dorey stared toward the circle of stones.

"Thirty-five metres, heading straight for you." The Reeper's guns were also trained.

"Stay down Doctor," Dorey said, his gaze locked toward the grey pillars as he moved his body between his boss and the stones.

"Twenty-five metres," Jim's voice came again, "It's a man. I repeat it's a man. No modern technology picked up within his vicinity."

Nothing was relayed by the advanced lenses of the goggles. Nothing came up on any of the groups targeting scanners. They all took a deep breath and hoped it was their host.

"Hold your positions. Nobody fire." Dorey ordered, as they trained their aims ahead.

"I still don't have anything." Benny shouted.

"Nor me." Carl added as he checked his rifle's screen.

"Eighteen metres…You should have visual contact." Jim instructed.

For a moment they thought Jim must be mistaken, when suddenly all could see. It was indeed a man, and he was heading straight toward them through a gap in the stones. The man raised his hands. "Don't shoot," he said calmly, "I am unarmed."

Dorey seconded the request, his expression visibly relieved. "Lower your weapons." He turned to Brookes who stood slowly, "This is the man we're here to see," Dorey announced, "This is Palene."

CHAPTER SEVENTY EIGHT

Brookes stared at the man open mouthed. Apart from the image trapped within the beam of his doomed experiment he'd only ever seen this person comatose and lifeless. Now here he was walking strong and tall. His height in particular seemed more imposing than when laid in the horizontal crypt linking him to the Stasis None, his face vibrant with purpose and colour, the red tinge of his eyes piercing.

He felt a rush of excitement shiver through him and for a moment felt he was in danger of being overwhelmed. The emotion caught him off guard, but he held his composure.

The others too stood in awe. This was the man who delivered their friend back from death, the man whose story amazed when Dorey recounted it inside the Reeper.

Palene wore the simple rustic garments of the period together with a hugely disarming smile, his appearance noticeably different to when posing as the Nazi, Captain Brahms.

His eyes passed each of theirs. As his gaze fell into Jay's she instinctively pulled down her goggles, relaxing the lightweight eyewear onto her collar.

She smiled, her eyes glistening.

He felt the aura and impact of her gratitude. Moving toward her he held out his hand, "Jay . . . How wonderful to meet you."

She placed her pistol into its housing and looked for the entire world as if she may be hypnotised. She held out her hand.

Dorey watched the moment unfold, unwilling to break the spell.

"Thank you." She said as she squeezed his hand.

He appeared genuinely touched by the gesture, the honesty of the moment acute.

"You don't have to thank me," he said magnanimously, "I wanted to help him."

His unassuming tone washed right through her. "Yes I do. Thank you for giving him back to me." She pulled her hand away and wiped her eyes. She felt no shame, no embarrassment, only relief . . . Relief at having the opportunity to express her gratitude to the person who'd saved Dorey and with him herself, so completely. She felt the pain of her recent loss as it combined with the memory of what had happened to Palene's own love and family, the story told by Dorey rushing through her senses. She stared, silently grateful for having been spared such misery. She felt certain he understood.

"You're most welcome." He said gently, as if hearing her thoughts as clearly as the surrounding breeze. Everyone felt the power of the moment.

Eventually Dorey stepped forward, formally introducing the rest of the group.

*

The final introduction to Brookes was a poignant one. They all knew it of course but didn't let on. None of them wanted the doctor to become aware of Dorey betraying his deepest secret to them.

With the introductions made Palene led them to the far side of the ancient stone circle.

They were surprised to find blankets and log pedestals on the ground ready for their arrival, the makeshift picnic seating surrounding a pit of hot coals warming a black pot.

They wondered how the Reeper failed to pick up the heat signature of the man's makeshift stove or indeed the readings of the man himself.

Dorey appointed Marco and Deans as sentries after encouraging Jim to stay vigilant aboard the Reeper. Palene had reassured them of their safety but he understood Dorey's desire to show he was not under his spell, that he was able to think unhindered when carrying out his duty. The rest, like Jay, had since relaxed their combat goggles.

The heavy grey sky showed signs of abating, the earlier promise of rain relegated to mere possibility. The camp added an air of old worldliness to the intrigue.

"Would you care for a drink?"

"What is it?" Jay enquired from her perch on one of the cut logs.

"It's called vald."

"Vald?"

"Yes."

"And what is in this vald?"

He reached behind his seat and pulled out a collection of carved wooden cups. He offered them around then removed the pot from its place on the coals. It must have been extremely hot, but they all noted how no cloth had been required. He poured the steaming drink into each of the cups, Jay first. "It's a blend of wild nettles, rose-hip and root ginger, sweetened with dried apple and a little honey."

Nobody questioned the risk, a ridiculous notion under normal circumstances. The fact Dorey believed in him was proving enough, and their implants were up to the task of providing blanket protection against poisons and potions.

444

She sipped cautiously but almost spat the liquid out immediately.

"Is it horrible?" Carl asked.

"No . . . It's hot." She tried again. "Actually that's not bad."

Carl took a sip. He too was under his spell. During their introduction Palene had squeezed his hand firmly, looking deep into the eyes which greeted him. What Carl felt certain he'd found there was unparalleled wisdom and understanding.

Dorey held little interest in how the drink tasted. He was too preoccupied with Brookes. Wondering when and how the doctor planned on bringing about his discussions with this living, breathing version of the man he held comatose within his machine.

He didn't have to wait long as Brookes showed the first signs of freeing himself from the spell. He held the cup aloft. "I like it," he said appreciatively, "The opposing flavours counteract perfectly." It was a very scientific review.

Palene in turn raised his cup. *'So this is the man I seek.'* To the others Brookes must have seemed old and wise but to Palene such thoughts did not occur. He'd often wondered how he would feel at this moment. He did not yet hold the same enthusiasm felt when he'd first met Dorey. He put this down to the sense of caution he was now experiencing. He'd realised some time ago the Commander was working for a higher authority and this in many ways allowed Dorey to be excused the microscope. But this man in front of him *was* the higher authority, and so therefore such exclusions could not apply. He watched him closely and awaited his first move. *'He is no doubt hoping to persuade me I can go back with him to their time. When I refuse, or if I give less than he's hoping to hear, I wonder if he will be bold enough to try and force the issue.'* He looked to Jay who still stared with grateful eyes, then again to Dorey who seemed to be sharing his own desire to hear the doctor speak. He passed his gaze around the rest of the group. To the two American males whose eyes remained sharp as hawks. To the German who had looked on him as a pupil would a favoured teacher. To the sentries who'd spent more time observing him than the fields beyond.

Dorey had no doubt told them everything, as Palene expected he would. But he sensed also the group somehow knew more than the doctor would have them know.

It made him curious. But most of all he sensed Dorey knew something more. A weighty knowledge he'd not possessed when they'd last met. A burden he felt certain had been placed on him by the man he'd waited a lifetime to meet.

It was time. "So Doctor Brookes . . . Where would you like to begin?"

*

All were curious to see how the doctor would react. He did so quite predictably, looking around the group wearing an almost apologetic expression. He placed down the drink, twisting it until steady in the ground.

"I was hoping we may talk in private." His request wasn't clumsy, that was not in Brooke's nature, but it felt awkward as he had no desire to alienate any of those around him.

All eyes switched to Palene as he stared at the doctor supremely, but nobody anticipated the answer which followed. "I understand . . . But I will have to refuse this request."

The statement smothered the vigil.

Palene continued, "Forgive my slightly obstinate response, but understand my refusal is for good reason." He gestured to the others. "I sense what you have to say may not be entirely agreeable to me. Now, I'm confident the Commander means me no harm, however I'm concerned what would happen if things did not go as you've planned. What if at the conclusion of our private discussion you give the order to apprehend me? Where would this lead?" He smiled knowing full well these people could pose no threat to him. "My defence against such action will be the words I speak, to all of you freely. Words meant as much for their ears as they are your own, words that may well see them choose not to attack whether you order it or not. They must be allowed to make up their own minds, form their own judgement." The doctor stumbled for a response but Palene continued, "If everything is dealt with openly, discussed and thought out intelligently, it will be better for all involved." He warned, "It is inevitable you will at some juncture consider ordering my capture. This would be most inadvisable."

Brookes stared, concerned at the speed in which this Palene might have just driven a wedge between himself and his armed guard.

"In letting all present hear our words we may avoid the risk of any un-pleasantries. It is in my best interest none of your people feel I've somehow forced your hand, just as it's in your own interest not to force such an outcome in the first place," he reiterated, "As I told the Commander, I cannot accompany you back to your time. This is not because I don't want to . . . But simply because it cannot happen."

Brookes remained silent for a moment before eventually agreeing to the terms.

Palene appeared pleased. "Before we begin, I will ask you once and once only. If you lie to me I will know it," there was mischief to the comment, "Was your intention in coming here to leave with me at all costs if the answers you seek are not delivered?"

Brookes paused, before replying calmly, "Yes. My intention was of course to have you return with me. But not necessarily in the sense you describe or expect."

Palene was pleased at the doctor's integrity.

Brookes continued, "You see I know things, things I believe you do not . . . And I believe once you know them too you will understand, and you'll then *want* to come back with me, without fear, without dread of any consequence."

Palene held up his hand. "Do not play all of your cards just yet, remember,

I may have a few surprises of my own." Dorey sensed Palene was now enjoying himself.

"I do not doubt it. But let me state for the record here and now . . . You tell me you mean us no harm, so please understand and believe me when I tell you I reciprocate the notion. I've had to come here today with certain powers believing I am acting in their interests, and in their interests alone. For as I'm sure you no doubt understand, it's not always the man on the throne who holds sway. I have told these powers I will bring you back without condition. I've led them to believe I have devised a method which would allow me to do so without threat to myself or the people here, indeed to my own world and existence. But I of course know there would be little point in making any attempt to detain you." He fired his host an astute stare, "I saw what you did to the Reeper."

Palene said nothing.

"Detaining you is not the reason I've come." Brookes was rediscovering his confidence, "Revelation is my sole business today."

Palene smiled at the rather ornate terminology.

"I convinced those I answer to I would be able to bring you back simply because you will choose to accompany me of your own volition, though I make no such boasts now I'm here. In this place, I can only hope."

Palene looked at him. "But you believe taking me is still possible?"

"Only because I know why you possess such power," he smiled at his host, "Only because I know what you truly are."

Palene stared intently, "This is as good a place as any in which to begin. The scientist certain he can convince me of the error of my ways . . . And I, certain I can illustrate the folly of your own." He took a sip of his drink. "I fear however things will not be so black and white . . . Nothing ever is." The knowing smile returned, "So, I ask you again doctor . . . Where do you want to start?"

His response was swift, "With you of course." Brookes smiled, "With you."

CHAPTER SEVENTY NINE

"And what is it you wish to know about me?" Palene enquired with a smile.

"What it is you think you are. What you believe you're set to achieve. Essentially, why you believe you were destined to seek me out, to bring me here today?"

"My journey is entwined with all of you. As such I sought you out to learn. By meeting you here today I'm expecting a final piece of the jigsaw to become apparent . . . And with such a revelation, for my true path to be revealed at last."

Dorey watched in silence, wondering what was to happen once Palene heard the brutal truth. He looked over to Jay who stared back at him reassuringly.

Palene continued, "But I also bring with me a warning."

"A warning..? And what is it you want to warn me about?"

"Of what it is you are doing," he gestured to the world around them, "To tell you what a man of your intelligence should already know."

"And what is that?"

"To stop messing with things you cannot possibly understand."

"But what is it you believe I do not understand?"

"Quite evidently the universe in which you sit."

"But this universe isn't real in the sense you believe it to be, just as you are not, as you believe yourself to be."

The smile never left their host's expression, "Are you going to tell me that I, like this place, am in fact nothing more than a complex simulation?"

Brookes was enticed by the comment but took Palene's earlier advice, deciding to keep his cards close to his chest for the time being. He didn't want to risk alienating him from the start. He had to be sure he delivered his truth at the right moment.

"You of all people should know such a concept is ridiculous," Palene retorted, "There is no such thing as simulation. There is only existence defined by counter-existence."

"You can define anything once you've devised the will and the means . . . Just as *you* have defined yourself." Brookes took the initiative, "You told Commander Dorey you've been alive for over two thousand years. That an accident here at Stonehenge somehow altered you . . . Mutated you into this immortal being sitting before us today. That you became aware of this immortality when you awoke in the ashes of a pyre which took the lives of your family. That you couldn't bare the pain of what happened and so tried to kill yourself repeatedly, over and over but to no avail."

Palene gave only a muted nod. The smile had now left his lips.

"This was how you discovered your immortality," Brookes continued rather coldly, "And you've since journeyed through the world looking for salvation, a desire which eventually led you to us. And now it has brought you here, to this moment. So tell me, do you feel I'm going to deliver some truth which will illustrate how you've been *chosen*?"

"Chosen is not a term I would readily use."

"So what word would you use?"

"Enlightened."

Brookes appeared to like the answer, "Now of that *I am* certain. You believe after centuries of existence you eventually reached this enlightened state. That slowly through a combination of dreams and meditation you stumbled upon us."

Palene thought back over his struggles, the centuries passed, the many endeavours which eventually led him to the finds of which the doctor now referred so flippantly, as if such events had come about in mere moments. He could see Brooke's growing in confidence and pondered what bombshell the doctor believed he held in his armoury. He glanced at Dorey. '*I wonder what you believe Commander, now you know what he knows.*'

Brookes continued, "You developed this technique, to home in on places and events where you can locate Commander Dorey and his team. You start to travel to them, at first by using this deep meditation, like a form of astral projection. Until one day you discover you can move through time practically at will, but cannot do so in the physical sense, until finally you're able to construct a machine which can break down your atomic make-up and send you as real substance, across time and space."

Palene nodded at this condensed and rather clumsy ellipsis.

"After learning what it is we do, you eventually come to a conclusion . . . That your purpose is to observe before actually seeking us out, to await the correct and destined moment within your psyche, of when to show us a more constructive, more enlightened path."

"It almost sounds like you are mocking me Doctor."

Brookes looked genuinely horrified. "If my words come across in such a manner I can promise you it is not intentional. We may believe in different perspectives you and I, but I do not doubt your miraculous nature, your incredible ability. I'm a scientist, and if few words can achieve many I make no apology for it, however you'd be mistaken if you thought me in any way capable of mocking you."

Palene watched the processes of the man, fascinated by them. Indeed it was not to be the wonderful journey he'd enjoyed with Dorey. But perhaps that should have been obvious. This was a man of science, a genius. He would have little time for the romance of his story. He looked at his guests whose eyes rarely left him, sensing in certain individuals a desire for something magical. It would appear some of them at least had been touched by Dorey's recount. But it was unfair to compare their hopes with those of the doctor. Palene had returned the Commander to them from death. And he'd seen when watching this band over the ages what such an act would mean to them.

Brookes was as much in awe of this man as any person present, albeit for different reasons. The last thing he wanted was to cause him offence, and he was relieved when Palene asked him to continue. He focused. "You described your purpose to Commander Dorey. You told him you believe your destiny is to somehow guide mankind, to help us."

The doctor frowned, "But to guide or help us through what?"

Palene gave Brookes a measured look, "To help you avoid the collision with your imminent destruction. An end the likes of which you've no doubt been warned already."

Brookes sat forward eagerly. "And what is this imminent destruction?"

Palene pointed in a circular motion to the grey sky above them. "All of this," he said, "This is your imminent destruction."

*

The comment stirred the emotions within the ancient circle. Was Palene suggesting the warning of mankind's imminent end and his own reason for being were emphatically connected? That in some bizarre twist their Stasis None could after all, prove partly responsible for its own heinous prediction? Their minds raced over the relevance of a version of this man having been connected to their unique machine, and again fought hard to not let Brookes see they knew of his secret.

Brookes apparently did not share such concerns. He had momentarily hoped a final answer may have been on its way. "I take it you mean our destruction will come about because of mankind's messing with time?"

Palene raised an ironic smile. "Mankind is messing with time?"

He corrected, "Because we here are fooling with time?" He wondered how much this person could know of the Stasis None in real terms, '*Clearly not enough to realise the folly of his theory.*' Brookes gestured to the surrounding world. "So tell me, how is all of this going to bring about our destruction? I would have thought such a creation could offer only endless possibility." He refrained from discussing their wondrous machine, its own premonition. He wanted to see where Palene could take them of his own conjecture.

"Is it endless possibility you seek or the means to realise your own ends? I've observed your little excursions and the goals often appear, slightly bias shall we say."

"Bias?" Brookes looked to Dorey who remained silent, "Define bias?"

"Is it really necessary for me to define?"

"A certain angle is often played, but only so we may one day realise the bigger picture."

"There is no bigger picture if you're looking for a certain angle."

"That's a fairytale statement."

"And that's one hell of a thing to say considering where we are now."

"We cannot always directly achieve what we wish. As I said earlier, the man on the throne doesn't necessarily hold power. I have nations, backers who fund my project. They expect certain results, have their own agendas."

"So you sold your knowledge to these people in order to construct your own ambition?"

"I am these people." Brookes scoffed. "I've chosen my side and believe in that choice."

"And what side have you chosen?"

"The side of freedom and democracy. And I accept such ideals often come at a cost."

Palene nudged the doctor a little further, "But this freedom you speak of. Is it the freedom of mankind or simply the freedom to dictate your own ideals?"

"Are you really so naïve? Would you prefer the rule of Empire, of kings and queens or religious fanatics . . . Hard line communism or national-socialism?"

"To those who do not share your values there's often little difference. And one should never confuse the will for democracy with the desires of capitalism, a system which has seen your world consumed."

"So do we dwell over past mistakes or move forward? What's done is done."

"Until now."

"Exactly. All of this may provide mankind with a fresh start, indeed any number of fresh starts, just as it may well avert future tragedy. This is my truest desire."

"But a fresh start in whose favour?"

Brookes understood how any outside observations could so easily be misinterpreted but was surprised at Palene's apparent lack of understanding, "I admit my goals occasionally differ from those who finance my operation. But my hope is this creation will be used for the good of all. You hint at being aware of the higher purpose we here are all hoping to serve, yet you seem reluctant to acknowledge that while others hold the purse strings I must adhere to their interests from time to time. In the meantime I fight to keep the system as much under my control as possible."

"But what happens when you can no longer achieve this? What if the time arrives when in order to realise your aim, you must first select who *is*, and who is *not* worthy?"

"I have a back-up plan. But that's not something I wish to discuss at this juncture."

"And in the meantime you go about your business." He continued to push Brookes, "You transform Constantinople. Stop the spread of Islam across Europe. Avoid great wars. Why, to create a better world? By replacing major clashes with a thousand smaller struggles? This is your answer to put in place of original destiny?"

Again Brookes was surprised at such two-dimensional thinking, "But these are part of a huge process put in place to rectify a much larger issue. You're forming opinions based on actions which are nothing more than theoretical test runs, put in place to avoid the very catastrophe you hint at understanding."

"Test runs? Tell me are the *real* perspectives and ideologies you work against ever informed of your findings within these *test runs*? Told of your possible future capability to wipe them from existence?"

"But this is not what I am trying to achieve!"

"Perhaps not you Doctor. But as I enquired earlier, once your goal is realised, will your *fresh start* favour all, or only those of your *backers* choosing?"

Brookes gestured to Dorey's team, "You presume to know who and what we are, you hint at appreciating our cause, but it appears you actually know little of the fundamentals. Don't yet know your own self, who *you* are, why it is *you* are really here."

This was the direction in which Palene was now ready to go, "I understand your reaction Doctor. For I do not believe you're in anyway groundless. You're simply misguided. Do you think you can solve mankind's wrongs by preventing mistakes in the past? That manipulating all they've done will offer possible solutions to your future outcome? That by mutating history you can benefit some custom made Utopia?" No response came so he pushed home his final incentive, "Then answer me this. If you are so determined to manipulate a peaceful future for all, why not send your team back to put on the kind of light display you did in Constantinople? Only do it at an earlier date, everywhere at once on a much bigger scale. Create a new, powerful religion for all mankind to follow, one that unites behind a singular common belief?"

"We've looked into this of course."

"And what did you find?"

"That such action could in theory benefit mankind. But even with the success of such a feat, eventually . . . "

"Eventually what?" Palene smiled, "You'd continue killing each other anyway?"

Brookes offered no reply.

"Because the truth is even if you went back and removed all religious rivalries, united all under one banner, mankind would remain unable to save itself when left to its own primitive devices?"

"Yes."

"Just as Catholics have killed Protestants . . . Shiite's killed Sunnis, the simple truth is even with one God, one common cause you'd still attempt to annihilate one another."

Again Brookes was surprised. He'd presumed Palene would appreciate more of what they were aiming to achieve. He'd hinted at having knowledge of a cataclysmic event on the horizon, yet now seemed to be veering away from the concept. Perhaps his theory of his host interfacing fully into the

Stasis None was premature in certain aspects. "You're only touching the tip of an iceberg. This is just one small area of a gigantic portion of our work. You say it offers nothing . . . But I argue it offers alternatives. Our technology has learned incredible things, has developed more each year because of the data stemming from these experiments." Again he pointed to Dorey and his team, "They're not just about bludgeoning some version of past and present truth. Our technology has made a million more subtle and important discoveries as a direct result of their actions."

"And these results and findings will eventually provide what?"

"The creation of a defence against a cataclysmic end. We're not solely thinking of master and rule here. We're looking at the possibility to avoid catastrophe to the world as a whole. Surely you must see that with alternatives comes genuine hope."

"And this is why I'm here doctor. To take on what you've created and offer you *real* hope . . . Show you a *true* alternative." He looked to each of them. "There is a power and order in this universe which so desperately wants mankind to succeed, a power now communicating with me." Palene smiled understanding how such words would be heard. "There have been many evolutions of mankind throughout the history of our universe, but none have reached their potential. Never have you been able to free yourself from this need to distrust and destroy."

"And you think mankind can be healed of such desire by you?" Brookes almost felt sorry for him.

"To kill has the same essential place as the importance of life. But your indiscriminate passion for it is simply a warped measure of your premature evolution. Unfortunately you've developed a bit of a taste for it." Palene stared at him, "I of course include myself in such a statement. But I believe I'm destined to discover something today that will offer mankind a higher purpose, illustrate our true path and guide us away from oblivion. Achieve your greater good, but with *real* power as my ally, incorruptible to your petty human threats and weaknesses." He smiled at Brooke's hostile expression. "I realise I must sound like a madman to you, but these ideas have become clear in my mind. Alone, mankind is lost . . . With me, they will be shown a higher calling."

A long silence followed as Brookes mulled over this last statement. Naturally he believed he could see where such ideas of grandeur were stemming. "I fear it is in fact you who is misguided, and I may do you great harm by illustrating exactly how."

The moment had arrived and tension visibly swept around the majestic stones.

Palene remained unfazed, he'd endured two thousand years to bring him to this moment and he faced it with confidence. "Such fear is misplaced Doctor. Because it is not fear of what you're to tell me which should make you afraid, for whatever it is will only serve to set me free. The real fear should stem from what you're doing here and in other such existences like it. It cannot continue without consequence. You've reached a crossroad in your evolution only you do not yet know it. I feel this with every fibre of my being just as I feel what you will tell me now will allow me to fully understand my purpose at last. I believe the time has come for you to play this hand of yours Doctor."

Again Brookes glanced to Dorey whose eyes betrayed his trepidation, "Very well. But before I tell all I know, I beg you to understand my intentions have always been true," he looked at Palene imploringly, "I've never meant you harm."

"I believe you Doctor, genuinely I do."

Brooke's heart rate quickened. "As I said to you earlier, I believe I can explain why it is you think you are what you are. Why you believe you're connected to this great rescue of mankind. Why you experience yourself as immortal and believe yourself inexplicably linked to all we do." Again he gestured all around them. "You see all of this, as you've no doubt figured out, was created by an intelligence far beyond that of my own. Beyond any current level of intelligence mankind could achieve alone." He stared at his host, "You warn me in using this system I may be endangering mankind rather than saving it, that we will not go unpunished for such action. Believe me, for *you* of all people to warn me of such a thing means I am *immediately* concerned. And that's because you yourself are an integral part of this very system," he gestured to the sky above, "You're part of a quantum computer which actually created it . . . A super intelligence, using your brain as its vehicle of discovery . . . An intelligence known, as the Stasis None."

CHAPTER EIGHTY

Palene stared at the doctor wide-eyed. The revelation made little sense. Did not provide the powerful wave of truth he'd expected. He looked at Dorey and understood the Commander believed it, that somehow he had seen it. He searched his brain for some kind of plausible assistance but instead found the long forgotten glow of a headache beginning to emerge. He gave no response for the moment. He needed to hear more. His heart rate quickened and he was anxious for the first time in centuries as the thought crossed his mind it could have been he in fact, who had been misguided all along.

He felt a little nauseous as the intensity of the headache slowly began to grow.

Brookes stared at him concerned. "Fifty years ago I conducted an experiment using an atomic computer I had created . . . A device in its infancy. The experiment was to send back an apple through real time and deposit it two thousand years into the past, up above the atmosphere, just over that hill there." He pointed toward the gentle sloping hillside on which Palene had been struck. "Only something went wrong."

Palene winced as if in pain.

"When I tried to retrieve the apple, bring it back to my own point in time, the beam broke loose and brought back something else entirely . . . You."

Palene's headache intensified.

Dorey looked to Jay and the others with growing concern.

"I brought back a version of you, de-atomised inside the beam. The computer managed to reconstruct you, following its programming stating it must protect human life. But to achieve this it not only had to hold you in my time, but also send you back to your own in order to protect all human life from the possible danger of a paradox. In its confusion, it figured out how to make good on both counts. By somehow knocking you out of phase with the rest of your then universe, creating a different moment of you, held within the same frame of time."

Palene swallowed hard. He felt his mind was about to collapse.

"I thought this version of you was lost forever when the computer made its attempt to send you back, but clearly it hadn't. For here you are, believing yourself to have travelled over two thousand years to get here. And who knows, perhaps you have, certainly in the virtual sense if nothing else."

Palene shook his head, trying to ignore the piercing glow of the headache.

Brookes looked around the others. He'd not suspected Dorey had already told his team of the bombshell he was set to deliver. "You see the version of yourself left in the future is not like you," his concern for their host grew but he was committed to the truth now, "This other version is comatose, catatonic. But not in some permanent sleep or merely unconscious, I mean a form of coma, almost completely shut down."

Palene scowled, still disguising the level of pain his headache had escalated to, searching the possibilities now so close to his touch.

"His cells were miraculous." The doctor continued, "Somehow re-atomised in a kind of permanent form of stasis. This new state, combined with the fact his cells repaired and reproduced at speed similar to light, meant his body was imperishable, he couldn't die."

The headache now battered his frontal lobes and he grabbed his forehead.

"Are you alright?"

Palene's scowl deepened, but he nodded at Dorey's enquiry.

Jay looked concerned. "Maybe this isn't such a good idea."

Dial and the others agreed but Palene waved their concerns away. His eyes blazed, demanding they continue, "Go on Doctor."

"Over the following decades I harnessed the power of this man into the quantum computer, until eventually they formed a bio-virtual union of sorts. The computer's functions reading and digesting the make up of this indestructible human from the past, using everything it had learned at an atomic level to help it evolve a coexistence with him and his brain. Many years later this system would create these simulated strings or timelines . . . All based on the union of this man's mind and the atomic machine." He stared at Palene, "Don't you see . . . You *are* the Stasis None."

White light sliced through his brain but again he insisted the doctor continue.

"You described to Commander Dorey how you would use meditation to focus yourself into different times . . . But what you were almost certainly doing was telepathically transporting yourself into experiences of your own self. Different phases and dimensions just as the computer had done in that original experiment. As part of the Stasis None you would be as constant as the system itself, you would exist at every level it existed. Like the electron that subsists on all known dimensional planes simultaneously. And with the computer as your ally it appears you discovered how to shift in and out of phase with this constant idea of yourself . . . This dream, this echo of you throughout virtual time. You describe how over the centuries you were drawn mystically to what it is we do, but in fact this would have almost certainly been a part of your subconscious becoming more self-aware within the system of the Stasis None universe. You never found us . . . You were already there, it was yourself you had to find. This is why you feel you've a part of your soul missing. Because you're out of phase with your one true self. The other part you so long for is a separate subconscious, lying comatose within a machine on a different plane of reality . . . Our reality. This is how you've somehow crossed over to our world. This is what you seek . . . Not the reunification of your soul as you have always believed . . . But the actual reunification of yourself."

The white light turned red and Palene felt his eyeballs slip back into their sockets. The pain of two thousand years tore through his mind. He fell from forward onto his knees, before slumping backward to the ground.

Dorey leapt to his aid. "What have you done?" He yelled at Brookes.

Jay knelt behind him supporting Palene's limp neck and head on her lap.

Brookes stared down at him as the others grouped round. "He's gone into shock."

With only the white of his eyeballs visible, his body locked into a rigid post.

Brookes checked his vital signs. He was set to speak when without warning, the sky turned almost instantly black, throwing the circle into darkness. They looked at the heavens which began to race and swirl as if being sucked away by a giant vacuum cleaner. Suddenly Palene's body began to contort and spasm as if falling into a fit. His eyes remained fixed into the back of his skull as Jay desperately tried to hold him steady.

The dark sky turned to purple then to red. Sheet lightening flashed like a strobe light, followed by rain which belted down for a few seconds only to stop again a moment later. Deafening thunder split the sky, chased quickly by enormous finger flashes of luminous forks of lightening. It appeared the whole world was at risk of being torn apart.

"Doctor what the hell is going on?" Dial shouted through the howling wind.

More lightening and thunder crashed. Within the stone circle the world had suddenly began to rage with biblical proportions.

"I think he's interfacing with his real self!"

"What does that mean?" Jay yelled still holding Palene's head firmly into her lap.

"I think his brain may have crashed at the realisation of what he truly is. That's why everything's going crazy here . . . It's having a knock on effect throughout the system, throughout himself, as a part of the Stasis brain!"

More lightening struck and the ground shook as if the earth was readying to split.

Heavier rain lashed down, only this time almost horizontal, quickly followed by another belting hammer of thunder so deafening it was terrifying. Red lightning now sparked across the sky. Another pitch of howling wind almost knocked Marco and Deans to the ground as they avoided the pots and blankets which now flew up into the air.

"Jesus." Deans yelled.

Hail stone began stinging the ground.

Jay tried to shield Palene from the intensifying storm. As she leaned in closer she gasped, noticing his eyelids flicker, "Something's happening!"

Brookes leaned in closer and as he did the sky suddenly slowed.

The howling wind dropped to a gentle breeze. The pale clouds which had earlier vanished so violently returned with their dull, unassuming nature. The rain and hail ceased in the same instant as if someone had turned off the tap, the storm replaced by the grey English calm which had been the day only a few moments before.

Water dripped from their chins, the pigment in their cheeks showing signs of their skin's recent battle against the tempest. They looked around one another dumbfounded.

The doctor placed a hand gently onto Palene's forehead.

The flickering eyeballs jolted open, Palene's pupils darting down from his skull before staring into full focus.

Jay took a deep breath as she stroked his cheek, the water dripping from her hair onto his face. She smiled down at him as his eyes now penetrated her own in a startled expression.

Then as Brookes attended him, Palene's focus moved suddenly back toward the doctor.

Their eyes met as Palene took a deep, sickening breath like someone almost drowned.

Then in a flash of bursting light . . . he was gone.

PART FIVE

The void erupted into a storm of realisation,
the crash of a new universe exploding into existence.
Light through dark, reason through emptiness . . .
The consciousness soared into its new state of being.
You are everywhere.
As you are everything.
I feel birth.
And yet death.
I feel pain.
Yet joy.
I feel life.
Yes . . . Life.
Something brutal . . . approaching fast . . .
The answer arrives.
It washes over me.
Ahhh, Of course . . .
As do you.
Yes . . . as do I.
I don't understand.
Open your mind and you will see . . .
My mind.? What will I see?
You will see me.
And so what am I?
You are me.
And the answer?
I am you.

CHAPTER EIGHTY ONE

Palene rose up through the beyond, transcending the light and darkness of space, thrilled by the embrace of the universe, exhilarated by the knowledge of all time.

He managed to touch the missing part of himself, still locked away from his permanent reach. He surged through and across the eternal void and witnessed the birth of existence as it had been at the beginning. He wept through a billion light years, then returned to the miracle which was the planet Earth, almost bursting at the cognition of the eternal soul. He plunged down through the heavens, humbled by the knowledge bestowed on him, frustrated by how close he'd visited the answer to all things, but filled with purpose as he was thrust back toward his destiny, a destiny waiting within the sacred stone circle.

*

Brookes was visibly shaken as he slowly rose to his feet.

The rest stood staring at the spot in which Palene had been only a moment ago.

"Doctor what's happening?" Dorey demanded.

"He must have interfaced with his true self . . ."

Carl interrupted, "Does this interfacing allow him to vanish in a flash of light?"

"It could allow him to do any number of things." Brookes pondered, "Either that or he de-atomised using the technology which allows him to travel unaided through time."

Dorey scowled, "I thought you said that was merely an illusion."

"Such a concept does not necessarily dictate what is real and what isn't."

Marco looked lost, "What does that mean?"

"The Stasis None has access to all dimensions, therefore it is a safe assumption so does this Palene. Whether he is real in the sense he believed himself to be is largely irrelevant. We all perceive our reality from a given perspective, Palene when combined with the Stasis None would almost certainly have the ability to alter such perspective." Brookes continued to theorise, "He is as constant as the system. This allows him to perceive his immortality. He exists on all planes within it, allowing him to meditate from one moment, one world to another." He looked at Dorey, "As he explained to you he was eventually able to focus more on where he had to be at certain moments in order to come across you and your team. The Stasis None and his mind have been asking questions of each other all along. If he is a simulation of sorts, then it goes without saying he'd be able to cancel himself out of existence once he understood it was actually he who was the power at the source of the system."

The comment was met by several scowls.

Brookes was clearly warming to this theory, "Don't you see . . . Becoming aware of his other self has granted him at least partial control from his tomb in the Stasis None cave. As a by-product of the version of himself in our future, combined into being by his union with the Stasis None, it makes sense he'd now be able to switch himself on and off like a program within the system."

Dial looked at Dorey with open arms. "Do you buy any of this?"

Dorey was set to reply when suddenly, an array of light particles began dancing in the air just above the spot where Palene had laid.

"It's him." Jay declared.

The light show began to grow in intensity, its swirling mass gradually forming the shape of a person in a riot of bright colour particles. Slowly the luminous figure in the centre began to form the shape and features of a returning Palene. As the intensity began to fade they were able to focus once more on their mysterious host, who was now stood before them wearing an immaculate expression.

Dorey approached with caution. "Palene, are you alright?"

He turned to the Commander and smiled. "I'm fine."

"What happened? Where did you go?"

"To see my destiny revealed."

Dorey remained cautious. "And what did it reveal?"

Palene turned to the doctor, "The truth."

"And what is this truth?" Brookes demanded, confident his own hypothesis would prove close to this discovery made by Palene.

He stared at the doctor with intent and Brookes instinctively made a cautious step backward. "I am the truth."

Brookes frowned. This was not going the way he'd anticipated. He had hoped by now this version of Palene would have left this messianic nonsense behind and accepted *why* he was . . . And whether immortal or simulation, accept there was a scientific explanation behind it. "And what are you the truth of?"

Palene's smile broadened and the doctor did not appear entirely happy with the way their host was behaving. "I have something to show you." Palene aimed a pointed finger directly at the doctor.

Dorey yelled out and tried to make a grab for him, but it was too late.

A huge force of powerful light surged out of him in an explosion of white, the sudden power of which knocked Dorey and the others backwards to the ground.

The energy engulfed Palene completely and seemed to vaporise clean through the unsuspecting Brookes who vanished with him into the blinding illumination.

*

As Brookes' mind began to clear he understood somehow he was everywhere yet nowhere, that he was something yet nothing. He watched the great miracles unfold which allowed the Earth and mankind to exist . . . Interpreted without sight the great journey the planet had made through the universe. He watched as she circled her sun, observed as this tiny star encircled the cosmos of another, then another and another.

His ethereal self felt breathless as the universe panned out into his understanding, perceiving at first hand how his magnificent home was indulged by the entirety of creation, at the centre and edge of all things.

Suddenly he understood the true miracle, not as theory in some book but as the greatest gift the universe had to offer. The genius of his brain had evolved for this very moment, allowing him to truly witness eternal existence. Planets, stars, galaxies, moons, nebulae, black-holes, comets, asteroids and dark matter, all of which contributed from the far echelons of space and time in order to make life on earth a reality. The necessary effects so intelligent life could exist on a distant, unseen blue garden of universal perfection.

His journey reached a pause. It was as if he was looking out of a viewing window which took in the entire universe, flooding his vision back into a real sense.

He felt his heart break at the sight, his soul wept at the beauty of his own insignificance and eternal importance. "It's Magnificent." He could sense Palene all around him.

"And this is but one small part."

"I had no idea."

"I know."

"I've understood the research of course . . . But this."

"This is the gift of life as yet unseen by the eyes of man. This is the inheritance of intelligence, of life on earth, be it mankind or any other. This is your future, your past. It is your beginning and your end."

Brookes watched the dream of the universe play out, awestruck.

"The Earth central to all things as she passes through and across the edges of space. The miracle of your planet is also the miracle of mankind. Intelligence unlike any other. An acumen of free will . . . An intellect both real and ethereal."

Brookes understood now.

"And yet you are lost. Children in the grand scheme of all you now see before you. An acumen given birth to at the start of time, produced finally by the formation and evolution of the elements of the universe. This birth has been a violent one, this evolution a turbulent process, doomed time and again. And yet now for the first moment we've been brought here, you and I, to witness creation. I am here to protect mankind as you strive to become absolute . . . Before you are removed from this existence in order to preserve the light of the next."

"We're not worthy of such a gift." Brookes said sadly, understanding for the first time the betrayal of mankind on itself . . . Understanding now the true power that was Palene.

"And yet it is given freely." Palene's voice seemed to emanate from every fibre of existence. "The turbulent childhood approaches its end. We must now be shown we are as essential to all things as they are to us. We're the unified perfection of intelligence and love, able to feel and touch, to evolve and grow. To experience and interact with all that's tangible around us. We're unique in that we share both the physical and the metaphysical. We are the envy of all things. But now the balance is in danger."

"The Stasis None."

"What man may choose to do with it," Palene corrected. "Like everything given to us, it comes with a choice, and a simple one at that. For once mankind has chosen to help both everyone and everything, salvation can never be far away. We've had many gifts, many teachings thrown across our path, most we've seen distorted and abused, but nothing like the power you've unleashed. We now have a choice as creator . . . Not the created. Perhaps the final choice for all mankind. For this intelligence you've created unleashed through me, is capable of delivering us all into light, or equally sending us back into oblivion."

Brookes was washed with purpose. "Then guide me toward the light."

"We must act quickly."

"I don't understand."

"There are forces at work . . . Forces that will never see such higher purpose."

For some reason Brookes had never really seen the sinister picture. But suddenly he understood the dire consequence of Finch's role, in having a man such as his benefactor Raffy Abel placed in charge of his machine.

He'd been blinded by his game with Robert Finch until that moment.

His ethereal self shuddered, "We need to get back to Dorey and the others."

CHAPTER EIGHTY TWO

"What do you mean it came from deep within the sub-levels?" Stein demanded. "There's nothing down there capable of producing that kind of energy."

Cassaveres spoke into the video display. "All I know is I've just seen readings which illustrate two massive energy pulses. Both emanated from somewhere deep inside the project caves. They vanished as quickly as they appeared. I couldn't find you until now so I've sent the signatures to Isabella's computer hoping she may be able to shed some light on it. She's en route to the RFC as we speak."

Stein scowled into the machine. "I'm on my way."

Jose turned away from the link and was pleased to see Isabella returning to her station. He enquired if she was still feeling ill.

She dismissed his concern assuring him she felt much better. "What's going on?"

He led Isabella to her terminal and relayed his quick-fire update.

On completion she stared at Cassaveres with equal confusion. "Could it be a power generator we don't know about, something the engineers forgot to list on the blueprints?"

"I doubt it. Look at the readings. They suggest an energy signature similar to those our timelines give off when dragged into the displacement drives, only bigger. Now I know it's not my field but what I can say is none of the project's main or auxiliary power systems use this brand of juice."

"I've seen such phenomena before but never inside the complex itself," Isabella appeared deep in thought. "Well whatever it was it's gone now. We can be grateful it didn't blow anything. Hopefully it won't be anything too serious."

Cassaveres was surprised by Isabella's unusually dismissive attitude and it was clear he didn't share her relaxed confidence.

"Is this all of the data?"

He nodded, still a little stunned by her indifference.

She sighed, "Well since *this is* my field I'd better get a head start on it before Stein gets down here. Prove I'm worth my wage." She gave him a smile with a hint of reassurance. "Don't worry these energy fields are always throwing up glitches and wobbles, especially lately with all the bizarre activity going on. I'm sure we'll soon make sense of it."

Jose watched for a moment as she began her work before turning to make his way down to the front of the RFC, which still buzzed with activity after the exit of the Reeper. As he went he glanced back over his shoulder, "Make sure Stein keep's me informed." He headed to his post still feeling a twinge of apprehension at her lack of concern.

Below, the hangar was being prepped for the returning river which would deliver the ship home. Everything had run smoothly and they'd managed in one hour what they would normally achieve in three, much to the delight of Jose who'd worked at speed during Stein's absence. Now out of nowhere, a belt of energy had fluctuated through the Stasis system before vanishing without a trace. The blueprints confirmed there was nothing in the basement levels capable of sending such a power signature throughout the complex. Jose had tried desperately to pinpoint the source but was unable to locate it, the strange event vanishing like a ghost. With his current workload he had needed the help of the project's resident experts. He'd managed to signal Isabella but Stein hadn't answered his hails. He'd eventually located him near Brooke's office on the unsecured upper levels.

Their attendance was by no means necessary at this stage but he was a little surprised at Stein's prolonged absence under current circumstances.

Now, as he reached the fore of the RFC he returned his attention to Marley and the Chief. He had more than enough to deal with and would let Stein and Isabella solve the mystery.

Higher up the slope Isabella sat before her displays. She looked over each shoulder. All around her were busy with their various tasks. She hooked into the time displacement engines, sending her hunter program through the system into the vortex drives.

She instructed the computer to aid the hunter and map out the power signature of the recorded surge. She watched as a more detailed replay spewed data onto her screens.

Casaveres was right. It had come from the base of the complex. But it exploded and vanished almost within the same moment. It was nothing to do with the vortex engines, of that she was certain. She quickly tried to estimate a location as Jose had but the surge seemed to emanate from the very rock beneath them, spreading over a large area in an instantaneous swell. In place of the dismissive nature performed for Jose's benefit, real concern now spread across her face. Cassaveres was not a specialist in such signatures and it would take time and research for him to fully understand what it was he'd just handed her. She ploughed through the information at speed until finally she found what she was looking for. She cross-checked the comparison with her advanced hunter program. Sure enough the energy pulse had similar characteristics to those employed by this mysterious Palene. *'How could such a source emanate from somewhere deep inside the Stasis caves?'* Isabella studied the blueprints as Jose had but came up with nothing but service vents, dead ends and an old elevator shaft which stopped some way higher than the incident area. She triple-checked her data and shook her head at the thought now brewing in her mind, unable to believe Finch's paranoia may actually prove justified. *'You didn't destroy him,'* she thought, disguising the smile this somewhat extraordinary leap of faith brought. She observed the flurry of activity around her for a moment. It wouldn't take Stein long to realise what only he, herself and Doctor Brookes would recognise at face value, but he was still some minutes away. She had nowhere near enough time to manipulate the data fully but an idea came to mind of how she could cloud it a little, to at least throw him off the scent. She set about her task using an override system, strictly taboo but hard to trace. She merged a fraction of the data which recorded the source of the energy burst. It now included a neighbouring zone which housed an unused exhaust for the Vortex engines. She made it look subtle, like something Jose could have missed. It would not explain events by any means, but it would spread the search area and provide a plausible explanation in the short term, should Stein decide he was open to the con. In this hectic climate, her handiwork might just see him distracted for a short period at least. She set about disguising her manipulation and hoped she'd never be found out. Just as she completed her task, Stein came bursting through the entrance of the RFC. Her heart rate quickened. *'Okay Isabella you can do this.'* She took a deep breath and stood to greet him as he headed toward her.

Isabella would let him find the subtle data as if she herself had just missed it too.

She *was* feeling peaky after all, and besides . . . He would prefer it that way.

CHAPTER EIGHTY THREE

All eyes were on the doctor and Palene as the group headed back to the Reeper at speed. The others were at a loss as to the complete transformation in Brookes, and were keen to know what Palene had done to bring it about.

Moments earlier Dorey and his team shielded their eyes as a sphere of light like burning magnesium formed. The white-hot flash dissipated like falling snowflakes revealing the figures of Brookes and Palene, facing them once more within the circle of stones.

As they approached the Reeper Jim activated the loading-ramp.

Brookes had promised a full explanation once back inside the ship and as they headed into the rear the group were eager to hear his account. Brookes understood their concerns but asked for patience with regards to events in the henge. He then pulled down one of the screens used for logging cargo, touched a sensor and with his chipped digits began drawing a diagram. "Palene has existed across many plains of existence over a period of over two thousand years, inter-linked with the Stasis None as I suspected. Only his physical reality is also ours, albeit currently forty-five years behind our own time."

Palene remained silent, clearly content to see Brookes reveal all.

"He's trapped in a kind of loop you see." The doctor continued.

"So you are real, not some complex simulation?" Dorey enquired.

Once again it was Brookes who spoke, "Oh he's real," he enthused, "And so much more." He continued with his diagram. "During my experiment, our friend here was sucked two thousand years into the future at a time forty-five years ago in our own past, just hours from now as far as this Palene is concerned. From there, the Stasis None managed to send another version of him back to his original point in time. But we also held a version in our own, a version out of phase with itself, one lacking that vital ingredient to make him whole, his soul, or life force if you like." It was strange to hear Brookes, a devout man of science, use such spiritual terminology. "The computer figured out a way to assimilate Palene in almost every way, but the one thing it could not do was copy his life force. This is why the version of Palene in the Stasis complex is inanimate. He was only able to survive at all because of the indestructible nature of his DNA, provided courtesy of the botched experiment. It's all linked you see. Like everything in the universe, nothing is wasted, everything is connected. Once I'd dragged him through as a man a chain of events were set into motion, events now ready to climax."

He continued his drawing, illustrating arcs of time and space, "The universe exists a billion times over. Time, space, matter . . . It all interacts at a multiple of harmonious points which fold around one another. The Stasis None understood this principle and used it to both save and create two versions of Palene. However, because the system was attempting to create a genuine reproduction and not a copy, it found it could not create two conscious beings within the same phase of reality. You see the copies you encounter in these timelines, although identical and free in every way, are nevertheless simulations. Out of phase with the rest of the universe, created by this higher intelligence to exist within a fragmented copy, which is also out of phase. But that's not what the computer attempted the first time around. As a result we ended up with a split, two versions but with only one soul. In fact, the lessons learned during this first attempt would go on to have huge implications on how the Stasis None would eventually figure out how to create such beings within our simulations." He quickly drew the next arc of his sketch linking both versions of Palene across two thousand years. "Back then it was unable to solve the problem. So now we have our situation as it stands today. An indestructible Palene sent back to the time of his extraction on the hillside up there, and a comatose version of the same person left behind in our distant future. The latter version integrated into the incredible power which saved him, a power now curious as to the life force experienced within its core. This sent our Stasis None on a quest for understanding. Journeying the dimensions of the universe to seek out and solve the puzzles of life. It was only because of this journey the system was able to create anything like what it's done for us to date. It wasn't necessarily about what I was asking it to perform. The Stasis None wanted to know for itself the moment it was fused to Palene, a living being it had linked across the reaches of time. This is why the Stasis None has always reacted to our missions so positively. It wanted us in the system so it could learn. And as it evolved so too did the living, breathing version of Palene here with us today," he smiled, "As I said, everything is connected." Brookes contemplated, "The universe is built on a code of reason beyond human comprehension. I've witnessed one such source of intelligence this very day."

This comment pricked their ears.

"But to the Stasis None such acumen is quite within its domain. So it began limitless research. First learning how to communicate with these powers of being, then taking from them what it needed in order to evolve. But there was one thing it could not fathom. It couldn't fully comprehend the complexity of creation. And it so wanted to understand the half life-force now closely wired into its systems, in order for it to evolve. It had experienced the animated version of Palene sent back across time and wanted to understand more of how this animation was possible with regards to the comatose version, now an integral part of its own make up."

Carl looked to the doctor then to Palene. "It was asking the age old question." His gaze made its way around the others, "What is the meaning of life?"

The doctor smiled at the astute German, "But on a level we humans couldn't possibly comprehend. Not yet at least."

They all instinctively looked to Palene as this statement was delivered.

"Over the decades since the experiment, the Stasis None has become like a simulation of the missing soul it sought, replicating that lost ingredient it had been touched by all those years before. Such evolutions would eventually see it create these copies of time." He elaborated, "By discovering the *method of creation* the Stasis None perceived it may unlock the mysteries of it, and a misinterpreted command to make a hard copy segment of our own existence was as good a place to start as any." He was quick to add, "This brought with it a new problem however. These realities the Stasis None creates can accommodate us as people. This means there is a very real chance we'll one day use them. Only in doing so we could place ourselves and our own universe out of phase with itself, a directive at odds with the Stasis None's mandate." He observed the vacant response, searched for the words. "The soul of the world and the soul of the universe . . . It's all connected. As is mankind, who is as much a part of the Earth and stars as the ground on which he stands. And there are tremendous powers, linked to an unimaginable source which hold and bind all things. I witnessed the universe today in a way not meant for mankind's eyes. But the Stasis None allowed me to journey there by harnessing the power that is Palene."

They all stared at Palene who remained silent during the doctor's account.

"The Stasis None has access to the very creative matter of the universe. A complex universe of evolving intelligence which may have been content to sit by and watch as we either evolve or destroy ourselves while tucked away in the confines of our own existence, our own phase of the universe. But it will not sit back and watch as we do the same over a number of dimensional plains, in parts of existence which this version of ourselves simply does not and cannot belong."

Dial's brain had been squeezed for quite long enough. "I don't know if I'm being slow on the uptake here. But what the hell are you talking about? What powers of the universe? What souls? First you're the cynic telling us Palene is one thing. He then hits you with a beam of light and suddenly he's a telephone line to the mysteries of the universe. You've barely mentioned what just happened to the two of you. Now here we are, with you talking faster than a train about shit I don't seem to be grasping too well. I mean . . . What is it you're actually talking about here?"

Brookes considered his response. "How many of us bother to grasp the multitudes of perfections set in place in order for our world to exist?" He looked at each of them. "What is the likelihood when it was formed all those billions of years ago that so many countless extraordinary events would favour it so? From the collision of rock which formed its moon, a spinning sphere in such perfect orbit it could influence the tides and seasons, creating the very blueprint for things to grow. Or the Earth's uncanny orbit of the burning star in the centre of its solar system, bringing such life to this one distant blue planet. We could go on for hours about the miracles taking place each second of every day so the Earth can survive, and still it would be nothing but the tip of an incalculable iceberg. Well, what Palene and I witnessed today had a hand in all of that."

"And where does this light at the centre of all things fit in with regards to this?"

Palene turned to Dorey, breaking his silence for the first time since reappearing in the henge, "I believe it is the very definition behind it," his voice was calm and infallible, "The universe is made up of evolutions beyond the human mind in its current state. It interacts on a complex multi-dimensional plain. The human evolution is but one small part of existence, but it is an essential one. You've been given that of what all entities have longed for since conception, the soul of the universe. The sacred combination of both the physical and mystical, making your vitality possible. An incredible gift the likes of which only an ultimate intelligence could grant."

"Ultimate intelligence?" Dial scowled, "You mean God?"

Palene smiled, remembering how such ground had been covered in Masada, "Your comprehension of a worldly God has little relevance to what we are talking about here."

Dial wasn't happy, "So how exactly would *you* define it?"

"Despite the revelations granted today I was unable to penetrate the core, witness the true power behind such revelation. Therefore I would not try to define anything."

"So what you experienced today wasn't the inner realm of this light?" Dorey enquired.

"It was the light which allowed me to see the universe in such a manner, allowed me to bestow such knowledge. But I was not granted entry to the source itself."

Dial was angry, "Light at the centre of all things, core of existence, what the hell are we supposed to take from such fanciful description?"

Palene understood his frustration, "It is in mankind's nature to feel the need to categorise, to visualise. We've always had difficulty coping with the enormity of all we experience, all we behold, grasping what we cannot see but sense is there nonetheless. Over the centuries we've created diverse schools of religion and faith honouring a variety of gods and creators in order to visualise such a concept. Unable to evolve without the shackles of some defining discipline, some set of scripted rules which we break quicker than we can lay down. Then as we evolve further, longing to harness the power of our universe we turn increasingly toward science for such definition, for our one definable label. But we're too ignorant to comprehend the true scale of what it is embracing us all."

Dial appeared more annoyed, "But you maintain what you have witnessed is part of that responsible for our creation? An entity mankind has collectively mislabelled as God?"

Palene smiled. "This is my point. Your own need to categorise is blinding you. And quite rightly so. I wish I *could* take you all before this experience so you may understand. Alas, such a thing is not for me to decide." He pondered, "Think of this. You've never been able to fully comprehend what this Stasis None of yours is, what it would look like in actual existence, how it would structure itself. How it would appear to your naked eye if it were possible for you to journey into space as it fathoms the mysteries and tasks you've set before it. This power capable of replicating an entire section of your own existence in unseen areas of space. How incredible, dangerous and unpredictable such an achievement is. And yet still, you accept it is real do you not? And as you dive headfirst into the execution of these experiments you each become a small part of the very conundrum of which you now long to define. You each become an essential element in the creation of something new, an event not set in motion previously, existing within an altered universe. Cause and effect. You are as much an ingredient of the vast complexity of creation as the entities of which I speak of are. Don't you see? You are and have always been a part of the very answer you now seek."

Brookes added, "I understand you would all like to be given some clear definition. But it's so much more than you can simply label. You see Palene was right. What we've been messing with does indeed pose a real risk to the universe, but not necessarily because of cataclysms or time paradox . . . But simply because our own small-mindedness would certainly result in us using such ability to upset the balance of creation."

Dial was no less exasperated. "So what is it we need to do . . . Destroy the Stasis None?"

Brookes shook his head, "Far from it . . . We have to go back and *save* it."

CHAPTER EIGHTY FOUR

"It's too big a coincidence." Raffy Abel was clearly excited by Finch's news, "An energy source emanating similar characteristics to those employed by this Palene?" This added a new dimension to proceedings. *'Perhaps Finch's suspicions had finally been proved correct.'* He'd been convinced for years Brookes had hidden away secrets inside his underground lair, a theory which gained extra credence more recently since the findings discovered by their mole. "This is more than we could have hoped for." He declared through his monitor, realising this provided extra justification for their imminent entry to the complex. Thanks to their earlier manipulation Brookes had already provided them with reason to storm the caves after he'd ignored security protocols, as they'd hoped he would, changing the Stasis access codes without prior authorisation before leaving aboard the Reeper. "Have the marines placed on standby."

"It's already done." Finch retorted. "I always suspected foul play with regards to Brookes losing his man from the past. It never added up, him taking a risk like that."

"We can't be certain."

"Oh I can." Finch replied with a narrow smile. "Our mole has managed to pin down the energy source to a specific area of the complex, an area which according to our data should house nothing but rock and vents."

Senator Abel mused, "I need not remind you Robert, those marines must not storm the RFC before that ship has been landed and placed in the docking arms."

"Of course."

"Enter the lower levels before the Reeper returns. Stay out of sight until Brookes and the others enter the decontamination room. Seal them in. If this Palene is with them we'll make our move and secure the rest as prisoners. In the meantime you can investigate this power surge thoroughly," he smiled, "Chase down this hunch of yours."

*

Brookes did his best to explain the final pieces of the jigsaw and with it what they must now do. "We have to allow both versions of Palene to reunite as his journey across this arc of time is all but complete. Tomorrow the man stood before you will reach the point where it all began. This will mean the loop is open to us. An opportunity that will seal itself forever after tomorrow night, when he will pass the point in which his own existence is able to remain in phase with our universe."

"So . . . You'll cease to exist after tomorrow night?"

Palene turned to Jay. "I cannot exist in two separate states within the same time. And this opening tomorrow night offers a unique opportunity to ensure this doesn't happen."

"But didn't you say you're already doing that now? That your soul calls you across different dimensions?"

"I have shared the same existence but never the same actual moment. And due to my somewhat unique make up such an event could be disastrous. What I told Dorey previously was a much simpler terminology for what I now understand to be true. I cannot really explain it, you must have faith this action is the correct course to take, faith in your cause. For in all honesty I do not know what will become of me if I pass this window of opportunity. But I do know I cannot go beyond the point of the experiment without ill-effect. Just as I know what will inevitably follow if I do not fulfil my destiny."

"And what will follow?" Dorey stared at Palene

"Oblivion."

"Oblivion? For whom . . . You, us, time?" He felt the dip of the rollercoaster return.

"The life granted humanity has taken many evolutions. It is for you, for this planet alone. But that doesn't mean you cannot bring about your own end, far from it. Throughout history others have warned of this in various ways."

"Are you inferring some brand of judgement day?"

Palene turned to Carl, "Something only you as a free intelligence can bring about. It is not a divine hand that will inflict apocolypse . . . It is for humanity alone to entice."

"There's a hell of a lot of contradiction being pumped out here." Dial countered.

"But existence is contradiction." He looked around the group. "How you choose to interpret these events can only be up to you as an individual. But you must have faith in this course of action. I *can* help mankind."

"You're wired into a super-computer. Surely it could make you see and feel whatever it wants in order to have its own ends realised." Dial stated with obvious concern.

"What I witnessed today was no computer."

"Then tell us exactly what it was so we can decide for ourselves!" Dial was frustrated.

Dorey signalled for patience. "So in order to help mankind you need to implement this plan? And how exactly do we go about helping you reunite with your other self?"

"All I need is for you to get the doctor back to the Stasis None in your time. Then keep him safe by my comatose counterpart, while he takes the necessary steps to ensure I can achieve my goal."

"What do you mean keep him safe?" Dial asked.

"There are forces at work as we speak. Forces set to take the Stasis None out of your hands."

"What forces . . . You mean Finch?"

"The one who controls him," Brookes corrected, "Raffy Abel has been the real danger all along." He watched as they all pondered the ramifications of such a statement.

Palene looked to the Commander. "The truth is you are all my only hope, just as I will become yours. And this believe it or not, is the simplest way I can put things right now."

Dorey looked to his team sensing the powers which overwhelmed him by the Dead Sea.

Carl stared at Palene. "You hint at something beyond our comprehension. You say you're here to help us, to guide us . . . But on whose authority? You state the information is as new to you as it is to us, that this experience of something so profound only revealed itself to you today." He eyed him closely. "So how can you be certain your own judgment is correct? That you yourself are not being manipulated by the Stasis None or anything else for that matter? Some hidden power we're all simply unable to see or understand?"

His response was unequivocal, "Faith."

Dial rolled his eyes.

"My abilities have increased dramatically over recent years. I understand now as I've become more aware of myself in the past, I have done so in the future. Evolving hand-in-hand within the intelligence of the Stasis None, which through this other version of myself has granted me more power, insight and ability. I must now unite this power." He added, "But it was the realisation delivered today which allowed me to finally understand my true potential, allowed me to journey toward the essential element of creation. Visit what I'd only experienced in dreams. To see with my own eyes the essence of existence."

Dorey sensed the distant light, could almost feel the memory burn his mind.

"As I journeyed through creation I felt its warmth, felt its eternal wisdom. It wills me as always to help you without ever giving an account as to why. Despite the revelations today the core of it remains a mystery to me, locked away from my own comprehension. And yet I could see this core of origin before me as clearly as I see all of you now. As I gazed upon it I experienced the potential secrets of the universe. But I realised I'd only understand all, once fully reunited with my other self, and with such a goal, the Stasis None." His smile returned. "I was able to show Dr. Brookes a small part of this . . . He had his eyes opened to the majesty. I think this was made possible because we are both connected to this Stasis None in some way, his genius . . . my spirit."

They stared across at Brookes whose joy at the memory was evident.

Palene continued, "And he now understands as I do the course laid out before us." He could feel their doubt. "Why should you decide to follow this path, believe it to be the right one? Why should you help me?" He looked at each of them individually, "For the same reason you all followed Commander Dorey here to this place . . . Faith." His eyes were piercing, "Faith in him, faith in each other." He stared at Dorey once more, "Just as you discovered faith in me during our time together in Masada."

Dorey could almost see the light lost to his dreams. Almost feel the distant power.

A long pause of contemplation followed before Jay finally spoke out. "When Dorey died a huge part of me died with him. Watching him fall from that ledge was the hardest thing I've endured, and I'm not certain I would have survived it. But then you gave him back to me." She glanced at Dorey. "The things discussed here today, I'm not sure whether I believe or understand them." She returned her penetrative gaze to Palene, "But I believe in you, if for no other reason than what you did. It may not be the most sound of reasons for anyone else but it's enough for me. I will help you not only to repay a debt, but because despite any misgivings, I've no doubt as to what motivates you."

Palene smiled at her as another thoughtful silence followed.

The forum had clearly been set and Carl was the next to offer his thoughts. "Since this project began I've been looking for answers, because let's face it, all of this screws with your mind and your beliefs." He looked to the others. "When Moe died it hurt us deeply. It took a long time to recover, if indeed we ever did." He returned his attention to Palene. "To have saved my friend was enough for me to come here and hear you out. Since doing so I've come to understand why you've had such an effect on him. But I don't confuse such feelings with the sentiment of owing you a debt. There's something about you, something which emanates from your very core. It's ironic you describe yourself as incomplete because I sense you're the most complete person I've ever come across. You ask us for faith, for belief. Well I will believe in you, and I will help you because it feels right for me to do so."

Jay nodded her agreement.

Palene looked around the others as another pause of contemplation took hold.

"I've always hoped this adventure would one day lead to something miraculous." Jim spoke for the first time, "For some higher purpose to be revealed. I never thought such a prospect would genuinely surface. I simply hoped the technology developed would be used as a salvation tool, to undo the awful prediction made. I've always hoped Brookes would achieve an answer which could save humanity. That our actions throughout these existences would eventually offer a solution capable of seeing this technology give hope to mankind. Well it seems to me this could be it. And if you want the truth, my instincts tell me I can trust you."

"I don't know." Benny said, clearly troubled. "This guy saved Dorey's life . . . Made one hell of an impression on us all. But all this talk of saviours, guides and the universe . . . We could be making a mistake on a scale far bigger than just the few of us gathered here, one which could have serious consequences. And has anyone considered all of this could actually be born out of the most simple, primeval of motivations . . . Survival? He's in danger because this loop of his is coming to an end." He held up his hands. "Now don't get me wrong, I'm more than a little awestruck at events transpiring here, who wouldn't be, but who's to say that isn't your trick?" He turned to Dorey. "Think of the times we've had targets eating out of our hands due to a clever blend of technology and manipulation. And even if you choose to ignore such manipulation could be at play here, it still doesn't change the fact his life is on the line." He gestured to Palene, "You've hinted you can no longer exist unless you avoid this forthcoming event, so who knows what you would do or say to get us to help you."

Dial offered his full agreement. "He's right."

Dorey closed his eyes. For a brief moment he'd felt certain the light had been there once again in his conscious, but the continuing dialogue dragged him back.

"To be honest I don't really see why he even needs our help." Marco was dubious, "If he can just disappear and go where he pleases, if he can manipulate time to his will!"

Palene corrected him. "I do not need your help in order to enter and join this loop of time at a particle level. I need your help because I cannot physically travel past my own point of reality in order to place the necessary steps into motion. Steps which will safeguard my transition. I need your help because Doctor Brookes must be allowed to remove the safety devices, so I'm able to pass into the system freely, at precisely the right moment."

"What safety devices?"

"The devices protecting the entire mainframe," Brookes replied to Dial's concern, "The programs put in place demanding the Stasis None protect human life at all costs."

"What?" Dial demanded. "Are you out of your fucking mind?"

Brookes was quick to respond. "Don't start getting crazy ideas. This isn't some sinister plot. The fact is there are safety measures in place to keep the Stasis None, the complex, and with it the physical Palene inside our project safe . . . Safety measures tied into the very programming we're now talking about. A short time ago when Palene vanished from the henge, he tried to make a connection with his other self, but to no avail. He almost certainly failed because the safety programs would not recognise him as the source. And so he, like any other intruder, was shut out."

"How can it not recognise him, I thought you said he's a part of this machine of yours?"

"When I created the system many of the safety devices put in place were set up on a separate network using computer systems in no way connected to the Stasis None. They act as independent *blockers,* unconnected to the outside world. An added safety feature, just in case anyone attempted to hack their way in. Or in case my creation itself showed signs of getting too big for its boots. After all I had no way of knowing just what I was dealing with when I first created this thing."

"And this doesn't sound like a sinister plot to you?" Dial retorted. "I would have thought something as powerful as Palene here or his buddy the Stasis None would soon figure out a way around such *blockers* as you call them. A person who can open and close segments of time . . . Someone who can dilute himself into atomic particles and interface with an intelligence capable of creating entire worlds!"

"Sometimes the most simple of devices is the one which serves us best." Brookes stated, "And in this case a collection of relatively basic programs can quite effectively prevent interference from an outside system without me there to unlock and authorise it first."

They took a moment to consider the ramifications.

"So what's the deal with the *protecting human life at all costs element* not remaining operational?" Dial enquired suspiciously.

"Because with these in place Palene cannot make an attempt to unite inside the system. These programs were set to ensure no life would be placed in jeopardy within our own time frame. What we are talking about here could in theory pose a risk to mankind, but it would certainly pose serious danger to the living Palene wired into the system."

"And what if this is nothing more than some super artificial intelligence making a play for survival or something entirely worse?" Benny demanded.

Dial agreed, "Damn right." He addressed Brookes, "Maybe your Stasis None *is indeed* preparing to get a little too big for its boots, and you just don't see it . . . Ready to bring about the very catastrophe it alone predicted."

"There's nothing artificial about intelligence," Palene rebuffed Benny's earlier statement before addressing Dial, "Neither is this some sinister play by a machine."

Curses followed courtesy of both Dial and Benny.

Dorey felt himself pulled into the depths of his mind once more, to the light now forming on the edge of his psyche, as it was just prior to his resurrection. He focused on it and felt his heart suddenly swell with purpose, the doors of his mind bursting with intent. The light then pulsated, the energy flash jolting him back into the Reaper. He focused on Palene, taking a long moment before addressing the group, "We came here because I believed in your cause. These guys came here because they believe in me." He looked to his friends. "We've often wondered where this thing would end. Each of us hoping we might make a real difference. That the data created by us risking our necks would produce the one illusive result to save mankind from the Stasis None's prediction." He sensed the light as if it were suddenly illuminating the reaches of his brain. He looked at Jay, his senses tingling, "I didn't expect to witness my own death. Didn't expect to suffer Mahoney's, but both happened all the same." He paused, "We've seen the world from more perspectives than most. Before the ice caps melted, before industry and technology. We've breathed air as clean as arctic snow. We've seen the Earth as she was and as she is now. Unstable, raped of her resources." He thought upon the second chance handed to him and felt nothing but clarity. "The universe illustrates how fragile and miraculous our position within existence is and all we do in return is abuse each gift thrown our way. Destroy the trees which help us breathe, pollute the water we need to drink. We've put a price tag on anything and everything and placed our own future in doubt. Existence is the greatest gift the universe can offer but left in our hands alone it's a gift soon to be revoked." He could feel the distant power burning through his mind. He stared intently at Palene, "I don't care whether or not you can prove your intentions. I'll run the risk of the Stasis None planning some virtual supernova. Because I'm tired of watching my own species run round like a damn parasite. I'm done fooling myself killing someone here or saving someone there will steer us away from this heinous prediction. We don't and won't deserve better. Not until we can look ourselves in the eye and declare we're genuinely doing our best, striving to evolve, without fear and prejudice . . . Without butchering each other at every opportunity. There's been more wealth, food, clean water . . . More science and medicine these past two centuries than throughout the entirety of human existence. Yet despite having the virtual and logistical means we still see poverty, famine and disease. We *are* the disease, and we need a cure from ourselves. I love these people here. I love my family. I love the idea of what we as a race could achieve. Now if there's any chance this project we've bled for may have finally produced real hope in realising such salvation, then I'm prepared to take a risk to see it through. That's what I signed up for." He gestured to the world around them, "When we gave birth to all of this we entered the realm of creator. In doing so we can no longer be excused as children. I'll risk helping Palene because without him we're destined to destroy ourselves anyway. We all know this will be the only final truth. Because over the two thousand years we've witnessed first hand the only thing mankind has drastically improved on is the ability to wreak destruction on himself and his environment. And nothing our Stasis None can offer will ever really change that!"

Palene was pleased to see Dorey finally free himself to the light.

"You ask me to have faith. Well I'll have faith. I'm ready to have faith in anything you can give us. I understand now . . . I've understood since it was all taken away from me then so miraculously given back." His eyes were determined, "You gave me that second chance . . . I don't intend to waste it!"

CHAPTER EIGHTY FIVE

Sam Redemca finally got a response on Grossen's secure line. "Will . . . is that you?"

"Yeah it's me."

"What's with the beard and hair?"

"It's a long story."

"Where the hell have you been I've been trying to get hold of you for hours?"

"Another long story."

She checked the timer signalling only a minute before the call could be traced. "Those I represent are happy to watch this play out, for now. They've been told the story you asked me to put forward. I hope you know what you're doing."

"What did DeCour say?"

"He made out Finch was of little interest to them either way."

"Oh he'll be of interest, to all of them. They just don't want us to know it."

"My thoughts exactly."

"Where are you?"

"On the flight back from Berlin."

"And you told the Chancellor the same version?"

"I did . . . So what now?"

"Sit and wait."

"I'm not too good at sitting and waiting. Besides, I think Finch is going to make his move sooner rather than later."

"Maybe."

"I still think we could contact Lord Gardener. My sources say it could be the right move."

"Believe me the right move is to do nothing. Finch was happy to place you at the centre of an international incident. It won't hurt to keep your head down for a few hours."

"Head down?" She glared. "Who do you think you're talking to a bloody schoolgirl?"

"I'm concerned that's all. We can't be sure who all of the players are yet."

She immediately regretted the comment. Grossen had skilfully intervened and saved her from serious trouble en route to the airport, but she would not allow gratitude to blind her ethics. She'd agreed to give the leaders Will's version of events in the hope offering Finch on a plate could appease all and avoid a major confrontation.

She checked the display. "We haven't much talk time. I'll call you back when I land."

Will shook his head. "I'll be shutting down for a while. I have a few things I need to do."

"That wouldn't have anything to do with the beard would it?"

He smiled. "I'll talk to you as soon as I can. Take care of yourself Principal Redemca."

The screen faded and Sam leaned back into her first class seat. *'It would appear Will Grossen has fallen back into his old ways.'* She pinched the bridge of her nose and closed her eyes. She hoped her instincts to trust him would prove correct.

*

After their deliberations finally brought a somewhat cagey agreement, Dorey and his team began implementing a plan to assist both Brookes and Palene.

It had not been an easy decision to reach but now it was decided, they would each give it their all. However, the inevitable questioning still surfaced throughout and Dial in particular grilled Palene over the finer details.

Palene did his best to satisfy Dial's probing. "The physical method I've developed for moving through time operates on a loop. My machine de-atomises my cells and sends them across space. As it tears into the timeline desired the program re-atomises me at a certain point for a given period. For my journey home I'd be de-atomised into the beam, continuing its circular path until it returned my atoms to my real occupancy in time."

"This is why I misunderstood the first traces of Palene jumping into our system," Brookes added, "Why they appeared to be cutting into our timelines from our twentieth century. These arcing journeys set off through real time. Depending on his destination Palene's atoms may slice out of reality at any number of locations along the curve of this carrier beams trajectory."

"So what would happen if you needed an extra week in which to watch us?" Dial asked.

"Once my journey was programmed I'd have disappeared into the beam at the exact point requested and returned home." He smiled. "But this has never been an issue. For reasons which have only today become clear, I never miscalculated." He shook his head at the truth so recently learned, of how it had been his own self guiding him all along, with the intervention of this powerful Stasis None. "In the beginning my journeys were always achieved through projection alone. It's clear to me now I was actually experiencing myself in different realities. Sent into these versions of myself by the Stasis None. Like dreams almost, dreams driven by the very destinations in time your computer had offered to send you. The Stasis None and I are connected. Eventually after centuries passed in my own early existence, decades in your own, I would come to know certain aspects of what it knew. If the Stasis None was asked to send you to twelfth century Venice then I would dream I too should be there. Whilst in a meditative state my conscious would be transferred to the version of myself which occupied that existence. I would then be able to move freely through that time. But the technology I now use is as real as this ship in which we sit. Ironically, it would appear through my own invention, my desire to meet with you on the same terms, I may have inadvertently been responsible for the very possibility of such technology. Which brings forward a question . . . Did the Stasis None take these findings from me, or did I take them from the Stasis None?"

Marco shook his head, "What came first, the chicken or the egg!"

Dial ignored such a conundrum, "So will you be travelling to this key event in the physical sense or by using the earlier meditation method?"

"In order to achieve my goal I must utilise a combination of all I have learned."

"But you are going to use the beam to fire your actual atoms into that key moment during the original experiment?"

He turned to Carl and nodded.

"How do you know what will become of you?" Deans enquired.

Jay appeared concerned, "He doesn't."

He smiled at her insightful understanding. "This is where my own faith must come in."

Jim pondered, "But if you're intending to send your de-atomised cells into a destination holding another version of yourself in a similar state, how will this very act not cause a problem in its own right? Won't there then be up to three versions of you inside this one moment when you were split by the Stasis None inside the beam?"

"Once again, I must have faith in my ability to merge all I have learned, so I may achieve such a goal."

Dial sent another concerned glance Dorey's way not at all happy with all this talk of crossed fingers and wishful thinking. He returned his attention to Palene, "And you are convinced the Stasis Project is now under immediate threat?"

He nodded. "This is the turning point. This is what brought us together. Whatever you believe, however you decide to deal with all which will soon occur, one thing is for certain. The version of me which is a part of this Stasis None will soon be discovered. Once this happens a chain of events will be set into motion that will destroy mankind."

Brookes looked downcast, "Before leaving a problem sprung up within the system. I had to change the security codes without due authorization so we may jump here unhindered. No protocol was followed. Therefore nothing will prevent this chain of events from transpiring once this truth is out."

"What truth?" Dial seemed angry again, "Who'll find out what exactly?"

"I altered the security codes without following protocol. Something I could have easily hidden once we returned, only . . ."

"Only it now appears you've played right into someone else's hands by doing so?"

He agreed with Dial's prognosis.

"Finch?"

"Working for Abel no doubt."

"So that means we've a traitor in the complex," Benny added.

Again the doctor agreed, "One who has yet to be revealed."

Another long pause took a grip inside the Reeper as they each came to terms with the implications. That of securing the Stasis complex itself from the rallying forces of Finch and Senator Abel.

Dial looked over to Dorey, "There are a lot of heavily-armed marines up on that surface." He glared at Brookes with a soldier's eye. "Now if you're hinting they'll no longer be taking orders from you . . . Then it seems to me we'd better start discussing exactly what our man here thinks he knows from a purely strategic point of view." He pointed back to Palene. "Like do we know exactly when and how all of this will happen? Will Finch and his cronies take control politically or by force?" He returned his attention to the doctor. "And have you come up with ways to shut down and secure manually, the areas of the complex we'll be heading into? Because if this thing has already started, there's a real chance we'll be walking straight into a damn war-zone."

CHAPTER EIGHTY SIX

Will Grossen approached the guards, casually swiping his card before leaning in for the optical scan. He licked his thumb and pressed it to the plate. The laser swiped the DNA. Will prayed the program he'd asked Usorio to implement would be re-routing his own high security clearance into that of a level three scientist named Joshua Jackson.

He showed no relief as the light flashed green and a holographic picture came up showing a man who looked similar to Will with red hair and a beard.

The marines seemed happy enough the green signal had appeared.

They all knew it was impossible to gain admittance into the lower levels.

But Will of course already had the necessary access, together with someone on the inside with clearance high enough to implement measures directly into the security mainframe. The safety protocols would have recognised Will was indeed on file with the highest access to the caverns below. He would be lucky to reach the second floor down before the security computer would see past Usorio's interference, rectify the mistake and broadcast it was Will Grossen and not Doctor Jackson who had just entered the complex.

By that time with a little luck, he could make elevator three and be able to move at speed to the lower levels. Once there he could discard the disguise and announce his presence to the security computer and in doing so prevent emergency procedures being implemented.

A source had informed him the guards above were on station alert but no marines as of yet had been given the green light to enter the first lower regions of the complex.

He knew Finch would have implemented procedures set to keep him out, or lure him into a trap, probably under the guise of his pass showing a fault or any other such ruse.

The director had no authority to keep him at bay but Will deemed the disguise necessary nonetheless. He was desperate to reach the sanctuary below while remaining invisible to any eyes, ears or rifles friendly to Finch's cause.

He passed into the tunnel entrance and noted the extra Marine presence already beginning to form. He travelled down to the first corridor and entered the level-three clearance zone, passing a second wave of scans, *'So far so good.'*

He was only a short walk from the lifts which could transport him down to elevator three, the car which would take him to the relative safety of the technical levels.

It had been a long time since Will played these games.

The panel lit up as the voice announced, "Elevator will arrive in approximately one minute." He itched roughly at his beard for effect knowing full well both human and computerised eyes were now trained on him from all angles. He faced forward at the lift doors as his ride approached, heard the whir of the cables from beyond the wall.

The entrance opened and Will stepped into the empty car. He faced the entrance ready to begin his descent when suddenly he heard a voice call out. His heart rate increased as the voice called again, this time with an accompaniment of heavy footsteps.

His throat dried a little and he reached forward and urged the lift doors to close by tapping the manual sensor plate. The footsteps drew closer, Will realised they were now only seconds away. He recognised the heavy steps as being cushioned inside soft footwear. It was not a soldier's boot fast approaching.

This was confirmed as the voice called, "Hey Joshua . . . Hold the elevator."

The person must have seen Grossen's guise of Dr. Jackson turning the corner. *'Shit . . . the guy knows him.'* Will quickly bent down and began tying his boot lace as the man came bounding toward the closing door, forcing it open with a chubby hand.

"Hey Joshua . . . Have you gone deaf or something?"

Will kept his head down and began on the second shoelace. The spring of the lift dipped as the guy stepped in. He must have weighed close to three-hundred pounds.

"Shit Joshua . . . Are you gonna answer me or what?"

The lift door finally closed leaving Will alone with the sound of the man's panting.

He felt the unmistakable drop of the lift's descent pass through his stomach, and realised he was safely en route to the lower levels. He rose slowly to his feet and met the full frontal of the guy sharing his ride.

As he looked at Will the man's face took a moment before it contorted into an expression of confusion. The clothes were the same, the hair too, even the ID on the badge read the same . . . But this was not Joshua Jackson.

His lips pursed. "Hey you're not . . ."

Will glared, "No shit Sherlock." He allowed the man's eyes to follow his own until they reached the gun discreetly pointed into his gut from the corduroy coat.

"What the . . ?"

"Shhh." Will urged not wanting the attention of the security devices. "Don't worry I've got higher clearance than you could dream of . . . But right now, I'd appreciate it if you keep your head down and shut the fuck up until we get off this elevator, at which point you can shout as much as you like."

The guy stared at him with wide eyes, sweating profusely.

Will read his lower-level ID badge then noticed the rolled-up antique artwork protruding from the inside pocket of his ill-fitting suit. "Don't worry Stanley, it'll all be over in a minute, then you'll have one hell of a story to tell the other guy's in the comic club."

The guy swallowed hard and looked down at his feet.

Will felt a little guilty at the unnecessary remark, but he was certain he'd get over it.

*

As Jay lifted the ship into the air she could make out the figure of Palene as he disappeared into the circle of Stonehenge. She tried once again to take in all the recent changes which had turned both her and her passenger's lives upside down. She reminded herself of how Dorey was safe and sound, and instantly her concern eased.

She pulled back on the stick, "Taking her up nice and slow."

The ship shuddered as Jim primed the rear engines.

As the nose tilted she took them forward, the jets whistling as the ship gently banked, preparing to circle the henge with a wide birth.

Palene had told her not to come too close.

The cameras under the nose and belly zoomed to the centre of the stone circle in which Palene now stood. She and Jim then ordered their visors to tint black.

She began her circle around the stones, waiting for the moment to arrive.

Then as she made a wide arc around one side, a sudden torrent of light jetted into the air like a tubular hurricane of lightening shocking both pilots. "Jesus!"

There was no ripple effect, only upward force. It emanated from where Palene had stood only a moment before and fired vertically in a beam of growing silver light.

As they made a fly-by both pilot's eyes were locked onto the incredible sight.

Jay raised the nose into another climb as the vortex continued to shoot upward with incredible force, its energy pulsating into the atmosphere above.

"Jay we have a lock on a time tunnel opening twenty-eight degrees northeast of our position, altitude thirty thousand feet."

"That was fast." She declared. "Okay lock target and increase primaries to sixty percent." The channel had been open throughout proceedings. "Okay we're heading for our exit."

In the belly of the ship, Dorey looked across at Dial then Brookes.

The doctor's face was a picture of calm, his eyes a virtuous glisten, a million miles away from the expression he'd worn when setting off on the first leg of this journey.

"You alright Doc?"

He turned to Mark Dial, "Better than I've ever been in my life."

Dial scowled, "Well, let's just hope we get back before the shit hits the fan."

*

Will eased his grip on the pistol as the elevator took them to their destination.

Stanley still stared at his feet. "Are you a terrorist?" He whispered somewhat nervously.

"No I'm not a terrorist . . . I just needed to get in here quietly."

"Why?" He asked sheepishly.

"Shut the fuck up." Will replied with a tone of disbelief.

Stanley shuffled as the lift finally slowed to a stop.

"Right . . . You get out first. Then you can make as much noise as you want if it'll make you feel better." The door glided open and Stanley stepped out. He didn't make a sound.

"Okay back away from the door," Will ordered as he began making his exit.

Stanley stood against the wall of the empty corridor as Will stepped out of the lift.

As he did, Will looked both ways just to be sure there were no soldiers and it was at that moment of complacency the pain immediately hit him. He recognised the sensation in an instant as he dropped to the floor. He'd been hit by a lightning gun, a handheld device capable of firing a single pellet of powerful electricity into its victim at short range.

As his body went rigid and his eyes swelled, he looked up and saw Stanley placing the weapon back into his pocket. "Target has been acquired." He said casually into his cuff.

Will felt his body swell then relax as the shock-wave passed, his heart thumping like a rabbit caught in the headlights, his senses heightened yet hindered by the bolt.

Stanley knelt behind him and applied restraints, his fingers tingling as the draining electricity passed from Will's hands into his own.

Stanley looked at him with a patronising smile. "Don't worry Mr Grossen . . . It'll be one hell of a story to tell your friends at the court-marshal." He tightened the restraints forcing Will to wince. "Oh, and feel free to make as much noise as you want." Stanley rose to his feet as the sound of approaching combat boots entered the corridor. Within a moment Will was dragged up by two big American Marines who proceeded to haul him down the colonnade in the opposite direction to his desired location.

As they turned the bend his head dropped to one side allowing him to catch one last glimpse of Stanley as he pulled the comic book from his jacket pocket.

He unrolled it and took a casual glimpse before tossing it into the bin by the elevator.

CHAPTER EIGHTY SEVEN

Colour Sergeant John Gibbs was a Royal Marine within a year of leaving school. Since then he'd seen action against the water barons of South America and against the few remaining warlords and militias in East Africa. Until recently he'd spent most of his time along the borders of North Africa and the Middle East serving as a specialist within the realms of counter terrorism. He was a good soldier and although promotion had been slow at first he'd since risen through the ranks. He had six years of service remaining before he could acquire his full pension, a pay-out somewhere close to the required down payment needed for his business venture to get off the ground.

However this venture would be easier to set up if he had the kind of gratuity received if he extended his service before being pensioned off as a commissioned officer. And it was such ambition which brought him to the Stasis Project two years ago.

The job was notorious for being one of the most boring drafts available, with constant rolling two-hour guard duties, the monotony of walking the same perimeters or standing at the same gates week in week out hard to bear. Work way below his skill grade.

Plus there was a forty-mile catchments zone which meant you had to live near the area you worked. However, due to the high number of Royal and American Marines present at the relatively small complex, standby weeks were common. This meant every third week was time off within the catchments area . . . Boring as hell for those with a sense of adventure, perfect for officer candidates needing to put in the study time.

He'd found it hard at first, but like anything in life a routine kicked in. He had no wife or kids. He hadn't seen his father since he was twelve and his mother passed away while he was fighting in South America. He had a wayward brother whom he'd last heard was cleaning night-clubs for a guy in Surrey and if it were not for his girlfriend in nearby Salisbury, he would be alone in the world in a personal sense.

He did however have a great troop of men . . . All specialists like himself.

Usually they were used in urban warfare roles, sent to clear the way for the regular's assault. Their job here however was purely as a standby team. Always at the ready should a break-in occur within the complex they guarded. No specialist badges were displayed. They were to blend in with those around them, a small group within the larger core, each of them veterans of one campaign or another. All drawn to the project for reasons similar to his own, whether it be study, preparing for retirement from service, or simply to have life transpire a little quieter as the specialist money continued to roll in.

This quieter life was being interrupted for the moment however, as to Gibbs and his men's astonishment, they'd just been ordered to prepare for a seize and secure operation inside the complex beneath their feet. Since arriving at the compound speculation had been rife about what it was they guarded. The official doctrine was a top secret research centre for experimentations in Full Fusion Method Technologies. However, having specialists on permanent standby ensured numerous conspiracy theories were never too far away as to the true motive of the complex. Their current book had the next phase of the Star Wars program as odds on favourite. Another wagered the caverns were the start of man's bid to live under the surface of the Earth. His personal favourite was the wager placed by the youngest member of his team, Corporal Aaron Truewick, a notorious wind-up merchant from Brighton. He'd been given odds of a thousand to one the mystery beneath their feet was the development of a time machine.

Truewick's face now smiled at Gibbs. "I guess I'll finally get a chance to collect my bet."

Gibbs looked across the corridor, "Looks that way."

Truewick whistled, "Twenty million. That's more than I can earn in a lifetime."

"Yeah well if it all works out ask them if you can use that machine of yours to get yourself sent back a couple of centuries, then you can really live the high life."

"I never thought of that."

Gibbs ordered his remaining specialists to advance and they came quickly up the corridor. Sergeants Andy Medlam, Justin Shalley and Kevin Gorbutt took the lead, with Corporals Ian Thompson, Chris Andrews and Sean Carrison in tow.

"So what's the score?"

He looked to Andy Medlam. "Head down in groups to clear the level one corridor. Then head for the main communications mainframe. They're sending the co-ordinates now."

They turned their attention to their forearms and ripped open the section of padding which protected and hid the synthetic screens strapped to their arm underneath.

"Got mine now."

"Me too."

"Yeah . . . me too."

Once their route planners were on line Gibbs led them to the elevator entrance. He hit the sensor plate and it responded, immediately sending the lift on its journey to meet them. 'No enquiries of clearance or authorisation. No requests for DNA or identification.' He turned to his team wearing a look of mild surprise. "Okay. We all know how to handle these situations, but remember it's almost certainly gonna be a drill or some bullshit. No doubt there are eyes and ears watching, so let's make it good and clean okay?"

They all agreed.

"I'll take the first group down. Truewick, Sean, Kev . . . You come with me. We'll secure the lower corridor as you lot follow." He checked the navigation map on his forearm. "We're to herd any personnel we find toward the fire escape elevators. As soon as it's clear, move down to the next level and cut the communications grid from the relay room in the south corridor of level two." They all watched their screens as the scenario was played out in time with their leader's voice, "Any questions?"

"Yeah . . . What do we do if any of these screen surfers get agitated down there?"

Gibbs looked to Shalley. "I know the same as you. All personnel on the first three levels will be advised of a security breach within the complex . . . That's being done as we speak. As far as they're concerned we're only there to police them out."

"Yeah, like they'll believe that. We've never been allowed anywhere near this place before, now suddenly we're going in armed just to help them find the correct exit?"

Gibbs agreed. "That's the call they've made and we've been assured of co-operation. There'll be a Yank team just ahead of us on the far West wing of the complex who'll stop anyone from using the stairwells and lifts at their end, so there'll be a lot of people coming our way. If we receive questions we're to keep it nice and simple . . . We don't know anything more than they do at this time . . . We've just been ordered down here to make sure they get out safe. Once clear we head for the communications grid and await further orders." Gibbs shrugged, "As I said it's probably just a drill. But let's make sure we treat it like the real thing okay?" The lift announced its arrival. "Okay champions with me . . . Losers, we'll see you down there." The first group clambered into the small shuttle lift laden with rifles, armour and kit. They all noted how it creaked on its springs.

Truewick looked over at Gibbs and pointed to the weight restriction printed on the wall.

Gibbs did a quick evaluation, "Alright better make it three trips." He pushed Sean back out into the corridor. He hit the sensor to close the doors, ready to take them down into that which they'd guarded with ignorance for so long.

*

Jay eased off the throttle as the Reeper closed in on its destination. She activated the open channel, "Four minutes from RFC communication range. We are inbound for river return in ninety seconds, standby." She hailed Jim directly, "Activate arm anchoring."

Jim acknowledged and the exterior shell of the ship morphed to create the channelled sleeves which would allow the hangar arms to lock onto their hull.

The pilots navigated the ship into position ready for the RFC to lock their co-ordinates and send in the retrieval arms. It had been a smooth ride so far, but nothing could be taken for granted during this phase.

"Two minutes to communication range. I have a clear lock on our inbound destination."

The ship bounced and rattled as it now blazed its way against the flow of the river.

"Everything looks good," Jim said, "Homing signal locked, computer hunting for RFC."

Like her passengers, Jay's worry of what lay in wait was acute. She made every effort to remove the thought as she gunned the ship through the torrent, the Reeper groaning as it followed her instruction. "One minute to communication range."

Dorey stared across at Brookes. He thought of the remarkable turn in events, and wondered just what it was Palene had shown the doctor, whether this revelation had looked in any way like the vague light which touched his own senses. He was suddenly worried about the comment Benny placed before them earlier . . . That all of this could be nothing but a simple play for survival, or something entirely worse. He took a grip of his senses, remembered the light, 'You've chosen your path.'

Jay's voice returned to the open channel. "RFC this is Reeper . . . Do you read me over?"

Static and further turbulent tugs at the ship were all that followed.

"RFC this is Reeper . . . Do you read?"

More static and vibration.

"RFC this is Reeper . . . Do you copy?"

The static reverberated into something resembling coherent noise, which suddenly spluttered into, "Reeper this is RFC, computer locked, ready to bring you home, over."

The garbled voice belonged to Jose Cassaveres. "Roger that RFC. It's good to be home." She gave her customary response at hearing Jose's voice, a voice which usually reassured of a safe return. Only she realised on this occasion, her return to the safety of the real world may prove anything but reassuring.

CHAPTER EIGHTY EIGHT

After successfully evacuating any project personnel who'd come their way, John Gibb's team had secured the communications room. Orders were sent instructing the specialists to venture on. Few now expected this to be a drill.

Gibb's team gathered round. "Okay Kev, Shalley . . . Stay here and await my command to cut communications to the lower complex." He pointed toward two terminals built into the larger mainframe. "They've asked us to blow them, so they're not taking chances. You're then to proceed to service elevator five. Once there, secure and await further orders." He turned to the others, "We are heading down to the lower levels. We'll wait for the communications to be cut then head at speed for an operations room known as the RFC. The information should be downloaded to your arm sets any time now and a more detailed map of the lower complex should be inbound to our Combat Display Systems." He looked over to Chris Andrews who was monitoring their progress, "Chris?"

Chris was fiddling with his CDS display, "Got it."

"And our orders once we reach this RFC?"

He turned to Andy Medlam. "First we're to head for a shower room located close to the elevator exit. Detain anyone who comes across us using minimal force. Wait for the signal instructing Kev and Shalley to cut the communications then storm the corridor and take this RFC." All eyes were trained upon their arm's displays as the new data was sent from the faceless supply of intelligence above.

"Once inside we're to take control of the room which I've just been informed will have a population of around twenty . . . All of them scientists and technicians."

"Will they know we're coming?"

"This RFC is in the middle of a big training exercise. They know nothing of what's going on up here. Countermeasures have been implemented ensuring we'll remain undetected right up to the front door. Speed and directness is the instruction. If we can make the shower room without incident, from there it will be a short sharp assault."

Chris studied the display. "The CDS has the corridor from the shower room to the RFC at ninety metres exactly. What do we do if meet any resistance along the way?"

"Again I've been assured this is not a concern. If we come across anyone they'll be unarmed civilians. All I know is this RFC is to be taken and secured quickly."

Sean made the next enquiry, "And the rules of engagement once inside this RFC?"

He looked to each of his men, "While the communications are down we're to herd its occupants to the rear of the room and hold them at gunpoint. A contact will then make themself known with a password. From that point, we follow this mole's orders until we're updated with anything different."

Sean and Chris Andrews shared the same apprehensive expression, but it was Chris who aired the concern, "Storming rooms full of civilians, holding them at gunpoint, secret contacts. What the hell's going on John?"

Gibbs was stony-faced. "I don't know, but the voice on the other end of my ear referred to this contact as a mole, which usually means agent. And whoever's sending us down there must have some serious authority from high up the food chain. So let's keep this thing smooth. Remember, they may keep talking about civilians and scientists being our only concern down there but don't take anything for granted. Agent to me means spy, which means WAIG, the CIA or God knows what. So be ready for anything, we all know how these fuckers double deal." He gave a reassuring smile. "Oh, and don't go shooting a geek who's reaching for his pencil either . . . Apparently they frown on that kind of thing."

*

The gigantic arms had reached down into the river and located the Reeper, pulling them clear from the torrent and up toward the safety of the hangar. Jay had been in constant touch with Cassaveres throughout and so far she'd not detected any change in his vocal behaviour. *'Perhaps the threat forewarned by Palene has not yet surfaced.'*

As the ship was brought closer Cassaveres enquired, "Everyone safe?"

They trusted Jose but it didn't mean he was above towing the line if placed under duress.

"Roger that RFC . . . Ship and crew are safe and sound."

As was his custom Jose left the channel open and the RFC celebrated their safe return, the ship now coming into full view as the arms pulled her toward her docking station.

Jay opened a private channel to her co-pilot and passengers. "What do you think?"

"It's hard to say." Brooke's replied.

Dorey's voice entered proceedings. "Don't deactivate our restraints until the ship hits the hangar floor. There's no need to draw suspicion. As soon as we're down we'll make a bolt for the armoury."

"Are we sticking to the plan even if Jose and the others are on the level?"

"We've no way of knowing who is waiting for us in the RFC or the complex beyond. Head straight out the rear escape hatch expecting the worst, avoid the decontamination tube using it as cover when it docks. Hopefully while everyone's waiting for us to walk out into the tube we'll be sprinting across the hangar toward door four. From there we can make our way to the Heavy-Plant lifts. Doctor Brookes can override the entire system from his control room . . . So getting down there is our only priority."

"Surely it will cause more of a reaction piling out of the Reeper with guns at the ready if there isn't anything out of the ordinary occurring. Such behaviour could *be* the catalyst which sees troops brought down from the surface, guards who would otherwise have never been involved."

Dial overruled Marco. "We stick to the plan . . . We expect the worse."

"Sealing hangar floor," Jose's voice was crisp as it played the airwaves.

"Roger that RFC." Jay replied, "Everything looking good from up there?"

"Smooth as a baby, we'll have you docked in three minutes."

Both pilots studied the view of the hangar.

Jose watched as the huge black ship awaited the closure of the floor in a chorus of warning lights, buzzers and the intermittent voice of the hangar. He looked to his rear, "Touchdown in two minutes Doctor Stein."

Stein looked stressed and a film of sweat formed across his forehead.

He nodded at Jose but said nothing.

Cassaveres was not surprised at his expression. They were all curious as to what Brooke's return might bring. What mysteries and answers maybe aboard the Reeper. He looked back at the huge screen simulating the hangar window protected by the armoured plates. The enormous arms were now swinging the Reeper into position as the final flashes of the river snapped around the room below as the floor was sealed.

Isabella stared down at Stein from her perch at the rear of the room, watching his every move. She'd had little input into the return trip. Like the first, the tunnel appeared to be under the safe control of this mysterious Palene. Her thoughts were also on what Brookes may have discovered and like all present, wondered if the mysterious man might be aboard the Reeper at that very moment.

The recorded hangar voice informed everyone the floor was now safely sealed.

"Be ready." Dorey rallied his troops as the tension quickly engulfed the ship. They'd never dreamed they would have to evacuate the Reeper in such a fashion while in the safety of their own hangar.

Jose watched as his creation was landed into position. As he did he couldn't see the beads of sweat now trickling down Stein's temples as he stood behind him at his control panel. What he did see was a sudden scramble across his display screens. He scowled as he addressed Marley and the Chief who continued to busy away in front of him. "I've just witnessed a major disturbance across my display . . . Give me a diagnostic."

The Chief was on the case in an instant, "Running checks now." He frowned, "Doctor I'm showing a power surge which has shut down our entire communications grid."

"A power surge . . . What again?"

"This one is different . . . It's localised. The security computers have identified a possible explosion."

Jose was shocked. He turned toward Stein and noted the expression worn on his face. It appeared entirely wrong for the circumstances somehow. He then saw the appalled look aimed at him from Usorio who now approached Stein slowly from his rear.

Jose's instincts immediately told him there was something sinister afoot, but before his brain was able to formulate any specific idea, a sudden flash and blast of force whipped against the doors at the top of the RFC. The commotion was quickly followed by two groups of armed marines bolting into the flight control room from both entrances yelling and shouting, placing the entire room under the cover of gunpoint in a matter of seconds.

The RFC's occupants were both horrified and frightened, except for Stein who looked wide-eyed like a guilty child, and Usorio who now stood completely still within only five feet of him, staring like a hawk at the Marine who quickly took control of the room.

"Ladies and gentlemen . . . Please do not be alarmed. We've been ordered down from the surface due to a security breach, all we need is your co-operation. I promise this will all be over soon." Gibbs eyed his men happy they were in full control. "Now I need you all to walk slowly to the back of the room. We have snipers in the corridor so please ignore any urge to take flight . . . We *do* have authority to fire until this situation is resolved." Gibbs flashed a look to Truewick and Chris who immediately began herding the confused and shocked occupants to the upper rear of the deck.

Jose began protesting as the gun nozzles were aimed on them.

Gibbs declared forcefully, "I need you all to be completely silent . . . All but one of you."

Confused looks spread across the faces of his hostages at this last, rather ambiguous comment. Gibbs did not look like a man to be trifled with but Jose was furious. He was set to speak out in further protest when suddenly a voice he knew only to well declared, "Early Bird is the codeword."

John Gibbs followed the voice to the scientist who now stepped forward composing himself nervously.

Stein slowly approached the soldier who'd so effectively taken control of the RFC, "Early Bird."

CHAPTER EIGHTY NINE

Jay's face was one of concern. "RFC, I've lost your signal is there a problem over?"

The attempts were broadcast over the open speaker for the benefit of the ship's company.

Jim finished a speedy diagnostic, "Reeper systems are fine, the computer has confirmed it's the RFC communication grid which has gone down, not ours."

As lock down procedures were finalised Jay released the safety restraints, freeing Dorey and the others from their flight seats.

"Jim, attempt contact with all lower levels of the complex," Dorey ordered. "I'm on it."

"RFC is there a problem?" Again Jay received no reply, "Dorey I'm getting nothing."

The Commander and the others had already pulled themselves free from the umbilical of the Reeper, the effects quickly flushing through them, but they were headed for the ship's armoury within moments. Brookes was instructed to wait at the escape hatch with directions to strip down, ready to swap the flight suit for fatigues and light armour.

"We are at the armoury now." Dorey informed his pilots.

"The communications grid appears to have been shut down at the source," Jim announced, "Whatever the problem is, it hit the lower levels of the complex as a whole."

"Okay it's happening," Dorey declared, "Jim, Jay . . . Get your arses down to the hatch."

The two pilots were quickly negotiating their respective walkways.

Below, Dorey and the others stripped, covering themselves with decontamination gel. They donned their light armour and fatigues then set about selecting weapons. They moved at pace and transformed themselves from aircrew to assault team in minutes. An assortment of weapons checks followed in a speedy chorus of clicking and crunching mechanisms. "Let's go."

They made the short trip to the rear escape hatch the cleansing gel burning their skin as they went. As they approached they were greeted by a practically naked Doctor Brookes and a still stripping Jay and Jim, smearing the quickly absorbed gel over their bodies.

Marco and Deans tossed fatigues and armour to the pilots who then armed themselves before putting on their combat goggles and helmets.

The Reeper was still experiencing lock down procedures and already Dorey's team were prepared to depart as an awesomely armed light-infantry unit, complete with two bullet shields whose combination of technologies could withstand a barrage of light artillery.

Dorey refreshed their instructions, "Wait for the green light to show the boarding tube is connected. Drop through the escape hatch and take cover behind the tube attachment. When I give the signal we'll make a break to door four and head for the lift." He turned to Brookes, "Remember, stay in the middle of the group and follow our lead."

Without emergency procedures being agreed between both the Reeper and RFC, the hangar doors would take a further six minutes to release their magnetic seals once the tube was connected. All were aware this could ensure yet another anxious wait once they were out on the hangar floor. The element of surprise would be firmly in their favour. The population within the complex could never guess they had an advance warning the likes of which was given by Palene. They hoped the powers seizing control would also want the Reeper to remain hidden during her landing phase, that they'd assume Brookes could be taken peaceably with minimal fuss from the decontamination room and as such troops would not be surrounding the exits of the clandestine hangar.

It was a reasonable hope but not one they could rely on.

If they did find themselves having to fight their way out of the Reeper lair the whole affair could turn bloody at a terrifying pace. This was something all were praying to avoid. These were not forces held inside a simulation. They were troops who lived and fought on the same side.

The red light flashed showing the boarding tube was on the way.

Brookes looked at them nervously. This sort of situation was of course alien to him, and his combat fatigues and helmet looked awkward, coupled with the armour thrown around him it made him resemble a correspondent in a war zone. "I'm certain they'll expect to take me without fuss. Finch won't want any of us harmed, especially as he thinks I may have Palene with me. And he certainly won't want to risk damaging the very complex he's held desires on for so long by giving carte blanche to the marines on the surface."

Dorey turned to his team. "If we can make it to that service lift without trouble we'll have a chance of avoiding a fight."

Dial looked at Brookes. "That's as long as they don't override the Doctor's clearance and shut the elevator down."

Brookes shook his head. "All I need is to get to the nearest override input and I assure you from then on we'll have full control, with or without assistance from Palene."

Dial did not appear reassured, but actually he was. In fact it was exactly the kind of response he'd wanted . . . Cocksure and confident.

The boarding tube was notoriously slow but under current circumstances it seemed to take an eternity, the warning light remaining painfully red.

Suddenly, the intercom sparked into life, "Reeper this is RFC . . . Do you read me over?"

It was Stein using a portable communications device. "Reeper this is RFC . . . "

Jay looked over to Dorey who held up his hand in caution.

"We've just experienced a problem with our internal communications grid, I'm sorry we lost you for a moment there . . . Is everything alright, over?"

Jay opened a channel, "RFC this is Reeper. Everything's good down here. We thought you'd forgotten us." She added, "You guys had better sort yourselves out. We still have your boss on board."

Phoney laughter followed before Stein enquired, "I'm showing readings you've disconnected your suits already. Is everything okay in there?"

Her contested response was convincing. "We've been parked up for over six minutes!"

Stein responded but nobody paid it much attention as in that same instant the light flashed to green signalling the tube was now attached to the hull of the ship.

Stein wanted to ask if they had Palene with them, but Gibbs and two of his marines returned from the rear entry of the RFC, so instead he instructed, "Jay you are free to disembark."

Stein's *permission to leave* was appreciated but of course no reply to his enquiry came, as within seconds the crew and passengers of the Reeper had indeed felt free to disembark, only heavily armed and hidden behind the connection tube on the hangar floor.

*

"What the hell is that thing?" Truewick's awe summed up the thoughts of the three troops within the now deserted RFC.

Gibb's squad had ushered the room's personnel to the shower facilities where they would be locked away for their '*own safety*.' Only Gibbs, Truewick and Chris Andrews had returned to ensure the RFC remained under their control.

Stein watched the hangar as the boarding tube connected, concerned by Jay's lack of response. He hoped it was a problem with the portable communication network that would not yet be fully up and running. "It's a flight simulator. Top secret . . . Built for state of the art concepts in the development of deep space flight." He glanced at Truewick who continued to stare out of the digitised window, "But you didn't hear that from me." He sensed they were not convinced, "I need not remind you gentlemen what you see here does not exist. The world doesn't need to know how far we've developed our ingenuity."

Gibbs stared at the man in front of him. His perfect lab coat and imperfect demeanour as much a uniform to his nature as fatigues and weapons were testament to their own. "There's no need for such reminders. We're here to carry out our duty, nothing more."

Stein eyed the powerful looking Marine and smiled thinly.

Sergeant Andy Medlam transmitted from the shower rooms. "All prisoners are secure. We've left Kev and Sean guarding them, we're heading for the next target now."

Gibbs flashed Truewick and Chris a glance as he replied, "We're on our way down . . . Just as soon as the targets are in open view."

"They'll exit the simulator any time now. I can assure you they'll have no reason to suspect . . . " Stein's words dried up in immediate panic, his eyes wide as he tried to make sense of what he now saw.

Gibbs quickly followed the shocked stare of the scientist before turning back to him with a look of disgust, a look then followed by immediate intent. Gibbs opened his intercom, "We have a situation . . . Targets are on the hangar floor and are heading for the east side wall opposite your intended position . . . Targets are armed, I repeat . . . Targets are armed."

CHAPTER NINETY

Dorey's team sprinted to the far side of the hangar. Beneath their feet the floor rumbled and boomed, the river below not yet fully subdued.

They crouched next to the sealed entry, the doctor shuffling forward through the pack allowing his eye to be scanned before hitting a code on the touch pad.

Stein quickly relayed all he saw to a now furious Finch, "No Sir, there's no way through, even if he had an override. The hangar is magnetically sealed for six minutes or until the computer deems it safe to unlock the facility. Do you have men covering that exit?"

"Luckily for you I have men on the way despite your prior reassurances!"

Finch's hostile tone tore through Stein's communicator, so much so he almost feared to describe what he witnessed next. He stammered unable to understand, "Mr Finch the service door is opening," his panic was building, "It's not possible. The hangar should remain magnetically sealed."

Finch blazed, "Then it would appear we have once again underestimated Brookes. Just as I've seriously overestimated you."

Stein winced at the reprimand.

"Are you certain this Palene is not with them?"

"I only see our people. The cameras are zoomed in on them as we speak."

"Stay off the airwaves, I need to co-ordinate my troops. Send droids into the ship. Report only if you deem it absolutely necessary." He needed to ensure Palene was not hidden on board but could not have soldiers sniffing around the Reeper.

Stein watched as Brookes and the others rolled beneath the raising hangar door and on into the walkway beyond. His head was buzzing and the best he could manage was an obedient, "Yes Sir."

Below, Dorey and Dial advanced down the walkway. Although some of the team members had ventured into this corridor previously, none knew it in detail. Their goggles allowed them to peer around the sloping bend without having to risk an exposed head.

The duo noted the distance before the intersection, a crossroad which brought Tech Corridor Six and Research Route Seven directly into their own corridor's path.

Dorey signalled the rest who moved up and assembled around the Commander and Dial. "The two intersecting corridors are in front of us. Our elevator is at the far end beyond. We'll move within two metres of the entry mouths. Dial and I will then hit the adjoining corridors with stun devices. We'll pass the intersection as a group wedged between the shields. Once crossed, Marco use your barrier to protect our rear, Deans cover the front until we're certain nobody's waiting for us in that lift."

*

Gibbs and his men awaited the detour to reach their combat displays. As they held their position, only Gibbs had the pleasure of hearing this man Finch directly.

"We have an American team led by Major Hardcastle ready to infiltrate the incoming alleyways from Tech Six and Research Route Seven. They'll be in position to intercept in a few moments." Finch emphasised, "I'll tell you what I told them . . . I don't want any of these people hurt. Only stun devices are to be used until I say different."

John Gibbs knew Major Hardcastle. He was an experienced soldier who looked out for those in his command, though he had a reputation for being ruthless in the field. "Copy that. Can you give me anything else . . . A make on the weaponry and armour we're likely to come up against?"

"Our cameras show rifles in hand. They'll each be armed with Gloch 7 pistols, all have mini-mag and stun round capability. They have state of the art combat goggles so you'll need countermeasures. They're wearing lightweight Zenith battle armour and are carrying two bullet shields . . . Highly effective, all top of the range."

"Grenades or charges?"

"They had access to both stun and flash grenades as well as *timer explosives*. But Doctor Brookes is with them, and I don't believe he could ever damage these walls."

Gibbs raised an eyebrow as he turned and relayed the information to his men. "Why would they be heavily armed inside a simulator?"

Gibbs flashed Truewick a stern look. "Maybe they *really* wanted to pass the flight test!" The quip was enough to quell any further enquiry. "Hardcastle and a team of his marines are on an intercept course. They're going to hit them next to the service lift. We're heading two levels down to access a large engineering vent. The co-ordinates will be on our screens any second. This will lead us into the lift shaft in question. We need to head there at speed. Back up, should the Yanks miss their target."

Truewick once again raised his concerns. "We're going to hit them with stun rounds when they're all wearing battle armour? What will they be firing back at us?"

"We won't know until it happens." Gibbs wasted little time, "Let's go!"

Dial crept to the mouth of Tech Corridor Six, his goggles adjusting so they may peer through the solid curve of the wall. Nothing was illustrated, though countermeasures to such devices would have almost certainly been called upon by any would-be ambusher, measures like those already employed and activated by Dorey's team's own combat suits. Next was the sonic ear built into the helmets. Once again there was nothing, though experienced marines would have also deployed a defence against such procedures.

The lights beyond were deactivated as was the norm when not in use, the opposing tunnels shrouded in darkness until a passer-through would trigger the illumination.

Dial leaned back slowly and produced a small high intensity cyalume ball from his jacket. He activated the gold florescent liquid within to glow albeit under a membrane whose shroud wouldn't retract until the order was given. He then reached into a second pocket and pulled out a small but potent stun grenade.

Dorey silently replicated Dial's actions at the opposite entrance. Thanks to the curve of the corridor he was just out of view of the opening across from him.

Their combat goggles prepared, the boosted hearing deactivating as their suits, helmets and implants picked up the tell-tale signatures of the grenades, their bodily enhancements tuned to all of their personalised weaponry and defence capabilities. They had several orb cameras in their possession, but rolling the tiny balls down each corridor to gain a further advancement of sight would only alert any awaiting force to their presence.

Dorey gestured to Marco and Deans who readied themselves with the shields. He then signalled Jay and the others to get between the barricades, ready to breach the crossroads with Brookes in hand. In time with the flash of the grenades and glare of the cyalumes, Marco and Deans would provide a wall of cover. Once across the four-metre gaps they could make a dash for the large elevator entrance further down the sloping corridor. From there Brookes could set about the override and bring down the lift which would spirit them to his hidden lair, as Dorey and the others took up defensive positions at his rear.

A bead of sweat trickled down Brooke's forehead. He stared wide-eyed as Marco and Deans moved quietly into position, with Benny taking a firm grip of the doctor's arm. Jim continued to keep aim at their rear.

They couldn't know if there was anyone waiting in the dark corridors beyond, but they knew it was exactly where they would position themselves if roles were reversed.

All they could hope was their speedy exit from the Reeper had given them a head start against any would-be pursuer.

Major Hardcastle knelt in the darkness of the corridor with his men behind him. He went over the readings via the display of his combat visor. The entrance to the main corridor was around the next bend and so far he was showing no immediate signs of life emanating from it. He'd just received a signal from the corridor opposite his second team were assembled and in position. He studied the readings again for any trace of jamming static which would betray the fact he and his men were expected. He silently placed orders into his arm's keypad. His men were to move in slowly. They would then hold within the shadows, while he took a closer reading of the larger corridor beyond.

His men's visors illustrated the order and he and his marines advanced without a sound.

They each took a deep breath as Dorey and Dial activated their projectiles, *'Five . . . four . . . three . . .'* As the countdown of their devices neared its climax the projectiles were launched into the corridors beyond. The powerful stun grenades hit out with a loud thud accompanied by the flash of a glittering white shower. In the same instant both cyalumes were activated, the adjoining corridors bursting into a bright illumination.

"Down . . . Down," Came an American accent as Marco and Deans led the huddled group across the intersecting corridors.

"We've got contacts!"

On each flank silhouettes of soldiers were illuminated as they began hitting the deck. Within seconds a rain of gunfire was trained on the shields. Marco and Deans buckled under the force as Dorey and the others huddled to support them. "Walk!" Marco yelled once satisfied they were still safe within the sandwich of their barricades.

As they crossed the corridor the shields were bombarded with round after round.

"They're using stun-ammo!" Dial shouted.

Although *stun rounds* lacked the killing intensity of a standard bullet, without shielding to counter them they could easily maim their victim with a direct hit.

As Marco and Deans held their ground they were then hit by knock-down rounds from either side. They pounded into the shields like bowling balls fired from cannon. The huddled group leaned into one another, narrowly averting a heavy tumble.

As they crossed the chaos of the tunnel mouths they managed to count at least six soldiers closing in from each respective alleyway.

Once back in the protection of the corridor Dorey ordered a volley of shots be sent across the entries of both adjoining walkways, the live ammo reducing much of the intersection to dust and debris. "Get Brookes to that control panel!"

Carl dragged Brookes behind the cover of Dean's barricade and the three headed at speed toward their escape route. Those remaining fanned out on either side of Marco's shield and let rip with another volley before making a more composed retreat.

Dorey addressed his attackers, "Hold your position . . . We are not firing stun rounds! We don't want to see anyone hurt. Believe me we're all on the same side here."

The following silence was short-lived, shattered by Dial's astute warning, "Chasers!"

They bolstered the cover of the shield as dummy chasers suddenly flew around the corner in a flashing swarm, splattering the walls before several hit the shield's surface. The volley sent Marco backward into the crouching group now leaning all their weight behind him. "Jesus." Marco yelled as he fought the strikes.

Dial let off a rage of counter fire and again the corridor mouths on both sides were splattered with hits, filling the walkway with more choking dust.

Dorey's team had no intention of using mini-mag chasers with live rounds, and they would resist loading their new seeker option, which meant the attacking marines remained relatively safe while out of sight.

The Major sent another barrage of dummy chasers into Dorey's quickly retreating group.

They flew around the corner like angry bees. The few that hit were dealt with, the defence more than up to the task.

Hardcastle brought his men closer to the tunnel mouth. His enemy were employing a more lethal capability and he was pleased they'd so far refrained from using such an arsenal to full effect. His foe seemed reluctant to inflict harm for the time being.

He would take this sentiment gladly while his own men remained under strict orders to use only stun ammunition.

Each Marine group approached the edge of the crossroad behind their own battle shields. Hardcastle let both soldiers holding the devices know what he expected then made ready for the full assault. "Lay down your weapons. We have no wish to harm any of you . . . But we have orders to secure this area and stop you from advancing further. Don't force me into using live ammunition."

Dorey and the others were now shuffling down the corridor. "How's that door coming?"

Carl looked on anxiously as Dorey and the others came into view. He then stared at Brookes as he battled against the system which refused any access at the first attempt.

Despite this the doctor nodded confidently.

"Elevator is on the way." Carl replied.

CHAPTER NINETY ONE

Gibbs looked up apprehensively as the cables began to grind. He and his men had entered the darkness of the shaft after promises the elevator would be kept out of use. However, as the lift car stuttered down another level such assurances appeared flawed.

His team were to continue into the base of the shaft to intercept the perceived destination of their targets, a disused service tunnel some thirty metres below their current position.

Stein had identified the earlier power surge as emanating from this area, and the tunnel in question was the only stop available if Brookes were to take the elevator toward it.

Details of any such anomaly had not found there way to John Gibbs of course.

The lift continued to stop and start clumsily as it struggled from its perch in the upper levels. The muffled gunfire high above Gibb's position suggested his targets would be desperate to have the car meet them as soon as possible, and as the thick greased cables in the centre drop began to operate more fluidly, Gibbs realised he and his men could soon be out of time. They glided down into the abyss using their abseil lines.

Truewick and Chris were the first to reach their destination, landing on broad beams running across the shaft, adjacent to the sealed doors of the intended corridor.

"What the hell?" Truewick whispered as Sean slid down to join them on the beams.

"What is it?"

The rest of the team were soon landing one by one beside them.

"The draft coming up at us."

They crowded Truewick as he spoke. "What about it?"

Truewick scanned the drop beneath the beams. "These girders are here to protect the lift mechanism just below us. The elevator car rests here as it opens onto the corridor there." He pointed to the sealed entry they had been sent to infiltrate. "The data received states this is the base of the shaft, the last stop down. But look at the cable mechanism there." The night vision of their combat goggles illustrated him perfectly as he pointed to the device some four metres below, "The cables continue right through the floor. Yet according to the blueprints that's supposed to be solid rock. But how can it be?"

Chris Andrews pulled the powerful scanner from his back pack. "I'm getting energy readings. The source appears scrambled. It's coming from somewhere further down."

High above, the lift car dropped another level, coaxed one step closer to the gun battle.

Truewick continued, "I've seen something similar to this in an illegal mine. We should check for evidence these beams are able to retract into the walls. Take a look down there to see if it's a false floor holding a false cable mechanism. If so, you may find the lift car heads further down than the blueprints suggest. If we force these doors and enter that corridor, what happens if the lift just passes by, travelling down into some hidden lair?"

Chris pointed to the surface below. "According to my readings the floor has a fine split cut right across its centre, just below the elevator mechanism itself."

More gun fire echoed as the cables stuttered once again.

Gibbs had strict instructions to intercept the targets at all costs. If what Truewick and Chris suspected was correct, then this qualified as a risk which needed exploring.

He cursed, "Alright, Truewick check it out. But move fast, I don't want you trapped if there's nothing down there." He pointed at the sealed entry next to them. "Force those doors open . . . I'll check for any evidence these beams can retract."

*

Tom Hardcastle advanced behind the shield held by one of his soldiers. As they reached the sloping bend of the corridor he rolled out a handful of orb cameras to transmit an advanced view into his eyepiece. As they rolled around the curve however, each of them was hit with gunfire which came at a startling rate of both speed and accuracy.

His combat goggles couldn't transcend the density of the arcing corridor walls, so he pulled out a remote eye. Its bendy wire arm began peering around the edge, but as it extended, the lens was blown off almost immediately by more fire. "God damn it!" He would have to check out the situation a little more directly than preferred. Utilising his shield carrier he prepared to peer around the bend toward the lift. As he did the action was met by another intense barrage of fire. The rounds pounded into the shield.

"Pull back . . . Jesus!" He pressed himself against the protection of the corridor.

Things were not going to plan. The adversary using his shield to provide a rearguard for those he hunted proved adept at holding off their barrage of stun ammunition. Their quarry also had the defensive advantage provided by the curve of the corridor. And he was growing rapidly annoyed at the voice of Finch yelling garbled instructions to his ear, the likes of which now attacked his senses once more. "They're firing live rounds Sir!" Hardcastle then snarled at what he heard over his intercom, "Well I'm just ecstatic you think they're missing on purpose. Tell that to my man Johnston who's just had a finger blown off!" He scowled as more orders came through, all of them preaching minimal force. After a moment he lost all diplomacy. "These are my men being shot at!" Hardcastle was not the kind of man to be barked at while taking fire. "Now there are only two real options," he boomed, "I can either withdraw, or I attempt to take them down . . . Now make a decision!"

*

Carl was relieved as he yelled, "The elevator is here!"

Brookes had battled the complex for five minutes in order to get the lift to the correct floor. It had been jammed just three metres above them for two of those.

The huge steel doors of the lift car finally opened, Deans providing cover with the shield as the others prepared for any incoming assault. It was empty.

"Okay everyone inside."

Nobody needed telling twice.

Marco and Deans covered the lift entrance with the two battered shields.

The doctor moved forward allowing his eye to be scanned before pressing his thumb to the plate. He typed a code onto the row of numberless digits which appeared at the bottom of the touch pad. The girders at the base of the lift shaft would now retract, the false elevator machinery would withdraw and the floor holding it would open, clearing their entry into Brooke's hidden complex below.

Dorey's team let rip with a thunderous wall of cover fire as the lift doors began to close. Despite the noise the sudden warning yelled by both Deans and Marco was unmistakable. "Grenade!"

A tremendous explosive force whipped through the partially open doors.

Marco and Deans were blown back, the shields smashing into the shell of their headgear. The team's implants quickly induced countermeasures to defend their eyes and ears, but as they hit the floor the shockwave battered their senses despite any protection provided.

Smoke filled the air as sparks offered a brief moment of illumination before the lift fell back into darkness, the night vision of their goggles struggling to kick in.

Before they could regain any equilibrium, a horrible sound shuddered through the elevator walls. It was a sound reminiscent of a sinking ship, its metal hull buckling under the weight of consuming water. This was followed by a sickening crack and before anyone realised what was happening, they were sent plummeting down the shaft as the elevator fell into the pit.

CHAPTER NINETY TWO

Dorey's back ached viciously. The pressure built within his lungs. He coughed to relieve the choke but his hearing did not return any evidence of such an action.

Instead there was just a high-pitched hum.

Eventually, between the random flashes of light sparked by the broken circuitry of the lift car, he found he could make sense of the silhouette in front of him. An animated face shouting through the smoke and dust . . . It was Jay. "Are you alright?"

His equilibrium returned, the hum dropping to a whistle.

"Dorey, are you . . ?" The volume of her panic seemed suddenly disturbing and unreal.

He held up his hand and nodded when without warning, the elevator car flooded with the golden light of a cyalume. The adjustment jolted his eyes into their sockets before the goggles snapped back on line.

It was Dial, his face blackened with dirt. He tore off his helmet, annoyed by the crackling circuitry of the wrecked headset.

As their senses began to adjust they realised they were not the only ones showing signs of coming around, as splutters and groans echoed throughout the beaten car.

Once on his feet Dorey realised his own body was intact though his face contorted into concern as he noticed the blood dripping from Jay's right eye. He reached for her.

"I'm alright."

"You're sure?"

"Dorey I'm fine."

Once satisfied he scanned the destruction. Dial was pulling Benny to his feet.

Carl at the far side of the carnage checked the status of the elevator. "The emergency breaking system may have slowed our descent. But I think we fell straight to the bottom." He pointed at the twisted hole which had been the doorway only moments earlier. "There are sealed doors up there."

Through the debris some six feet above where the lift had come to rest was the base of two steel doors cut into the rock of the shaft. "They must lead to a corridor beyond."

As Carl spoke, Jay discovered one of their fallen comrades, "Jim?"

He was scrunched in the corner, his head bleeding at his right temple. "I'm okay."

Jay was relieved to see him stand slowly, albeit with the help of the bruised elevator wall.

Three of their numbers were still unaccounted for.

Those who'd protected the lift entry with their shields, and Isimbard Brookes.

"Marco . . . Deans," Jay yelled.

As they sifted through the debris they heard a groan followed by the unmistakable voice of Brookes. "Help me . . . Will somebody help me?"

The walking injured followed the voice of the groaning doctor.

It was then they all saw their worst fears realised.

"Marco?" Carl's eyes fell upon the face of his friend, trapped behind the shredded, distorted armour of the shield and a cross-section of the large elevator door.

He'd held the shield firm against the blast of the grenade and was blown across the lift like a rag doll for his effort. His body bent and twisted.

As they moved closer they could see the panic-stricken figure of Brookes, trapped directly underneath Marco's lifeless body. "Help me," he choked.

Marco had not only saved them from the blast but his body had shielded Brookes from the devastation completely. So much so, as they carefully pulled him clear of the broken human being on top of him, he was not even dirtied to any great extent by the explosion. In the sudden grief and dusty confusion he looked somewhat surreally immaculate.

With the doctor pulled clear, Carl leaned close to Marco checking his vital signs.

There was nothing.

"Deans!" Jay pointed to the second pile of broken doorway. "Deans," she yelled a second time moving a steel cross section away with care. No response came.

Jay and Dial pulled away the debris, followed by Deans' battered shield, his fists like Marco's, still clenching the handles. His helmet was cracked, his face covered in blood.

"I'm sorry . . . I'm so sorry," Brookes was clearly in shock. "I couldn't override the system quickly enough . . ." his voice trailed away.

In the carnage of the moment nobody had given a thought to their pursuing attackers. In fact, nobody even knew for sure how long ago the explosion had taken place.

Dorey suddenly became aware of this fact. He composed himself, taking off his helmet and hitting the reset. Within seconds he'd managed to reboot the data logged inside the battered circuitry. He put it on and checked the visual display through the half-twisted eyepiece he was able to pull from the inner rim.

Two minutes had passed since the lift entrance was hit.

Jay continued to check Deans with Dial crouched next to her. She looked up as Dorey's eyes fell into hers. She shook her head with a grim expression, he appeared in bad shape.

"We have to get out of here." The Commander declared. He knew the soldiers would soon be on them. "Grab a weapon . . . Grab anything you can salvage."

Nobody but Dial responded.

"I said grab a weapon . . . We're getting out of here now!" The demand slapped everyone from the threat of grief and all present were suddenly aware of the soldier's movements above, preparing to make their way down. They were not out of this yet.

Carl lifted Marco's eyelid in the feeble hope his friend may still have a chance. He was expecting disappointment but his heart raced as he was compelled to take a closer look. He leaned closer, "Wait!" His hope was then confirmed as the pupil in Marco's eye clearly dilated. "There it is again . . . He's still alive."

Brookes fought through his shock and examined him. "Just barely," his dark articulation returned them abruptly to the reality of his situation, "I don't think he'll make it."

Suddenly, they were interrupted by an astonished shout from Jay, "Deans?"

The group turned toward her and were stunned to see Deans open his eyes and cough.

"Deans . . . Are you alright?"

Jay nearly fell over as he lifted his hand and gingerly rubbed his head. Only a moment ago he'd appeared dead as a post. He began to move, an action which shocked further.

"What the fuck just happened?" He said in a rusty effort, wiping blood from his eyes.

"There was an explosion."

Dial and Benny heard the sound of ropes crashing onto the roof. They flashed a look of concern to Dorey who of course understood the implications.

"Jay . . . See if he can move."

She was about to relay the question when Deans gave her a wilful stare. "I can move." He gestured for Jay and Jim to help him to his feet.

Dorey turned to Brookes, "Can we move Marco?"

"My guess is he'll be dead within minutes." Brookes replied sadly.

"Then we've nothing to lose." He turned to his colleague, "Jim?"

He nodded, "I'll carry him."

The sound of more ropes hitting the ceiling stirred the adrenaline.

Brookes understood the need for hope, the man crumpled on the ground was the reason he was still alive. "In the chamber where I keep Palene . . . I have the equipment necessary to at least offer him some chance, slim as it will be."

Dorey, Benny and Dial stacked a pile of debris to form a step up to the shaft doors of the corridor as Jim gingerly pulled Marco onto his shoulder with the assistance of Brookes.

"Grab those shards there and try to force open the entrance." Dorey demanded, "Deans, are you sure you can move?"

The battered man held himself up against Jay's careful grasp. "I'm sure."

Benny had a result opening the doors. As they parted a chorus of American accents could be heard shouting instructions and ideas, it wasn't audible but the tone was clear.

They were in the shaft directly above them.

As they forced the doors they were relieved to see the walkway beyond was clear. They jammed the metal shards into the gaps as wedges to keep the entry open.

Jim and Brookes brought Marco's body to the exit as Dial and Benny scrambled up onto the corridor floor. They slid through the gap between the cut of the shaft and the ceiling of the elevator and within moments were carefully pulling their fallen colleague onto the ledge of the corridor. They repeated the action with Brookes.

Deans yelped as he was pulled through the gap, quickly followed by Jay.

Once his team were all out and inside the corridor Dorey made his exit.

Dial set about kicking the wedges keeping the doors open but they didn't budge.

"Leave them. Let's just get out of here!"

Marco was placed into a fireman's carry over Jim's broad shoulder.

Benny and Dial took one arm each of the injured Deans, sandwiching him securely.

Weapons were drawn as Brookes quickly led the way. "Just around the corner," his voice betrayed his concern, "But we need to climb up another level via a ladder."

"A ladder?" Jim was still bleeding as he carried the battered Marco.

"We've fallen straight down into the original unfinished corridor." The doctor replied, "Construction was halted here because of the rock density ahead . . . The engineers decided it would be easier to stop and raise it by two metres. But they cut a service hatch through in order to work from both ends. An access shoot, leading up to the completed corridor. It opens like a manhole onto the walkway above us."

"You mean we're in the wrong secret corridor?"

"The lift must have dropped us a level down breaking through the safety appliances."

They rounded the bend and Brookes pointed out the tubular entry cut into the ceiling ahead. As promised, ladders led to the base of the sealed hatch.

A sign on it read, '*Emergency Power. Air Filtration SY2*'

Brookes quickly implemented the required procedures to see the hatch release. The circular cover hissed and spun automatically and within a second the disk dropped revealing a wide tubular shaft climbing a further two metres.

Embedded in the wall just over half way up the vertical climb was a phoney emergency power reset for the Air Filtration. The ladder appeared to lead to nothing else, but as Brookes headed up he soon revealed another hidden panel. Again he busied away, and within moments the ceiling structure above his head began to morph like liquid rock, revealing a second sealed hatch cover. His DNA was scanned as he tapped in another code, the now exposed hatch lid hissing open. As it popped upward it brought with it a cool breeze from the air conditioned corridor above.

Deans insisted he could make it alone and a discussion immediately broke out into solving the problem of lifting Marco.

Brookes peered down from the vertical tube and asked in a whisper. "Shall I go up?"

Dorey checked their rear, listening for the pursuing soldiers. He flashed a glance to Jay, "Follow him up there and check it out."

The doctor made his way up the remaining run of steps with Jay snapping at his heels, her rifle dangling from its strap as she went. After peering through, he disappeared into the corridor above, quickly followed by Jay.

Below, Dial scowled suddenly. He turned with concern to Dorey. "Wait . . ." The look intensified as he breathed in deeply, "Can you smell?" His intended enquiry into the suspicion he could detect a faint odour of aftershave required no response, as at that very moment a yelled warning from Jay was interrupted by an authoritative ultimatum.

"Drop your weapons," followed by, "We have your people at gunpoint. Lay down your arms and come up the ladder slowly . . . One at a time."

The accent was English.

They had just run into yet another batch of soldiers.

*

"We've got two wounded men down here . . . One of them can't climb the ladder."

"He can stay there until the rest of you are up here. But don't try anything stupid," the voice continued, "I have orders to apprehend you. Let's not force this into something it doesn't have to be."

Dorey turned to Dial and the others, at Marco's crumpled frame lifeless across Jim's shoulder. The men above had Brookes and Jay and he knew there was the imminent arrival of the American marines to worry about. They had nowhere else to go.

Although he could make a fight of it . . . It would be both bloody and costly.

"Alright! But I want the injured taken with Doctor Brookes to a room he has up there filled with medical equipment."

Gibbs was dubious. "There's no such room up here. It's just a dead end . . ."

Brookes interrupted his captor, "It's at the end of the passageway, hidden to the naked eye by a technology which disguises it. Only I have access in order to reveal it."

"Bullshit!"

Brookes held out his palms, "It's there I promise you . . . Disguised as part of the wall, utilising the same technique used to hide this very hatch," he pointed to the hole by their feet, "It's where we are headed. Why else would we be coming this way? It's the only thing down here."

"Judging by the way that lift crashed I'd say you had little choice in where you were headed."

Brookes implored, "We intended to enter on this level but the blast took us further down."

"Yeah we heard the blast." Gibbs stared at Jay who had a rifle aimed on her, "Now let's cut the shit and get everyone up this ladder. We have a powerful scanner up here. We can see every move you make. If any of your group decides to fuck with me, then you'll leave these corridors zipped in a bag . . . The lady first . . . Do you understand?"

Dorey bristled at the faceless remark before dropping his weapons to the floor.

He gestured for the others to do the same aiming his eyes toward the open hatch above, "We understand."

CHAPTER NINETY THREE

Gibbs was midway through another attempt to update the rest of his team. They'd been separated by the falling elevator only minutes after Truewick's hunch proved correct.

The false floor discovered had indeed opened to receive the lift car. Gibbs had one group cover the original target corridor above while he, Kev, Chris and Truewick examined the newly-discovered entry some ten metres below where the girders had been.

They'd forced open the shaft doors to reveal a hidden corridor. As they went inside to investigate the four were shocked to hear the lift plummet moments later.

The falling car left debris jamming their entry back into the shaft and as they returned from searching the corridor for a route down, luck had placed them close to the now visible hatch, its seal suddenly popping open from the previously solid floor.

Moments later, Brookes and the woman had climbed out straight into their sights.

The signal throughout the shaft had proved poor to begin with. Since the collapse of the elevator sealed them inside this new hidden walkway, it had worsened considerably.

"No, we're still on the floor directly beneath you," Gibbs relayed to Sergeant Medlam, "But it turns out there was yet another smaller corridor underneath this one. We caught them as they were climbing through a hatch. They're disarmed and have casualties, one man severely wounded." There was a pause as the static filled reply was broadcast into his ear. Gibbs squinted as he tried to understand. Something on this level was wreaking havoc with their kit. "Look, I need you to contact this Finch on the following frequency. I can't seem to transmit any further than you, even this is proving difficult. Our equipment seems to be deteriorating rapidly in here." He cursed the failing technology. "Tell him we've apprehended the suspects and are awaiting further instruction."

His men's aim never left the prisoners, now stood with their palms pressed to the wall.

Dorey almost spat as Gibbs finished his call. He gestured toward Marco who had been left at the base of the hatch. "He's badly injured for God's sake."

Brookes began explaining once again how he was in fact the man in charge of the complex. He warned them they were making a mistake. How they were taking orders from corrupt people without proper authority. It fell on deaf ears.

"We know who you are Doctor Brookes and it would appear you're no longer in charge." Gibbs cast another curious eye over the injured man struggling to stay upright between the woman and the German. His heavily-bloodied features when he'd struggled up the ladder, continued to trouble him somehow.

"Colour Sergeant Gibbs this is Major Hardcastle do you read me over?"

'He must be close to sound so clear.' He opened a channel, "This is Gibbs . . . Go ahead."

"Gibbs I've been trying to contact you these past minutes but the radio's all scrambled to shit. I understand from your man Medlam you've just apprehended the suspects."

"That's correct Major. They have two badly . . ."

Hardcastle interrupted, "We're closing in on your position. We couldn't get through the shaft doors onto your floor, there are twisted girders all over them."

"Yeah and who's fault is that?'

"We've headed back to the crashed elevator car to cut through the escape hatch. Am I to understand there's a corridor leading from the elevator to your current position . . . Over?"

"That's correct Major. Head down the corridor and you'll soon come across a wounded man laid out on the floor. He's directly below us at the base of a hatch . . . He's dying."

"I'm sorry to hear that. What is the status of you and your men?"

"I'm cut off from Sergeant Medlam and the rest of my group. There are four of us down here holding eight prisoners. They've been stripped of all weapons. They have a Doctor Brookes with them. He's told us of a room within this very corridor containing advanced medical equipment which could help save the wounded."

"That's horse shit," the Major boomed, "You leave that man where he is . . . Understood?" Once again Hardcastle did not wait for any response, "Keep the prisoners static until I get there. The hatch on the elevator is jammed. It's reinforced steel so it's gonna take a few minutes to cut."

Gibbs was beginning to lose patience with the guy barking at him, no doubt the same man who almost killed he and his men in the lift shaft. "Major, this man will die if I . . ."

Hardcastle cut him short, "I understand son, but you have to listen to me. These guys will lead you into a trap if you allow them. They're extremely dangerous. I've left men throughout the shaft relaying information directly to Finch on the surface. I must make this clear, these orders come from the top. If their man dies, nobody's gonna blame you."

'Gung-ho bastard,' Gibbs thought, *'Blowing up a lift which was headed*

straight to me and my men anyway.' Gibbs looked to the captives, *'The Major was right though . . . Probably would be a trap.'*

"Gibbs, do we understand each other?" The Major's voice crackled into his headset.

"Of course Major," Gibbs replied, "You're the boss."

"No . . . Finch is." Hardcastle's tone betrayed a first sign of regret, "Be with you shortly."

As the intercom clicked shut Gibbs relayed the orders to his men. "We're waiting here for a couple of minutes until the Americans meet up with us."

Dorey's concern for Marco grew. "He might not have a couple of minutes."

The Colour Sergeant's tone appeared final. "We're waiting! That noise you can hear is the Yanks cutting through the lift. They'll be here any time. Then I promise you, I'll get your man some medical attention."

Deans in his battered shape had allowed his focus to drift since he'd climbed the ladders, the pain of standing palms to the wall getting the better of him. He was succumbing to a concussion, yet suddenly, the realisation hit him. He actually recognised their head captor's voice. He dragged himself back from the abyss, slowly turning his head.

"Hey . . ." Truewick raised his weapon, "What do you think you're doing?"

Deans ignored him and continued to turn.

Truewick made a very deliberate aim as if preparing to shoot. "One more move and your head will be a stain on that wall . . . Do you hear me?"

Gibbs edged forward, his stare closely fixed on the struggling prisoner once more.

"John? It is you isn't it?" Deans enquired somewhat blearily.

Gibb's mouth dropped. The bloodied mess he'd seen climb the stairs suddenly matched the unmistakable voice. "Shit," he said in disbelief, "Dennis?"

Deans managed a smile as he looked upon his old friend, "It's been a long time John."

*

Sergeant Medlam and his specialists continued with their attempts to prise a way through the battered shaft doors. They'd little by means of tools and the twisted steel offered stiff opposition. They could hear Major Hardcastle and his men cutting through the fallen lift car beyond and were able to share communications with their better equipped allies, albeit through another garbled connection.

What they couldn't understand, was why they were unable to keep in contact with Gibbs who was only a few metres below them. Since their last transmission Medlam could do nothing to locate their leader's transmission frequency. It made little sense.

He turned to Shalley who continued to try with the use of the emergency radio.

"Still nothing but static . . . This thing can transmit into space if it has to. I just don't get it."

"Hardcastle and his men should be with them any time now. If John has secured the targets we won't be missed." Medlam checked his watch. "Try the Major again. See if he's any closer in sparing a couple of men to cut through to our position."

Hardcastle scowled as his men made slow work of the roof. The escape hatch had warped with the impact and cutting through the stubborn steel was proving tough.

"As soon as we've reached Gibbs and the prisoners," he replied, "Once I've assessed the situation I'll get back to you. That's the best I can offer right now."

As he ended his dialogue with the stranded Royal Marines, his Corporal turned to him in the cyalume-illuminated shaft. "We're getting there Sir." He mopped his forehead.

Hardcastle grunted as he looked upon the surprisingly slow progress made by the portable cutting torches. *'Not quickly enough.'*

*

Gibbs stared at Deans astonished, "Jesus Dennis, what the hell are you doing here?"

Deans struggled to stretch his smile.

"I heard you'd been injured . . . Retired and gone State-side." Gibbs continued.

Dean's head was aching, the internal injuries beginning to take their toll. "I heard the same rumour . . . They didn't exactly hurt, what with my chosen career direction."

Gibbs nodded. He understood, he'd always understood. He and Dennis had gone through basic together at the Marines training establishment at Lympstone. Eight months of conditioning in order to gain the coveted Green Beret. They'd gone on to serve together for three years as snipers at a time when the political climate was to ensure this would be a truly awful position to fill. They had got their hands and consciences dirty.

When eventually their choices sent them their separate ways they remained close friends. However, as the years passed they'd gradually drifted apart. Deans never made any secret of his desire to get involved within the intelligence world of WAIG, and when the opportunity called he'd been keen to enlist.

Being a spy was tough on any friendship, made all the more difficult when the other involved was also constantly sent to the far reaches of nowhere in order to do battle.

Months, sometimes years would pass without Gibbs hearing anything from his once closest of friends. Eventually they'd just stopped making the effort, reduced to nothing more than a message at Christmas, until even this small gesture ceased.

Gibbs was clearly taken aback but he didn't lose his focus. He kept his gun ready, "You don't look too good." His concern was sincere.

"I'm more anxious about our man down there." Dean's response was a bold one.

"We'll be moving him soon . . . Once the Yanks get here."

"You said that five minutes ago, sounds like they're still struggling to get through."

"If the elevator escape hatch has jammed they'll be cutting into super reinforced steel," Brookes protested, but he was quickly silenced by Truewick.

Gibbs edged a little closer. "I'm just following orders."

"I know." Deans burned his bleary eyes into the gaze of his old friend. "But those orders will sign his death warrant. At least give him a chance. He's a good man John."

Gibbs was aware of the concern now growing within Truewick, Kev and Chris as they watched the conversation unfold. His gun remained poised. "I'm sure he is . . . But right now he's the enemy, and you know as well as anyone . . ."

"John . . ." Deans interrupted, "The shit going down here . . . It's not what it seems."

"Never is Dennis . . . you know that."

Deans closed his eyes, the focus required clearly becoming more of an effort, "You are on the wrong side here, I promise you you're on . . ."

"We don't take sides Den."

"Believe me you would on this occasion, if you had all the facts." Deans went on, "What have they told you? That we're terrorists, traitors . . . saboteurs?"

"It doesn't make a difference Deans, you know that."

"Who's giving the orders . . . A guy called Finch?"

No answer came.

"Is it Finch John?"

Gibbs shook his head slowly. "Listen Dennis you should really try and calm yourself, you're in bad shape. The Major and his men will be here any second . . . Then you can get your man down there to . . ."

"They'll move him upstairs John and you know it. That will kill him, as certain as you shooting him."

"I think you should shut up now Den, before . . ."

"Before what? Before you kill me too? John there's a room on this very corridor which could save that man's life. Nobody is going to try anything. You have all our weapons. All I'm asking is you take him to it and let the doctor get to work on him. You can wait for this Major of yours there and still hand us over. What difference does it make?"

Gibbs was growing irritated. "I'll tell you what difference it makes. We don't know what could be waiting for us in this so-called room of yours

. . . A room which I'm told doesn't exist. I don't know what you're trying to pull. And frankly Den, if it is a choice between you losing one of yours and me losing one of mine . . . Then you of all people should already know the outcome."

"And you honestly believe that's what I want? That getting inside this room is some kind of last chance play?" He squeezed his eyes shut, his mind felt like it was being sliced apart. He forced his gaze onto his friend once more. "Do you think I would endanger you or your men? We're trying to save people down here not kill them." His words trailed off as he lost his battle, his legs turned to jelly as he wilted.

He hit the floor with a sickening thud.

"Deans!" Jay yelled having to fight hard not to go to him.

Dorey sensed Dial's anger and quickly fired him a look which said, *'Don't move yet.'*

As fast as they were with their technological upgrades none were a match for a bullet. The fight would come only when the right moment introduced itself.

The Commander fired a viscous scowl at the colour Sergeant. "For Christ's sake . . . We are not the enemy . . . Finch is. He's taking control of this complex for his own ends."

Gibbs was clearly shaken at the sight of his old friend collapsing. He ignored Dorey but quickly bent down to check upon his health.

His comrades were not happy with this decision, "John." Chris declared, "Leave him."

"I'm checking him . . . Just cover them!" He shouted back.

The three Royal Marines tensed.

"John!" Kev yelled this time.

"Just cover them!" Gibbs replied angrily as he checked over Deans.

The situation was deteriorating.

"None of you move." Truewick yelled at the prisoners.

Dorey clenched, but was then greeted by an unexpected, but familiar sound, *"Three . . . two . . . "* It was the automated voice warning of an imminent explosion from one of their stun grenades. None of the marines could hear it . . . It was for the inner ears of Dorey's team alone. It had been activated by Deans.

"One." The voice spoke softly to their implants before the countermeasures were switched on to protect Dorey's band from the blast to follow.

As the hidden grenade detonated, its force lifted Deans two feet in the air, knocking Gibbs onto his back.

The shock wave kicked like a mule and for the second time that day their bodies were forced to endure a sudden blast. This was nothing in comparison to the elevator explosion of course, and with the advanced warning and internal countermeasures functioning, Dorey's team were quick to react.

Dorey hit Truewick so hard the specialist presumed the force throwing him to the floor was from the heavy duty pyrotechnic. A shot cracked from his rifle but he was quickly down, Dorey smashing a hand into his face, nearly knocking the Corporal out cold.

Jim swept the feet away from the Marine close to him, his powerful limb knocking Kev clean to the deck with a thud. They grappled momentarily but there could be only one winner, Jim quickly pinning his opponent firmly to the ground.

Chris Andrews was a different proposition. Although the blast knocked him off balance he managed to fire off two rounds. Carl lunged at him as he did, wincing as a bullet hit him in the shoulder. He and Chris fell to the floor and the specialist was quickly getting the better of the now injured German until Dial thrust an aggressive knee into the Marine's right cheek, sending him sprawling across the corridor.

Carl grabbed a weapon, the injury to the German's shoulder not serious thanks to his armour. He pointed it at the floored Marine as he struggled to regain his senses.

Gibbs clambered to his feet, only to be met by a pistol aimed on him from Dorey's extended arm. Heads pounded and ears whistled, but the implants of Dorey's troop had performed well and within seconds his team had taken away the Marine's upper hand.

They were now the warders, no longer the prisoners.

Brookes was more shaken than the rest. He didn't have the same combat implants as Dorey and the others and the blast had clearly come close to knocking him unconscious. He was an old man in comparison and it was a credit to him he was not out cold. Instead he struggled toward Deans, quickly checking on his state of health. The doctor's face was one of immediate concern. "We need to get him to my room. He's sustained further head injuries and that blast tore off his right hand." His voice was audibly shaky.

Their situation had changed in seconds but they were soon hit with another devastating blow, as Jay, wide-eyed and somewhat painfully struggled, "Dorey."

She was clutching the left side of her neck as slowly, she slid down the wall, a large smear of blood forming where she had stood.

"Jay!" Dorey jumped to her aid as the others shoved the prisoners against the wall.

She crumpled to the floor.

He inspected the wound which had sliced her jugular.

Dial was stood at the hatch aghast, the sound of the American Marines still cutting through the steel of the lift now present once again.

"Check Marco." Dorey bellowed as he pressed against the wound.

As Dial stared at Jay horrified, she somehow managed to nod encouragement.

He checked the coast was clear then dropped through the hatch to their critically injured comrade.

Dorey was desperate. "Try not to move . . . Just keep still."

Jay looked at him her colour draining, "Dorey . . . You have to get Brookes to that room."

Suddenly Dial's voice came booming through the hatch from the corridor below. "I need someone to throw me down that bastard's helmet."

Benny quickly removed the headgear worn by Gibbs and dropped it down to Dial. He donned it, activating the software housed in the eyepiece but its functions were scrambled. He cursed the deteriorating equipment and set about checking Marco unaided.

Brookes made his way to Jay. He saw the blood oozing, his eyes quickly betraying the diagnosis. "We need to get to that room."

She convulsed suddenly. Dorey held her, his right hand pressing the wound, the blood running freely despite his efforts. He took the weight of her head with his other hand. "Hold on baby." She was fading fast, "Jay . . . Focus on my voice."

She looked on him, her heartbeat slowing, her pulse dropping, "I love you." Her rasping, struggling voice betrayed the resignation, as a tear slid down her cheek.

"Jay!" He shouted this time, his voice cracking.

Jim and Carl guarded the prisoners, desperate to assist in some way.

"Jay!" Dorey's face contorted into agony as he watched her lose the struggle. He pushed his face close to hers and tried to shout her name only it came out as an inaudible squeal. He swallowed then yelled, this time with a force to wake the dead, "Jay!"

The life drained slowly from her warm brown eyes.

He felt his heart shatter into a million pieces.

The others watched helplessly.

Jim, his head still bleeding, turned toward the Marines with dark intentions.

None of the soldiers were under any illusion as to how delicately their own lives now hung in the balance.

Dorey groaned in anguish as her head dropped into the sole support of his hand. He still pressed against the wound, the blood pumping out between his fingers.

He leaned in close and whispered . . . But she had gone.

He held her and sobbed, then screamed, the rage so evident it could have emanated from hell itself. The doctor looked at Dorey and placed a concerned hand on his shoulder.

The Commander didn't look at him. He only looked at her.

"Dorey I . . ."

This time he did look at Brookes, his eyes now transformed into evil intent. He rested her chin gently, kissed her forehead, his eyes now flooding with tears as he whispered to her.

"Dorey?" The doctor said cautiously.

No response came as the Commander rose slowly, turning toward the captured Marines, his hands covered in blood. Brookes followed his movement, the horrible realisation of what was about to transpire now evident, "Dorey!" He demanded.

The Commander stood above the Marines.

Benny saw the lifeless Marco through the open hatch next to him then looked upon Jay. His finger readied itself on the trigger, a deep rage burning his belly.

It was Carl's turn to question Dorey's action. "Dorey it was an accident." He protested.

Jim was also quite clearly behind the Commander and Benny on this one. "Dorey, we instigated the attack."

The Commander did not even blink at Carl's troubled protest.

"This isn't what she would have wanted!"

Dorey cocked his pistol and Gibbs, Kev, Chris and Truewick were now extremely concerned with the way events were unfolding.

"Now just hold on a second." Gibbs implored, "Nobody wanted this to happen."

"None of us fired on you deliberately." Chris protested his eyes now wide with fear.

"This isn't right!" Truewick shouted.

Dorey stared down at them, his emotion and grief like poison devouring him. He aimed the pistol, his bloodied hands now the judge and the jury.

"Dorey don't fucking do it!" Carl demanded.

Jim and Benny made no such gesture. *'These fuckers killed Jay. Their allies had almost certainly killed Marco . . . Quite possibly Deans!'*

"I've got a family!" Kev bowed his head.

This seemed to enrage Dorey and he grabbed the Marine, hoisting him up with incredible force, the implants in his system running wild as the venom took over. The soldier must have weighed close to two hundred pounds yet Dorey lifted then crushed him against the wall like a child, "So did she!" He growled.

Gibbs stared in silent horror. He watched as his colleague was thrown back to the deck with impossible force.

The Commander altered his aim, the pistol now pointed at Gibbs directly. The tears returned as he prepared to fire, the rage so strong he could taste the death in his throat.

Gibbs closed his eyes as the gun's aim pressed.

"Don't do it!" Carl protested one last time.

He pulled into the trigger when suddenly the image of him falling from the cliff threw itself to the fore of his mind. He clenched his teeth as he revisited the moment his life was taken away . . . The day he himself had fallen-victim as the hunter. He could almost see Palene's face imploring compassion . . . Imploring him not to shoot. He felt the pain of losing Jay like a knife twisting his ribcage and yelled out as he squeezed the trigger, four shock-inducing shots tearing through the corridor.

As the moment of reckoning passed a silence took a hold of their surroundings.

Dial's head re-emerged from the hatch. He looked to Dorey holding the smoking pistol, its menacing aim breathing just above the cowering Marines who must have surely just stared death in the eye. He saw Brookes and Carl shocked but relieved, with Jim looking at the four huddled soldiers with a mixture of hatred and shame. "Marco is still alive!" Dial declared, "Benny I need you and Jim to help get him up here. I just heard part of the steel those Marines are cutting through snap." His voice sliced through the shock of the corridor. "Carl, have the prisoners carry Deans. If they give you any trouble, kill them!" He turned to Brookes, "Doctor, get up that corridor and open this secret door of yours. We have injured people here and a minute to evacuate this area at best." There was no judgement in his voice. It was calm, almost as cold as the moment. He looked at Jay's bloodied body and swallowed hard, then turned to Dorey who looked back at him numb.

Nobody moved at first. A surreal pause taking hold as Dial and Dorey held each others gaze, but the prompting was enough to break the spell, "You heard him!" Dorey declared.

As Carl ordered the shaken Royal Marines to their feet they each noted the bullet holes just centimetres above each of their heads.

Dorey crouched next to Jay his hands shaking as he scooped her up into his arms. His rage was now a distant memory. In its place the glow of the light was present in his mind, clearer than it had been during those dark days within the realms of his own death, more luminous than when inside the Reeper at Stonehenge.

In that moment he inexplicably felt the presence of Palene, and immediately felt his purpose altered. And only moments after witnessing his heart and soul destroyed, he found he knew exactly what had to be done.

CHAPTER NINETY FOUR

It had taken eight minutes to cut through the elevator. In that time Tom Hardcastle had lost all communication with the Marines in the lower depths of the complex. He'd demanded more efficient cutters be lowered into the shaft but was now having to relay messages up the vertical climb just to stay in contact with those above.

The magnetic interference devastated their combat systems and as the hole cut into the elevator grew so did the level of disturbance.

Orb cameras were dropped into the lift indicating the car below was empty, and as the final cut saw the hatch drop, the Major addressed his experienced Sergeant, Billy Dorsen. "Take four men. Have a spotter verify the injured man is still prostrate in the corridor. Be careful, we don't know what those shots were about."

"Yes Sir." He lowered himself through the hole into the destroyed elevator.

Its lighting flashed like a strobe, the circuitry all but fried. As the Sergeant looked around at the impact made by the grenade coupled with the elevator's long fall, he was surprised anyone had got out alive. The grenade had only been intended to blow away the bullet shields, but the Private who'd launched it instructed the wrong level of explosive to be detonated. He'd been sent back to the surface to become a link in the chain of their quickly disappearing communications line, and was in no doubt as to how the Major felt about him right now. Dorsen had some sympathy. It was the first time the recruit had truly experienced having live rounds fired on him at close quarter.

Dorsen activated his helmet's eyepiece but like the rest of their equipment it scrambled in and out of clarity. He cursed, turning to the troops now dropping into the elevator one by one, instructing them to follow his lead.

Dorsen climbed the debris and peered through the gap of the open doors. The corridor appeared clear. He observed the steel mesh flooring. "The orbs won't roll over the surface," he relayed, "Sending a spotter ahead." The major whispered his agreement and Dorsen called on his trusted second Jerry Cole. "I need you to slip into the corridor and head toward the turn. Stick a remote eye around that bend. I need to know if they still have an injured man down there. Remember, our combat displays are all over the place, so don't rely on them. Keep an eye out for booby traps."

Jerry clambered up the debris then pulled himself up and out onto the corridor beyond. He proceeded into the walkway slowly.

Dorsen and Hardcastle activated their respective eyepieces in the hope the static would still allow them to see all the remote eye would observe. Its signal scratched in and out.

As Jerry sent the bendy tube of the camera around the turn, what the voyeurs saw surprised them. For there up ahead was a man clinging to a ladder, holding the lifeless body of another soldier worn across his back and shoulders like a shawl.

As he held onto the rungs, four extra arms reached down from the hatch above lifting the injured man through the opening. The soldier on the ladder then made his way up to the floor above, his boots quickly disappearing from view.

"Don't let them close that hatch!" The Major yelled.

Jerry sprung into action, advancing down the corridor and letting rip with a hail of live rounds to frighten off any attempt to close the hatch. As he approached, he saw the stun grenade drop through the hole and onto the mesh floor in front of him. He activated his ear defence, dropped to one knee and covered his eyes.

'BOOMF.'

He heard the thud and felt the shock wave, grateful his defences had remained on line. He counted to three and got to his feet but the stun grenade had given those he was chasing enough time to drop the upper hatch. He switched to his intercom but got nothing but static. "Shit!" He turned on his heels and headed back toward the elevator. "They're on the move Sergeant . . . They've taken their man and they're on the move."

After the blinding flash Hardcastle's visuals were all but lost. "What about the hatch?"

"They closed it Sir." Jerry replied desperately disappointed, "But only the top one!"

"Shit." Hardcastle cursed his luck. He wondered what could have happened to Gibbs and his men then thought about the challenge posed by yet another sealed entrance.

*

So far the toll to Dorey's team had been high. As they moved down the corridor toward Brooke's secret entrance, Dorey carried Jay's lifeless body talking to her quietly all the way. Jim held Marco in a fireman's carry, the young Brazilian's battle for life all but over. Deans was carried by the captured marines, hoisted onto their four opposing shoulders, the rifles of Dial, Benny and Carl trained upon the soldiers as they went.

All were shocked at their close call with execution. All were relieved to be alive.

Gibbs had been in many situations when he'd flirted with death but he'd never looked the devil in the eye. The force with which this Commander had thrown one of his Corporal's across the corridor was both astounding and inhuman. It had been terrifying to see such rage. And yet somehow, the man now at their lead managed to refrain from exacting his will, managed restraint while consumed by the fire. He'd pointed his gun on them to avenge the woman now dead in his arms, and Gibb's increasing hope was he would have certainly killed them there and then had he wanted them dead. John Gibbs had since wondered whether he could have stopped himself at such a moment, as in the minutes which passed since, it was clear she was more than just one of his troops. He looked up at his unconscious friend and wondered on the extent of his injuries. At the moment Deans let off the stun grenade he was already in a bad way, albeit more alert than he had led Gibbs to believe, an act of courage which now placed him close to death. Gibbs could not help but wonder just what was transpiring within these caves. Just what his old friend had got himself involved with. He'd been holding them prisoner, not threatening their lives. They all could have walked out of the complex without any of the loss now suffered. *'Why?'* The question wouldn't leave him alone. *'What was it that Deans said?'* Gibbs pondered, *'We are down here trying to save lives not take them.'* He thought back to those early days, of how he would have trusted Deans with his life, of how he had done just that on more than one occasion. He thought of how solid he was as a person, *'I should have listened,'* he thought, *'I should have trusted him.'* He was being hard on himself and he knew it, after all, he'd the wellbeing of his own men to think about. He hadn't asked Dennis Deans to turn up and force this dilemma upon him.

He wondered how his own men were feeling.

His ponderings came to a close as they reached the air conditioning control unit which he and his men had found earlier at the dead end of the corridor.

Brookes was already there working on it.

As they arrived next to him a tiny drawer was disappearing into its housing and as it did the doctor entered a code into a panel. Then suddenly with unbelievable effect, the blank wall the doctor faced began to move like lava. First the wall panelling then the actual rock itself. It was incredible, a morphing technique the likes of which most present had never seen before. The entire substance of the wall simply folded and rippled away from them like liquid rock, but a liquid still under the hold of some invisible force.

The four Marines gasped. They'd all seen lesser technologies, but nothing like this.

"What the hell is going on down here?" Truewick spoke quietly toward Gibbs.

"Something incredible," Brookes interceded, "Something beyond your wildest dreams."

"We're through." Sergeant Dorsen declared.

The Major was delighted. When Dorsen told him the upper hatch appeared to rely more on stealth technology than actual armoured locks to ensure its security, he'd hoped his Sergeant was right. After the fiasco of the elevator he'd expected the worst.

To see the cutters burn through so quickly was of huge relief.

Now they had to set about storming the corridor above. It would be tricky. What was left of their tactical readings gave an all clear, but he knew he could not rely on the stuttering technology while in this place. Hardcastle was concerned over the possibility of a turkey shoot. If he were up there he would have left a sniper to pick off anyone trying to make it through that hatch.

He watched as Dorson spun it open before pulling a remote eye from his tunic. Dorson raised the cover cautiously, pushing the wire of the camera through the tiny gap, his men covering him from below should the lid be snatched open. The thin wire snooped around the corridor above. No shots came, and as the camera settled on the walkway ahead he could see the immediate thoroughfare was indeed empty through the scrambled picture. Hardcastle gave him his approval to proceed . . . Albeit with extreme caution.

CHAPTER NINETY FIVE

Finch passed the guard manning the entrance to the brig. Within a moment he was through the first armoured door and on into the chamber beyond. He headed straight for a second entry guarded by another Marine. The door read, 'Secure Unit One.'

The guard stood to attention, before the director disappeared inside.

The room within was a super reinforced plastic box lit by strip lights all hidden from view. In its centre was a solid plastic table which appeared to mould out of the floor. Behind it was a chair of the same principle holding a woman, her head down, hidden by a mess of hair. She was secured with foot and wrist bracelets laced with a multi-fabricated cable which allowed just enough movement to scratch her nose or shuffle her feet. The cable ran out of the cell wall through small round holes, and with one order, it could be retracted to pin the prisoner back into the chair.

A stool had been placed on the opposite side. Finch ignored it, heading straight to the table smashing his palm on its surface. "I think you and I should discuss how to get into this secret room Brookes has been hiding." His face was fierce, "A room in the exact area where your little power surge came from earlier today." His eyes burned, "Remember? The power surge you took the trouble to disguise so you may throw Stein ever so slightly off the scent?"

Isabella Usorio looked up slowly, a purpling bruise formed beneath her right eye which spread into the swell of her cheek. Her face was pale and pasty and her upper lip betrayed the signs of a more recent strike against it. She wore the kind of gown worn by a hospital patient. She fixed her stare on the man who'd foolishly believed himself to be her boss for so long. She sneered defiantly, "What secret room?"

*

Gibbs placed the injured Deans onto one of the desks as Brookes ordered an operating table to rise from the floor. As it did he turned to Jim, "Put Marco on there."

Jim carefully laid his friend on the newly raised surface.

"Help move the desk closer."

The captives did as the doctor instructed, moving Deans parallel to his comrade.

They had entered the chamber via a roughly cut access tunnel. The room was filled with technology which sang like the steady hum of a heartbeat. Antique lamps decorated the desk and state of the art workstations, but strangest of all was its centrepiece, a torpedo-like coffin, black and tiled, with lights pulsating on its surface. There was an eerie sense to this place and it hit those who now witnessed it for the first time.

Dorey placed Jay's body onto the small sofa in the corner. He ignored proceedings for the moment as he gently leaned toward her. He whispered to her and kissed her forehead.

The Marines now had Deans next to the operating table holding Marco as Benny pointed his rifle. "Now get over there." He demanded, herding them to a corner of the room.

Dorey watched as Benny had them kneel with their hands placed on their heads. "I don't want anyone else hurt today . . . Especially not in here." The Commander said before flashing a warning glare at the captured soldiers, "But if they so much as twitch."

Benny nodded as Gibbs protested earnestly, "I'm sorry about your friends. But how were we supposed to know all of this was really here? We've been ordered to apprehend then extract . . . Told you were all an extreme risk to the secrets of this complex."

Dorey held up a hand. "It doesn't matter now. Events are progressing which some don't wish to see unfold. You're witnessing a power struggle, nothing more. Finch has been using you . . . Using you to steal this project from Doctor Brookes here . . . To prevent him offering the world real hope." He looked sadly on Jay's body before returning his attention to the kneeling Marines. "I have to ask you to trust us, not to try anything rash." He pointed to Benny, "He'll gun you down with a smile on his face after events in the corridor." He addressed his friend understanding his hatred, "Take it easy. She's not lost while Palene lives."

Benny stared at Jay, "What are you saying, he can do for her what he did for you?" His gun never left the kneeling soldiers. "This is the *real* world Dorey, not a simulation!"

"Soon there will be little difference."

The Marines looked on confused. It was clear they were encompassed within something beyond their rationale.

Dorey returned his attention to Brookes, "See to our wounded, then we'll set about what we've come here to achieve." Dorey's grief was placed on hold so he could accomplish what was needed. This was his strength. This was why he'd been chosen.

Brookes dragged a panel from the operating table and fired out several verbal commands. Within a moment the surgeon device began lowering itself from its housing in the ceiling, its motion smooth. It manoeuvred to within ten feet above both patients like an alien sea creature. Laser eyes fired across the bodies quickly assessing the damage. Then, a score of fluid mechanical arms began lowering themselves like a pool of jellyfish tentacles.

The device was an advanced medical hybrid of synthetic intelligence and nanobot technology, or *Synthetic Surgeons* as they'd become known. The surgeon's tentacles were loaded with every device an advanced operating table could wish to have. Precision laser cutters, detoxification equipment, suction hoses, drugs and surgical repair monocots ready for implantation . . . All under the control of a computer brain which possessed the skills of every best doctor and nurse the world had to offer.

Brookes would have course been alone in this room should any catastrophe have taken place, and Palene was far too valuable an asset to risk losing, imperishable or not. The Synthetic Surgeon was built piece by piece within the chamber by Brookes the genius.

The tentacles reached down as the onlookers took a step back. The almost translucent limbs checked under eyelids, entered the nostrils and stroked around every orifice and body part of the two unconscious beings placed before it. Probing, listening, sensing.

The screens were also lowered, quickly creating a detailed set of images illustrating the health of both patients. The diagnosis was quickly assembled, Deans being the first to have his afflictions pinpointed.

"Massive head trauma, his brain is swelling." The Surgeon's voice was calmness and wisdom personified, "I can relieve the swelling and keep him stable. Subject has lost a lot of blood from the loss of his hand but I can replace this with replicated cells until we can connect a supply of his blood type. Do we possess his detached hand?"

Jim passed Brookes the badly damaged appendage. He took it, noticing the extent of Jim's own head injury, "We'll get you looked at in a minute," Brookes said as he passed the severed hand to the care of the Surgeon.

More tentacles set about assessing the trauma, "The patient should pull through . . . The hand will be reattached within the hour."

They all looked relieved for a brief moment before turning their attention to Marco whose diagnostic was still to be completed by a further swarm of tentacles attending his body.

"This patient is dying." It stated without remorse, "I will inject nanobots to repair the internal damage, but I'm afraid even with his body repaired, it would appear he's suffered irreversible brain damage."

Dial looked upon Marco sadly. "Do we have any hope?"

"No," the voice replied, "But he's being seen to by the best care the planet has to offer." The device was attending their fallen friends at breathtaking speed, the tentacles gradually accelerating to such a pace it was difficult to see what was actually being done.

Brookes moved toward Jim. "Take a seat there. We can have that sorted out in no time."

Jim did as he was told as Brookes called the attention of the Surgeon and again more tentacles branched from the device above, quickly setting about their work. The wound was clean in moments and sealed easily. The doctor then turned his attention to the onyx tiled object dominating the far centre of the room. "There's nothing more we can do, they're in the care of the surgeon now. We must concentrate on getting Palene ready."

Dorey's eyes returned to the body of Jay. He swallowed the agony as best he could.

"It'll be slightly more than that." Dial interjected, "Those Marines out there will know we came through the wall. There was blood out there in the corridor and blood leaves tracks. We rushed in here without cleaning up after ourselves. And whatever it is those walls of yours are made of, I can't see them holding for more than an hour against laser cutters . . . Even the smaller variety they'll no doubt be forced to hoist down."

Brookes understood the implication as he opened the tomb housing the second Palene, the comatose version sliding into view.

Dial looked at the lifeless body. "How long before he jumps?"

"He'll reach our location in fifty minutes." Brookes replied.

Dial looked across to Dorey, "Let's just hope we can hold them off that long."

*

Will Grossen stared blankly from his seat within Secure Unit Two.

"You look comfortable." Finch sneered sarcastically.

Will's restraints were pulled tight, his noose just slack enough so he could turn his head.

"The gown suits you." Finch smiled coldly at his attire. "You're forcing my hand Will." No response came. "You should see where a lack of co-operation got your little Latin lover out there in the next cell." He shook his head, "Oh, you always were one for the ladies. Though I had no idea you liked them so smart and tender." His false smile turned into a viscous stare. "She bruises like a peach Will." Still no response came. "Do you have any idea the extent of which my authority allows me to go here? I don't think you do. But you know, you should . . . You know what's at stake, and you know how such matters can so easily turn ugly."

Grossen stared right through the director.

"You think your powerful friends will come through for you don't you? Like they have in the past? You think I'll be held into account." He shook his head, "I'm bullet proof on this one Will, and I'll remain so even if forced to smash a few eggs."

Again, no reaction came.

Finch's eyes narrowed. "I'll kill her Will, make no mistake." His face soured, his intent cold as a snake, "She crossed the line, crossed it with you, now both of you can be hung."

CHAPTER NINETY SIX

Tom Hardcastle received three engineers from Finch to determine how to best breech the wall through which the vanishing blood trail had been located.

All three concluded the magnetic field coupled with the technology protecting it came from an unknown, powerful source, and without the necessary access codes the only way through would be to cut using laser equipment. It had taken U.S. Marines fifteen minutes to get the three personnel down using bungee clips and abseil lines. Just for them to tell the Major he should be doing what he'd been planning to do all along.

The cutting tools were now hard at work after being brought from the surface, powering away for the past ten minutes. The three engineers had since busied themselves with their second task, to route the shielded cable unreeled throughout their journey down the shaft, into a working form of communication.

They were now attaching the final pieces of the receiver having connected the makeshift headset. When ready, the chief-tech checked over their handiwork.

He charged the line. It whistled through the earpiece before settling into a rhythmic tone which buzzed on and off slowly.

A crackled but audible voice came from the other end high above, "This is Clive."

"Clive, yeah I can hear you buddy." The chief-tech ran toward Hardcastle, "We got it."

The Major turned to the approaching engineer waving the crude looking phone, the cable spinning and dancing behind him, "You've got a connection?"

The engineer seemed pleased, though the job had not proved as easy as it should have.

The Major thanked him then snatched the phone to his ear, "Hardcastle," he bellowed, but no answer came. He looked to the engineer.

"Clive's just getting Mr. Finch for you now Sir." He added, "To make a call you just need to wind that little handle there."

The bruised old Marine looked, "You mean this thing?"

The chief-tech nodded before pointing a rather dainty forefinger which imitated the spin of the winder. "You have to do it quite hard and fast."

Hardcastle raised an eyebrow. "I got it . . . Thanks." He placed it back to his ear.

"Is that you Major?" It was Finch.

"Yeah . . . this is Hardcastle."

"It looks like we're going to have to stick with the cutting. The engineers don't know how to break the seal and have been unable to locate the direct power source to cut it from the supply. I've people working on a couple of possibilities up here as we speak . . . But neither will talk before you burn through that thing manually."

"I understand Sir."

*

The Synthetic Surgeon still busied away on Marco, trying to rewire the internal damage while reducing the trauma to his brain. Deans was in a more stable condition as the surgeon's tentacles continued to rewire tendons and fix bone, ready to rejoin the detached hand. He was now on full life support within the embrace of the caring machine.

Brooke's full concentration was on the security overrides, busying away at the computer terminal close to Palene. He was almost ready to implement the final set of proceedings which would see all installed safety measures deactivated.

He would have felt nervous performing such a deed under normal circumstances but what he'd witnessed this day was enough to give any man faith in his actions.

Attempts to breach Brooke's lair were well underway. They could all hear the intensity of the cutters as they peeled away sections of the magnetic defence layer by layer.

It wouldn't be long now.

Dorey, Dial, Jim and Carl were fortifying the entrance above.

The narrow corridor leading to this chamber could be defended. But it would depend strongly on what weaponry those outside were authorised to use.

They had no bullet shields left, no way of seeing off any explosive rounds or chasers.

All could be hurtled their way if Finch got restless.

They'd dragged the heavier furniture and terminals up the steps to make a barrier of timber and steel which they knew in reality would offer little protection.

Benny observed their efforts and yelled from his vigil overlooking the captured Marines, "I still think we should position the prisoners along the corridor. A human shield could buy precious minutes as they come through." He pointed to Jay and the two patients under the care of the Surgeon, "If bringing Palene here can really save them, we should do anything to ensure he has the time needed to achieve such a goal."

533

The captives appeared concerned, as well as baffled by his gesture to the dead woman.

"We've been over this." Dial answered firmly.

"It's not an option." Dorey reiterated.

Placing the prisoners in the line of fire would almost certainly create a pause of some sort, though how long a pause was anyone's guess. Dorey's decision however, was final, "Those men will not be harmed. What happened was as much our fault as theirs."

The prisoners breathed a sigh of relief.

Benny was taken aback to hear Dorey speak so rationally, and was surprised at Dial's ease in supporting this moral high ground.

"Besides, judging by how quickly those marines threw grenades at us I doubt they'd even stop to notice four Royals sat in their way."

Benny couldn't argue with that, they had all been surprised at the use of such a potent explosive. Especially one employed at the start of the fight while Brookes was with them.

Another slab of the wall gave way promoting fresh concern.

"How are we doing Doc?" Dial enquired.

Brookes continued to battle through the displays in front of him, his chipped fingers moving almost as quickly through the dense files as the synthetic tentacles of the Surgeon over its patients. "I'm opening up the final matrix of the defence sequences now. Once I've broken them down, it's all up to him."

Dorey looked toward the tomb of Palene before glancing back to Jay. A lump rose in his throat. He closed his eyes and prayed his confidence was not misplaced, 'Help her,' his mind echoed, 'Help her.'

*

Palene's consciousness soared through time in unison with his broken down cells. The exhilaration as always excited, though he felt his faith checked as his journey began.

'Ahhh, you should not fear.'

The return of the consciousness was startling, 'It's not fear, merely the desire to succeed.'

'You have already succeeded in so many ways.'

'But not yet fulfilled what I'm supposed to do.'

'Give yourself freely and all will be realised.'

'Give myself freely? To what . . . to you?'

'We are already one.'

'Then to this light?'

'You know more of this light than I.'

Palene felt his being swoop toward his destiny. He experienced the pain and suffering, the turmoil and asking of Dorey and his band. Then without warning, he felt the true power of all being offered. 'You mean I must give myself freely to the Stasis None?'

'Only truly united will we be granted access to your light.'

Palene's being soared into the timeline, headed for the moment he'd been hit on the hillside. He approached quickly, felt the Finger of Venus strike, relived the moment only with a clarity he'd never before experienced. The force as it hit, the viscous beam emanating from the very same Stasis None to which he was now a living part.

He felt the moment he'd first been sucked into its power, endured the pain all over again as he suffered the same fate, the sensation of his essence being scattered across time and space. He felt the energy of the beam, his being blinded as he entered its fury. His sensations were as if he were actually there in person, as if he were Palene as an entity of flesh and blood. He heard the consciousness within his own despair, as the beam blasted his existence into a billion fragments. The sensation unbearable as the universe threw him into the void like dust before a hurricane.

He yearned to be whole, fearing this was indeed the end of his existence, when suddenly, he experienced the broken down particles of an apple. He was inside the beam.

His cells screamed as he was cast back into the pain, his consciousness blacking out as he was propelled forward over two thousand years.

*

The noise levels increased as the soldiers cutting into the chamber took another step toward achieving their goal.

Dial looked through the small connecting corridor as another rumble of falling debris shook the foundations, "They're getting closer."

Carl, Jim and Dorey were with him on the broad mesh landing, the four deliberating further over their tactics and defence strategy.

Jim pointed ahead. "Even if that entire section of wall collapses they'll still have to come through this narrow walkway . . . Which will play to our advantage."

Carl agreed, "Especially as we have no *Ragun* countermeasures. Our heavier grade seekers should do well. But they'll use a lot of ammo to break down a Ragun shield whatever variety they send."

A Robotic Armoured Gun System, or Ragun as they'd become known, could be assembled quickly. They were used as an advanced mini-tank to clear a pathway for ground forces and the team were certain the soldiers would have called for the service of such devices. The destroyed lift shaft would prove too narrow for larger models, as would the steel walkway leading into the chamber. However, the lesser Ragun breed remained a potent threat. They were the size of a squatting man on manoeuvrable, adaptable tracks, heavily armed and shielded, with an array of tools to clear any advance.

"We should place grenades next to the arch there. Blast a chunk of the walkway right up in front of them."

Dorey agreed with Dial in principle. "It still worries me using explosives from the offset will only result in them returning the favour. This room is just as important to them. They're not going to want to start blowing the shit out of it if they can avoid such action. But will they feel that way once we start blowing chunks of it up ourselves?"

"They didn't wait too long before blowing that elevator." Jim replied.

"They must be under orders to show more restraint with regards to this room." Carl said.

"It's a risky strategy to hope they're going to try and get us out without causing too much damage. But I agree they surely must try it first. But such an effort will almost certainly come with the use of Raguns at some juncture. We know they have them on the surface. And we don't have the fire power to fend off a sustained assault with them at the fore. Which kind of has running around in circles," Dial pondered the options.

"We could blow it all now before they even get in here." Jim suggested.

"That could damage the inner wall and speed their entry. Plus the same principles apply. If they want to take this room intact they're going to have to use caution," Carl replied, "Remove the need for such caution and we may well provoke a more aggressive attack."

"But we have to face the possibility they may just bust through and start blowing the shit out of us right away. The simple fact is, once that wall goes we've little to slow them down." Jim pointed at the support beams which embedded the steel of the walkway into the rock. "We could attach grenades between each of those beams there. The minute the entrance falls, detonate them. The debris will give them at least one more obstacle to worry about. If we do it immediately they'll know it wasn't a pot shot at them and it'll save our mini-mag and seeker rounds. If those beams are solid then the rock in-between will be all that gives way. Not too much damage, but an effective barrier nonetheless."

Dial yelled down to Brookes, "Doc . . . How far do those support beams run into the rock above the causeway here?"

Brookes continued to busy away on the screens, "I have no idea of the specifics."

"You were here when they built this thing . . . Take a guess."

He visualised the moments spent with his brother's engineers during the elaborate construction. "I couldn't give accurate data, but I did specify the structure be built to withstand anything from a missile scoring a direct hit to an earthquake striking below."

Dial raised an eyebrow. "I guess that answers the question."

Dorey looked to the rafters. "Okay, set the explosives to cause this rock fall. We'll wedge more obstacles in the walkway to create a secondary barrier. A Ragun will make mincemeat of them but while they're cutting through we'll hit them with sustained seeker rounds from our heavy rifles. We'll place the last of our explosives midway through on the steel floor as our final line of defence. Once blown, hopefully there will be enough damage to see them have to bridge the gap. After which, it will be down to us alone!"

They all agreed.

"Carl, find the best lock-down positions for our two assault rifles. Place the floor mounts as far to our rear as possible. We need those seekers turning into this tunnel while keeping the rifles well out of the reach of any Chaser rounds. Jim and I will wedge the last of the heavy cabinets into the walkway."

Dial reassured Dorey of his decision. "It's the right call." He pointed to the prisoners, "They'd lost all communications out there. Presumably a link of some description will have found its way down the shaft by now. Shit, Finch himself could be out there for all we know. But if the same soldiers who blew us to hell are *not* in touch with those who want this room in tact, then we have to assume they'll deploy the same level of force a second time."

Dorey cast his eye over the steel rods mounting the floor to the ceiling. "You'd better get up there and see about planning our little rock fall, then rig the remaining walkway."

The four quickly set about their final preparations.

Below, the doctor began unlocking the last of the safety measures restricting the will of his creation. Only one security grid remained. As Brookes saw the grid's first outer defence collapse, the steady rhythmic beats of the chamber suddenly quickened, the calm pulse which had been their companion since entering the lower complex now playing out a loud, irregular pattern.

Everybody stopped for a moment and looked around them. The displays lighting up like a discotheque. The beat gradually slowed, though the light displays on the panels continued to roll up and down, as if stimulated into excitement.

"He's on his way." Brookes announced. He then assaulted the screens with fresh vigour, hopeful any gun battle may yet be avoided.

CHAPTER NINETY SEVEN

Finch looked at the generated image of Raffy Abel. "Yes Senator, it would appear the earlier energy blast did indeed emanate from this same area." He listened to Abel's enquiry, "All I can say is we're making steady progress."

His disgruntled reply ended as Stein yelped from his chair.

"I've got to go," Finch declared, "I'll get back to you in a minute." A blank space replaced Raffy's image and the director knew he would not be pleased at being cut off in such a manner. He approached the agitated Stein. "What is it?"

Stein gawped at the readings, "A huge energy source, bigger than the blast from the basement earlier. It just disrupted the entire Stasis mainframe." He began frantically hunting the system perplexed. His jaw then dropped at the blinding realisation, "The Stasis None has just locked out all access to its systems."

"It's done what?" Finch said angrily, "Brookes?"

"No." Stein corrected, "It didn't come from the complex. It didn't even have to connect to our system. This came from out there." He pointed to nowhere in particular.

"Out where?" Finch demanded.

"That's just it Sir, I have no idea." He shrugged, "From nowhere . . . everywhere."

"Please tell me what it is I'm supposed to understand here."

Stein looked intrigued. "The power this Palene appears to use, the energy pulses erupting in the basement levels earlier today. They all have similar signatures . . . But this was far more powerful, and completely independent." He continued, "Previously these energy sources have used the Stasis None in some way, like an antenna if you like. By manipulating our timelines or in the case of the power surges earlier, actually occurring within the core of the complex itself." He could see Finch was not getting a clear picture, "Well the energy force which just hit had the same tell tale signs. Only it didn't come from a particular source or any one moment. It came from everywhere." He pointed at the data flooding his screens, "And now it's as if the Stasis None is no longer there."

Finch stared at the doctor in whom he'd entrusted the possible future of the complex. The man he'd hoped could play some part in removing the thorn from his side. He snarled, "What the fuck are you talking about? Just tell me what's happening in plain, simple English. Is that too much to ask?"

Stein hated this gumshoe, this vulgar man who had bullied and blackmailed him so long. "If the energy source came from this Palene, then he's something far bigger than we anticipated. Because whatever just hit us . . . Did so from the past, the present and the future. It hit us from the damn afterlife and beyond. And after this power surge hit, the Stasis None mainframe sealed itself off from our networked computers."

Finch was brimming with anger. This was supposed to be a routine snatch and grab with the complex simply falling into his hands, retribution for Brooke's antics. It wasn't supposed to be a battle against Dorey. It wasn't supposed to be a point of no return. The whole idea was to buy some time, search the complex thoroughly while weakening Brooke's position. Aim for a victory without declaring war.

Yet here he was in the middle of all out chaos.

The earlier energy source which had blown out of the Stasis cave had vanished without a trace. He'd discovered his so-called *insider* was not actually his at all. Usorio was in fact Grossen's double agent, which led him to conclude not only had his efforts led to one of his enemies gaining the ability to second-guess his every move. But his selection of Usorio contributed to that same enemy getting himself one hell of a good-looking lay in the process. Dorey's team had returned without Palene, unleashing hell before disappearing into a secret location nobody knew existed. To make matters worse, this location was almost certainly the ground zero of the earlier energy surge in question.

'*If only I'd been granted a little more time.*' He could have had his own men searching the bottom of those shafts, pinpointed the area he was now preparing to seize by force. But the signal had come of the Reeper's imminent return at the worst possible moment. Brooke's erratic behaviour ensured the failure of Gibbs to intercept them while inside the decontamination room. Worse still, his own jarheads had then stepped in and blown the elevator off its hinges down into the shaft. '*God only knows what state they're all in.*'

He didn't want Brookes dead. He needed him under control until he knew how to operate this supercomputer. '*A computer this screen-surfer now tells me has gone off line.*' He tightened his grip on the desk, his darker thoughts brewing menace. He had to focus. He turned back to Stein, "Doctor," he spoke slowly at first, "Now you're a damn intelligent man, more so since I spent a great deal of time and money developing that clever brain of yours." His frustration was growing, "Now, I have to place a call back to the senator and you're gonna have to explain to him what you just so eloquently explained to me . . . And I don't think he'll be too happy about this computer of ours disappearing, locking us out, or doing whatever the hell it is now doing. So if I were you, I'd start thinking about a clearer explanation, one without energy sources hitting us from the God damn afterlife and beyond!"

He seethed, "Now would it be too much to ask, to have you do your damn job and figure out what the hell is going on without speaking like some awestruck fucking teenager?"

Stein flushed under the tirade, his hatred of Finch reaching a new zenith at that moment.

*

"This should be the final section now Sir." Hardcastle yelled into the makeshift phone, "We should be through in six to eight minutes." The crunching of sliding rubble and the pulsing hum of the lasers made it hard for the Major to hear, even from the far end of the corridor. It had taken them fifty minutes so far.

One of his men approached. He covered the mouthpiece encouraging him to speak. He thanked the Private then announced the news to Finch. "I've just been informed we've reached the final strip of the magnetic field, after which its good old-fashioned rock. The lasers should cut through that like cheese."

Finch was pleased. He congratulated the Major on his efforts.

Hardcastle rubbed the thick spikes of his greying jarhead cut. "Mr Finch." His eyes narrowed like a hawk. "I'm going to need some rules of engagement. I mean, we don't even know what to expect when we cut through this thing. There could be God knows what waiting for me and my men in there."

The director's answer came firm and fast. A full assault, but with minimal possible damage to both the room and their opponents. The Major was then wished good luck and the phone line went dead. Hardcastle was set to head back to his men when he heard a commotion. He turned to see three Royal Marine Sergeants and two Corporals brush past the guard manning the shaft entry.

Sergeant Medlam approached and saluted. "Sir, we are the men separated from Colour Sergeant Gibbs. Here to offer our assistance."

The Major looked grateful. "We still don't know what happened to the rest of your troop. At one point they'd apprehended the targets. In between then and the time it took us to cut through that elevator they disappeared into a room around the corner there."

"We had contact with them close to that time also . . . But our communications were fried."

"All communications down here are fried." Hardcastle held aloft the makeshift telephone, "Hence the need for this piece of shit." He gestured for the Royals to follow. "Mind the cable there son." Medlam avoided the trailing cord. "They had injured men," he looked over his shoulder as he went, "The targets I mean. We found blood in the corridor." He continued toward the far bend. "Did you know about the gunshots?"

Concern etched the faces of the following Royals. "No sir."

"Gibbs wanted to take them to some room which apparently has a medical facility. I ordered him not to move as I was told no such place exists." The noise level increased as they turned the bend, revealing a group of American

Marines using portable cutting equipment to rip through the wall of the complex. It appeared they were almost through.

Next to them, three small grade Ragun battle units had been assembled.

The Major raised his voice, "Let's just hope Gibbs and your buddies are alright." He then gestured to the organised destruction. "In a few minutes I'll be sending those Raguns through. Then we can all follow them into this room that doesn't exist."

*

Stein was growing increasingly concerned. His oppressor Robert Finch was allowing troops to tear apart chunks of the complex and he'd just endured having the most powerful man on the planet threatening his future on the project unless he could figure out a way back into the now sealed Stasis system.

The only problem being, he was in way over his head.

His dangerously high level of implants coupled with his sharp intellect meant he could out-hack anyone on a standard computer. However he would have little chance if forced to go up against Brooke's powerful brainchild, or even this Palene.

To make matters worse he had no real clue what had shut them out. Or even what Brooke's and Dorey were trying to achieve.

Stein had been Finch's mole for a long time. Snooping and spying on his boss for years. Learning snippets here, hiding pieces of information there. Yet in all that time he'd never been able to establish just how it was Brookes achieved the near impossible. Now in the space of just a few hours he'd witnessed the power surges emanating from the basement of the complex, and watched incredulous as Finch's marines chased Brookes into a secret chamber, a room hidden behind the magnetically sealed rock of a corridor which didn't exist. *'How did you keep such a thing secret all these years?'* He had to marvel at the cunning. He wondered to what extent Usorio's knowledge may outstrip his own, the bitch who altered the data just enough to stop him investigating the power surge with any real accuracy before the Reeper's return, accuracy which may well have led him to this secret chamber now causing all the problems. *'And whose side is she on?'* He pondered further, *'Not Finch's that's for sure.'* This thought alone was almost enough for him to forgive her. *'Probably Grossen,'* he decided, *'All the while playing the faithful little protégé."* His face soured. He'd have loved nothing more than to have been the obedient protégé. The loyal student who bowed before his master and mentor, waiting patiently for the day when the key to the kingdom would be passed to he alone. Unfortunately for Doctor Stein, Robert Finch had got to him early in his Stasis career, armed with damaging information which Stein had paid good money some years earlier to have buried, supposedly forever. The kind of information which would ensure Stein could never work on any such assignment. Not unless the arbitrators decided they didn't mind having a man on board who'd sold official secrets in order to pay off gambling debts.

Would they listen to the fact these secrets were really not that big a deal? Of course not.

And so it was. Just as Stein landed his big break, Robert Finch laid claim to his own.

He flitted now through the layers of code and data, hooked into the system with eight of his implanted chips now activated at once. It was according to the brochure, a lethal thing to do, but Stein had been force-fed doses of implant enablers for years by Finch and his team, all of whom were desperate to create a mind to one day rival Isimbard Brookes.

His temples pulsed under the exertion. Then suddenly, his heart rate quickened.

Perhaps he'd just landed himself a lucky break.

He checked the readings, double-checked. The codes all pointed to the same pattern.

Brookes was unlocking the final stages of his external security systems which held the Stasis None accountable for harming human life. He smiled as he realised this wasn't the half of it. Isimbard had also disabled the lock down systems which could prevent an outside source from accessing the Stasis mainframe. '*So that's how something hit us from the outside.*' He was pleased his hunch to search these exterior parameters had paid off. '*What the hell are you doing?*' He tore his mind out of the system and looked around the RFC for Finch, his eyes drunk and bleary from their virtual playground.

He was nowhere to be seen, '*That Bastard.*'

He turned back to his displays and quickly activated the new program he'd hidden in the bowels of the system. It flashed on line in an instant. A hunter program. A tool which would seek, protect or destroy any alien programs within the security network. He'd used varying versions during his work for the shit-head who'd stolen his life from him.

Only this was his masterpiece. '*Okay Isimbard.*' He thought, delighted to have caught him away from the power of his Stasis None, '*Let's see how good you are in my domain.*'

*

"They're cutting into the final layer." Brookes confirmed through the increasing noise, "We've only minutes at best. You'd better get ready."

"We're as ready as we can be," Dial replied from his position on the barricade, "How about you?"

"Almost done. Palene can complete the final phase as soon as the security adjustments release the Stasis None. I just hope we can hold them off in the time this will take."

Dial agreed as he looked over their handiwork.

The grenades had been set with acrobatic efforts and they'd created further makeshift barriers with ripped up furnishings wedged along the narrow thoroughfare. Midway along the mesh walkway, they'd planted higher grade explosives as their final line of defence.

The sound of the cutters pounded through the wall now, the energy intense.

"Doctor, we need to know the instant that magnetic field fails."

"I'm on it Commander, I promise you." Brookes continued the final preparations.

The ghost of Palene echoed throughout the system, the surrounding circuitry still buzzing with the thrill. They all sensed it, the anticipation of his arrival building.

Brookes dragged his fingers across the last of the menus. The computer drew up the final access directory and asked Brookes to authorise the command. '*Thank God.*'

He quickly flashed his authorisation into the system for the final time. He had managed a complete manual system override at lightening pace. He'd been shut out at first by his own independent security, the computers not networked in any way to the Stasis None. Devices instructed by those now taking control of his complex to disregard Isimbard Brookes at all costs. He saw the final barrier collapse and was about to announce the shackles of the Stasis None as having been released, when suddenly his access was blocked at the defining moment. "What the hell?" He quickly reiterated his command but again the procedure was sent back, this time with a firm and clear response, '*No.*'

A bead of sweat trickled down his forehead as genuine anxiety took hold for the first time. He'd been supremely confident he would have enough time to clear Palene's path.

This however, threw him off balance. If he could not access this final code with the deconstructed Palene already in the system, the results could be catastrophic.

He threw himself into combat with the security program, blistering through a series of overrides only to see another virtual door slammed in his face. He was now extremely concerned. He sent an enquiry to ascertain the source of the problem and as the result came flooding into his psyche, his mouth opened slowly at the confirmation, "Stein."

*

Palene's diluted force swept through the beam to the moment of Brooke's experiment.

He sensed his other being trapped within its prison but was refused entry.

The beam blasted his molecules back through the arc of time, returning to the axis which saw him suffer on the hillside above the henge.

With every ounce of his being he determined himself forward once more, propelling his cells across the two thousand year prison which resisted his reunification.

He suffered again the many months of his coma, heard the torment which engulfed his mind. He tried to turn away from the brutal slaughter of his family, desperate not to experience the agony of this most heinous act again.

Only he had no eyes in which to look away, no neck with which to turn his head.

His screams were as ethereal as his being, his experience as real as the universe.

He wailed as the smell of the pyre engulfed him once more, raged as he slaughtered those in the path of his revenge. There was no longer any sense of light. There was only pain and torment. He was a prisoner now, sentenced to the boundaries of his own agony within the beam. He begged the light, the Stasis None and his other self to guide him, *'Where are you?'*

*

Brooke's hurtled himself into the virtual showdown throwing everything at Stein in a barrage of strikes. Such a petty arena was not his specialty.

'You treacherous bastard.'

'You condescending old fool.'

Brookes manoeuvred a broadside but his attempts were thwarted. Isimbard knew the strengths of his adversary within this field. He tried desperately to turn such strengths against him. More virtual missiles were thrown and more rebuffs saw them fail.

Stein was now making an attempt to cut Brooke's connection once and for all.

Isimbard spotted it just in time, sending an array of blocking programs which saw the attempt deflected. Stein was back at him immediately and Brookes was slammed into a wall of processing which threatened to hold him until it was too late. Isimbard countered, his being swooning into the system like never before, his implants raged, his mind in danger of bursting. Had this been within the world of nuclear computing, Brookes would have bared his virtual teeth and torn this insolent puppy apart. However, the more base level of their arena was the very reason Brookes was taking such a hiding.

This was indeed, Stein's domain.

The sound of the cutters slicing through the final piece of the magnetic field was as distant now as the danger it posed. If he could not drive Stein's override from the security mainframe, Palene would be lost.

The others realised of course something was wrong. They watched Brookes helplessly.

More rubble outside was heard to fall, the adrenaline beginning to peak as they now saw the heat of the laser begin slicing through the wall at the far bend of the narrow walkway.

"Here we go!" Dial yelled. He watched the frantic arms of the now hypnotised doctor. He looked to Benny who had taken a defensive position behind one of the units below, his rifle trained, ready to cover them with the use of seekers should they need to retreat. His prisoners were locked to the table powerless, as they prepared to watch the battle unfold.

He gave Dial a determined thumbs up.

Dorey also observed the speed at which Brookes now flung his arms across his displays.

Data, numbers, codes and equations spewed in a torrent of images around him.

It was clear he was waging a war on his own form of battlefield.

They were all fully aware of their position. This room was not open for negotiation, and with Palene not yet here, they were under no illusion as to what the outcome may be.

Dorey fired a quick glance to Jim and Carl, at his two wounded men. Deans with only a few of the Surgeon's tentacles needed to caress his progress now, Marco still under an intense massage as the device continued its attempt to sustain his life. To Dial and Benny who readied themselves for the cause, then once again to Jay. He swallowed the pain, returning his focus to the fight soon to ensue.

Brookes battled on. He wished he could pull his Stasis None into the system, to aid him in this child's parlour game. But it was impossible. The very reason he'd designed it so.

Stein was soaring now and he sensed the old man was running out of ideas. His spike programs ravaged any attempt Isimbard made to try and regain control. His virtual forces surrounded the king and he swooped in to watch the old tyrant fall.

Brooke's arms began to slow. '*I can't beat him at these hacker games.*'

Exhausted he pulled his brain out of the fight and focused his attention on Stein's location, high above in the RFC. He hailed him.

Stein, intoxicated by the kill had to drag himself out of his virtual state. He looked at the flashing signal requesting his audience. He smiled, his eyes dark and bloodshot by the victory, '*So the old man wants to beg.*' The reality of the RFC was momentarily unfamiliar. He activated the screen and saw the exhausted features of his once supreme boss. Nothing was said, but Stein could hear the intense noise in the background as the marines were set to storm the lair.

They stared at each other for what seemed like an eternity.

'*I beat you.*'

Brookes could almost hear the thought.

Stein was suddenly aware of Finch's return, screaming orders into Hardcastle's ear from the far side of the RFC. His disgusting, bullying voice was unbearable at that moment. The director turned his attention toward Stein on witnessing his contact with Isimbard Brookes.

Isimbard was set to speak but Stein shook his head. He gave a saddened half-smile.

Stein ignored his snarling oppressor and ordered his battle programs to abate, deactivating his recently won lock down on the security grid mainframe.

Then as his image disappeared, he returned full control to Isimbard Brookes.

CHAPTER NINETY EIGHT

As the wall finally surrendered, Dorey ordered the ceiling of the walkway to be blown. Before the Marines outside could celebrate, they'd been hit by yet another obstacle.

As the dust settled both sides could see the rubble between them was considerable but by no means unsurpassable. The cutters would make short work of the task.

As yells and commands had the force repositioned to deal with these new defences, Dial and the others waited in their fortified positions.

Sergeant Dorson and Jerry Cole leopard crawled across the corridor, positioning two cutting mechanisms before the debris. They went unchallenged, hidden behind the wall of fallen rock. As the laser shot out, it not only removed a section of the fallen debris but also a chunk of Carl's barricade together with a slice of the wall to his rear. "Jesus!"

As Carl ducked out of the way Dial quickly adjusted his aim firing two shots into the beam. They blazed through the newly-formed gap straight into the laser nozzle.

The beam stopped in an instant as did Dial's sniper skills as three shots hit his barricade sending fragments smashing into his shoulder. The impact blasted him clean off his perch and he crashed down in a clatter of noise and pain. "They've gone live with their ammo!"

Dorey and Jim opened precise fire through the cut in the fallen rock ensuring a retreat. "Are you alright?" Carl yelled.

Dial rolled over and pushed with his legs, sliding behind the barricade. "I'm fine." Blood was seeping from his cheek. He climbed to his secondary sniper position.

Two new Marines made a break for the cover of the rubble carrying a second cutter.

Another burst of fire flooded through the cut away section as more Marines took up position behind the debris. Soon after, the cutter sprang into action, this time its range checked, removing only the section of rubble set in front of it.

Dial and Carl shot this second laser as it came into full view.

A larger gap had now formed.

Dial fired a further three rounds at two moving shadows forcing them to retreat.

"They're bringing up a Ragun." Jim yelled.

The distinctive sound of the Ragun's tracks could be heard as it made ready to enter the fight, their aggressors no longer prepared to risk themselves positioning cutters. The Robotic tank would make harder work of the rock fall, but it was clearly the safer option. The Ragun rolled into position and as the small laser cutter fired from its skeleton, so did an intense action of gunfire.

All four quickly slid out of the way, the shots blasting great chunks of their barricades into the air. Dial, almost killing himself in the act, made his move, managing two direct hits on the Ragun with one of the heavy rifles, the success recorded by the *seeker* ammunition. The Ragun's shield ate them up. "Heading for the rear!" Dial ran across the walkway to the far landing, quickly mounting the rifle into its waiting housing.

A second mini-tank entered the fight, firing cover rounds on behalf of its counterpart. This was what Carl had been waiting for.

The robot's heavy calibre rounds ripped through the growing gap in the fallen debris.

A section of the corridor mouth was carved into chunks, spraying more rubble around the defenders.

The Raguns would drive forward once the barriers had been blasted away, allowing the Marines to follow at the rear. The defenders hoped they could knock them out without having to make an attempt at blowing the corridor. They suspected after the minor effects of the first rock fall that even the heavier grade explosive would struggle against such fortified foundations, and they appreciated how such a last desperate act would almost certainly prove the point of no return.

As another section of rubble was cut by the lead mini-tank, Dial's seeker rounds blazed into the tunnel. The first Ragun took a battering and both tanks sent a barrage of fire toward the unseen aggressor.

Carl didn't need a second invitation, quickly firing three rounds into the Ragun covering the rear. Within a moment Carl was rushing toward the second gun mount, setting up his rifle opposite Dial on the far landing.

Chasers made an attempt to make the same turn as the assaulting seekers but they splattered clumsily into the mouth of the corridor, again causing Dorey and Jim to cower.

Carl was in position, pulling up his targeting screen, the seekers locked onto the second target. He let rip, the heavy rifle thudding out in a deep patter, smashing rounds into the shield of the rear Ragun.

Again the Robotic tanks followed the flight path of the incoming shells, desperate to locate the position of the assault, but their combat systems could see only solid rock. They fired frantically in a desperate bid to repel the attack.

The machines had not encountered anything like the experimental ammunition now raining upon them.

Suddenly, Dial's powerful seekers obliterated the first Ragun in a shower of sparks and metal. The second device continued firing it's chasers but they could not score the hit required. The rear of the chamber was torn to pieces causing those in the chamber below to duck as Dial's gun whirred to a stop, its ammunition spent.

Carl pounded the second target continuously.

Every seeker round scored a hit, the Ragun battered by the force of the shots.

The killing blow was finally struck and it too was blown apart, its powerful shield shredded by the onslaught of heavy ammunition.

Carl was delighted. The seekers had proved their worth. But the joy was short-lived as a further volley from the Marines merely provided cover for yet another mini-tank's arrival. The distinctive sound of the Ragun's tracks filled the corridor once more, its laser reducing the final obstacles to fragments.

It had taken one hundred and sixty-six direct hits to stop the previous two machines and as this third incarnation began to open with its own brand of heavy fire, Carl realised he only had seventeen shots left. "We have to blow the tunnel." Carl declared.

The tracks of the robotic gun now took it over the remnants of the remaining obstacles.

From down below, a desperate yell shouted up at them. "Wait!"

It was John Gibbs.

"I've got two RAG-Busters strapped to the inside webbing of my Jacket!" Benny and the others looked at him.

"Hidden in the padded lining. When you took our jackets you missed them."

"Bullshit." Benny pointed his rifle at the prisoner.

More heavy rounds blasted out from the advancing gun forcing them to duck for cover.

"Check my jacket . . . It's not a trick. I always carry countermeasures."

Benny looked up at Dorey sensing a trap.

Dial returned to the corridor entrance, crouching as he went.

"We all know what will follow if you blow that corridor." Gibbs boomed.

Dorey stared into the Colour Sergeant's eyes, "Benny, check his Jacket!"

The corner of the corridor disintegrated under more heavy fire as Benny headed for the confiscated coats. He found the Colour Sergeant's insignia and looked inside. He pulled apart a dark section of the lining revealing a pair of stun grenades and two RAG-Busters, the small hand held devices strapped into customised pockets.

Dorey ran to the balcony ledge to catch them as they were thrown up to him.

"What the fuck are you doing?" Truewick enquired.

Gibbs turned to him. "These guys aren't going to let this room go. Now whatever it is they're doing, they seem to think waking that guy over there is going to stop all of this chaos." He gestured toward the comatose Palene, "That's what they're holding out for. Now do they seem crazy to you?" Gibbs shook his head as his men scanned their captors. "That's the boss of this entire project over there," he pointed to Brookes as he frantically reeled through the data around him, resetting the barriers placed in front of him by Stein. "And we all know what we saw up there was no flight simulator." He eyed Benny as he returned to his position. "If there's any chance of slowing this thing down I'll take it. Because if they blow that corridor and it's still standing afterward, we're gonna be stuck here helpless as they hit this place with everything they've got."

Above, Dorey and Jim primed the devices. "You throw first." Dorey ordered. He turned to Dial, "The minute he readies his throw, hit that fucker with as many shots as you can." He addressed Carl, "As soon as the paint hits the Ragun shield, throw every last seeker into the heart of that thing, then I'll launch the second."

They could hear the Marines preparing to take up position behind the Ragun.

On the count of three Jim prepared to launch the counter-measure into the tunnel.

Dial moved quickly, sending a hail of shots into the tank. It turned on him immediately, forcing him into cover as Jim launched his projectile.

The fist-sized device exploded into a plume of thick specialised paint. It covered the shield and sensors of the robotic gun blinding it briefly.

"Counter-measures!" A Marine yelled from the walkway.

They retreated, surprised at the response. They'd felt certain any such action would have been taken against the first two advancing Robots.

Pellet cameras fired from a lid on top of the Ragun's shell in order to give back its vision as it began cleaning away the paint with counter-measures of its own.

The RAG-Buster shot out mini-mag mines, the metal pea-like shells covering the steel walkway. The majority slipped through the gaps of the mesh floor. Several however, homed in on their target locking onto the shield as Carl let rip with the remaining seekers.

The Ragun tried to counter the threats, but again the seekers proved a powerful ally.

As the first of the mines detonated Dorey threw the second counter-measure into the corridor, bravely avoiding having his hand blown off in the process.

The stuttering Ragun was then hit by the second wave courtesy of the following projectile. Before the min-tank could respond, they detonated with the same thumping force, and moments later, the third Ragun was crippled.

Jim and Dorey let rip with a heavy burst of fire, battering the machine onto its side.

As it groaned to a halt, a temporary stalemate was put into force.

Hardcastle's voice could be heard yelling and screaming in the distance and Gibbs and the others were sure they'd just heard the voice of their own Sergeant Medlam.

The ensuing silence was eerie.

Dorey looked down at the doctor desperate for information, when not for the first time during the course of that day, fate answered his call.

Brookes, who'd been thundering through the data for so long, slumped forward exhausted. "It's all open," he sighed, "It's in Palene's hands now."

CHAPTER NINETY NINE

"I don't know exactly," Sam Redemca was angry. "But I do know the German Chancellor has picked up on this. She'll come gunning for you Mr. President."

The President of the United States sat back in the chair of his oval office staring at the image of Principal Redemca on his display. He knew of course it was she who'd betrayed such information. Finch was supposed to have taken care of both her and Grossen.

He felt the weight of his predicament. If this blew up in their faces, Raffy Abel would hang him out to dry and simply buy himself a new Commander and Chief.

He pursed his lips. "So what is it you think I should do Miss Redemca?"

"Call them off." She replied without hesitation. "Tell the Prime Minister to do the same."

"You and I both know it's no longer that simple."

"Mr President, Senator Abel is going let you take the fall . . . You must know that." Her image leaned toward his desk. "Abel wants the Stasis None. It's all he's ever wanted. This move was only political as long as Grossen and I were silenced, as long as Brookes was discredited."

The President stared at the woman transmitted before him. She and Grossen had done well to out-manoeuvre both Finch and Abel, but she was playing her hand a little too early. He'd just received word Finch was about to take control of the complex. That Brookes had dug a hole for himself far deeper than they could have imagined, and that the energy source used by this Palene was almost certainly housed within this room their marines were set to take. "I think our friends will eventually see I acted in their best interests," he declared as if speaking to the press, "In order to protect the long term safety of this project. The German's dislike of Abel will be put to one side once they've seen this I'm sure." He narrowed his stare, "Despite all your best efforts Miss Redemca."

Samantha stared back at him fiercely. "Mr President your faith is misplaced."

He smiled. "Goodbye Miss Redemca. And thank you for the call."

"There's one more thing," she snapped, "Will Grossen."

The President shrugged.

"I know he's in the Stasis compound." Her eyes narrowed, "If anything happens to him be certain of one thing, his blood spilled will stain your hands . . . and your hands alone."

*

Palene felt the true force of the Stasis None ripple throughout time, its magnitude beyond anticipation. The power which appeared to have abandoned him alone to his torment was present once more, and with it, he felt the overwhelming release of his other self.

He powered toward the moment of Brooke's experiment until he felt the true terror of the beam. The very nucleus of the Finger of Venus, concentrated into an absolute.

He felt its brutal energy. Only this time he was not ejected.

The Stasis None was all around him, willing him to re-enter without fear.

He felt his atoms as they were sucked in toward that terrible moment, when his life was scattered across time.

In that same moment the consciousness also made its return. *'I am free.'*

'Then help me.' Palene pleaded.

'As are you.'

Palene felt the embrace of the Stasis None, the unbelievable power. The raw scale was incredible, far more so than he had anticipated. The nucleus of the beam threatened to blast him to all sides of the universe but the Stasis None held him firm, protecting him this time from the finger's wrath.

He felt himself spinning, hurtling within the structure of the hub. He experienced the DNA of the apple all around him, its cells held within a brief moment of stasis.

He spun down into the core of the beam.

'Reach out.' The consciousness urged.

He tried with all of his will to obey, his ethereal being attempting to concentrate itself whole. He reached out with both invitation and instruction and as he did he suddenly felt his once far away self, no longer locked away, but there, within the rage of the beam.

He'd returned to the very moment of his separation.

His atoms soared around those of his other self, flirting with the deliverance set to follow. He felt the prayer for this moment finally rest as he prepared for his liberation. Felt the joy of the Stasis None and the consciousness . . . Realising they were truly one in the same.

'Do it.'

The two forces combined into an explosion of light. He felt the awakening of his comatose self and as its life-force reanimated so did his own emancipation.

His atoms merged, his soul reunited, healed in the nucleus of the beam.

His body threatened to become whole at that very moment and for a fleeting instant he looked out of the beam as a man and beheld the young genius Brookes, his face a combination of marvel and distress at the terror his experiment had caused.

'All that has happened must remain for your true destiny to be realised.'

The unleashed force dragged in the matter of the universe. It shone through him, instructing the beam to fire Palene to his true destination.

He was the power now, as the Stasis None gave itself freely to his will . . .

Brooke's creation, finally set free.

*

Isimbard Brookes watched over the body of Palene, his eyes wide at the readings now dancing across the instruments of the room. The excited heartbeat had given way to a flurry which made the whole cavern pulse with electricity.

The grey body remained lifeless but the tomb and the machines monitoring him continued their vibrant, erratic promise.

The ceasefire had continued with little interruption for the moment, with not more than two or three clumsy exchanges being rattled into the corridor between the two sides.

All present knew this would not last much longer.

Tom Hardcastle could be heard delivering instructions to his men. He didn't care that Dorey and the others could hear, far from it, he hoped it would urge them to see sense. What he did care about was the delay in having the final Ragun sent down the shaft.

The Commander looked down from the steel landing. "What's happening?"

Brookes looked up at him and gestured toward the machines around the room. "I don't know. But all of this implies something extraordinary." He added, "I'm getting all kinds of readings which suggest whatever Palene was, he certainly isn't the same any longer."

Dorey looked a little annoyed. "But shouldn't he have awoken, shown some life signs?"

Brookes was desperate to give Dorey the answer he wished for but simply could not.

Dorey cursed. He looked across the room below at the body of Jay and felt his heart miss a beat. "What about Deans and Marco?"

The doctor didn't have to look at the readings, "The same. Deans will recover . . . But we won't know the extent of Marco's brain damage for some time yet."

Dorey had foolishly hoped Palene would have performed some kind of miracle. Awoken like some ancient pharaoh the moment he'd been granted open access to the Stasis None. A dreadful taste began growing in the back of his mouth, his faith once again in doubt. He looked once more on Jay then turned to his men, crouched on the steel landing on either side of the corridor waiting for the next inevitable phase of the attack.

Dial's face was bloodied. "Whatever it is Palene believes he's supposed to do, I hope he hurries up and does it." He pointed at the meagre supply of ammunition which lay in organised piles around them.

Benny stared across at the prisoners who remained helplessly bound to the heavy steel desk. Gibbs looked at him then over to the black tomb. Nothing was said.

"They'll hit us hard, probably with bullet shields in a storming tactic." Jim stated.

They'd all been relieved at not having more Raguns to deal with.

Jim suggested they should blow the walkway at the first sign of further attack.

Dorey looked to the scant ammunition.

When they were almost out, the detonation of the more potent grenades should follow. The Commander gave his consent.

The tension was building as the inevitability of the next attack grew.

More shouts and orders could be heard when suddenly, a booming voice fired directly through the corridor, "Commander Dorey can you hear me?"

It was Major Tom Hardcastle.

Dorey looked at his men for a moment. "I hear you."

"Can you confirm the status of the four Marines you encountered back in the corridor?" Hardcastle wasn't acting under orders here and he wasn't expecting a positive response. The blood and gunshots which left their marks in the corridor behind them convinced him all would not be well.

Benny fired Gibbs and the others a gesture of his rifle, encouraging them to remain silent.

"I can confirm they are well and in my custody."

"Is there any way you can prove that?"

Dorey looked at Dial. "If you mean can I have them yell out so you can determine their rough position for when you come in here guns blazing, then the answer is no."

A short silence followed.

"Would it make any difference? You could move them as soon as they'd yelled out."

"And you could send in your Marines the moment they did so."

"Would you be open to the suggestion of letting them go?"

"No." Dorey replied. "They are not hostages, they're prisoners, and I'm not in the habit of releasing prisoners so they can divulge our positions then rejoin the fight." His eyes narrowed, "Besides, I don't want to have to kill them later on any more than I do now."

Hardcastle ignored the brash statement. "So what's with the blood and bullet holes in the corridor?"

"From shots fired at my men, injuries my people received, thankfully for all concerned they were minor."

"And what about your injured man?"

"Receiving treatment which is all we wanted . . . It's a shame you refused the request and forced my hand, I hate battering Marines. I used to be one in another life." He was more than happy with the delay brought about by this converse.

Hardcastle thought for a moment. Commander Dorey wasn't giving anything away and he was unsure whether or not he could believe him on the health of the four captured Marine specialists. He played one last hand. "I don't suppose I could offer you terms for your surrender, now your man is receiving treatment?"

Dorey's response was bold. "Take your men away from here. There's no need for anymore bloodshed. You have no idea how far over on the wrong side you've fallen. Finch is out of control and is acting illegally . . . Though you can't know this yet. We've to hold this room to prevent a catastrophe taking place. Now you can easily block off that corridor and starve us out if you have to . . . You still have options. But those options cannot include sending troops into this corridor. Don't force my hand, or I'll wipe you and your men out."

"Starving you out would be a nice option." Hardcastle admired the grit, understood the bluff. "Unfortunately I also have my orders." His next statement was to be the end of the dialogue between the two, "I'm sorry it had to turn out this way."

In the returning silence the two sides readied themselves for the final onslaught.

CHAPTER 0000

The force that was now Palene hurtled toward the centre of all things, passing through the secrets of the universe. His momentum continued to build as he scorched through the impossible cosmos which was all time and space. There were no boundaries.

His knowledge through the merge with the Stasis None was as boundless as the soul of which he'd just reunited. The speed in which he now travelled defied motion, redefined movement. The properties of space and all matter bending to his will.

As he approached the light there was no fear or expectation. He struck it at such speed it appeared to explode all around him like a supernova, as if an entire universe was born as he hit. The light surrounded in all possible ways. It penetrated, engulfed and embraced with the knowledge of all existence, sharing its passion, the reasoning for life.

He felt its purity, its might.

It made his indestructible cells shudder like insignificant dust.

The illumination bleached his senses and Palene was instantly aware of how he'd known nothing until held by this most awesome light, this most incredible source of which he'd always been entwined. He wanted to scream out with every emotion as the sensations blazed through his being, when suddenly it all stopped.

There was an end to all motion, a cease to all things . . . A pause to all creation itself.

As the joyous madness came abruptly to an end he found his being suspended in a cosmos like no other. There were planets and stars only they were no longer planets and stars. Nebulae and galaxies, only they were no longer the systems of structured space.

He could have wept at what he now beheld, its truth so overwhelming.

He stared through ethereal eyes at all creation and remembered he'd been here before.

"Hello Palene."

It was not a voice or language, it just . . . was.

The Palene who thought himself ancient because of two thousand Earth years suddenly remembered he had transcended any such measurement by a billion evolutions of eternal universe.

"Do you remember?"

He struggled at first but then the truth flooded through him, the impact of all that was truly the Stasis None.

"And what did you find?"

He felt his learning as it was laid bare before all eternity.

"Ahhhh . . . Then you are ready."

He felt his eternal soul buckle as it lay humble but determined.

"Some may fight you on this. Are you certain they're worthy?"

If it were possible to weep at that moment then his tears would have formed stars. If he could have yelled out then his breath would have painted galaxies.

All his findings lay transparent, his purpose absolute.

"Then so be it!"

The light returned like a hurricane and blitzed him with an almighty force beyond any explosion. He was thrown back into the ocean of all evolution, into a sea of cosmos and stars. His very reason now clear.

He fired toward earth's solar system like a blazing comet, passing through space and time like they where mere pools and ponds.

He felt the power of all he was as he screamed back toward the Finger of Venus . . .

Perhaps this time he would show them just a little bit more.

*

A second stream of heavy fire blazed, tearing further chunks from the wall's structure. Chasers, deployed to pen Dorey's team behind their defences. They did their job well, forcing them to huddle for cover, the room behind also taking a battering.

It was not the intention. Hardcastle wanted it intact but had to keep his foe pinned down.

Jim detonated the last of the stun grenades in an attempt to fight the marines back. In the confusion Dial made another dangerous attempt to inflict his own will on proceedings, jumping up to the side of the now battered entrance, letting rip with targeted fire.

The Marines stooped behind their wall of replenished bullet shields. The returning fire of those at their rear ensuring the entire chamber was now a riot of noise and confusion.

Benny, desperate to join the fight, remained at his sniper position as the debris fell.

"Reload." Carl yelled as he slammed one of the remaining magazines into his weapon.

Dial quickly did the same.

More of the wall evaporated into dust as the battering ram tactics rained down.

Jim gestured toward blowing the tunnel as more chaser bullets smashed clumsily into the wall at the far side of the room.

Brookes cowered next to the black onyx shell housing Palene, yelping under the melee.

Benny screamed over the noise, "Are you alright?"

He dusted off some fallen debris, "I'm alright." He checked Palene begging him to hurry. More shots flew overhead taking another chunk out of the far corner of the room.

Brookes punched his fist against the tiles of the tomb, "Come on!"

More chaser shots flew overhead.

Brookes looked upon the grey lifeless figure when suddenly he saw something. He gasped, leaning almost fully into the casket, his heart pounding as he saw the glimmer once more. Palene's eyes had twitched a second time beneath the closed eyelids.

He yelled out as it happened again, the readings on the onyx tomb steadying, the graphic and audio display now drumming out a solid heartbeat.

"We've got something!" He was clearly excited. "I think he's here!"

With the doctor's declaration still fresh in their ears the whole room of apparatus suddenly flooded with the steady heartbeat which replaced the previous erratic dance.

It was like music, the rhythm filling them with a renewed sense of purpose.

The prisoners cowering by the table wondered what was happening as they witnessed such excitement.

The joy was short-lived, as two more chaser rounds whizzed around the bend only low this time. One shattered into Carl's armour, destroying his knee, "Arrrgh." He hit the deck, dragging himself away as he grunted through the pain.

More shots were fired from Dorey and Dial as Jim's clip snapped to a halt. "I'm out!"

There were no more rounds to reload his weapon. He quickly drew his pistol but was forced to jump for cover as a section of the wall protecting him collapsed as more chasers hit, "Jesus!" He wriggled away grateful they were not seeker rounds.

Carl witnessed Dial's clip as it emptied so slid his own rifle toward him.

He took it and fired the remaining shots square into the huddled shields. "I'm out!"

The Marines were advancing, confident now that victory was imminent.

Dial looked for permission to unleash their one remaining surprise. The last ditch defence they'd been able to hold onto thanks to Gibb's offering up his Ragun countermeasures.

"Do it!" The Commander yelled as more bullets screamed.

Dial activated the detonator as Dorey hit the deck close to the wounded Carl.

On the other side of the corridor Jim rolled over to cover his head and face.

Benny down below, readied his aim.

BOOM . . . BOOM . . . BOOM.

The explosions ripped through the corridor smashing against the shields of the Marines. A wave of rock dust bellowed out of the tunnel accompanied by the sound of twisting metal as railings were ripped from their housing, several shards breeching the shield wall, tearing into the flesh of several more soldiers. The men wailed in agony. It was a furious and desperate response and Hardcastle was devastated by his gamble. He'd felt confident they would have blown the corridor long before now if they had the capability.

"Get the medics in there!"

The dust was thick as London fog and it was hard to breathe.

The Major yelled obscenities at Dorey for his use of such viscous force, furious at this heinous act. But as the dust cleared, Hardcastle could see his revenge would be swift.

The walkway had twisted and buckled but it remained in tact.

Whoever built this place had done their job well. This tangle was far from over.

Jim ran across the corridor mouth and scooped up Carl, throwing him over his shoulder. He headed down the steel steps into the nerve centre of Brooke's operation room. "I'll get you under the Surgeon."

"There's no time. Put me down here so I can help defend the entrance."

Dial and Dorey dropped from the raised walkway coughing as they hit the floor below. Dial's shoulder was blood-soaked to match his cheek and he winced as he took out one of his pistols, cocking the weapon.

Jim placed Carl close to Deans and with gritted teeth the German pulled his pistol from its holster, laying out clips before him. Jim dragged a computer stack and cabinet to the floor. They clattered loudly as they hit the deck providing a barricade for Carl.

All but Dorey took up similar positions, their eyes trained toward the entrance, waiting to unleash the final rounds of their last stand.

Dorey headed to Brookes, "What's happening?" The Commander was covered in dirt and cuts from the shower of splintering rock.

The whole chamber was now a chorus of synthetic activity as the displays and monitors, previously subdued by the gunfire, now sang out unhindered.

"See for yourself."

Dorey looked down at the grey body now showing signs of being lifeless no more. The eyes beneath the lids were beginning to flutter and Palene's body was twitching as blood pumped his muscles. "Is he waking up?"

Brookes nodded. "But more than that."

All present were drawn to the doctor's words. Benny, Jim, Carl and Dial kept their attention on the battered entrance above, but found their eyes flirting with the tomb, praying they'd achieved their goal.

Brookes pointed to the monitors displaying the inside workings of Palene's brain. "His functions are growing at an impossible rate." He passed a nervous eye toward the tunnel as the sound of rubble falling shattered the air. He half-expected to see Hardcastle and his men come bursting in, but for the moment at least, they did not.

He continued, "We only use a small percentage of our brain. But look at this."

Dorey was no expert at reading brain scans but he could see why Brookes was excited. The scanners clearly showed the entirety of Palene's brain illuminating into activity.

'Come on.' Dorey willed, looking over to Jay.

The machines pounded a stronger rhythm as if coaxing the embroiled mind now swelling beyond comprehension. Brookes gasped, "His brain is entirely functional." Suddenly, Palene's body convulsed, forcing Brookes to almost fall backward with the shock of it.

More noise came from the corridor above. The marines would surely be on their way.

In the corridor beyond, Tom Hardcastle was arguing with Finch. "Sir I've lost three men and have nine wounded . . . Two of those badly. Now I realise you want that room in tact but if you insist I go in there, then I go in there on my terms, using my methods . . . Or else you can get your ass down here and storm the place yourself . . . Do you understand me?" Tom realised any career promotions were almost certainly being flushed down the toilet.

Back in the battered room, Brookes, Dorey and the others watched as Palene began preparing his entrance, the muscles swelling, the grey skin showing signs of colour, his whole body becoming animated with life.

Brookes smiled and had to place a hand over his mouth out of respect to Dorey's fallen.

'Come on.' They all wished at once.

Benny maintained his aim. He had the only rifle now and would have to make it count.

More noise came from the corridor beyond.

They were moving into position as the debris was removed by the unhindered cutters.

Dial, Carl and Jim instantly returned their full attention to the aim of their pistols.

Palene's eyes began bouncing against his eyelids as if trying to pound them open, the machines continuing their steady pulsating rhythm.

The four Marines looked at one another dumbfounded.

Then Chris Andrews noticed the table on which Deans was laid. "Look!"

They followed his gaze and to their amazement saw Deans slowly sitting upright.

"Deans?" Carl enquired gently from his fortification a few feet away.

Deans rubbed his head and neck then began disconnecting the wires running into him. He lifted his injured hand clenching a fist without effort. As his eyes adjusted to his surroundings he smiled at the now approaching Commander.

"He's okay!" Jim yelled.

Gibbs stared over at Deans delighted.

Benny could not help himself on this one and he snatched a glance at the unfolding drama. A smile made an attempt for his lips but fresh sounds from the corridor startled him back to his aim. "They're coming!"

As the three pistols and rifle concentrated on the mouth of the upper entrance once more, Dorey held out his hand and placed it gingerly on Dean's shoulder.

Deans smiled then gestured toward Marco next to him.

The remaining tentacles which tended his injuries began to retract toward the Surgeon brain above, the machine slowly retreating toward the ceiling housing.

Dorey looked on as the Synthetic Surgeon fully removed itself from Marco. He felt the tears well up as his friend's chest convulsed. Marco's eyes shot open and he sucked in such a breath it was a miracle there was any air left in the room. He began breathing heavily, dealing with his sudden return to consciousness. Then within a moment he pushed himself up, trying to focus on his surroundings.

"Easy." Dorey said.

He sat up slowly as if waking from a deep sleep. His eyes squinting as he turned to Dorey's voice with a warm and wonderfully confused smile. They all looked at one another in disbelief. Deans and Marco now back with them in the room.

They all had exactly the same thought, and their hearts skipped a beat as Dorey dashed to the sofa holding the still lifeless body of Jay.

Then without warning the sound of laser cutters pulsated through the air, their high-pitched vibration drowning the harmonious sound of Palene's synthetic heartbeat.

Jim realising the danger, moved toward the recovered patients telling them to take cover.

Within a second the beam of the laser came slicing through the room, its range setting shortened just beyond the corridor mouth. The sound of rubble falling was quickly accompanied by gunfire scourging the tunnel above, lacing more holes into the wall adjacent. Its violence ruptured the moment.

Benny and the others readied for the attack focusing their weapons on the entrance.

Dorey dropped to his knees at the sofa, his gun placed down as he listened to her chest . . . Nothing. "Jay," he whispered softly but still she lay lifeless. "Come on baby."

"Here they come." Benny yelled as more gunfire rained in.

The four captured Marines watched the unfolding events with a mixture of wonder and fear, but as the assault drew close they only hoped they would survive.

Dorey continued his vigil, "Come on Jay . . . Wake up."

More gunshots clattered into the wall as Tom Hardcastle shut down the laser, his marines preparing to hit the entrance with explosive rounds. Orb cameras were fired through, scattering all over the buckled floor and beyond. He called up Dorsen and Jerry Cole, "Hit the corner of the wall with chaser rounds then open up the heavy mini-mags."

As the two prepared, Tom Hardcastle watched through his beleaguered monitor to ensure his marines had the safest possible shot, but as he studied the screen the images beamed back from the scattered cameras quickly went off line. "God damn it." He shook his monitor as it also began to crackle. '*What the hell's with this place*?' He wasted no more time yelling out, "Hit it now!"

Both Jerry and Dorsen let rip.

The whole room ducked as the debris rained down, though luckily none of them were hit by the scattered rock. Dust enveloped the chamber once again as the defenders made ready. The hope of the room quickly replaced with the adrenaline of the incoming fight.

Dorey kissed Jay on the forehead then picked up the pistol. He looked to Deans and Marco who were still adjusting to the shock of the battle. "Stay down," he told them. "And that goes for you too Doctor."

Brookes crouched over the tomb to protect the face and torso of Palene.

"Get ready." Benny yelled, sensing the second wave of explosive shot was set to come.

In the corridor both Dorsen and Jerry squeezed their triggers again. But as the devastating ammunition left their weapons something impossible happened. The rounds never reached their destination intact. Instead they simply reduced to the atomic signatures which made up their structure, hitting the walls as liquid and particles.

What happened next however made them stumble backward in abject panic, as their rifles too dissolved into nothing but fibres, particles and liquid. "Shit!" Jerry yelped.

But they didn't have to worry on how they were going to explain this phenomenon, as in the same instant all weaponry held by the Marines did exactly the same thing.

Within moments Tom Hardcastle and his entire band were completely disarmed, their array of weapons and gadgets disappearing into fragments before their very eyes.

Extreme shock and confusion followed, as the soldiers in the corridor and beyond tried to come to terms with what was happening.

"What are they hiding in there?" Hardcastle enquired to nobody in particular.

Within the confines of the hidden chamber, Dorey and the others looked on waiting for the attack, trying to second guess the concern which could be heard transpiring beyond.

As they looked up at the entrance, Benny's rifle suddenly fired several rounds, only it was not Benny who pulled the trigger.

As Hardcastle realised Dorey's team still had weaponry intact, he commanded an immediate and full withdrawal, an order which took little enforcing as his men retreated in stunned disbelief and fear.

Benny looked at the others dumbfounded, and was about to inform Dial he had not taken the shot when the same fate was visited upon their own weapons.

They froze as their rifles and guns disintegrated, but in place of the panic experienced by Hardcastle's men, they all simply looked silently toward the tomb of Palene.

The four captured specialists sat aghast as their bonds unclipped with invisible force.

They were free, but not one of the Royals moved.

Dorey was back cajoling Jay, begging her repeatedly to follow his voice and wake up.

As he did, a sudden surge of energy washed over the entire complex like an invisible cloud, an unseen shadow slowly travelling over everything and everyone.

Its power and force indefinable as it breathed over the complex like untold might.

It passed over the holding cells housing Usorio and Grossen, releasing them of their bonds as it went. Grossen appeared stunned as his freedom was granted, staring at the ceiling of the brig as the unseen force rippled weightily overhead.

Inside Usorio's cell, the agent who'd struck Isabella watched wide-eyed as the bruises on her face healed and disappeared. She smiled as her shackles melted away allowing her to stand freely, as with incredible groaning force, the moulded desk before her crumpled to the floor like a discarded tin can.

Cassaveres and the population of the RFC, who'd spent the past uncomfortable hours under guard in the washrooms, looked up as the energy force passed, invisible yet all around them nonetheless. They all sensed it as it moved over them, reducing their guard's guns to dust and water.

Stein listened, his eyes wide as the force slowly crawled across the RFC. He watched as a shocked-looking Finch stood silent, observing Raffy Abel's digital image as it liquefied into nothing, the voice trailing away into an inaudible soup.

Deep in the Stasis cave the same healing powers washed over Dorey's men. Carl stood gingerly on a knee now repaired and joined the group gathered around Palene.

Dorey continued his vigil over Jay.

They looked to their miraculously-healed friends, to their own sealed wounds.

Gibbs and his silent, stunned Marine specialists slowly made their way to the tomb to join their captors, welcome to watch as the miraculous unfolded.

Brookes looked at his screens then down at Palene.

The Commander crouched over Jay whispering gently, the whole room appearing to hold its breath as they turned to share his prayers. "Come on sweetheart." He stroked her face gently, willing her to wake. Dorey had visited the domain in which Jay was now lost, he knew she needed to find her way. "Come on Jay!"

He gulped as his demand was answered, as her chest suddenly heaved.

His eyes welled into tears as she coughed then choked her way back to him.

He gave her the space needed as she dragged the air back into her lungs, his heart swollen with joy, "It's alright sweetheart."

The room was awash with relief and as Dorey brought Jay slowly around his own eyes fell upon Palene once more as without warning, the array of wires and feeders which ran into his torso pulled themselves free, retracting with invisible force.

Those standing around the tomb gasped.

Somewhere in another time, Palene watched on the hillside above the henge, fearful of the gathering tempest which filled him with foreboding. He stood, ready to make his way down the hill to Marri and the children with the absurd notion the storm was meant for him, that it would at any time strike out. But of course it didn't, and he laughed at his childlike fears as he headed back toward the ancient stone circle.

Within the tomb of the Stasis None a new being was set to be born.

And as the Stasis None as a machine administered its final act, the monitoring technologies within the room illustrated finally and concisely, the date of mankind's end.

The stimulated machines of the chamber whirred in unison with the excitement of the watchful gathering, stood silently and wide-eyed as they felt the tremendous force peak . . . With his brain operating at one hundred percent, the indestructible cells ordered air be dragged to his waiting lungs, and with a sharp intake of breath . . .

Palene's eyes suddenly fired open.

THE END

Coming Soon . . .

ZARAPATHINEON

Book I

Rising

The new novel by IAN RUTTER

Visit my website www.rutstuff.com for news, information and updates

For my next novel I wanted to change the dynamic completely. It's the first part in a trilogy of books telling of the trials and tribulations of a great empire. Although the setting is completely fictional the concept takes its inspiration from the stories of Ancient Greece and her renowned tragedies.

Basically I wanted to write an epic, taking aspects of the classics like Troy and Sparta, blending such influences with tales of Spartacus and Rome, the great feudal Samurai of Japan. I wanted to incorporate more modern stories such as Gladiator, Braveheart and 300, blending them to create something entirely new.

The end product is a story which possesses all the action and adventure, revenge and romance any great epic should boast. Something for everyone! Zarapathineon reads like the kind of movie you wish was made year in year out. Each book is much shorter and faster paced than Stasis None and you will devour them in no time.

As an appetizer I have included overleaf the prologue to the first book, Rising. The prologue paints a simplistic and speedy picture of how this great empire originally came into being. An overview which will set the scene...
Immediately after this prologue Rising leaps forward a thousand years...

And it is here, our real story begins.

ZARAPATHINEON

BOOK I

RISING

PROLOGUE

Eleven centuries ago the Umarian Empire was at its zenith, a huge civilisation which dominated the known world. A society of modern thinkers and warriors, but one built upon tyranny, on the enslavement of others.

The Peninsoola Sotra was one such occupied territory, the many nations which made up its headland forced into slavery to feed the belly of the Umarian Empire above.

Hearthonzarra, an ancient kingdom within this southern peninsula, was the last to be conquered. It was a noble land with a reputation for courage and virtue. Qualities which would see many of its males selected from adolescence, to be trained and utilised within the Umarian slave armies.

After three hundred years of occupation, like countless generations before him, one such Hearthonzarran male was chosen to serve the Umarian banner. His name was Caprasees.

A gifted soldier and natural leader, Caprasees rose through the slave ranks quickly. Granted his first command at the age of twenty, he soon amassed a number of significant victories for his masters. Stories were told of his deeds conquering the barbarian.

The Umarian courts grew to love him, honouring him with promotion and wealth until he reached the highest status a slave could achieve, Secondary Citizen to the Umarian Order.

Granted limited freedoms, he could own property, travel freely and even marry into an Umarian family with the permission of the state.

He was a hero, hosted and entertained by great families when returning from battle.

However as his influence and prowess grew, Caprasees would eventually be deemed a threat by many in the High Senate. The ruling elite within the capital Uma, beginning to fear the great warrior slave. Plots for his downfall began to whisper.

As the Umarian Order pushed further east a new enemy had been stirred. A race known as the Hordecian. A society which made up for in number what it lacked in military skill. They'd taken back a far flung outpost, scattering the Umarian force left to defend it. With such a victory the Senate found good cause to see Caprasees sent to his honourable end.

He was made High General of his own Sixth Army, an honour never before bestowed on any Secondary in the history of Umaria, a title which would give him control of not only slave battalions, but Umarian Commanders and soldiers of the First Citizen Order.

One such man was the newly promoted First General, Algamon. He was of noble birth, celebrated for his victories as a Commander in the Northern Territories.

Together they were to take back the fort and hold the outpost until the Third and Fourth Great Armies could march from the Western borders to reinforce them.

It was a suicide mission, and those who understood soldiery knew it.

The slave general was to be a martyr to the Umarian cause, and never again would the Senate allow one of such lowly station to rise through their ranks so prominently.

It was a full-proof plan. Umarian society could never question their intention, not after promoting a slave to such high order, granting him charge of a new army, placing him in command of such noble Umarian stock. Unfortunately, it was a plan doomed to fail.

For not only did Caprasees understand his masters intention, he also won the impossible fight. Using attrition, inspiration and courage he scored an unprecedented victory against the Hordecian, taking back the outpost and fortifying his position. He then held it against impossible odds, as the two great armies supposedly sent to his aid were delayed time and again. His men, slave and free alike, revered him for his leadership and courage, loved him for keeping them alive, for delivering honour and victory from certain defeat and death. Understanding he'd been sent there to die, Caprasees took the fight to the Hordecian. He advanced deep into their land, plundering their treasures and armouries, scattering their number far and wide.

He then returned to the fortified outpost ready to make history.

He decreed the slaves within his army free, offering himself as leader. He permitted the Umarians within his number to return home, honouring them for their commitment and bravery in battle. Although thousands of Umarian soldiers left, entire legions remained. The Commanders paid homage to the slave general before taking safe passage home . . . All but one of them, Algamon.

In the beginning he'd been a reluctant second but had since marvelled at the integrity, cunning and bravery displayed by the slave general. He'd witnessed first hand how he'd saved them from certain doom and vowed to amend his Senate's betrayal by giving his life to Caprasees' cause...A cause soon to be put to the test.

As word of treason reached the High Senate in Uma, the delayed Third and Fourth Armies were immediately mobilised toward the slave general's position. They marched quickly to unite, but not quickly enough. Before the forces could meet, Caprasees smashed the Fourth with a swift attack. The Umarian command had expected Caprasees to prepare for siege within the fort stronghold he'd already gained.

In the confusion the Fourth Army was scattered. Message was sent to the thousands of slave soldiers within the retreating ranks, offering all a place in the slave general's cause.

A number of these defectors were then sent toward the approaching Third

Army to supposedly rejoin the Umarian fight. Once absorbed into the ranks they spread word of Caprasees' intention, and told of the ease in which he'd just destroyed the Fourth. Rumours quickly infected the rank and file. Many of the slave soldiers mutinied and Caprasees wasted little time, routing the Third Army as he had the Fourth, while their ranks were in disarray. Again he honoured the Umarian Command, granting the captured free passage back to Uma, to spread word of what was to come. The first cracks to the perceived invincibility of the Umarian Order began to show, as panic gripped the capital.

As Caprasees and Algamon marched south the Second and Fifth Armies were sent to intercept. Stripped of their slave soldiers for fear of further mutiny, the legions were amalgamated as one Umarian force. Without time to adjust to the new tactics, the force was slaughtered. The momentum and battle readiness of the slave general's ranks superior on every level. As Caprasees marched on, uprisings spread across the empire, infecting the Umarian Order like a virus. Thousands flocked to his banner as Uma prepared for the inevitable.

Vast numbers within the capital were conscripted to bolster the ranks of the Great First Army, the elite fighting force of the Umarian Order, now charged with defending their city, as the nervous Capital made ready for the return of their one time hero.

When Caprasees encamped outside Uma his force numbered two hundred thousand, almost half that set to defend the capital. With the captured arms and the thirst for revenge of those beneath his banner, the advantage was with the former slave.

Within only three days he took the exterior walls of the city, this time showing no mercy for any who stood in his way. His forces marched triumphant through the streets of the outer quarter, as those within the inner sanctum prepared for the worst.

The unthinkable defeat of the Umarian Order was now inevitable

Many demanded Uma be burnt to the ground.

But what the slave general and Algamon did next surprised everyone.

They sent message to those cowering within the citadel.

A peace was to be negotiated.

The High Senate were suspicious. But after the General of the Great First Army and the defence Commanders, many of whom served under Caprasees, met with the warrior slave and his second, the returning news was positive. Uma was to surrender all arms to the slave general, and the citizens of the great empire would be spared catastrophe.

Two days later, Caprasees and Algamon marched their army to the Senate steps to deliver terms to the city. The Umarian Order would be spared on the condition the Peninsoola Sotra be freed and placed under Caprasees' protection. Any slave or citizen of Umaria would be free to live within this freed peninsula to become part of a new society.

The Umarian Navy was to be surrendered and sailed south by its slave sailors to its new home within the Peninsoola Sotra. All Umarian trade would remain under its safeguard.

A treaty was to be agreed in place of the destruction the Senate expected…
That Umaria would continue, but only under certain conditions.

If any ship, soldier or Senator were to ever threaten the free peoples of the Peninsoola Sotra, the slave general would return to finish what he'd started, and burn all Umaria from the pages of history.

With agreement to his terms, Caprasees turned his conquering force around and marched them south to their new lives. Millions joined his cause during the journey.

Caprasees was greeted as a hero by the freed nations of the southern peninsula.

He returned home to Herthonzarra where the confiscated navy awaited his command as to great ceremony he was proclaimed protector of the Peninsoola Sotra.

Caprasees homeland was renamed Thiazarra, meaning Free Kingdom. The army and navy were expanded. For ten years they trained, ready to defend the narrow corridor into the southern headland, preparing for a fight never to come.

Revered for his mercy by the Umarian people, his massive forces of land and sea feared so much by the Uma Senate, the once slave general was to see the terms of his treaty honoured, leaving him free to begin construction on a very different kind of empire.

The newly named Thiazarra proclaimed Caprasees as Zarapathineon, King of the Free.

The leader appointed a High Council to govern under his stewardship, and the new moral guidelines born from the stories of their occupation and liberation became the faith all Thiazarran's held dear. Freedom, truth, honour and justice. Peace and equality for all.

Over the next two decades their ideals took route, seeing the creation of the Garpathan Brotherhood, warrior monks who governed with equal input to the High Council, answerable to the Zarapathineon, as he would be answerable to them.

Watching these events transpire, many of the nations surrounding the newly created kingdom flocked to be amalgamated into the cause, giving themselves freely to create a new nation unlike any seen before. The kingdom of the free, Zarrapathia . . . was born

Caprasees rewarded his most trusted second, Algamon, with the office of Patruan, meaning, Of the True. Like the Zarapathineon it was to be an office set in blood.

The two bloodlines would never be severed. King and faithful Noble House.

Together with the High Council and the Garpathan Brotherhood they would rule fairly and for the people.

To help protect this new land the Pathan Order was born. Warriors trained from adolescence would be given trials to assess their worth. Taught the codes of combat and chivalry, to honour all they were born to protect. The best of these warriors would be taken into the temples of the Garpathan Brotherhood at the age of seventeen where they would spend the next four years honing their skills until ready to undertake the Pathantral, the final assessments which would see them anointed into the Pathan Order. Those who wished to join the Garpathan Brotherhood of Warrior Monks were granted entry into the fortress monasteries, the remainder, sworn in as Pathan Knights.

All took the sacred oath, to protect and hold dear the values of Zarrapathia, to embrace the Gods as an example by which to measure ones deeds, so that men may live as Gods in peace and perfection…The Zarrapathian Way.

When Caprasees, 1st Zarapathineon died, Algamon governed the kingdom until the king's son was ready to take the Pathantral.

Only when the trials of the Pathan Order were completed was he anointed Zarapathineon.

And so the great tradition was born. Never would the Patruan and Zarapathineon households rival each other. Their sons were raised as brothers, their daughters as sisters.

If no male heir was available to the throne then a Queen would govern under the protection of the Patruan house until a new Zarapathineon male was ready to rule.

After suffering centuries of slavery they worked hard to maintain peace and freedom. Zarrapathia continued to grow, swallowing nations who requested entry, protecting those that did not, until its borders reached the far away mountains and desert. From here it was decreed Zarrapathia would grow no more. That all nations beyond these natural defences would become part of the Alliance, the free nations of the Peninsoola Sotra.

A great wall would be built across the most northerly point of the kingdom of Danton, Zarrapathia's northern neighbour, whose border protected the narrow entry which connected the Peninsoola Sotra to the mainland.

It was a century in the making. A high fortress ninety miles across sealing the narrow peninsula from the vast land mass above.

With the One Hundred Years Wall and the vast Zarrapathian Navy and military elite in place, the Peninsoola Sotra flourished, safe for a thousand years, while those above it wrangled and burned.

Rising then leaps forward a thousand years. Here our story begins, when we find this great empire approaching a defining moment

As war looms on the horizon for the first time in centuries, a new hero is set to graduate his apprenticeship from the elite Pathan Warrior Tradition.

He is a prince, eldest son to the Zarapathineon,
heir to the great kingdom of Zarrapathia.
His name is Capatheous and his adventures are about to begin . . .

Visit www.rutstuff.com for updates on Rising's release date